SCARLET WOMAN

Shivers coursed through Melinda as Blake locked her to him. For a brief, poignant moment he stared down at her. Open. Pliable. Susceptible to her. His tremors shook her, and her nerves tingled with exhilaration when she heard his hoarse groan of capitulation. Then his mouth was on her and his tongue stabbed at her lips until she opened and, at last, had him inside of her. His big hand gripped her buttocks and she undulated wildly against him as his velvet tongue promised her ecstasy, plunging in and out of her and testing every crevice of her mouth. Strong and commanding like the man himself. Hungry for all of him, she spread her legs and he rose hard and strong against her. She slumped into him and might have fallen if he hadn't lifted her, carried her to the sofa, and sat down with her in his lap. For a long while, he sat there, rocking her and stroking her, soothing her with a tenderness she'd never known.

SCARLET WOMAN

Shivers coursed through Melinda as Blak
For a brief, poignant moment he stared d
Pliable. Susceptible to her. His tremors s
nerves tingled with exhilaration when sh
groan of capitulation. Then his mouth was o
stabbed at her lips until she opened and, at
of her. His big hand gripped her buttocks
wildly against him as his velvet tongue pr
plunging in and out of her and testing e
mouth. Strong and commanding like the n
for all of him, she spread her legs and he
against her. She slumped into him and mi
hadn't lifted her, carried her to the sofa, a
in his lap. For a long while, he sat the
stroking her, soothing her with a tendernes

SCARLET WOMAN

Gwynne Forster

ARABESQUE

BET
BOOKS

BET Publications, LLC

ARABESQUE BOOKS are published by

BET Publications, LLC
c/o BET BOOKS
One BET Plaza
1900 W Place NE
Washington, D.C. 20018-1211

ISBN 0-7394-1909-9

Printed in the United States of America

ACKNOWLEDGMENTS

To Brother Simba, co-owner of Karibu Books, Hyattsville, MD, and an exemplary man of strong moral fiber. In my research for this book, Brother Simba shared with me his experiences as a volunteer teacher and counselor to African-American youths during their incarceration at the District of Columbia's Lorton Prison and after their return to society. Brother Simba inaugurated a study group at Lorton (The African Development Organization), and he remains a mentor to those young men who accept his counsel. My thanks also to my husband who supports and encourages me in everything that I undertake.

ACKNOWLEDGMENTS

Prologue

Melinda looked out of the only window in her tiny one-room apartment and saw nothing. Not the children jumping rope and playing hopscotch, nor the single mothers who sat on the stone bench beneath a big white oak tree escaping the late-August, Maryland sun. Over and over, her mind replayed Prescott Rodgers's proposal. Marry and live with him in his home and brighten his life by doing for him what he couldn't do for himself. He wanted her to read to him the classic literature of the English language. Although he was a brilliant man, dyslexia had deprived him of the pleasures of reading and writing. He had contacted the high school at which she taught English, offering to pay a student to read to him. None found the idea attractive, and she eventually volunteered to do it one or two hours weekly at no charge. But his tales of his world travels, especially his wanderings through Italy, so intrigued her that the few weekly hours soon became a daily ritual, a treat to which she looked forward each day.

A self-made man, inventor of a film-developing process, a fluid for contact lenses, and a type of eyeglass lens, all of which yielded hefty royalties, Prescott Rodgers had amassed a fortune. He lived a reclusive life, fearing scorn because he could not learn to read.

"We're both lonely," Prescott had argued, "and we have much to give each other. I know the chemicals I've worked with all these years are shortening my life, and I'd like to spend what's left of it in your company. Marrying me would still the tongues of those curious about your daily visits."

"Well, I . . . I don't know—"

"Will you accept a marriage of convenience? That's selfish of me, I know, because you're young, and I'm sixty-eight years old."

As a married woman, she would escape much of her father's intolerance and authoritarianism, and she would have a companion. Musing over her own life of loneliness—for which her father's self-righteousness and his indictments of all who disagreed with him were largely responsible—she reasoned that at last she would have a niche. She would belong with someone. Melinda added up the advantages, shoved the doubts and disadvantages out of her mind, and agreed.

She married Prescott Rodgers in a private ceremony in the office of Blake Edmund Hunter, Prescott's lawyer, with only Hunter and her parents as witnesses.

Prescott gave her a monthly allowance of $1,100 for her most personal needs, provided her with a housekeeper, and bore all other expenses. She read to him each morning, entertained for him, sparing though it was, and enjoyed the remaining four and a half years of his life as his wife.

Chapter One

Melinda Rodgers sat in Blake Edmund Hunter's law office on that damp, mid-May morning, dumbfounded, as he read aloud her late husband's will. She was to set up a foundation for remedial reading and the acquiring of literacy that would meet the needs of both children and adults and have it fully operating within a year of his death. She must also marry within the year.

If she failed to fulfill either requirement, the house in which she lived and everything else—except for one million dollars to rehabilitate homeless people—would go to a charity of Blake's choice.

"It doesn't surprise me that he'd want that foundation," Melinda said to those present—Blake, her parents, and her best friend—"but as much as he valued individual freedom, I can't believe he'd attempt to force me to get married."

"You just have to carry out his wishes," her father, the Reverend Booker Jones, said. "You wouldn't be foolish enough to throw away all this money. The church needs some repairs."

"Now, dear," Lurlane Jones said, in a voice soft and musical. "Our Melinda is in mourning; we mustn't push her."

Melinda watched Blake Hunter lean back in his desk chair and survey the group, his sharp, cool gaze telling them that he judged them all and found them wanting. She tried not to look at him, lest she betray her feelings.

"I really wouldn't have thought it of Prescott," she said, "but I guess you never truly know a person."

She glanced toward Blake, and her heart turned over at the softness of his unguarded look. She told herself not to react, that she had to be mistaken. He had shown her respect but never liked her, and she doubted he had or ever would have any feelings for her, though Lord knows he lived in her heart and had since the minute she met him.

With his cool, impersonal gaze back in place, he immediately confirmed her thoughts. "Don't think you can play at this, Mrs. Rodgers, and you're not allowed to hire anyone to do it for you. You have to do it yourself and to my satisfaction."

His sharp words and unsympathetic attitude surprised her, for he had always appeared gracious and considerate toward her during her husband's lifetime. "As my husband's close friend, I expected that you might give me some advice, if not help, but I see I'm on my own. I'll be in tomorrow morning to talk this over with you."

His left eyebrow shot up, and he nodded in what appeared to be grudging appreciation. "I'll be here at nine."

"Let's go, Rachel." Melinda said to the friend she'd asked to be with her when the will was read. But she noticed that the woman got up with reluctance, almost as if she didn't want to leave.

"You do what that will says," Booker Jones roared in the

descending elevator. "We can't afford to lose one brown cent of that money. We need it to do the Lord's work."

"Melinda will do what's right. So stop fussing," Lurlane said.

Melinda didn't respond. Her father taught his parishioners that money was the root of all evil, but he never said no to it.

"Is he like that all the time?" Rachel asked Melinda as they walked down one of the main streets of Ellicott City, Maryland. "My father hardly ever raises his voice."

"Your father isn't a preacher," Melinda reminded her. "If other pastors are like my father, they're always right. He talks over everybody and across everybody, because when he opens his mouth the world is supposed to shut up and take heed."

"Girl, you go 'way from here," Rachel said. "He's a good man. Last Sunday, he preached till he was plain hoarse and couldn't say another word."

"Yes, I know he's good, and I bet he started whispering into the mike. Nothing shuts up my father."

"He's a righteous man."

"You're telling me? He's the only one on earth. I wish he'd understand that he can't mold people as he would clay figures just because he believes they'd be better off."

"Now, Melinda. You don't mean that."

She did mean it. Her father believed in what he taught, but he was driven by a secular monster, the one that made you want praise and acceptance. Tired of the subject and uninterested in Rachel's views of Booker Jones, Melinda stopped talking. Who knew a man better than his family?

"Rachel, why do you think Prescott put that clause in his will forcing me to remarry? I just can't figure it out."

"Me neither, girl, and Blake Hunter is going to see that you do it or lose everything, including your house."

Melissa shrugged. "I'm not worried about that, because I never intend to remarry."

Rachel stopped walking. "Was Mr. Rodgers mean to you?
I'd have thought an older man would be sweet as sugar to a
woman less than half his age."

Melissa smiled inwardly, aware that the comment reflected
the local gossip about her and Prescott. "My husband treated
me as if I were the most precious being on this earth. He . . .
he was wonderful to me. Those four years were the happiest
of my life."

"Well, I'll be! I guess there's no telling about people. Maybe
I'd better start looking for an older man. I'm thirty-two. With a
fifty- or sixty-year-old man, that ought to stand for something."
Rachel didn't say anything for half a block, and then she spoke
with seeming reluctance. "How old do you think Blake Hunter
is? And how come he's not married?"

"Why would I know?"

"He was your husband's close friend, wasn't he?"

"They never discussed the man's private affairs when I was
around. I know practically nothing about him."

"I'll bet you know he's a number ten."

"A what?"

"A knockout. A good-looking virile man who makes you
think things you couldn't tell your mother."

So she'd been right. Rachel hadn't wanted to leave Blake's
office. The woman was after Blake. She told herself to forget
about it. Nothing would ever happen between Blake Hunter
and herself.

Melinda walked into the redbrick colonial she'd shared with
Prescott and froze when she realized she'd been expecting to
hear his usual, "That you, dear?" *Get a hold of yourself,* she
said aloud, squared her shoulders, and headed for her bedroom,
determined to meet the rest of her life head-on. The sound of
Ruby vacuuming the hall carpet reminded her that the upkeep
of the house was now her responsibility.

"We have to talk, Ruby," she told the housekeeper. "I don't

understand it, but Mr. Rodgers didn't provide for you in his will, and I can't keep you on here. I'm afraid we'll have to separate."

"He paid my wages for the entire year after his death, Miz Melinda. And last year, he drawed up a real good pension plan for me. Only thing is, I has to work here for the next twelve months. He done good by me."

Melinda swallowed several times and told herself it didn't matter that Prescott had left his housekeeper better fixed than his wife.

"Is Blake Hunter in charge of your pension and wages?"

"Yes, ma'am. My pension starts thirteen months from now, and Mr. Blake will send me my salary every Friday, just like he always done." She coughed a few times and patted the hair in the back of her head. "If I was twenty years younger, that man wouldn't be single. No siree. That is one sweet-looking man. A face the color of shelled walnuts." She rolled her eyes toward the sky and wet her lips. "Them dreamy eyes and that bottom lip ... *Lord.*" She patted her hair. "Honey, that is *some* man."

Imagine that. "He's a hard man," Melinda said, thinking of how lacking in compassion for her he'd seemed when he read the terms of her late husband's will. Harsh terms, and so unlike Prescott. "But if anybody could break through that wall he's got around himself, Ruby, I expect you could."

Ruby put the can of furniture polish on the table and shook out the chamois cloth she used for polishing. "Miz Melinda, that man just can't help being hard. He done nothing but work from daylight to dark six days a week from the time he could walk till he finished high school. His daddy cracked that whip."

She stared at Ruby. Surely the woman was mistaken. "He told you *that?*"

"No, ma'am. He sure didn't, but I heard him telling Mr.

Rodgers that and a whole lot more. That man been through somethin'.''

Melinda's eyes widened, but she quickly replaced that with a bland facial expression. No point in letting Ruby know that anything about Blake interested her. She'd had two shocks in two minutes, and she had a hunch she'd get more of them. She leaned against the wall and waited for Ruby's next shot. Her impression of Blake had been of a privileged youth from an upper middle-class family. How had he become so polished? Ruby's high-pitched voice interrupted Melinda's musings.

"Working a boy like Mr. Blake's daddy done made him work would amount to child abuse these days," Ruby said, warming up to the subject. "He said his folks was poor as Job's turkey."

"Well, he certainly overcame it," Melinda replied and walked rapidly up the wide stairs, richly carpeted in Royal Bokhara. However, realizing that she'd practically run from the talk about Blake because she didn't want to think of him, she slowed her steps. As executor of Prescott's estate, the man would be a fixture in her life for the next twelve months, and she'd better learn to handle the consequences.

Blake Edmund Hunter looked from one woman to the other as Melinda stood to leave his office and Rachel Perkins remained in her chair gazing at him. Another one of nature's stupid tricks! Rachel wanted him so badly she was practically salivating, and Melinda Rodgers didn't know he was alive. His gaze followed Melinda's svelte physique, straight, almost arrogant carriage and sweetly rounded buttocks as she strolled out of his office. He wanted her and had from the minute he first saw her, but he was Prescott's friend, so he hadn't let himself give in to it when Prescott was alive. He was damned if he'd succumb to it now.

If anything turned his stomach, it was a gold-digging woman, an unfaithful wife, or a treacherous friend. She hadn't given him reason to believe that she would be unfaithful to Prescott, and he was grateful for that, because she'd been temptation without trying and he wouldn't have considered disloyalty to Prescott.

Yet, as much as he desired her, he had reservations about her. For instance, that virginal innocence she wrapped around herself didn't fool him. She was less than half Prescott's age, and nobody could make him believe a young, gorgeous woman like her had married an old, solitary recluse for love. She'd married Prescott Rodgers for his money, and Blake would see that she carried out the terms of that will, *or else*. That clause Prescott had inserted requiring Melinda to marry within a year or lose her inheritance . . . He squeezed his eyes shut, and told himself the lump in his throat had nothing to do with that.

He answered the phone, grateful that its ringing had derailed his thoughts. Dangerous thoughts.

"Yes, Lacy. Look, I'm sorry but I have to deal with this will."

"But you can leave it long enough to have lunch with me."

He glanced at his watch and banged his left fist on his desk. Softly. Reaffirming his intention to stay away from her. "I'm having lunch at my desk today, and for goodness' sake, Lacy, please don't pout. It's so childish." He could imagine her lower lip protruding in what she considered a sexy come-on.

"You're busy every time I call."

Leaning back in the chair and closing his eyes, he told himself not to show annoyance. "Lacy, I told you I'm not ready for a relationship, and I haven't said or done anything that would make you think otherwise. I'm sorry."

In his mind's eye, he could see her lighting a cigarette and taking a long drag, a habit he hated. "Maybe this weekend?"

She had the tenacity of Muhammad Ali smelling victory, but he refused to be roped in.

"I'm longing to see you," she whispered.

He wished she wouldn't beg. Three dates didn't amount to a commitment. "Yeah, right! I'll . . . uh. Look, Lacy, I wish you well. I'll see you around."

He hung up, but he doubted that ended it. Any other woman would know that he'd just broken ties with her, such as they were, but not Lacy Morgan. He'd never seen a human being with thicker skin.

He walked over to the window and looked down at the flowering trees, but they didn't engage his thoughts. What would happen to Melinda if she couldn't do as Prescott's will required? His long, tapered fingers rubbed his jaw, and he shook his head as if to clear it. The Rodgers account was but one in his portfolio, and several others required his attention. He pushed the intercom button.

"Irene, could you come in and take a letter to Folson?"

"Yes, sir."

Now here was a woman he admired: always professional, and she expected him to be the same. So he wasn't prepared for her comment.

"Blake, I don't see how Melinda is going to set up that foundation. People here don't think highly of her since she married Mr. Rodgers. And to make things worse, she never once went anyplace with him from the time they married till he died. Some say they weren't really married, that she just lived with the old man."

His jaw twitched, and he knew he grimaced, for her blood reddened her light skin and she lowered her eyelids. *So much for her unfailing professionalism.* He looked over a few notes and dictated the letter.

"Anything else, sir?"

With his elbows propped on the desk, he made a pyramid

of his ten fingers and looked her in the eye. "Yes. There is. I was Prescott Rodgers's witness when he married Melinda Jones in this office in the presence of her parents. That's all."

He didn't care for character assassins any more than he liked gold diggers, and he hated feeling protective toward Melinda, but he did. Feeling a flush of guilt, he tapped his Mont Blanc pen on his desk. If she couldn't establish that foundation, he wasn't sure he'd be able to live with himself. He'd insisted that Prescott include that provision in the will and had worded it himself. If she ever found out . . .

Melinda dressed carefully that morning, choosing a white linen suit—she wasn't going to mourn in black; Prescott had made her promise she wouldn't—a blue and white striped linen blouse and navy accessories. She wanted to look great, but she didn't want Blake to think he'd ever entered her mind.

"Come in, Melinda, and have a seat," Irene said, when she opened the door. "He'll be with you in a second."

Looking around the reception room, she marveled at its decorations, carpets, paintings, and live green plants—elegance without ostentation.

"Good morning, Melinda. Nothing pleases me like promptness."

She stood, accepted his extended hand and wished she hadn't, as her heart lurched, and fiery ripples spiraled up her arms. His gaze seemed more piercing than ever, or had he noticed what that physical contact with him had done to her?

"Hello, Blake. I've thought this over and figured that I can either try to comply with this strange bequest or walk away from the entire thing." At his quick frown, she added, "Neither one of those provisions is easy to comply with, but I've made up my mind to do all I can to get that foundation up and operating. Reading is what brought Prescott and me together, and I know how dear this project would be to him.''

His frown deepened. "What do you mean by that?''

So Prescott hadn't confided that problem! She lifted her left shoulder in a dismissive shrug. "Long story. Let's get started on this.'' Something flickered in his gaze, but she discounted it as being impossible. Blake Hunter had no feelings for her.

She made notes as he talked, suggesting names of people she should contact, and providing her with tips about their personalities and attitudes. Once, when she glanced up at him and saw the softness in his fawnlike, brown eyes, she had to stifle a gasp and quickly turned her attention to the tablet in her lap.

"Your father wants to be on the board,'' he said. "I can't advise you about that, but I'm sure you'll want board members who can get along with each other.''

Laughter flowed out of her at the thought of her father cooperating with any group of eleven people anywhere in the world. She looked at Blake. "Do you know anybody in this town who can swear to having had a gratifying conversation with my father?'' She'd often thought the problem with her father was his longing for acceptance, but she would never allow herself to say that.

What was certainly mischief gleamed in his eyes. "I didn't know you knew that. What he's like, I mean.''

"Blake, I lived in the house with him until I went away to college.''

His big body settled itself in his desk chair, relaxed, and he twirled a pencil, the only playful thing she'd ever seen him do. "I'll bet you thanked God for college.''

She leaned toward him, enjoying this unfamiliar side of him. "Did I ever! I put on some lipstick before the train left the station.''

A smile played around his lips, mesmerizing her. "What

about your soul? Weren't you afraid you'd burn in hell for that worldly deed?''

"Tell you the truth, it didn't cross my mind. Do you think a bird worries about the cage after it flies out? Not for a second. I thought, *'Free at last!' ''*

Suddenly, his demeanor changed, and she supposed he'd only temporarily forgotten himself, that it was back to business.

"I'll ask Irene to type out this list of prospective board members along with their street and e-mail addresses and their phone numbers. This will take time, so the sooner you get on it, the better.''

"Yes, *sir!''*

His eyebrows went up sharply, but she didn't care if he recognized her insolence. He couldn't change faces with her like a chameleon and expect her to accept it.

"You're not as easygoing as you appear to be, are you?''

She put the tablet in her pocketbook and stood, preparing to leave. "I didn't know anybody thought me easygoing. That is a surprise.''

"Real little tiger, eh?'' he said, walking with her to the door.

She whirled around and he towered over her, inches from her body. *Get a grip on it, girl.* "Tiger, lion, or leopard. Cross me, and I claw. But unless you step out of line, you'll never get so much as a hint of my feline side.''

She wanted to back away from him, but the door trapped her. She didn't like the feeling that pervaded her body, a strange hunger that she suspected had nothing to do with food. He didn't move, and she didn't want him to know what his nearness did to her. Then his pupils seemed to dilate, and his nostrils flared. *Oh, Lord, please let me get away from here without making a fool of myself.*

Summoning all the strength she could muster, she whispered, "Would you please open the door?''

He reached around her in what felt like a half caress, though she knew it wasn't, and turned the knob. She stepped backward and nearly lost her footing, but he grabbed her and pulled her toward him.

"What . . . ?"

She glanced over her shoulder as Judd Folson walked in for his eleven o'clock appointment. And from the man's knowing expression, she didn't doubt that he assumed he'd caught her in Blake Hunter's arms a week after she buried her husband.

She raised herself to her full height—nearly six feet if you took into account her three-inch heels—and looked him straight in the eye. "Good morning, Mr. Folson. Lovely day, isn't it?"

The man nodded in reply, gaping as he did so, and she realized that Blake's arm remained around her waist. She stepped away, stood against the doorjamb, and made herself smile.

"Thanks for your help, Mr. Hunter. I hope Irene can get that list to me in a day or two and I can get started." Nervous words, and she knew it.

But he didn't answer, only stared at her with those piercing eyes and nodded his head, before turning to Judd Folson.

"Have a seat, Judd," Blake said to his visitor, though his thoughts remained with the woman who'd just left. "I just looked over your suit."

"Man, if you could work with that nice little tidbit hanging on to you, I take off my hat to you."

In the process of sitting down, Blake stopped seconds before touching the chair. "What tidbit are you talking about?" Folson was a good client, but that didn't mean he could make a rude statement about another one of his clients. About to slap his right fist into the palm of his left hand, he caught himself and sat down.

Folson shifted uneasily in his chair, and Blake didn't have

to be told that the man noticed his testiness. "Well, I thought you and she were . . . not that I blame you. She's just about the best-looking . . . uh . . . woman around here, and after four or five years as Mrs. Rodgers, she must be—"

Blake interrupted him, because he knew that if he heard him say it, he'd pick him up out of that chair and . . . He told himself to calm down.

"Mr. Folson," he began, though he normally addressed the man by his first name. "I was opening the door for Mrs. Rodgers who stood with her back to it, and when you almost knocked her down, I grabbed her to prevent an accident. I assume you would have done the same."

"Well, sure. I . . . I just thought. Never mind. What do you have for me?"

Blake opened the file and outlined for Folson his options in respect to property he wanted to sell. "You'll get top price for it now, but it's impossible to predict its future value. Depends on property changes in the neighborhood and whether we get aggressive growth in another part of town. My advice is to sell now, take your three hundred percent profit, and consider yourself lucky."

"All right, let it go. I need to get rid of some holdings anyway."

"I'll keep you informed."

He wanted the man to get out of there. He bowled and played soccer and basketball at the same club as Folson and sometimes with him, though he wouldn't call him a friend, but right that minute, he wanted the man out of his sight. He stood, signaling the end of the appointment.

Folson shook hands and went on his way, but Blake walked back and forth in his office until he forced himself to sit down. He let out a sharp whistle as the truth exploded in his brain. Melinda Rodgers's behavior as she walked toward that door was solid evidence that she reciprocated what he felt, and she'd lie if she disowned it. Now, how the devil was he supposed to handle that?

He answered the intercom buzzer. "Yes, Irene."

"Melinda Rodgers on two."

"Hello, Melinda. What can I do for you?"

"Hello, Blake. I have some questions that occurred to me since I left your office. First, is that clause stipulating that I have to marry within a year legal?"

What was she getting at? "It's legal. Why do you ask? You thinking about contesting it?"

"Contest it? Why should I do that? He was entitled to specify his wish. I just don't understand it."

Angry now at himself for his softness toward her and for having reprimanded Folson in her defense, he spoke sharply to her. "It shouldn't be difficult for a woman like you to find a husband. If it's known that you're looking for one, you can have your pick. So, that certainly won't be an obstacle to your inheriting Prescott's estate. Your problem is setting up that foundation."

Her lengthy silence was as much a reprimand as any words could have been. Finally, she said, "And the foundation. Are you sure someone else can't set that up and I approve it?"

"Trust me, you'll do as the will states. That, or nothing. If you want that inheritance, get busy."

He thought she'd put the telephone receiver down and left it, until he heard her say, "Is there a provision in that will that allows me to replace you as its executor?" Her tone, sharp and cold, was meant to remind him that he was her husband's employee, a fact that he never forgot.

He looked down at his tapered and polished fingernails. Perfect. You could even say he had elegant hands. But at that moment, he wanted to send one of them crashing through the wall. Replace him, indeed!

"For whatever reason you'd like to have my head, Melinda, don't even think it. You and I will work together until this is settled."

"I don't suppose you're offering to help me fulfill that second clause in the will."

She let it hang, loaded with meaning and the possibility of misinterpretation. Thank God for the distance between them; if he'd been near her, he didn't know whether he'd have paddled her or . . . or kissed her until she begged him to take her. He told her good-bye at the first opportunity and hung up, shocked at himself. Prescott was dead, but even so, he didn't covet his friend's wife. Melinda had pushed his buttons, but the next time, he'd push hers. And she could count on it.

If she wasn't mistaken, something had happened between Blake and herself while they stood at his office door. For a few seconds, her whole body had anticipated invasion by the wild, primitive being within hand's reach, and she'd been ready to open herself to him. Men who stood six feet four inches tall and had a strong, masculine personality weren't all that uncommon. But add those warm fawnlike eyes that electrified you when he smiled and . . . She grabbed her chest. Oh, Lord. . . . If she could only avoid him.

Melinda dreaded going to church that next Sunday. Custom allowed her to stay away the first Sunday after becoming a widow, but not longer. After the service, she went to her father's office on the first floor of the church, not so much to visit with him as to avoid the condolences of her father's parishioners who huddled in groups at the entrance to the church and on its grounds. She knew what they thought of her, that they believed only wicked women wore high heels, perfume, and makeup and that she had married Prescott for money. For all their righteousness, only one of them had come to sit with her during her husband's final illness.

"You seem tired, Papa," she said. "Maybe you need a vacation."

"Can't afford it. You get busy and set up that foundation, otherwise you'll lose that money."

He wasn't going to inveigle her into putting him on that board; once the word was out, no one else would sit on it.

"I'll get started on it, but I wish everybody would remember that Prescott hasn't been gone three weeks. I need time to adjust."

"Didn't mean to rush you, but you have to make hay while the sun's shining, and people will be more likely to help you now while your grief is fresh."

Melinda hadn't associated her father with greed. Maybe he really did need money for the church. Best not to comment on that. "Yes, sir. I'd better be going. See you soon."

She patted his shoulder and jerked back her hand, remembering that he didn't like being touched. She'd like to know what would happen if he unlocked his emotions, but she wouldn't want to be there. The thought brought Blake Hunter to mind. Now, there was a man who probably controlled the blinking of his eyelids.

After parking her four-year-old Mercury Sable in front of her parents' house, she went in to see her mother. "Why weren't you in church this morning, Mama? You aren't sick, are you?"

"No, honey. Your father had a miniconvention yesterday, and after cooking and serving that gang, I was too tired to get out of bed this morning."

"Papa ought to get you some help. You're practically a slave to those preachers and the members of that church."

Lurlane Jones rolled her eyes and looked toward the ceiling. "Bring me Aladdin and his magic lamp; I'll get some help a lot quicker that way. Your father does what he can."

Her mother had the looks and bearing of a woman of sixty, though she'd just turned fifty, and her father looked as if he hadn't lived a day longer than forty-five years though he'd recently passed his sixtieth birthday.

"It's sapping your life, Mama. The hardest work Papa ever does is preach his sermons, and since my brothers and I are no longer here to help you, you're slaving here all day and half of some nights. You won't catch me doing that for any man. Never!"

Lurlane tightened the belt of her robe and began brushing her long hair in a soothing, rhythmic fashion, as if expressing pleasure with her life and all around her. "We're of different generations, Melinda. When you find a man you love the way I love your father, you'll understand."

Melinda's head came up sharply. "Are you suggesting that I didn't love Prescott?" It hadn't occurred to her to wonder what her parents thought of that marriage, and they hadn't let on.

"You loved him as a friend, a pleasant companion, and only that. You're still an unbroken colt, as your grandfather would say, but that'll change before long."

"My life, the part I held to myself, wasn't secret after all," she said to herself, walking rapidly out of the dining room to escape the sound of the ticking clock—a source of irritation for as far back as she could remember—knowing that her mother would follow. She wrapped her arms around Lurlane, kissed her, and left.

Driving home with her mind on her options, she was glad she'd invested in blue chip stocks most of her teacher's salary and every penny of the allowance that Prescott gave her each month. The payoff was having enough money to support herself while she studied for a Ph.D., and enjoying the choice of remaining among the gossipmongers of Ellicott City or leaving the town. But she could not dishonor Prescott's wishes that she set up that foundation, so school would have to wait one more year.

As she entered the house, she heard Ruby say, "She's not back yet, Mr. Blake. Maybe she stopped by Reverend Jones's house. She does that some Sundays."

Melinda rushed to the phone that rested on a marble-top table in the hallway. "Hello," but he'd already hung up. She looked down at the receiver she held, while disappointment weighed on her like a load of bricks.

Every molecule in her body shouted, "Call him back," but he would want to discuss business, while she . . . She went into her room, threw her hat and pocketbook on her bed, and looked around. Blake Hunter had aggravated her nerves and irritated her libido for almost five years, and it hadn't gotten the better of her. She wasn't going to let him mess up her mind now.

She ignored the telephone's insistent ringing. "Yes, sir, she just walked in. Yoohoo! Miz Melinda, it's Mr. Blake."

"Hello, Blake." Did that cool, modulated voice belong to her?

"Hi." A pause ensued, and she wondered why, as her heartbeat accelerated.

"What is it, Blake?"

"I hope you didn't decide to put Reverend Jones on the foundation's board of trustees."

She stared down at the phone. "I thought we had an understanding about that."

"Yeah. Well, I wanted to be sure."

"Not . . . to worry." The words came out slowly as she realized he'd changed his mind about something, and that her father's membership on the board was not the reason he'd called. She sat on the edge of the bed, perplexed.

"Why are you calling me, Blake?"

"Didn't I just tell you—"

"No you didn't," she said, interrupting him. "But if that's

the way you want it, fine with me.'' Angry at herself for seeming to beg the question, she added in a voice that carried a forced breeziness, ''Y'all have a nice day.''

''You bet,'' he said and hung up.

Pressing him hadn't gained her a thing; she might even have lost a few points with him.

Chapter Two

The biggest error he'd ever made. What the devil had come over him? He'd feasted his eyes on her, eaten at her table, wanted her for nearly five years and kept it to himself. Not once had he done anything as stupid as making that phone call. He'd swear that, until yesterday, she hadn't had an inkling as to how he felt about her. The thing to do was get his mind on something and somebody else. To make himself useful. He put on a pair of jeans, a T-shirt, stuck a baseball cap on his head, got into his Mercury Cougar, and headed for Metropolitan Transition Center in Baltimore, a state facility for short-term prison inmates.

As he entered the institution, he met a priest he'd often seen there. "Got three new ones today," the priest said. "Tough kids. I expect you can do more for them right now than I can."

Blake didn't like the sound of that. "Where are they?"

"Up on 9XX3. Jack will send them down."

"Thanks. As soon as one leaves here, two or three replace him."

The priest shook his head. "And they're so young."

Blake sat on the uncomfortable sofa, drabness facing him from every angle, and waited for the young men. Why would a person risk going back there once he regained his freedom? Yet the prison held dozens of repeat offenders. Finally, the boys arrived, none of them over eighteen.

"I'm Blake. A lot of the guys here take my course in criminal law. Would you like to join?"

"School? Juku, man," the oldest one said. "Man, that's like an overdose of Nytol."

Blake shrugged and pulled his cap further down on his forehead. "I make it cool, man. One of the brothers learned enough law to get his case reopened. I wouldn't think he's any smarter than you."

"I gotta keep my lines open, man. Otherwise, while I'm in here, my territory'll go up for grabs."

The youngest of the three looked at Blake, attentive, but unwilling to cross the leader.

"How long are you in for?" Blake asked the older, talkative one whom he'd sized up as the leader.

"Eighteen months. Why you take up your time coming out here?"

"We brothers have to hang together," Blake said. "The street's mean; it can suck every one of us in like quicksand."

"Man, I ain't fooled by your jeans and sneakers," the older one said. "You don't know nothing 'bout the street, man. It's a pisser out there."

Blake had been waiting for that. It always came down to *are you really one of us?* He rested his left ankle on his right knee, stuck his hands in the front pockets of his jeans, and leaned back.

"I hustled the streets of Atlanta till I owned them. You name it, I did it—running errands on my bike, shining shoes, selling shoestrings, peddling books, peanuts, even the Holy Bible. I delivered packages, did whatever I could to make a living and keep myself in school." He had their attention now, and he'd keep it. "Every cop knew me, and I knew every junkie on the street, but I wasn't their customer."

"Did you rat on them?"

Blake raised an eyebrow and pasted a look of incredulity on his face. "I'm sitting here talking to you. Right?"

"Cool, man. My name's Lobo." The older one held out his hand, palm upward. "Put it right there, man. You're mega."

He supposed that was a compliment, so he thanked Lobo.

The others introduced themselves as Phil, who hadn't said anything previously, and Johnny, who was the youngest of the three. Two potential gang members if he'd ever seen any.

"I'll be here next Saturday at three o'clock when I teach criminal law. Hope to see you brothers in the class." He picked up the bag he'd rested on the floor. "Meanwhile, I brought along a few things you might like to share—some chocolates, writing pads and pens, deodorant, soap, aftershave, things like that. See you Saturday." Rule number one, never overstay your visit.

Lobo extended his hand, and Phil and Johnny did the same. "Chill out, brother," Lobo said. "You da man."

Blake let himself grin. Getting their confidence was the first step. Later, he'd try what the correction institution didn't bother to do—work at correcting them.

When he got outside, it surprised him to see the priest sitting against the hood of his Cougar. "How'd you make out?" the priest asked him.

"I made a dent, but not a very deep one. They've been there less than a week and already they're a little gang."

"Not very encouraging," the priest said. "How'd you get into this?"

Blake walked around to the driver's side of his car. "I'm going to Ellicott City. If you're headed that way, I'll give you a lift."

"I'm going to Baltimore."

"A couple of years back," Blake said, as he headed into Baltimore proper, "I had a client, a young Moslem man, who told me he'd managed to turn some of the brothers around, giving up one day each week to teach in the Lawton Prison Program. He impressed me, and I decided to do something similar."

"I wish I knew how he did it."

"He had his successes as well as some failures, you know." He slowed down to avoid colliding with one of Maryland's road hogs. "By the time we get to these criminals, most are too far gone for help, but I decided to try with the young ones." He paused for a minute. "I'm not being disrespectful, Father, but it might help if you learned the language of the street and took off that collar. They don't want to be corrected, so you have to be subtle."

"Thanks. You don't play golf by any chance, do you?" the priest asked him.

"You bet. I'm no Tiger Woods, but I occasionally shoot around par."

"Then maybe we could go out together some Saturdays after your class. My name is Mario Biotti."

"Blake Hunter. It'll be a pleasure."

He dropped the priest off in Baltimore, and headed home. He loved junk food but didn't allow himself to have it often. Today, however, he pulled into Kentucky Fried Chicken and ordered a bucket of southern-fried buffalo wings, french fries, buttermilk biscuits, and coleslaw. Walking out with his treasure, he patted his washboard belly, assuring himself that he could occasionally indulge in junk food and keep the trim physique in which he took pride. As he opened the door of his car, he heard his name.

"Mr. Hunter. Well, this is a pleasant surprise."

Rachel Perkins. Just what he needed. "Hello, Miss Perkins," he said, remembered his baseball cap, and went through the motion of tipping his hat. "Great day we're having," he added, getting into his car as quickly as he could and igniting the engine.

Her obvious disappointment told him he'd escaped an invitation that he wouldn't have wanted to accept, and a grin crawled over his face as he waved at her and drove out of the parking lot. He'd always enjoyed outfoxing people, and Rachel Perkins was outdone.

At home, he put the food on the kitchen counter, washed his hands, and was preparing to eat when the telephone rang.

"Hi, Callie. What's up? I was going to call you as soon as I ate."

"Nothing much. Mama said Papa's still poorly, but I haven't been down there since we last talked. He keeps driving himself just as he always did, even though we send him money and he doesn't have to do it."

"He's a hard man, and that extends to himself. Thank God I got out of there when I did."

"Tell me about it. I have to thank you for insisting I get my General Education Diploma and for sending me to college. No telling what I'd be doing now if you hadn't."

"Water under the bridge, Callie. You only needed a chance. Why don't you come up here for part of your vacation? You haven't seen my house yet."

"Maybe I'll do that. Don't forget to call Mama."

"I won't. Hang in there."

He hung up and walked back into the kitchen with heavy steps. He dreaded going to Six Mile, Alabama, but no matter what his father's shortcomings, his mother needed his support, and he'd have to get down there soon. He sat against the kitchen counter, propped his left foot on the bottom rung of a step stool, and bit into a piece of chicken. Somehow, it failed to satisfy him as it usually did on those rare occasions when he ate it. He put the food in the refrigerator and went out on his patio. What the devil was wrong with him? He was hungry, but had neither a desire nor a taste for food, and that didn't make sense: he loved to eat. Maybe he needed a check-up.

The phone rang again, and he raced to answer it. "Hello. *Hello?*"

The caller had the wrong number. He slammed his left foot against a leather puff that he'd bought in Morocco and considered himself fortunate to have chosen that rather than the wall as a means of relieving his frustration. *Damn her, anyway.*

Melinda looked over the list of people Blake suggested for membership on the board of the Prescott Rodgers Foundation, as she'd decided to call it, and ran a line through the name of Andrew Carnegie Jackson. The man's parents named him Joseph, but he changed it, claiming that Joseph reminded him of the song "Old Black Joe." A man with money, he'd said, ought to have a name to go with it. Hardly a social event took place in Ellicott City that someone didn't make a joke of it.

She stared at the name Will Lamont, and grabbed the phone with such recklessness that she jerked it off the table and the receiver fell on the floor.

"What are you trying to do to me?" she asked, her voice sharp and cutting, when Blake answered the phone. "Will Lamont is head trustee at my father's church. I can't put him on this board unless I appoint my father too."

"Then scratch off his name."

"That's exactly what I did. How could you—"

"If he's off the list, what's the problem? I gave you a bunch of names. Do what you please with them."

Her fingernails dug into the flesh of her palm. "Thanks so much. You're supposed to be helping me, but it's clear you're waiting for me to blow the whole thing." She held the phone in her left hand and pounded softly and rhythmically on the desk with her right fist.

"So you think I'm an ogre? Fine. I like that; it means I don't have anything to live up to."

She wanted to . . . What *did* she want? She'd better rope in her thoughts. "Prescott talked about you as if you could change the direction of the wind. I wish you'd show *me* some of your virtues. So far, you're batting pretty low."

"Well, I'll be doggoned. You want to see some of my virtues. Why didn't you say so? I'll be happy to oblige you."

She looked down at the print of her little fingernail in her right fist and shook her body, symbolically shedding the goose pimples that his words brought to her arms. Suggestive words that imbedded in her brain images of his beautiful fingers stroking her flesh.

Angered that he seduced her so easily, she said, her voice crusted with ice, "What are you talking about?"

"Me? Same thing you're talking about. Why?" The words came out almost on a laugh. Mocking. Yes, and accusing. "Did I say something wrong?"

She escaped to the safety of talk about the foundation and the list before her. "Who drew up this list, you or Irene?"

"I gave her the names. She did the rest. She's extremely efficient."

She didn't give two hoots about Irene's efficiency, and she was sure he knew it. "Did you put these booby traps in here intentionally, or did you have temporary lapses of political savvy?"

"I don't have such lapses. If you see a name on that list,

it's because I intended for it to be there. I don't mix foolishness with business.''

''I see.'' She couldn't help needling him, even though she knew that was a substitute for something far more intimate. ''One of your virtues. Right?''

She heard the wind swoosh out of him and prepared herself for biting words, but the expectation didn't materialize.

''Think over this conversation, Melinda, and let me know what you make of it. Any disinterested person would think you're after more than you're receiving. Think about what you want before you get in too deep.''

She had to let that stab go by, because he'd changed from teasing to baiting, and she refused to bite. ''Since I'm not a disinterested party, I won't be able to judge. Right?'' She began walking back and forth from her desk to her bed. ''The will says you're to help me; if you don't, I'll do it without you.''

''You might as well cooperate with *me;* it will be done to my satisfaction or there'll be no foundation and no inheritance.''

She swore under her breath. ''A person with a flea brain could see through what you're doing. I refuse to fail, because that would make you happy.''

She imagined that one of his mesmerizing grins had taken possession of his face when he said, ''You don't want me to be happy?''

''Does the sun rise in the north?'' she asked him. ''This isn't getting me anywhere. See you.'' She hung up and immediately wished she hadn't. Jostling with him had been fun, and while they were at it, she'd had a warm, cozy sensation, far from the forsaken feeling she had now.

An hour later, his belly full of calories, Blake lay flat on his back on his living room floor listening to Ledbetter sing the blues. He wasn't contented, but he felt a lot better than he did before she called to chew him out. If only he had a firm handle on whatever was going on between them.

He voiced his frustration with a satisfying expletive. She could raise hell and threaten all she pleased, but she'd fulfill the terms of that will or she'd be just another widow. She married Prescott for money, and if she wanted to get it, she'd have to earn it. She could heat him to boiling point; it wouldn't make an iota of difference.

Melinda decided to tackle Judd Folson first and get that over with. Too bad that he'd misunderstood the scene with Blake and her when he'd walked into Blake's office.

"Good morning, Mr. Folson. This is Melinda Rodgers. I'm calling to—"

"Oh, you needn't worry, Melinda. Blake explained that he had to catch you when he opened the door. I didn't—"

The nerve of him. She told herself not to react. "Mr. Folson, my late husband's will requires that I establish a foundation to support remedial reading here in Ellicott City, and I'm inquiring as to your willingness to serve on the board. I'm canvassing twelve of the town's leading citizens. It's a charity foundation, so there's no honorarium for this." She heard a sound like someone clearing his throat and waited for the verdict.

"The leading citizens, eh? Well, now, that's right decent of you. You can put my name down."

Martha Greene agreed to serve, but not before she let Melinda know what she thought of the Reverend Booker Jones. "That man thinks everybody's headed straight for hell, everybody but him, that is. It's a wonder you turned out as well as you did."

Melinda closed her eyes tight. Ten more to go, and she could shake Ellicott City dust from her feet, except for Christmas and Mother's Day. *Turned out as well as you did! Grin and bear it, girl,* she admonished herself. *It'll soon be in the past.*

"Then you'll serve, Mrs. Greene? Thank you so much. My husband would be pleased."

"You think I'm doing it for him?" the woman shot back. "I'm signing on because of all the people around here who can barely read a street sign. Prescott Rodgers stayed as far away from the citizens of this town as he could get. Anybody would have thought he was scared we'd absorb some of his money."

Just a sweet, loving human being. "Whatever your reason, Mrs. Greene, I do appreciate your help."

She hung up. "Whew." That was as much as she could take for one evening. She went over the lesson plans for her classes in American literature and contemporary fiction writing, got ready for bed, and put on a Billie Holiday CD. Jazz, Mozart, and Brian McKnight ballads could lull her into contentment every time. She sat on the floor with her back against her bed and closed her eyes to let the sound of Billie singing "Why Not Take all Of Me?" wash over her. Within seconds, Blake Hunter filled her thoughts, and then she could feel his fingers gently loving her neck, face, arms, her belly, thighs, all of her. She gripped the coverlet on her bed as he hovered above her, and when he wiped tears from her eyes, she felt the dampness on her face and knew that she cried.

Melinda got to school the next morning, but she'd tossed in bed all night begging for the sleep that never came, and every muscle in her body ached. When questioned about her obvious fatigue, she explained to Rachel that working on the foundation had worn her out.

"I thought maybe you'd been out with that fine brother who's handling Prescott's will."

"You saw him the last time I did."

Rachel lowered her gaze, and Melinda couldn't help noticing

the look of embarrassment on the woman's face. "Are you suggesting that I'm seeing Blake socially?" she asked Rachel. "Well . . . uh . . . no, but you know how people talk." Melinda didn't press Rachel, but the woman's words failed to placate her. She'd noticed her fascination with Blake, and Melinda didn't blame her. Who would? Blake Hunter wasn't just handsome; his tough, masculine personality and riveting presence jumped out at you, and you had to pay attention to him. Any female between the ages of eight and eighty with warm blood running through her veins would give the man a second look.

"What are they saying about me and Blake Hunter? What *can* they say?"

Rachel patted Melinda's shoulder and looked as if she wanted to deny her statement. "Girl, our folks love to gossip. You know that."

She stared down at Rachel, who stood little more than five feet five inches in her three-inch heels. "It isn't just 'our folks' who gossip; all small-town people gossip; they don't have much else to do." Seeing the relief on Rachel's face, she knew the woman had been saved from embarrassment. Or maybe from lying.

Later that afternoon, the school's superintendent called Melinda to his office. "Mrs. Rodgers, I understand your late husband's will contains provisions that aren't favorable to you. I was—"

"Who told you that? As far as I'm concerned, there's nothing bad in that will."

"But I heard you'd been disinherited, and I thought you might ask Mr. Blake to settle some money on the school."

She propped her hands on her hips and glared at him. It wasn't easy to ring her bell, but he'd just managed to do it. "Is that all, Dr. Hicks?" Without waiting for his answer, she spun around and left.

On an impulse, she stopped by Blake's office on the way home. If he couldn't do something to arrest the awful gossip, she'd chuck the whole thing.

"Melinda. What a surprise," he said and stood when she entered his office. "What can I do for you?"

She explained the reasons for being there. "It started yesterday with Judd Folson. Even Rachel's repeating these stupidities. I'm fed up."

The tips of his fingers warmed her elbow. "Come on in." He didn't go to his desk as she would have expected, but led her to the leather sofa that rested beneath a collection of paintings by African-American artists and sat there beside her.

"Tell me about it." His voice conveyed an unfamiliar softness, a tenderness, maybe even an intimacy. At least she thought so.

"It's . . . I know a lot of people don't like my father, and I understand that. I even accept it, because he's a big dose for me sometimes, but what did Prescott ever do to anybody?"

"Ordinary people envy the rich, Melinda. He didn't have to do anything to anybody."

Her eyes widened, and her pocketbook slipped from her lap to the floor. She caught herself, but not quickly enough to hide her shock. He picked up her pocketbook and put it on the sofa beside her.

"Why are you surprised? The poor have hated the rich since the beginning of time."

She couldn't help staring at him. "Rich? What do you mean, 'rich'? I know Prescott was well off, but rich?"

Now, she had obviously surprised *him*. "Prescott Rodgers was worth millions, and his estate will earn royalties probably for as long as people wear glasses and use cameras."

She slumped against the back of the sofa and slowly closed her mouth. "I never dreamed . . . Prescott never talked about his finances, and I didn't question him about them. I knew we were well off. We had what we needed, but if he hadn't given me anything more than the first real peace I'd had in my life, I would have been contented.''

He stared at her for so long that she decided she'd lost his sympathy, that she'd better leave. But he restrained her with a hand on her shoulder, a hand whose warmth she felt to the marrow of her being.

"Don't go. Please. This takes some getting used to.''

"Why? What did you think? That I—''

He cut her off. "Don't say it. Right now, I don't know what to think. Prescott talked freely to me about his affairs, or at least I think he did, so it didn't occur to me that he didn't share them with his wife.''

She didn't like the chill that settled in her chest. "There was no reason why he should have.'' She stood and walked to the door, giving him no choice but to follow her.

"If you want to take over the matter of that foundation, it's all right with me,'' Blake said.

"You know I can't do that. I've sworn to do as he wished, and I can't sidestep my integrity and live with myself.''

His voice behind her, so close to her ear, sent shock waves throughout her body, and she had to will herself not to turn around.

"I . . . I'll help you with it. Maybe . . .'' His breath seemed to shorten, and his words became rasping sounds. "We'll . . . like I said, I'll help you.''

And then it hit her. His opinion of her didn't differ from what the rest of Ellicott City thought about her. "You don't believe me, do you? You think I knew and that I can't wait to get my hands on Prescott's money, don't you? Isn't that right?''

The sudden coolness of her body told her he'd stepped away from her back. She saw his hand on the doorknob and remembered that moment two weeks earlier when it had rested on her waist. Protective. Possessive. He turned the knob, and when

she risked a glance at him, she bit back the gasp that nearly
sprang from her throat. Desire, fierce and primitive, shone in
his eyes.

"What do you want me to say?"

The words seemed to rush out of him. Perhaps he'd found
some kind of reprieve, had grabbed the opportunity to reply
logically, but without saying anything meaningful. She didn't
answer. But she hurt. Oh, the pain of it, shooting through her
like a spray of bullets tearing up her insides. The ache of
unappeased desire, and the anguish of knowing he thought so
little of her. With her hand covering his, she pulled open the
door and rushed down the corridor to the elevator. He didn't
think well of her, but he wanted her. She didn't know if she
could stand it.

He watched her rush away from him, her hips swaying almost
as if in defiance above the most perfect pair of props a man
ever looked at. Seconds earlier, he'd come close to doing what
he'd sworn never to do. As she reached the elevator, he closed
his door and leaned against it. It wouldn't do for her to look
back and find him watching her. She needed his help; without
it, the good people of Ellicott City would laugh at her, and he
couldn't bear to see her ridiculed.

A man confided things to his lawyer, but to keep his wife
in the dark about his wealth . . . He ran his hand over the hair
at the back of his head. He didn't believe she was lying, but
something didn't jell. A woman who'd been married for almost
five years ought to know how to finesse a man's revved-up
libido. Any man's. But she didn't make small talk, didn't joke,
didn't say anything that would have cooled him off. That level
of naivete in a twenty-nine-year-old widow was incomprehensible. He should keep his distance, but he didn't see an alternative
to sitting with her while she contacted the people on her list.

She'd had time to drive home, so he called her. "Melinda, this is Blake. Suppose you stop by after school, and we'll go through your list till we get twelve people to agree to serve. The sooner we do this, the better."

Her long silence annoyed him until he let himself remember that she was probably as shaken by their near-encounter as he. "All right," she said at last in a voice that suggested disinterest. "I want to finish it as soon as possible."

He believed that, but not her feigned disinterest. "Till tomorrow then."

She hung up, obviously discombobulated, and he was certainly at the root of her discomfort. While he tried to think of a way to smooth their relationship without indicting himself, the phone rang.

"Reverend Jones on one," Irene said.

"Hunter. What may I do for you, sir?"

"I just talked with that daughter of mine. She doesn't seem to understand my position in Ellicott City. If anybody should be on that board, it's me. You're her advisor, so I'm depending on you to set her straight."

Here we go! He sat down and, to make certain he stayed calm, he picked up a red-ink pen and began doodling. "Reverend Jones, my job is to advise my client, not to dictate to her, but I've warned her that it's best not to give either a political or a religious flavor to the board. Further, I've suggested that she exclude from consideration members of her family and of Prescott's family." He hadn't, but the words might convince Jones not to ride hard on Melinda.

"That's bunkum. Rodgers didn't have any family. At least not that anybody around here ever heard about, and they can't come in now and start demanding the man's money when it belongs to Melinda."

"You needn't worry about that, sir. Have a good day."

He hung up and considered the pleasure he'd get out of

pitching something—*anything*—across the room. Booker Jones planned to aggravate him to distraction, and he'd probably do it from the hallowed perch of his pulpit.

His anticipation of Booker's tirade proved prophetic. Melinda forced herself to go to the Third Evangelical House of Prayer—her father's small church—the following Sunday morning and hadn't been seated for ten minutes when she realized that her personal affairs would be the text of her father's sermon.

"Children, obey your parents. That's a commandment. But does my own daughter obey it? I say to you, parents, don't be discouraged, as I am not discouraged. They will perish, every last one of them. But our reward will come, and oh, how beautiful it will be. Let them know that money is the root of all evil. Let them know that they will burn in hell. And brothers and sisters, it won't be a little blister, and there won't be any salve to put on it . . ."

Tuning him out, all she heard was the drone of his voice. Getting up and leaving wasn't an option, so she sat there and let herself think of pleasant things. Her life with Prescott and the peace and contentment she'd known with him. But as she reminisced, it came to her forcefully that Prescott had treated her as if she were a child, taking care of her material needs, giving her an allowance, never broaching the subject of sex— not that she'd have welcomed it. She'd gone from one father to another one, and neither had prepared her for her encounters with Blake Hunter. A tough man with a soft core, she surmised, and a masculine persona that fired her up and awakened the womanliness in her. She hadn't known the meaning of the word *lust* until she first looked into his eyes and he stared at her until her nipples tightened and her blood raced as if she were in a marathon.

She wanted to close her eyes and think about him, but didn't
dare for fear her father would think she slept during his sermon.
At last the choir sang the closing hymn, and she rushed out of
the church.

"Didn't Reverend Jones really preach today? Bless the
Lord," one of the sisters said to her.

No way was that woman going to make her concur with her
father's accusations. "My father speaks his mind," she told
the startled woman and brushed past her.

With her heart lodged in her throat, she knocked on Blake's
office door the next afternoon at three-thirty. He opened the
door, smiled, and her pulse kicked into overdrive.

"Hi."

Not *hello,* but *hi.* She looked up at him and tried to smile
back, but she suspected she hadn't succeeded. What had caused
this about-face?

"Hello. Uh . . . hi."

If he noticed her lack of composure, he didn't let on. "I
wish you'd brought some fries or something. I didn't get any
lunch. Been preparing for a trial tomorrow morning."

"I could go get some," she said, wondering at his turn of
mind.

His fingers touched her elbow, and he walked with her to
his desk. "No need for that. I'll order something by phone.
What would you like? I'm having french fries and ginger ale."

"You haven't eaten since breakfast, and you're ordering
french fries?"

A sheepish expression flashed across his face. "Come to
think of it, all I had for breakfast was a glass of V-8 juice."

She shook her head in wonder. "How can you look the way
you do if you don't eat properly?"

His eyebrows went up, and she knew she'd said the wrong thing.

"How do I . . . Never mind. Most days I eat bran flakes and a banana. That better?"

"Decidedly," she said and put forth a lot of effort to prevent his seeing how relieved she was that he hadn't finished that sentence. When he'd eaten the french fries, he opened both bottles of ginger ale, wrapped a napkin around one, and handed it to her.

"Ready?"

She nodded. "Ready as I'll ever be."

A grin converted his whole face into a thing of beauty. She'd better concentrate on that board of directors, or anything other than him that would occupy her mind. The man was safer in a less jovial mood.

"Let's try Alice Pride first," Blake suggested. "She craves social status, so she ought to be a shoe-in."

And indeed she was. "I'm just too glad to do some good for my town," Alice said. "Just let me know when you're calling the first meeting. I'll be there."

And so it went for the first two calls. Then Melinda dialed Luther Williams and told him the purpose of her call.

"What?" she asked, and her face must have mirrored her horror at Luther Williams's indictment of her, because Blake snatched the phone.

"This is Blake Hunter. We're working on setting up this foundation according to Rodgers's will. What's the problem, Luther?"

"Well . . . I . . . You know what everybody says. I mean, you don't expect me to join in with a kept woman to—"

"What the hell are you talking about, man? This foundation was Prescott Rodgers's bequest. And what do you mean by trashing a woman's reputation on the basis of gossip? That's slander."

Melinda put the list on the desk, picked up her pocketbook that she'd placed on the floor, and started for the door.

"Oh, no, you don't," he called after her and slammed the receiver into its cradle. "Is that all it takes to make you tuck your tail in and run? Is it?"

She whirled around and slammed into him. "You don't know what it's . . . like," she whispered, as the fire began to blaze in his eyes. The belt on his trousers touched her belly. So close. Lord, he was there, and she could have him. She closed her eyes to hide the temptation before her.

"You're not a coward, are you? You won't let them beat you down. I won't let you run. Do you hear me? Stand up to them. Show the bastards you don't care what they say."

"Bu . . . bu . . . but I . . . I *do* care. I do."

Shivers coursed through her as he locked her to him. Startled, she looked into his fierce eyes, then dropped her gaze to his mouth and parted her lips. For a brief, poignant moment, he stared down at her. Open. Pliable. Susceptible to her. His tremors shook her, and her nerves tingled with exhilaration when she heard his hoarse groan of capitulation. Then his mouth was on her, and his tongue stabbed at her lips until she opened and, at last, had him inside of her. His big hand gripped her buttocks and she undulated wildly against him as his velvet tongue promised her ecstasy, plunging in and out of her and testing every crevice of her mouth. Strong and commanding like the man himself. He held her head while he plied her mouth with sweet loving, stroked her back, her shoulders, and her buttocks until she sucked his tongue deep into her mouth and feasted. When his hand went to her breast, she pressed it to her while his fingers twirled her turgid nipple. Hungry for all of him, she spread her legs and he rose hard and strong against her. She slumped into him and might have fallen if he hadn't lifted her, carried her to the sofa, and sat down with her in his lap.

For a long while, he sat there, rocking her and stroking her, soothing her with a tenderness she'd never known.

"It wasn't any use, was it?" he said at last.

She knew what he meant and didn't pretend otherwise. "Looks that way. But it shouldn't have happened. I have enough problems as it is."

"I won't argue with you about that. We have to work together on this foundation, and don't forget, there's one more clause."

"How could I forget *that?*" she asked, getting to her feet. "I think I'd better go now."

"Do you want me to . . . Can I drive you home? I mean . . . do you need me for . . . something?" He gasped it, as if releasing the words pained him all the way to his gut.

She shook her head. "I drove, but thanks."

He walked with her to the door and stood looking down at her. Nobody had to tell her what he was thinking or what he wanted. Suddenly, his right shoulder lifted in a quick shrug, and she knew he'd won over temptation. At least one of them had sense. If he'd kissed her again, she wouldn't have left the way she entered. That much strength she doubted she had. But what about tomorrow and the next day and the next?

He winked at her and grinned. "Don't worry, Melinda. There isn't much I set myself to do that I can't manage. See you tomorrow."

By the time she reached her car, her breath came in short gasps, but that didn't explain her inability to steady her fingers enough to get the key in the ignition and start the vehicle. After a few minutes, she gave up. Why had everything become so difficult? She wanted to lay her head on the steering wheel and wake up in Italy, Switzerland, Kenya, or anywhere but Ellicott City.

The people had the same character as the town: museum pieces, all show and little substance. If she got involved with Blake, the busybodies would assume they'd been right all along, and if she stayed in Ellicott City, she didn't see how she could avoid it. He might have the mental toughness of a samurai warrior, but she'd been in his arms, and she knew how badly he wanted her. The next time . . . For five years, she'd hungered for him, locked him in the privacy of her heart and the recesses of her mind, never revealing to anyone what she felt and how it pained her. And now, he'd transformed her into a hot and passionate woman, a willing lover. She didn't believe in lying to herself, so she didn't promise herself she'd resist him.

Blake stood at the window in his office and looked down on Old Columbia Pike where he could see the top of Melinda's green Mercury Sable. Why didn't she drive off? He didn't want to become involved with her, but he'd had her in his arms, felt her tremors, smelled her heat and tasted her sweetness, and he wouldn't bet five cents that he wouldn't touch her again. When a woman wanted him as badly as she did . . . He swallowed hard. His hands had roamed her body and she'd relished it, had opened herself to him, as uninhibited as a tigress in heat. And he was starved for her.

"Blake, I've been buzzing you," Irene said, and he turned to see her standing in the doorway between their offices.

"Oh, thanks. What is it?"

"Lacy Morgan's on line one."

He swore. "Tell her I emigrated to Alaska."

"What? I beg your pardon."

What a great idea. "You heard me. Tell her exactly that."

"Bu . . . but . . . How do I phrase it? I can't just lie."

"Tell her I told you I moved to Alaska." He snapped his finger. "Oh, yes, and I didn't leave a forwarding address, a phone number, fax number, or an e-mail address."

She stared at him as if he'd lost his mind. "That is an order, Irene."

"Yes, sir ... I mean, Blake."

His laughter followed her rapidly retreating figure, a cleansing release that he'd needed and needed badly. With luck, Lacy Morgan would consider herself insulted. Now, if he could just straighten out the rest of his life that easily. Not a chance. He grabbed his briefcase, got in his car, and drove to the Patapsco River where the swiftly moving water never failed to soothe him. He looked at the late-day sun, slowly dying, its rays filtering through the leaves of the oak and beech trees that towered in the distance. A light, fresh breeze frolicked against his body, cooling and refreshing it. Pretty soon it would be night and, as on every other night, he'd be all by himself. He took his cell phone out of his briefcase, pulled air through his front teeth, shrugged, and put the phone away. He didn't want to hear any voice but hers.

Chapter Three

"Who is it?" Melinda called downstairs to Ruby when she heard the doorbell.

"Uh, it's . . . Mr. . . . What did you say your name was?"

"Humphrey. Jonas Humphrey."

"Jonas Humphrey, ma'am."

Now, who could that be? She knew Prescott's few associates, or thought she did. During the last two years, Blake had been their only visitor. But after that bombshell Blake had dropped about her late husband's finances, she couldn't be sure about anything concerning Prescott. She kicked off her bedroom shoes, stuck her feet in a pair of loafers, and went downstairs.

"I don't think we've met, Mr. Humphrey. What can I do for you?"

"Well, miss"—he looked around, shifting his gaze from

place to place as if appraising the room's appointments—
"could we sit down, perhaps? I'd like a soda or anything cold,
if you don't mind."

She knew a shifty look when she saw it, and she wasn't
going to be taken in by this interloper. "Would you please tell
me why you're here?" she asked the man. Around forty or
forty-five years old, she supposed, he projected self-confidence,
though she wouldn't have credited him with a right to it.

She leaned against the piano and trailed the fingers of her
left hand rapidly over the bass keys in a show of impatience.
"Well?"

He cleared his throat and looked approvingly at the Steinway
Grand. "I don't suppose you know it, but my beloved Heddy
passed on about six months ago, and I find the burden just too
heavy to bear. When your dear father was preaching night
before last, it came to me clear as your hand before you that
he was leading me straight to you. I own a little shop down at
the end of Main Street." He took a card from his pocket,
handed it to her, and she read *Humphrey's Firewood*. "It's not
much, but everybody around here needs wood."

Where was this leading? "What does all that have to do
with me?" she asked him, though she'd begun to guess the
answer.

"Reverend Jones said a woman shouldn't be alone, that she
needs a man's protection. I'm sure he taught you that from
childhood. Well, since we're both alone, and . . . well, I thought
we might get together. I see you like music. I do, too." He sat
down and crossed his knee, though she remained standing. "I
got all the records Sister Rosetta Thorpe and Hank Williams
ever made. I had one by Lightnin' Hopkins, but my dear beloved
smashed it one day when she got mad with me. God rest her
soul."

She'd had enough. More than enough, in fact. "Mr. . . . er

. . . Humphrey, did you say your name was? I am not interested in getting married. Now, I'd appreciate it if you'd excuse me." She called Ruby. "Would you please let this gentleman out? And, Ruby, don't let anybody else in here unless you know them."

The door closed, and Ruby called up to her. "All right, ma'am. He said he knowed Mr. Rodgers. I'm telling you some of these mens is the biggest liars."

Had her father put that man up to proposing to her? She sat down and telephoned him.

"Jonas Humphrey?" he asked her, a tone of incredulity in his voice. "You mean that thief down on Main Street? Why, he'd steal a cane from a blind man. Of course I didn't send him over there. You watch out, girl, because they'll be hearing about that will. Not that it would hurt you to get married. A woman shouldn't be alone—"

She'd heard that a hundred times already. "Sorry, Papa, but I have to go. Talk to you again soon."

"All right, but you come to prayer meeting tomorrow night."

She dressed and rushed to meet Rachel at Side Streets Restaurant. The historic old mill pleased her more than the wonderful seafood served there. Its quaintness gave her a sense of solidness, of permanence. They had barely seated themselves when Ray Sinclair entered with his latest girlfriend. In her single days, she'd been enamored of Ray, but he had ignored her, often seeming to make a point of it. The day he stepped in front of her and got into the taxi she'd called, her affection for him dissipated like chaff in a windstorm. But on this occasion, he seated his date, left her at the table, and walked over to speak with Melinda.

"Terribly sorry to hear of your great loss, Melinda. If I can do anything to help, just snap your fingers."

She leaned back in the booth and spoke with dispassion. "I don't need anything, Ray. My husband provided well for me and, if he hadn't, I provide well for myself. Nice seeing you."

Rachel's eyes seemed to have doubled in size. "Why'd you dust him off like that? He's the most eligible man around here. If that doesn't beat all—"

Melinda threw up her hands. "When I had a crush on him before I got married, he flaunted it, showed me as often as he could that he thought himself too good for me. Now he wants to know what he can do for me. I guess he's been listening to all the gossip, or maybe he's heard about the will. That poor girl he's got with him is welcome to him."

She'd hardly walked into her house when her phone rang. Ruby had left for the day, so she waited for the voice on her answering machine.

"I was wondering if you might like go with me down to Lake Kittamaqundi for the Fourth of July celebration. It's nice and casual. Give us a chance to get reacquainted."

Why was she supposed to recognize his voice? She did, but he didn't need to know that. "Who is this?" she asked.

"This is Ray," he said, obviously crestfallen.

"Now let me see, hmmm. I'll have to let you know."

"We'll have a good time. I'll order a picnic basket, some wine, and . . . Listen, we'll do it up big."

"Are we still talking about watching kids shoot marbles and dogs play catch down by that lake?"

"Uh . . . well, there's the fireworks, you know. Anyhow, I'll call in a day or so to see what you decided. I'm glad you're going. It'll be great."

It wouldn't hurt him to hope; he might recall the many times he'd let her hope and pray, and all to no avail. Of all the men in Ellicott City, Ray Sinclair was least likely to get a second glance from her.

If she were certain of the reason for his sudden interest, she might be amused, but she remembered Luther Williams's insulting suggestion, the awful accusation that had brought her into Blake's arms, and she no longer felt like playing games with Ray. Who knew what he'd heard or what he wanted? Tomorrow, she'd work on that foundation, much as she hated doing so. But the sooner she finished it and got out of Ellicott City, the happier she'd be.

He knew it was a dead giveaway, opening the door before she'd hardly had time to ring the bell, but the entire day had been one long wait for three-thirty.

"Hi." He meant it to sound casual, and he hoped it did, but he didn't feel one bit nonchalant about her. "Ready to tackle that list?" he asked, mostly to remind her, if not himself, that they were together for business and not social purposes.

"That's why I'm here. Whether I'm ready for it is something else." She was looking directly into his eyes as if searching for something important. It wasn't a stare, more like an appraisal. Or a question, as if she didn't really know him and wanted answers about him.

And she was getting to him, too, so he made light of it. "I don't have crumbs around my mouth, do I?"

The back of her right hand moved slowly over his left cheek in a gentle, yet astounding caress. "Your mouth is perfect. Let's tackle the mayor first."

"What do you mean by that?"

She threw her briefcase on the sofa and walked away from him in the direction of his desk. "I mean the mayor will probably be difficult, so let's call him and get it over with."

He caught up with her and stopped her with a hand on her

right shoulder. "Baloney. You know I wasn't talking about the mayor. You walk in here, make a suggestive remark, caress me, and then stroll off as if all you've done is toss a piece of paper into the wastebasket." He pushed back his rising irritation. "Honey, you play with me, and you will get burned as sure as night follows day."

She stepped away from him. "Oh, for goodness' sake. I was just being pleasant."

He imagined that his face expressed his incredulity; he refused to believe she didn't know a come-on from a pleasant pat. "Pleasant? Yeah. Sure. And I'm standing in the middle of the Roman Forum."

"Oh, don't make such a hullabaloo over a simple, friendly gesture. If you wanted to hear some real corn, you should have been in on the conversations I had with two would-be suitors today."

His head snapped up. "Who? You mean—"

"One guy proposed marriage, and the other one's an egotist who thinks all he has to do is phone me. Biggest laugh I ever got."

She could see the perspiration on his forehead, and he knew it, but he couldn't do a thing about it. He couldn't even reach for his handkerchief, because she'd glued her gaze on him. He laid his head to one side and decided to go for broke.

"Not bad for one day. At this rate, you can't miss. If we can finish this list, you'll be free to get on with that other business."

Now what had he done? She'd wilted like a crushed rose. He looked downward and kicked the carpet with the toe of his left shoe, ashamed that his words—spoken to hide his own feelings—had bruised hers. The urge to take her in his arms and soothe her almost overwhelmed him, but he knew the consequences if he gave in to it. He'd tempered his opinion of her, but too much remained unexplained, and not all of it was pretty. The wisest thing he could do would be to keep a good solid distance between them. With her standing there open and vulnerable, a defenseless beauty, he laughed to himself. If he was serious about staying away from her, he'd better pray for sainthood.

She straightened her shoulders and sat down, and his admiration for her soared.

"Good afternoon, Mayor Washington," Melinda said, and continued with her reason for calling. "I hope I can count on you to serve."

She held the phone away from her as if to protect her eardrums, and he took it. He'd rather not get on the wrong side of His Honor, the mayor, but he said, "Frank, this is Blake Hunter. I'd be careful about that kind of talk if I were you." He winced as he thought of Melinda's ordeal with the people of Ellicott City. "Mrs. Rodgers is setting up a foundation as prescribed in her late husband's will. If you slander her as you were doing, she'll sue you, and as representative of her husband's estate, I'd have to take you on."

"*You?*" The mayor sounded as if he was stunned.

"You got it. I'd rather not do that, buddy, but you know me. I'll bite the bullet every time."

"Sorry, brother," the mayor went on, "but . . . you know she's not fit for something so important as that foundation is to this community."

Blake tightened his fist, then he ground his teeth. *Count to ten, man,* he told himself, loosening his tie. "Have you forgotten that there won't be a foundation unless she sets it up?"

"In that case the money goes to the city. Right?"

"A million will go to the city for the benefit of the homeless alone and the rest to a charity event or organization of my choice. It will pay for you to cooperate."

"That's not the way I read it. If necessary, we'll go to court."

"Forget that, buddy. You'll only be wasting time and money."

Melinda grabbed the phone. "Excuse me, Blake, but I just want to tell the mayor that he will not serve on this board, not now or ever. That's right, sir." She hung up.

"You just made an enemy, but he deserved it. Let's get on with this."

Well after seven that evening, they could count twelve people who were willing to serve on the board. Melinda leaned back in the chair, locked her hands behind her head, and blew out a long breath.

"I'm pooped."

He didn't doubt it. "Me too. How about something to eat? Let's go around the corner to Tersiguel's. I feel like some decent food."

"Fine. Where's the ladies' room? I need to freshen up. I'll eat what Ruby cooked for me some other time."

"There's one just off Irene's office. I thought you were too pooped to bother with hair and lipstick and things like that."

"Mr. Hunter, I never get that tired."

They'd barely seated themselves when Martha Greene paused at their table. "Oh, how nice to see you, Mr. Hunter! Good evening, Melinda." From hot to freezing in less than a second.

Melinda searched Blake's face for the question she knew she'd find there. "What is it?" he asked her.

"As far as I know, I've never done anything to offend her, but she seems to enjoy being rude to me."

His eyes softened with what she recognized as sympathy, but she didn't want that, not from him or anyone else. He reached across the table, evidently to take her hand, but withdrew before she could enjoy the warmth of his touch.

"I believe I reminded you once that most people envy the rich, but when a woman is both rich and beautiful, women will dislike her and men will turn cartwheels for her. Even so, Martha Greene isn't known as a charitable person."

Flushed with the pleasure of knowing that he thought her beautiful, she lowered her gaze. "You don't know how happy I'll be when the will is settled and this business is history."

The expression in his eyes sliced through her, and she knew that somewhere in those words, she'd made a blunder. A serious one, at that.

"I imagine you want to get on with your life," he said, "especially after having spent almost five of your best years in semiretirement. But don't forget that when you finish this round, you've got to show me a marriage certificate."

She knew that she gaped at him; she couldn't help it. Her fingers clutched the table, knocking over the long-stem glass of white wine that soaked the tablecloth and wet her dress.

"You kissed me and held me as if I were the most precious person in the world, and now you can say that to me. You're just like all the others." As though oblivious to the wet tablecloth and the dampness in her lap, she gripped the table and leaned toward him.

"You at least know that Prescott was happy with me, that I made his life pleasant, and that I was loyal to him. You know I never looked at another man, because I didn't look at you."

"Look! There's no need to—"

"Yes, there is. You listen to me. It happened the minute you opened your office door for Prescott and me when we went there to be married. And the first time you came to our home I knew that what I felt for you twenty minutes before I took my marriage vows was definitely not superficial. From then on—at least once a week for almost five years—I had to deal with you. But you didn't know it, and don't tell me you did. You don't know what it cost me, and you'll never know. So don't sit there like a judge-penitent and pass sentence."

She tossed a twenty-dollar bill on the table, grabbed her purse and briefcase. "I'll eat whatever Ruby cooked. I'll . . . I'm sorry, Blake."

Walking with head high, away from the source of her pain, her eyes beheld only a blur of human flesh and artifacts. She didn't see the gilded candles on the hanging chandelier, the huge bowl of red and yellow roses on a marble stand beneath it, or her reflection in the antique gold-framed mirrors that lined the walls. Only the gray bleakness of her life. But none of those who accused her would ever see one of her tears. The gossiping citizens of Ellicott City irritated her. But Blake's words bored a hole in her. She got into her car and sat there, too drained to drive. Should she fault herself for having let him hold her and show her what she'd missed? Maybe she shouldn't have allowed it. *But I'm human, and I've got feelings.* After a while, she started the car and moved away from the curb. "You're dealing with your own guilt, Blake," she said aloud, and immediately felt better. "You wanted your friend's wife; well, take it out on *yourself.*"

Blake washed his Maryland crab cakes down with half a bottle of chardonnay wine and considered drinking the whole bottle but thought better of it. He shouldn't have plowed into her, knowing he'd hurt her, but she had infuriated him with her tale about the men who wanted to marry her. He knew she'd attract every trifling money hunter and womanizer in Howard County and maybe farther away than that.

As much as he wanted her, he didn't intend to get in that line. Her apparent eagerness to gain control of Prescott's millions didn't sit well with him, especially since she hadn't once shown the grief you'd expect of a woman recently widowed. His left hand swept over his face. It wasn't a fair accusation, and he knew it. Not everybody grieved for public consumption. He didn't covet another person's wealth; he made a good living and had every comfort that he could want, but he'd earned it. He'd worked for every dime he had, and he couldn't sympathize with, much less respect, anybody who didn't work for what they got. He let out a long, heavy breath. How had it come to this? She was in him, down deep, clinging to the marrow of his being, wrapped around his nerve ends. Way down. Right where he lived.

"Oh, what the hell. If it hasn't killed me so far, it won't!" He paid the check and left her twenty-dollar bill on the table for the waiter.

He walked into his house, threw his briefcase on the carved walnut dining-room table, and looked at the elegance all around him. Thick oriental carpets covered his parquet floors; Italian leather sofa and chairs; silk draperies, fine walnut tables and wall units and fixtures, and fine paintings adorned his living room. All of it aeons away from the days when water soaked his bed every time it rained, and wind whistled through the cracks of the house in winter. The memory depressed him, and he wondered if the hardships of his youth had made him a tough, cynical man. He hoped not. Shaking it off, he telephoned his mother in Alabama, his thoughts filled with the one problem he'd never solved. His relationship with his father.

"How's Papa?" he asked her after they greeted each other.

"Just fair. I think he's tired, and I don't mean ordinary tired. I sense that he doesn't feel like going on."

"You serious?"

"I wish I wasn't, son."

"I don't like the sound of it," he told her. He'd gotten the same feeling when he spoke with his father the previous morning. "I'll be down there tomorrow."

After hanging up, he remembered his promise to visit Phil and Johnny. The warden had separated them from Lobo, who'd set up business as usual there in the jail. Blake called the warden and asked him to explain to the boys that he'd see them on Sunday.

"I'd hoped to hold my grandchildren," his father told him, "but none of the three of you bothered to get married yet." His thoughts appeared to ramble. "You had a tough life, but you made something of yourself, and I'm proud of you. I know I seemed hard, maybe too hard, but we had to live. Make sure you find a girl who'll stick with you through thick and thin. One like your mother."

The old man's feeble fingers patted Blake's hand. He'd never thought he'd shed tears for his father, but when he walked out of the room, they came. And they flowed.

He didn't want to use Melinda, but when he boarded the plane in Birmingham, his only thought was to have her near him. It might be unfair to her, but life wasn't fair. Right then, he knew he could handle most anything, if she was there for him. As soon as he walked into the terminal in Baltimore, he dialed her on his cell phone, and when she didn't answer, he felt as if the bottom had dropped out of him. Surely she didn't mean that much to him.

"It's because I know I'm losing my father," he rationalized. As a child, he'd almost hated the man who'd driven him so relentlessly. How often he'd wondered if he worked so hard to save young boys from a life of crime because he'd had neither a childhood nor the freedom that adolescence gives the young. What the heck! He put the car in drive and headed for the Metropolitan Transition Services Center.

For the first time, he thought his private visit with the young boys—this time, Johnny and Phil—was less than rewarding, because he didn't feel enthusiasm and couldn't force it.

"You got a load, man?" Phil asked him.

He shrugged; it wasn't good policy to share your personal life with the prisoners, who tended to focus on themselves.

"You not sick?" Johnny's question surprised him, because the boy hardly ever showed interest in anyone.

"I'm fine. But I think my father is dy . . . isn't going to make it."

"That ain't so good," Phil said and, to his astonishment, the boy put an arm around his shoulder. "It sucks, man. I know how you feel."

Another time, he would've asked Phil about his father, but right then, he was grateful that at last he had a bond with the boys, even if that progress grew out of his own grief. At the end of the hour, he knew their time together had been productive. Driving home, it came to him forcibly, a blast like a ship's signal in a fog: he'd reached them not because of any ingenuity on his part, but because he had needed their comfort. They understood that and accepted him because *they* had been able to give something to *him*. It was a lesson he hoped never to forget.

Shortly after he got home, he answered the phone and, to his disappointment, heard Lacy's voice.

"I called you half a dozen times," she said in that whining voice that made his flesh crawl. "At least six times."

"Right. You said that a second ago. I was at the prison with two boys I'm working with."

"Why would you waste time with those thugs? When they

get out, they're going right back to dealing drugs and shooting innocent people.'' As if she'd been wound up like a top, she held forth on the subject of bad, hopeless children.

''I think every kid deserves a chance to make something of himself, and I'm doing what I can to help.'' He looked at his watch. With more things to do than he cared to contemplate, wasting ten minutes listening to Lacy's prattle didn't please him. He closed his eyes, exasperated. ''These two boys are serving time for petty theft, and there's hope for both of them.''

He imagined that she rolled her eyes and looked toward the ceiling in a show of disinterest when she said, ''If you say so.''

''Lacy, this is one more way in which you and I are as far apart as two people can get. You don't care what happens to those kids; I do.''

''Oh, for goodness' sake! Are you taking me to Lake Kittamaqundi on July Fourth for the Urban League picnic?''

''I have no plans to go, Lacy. Count me out.''

''But everybody's going, and I don't want to miss the fun.''

She still hadn't gotten the message. He didn't want to hurt her, but he wasn't going to that picnic with her. ''I'm sorry, Lacy. If you want company at the picnic, you'll have to ask someone else. Okay?''

After a few seconds of silence, her breathy voice with its sexual overtones bruised his ears. ''I don't want to go with anyone else, but I can't drag you over there.'' A long pause. ''Can I?''

''No, you can't. See you around.'' For a woman of classic good looks, he couldn't figure out why she sold herself so short, insisting on a relationship with him, although he told her in many ways that it wasn't going to happen.

He thought of calling Melinda, apologizing to her and telling her he needed her, but he couldn't do that. In his whole life, he'd never let anybody see him down.

"Hold your head up and push your chin out even if you're dying," Woodrow Wilson Hunter had preached to his children, drilling it into Blake, the last of the three to leave home. There had to be a gentler method of nurturing a boy into manhood; at times, he still felt the pain. He ate a sandwich and stretched out in bed to struggle with himself and his feelings for Melinda until daylight rescued him.

The telephone rang as he walked toward the bathroom to get his morning shower, and thinking it was probably Lacy, his first inclination was to ignore it. But he heard his sister Callie's voice on the answering machine and rushed to lift the receiver.

After listening to her message, he asked, "When did it happen?"

"About half an hour ago. I'm on my way there now."

He hung up, slipped on his robe, and walked out on the balcony just off the dining room. An era of his life was over, and yet it hung ajar. Unfinished and devoid of the explanation he needed but would never get. He stared out at the silent morning, at trees heavy with leaves that didn't move. Air still and humid. Heavy, like his heart. Everything appeared the same, but it wasn't. He went inside and telephoned Melinda.

Melinda dragged herself out of the tangled sheets and sat on the side of her bed. If she packed up and left town, she wouldn't miss the place or the people. However, the losers would be those who lived in a world of illiteracy and who relied on information that they couldn't evaluate and thus rarely questioned. If only she could avoid Blake Hunter until that board was operating to his satisfaction, the gossipmongers would have to find another subject. Weary of it all, she decided not to bother with the board that day.

"Now who could that be at eight o'clock in the morning,"

she said aloud when the phone rang. "Not Ray Sinclair again, I hope."

"Melinda, this is Blake. I can't help you with that board meeting today. I have to cancel our appointment."

"But . . . What's happening, Blake? You told me I should go ahead with it, and I figured I was on my own from now on. What's going on?"

Strange that he'd forgotten that; he took pride in having an almost infallible memory. "I'm sorry I plowed into you the way I did the other night when we were supposed to be having dinner. I shouldn't have said those things, and I don't know why I did because I didn't believe them." He supposed he'd surprised her, because she considered him a hard man.

"Something's wrong. I know it is. What's the matter, Blake?"

Her words and the compassion in her voice took him aback. He didn't want to unload on her, but if he started telling her about the hole that had just opened in him and that grew bigger by the second, if he told her what he felt . . . "My . . . my father died, and I have to go to Alabama for a few days."

"Your father? I'll be right over there."

"Melinda—"

"You . . . Maybe you shouldn't be alone right now, and anyhow, I want to be there with you until you leave."

Those words caressed his ears like a sweet summer breeze. He couldn't discourage her, because he wanted, needed to see her.

"You might need me for something," she went on, as though oblivious to his silence. "I'm coming over."

He sucked in his breath. If she knew how he needed her . . . He hardly trusted himself to be alone with her. "I'll be here." was all he managed to say.

He showered quickly and dressed, certain that if he opened

the door for her while still wearing only his robe, he'd destroy what there was of a relationship with her.

Twenty minutes later, he opened the front door, and the rays of her smile enveloped and warmed him like summer sunshine. Without a word, she reached up, and he knew again the delicate touch of her lips on his mouth, warm and sweet. But he didn't kiss her; if he did, he wouldn't stop until they consummated what they felt.

"No point in saying I'm sorry. You know that," she said. "I just . . . well, I needed to be here with you."

His heartbeat accelerated so rapidly that, for almost a full minute, he couldn't catch his breath. He shouldn't encourage what was happening between them, because he was neither sure of her nor of himself.

"I'm glad you came. It's so strange, knowing he's gone and we never resolved our differences. After I matured enough to understand him and why he drove himself and everyone around him crazy the way he did, we ignored the issues between us, pretended they didn't exist and got along with each other. I wish I'd confronted him."

Compassion for him shone in her eyes with such fierceness that he had to steel himself against the feeling that slowly snaked its way into his heart.

"Didn't he love you?"

His fingers pressed into his chest as if he could push back the pain. He wished she hadn't asked that. "I don't know. I wish I did. Yesterday. I was down there yesterday, and he told me he was proud of me. So, maybe. I don't know."

With a tenderness that shook him, her arms wrapped around him, held and caressed him, and he closed his eyes and let himself relax and absorb the loving she offered. She seemed to be telling him that he needed love and caring and that she wanted to give him that. Her fingers squeezed him to her, and then she released him and stepped back.

"What time is your flight?"

He studied her eyes, needing badly to understand what he saw there, and he didn't want to make a mistake. "That reminds me, I have to check the Baltimore-Birmingham flight schedule."

She patted him on the back. "I'll do that. You pack. See? I told you you might need me for something."

He had to get out away from her before he did something foolish. "I . . . uh . . . there's a phone out in the hallway." He grabbed a suitcase from the closet in the foyer and headed for his bedroom without looking at her.

"There's a Delta Airlines flight at eleven-forty. I'll drive you."

"I was going to drive and leave my car at the airport."

"And it probably wouldn't be there when you got back."

He shrugged. "This is true, but if you drive me, how'll I get home when I come back?"

She didn't look at him when she said, "You'll call me, tell me when you'll be back, and I'll meet you. Simple as that."

He didn't know her reasons, and he didn't want to ask, because he wasn't sure he had anything to give in return. "I can't let you do this, Melinda."

"Why? You want an affidavit stating that you're not obligated to me? Give me a pen and a piece of paper."

When he grabbed her shoulders, he surprised himself more than her. "It isn't that I don't trust you—"

"What about my integrity? Do you believe in that? Do you?" Her lips trembled, and her eyes held a suspicious sheen.

His fingers moved from her shoulders to her back and then gripped her waist. "Yes. Yes, damn it. Yes!"

Her lips parted to take him in, and desire slammed into him, hot and furious and overpowering. The sound of her groans of sexual need shook his very foundation, and against his powerful will, he rose against her hard and hurting while she feasted on his tongue. He had to . . . Caught up in the fire she built in him, he wrapped an arm around her shoulder and the other around her buttocks and lifted her to fit him. She straddled him, hooked her ankles at his back, and moved against him with a rhythm that sent hot needles of desire showering through his veins.

"Melinda. Melinda!"

"Huh?"

He set her away from him as one would a pan of boiling lye. Then, realizing that he might have hurt her, he folded her in his arms and hugged her. Her breath came fast and hard like that of a marathon runner at the end of a twenty-six-mile race, and he held her as he strove to regain his own equilibrium.

After a few minutes, he trusted himself to speak. "Something's happening here, and it . . . it doesn't want to be controlled." A half laugh tumbled out of him; he'd never been one to dodge responsibility, and when it came to fanning the fire between them, he was the guilty one.

"I'd like to know what's funny so I can laugh. It's gotta be an improvement over what I feel."

She'd begged the question, so he had no choice but to ask, "What do you feel?"

She looked at him with the expression of one staring at the unknown. "Need. Confusion. Loneliness. A lot of stuff that makes me feel bad."

He had almost relaxed when she said, "And I feel something for you that I shouldn't, because you don't want me to feel like this. But don't worry; you're as safe with me as a lion cub surrounded by a pride of lions."

He wasn't sure he wanted all that security, but it wouldn't hurt to have it while the coming eleven months revealed her future.

Her father raised her to want only what was good for her, and though years had passed since she'd believed his every word, she conceded at the moment that she'd be better off if she'd never wanted Blake Hunter. But on the other hand, she was glad she hadn't died without feeling what she experienced when he had her in his arms kissing and loving her.

Get your mind on another level, girl, she told herself as she let him ponder her last words. "We'd better get started," she said after minutes had passed and he hadn't responded to her assurance as to his safety. "No. Wait a minute, is there anything in the refrigerator that will spoil? Any plants? Pets?"

A frown clouded his face. Then he smiled, and she wondered if he'd done that intentionally to make her heart race and butterflies flit around in her stomach.

"I forgot about the refrigerator." He dumped the handful of fruits into the garbage disposal. "That's it. I'm the only thing here that breathes. Come on."

He picked up his suitcase, took her hand, and walked to the door. "You're a special person, Melinda. Very special." He looked beyond her and spoke as if to himself. "And very dear." She didn't speak. How could she when she didn't know what those three words meant? They walked to her car, and when he paused at the front passenger's door, she handed him the car keys.

"Since you're apparently not a male chauvinist, why don't you drive?"

He stepped around to the driver's side and accepted the keys. "You mean if I'd asked to drive, you would have objected?"

"You got it."

"You think that means I'm not a chauvinist?"

She got in and closed the door. "It's a pretty good indication. But if you are, you'll let me know; that's an ailment a man can't hide."

"Now wait a second. Who's being a chauvinist?"

"Not me, I was just stating a fact."

"That so? Do you know that much about men? I wouldn't have thought it."

"Whoa. I didn't realize a married woman—or a widow for that matter—was expected to account for such things."

He looked over his shoulder, moved onto Route 144, and set the car on cruise. "And I didn't ask you to, but you have to admit there's a certain freshness, an innocence about you that one doesn't associate with a woman who's had almost five years of marriage. But maybe this isn't the time to get into that."

How much did he know about her marriage to Prescott? "I'm not sure I follow."

His quick glance sent a chill through her. A man didn't discuss his marriage with his attorney, did he?

"You mean about the innocence? Could be it's just the way you are with me. Whatever. I like it."

She folded her hands in her lap, stared down at them, and made herself relax as he turned into the drive leading to BWI airport. "No comment?" he asked.

"Some other time. No point in getting into a deep discussion that we can't finish."

A grin danced off his lips. "In that case, I'll repeat those words the minute I get back here. Be prepared."

They walked into the terminal minutes before his flight was called. He put his ticket in the breast pocket of his jacket, took her hand, passed the security checkpoint, and reached the gate as boarding began.

Blake dropped his suitcase on the floor and clasped both of her shoulders. "I'm never going to forget this, Melinda. Never. You can't possibly know what your being with me these past couple of hours means to me. I'll call you."

She hardly felt his kiss; it passed so quickly. But she recognized in it a new urgency. Or maybe it sprang from a deeper need. She didn't know, and she was afraid to guess. She walked slowly back to her car thinking that she had no idea where in Alabama he was headed.

Chapter Four

Callie ran to him with arms open and tears glistening in her eyes as he stepped into the terminal. Wordlessly, they held each other, seeking comfort in shared sorrow. Although she was two years older, once they became adults he'd treated her as a younger sister. He'd always loved her, and as a small boy, had followed her constantly unless there was work for him to do. He picked up his suitcase, and they walked arm in arm to her car.

"Thanks for meeting me, Callie. How's Mama doing?"

"Pretty good. She said she expected it, though she hadn't thought it would be so soon."

"Neither did I, and I was with him yesterday. How'd you know I'd be on that plane?"

"It was the next one in from Baltimore, and I knew you'd make that one if you could."

He remembered Melinda's comment about his lack of male chauvinism just as he was about to ask Callie for the keys to her car, and he smothered a laugh. Instead, he asked her, "You want to drive, or you want me to drive?"

The startled expression on her face was evidence that he ought to mend his ways. "You're going to sit in the front seat beside me while I drive?"

The laugh poured out of him, until he stopped trying to stifle it and leaned against the car, enjoying it.

"What on earth are you laughing at?"

He told her, leaving out what he considered irrelevant. "Maybe she was telling me something. Do you think I don't have enough respect for women?"

Both of her eyebrows shot up. "You? No, I don't think that. You're a man who takes charge, and I expect you'd want to drive even if it was John's car."

He opened the driver's door and held it for her. "You drive. As for me driving John's car with him sitting there, you and I both know he'd have to be deathly ill. Did he get in yet?"

"He'll be in tonight."

Much as he disliked facing what he knew awaited him, it was nonetheless good to have the affection and support of his siblings, John and Callie. He knew they'd all be strong for their mother, but did they hurt as he did and did they feel cheated of a father's love? Maybe some day they'd talk about it.

Whatever he'd expected, it wasn't the smile with which his mother greeted them. "I'll be lonely when y'all leave," she told them, "but he wouldn't want us to sit around with long faces."

He hugged his mother and walked into the house, feeling the difference the second he stepped across the threshold. The windows were wide open, and the curtains flapped in the breeze that flowed through the rooms. He turned to look at his mother with what he knew was an inquiring expression.

Her smile radiated warmth and contentment. "The last thing he said to me was 'enjoy what's left, and let the sunshine in.' I'll love him as long as I breathe, but I aim to do that starting now."

The pain began to crowd his heart. Maybe it wasn't the time, but he couldn't hold it back. "You loved him so much, as hard a man as he . . . he was?"

With a vigorous shake of her head, she said, "He wasn't hard. I know he seemed that way to you children, but the day he married me, he promised I'd never want for anything. Sometimes he worked all day and most of the night to keep that promise. I hurt for you all when you were growing up, and I didn't like to see how you felt about him, but he taught you the values that would see you through life."

"Mama, when I was ten or eleven, I'd get so tired I couldn't even run."

"I know, son. And I remember how he held my hand and cried at your college graduation as you stood up there and gave that speech, top student in your class."

She turned to Callie. "When you got your degree, he said we'd go to your graduation even if his strawberries rotted on the bushes while we were gone, and you know the value of those berries and what they meant to him. He loved all of you." She sniffed and blew her nose, fighting back the tears, but her eyes remained dry.

"John surprised us with these air conditioners he designed for his company," she went on, "and your father walked all the way to Mr. Moody's house and asked him to come down and see what John did. He was so proud of you all."

Her arms wound around his shoulder, reminding him that he could count on her when everything else failed, and it had always been that way. "You were the one he worried most about," she said with a wistful smile, "because you are so strong-headed, and you were so angry with him. Let it go, son.''

Why did the price of forgiveness have to be so high? He looked at his mother with new insight about the way their family life had been when he was young and bitter, and now he had to know more. "Did he ever tell you he loved you?"

Her lips parted in what was clearly astonishment. "Yes. All the time. Not always with words, maybe, but in numerous other ways. Let it go, son. Let the sunshine in.''

Blake lifted his shoulder in a shrug. "I guess I have to. The trouble is I wanted to love him.''

"You children made his last years beautiful. He had a lovely home, more than enough for us to live on even if we didn't work, and for the first time in his life, he had a little leisure time.''

"I'm glad we could do it.''

John arrived that evening and they finished the funeral arrangements while they reminisced about their childhood. Blake didn't like the drama and commotion that accompanied southern mourning, and he was glad to have a moment alone. He walked out to the front gate where the summer breeze carried the scent of roses and the clear moonlit night brought him memories of his childhood. And loneliness. He went inside for his cell phone, came back and telephoned Melinda. Maybe it didn't make sense, but he needed to hear her voice.

"I've just been thinking that I had no idea where you are,'' she said after they greeted each other.

"I'm in Six Mile, about twenty miles outside of Birmingham. It's small, barely a hamlet. Here's my cell phone number. Call me if you want to.''

"I will, and I'm glad you called me. How's your mother taking this?''

"Philosophically as usual. I guess it's worse for me than for Mama and my sister and brother, because my relationship with him was so much poorer than theirs, but I'm making it. Being with John and Callie, my older brother and sister, and talking things over with them puts a clearer perspective on my childhood. I'll be fine."

"How'd you get there from Birmingham? Rent a car?"

He leaned against the gate and inhaled the perfume of the roses. Strange how the floral scene reminded him of Melinda. Bright. Cheerful and sweet. "I'd planned to rent one, but Callie met me." He told her of Callie's reaction when he asked her whether she wanted to drive her own car. "I'll have to be more careful. Callie says I'm just a guy who takes charge, but that can seem overbearing. What do you think?" He realized that he wanted her to think well of him, and that surprised him, because he didn't remember ever caring whether anyone liked him. He had to do some serious thinking about what Melinda Rodgers meant to him and what, if anything, he'd do about it.

Her voice, soft and mellifluous, caressed his ears and wrapped him in contentment. "I think you're tough, and I imagine you can be overbearing, but you haven't treated me to any of that, so I don't know."

"What were you doing when I called?"

"I . . . uh—"

"What?" He told himself to straighten out his mind, lest his imagination get out of control.

"Well, I was lying here looking up at the ceiling, and don't ask me where my mind was."

"Would I be presumptuous to think your mind might have been on me?"

"Roses are red and violets are blue."

He laughed because he couldn't help it and because so much of something inside of him strained to get out. "I wouldn't take anything for that. Go ahead and keep your secrets."

"Are you going to let me know when you're coming back so I can meet you?"

He closed his eyes and let contentment wash over him. In the seventeen years since he'd left his paternal home and the mother who'd nurtured him, he'd forgotten what it was to have someone care about his comfort and well-being. Irene made a stab at it, but he didn't cooperate because he didn't want an office wife.

"I said I would, and when I tell you I'll do something, I do it if it's humanly possible. Remember that. I'll see you in a couple of days."

"Can I do anything for you while you're away?"

"Thanks, but . . ." It occurred to him that she could, but he hesitated to involve her. He hadn't heard from Ethan in over two weeks, and if the boy got into trouble again, he'd be a three-time loser, which meant he'd be an old man before he got out of jail.

"If you don't mind, call this number, ask for Ethan, and find out how he is. Tell him where I am and that I want him to call me tomorrow night. Don't give him your name, telephone number, or address. Just say I told you to call him. If he's in trouble, call me back."

To her credit, he thought, she didn't question him about his relationship to Ethan, but promised to do as he asked.

He didn't want to leave her with a cold good-bye, but their relationship didn't warrant much more. So he merely said, "Talk to you again before I leave here," and she seemed to understand.

"I'll expect that," she said. "Take care of yourself."

He hung up and went inside. He didn't feel like dancing, but he walked with livelier steps.

Two days later, Blake stood at his father's final resting place, dealing with his emotions.

"If you had wound up in jail or as an addict," his mother

said, "maybe you'd have grounds to hate him. But look at you.
He must have given you something that inspired you to reach
so high and accomplish so much."

What could he say? She looked at it with the eyes of a
woman who loved both her husband and her children; she
wouldn't lay blame. He wished he were in the habit of praying,
because he could use some unbiased guidance right then.

Gloria Hunter's fingers gripped his arm. "Let it go, son. If
you don't forgive your father, you'll never be able to love
anybody, not the woman you marry, not even your own children." His mother tightened her grip on him as she whispered,
"Please let it die with him."

Strange that he should think of Melinda at a time when he
was finding his way out of the morass of pain and bewilderment
that dogged him and had been a part of his life for as long as he
remembered. What did she feel for her father? It was suddenly
important for him to know if she loved Booker Jones, a man
who few people in Ellicott City, other than his family and
parishioners, seemed able to tolerate.

His mother's words bruised his ears. "Son, you've got to
let it go."

In his mind's eye, he saw again his father stand, tears streak-
ing his cheeks, when Columbia University conferred the doctor
of laws degree on his younger son. As pain seared his chest,
he knelt and kissed the sealed metal casket. When he stood,
his mother's arms enfolded him, and he didn't think he'd ever
seen her smile so broadly or her eyes sparkle so brightly with
happiness.

Melinda waited until late the next morning before she tried
to locate Ethan. She supposed he might be a relative, since
Blake didn't have any children. She amended that. He didn't
have any that she knew of.

"Ethan ain't here," the voice of an older female said in answer to Melinda's question. When asked where she could find him, the woman advised, "Look down at Doone's poolroom over on Oela Avenue facing the railroad. If he ain't there, I couldn't say *where* he is."

She couldn't find a phone number for Doone's, but though she was wary as to what she might discover there, she got in her car and drove to the place.

"Whatta ya want, miss?" a big bouncer type of a man asked her.

"I'm looking for a boy named Ethan."

He pointed to one of the pool tables. "Right over there. Hey, Ethan, a lady's here to see ya."

Melinda watched the boy amble toward her. An attractive, neat kid whom she imagined was about sixteen years old, she wondered what he was doing in a poolroom so early in the day.

"Ethan, do you know Blake?"

Recognition blazed across his face, and since he showed interest and wasn't hostile, she decided to smile to indicate her friendliness.

As quick as mercury, his look of recognition dissolved into a frown. "Yeah. I know him. What's the matter with him?"

"He has a family emergency and had to go out of town. He wants you to call him tonight. And please do that, Ethan, because he's worried about you."

Ethan looked hard at Melinda and narrowed his eyes as though making up his mind about her. "You sure he's all right?"

She nodded. "I'm sure. Will you call his cell phone number?"

He stuffed his hands in his pockets and looked past her. "Uh . . . yeah. I shoulda called him, so he'd know I wasn't in no trouble. But I got this job staking balls late nights to early morning, so . . . I shoulda called and told him. Tonight, you say?''

"Yes. Tonight."

"Okay. See you." He started toward the table, then turned back to her. "Oh, I forgot to thank you for coming by."

She told him good-bye, but she couldn't get him off her mind. He didn't seem like a criminal, but she supposed that wasn't something obvious to the eye.

When she got back home, Ruby accosted her right at the door. "Miz Melinda, how come all these mens calling you? I left the messages on your desk, but it don't look good to have all these mens calling here when you just been a widow. Six months from now when you needs one, that'd be a different matter. Oh yes," she called, as Melinda walked up the stairs, "Miss Rachel said for you to call her. That woman sure is nosy. I told her I ain't seen Mr. Blake in this house since poor Mr. Rodgers passed. God rest his dear soul."

She looked at the names of her callers: Leroy Wilson, Frank Jackson, Roosevelt Hayes, Macon Long. She didn't know any of them, but she knew what they wanted: a chance to help her spend her late husband's money. She tore up the messages and telephoned Rachel.

"Hey, girl. What's going on?" Rachel asked.

"Good question, Rachel. Any time you want to know what's going on here, who's been here and what I'm doing, ask *me*. That'll save Ruby the trouble of telling me what you asked her."

"Tight-lipped as you are? I wanted to know, so I asked. Really sorry, Melinda. I—"

"Now that we've got that settled, Blake hasn't been inside this house since Prescott passed. Should I tell him you asked?"

"Of course n . . . Well, if you want to."

She didn't intend to play games with Rachel. They would either remain good friends or they wouldn't, but she was a grown, unattached woman and she didn't have to answer to a soul.

"Rachel, I'm meeting Blake at the airport in Baltimore tomorrow, and I can't swear he won't come into my house or that I won't go into his and stay awhile."

Silence hung between them. "Then you *have* got something going with him," Rachel said after some minutes, her voice arid and hollow. "I thought so." Suddenly, she appeared to brighten. "Well, if he makes your top twirl, honey, go for it."

She didn't believe her, but neither did she blame the woman for a gracious stab at face-saving. "Say, have you ever been to that Great Blacks In Wax Museum in Baltimore?" she asked, deliberately changing the subject.

"No. Want to go tomorrow?"

Melinda couldn't help laughing at Rachel's transparent effort to go with her to the airport to meet Blake. "Sorry, I can't go tomorrow. I'm meeting Blake. Remember?"

After making small talk for a few minutes, they hung up. But before she could pull off her shoes, the phone rang again.

"Melinda, honey, this is Ray. I'm just confirming our date for July Fourth."

She gripped the receiver and considered slamming it back into its cradle. The nerve of him trying to force her to let him display her at that fair for the benefit of local citizenry. "We don't have a date, Ray. I told you I'd think about it. I've done that, and I've decided not to go with you. Thanks for being in touch after all these years. Now, if you'll excuse me, I have a lot to do." She hung up. Five of them in one day, and Lord knows how many more such overtures she could expect. She didn't wait long for the next one.

Minutes later, a man identifying himself as Salvatore Luca claimed to have seen her on Main Street, inquired as to who she was and was anxious to meet her. At least he hadn't come right out and applied for the job of husband.

"There must be some mistake, Mr. Luca," she said in her sweetest voice. "I haven't walked along Main Street in I don't know when. Hope you find her."

She settled down to study the list of twelve people whom, with Blake's help, she'd chosen for the board, but she couldn't get interested in the task of selecting the board's officers. Why had Prescott saddled her with something for which she had no taste and worse, with the stipulation that she marry within the year or lose the inheritance, a modern-day coup de grâce?

Cold tendrils of fear shot through her. She got up from the richly inlaid walnut desk, walked to the window, and looked down at the goldfish pond in the back garden, but the colorful creatures didn't amuse her. Not even the gentle breeze that brushed her face when she stepped out on the porch off her bedroom gave her pleasure. Maybe nothing ever would again. She turned away from the blackbirds that perched on the porch swing waiting for the crumbs she usually enjoyed feeding to them and walked slowly back into the house. It couldn't be true; she wouldn't let it be true. Blake couldn't be like all the others, maneuvering for the money her husband had earned despite a handicap that would have bested most women and men. She didn't want to think that of him, but he was certainly making the road rough for any other man.

She picked up the tablet containing the names of the board members they'd selected, and her gaze fell on Salvatore Luca's name. She'd written it there, idly, as she spoke with him. She pitched the tablet away from her, lifted the receiver of the ringing phone, and slammed it back in its cradle without answering it. Fed up. With no school until September, she didn't have to stay in Ellicott City. Not once in her life had she had a vacation, and she was due one. When the phone rang again, she ignored it.

"Miz Melinda," Ruby called, "Mr. Blake's on the phone."

What timing! "Hi. What time shall I meet you?"

He seemed to hesitate. "You sure you want to?"

Taken aback by his perceptiveness, or maybe it was his sixth sense, she softened. "Of course I'm sure. What time?"

"Four-twenty. Delta."

"How are things with . . . with your family?"

"About what you'd expect, I suppose."

"You. What about you, Blake?"

"I don't know. Burying your father makes you look at yourself and your life with a critical eye. Let's say, I'm making it."

She didn't know how to take that, but she suspected that he was being brutal with himself, judging himself in the harshest terms, and she hurt for him.

"Don't judge yourself unfairly. You're one terrific guy. Come on home, Blake, and stop thrashing yourself. You don't deserve that."

"I wish it was that easy. See you tomorrow."

She'd pulled back, and nothing would convince him otherwise. That was her right, but he wished she'd done that before he began to need her. He didn't want to misjudge her, and he was fairly certain that he didn't, but at gut level he sensed a coolness definitely at odds with the warmth that leaped out from her to him the morning he left Baltimore for Six Mile. Hell, he'd handled worse, and this wouldn't break him. As he strode into the terminal, he wouldn't have been surprised if she'd changed her mind and decided not to meet him.

She rushed to him, but her arms weren't open wide to receive him. He walked now with heavy steps, as though moving against a strong force. The uncertainty of what awaited him and the pain of what he'd left in Six Mile crowded his thoughts and weighed him down. He hadn't realized what he felt for his father . . . and for her.

"Hi." She reached up to hug him, and he drew her close and soaked himself in her sweetness.

"Hi, yourself," he said, substituting those words for genuine communication. "Thanks for meeting me."

She smiled at him, and he saw warmth in her eyes, but not the intimacy that had burned in her gaze and sizzled in her arms when she'd held him that morning in his apartment.

"Don't thank me. I couldn't have stayed away."

Four days earlier, she'd said, "I need to be here with you." He digested the difference, hooded his gaze, and picked up his bag.

"Let's go," he said, and she reached for his free hand. He let her hold it.

"So what happened since we talked the other night?" he asked her as she headed out on Route 144. "Been doing some thinking?"

"You could say that. Five strange men and one not-so-strange called me yesterday, and none of them gives a hang about me." She swerved to avoid a van when it moved into the center lane. "Somebody told those guys about that stupid clause in Prescott's will, and they're all after money at my expense. It's never going to happen."

So that was it. "And you soured on all men, including me, just because some of the brothers see a good thing and go after it?"

Her quick glance was less than flattering. "One of them wasn't a brother. 'I saw you on Main Street and had to know who you were,' " she mimicked. "I haven't been on Main Street in a solid year. The guy's never seen me. A good lie, though."

"What do you mean?"

"He was prepared to spend time with me and get me to fall for him. Trust me, that beats guys like Jonas Humphrey, who just dropped by my house and said he was prepared to marry me. He should live so long.''

Before he could respond to that, she changed the subject. ''I've decided I need a vacation, and I'm going to take one. I need to get away from all this. Time enough to worry about that board when I get back. Of course, if you feel you'd like to set it up, be my guest.''

So they were back to that. The passion that consumed him while the plane crept at a snail's pace from Birmingham to Baltimore had already begun to cool, but now it deserted him.

''If you don't want Prescott's estate, at least consider the people in this county whose lives will be enhanced if they develop good reading skills.''

She drove up to his house and cut the engine. ''I'm going to see it through if it takes me five years.''

He knew his bottom lip dropped, and he stopped himself when he started grinding the teeth on the left side of his jaw. ''You can be exasperating. In all the years I visited Prescott, I never saw in you any semblance of belligerence. Always the gentle, smiling hostess.''

She turned to face him and lifted her shoulder in a shrug. ''Things have changed. I'm on my own now.''

While he stared down at her, he had the pleasure of seeing her eyes darken in recognition of him as a man. ''Yeah. Well, don't go overboard, and it wouldn't be a bad idea to examine your tires when you get home.'' He couldn't help grinning when she raised her eyebrows and parted her lovely mouth, clearly perplexed.

''Why?''

''Considering how you took that curve when we came off the highway, your tires are probably split. I wouldn't make a habit of that, if I were you. '' He opened the door and paused. Small talk. A sure sign that he wasn't saying what he felt any more than she was.

"I . . . uh . . . suppose you'll let me know your plans?"

"Sure I will." Her airy tone was forced or his name wasn't Blake Hunter.

So be it. He didn't say good-bye, because he didn't feel like it. Once inside his house, he dropped his suitcase on the floor and paced back and forth along the hallway connecting the foyer and dining room. He'd been on fire, and she'd cooled him off as thoroughly as if she'd sprayed him with ice water. She wouldn't have to do that a second time.

Melinda had prowled from room to room in that big house ever since finishing her supper. The darkened skies heralded an approaching storm but, uneasy, as she tended to be during storms, she walked around her bedroom looking at its mauve and lavender silks in the romantic setting that had never witnessed romance.

Without considering what she did, she sat on the edge of her bed, reached for the phone, and dialed Blake Hunter's number. Her heart palpitated at the sound of his deep, sonorous "hello," stunning her into recognition of what she'd done.

"What is it, Melinda?" His voice had the tone of a command as if he knew she'd started to hang up and forbade her to do it. She'd forgotten about caller ID.

Frantically, she searched her mind for a reason to have phoned him. "Uh . . . I wanted to know if Ethan called you."

"Yeah. Right."

"What does that mean?"

"He called. Thanks for finding him. I'd rather he wasn't working in a poolroom, but at least he has a job and he gets to it on time."

Since he didn't believe her, she'd lay the onus of the conversation on him. "Ethan interested me. Who is he?"

"Ethan is one of the young boys that I'm trying to help

straighten themselves out. He's fifteen, and he's already been in jail twice. He promised me he's going to school in September, and keep at it till he gets his high school diploma.''

"He showed genuine concern for you, asking me repeatedly if you were all right.''

"Not many people have shown an interest in him.''

"*Oh!*''

"What is it? What's the matter.'' The urgency in his voice said he cared and cared deeply. "I ... uh ... Isn't that thunder?''

"Sounds like it. Best not to use the telephone during electric storms. I'll—''

"Wait. I think somebody's at my front door. But at this time of night ... I don't know who it could be.''

"Check it. I'll wait.''

The thunder loomed closer and louder, but she forced herself to creep down the winding stairs and turn on the camera that hung just below the eaves at the front door and displayed the visitor on an indoor screen while taking his picture. She didn't know who that man was or why he'd come, uninvited, to her home. He rang the bell, this time following it with a heavy knock on the door. She checked the locks and alarm system and raced back upstairs.

"I've never seen him before,'' she told Blake after describing the man.

"You're sure the house is secure?''

"I think so. Prescott installed a very expensive system, though we never had to test it.''

"Relax. I'll call you later, but wait till you hear my voice on your answering machine before you pick up. All right?''

He hung up before she could answer, leaving her to wonder why he would concern himself when, only a few hours earlier, she'd deliberately thrown cold water on their budding relationship. The doorbell rang persistently, but she ignored it, knowing that the camera would document the caller's every move.

A clap of thunder, a flash of lightning, and tremors raced through her body. Another sharp crack of thunder and she covered her eyes with her hands, but between her fingers, she saw the flashing light. When the telephone rang, she raced to it but, remembering Blake's warning, waited until she heard his voice.

"I'm parked across from your house. A man dashed away from your front gate, but I didn't see his face. Anyhow, he's gone." Flashes of light almost blinded her, and thunder bellowed like a foghorn in her ear.

"We'd better hang up," he said. "It's dangerous to talk by phone during this storm."

"I'm coming down to let you in."

"Melinda! I don't think—"

She hung up and ran downstairs. Whether to have company during the frightening storm or because she longed for him, she didn't know and didn't want to question her motives. She peeped out of the window as he streaked through the rain, and opened the door as he reached it.

Nearly soaked, he stood before her, gazing down at her. She didn't look at the door as she slammed it shut with her left hand, because she couldn't take her eyes from him. He wouldn't let her. His aura possessed her as he stood there wet and wild, his legs wide apart and his hands balled into tight fists. Shaken, she moved to him and lay her head against his chest. He let her wait and then, as if driven to it against his will, crushed her to his wet body. She wanted his mouth on her, but he denied her, though he held her now as if he cherished her.

"Why did you want me to come in here? Why?"

"I . . . I didn't think—"

"Well, think about it right now. What do you want from me?"

"I wanted a reconciliation, some evidence that . . . that—"

"That I want you? Is that it? Evidently, you didn't need that when you met me at the airport today."

She shook her head. "I'm . . . I'm scared of lightning, and I—"

"Not good enough. If all you wanted was company, you could have opened the door for that man who was so anxious to get in."

"That's not fair, and it's unworthy of you."

"But it's all right for you to try dangling me as you would your little puppet, huh? Don't even think it. I could die wanting you, before I'd put up with that. I meet a woman as an equal. Period. Tell me why you asked me to come in here."

" 'Cause I . . . Oh, Blake. Hold me and . . . and—"

His mouth possessed her, hard and demanding, but when she parted her lips for his tongue, he stepped away.

"You and I have to decide where we're heading, and this isn't the time. I sensed when you met me at the airport this afternoon that you've developed strong misgivings about me. Brand-new ones. I don't know why, but it's the reason you backed off."

He rubbed the back of his neck and closed his eyes briefly before reclaiming her with a mesmerizing gaze. "I admit I'd rather not get involved with you, at least not now, and you can figure out some of the reasons. We're both ambivalent, so what do we do about it?"

"Who's the . . . the woman who interests you?" She hadn't planned to ask him. Not ever. But there it was.

His eyes widened at her boldness. "No woman has a claim on me."

She didn't want him to leave, and she didn't know a graceful way of keeping him there. "There's a dryer downstairs, if you want to dry your clothes."

She wanted to wash the grin off his face. He had an irreverence, a wickedness that excited her. "What's amusing?"

"You are. I'm your guest. Sure you don't want to dry them for me?"

Annoyed at his brazenness, she cocked her head to the side and let her lashes lift at snail's speed. "I don't mind looking at your washboard belly and those fabulous biceps or anything else you care to display. As far as I'm concerned, the male body beats the female's by miles."

Emboldened by her own words, she pinched his cheek as she strolled past him on the way to the door that led to the basement. "A man like you? God's perfect art? Go ahead and strip; I sure as heck won't turn my head."

His words stopped her. "I've done things I regretted, Melinda, and I probably will again. But I think you ought to know that whenever I step out of line, I know full well what I'm doing, and I'm prepared to take the consequences, regret or not. Keep that up, and in a minute I'll have you on this floor, buried as deep into you as I can get."

She imagined the lover he'd be and could hardly contain herself, but she bluffed. That was all she *could* do. "You'd need my cooperation for that."

The fire of desire blazed in his eyes. "And I'd have it. You know I would."

Knowing that her feelings for him were so transparent distressed her, but she held her own. "If you could read my mind," she said cryptically, a smile shimmering around her lips, "you wouldn't be standing over there. Maybe you want to dry off at home." She hoped that would bring him down a peg.

But it didn't. He half laughed. "I was planning to do that all along. You may be immune to male nudity, but when I strip in a woman's presence, baby, I mean business." His grin, devoid of warmth, told her he wasn't amused. "Be sure and keep a good watch," he said. "If that guy shows up again tonight, call me."

"Why?"

"I'll enjoy dealing with him. Sleep well."

"You too. And, Blake, thanks for coming over here."

He opened the door with great care, stepped outside and looked around; then he was gone.

She slept fitfully as Blake Hunter danced in and out of her dreams, mesmerizing her with the heat of desire in his hypnotic eyes, walking away from her with long strides. Never looking back. Then he held her hand as they strolled down Rome's Via Veneto while Prescott described the pleasures to be found in Rome, Florence, and Venice. She began thrashing in bed when Blake laid her beside the Trevi Fountain and rose above her as she prepared to receive him. His moans of pleasure awakened her.

Startled by the implications of her dream and by its vividness, she got up and sat on the side of her bed. How had such a strange and tantalizing experience lodged itself in her subconscious? Rome and Venice were Prescott's favorite cities. He told her so many intriguing tales about them that she felt as if she'd been there. Could her intuition be telling her that she ought to get away from Blake or, perhaps, from Ellicott City? That she needed to witness life from another corner of the world? She walked to the window and looked out at the full moon. Didn't she deserve to be more than a monument to a memory?

"Italy?" Her father roared when she told him of her plans. "You can't go over there. I hear tell those men walk behind women and pinch their backsides. I won't have my daughter—"

"Papa, I'm going to Italy. Prescott told me so many wonder-

ful stories about it that I feel as if I've been there many times.
He'd close his eyes and paint the most wonderful pictures of
Rome and Florence for me. Other places, too, but especially
those two cities. Don't worry about those guys; I'll wear a
girdle and frustrate them like the devil.''

''You'll wear ... Girl, do you know who you're talking
to?''

''Yes, sir.''

''And what about that board you have to set up and the
husband you're supposed to be finding. Melinda, girl, you're
going to fool around and lose millions. You get busy, and don't
bring me no Italian son-in-law. You hear?''

He passed the phone to her mother. ''Enjoy it while you
can, honey,'' Lurlane advised, ''and bring me some pretty
postcards.'' Melinda said she would.

Shortly after noon, she stepped out of the front door to see
whether the storm had damaged anything. Only the limbs of a
young crab apple tree lay on the ground, for which she was
grateful. The big footprint in the middle of the patch of begonias
she'd set out the day before reminded her of the previous night's
visitor, and she phoned Blake to ask if he'd like to see the
man's picture.

While she waited, she mentioned the incident to Ruby.

''Don't no mens come here to see me. I values my neck too
much to let that happen. My husband wouldn't hold for no
stuff like that.''

''Well, what do you think he was after? It was late, and he
didn't want to leave.''

''I guess they thinks widows is needy. Like my husband
says, though, there's women and then there's *women.*''

Later, Ruby looked at the pictures. ''I seen eyebrows like
them before, but otherwise I ain't got no idea who he is. I tell
you one thing, though; that man's nervous and shifty, which
means you don't want him 'round you. I'd keep them pictures

for the police; they might come in handy." She answered the doorbell. "It's Mr. Blake, Miz Melinda."

"I . . . uh . . . I'm going downtown in a few minutes to book a flight to Italy. I need a change," she told him after they'd talked for a while.

"Italy? Why on earth are you going *there?*"

"Prescott talked about that country and the people so much that I imagined being there. I need a change, and I . . . I've decided to experience the place for myself."

His intense stare was just short of intimidating, but her father had given her plenty of opportunities to fold up, and it had yet to happen. If he couldn't manage it, no one could.

"You can't hide from life, Melinda. If it's a change you need, I'd say go and have a great time. But if you're trying to escape the reality of your circumstances, nothing will have changed when you get back here. If you need me, you have all of my phone numbers. I'll be here for you."

Her face must have mirrored the question in her mind, for he added, his voice somber and minus its velvet beauty, "That's right. I'll be here for you. I'll always be here for you no matter what. I'd appreciate knowing when you plan to leave."

"I'll call you."

Two weeks later, having already imprinted Florence in her memory for all time, Melinda strolled down the Via Veneto, Rome's most famous street. Her mind bulged with memories of the vivid dream in which she walked that street hand in hand with Blake.

She felt a rubbing on her buttocks and whirled around. If one more man made a pass at her or tried to pinch her, she was going to collapse in giggles. Flirting had to be the national pastime. A country full of handsome men, but she saw and didn't see them; Blake had taken a seat in her head and refused to move. She sent him an e-mail: *If you were here, this would be the time of my life.*

When she got up the next morning, she found a computer reply on the floor just inside her room door. *If I thought you meant that, I'd be tempted to take a much-needed vacation.*

She replied: *You'd be tempted, but your self-control would take care of that. See you when I get back.*

But he didn't give her the last word: *If you ever learn how to handle my self-control, we won't be having exchanges such as this one. See you when you get back.*

Chapter Five

The next day, Melinda strolled through the Vatican Museum with Winnie McGhee, an American woman she had met on a tour the previous afternoon. Having agreeable company added another dimension to her stay in Rome, especially while sightseeing and that all-important Italian pastime, dining. Italians treated food with the respect due it and dined with gusto. But when it came to art, it was so much a part of their lives that they seemed to leave the museums to the tourists. Nothing she'd read prepared her for the beauty and richness of the Vatican Museum's art collection, and she said as much to Winnie.

"And nobody told me I'd probably walk at least ten miles while I was in here," Winnie said of the museum. "If they had, I would've worn my Reboks. Lord, but my feet are killing me," she moaned, for at least the third time.

"Maybe you'd better rest tonight. We can see the night life another evening."

"They don't hurt *that* bad. My cousin works at the U.S. Embassy, and he said if we meet him there at five o'clock this afternoon when he gets off, he'll take us for cocktails and then to dinner. Dress up. Michael is real fancy."

Melinda put on a short black dinner dress and brightened it with a rose quartz necklace and earrings. Black shoes and bag and a black cut-velvet stole completed her attire. To her amazement, Winnie had dressed entirely in apple green, a color Melinda detested. Michael waited for them in the embassy's reception room—an ordinary-looking chamber dominated by a huge American flag and an imposing marine—along with an Italian who worked at the embassy as an interpreter.

The Italian's eyebrows shot up in appreciation when he saw Melinda. *"Ehhhh! Bella!"* he whispered as he kissed her hand. If cousin Michael had intended the Italian for Winnie and himself for her, the Roman had quickly changed that scenario.

The quintessential Italian male. A number ten if she'd ever seen one, and like all Italian men of his ilk, he knew it. Evidently, Enrico didn't like apple green any more than she did, because he made no secret of his preference for her.

As the evening progressed, she decided that nothing could compare with the Italian passion for people watching or with their food, which the four of them enjoyed in an upscale restaurant that featured gourmet delights.

"I will show you the whole world," Enrico assured Melinda as they walked down the Via Veneto that night toward her hotel, which faced the Borghese Gardens and the famous Villa Borghese. He spread his hands in an expansive gesture. "The whole world."

Deciding to go with her wicked streak, she replied, "But I only have another week of vacation. We can't see the rest of the world in one week."

Obviously feigning shock, he clasped his hands to his broad chest. "Ah, signorina, I could live with you a lifetime in one day." They entered her hotel and he stopped walking, looked down at her, and frowned. "You would desert me when I have at long last found you? All my life, I have been searching for you."

She patted his arm. "Same here, so I guess we're both lucky I took this vacation. Thanks for a great evening." She took a step toward the elevator.

His dark eyes seemed to get blacker, then flash with fire before he half-lowered his long, curly black lashes. *"Cara mia, what kind of men do they have in the United States who don't teach a beautiful signorina how to tell a man good night?"*

She wouldn't laugh. She wouldn't let herself. But her lips parted in a full grin, which Enrico accepted as acknowledgement of his wisdom.

"I know one man back in the States who I'm going to ask that question, and he'd better have the answer."

He grasped both of her forearms. *"You are not married?"*

"Not anymore."

He crossed himself, looked toward heaven, and let out a long breath of relief. Then he seemed to panic. "But if you are divorced, the Blessed Mother will not countenance my . . . er . . . loving you."

She swallowed a laugh, though she sympathized with him because he'd just shot himself in the foot. "I was thinking that, too, Enrico, and I'm so glad you're such a wonderful, righteous man. I'll say good night." She squeezed his fingers, and made it into the elevator before he could recover from his enjoyment of the halo she'd draped over him.

She walked into her room, kicked off her shoes, and fell back across the bed, exhausted by the day's activities. From the corner of her eye she noticed the flashing red light on the telephone and considered not answering it. She'd had enough of Enrico's delicate, less-than-serious pursuit for one evening, though he was fun and she suspected his antics amused even him.

Melinda considered erasing the message without playing it, but it occurred to her that many women would love to have Enrico's attention. *I'm in Rome,* she remembered, reason enough to cut the Romans some slack.

"Hello."

"Signora," the front desk clerk said, "I am sorry to bother you, but please check your messages. The same gentleman has called you three times this evening. Buona notte."

"Good night."

Now who could that be? She lifted the receiver and punched the red button. "You must be having a great time." Blake Hunter's voice caressed her like layers of soft satin. "When you get in, call collect."

Hearing his voice stirred up conflicting feelings in her, reminding her of what she'd left behind and what she'd have to deal with the minute she set foot back in Ellicott City. Not to speak of her deep and unsatisfied longing for him. A glance at her watch told her that if it was midnight in Rome, it was six o'clock in the morning in Ellicott City. But he'd said call him, and though his voice didn't convey a sense of urgency . . .

She dialed his number. "Hello, Melinda."

"Is there anything wrong, Blake?"

"Not that I know of. Why?"

She rolled her eyes toward the ceiling. The man could be so exasperating. "You called me three times?"

"Yeah. I wanted to talk with you. Rome's a fast city; should you be out at midnight?"

"I wasn't hanging out on the street all by myself. Is that what you wanted to talk with me about?"

"I'm glad you found a friend to do things with. Sightseeing

can't be too much of a thrill all by yourself. Is this friend an American?''

Might as well have a little fun. "Well, yes and no.''

"Yes and . . . Run that past me again.''

"I said—''

"I know what you said.''

She smothered a laugh. "She's an American, and he's . . . uh . . . He's Italian.''

"At least you don't have to worry about the language. Are they married?''

The laughter broke through, and she had to let it roll. "Not that I know of.''

"What's so amusing?'' His voice didn't indicate that he found anything to laugh at. He'd switched from hot to cold as quickly as that, and the teasing lost its appeal for her.

"I was having fun. I'm glad you called me, Blake.''

"I'll try to believe that if you give me some more evidence.''

"There's plenty of that, but you don't want it. Remember?''

"Hell, Melinda, let's cut out this circus. I miss you.''

"Uh . . . me too.''

She heard the sudden thumping of her heart, and the marbles jockeying for position in her belly made her dizzy. Giddy with expectation, she clutched the receiver and waited.

"When are you coming home?''

"Next Sunday.'' He already knew that.

"I'll be waiting for you.''

He wasn't getting away with that. She detested misunderstandings, and that sentence reminded her of a molted animal; it was and it wasn't.

"Do you mean you'll be waiting for me at the airport?''

"That and more.'' The slight unsteadiness of his voice, deep and suddenly hollow, set her heart to thudding so hard that it frightened her, for she could recognize the truth when she heard it. And what was *her* truth? She had six days in which to settle that with herself.

"I'll be there Sunday."

"All right. Good night, babe."

The next afternoon, Melinda joined with Winnie for an organized bus tour of Ancient Rome. "Stay as close to me as you can get," the guide told his group, as the thirty-some tourists assembled in front of the Catacombs at San Sabastiano just off Via Appia Antica, the Appian Way, near where, it is said, Christ appeared to Peter.

"I thought this was where the Christians hid out during the Inquisition," Winnie said upon learning that they were about to enter the underground Christian burial site.

"No way. When they got here," Melinda explained dryly, "they'd finished hiding. Trust me."

The group followed the guide into the black labyrinth of the past along path after path of rows upon rows of boxes, the final resting places of the long-ago departed. "I'm getting out of this dump," Winnie said. "Ain't been no air in this place in eighteen hundred years."

"Hurry up, Winnie. If we get left down here, we'll never get out."

"Both of my feet hurt. I'm walking fast as I can."

Melinda didn't want to panic, but dread and unease had settled over her. "I don't even hear the others, Winnie."

"I know, but I have to rest."

"Go right ahead, you'll be in good company. Some of these good people have been resting down here since the second century A.D. According to my guide book, this is the only cemetery in Rome that was available for Christian burials throughout the Middle Ages."

"Well, I hope they've been happy down here. I hate this place."

"In that case, walk faster or you may never get out."

"But I—"

"We're way behind. I can barely hear the guide, and I can't see a thing. I'm going to walk faster. If you park yourself down here to rest, girl, I'll see you in heaven."

"You can't leave me."

"Not if you keep up with me, I can't. But I'm not getting left down here, so come on."

She grabbed Winnie's hand and all but dragged her along the dark, dank path. Seeing a shaft of light, Melinda decided she was getting out there; she didn't care where the guide and his followers were.

"So there you are," the guide said as they emerged into the glaring sunlight. "I was afraid we would have to leave you."

Melinda remembered that standing akimbo with *both* fists on your hips was supposed to be unladylike, but that didn't cause her to desist. "Are you telling me you would have left us down there to rot?"

The man lifted his right shoulder in a lazy shrug. "I had a one-way ticket. To go back for you would cost me six hundred lira. With that, I can buy bread."

You could have bought a lot more than that with the tip I'm not giving you, Melinda said to herself. Noticing that the group listened to their conversation, Melinda turned to them, raised her arms as if in surrender, and said, as dramatically as she could, "Imagine! My life for a loaf of bread." The group rewarded her with a spirited ovation.

"What am I going to do?" Winnie asked no one in particular. "My feet feel terrible."

"Buy another pair of feet and quit griping," a woman of around eighty advised.

"Or find another way of calling attention to yourself," a Scandinavian blonde said in an air of disgust.

"Wasn't it great?" Winnie asked when they were back on the bus and headed for the Quirinal, the highest of Rome's seven hills, for a view of the city at sunset, renowned as an awesome sight.

Melinda stared at Winnie with what she supposed was a withering look. "Sure, and you're in Germany right now reclining against the Brandenburg Gate."

"Oh, pooh," Winnie said. "It was fun. Where'll we go tomorrow?"

Melinda leaned back in her seat, took a deep breath, and let a grin creep over her face. "Tomorrow, I am going to let you give your feet the rest they deserve."

For the next five days, Melinda drifted around Rome, partly in awe of the art, architecture, and remnants of Roman glory and partly dazed by Blake's subtle promise. She'd withstood so much adversity that she couldn't think of anything she feared, except lightning and coming to terms with Blake. A strong, sensual and possessive man, nobody had to tell her that if he made love to her, he'd own her heart and her whole being. And she was hungry for him, had been for five years, starved to come alive in his arms, to know at last what she'd missed.

The trouble was, he wasn't sure of her honor; at least, he hadn't been the last time she saw him, and eight or nine days alone with his thoughts wouldn't likely have changed that. What had changed, she figured, was the seesaw between his intellect and his libido, and his intellect wasn't winning this one.

Melinda's dilemma didn't approximate Blake's battle. "I know I'm not cheating Prescott, that if he were alive, I wouldn't contemplate any kind of intimacy with Melinda," he said aloud in the privacy of his bedroom. "Then why can't I just let go and enjoy what I want so badly that I can't sleep at night?"

"Your honor is all you have," his father had preached to

him and his brother. "Don't touch another man's wife." It was as much a part of him as his name.

He finished dressing in jeans, a Chicago Bulls T-shirt and sneakers, got his baseball cap, and headed for the Metropolitan Transitional Services Center in Baltimore. Thinking of the place, he shook his head. It was an institution for inmates with short-term sentences, and no ambiguous title would change that. He parked, went inside, and signed in at the warden's office.

"How's Lobo doing?" he asked the warden.

The man pursed his lips and moved his head from side to side. "Rotten. The kid's trouble waiting to happen. He knows it all. Would you believe he started organizing a gang right in this prison?"

"Yeah. I believe it, but that doesn't mean he's hopeless."

"He can serve the rest of his time over in Hagerstown. I got enough problems."

"He was a bad influence on Phil and Johnny, but I hate to see him go to Hagerstown."

"The boys'll be down in a minute. By the way, you seen Ethan?" The warden's cynical attitude toward youthful criminals was one of the reasons why so few at that institution made an effort to reform.

"I saw him a few days ago. He has a job, and he's trying to stay straight." The disbelieving stare the warden leveled at him didn't surprise him.

"You talking 'bout the same Ethan? Well, that's a miracle if I ever heard of one."

Blake raised his shoulder in a quick shrug. "No miracle whatsoever. He just needed a little help."

Blake took a seat. He'd learned not to stand when the boys came down to meet with him. Most were short, and his six-feet-four-inches height seemed to intimidate them. When he was sitting, they were equals. He didn't have a long wait for Phil and Johnny.

"Thanks for getting that school to take us," they said in unison. "The principal interviewed us and said we could stay together," Phil added. "He said we'd keep each other out of trouble."

"In two years, you'll finish high school," he told them. "You're getting another chance." He looked at Johnny. "Pretty soon, you'll beat me at chess; there isn't much more I can teach you. So I found a chess instructor for you when you get out. You could be a champion if you work at it."

"Oh, I am. I can beat every guy in here now. Who woulda thought a game like that could be so much fun?"

"What happened to Lobo?" Phil asked Blake.

"Seems he doesn't want to get his act together, so they're sending him to Hagerstown."

"Whew. That brother's full of it, man," Phil said. "He wanted to organize a distribution ring for when we get out, but I told him no way. I'm in here for snatching a woman's pocketbook; that heavy stuff could get me sent to Westover."

He'd never asked them why they were incarcerated, not wanting to put a wall between himself and the boys, but he had their confidence now, so he felt comfortable asking Johnny, "What about you?"

"I was shoplifting, but what I got wasn't worth this trip." His shoulders sagged. "Nothing woulda been. No matter how hungry you get, man, in here you gotta wait till somebody feeds you."

Blake watched, awed, as Johnny sliced the air above his head. "I had it up to here, man." What a difference from the day he met them!

Sweet music to his ears. Some of the boys he worked with changed their lives, but a lot of them went back to jail. He consoled himself with the thought that it was worth the effort if only one became a successful citizen, husband, and father.

"I can't stay long today," he said. "I have to meet someone at the airport." And he had to go back to Ellicott City and dress, because he wouldn't have dared visit those boys wearing a business suit, shirt, and tie. They threw him a high five, and he headed for home and then—Melinda.

"You look good," he said, taking her bags. She didn't offer him a kiss and he didn't expect her to. "Relaxed and refreshed. Yeah. You look . . . great."

Her smile was what he'd waited for. Warm and generous. "There aren't any flies on you," she said. "You look terrific, and you haven't even left town." She stopped and worried her bottom lip in that way she had just before one of her wicked utterances.

"Hmmm. You didn't leave town, did you, Blake?"

He felt good. Lord, he felt good. He was living and breathing again. The hell with it. He put his free arm around her and squeezed her to him as they walked through the terminal.

"I went to Baltimore."

"Silly. That's not what I meant and you know it."

He moved his arm from her waist and took her hand. "You know how it is, sweetheart; when the cat's away . . ." Enough of that.

The happiness he felt nearly overwhelmed him. He wasn't used to it. At the bottom of the escalator, he stopped and stared down at her. He didn't know what she saw in his face when she looked at him, for he had never felt so vulnerable. She sucked in her breath and wet her lips and he bent to her mouth. Her arms crept up his chest to his shoulders, and then he could feel her fingers at the back of his head just before she parted her lips and invited him in. The heat of desire, frustrated, long bottled up, plowed through his body, and he locked her to him and plunged his tongue into her sweet welcoming mouth. She sucked on it, pulling it deeper while her hands caressed his head and the side of his face, and the sound of her moans excited him until his libido warned him of what would come next. He wanted to let himself go, but it wasn't the time or the place.

It wasn't easy to release her, but what choice did he have? They were in the airport, even if the escalator shielded them. But he knew that if they'd had privacy, he wouldn't have stopped unless she asked him to.

He did his best to reduce the sexual tension, putting his arm loosely around her waist and continuing toward his car. "Is that Italian fellow expecting to see you again?"

He nearly stopped walking when a burst of giggles escaped her. That was one trait he would never have associated with Melinda Rodgers.

"What's cracking you up?" he asked, putting her bags in the trunk of his car. He opened the passenger door for her, hooked her seat belt, and got in. She laughed aloud.

"What's funny?"

"That Italian will not be looking for me because he's under the impression that I'm divorced. He's a practicing Catholic and isn't about to get mixed up with a divorced woman."

He quirked an eyebrow and told himself to keep his gaze on the highway, but he'd give anything for a good look at her right then. "Why did you tell him that?"

Her laughter rolled over him, the sweet music of a master musician. "He asked if I was married, and I said not anymore. I guess I don't look old enough to be a widow, or maybe the world thinks we Americans get divorced whenever we're bored. I don't know."

"You could have straightened him out."

"I congratulated him on being a religious gentle— What *is*

this? He wanted an affair. Are you saying I should have encouraged him? Pull over to the shoulder and let me out of here.''

"Hey! Do you think I'm crazy? I just wanted to satisfy myself that you didn't want the guy.''

"Didn't want him?" she fumed. "I was in his company one evening. Is that what you think of me?''

He couldn't help laughing though he knew she'd get madder. "If truth be known, it happened to me the first time I looked at you, and it's only gotten worse day by day for the five years since.''

"Humph. You're a man. That's the way men do things.''

He pulled up to her house, cut the motor, threw his head back, and roared with laughter. "And you sure are a female. Lord, I missed you, and I didn't even know why.''

Her head snapped around so that she faced him. "If you know now, be sure not to keep it to yourself. I hate the darkness, real or imagined.''

He looked at her and allowed himself a grin that dissolved into a laugh. "A great philosopher once said, 'Knowledge is truth; nothing can be known.' I'm with him.''

She stared at him for long minutes before swinging her long legs around and getting out of the car. "You're crazy. You know that?''

"Maybe. I don't know. Something's happening.''

She reached in her pocketbook for her door keys, put the key in the lock, stopped, and turned around to look at him, amazement splashed over her face. "You have laughed more since you walked into that airport terminal than in all the years I've known you. At least, around me.'' Her voice softened. "Do you . . . uh . . . have any idea why?''

Maybe because he was so glad to see her, but he certainly wasn't going to tell her that. Her question sobered him. "Beats me. I'm not in a habit of analyzing myself.''

She turned around, opened the door, took a few steps inside, and stopped.

He sensed that something wasn't right. "What's the matter?"

"I smell a cigar. Nobody's smoked a cigar in this house for as long as I've lived here. And this is definitely the odor of a cigar."

He sniffed the air. She was right. "Maybe Ruby had company."

"Blake," she said, her voice strained, "I gave Ruby a vacation. She's in Virginia visiting her mother, and she left the day before I did and won't be back until day after tomorrow. Ruby's husband doesn't smoke. So what can this be?"

He unhooked his cell phone from his belt and dialed the police department.

Two officers searched the house, the gardens, and the pool, but didn't find anyone, nor did they find evidence of tampering. But they confirmed that the smell of cigar smoke also permeated the den upstairs.

"Don't stay here tonight," Blake said. "Until we can get a guard posted here, I want you to stay in a hotel."

"That's not a bad idea," one of the officers said, as they walked to the front door. "If the guy didn't find what he was after, he'll be back. If you need us, call. Meantime, we'll cruise by ever so often to check things out."

She thanked them and dropped into the nearest chair, the euphoria in which Italy had draped her no longer evident. "I don't want to go to a hotel. How could anyone get into this house without leaving some evidence of forced entry?"

He knelt before her on his haunches. "That person could have a key, could have had one for years. Consider changing the locks and the security system." He jumped up. Where was his head? "Wait a minute? Did you leave that security camera on?" He knew before she spoke, from the expression on her face, that she hadn't done it.

"What about the man who wanted to get in here that night just before you left for Italy. Did you get him on camera?"

She sprang from the chair, ran to the front door, and rewound the camera. *Not an inch of film, used or unused, remained.* Panic streaked across her face. "It's empty. Oh, my Lord. That's what he came in here for."

He rushed to her and put his arms around her. Logic said that was only one of the things the man had wanted. The point was, what did he want that night and why did he go in the den and no other room?

"Did Prescott have any relatives that you knew of? He told me he was adopted, an only child, and that both of his adoptive parents were dead. Is that what he told you?"

Though she tried to hide it, he could see fear in her eyes, stark and real. "That's what he told me. He said he was lonely as a child and always wished he had siblings or cousins." She frowned, obviously searching her mind. "Maybe you should check his past business associates. Did anyone ever stay here with him? This . . . this beats me, Blake."

"Tell you what. Let's put a roll of film in that camera and set it. I'll have a guard stationed front and back tonight. You can stay with me . . . if you're willing to chance it, or—"

"What do you mean if I'm willing to chance it?"

It wasn't a moment for comedy, but the way she stood there, hands on her hips, ready to take a dare, he couldn't help grinning at her. "You can risk the tongues of the local gossipmongers, or . . ." He stopped laughing and let all that he felt for her shine in his eyes. "Or you can risk me."

After contemplating his words, she let him know what she thought of her own strength as well as his character. "Since Prescott died, I've realized that the good people of Ellicott City think I'm tarnished and they'll probably always think it."

Her lips worked furiously, almost trembling, and he could see how close she was to tears. But she pushed her shoulders back and raised her head, ready to deal with the problem *and* with him. "Truth is, *you're* not even certain that I'm not what these people think I am. But I can stay with you in your house without risking anything. I'm never going to let myself down, and I'd bet on your pride and that awesome self-control of yours anytime."

Maybe she was sure; he certainly wasn't. He might be uncertain about his attitude toward her but definitely not about want he wanted and needed. "I think it's best you have the house secured. I can take care of that tomorrow morning, if you'd like."

But she seemed preoccupied. "That man was about . . . I'd say around fifty-five or sixty, from the picture the camera took. I'm not too good at drawing, but I think I could sketch him near enough."

He stared at her. "You mean you looked at the pictures and rewound the film?"

"Yeah. I did."

She sketched the man as she remembered him and gave the drawing to Blake. "I think I'd better stay in a hotel tonight."

He handed her his cell phone, and with the operator's assistance, she called the Sheraton and reserved a room.

"I'll drive you. Call me in the morning when you're ready to come home."

On the drive back to Baltimore, he kept thinking about the sketch. He'd never seen the man, who probably wasn't a relative. The answer was right at the forefront of his mind, but he couldn't pull it out. He would, though.

Her words interrupted his thoughts. "Prescott never told me much about his business, and I didn't ask. I knew he'd closed his laboratory and that he couldn't work with chemicals any longer. But that's about all. Ruby answered the phone, so I didn't know who called him."

It didn't make sense to him that a wife wouldn't be interested in her husband's affairs. "Didn't you ever ask him about his friends and associates?"

"You're the only one of his associates that I met, and if he had any other friends, I didn't know about them. When we met, I suspected he'd been very lonely, and little things he said gave me the impression that many of the movers and shakers in Ellicott City resented him."

A glance told him that she'd drifted into the past. "He was such a great storyteller; through his reminiscences, I saw the world. As I told you, it was his tales of Italy that prompted me to go to Florence and Rome." She settled down in the leather-cushioned seat and sighed. "He was a good provider and a wonderful companion. I was contented."

He nearly hit the brakes. What a way for a woman to speak of her husband! Not a word of love or affection. A young, sensual woman who got scorching hot whenever he touched her. It didn't make a bit of sense, and he'd have to give it a lot of thought; if she hadn't married for love, then what for? He'd spent the past week grappling with his doubts about her motive for marrying Prescott and had decided to give her the benefit of the doubt. But she'd just popped that balloon. His gaze drifted to the speedometer, and he lessened the pressure on the accelerator. It wouldn't do to get a ticket for driving seventy miles an hour in a fifty-five zone, but the shock of her words had taken his mind off the need for careful driving. He was a lawyer, and investigating people was a part of his business. He didn't intend to continue in ignorance about a woman who, if she knew it, could bring him to his knees.

The next morning, Melinda stood in front of the Sheraton waiting for Blake and hating herself for not haven driven to Baltimore in her own car. She'd spent half the night trying to figure out the reasons for his on-again off-again passion. In the airport terminal, he'd kissed her as if he were afraid she'd evaporate, but a couple of hours later at the hotel registration desk, he'd forced a grin and said, "See you in the morning." *And what about your own indecisiveness,* a niggling voice demanded.

Before Blake could get out of the car and walk around to her side of it, she opened the passenger's door, threw her small hand luggage in the backseat, and got in. "Thanks for coming."

"My pleasure. I've had a guard posted around the house, and as soon as you get home, we can call a security agency."

"You don't think I should keep the one I have?"

"Whatever you think best," he said, surprising her by leaving the decision up to her. "Might be a good idea to change though, because there's no telling who the culprit is."

During the trip home, their conversation consisted of banalities, impersonal words to cover self-consciousness and fill the space vacated by intimacy. At the front gate, he introduced her to Tillman, the guard, and walked with her through the downstairs portion of the house where she met Hawkins, who'd posted himself on the back porch.

"You ought to be safe with these fellows here." He gave her the phone number of the security company. "This one has an excellent reputation; Tillman and Hawkins are their men." She made an appointment for later that day and thanked him.

When he looked at her as though scrutinizing every pore of her face, she could see the conflict in him and his unwillingness to let go whatever misgivings haunted him at the moment and prevented him from taking her in his arms. Self-control was a thing to admire, but as far as she was concerned, that much of it could shackle a man. If he ever let himself go, she wanted to be there.

Suddenly impatient with his uncertainty, she started for the front door. "I may call you this afternoon after I work out a slate of officers for the board. I'm anxious to get this over with."

This time, it would be she who did the brush-off. "Thanks for the lift." She opened the door and waited.

But he wouldn't be rushed or dismissed. "Call me as soon as the security man finishes. I want to check it out before he leaves."

At her raised eyebrow, he said, "As executor of this estate, I'm responsible for it until I can legally turn it over to you. See you this afternoon."

Displeased because he'd had the last word, she saluted him. "Yes, sir." But if it nettled him, he didn't let her know it.

She watched him drive off and wondered if she'd ever be a normal woman in a normal relationship with a normal man. When he'd laughed so happily after they met in the airport and been so sweet and loving, she'd begun to hope he'd won his battle with his conscience or whatever objections he had to their relationship. But he hadn't changed—or maybe he'd backtracked—and if she didn't get that board in order and get out of Ellicott City, she didn't know what she'd do. The phone rang, and when she heard her father's voice, she actually welcomed it. How could she be so forlorn that she welcomed the lecture she knew he'd give her?

"You're back. Weren't you going to call your parents?"

"Hi, Papa. I stayed in Baltimore last night, and I was so tired I crashed the minute I got in my hotel room. How's Mama?"

"Just fine, thank the good Lord. What's wrong with your big house you couldn't stay there? You were by yourself, I hope. I don't trust Hunter. The man sees a chance to get rich just like all these other good-for-nothing gigolos. You watch that fellow."

"He's legally responsible for this estate, Papa. That's all."

"I'd like to know why he's so dead set against having me on the board."

"Papa, if I put you on the board, I have to put a clergyman

of every other faith and denomination on it. This isn't supposed to be a board composed of religious advocates.''

''We're outstanding citizens, and that's all the will specified. If a man of God can't be trusted, who can?''

She rolled her eyes toward the ceiling and resisted pulling air between her teeth. ''Twelve of you together would be a twelve-man wrestling match. Prescott would have hated it. The list is complete, and not a man of the cloth is on it, Papa.''

She could imagine that he frowned and rubbed his chin as he did when frustrated. ''Well, at least you didn't embarrass me. But you come to prayer meeting tomorrow night. You got to feed your soul, child, you hear?''

''Yes, sir. Love you, Papa.''

''I know, girl. I know. Bye now.''

She phoned Rachel. It was a loose friendship, but she valued it nonetheless. At least Rachel didn't blame her for Booker Jones's arrogance.

''Hey, girl! You back? Tell me you brought one of those tall, dark, and handsome Neapolitans with you.''

''I didn't go south of Rome, and if I saw a Neapolitan, I didn't know it. What've you been up to?''

''You know me, girl. I do as little as possible when it's hot. I've been looking for a date for the fair, but not a single nibble so far. You wouldn't by chance be going with a certain sexy lawyer, would you?''

In the six years she'd known Rachel, the woman had yet to show an interest in a man who was interested in her. It was incomprehensible that Rachel, a feminine, chocolate-brown woman with large dreamy eyes, couldn't find a man to love and who would love her. Of course, she had flitted away five of her best years with Ron, and not because she loved him, but in order not to be alone. From where Melinda sat, having Ron would be worse than being alone.

She'd better discourage Rachel. ''Why do you want to know

about Blake? You spent a couple of hours sitting across his desk from him when he read Prescott's will to us. If he was going to make a move, he'd have done it by now. Rachel, learn to like the men who like you; if you don't . . .'' She let it hang.

"I know. But you can't blame me for . . . Oh, what the heck, I'll ask Ron to take me."

Ron. Melinda hurt for her friend. "Honey, it's time you did something about him. I've got to get to work on this board. See you later."

"I'm sure glad you're back home, even if you did come back by yourself. See you."

One by one, she rejected as chairperson of the board each of the individuals she and Blake had considered. Then she remembered that when Prescott died, Betty Leeds called to ask if she could help her and sent a basket of flowers to the memorial service. The only one who did so. As she reflected on that period, she realized for the first time that many people resented her husband's wealth and accomplishments. She'd thought they snubbed her because she'd married a man more than twice her age and assumed she did it for his money, but she was learning that they didn't like him, either. For whatever reason, their harsh judgment hurt.

The security company's man replaced the security system and knocked on the door of the den where she worked. "I've finished, ma'am. Nobody can get into this house without a key or sounding a loud alarm that rings here and in our office, in which case, the police will be here in ten minutes."

She remembered that Blake wanted to look over the system and called him.

"I'll be there in a few minutes."

Her call surprised him, because he'd expected her to ignore that request. He'd meant it, but he'd also needed an excuse to go back to her, to be near her. He rubbed the back of his neck and walked from one end of his den to the other, back and forth. It was moving so fast, too fast, and yet, he couldn't stop it. Didn't want to stop it. And why should he?

His gut instinct told him she was honest. She had to be; if she'd told him the truth, she'd wanted him for almost five years. He'd been in her home visiting with her husband, and he'd dined at her table more times than he could count, and not once had she let him know that he attracted her. Yet, now she admitted wanting him from the minute she laid eyes on him. And he believed her, because he only had to touch her and she became a torch in his arms. He needed her. That sweet, innocent smile could seep into him and tie him in knots.

But so much about her mystified him, and he was too smart to get entangled with . . . Hell, he *was* entangled. He . . . When he saw the sunset over Lake Kittamaqundi, he longed to share it with her. Something so ordinary as his brioche and morning coffee would fail to satisfy him when he longed to let her taste it. And he no longer found solitude when he sat alone at the edge of the lake with the breeze whipping around him.

He sat down and dropped his head in his hands. How long had he loved her? And he loved her. Oh, yes. No mistake about that. For what other reason would he think about her when he was arguing a case and writing his briefs? Why would he lie awake at night aching for her, and why didn't he ease that ache with another woman?

For a full fifteen minutes after he reached her house, he sat in his car, telling himself to cool down, that loving her didn't mean he had to lose his perspective.

Finally, he went inside, checked the doors, windows, and gates as well as the additional cameras installed at the front and back doors. "It's sound," he said to the man and gave him his business card. "Send the bill to me at this address."

"Right. I'm glad you're pleased."

* * *

"Wait a minute," she said to Blake as he started down the stairs. "There's supposed to be some kind of alarm in this walk-in closet. I should have told the security man about it. At least, I think Prescott said it's an alarm."

"Which closet?"

She pointed to a door in the hallway next to the den. "This one right here. It's full of stuff Prescott stored in there. I've opened the door and looked, but I've never been in it."

Slowly, tentatively, her hand turned the knob, and she opened the door and stepped inside. A box fell, and then another and another. *"Blake!* Help me with this thing!"

He was already there, pushing the box back on the shelf. "I've got it. Find the light switch."

It was then that he felt her hips cradled against him. Then she turned, and her breasts flattened against his chest, her breathing accelerated, and when he tried to twist away from her he knocked over a stack of heavy boxes. Fearing that they might have hit her, he grabbed her. And then her scent filled his nostrils, her breasts heaved against his chest, and he could feel her tremors. He had to get away from there. He had to . . .

"Melinda where is the li . . ." Good Lord. Her mouth was there, the hard tips of her breasts teased his pectorals, and she shifted her body against his. His blood thundered in his ears, and then . . . She clicked on the light, and he looked down at the wild, hungry woman in his arms. He supposed she saw the inevitable staring her in the face, because she bolted from that closet, and he followed her out of it to where she leaned against the wall, panting, her eyes closed.

They stood there as if in a trance until she opened her eyes, and his gaze followed hers as she looked across the hall at the open door of her bedroom.

"He . . . uh . . . You think that man did a good job?" she

asked him. "I mean . . . he . . . uh . . . wasn't here but three hours."

She rubbed her hands up and down her sides almost rhythmically, and he watched their movement fully aware of the significance. As if seeking privacy or a means of escape, she half-turned from him.

But he'd seen her tight nipples outlined beneath her jersey T-shirt, pointed and erect, and when she swallowed not once but several times, his blood began to race and his heart slammed against his chest, pounding like a pagan drummer. He should get out of there, but he knew he wouldn't.

"You want me to leave?"

Her shoulders jerked forward as if he'd frightened her, and she stopped stroking her thighs, folded her arms and rubbed them almost as if she punished them.

"I said, do you want me to leave? Do you?"

When she spun around to face him and gasped, he knew his emotions blazed on his face.

He jammed his hands into his pockets and stepped closer to her, knowing that if he put his hands on her he'd have a hard time removing them. She still hadn't answered him.

"I'll leave this minute if you want me to. Tell me what you want."

"I . . . I . . . Blake, for heaven's sake, what do you want from me?"

Her trembling body swayed toward him, but he kept his hands in his pockets. He'd fought it until he couldn't. He was tired and . . . he loved her . . . and . . . and needed her as he needed his beating heart.

He barely recognized the dry, hollow tones that came from the depth of his being. "I want you. That's what I want, and if you don't tell me to leave here, I'm going to have you. You want me. I can see it. I smell it. I've needed you for years. All you have to do is say the word *go.*"

Over his shoulder, she looked at the mauve and lavender bedroom in which she'd slept alone for almost five years, and the pain and loneliness of it settled on her once more. All the nights of tossing in that bed while he'd loved her only in her heart and mind came back to her with punishing force. And she loved him and had for . . . for so long. When he stood before her like that, strong and manly but vulnerable, open and pained, she could neither deny him nor herself.

"You . . . first you want me and then you don't. I'm human, Blake, and . . . and I hurt . . . I—"

He interrupted her. "And I hurt. Either tell me to leave or come here and put your arms around me."

She looked at his outstretched arms and forgot about reason. Forgot that tomorrow he'd be sorry. Forgot about what the people thought of her and what he probably thought. *I'm twenty-nine years old, and he's the only man I've ever wanted, ever loved. I'll regret it, but I don't care. At least I'll know what it is to lie in his arms.* She made herself look into his eyes and the expression in them nearly unglued her.

"Melinda!"

He spread his legs, emphasizing his manliness, and his nostrils flared as his aura seeped into her. She swallowed the liquid that accumulated in her mouth, inhaled his scent, tasted him, and her blood roared in her ears as she stared at his outstretched arms.

Maybe she moved on air; she didn't know how she got to him, but his big hands were locked on her, holding her. She raised her face and knew the power of his unleashed passion as his mouth possessed her. She parted her lips and his tongue danced in her mouth, mating with every crevice of it, taunting and teasing. Laying claim. And possessing. His hands claimed her buttocks, then skimmed over her arms, her neck, and her back. Her heart began to hammer out an erratic rhythm as he twirled his tongue in her mouth. His lips. His smell. His hands. All of him. He possessed her.

Her breasts ached so badly. Why didn't he do something to them? She needed ... Grabbing his hand, she rubbed her left nipple with his palm and moans pealed from her throat. When he attempted to raise her T-shirt, she jerked it over her head and threw it across the room. In seconds, her bra was on the floor, his hot mouth opened over her nipple, and spirals of unbearable tensions shot through her, straight to her heaving center until she let out a keening cry of helpless surrender.

"Take me to bed," she pleaded, as he suckled her. But he moved to the other breast and nourished himself until she cried out, "Blake, something's happening to me."

His head snapped up, and he stared down at her, but she pressed her face to his chest. His hands stroked her back with such tenderness that she almost cried.

"That's my room right over there," she whispered. He couldn't leave her. Not now.

He took her hand and stopped at her bedroom door. "Are you sure? If we go any further, I don't know if I'll be able to stop."

She did her best to smile. "I won't want you to stop."

He threw back the covers on her bed, stepped behind her, and caressed her breast. At the touch of his fingers on her naked flesh, hot darts of desire zoomed straight to her love portal. Shaking, she turned around to face him. He lifted her and laid her on her bed, and when she made as if to remove her pedal pushers, he stilled her hand. While he pulled them off slowly and methodically, her nerves rioted in her body. He stood there looking down at her, as she lay there nude but for little more than a G-string, and desire roared through her with awesome force.

She watched him disrobe, impatient for what was to come. When he knelt beside her bed and kissed her from her head to her feet, her hips swayed involuntarily, but he wouldn't be rushed. At last, she spread her legs and raised her arms to him in a gesture as old as woman.

"Honey, please. I'm going out of my mind."

But he kissed her thighs, moving to the inside of them slowly upward until he reached her woman's secret. Methodically, as if they had always been his to love, he opened her folds and kissed her until her hips moved upward to meet his rapacious lips.

"Blake," she moaned. "I can't stand it."

"All right, love." He climbed into the bed beside her, gathered her into his arms, and let her feel all of him, from his powerful shoulders to his full hard length, and she gasped in surprise. His kisses were showers of fire, and with his lips locked to her nipple suckling her, draining her of will, her womb contracted. Frantic for relief, she lifted her hips to receive him, but he wasn't ready. He pulled her nipple deeper into his mouth and let his fingers drift to her petals of love, where he teased, stroked, and tantalized until she screamed aloud. She felt a gush of liquid, and he rose above her, sheathed himself with a condom, and stared down into her eyes.

"Look at me, Melinda. I want you to know that it's me loving you. Think about me and nobody and nothing else."

"Yes. Oh, yes."

His lips brushed hers. Then he twirled his tongue around her nipple and suckled her while his fingers stroked the most intimate part of her until she writhed beneath him. Frustrated, she reached down and took him in her hand.

"That's right, love. Yes, oh, yes. It's what I want you to do. Take me in, sweetheart."

She brought him to her, lifted her hips for his entry, and a scream tore from her lips as he drove home.

He stared down at her. "What in the name of . . . What happened? You couldn't be—"

She nodded as he kissed the tears that streamed from her eyes. "Ours was a marriage of convenience. I was lonely, and he needed a companion."

"Well, I'll be."

"Blake, don't. Please don't leave me like this."

He gathered her to him and buried his head in the curve of her neck. "I'm ashamed. I've done you such an injustice."

"It's all right. I . . . I just want you to love me. It's all I ever wanted from the minute I saw you."

"And it's all I wanted. You're precious to me. Do you understand? How do you feel?"

"I feel like I need something to happen."

He levered himself on his forearms and kissed her eyes, her cheeks, her nose, and the curve of her neck. She turned her head in the hope of feeling his lips on her mouth, but they caressed her chin. At last, he gave her the thrust of his tongue, deep, commanding. Laying a claim. He smiled down at her, a tenderness in his eyes that she hadn't seen before. And then his lips closed over her aching nipple, and he pulled, tugged, and suckled until she contracted around him. He reached down and stroked the nub of her passion until her hips undulated, heat seared the bottom of her feet, and jolts of electricity whistled through her veins as a strange pumping and squeezing began in her center.

"Blake, please. I think I'm going to die right now."

He began to move, slowly and carefully, as if testing, but she didn't want that; she wanted to explode. "Honey, please."

"Are you okay?"

"Yes. Yes."

He thrust slowly, then faster and faster until, finally, he let her have his power. With one hand beneath her buttocks, he stroked, then teased, moving in circles.

"Tell me what you feel. Do you think I'm hitting the right

spot. It should get more urgent with each stroke. Tell me what's happening, baby."

"I don't know. I think if I don't burst wide open, I'm going to die. It's terrible and it's ... Oh, honey, it feels so ... Oh, Lord!"

He increased the pace, kept his hand between them and stroked her until the squeezing, pinching, and pumping shook her from head to feet and her whole being erupted into a vortex of ecstasy, and she released a keening cry.

"Oh, Blake. Blake. What are you doing to me?"

"I'm loving you." Then he drove masterfully, and when the rhythmic movement around him ceased, he gripped her to him and, with a powerful shudder, collapsed in her arms.

They lay locked together as one, his body within hers. Speechless. Undone by the force of what they'd just experienced. She prayed that he wouldn't tell her he was sorry.

After a few minutes he separated them, but continued to lie above her. "Are you all right? Tell me how you feel."

"I'm ... I guess I'm kinda in shock. If I'd known that I'd be this way with you, I wonder if I would have been a virtuous wife. I feel ... liberated. A whole woman. I feel fabulous."

He stared down into her face. "You're not sorry?"

She shook her head. "No. How could I be? What about you? If you are, I don't want to know it."

"I'd have to be an idiot to regret an experience like this. No, I am not sorry." He seemed to search her, looking for she couldn't imagine what.

"What is it?"

"I never dreamed you were ... uh ... untouched. Why didn't you tell me? I would never have been so careless. I would have taken pains not to—"

"You couldn't avoid hurting me. At least it was over in a second."

He grinned in that way that she loved. "We're going to readjust this whole scenario."

"What do you mean by that?"

"When I look at you, think of you, I don't want to associate you with Prescott, because you were never his, and now . . . now, you'll never be any man's but mine."

Not associate her with Prescott Rodgers? Her eyes widened. He was kidding himself.

Chapter Six

When he would have separated their bodies, she locked her legs around his hips and held him to her. Though shaken by the enormity of what he'd just experienced, a sadness pervaded him at the thought of what had *not* happened. He looked at the woman who smiled up at him, sweet and trusting, as if he were her whole world. She'd given him everything, and he had felt her love and trust, but he hadn't been able to let himself go, to give himself up to her, open and exposed. He'd never been able to do it, not once with any woman, because that meant baring his soul, exposing his insides. But this time, he'd been so sure . . . because he loved her. For the first time in his life, he loved. And still . . . He closed his eyes and tightened his grip on her, fighting off the loneliness he suddenly felt. She would accept and cherish whatever he gave her, however he gave it, at least for now, because she loved him. But the time would come when she would need all of him. He kissed her eyes and her sweet lips and thanked God that he'd brought her to a powerful climax. He'd done his best to give her everything, and he had. *All but myself.* He knew now that until he resolved his conflicts about her, he couldn't give more.

"You're so pensive, Blake."

He tried to make light of it. "This is a time for reflection. First time I've . . . uh . . . initiated a woman, and believe me, sweetheart, it takes a mental adjustment."

"Is that bad?"

So she was anxious. "Would you call being alive with every atom of your being shouting to the heavens a bad thing? How could you think that?" he asked, striving to put her at ease.

"I'm not an expert on the minds of men. Just about everything they do surprises me."

He made himself grin, though he wasn't in a grinning mood. "Whoa. That's a man's line. Are you telling me—"

She interrupted. "Do you think I expected ever to be in this bed with you? Not even after you kissed me until I got the shivers. You said it wouldn't happen, and I believed you."

He could almost see his gloom evaporate. He laughed. Laughter was one of the gifts she'd given him. And how precious it was!

"I believed me, too," he said when he could stop laughing. "I'll have to learn to be more reliable."

Her fingers moved slowly over his face, as if seeing him with her senses rather than with her eyes. "Not about this, I hope. But I don't suppose I have to knock myself out thinking about it. Once the genie is out of the bottle . . ."

Lord, he loved her. If only . . . Until he could master himself, he'd make sure she didn't want or need any other man. He sucked her nipple into his mouth, put one arm around her shoulder, a hand beneath her hips, and began to move.

* * *

Hours later, he walked with her down the stairs holding her fingers so tightly that they hurt, but she didn't remove his hand because she knew he was fighting with himself. He had the proof that Prescott had not consummated their marriage, but did he believe the reason she gave him? The truth? And if he did, would he punish himself with the notion that he'd taken his friend's wife? When he'd been loving her, she'd never felt so cherished, and when she'd exploded beneath his driving passion, she knew she'd never stop loving him. He'd made her feel like a queen, the only one alive, but right now something separated them and she suspected it was his conscience.

At the door, she said, "You know Ruby's off today. I could cook you something quickly."

He shook his head. "I'll get a sandwich when I get home." Then he gazed at her with a look that said he wanted something, but she couldn't imagine what because she didn't feel his sexual tension. Perhaps he was trying not to show it, she mused, for he'd moved back from her.

"You said you weren't sorry."

He shook his head as the fawnlike eyes she loved let their brilliance bore into her, seeming to penetrate her soul. "I am not sorry, Melinda, and I never will be. We'll talk tomorrow." His kiss on her lips fired her for a second, and then he was gone.

Several mornings later, reading her mail, Melinda stacked seven letters in a pile and considered throwing them out. Reading them would be a waste of time; every letter would reveal a man who wanted to ride Prescott Rodgers's gravy train.

The handwriting on one letter persuaded her to open it. Goose bumps popped out on her arms when she read, *One of these days, lady. One of these days.* There was no signature, only a post office box number that she suspected would prove phoney. Maybe she should show it to Blake. However, after a minute, she discarded the idea; she'd fight her own battles.

"Miz Melinda," Ruby called. "A gentleman says he wants desperately to speak to you. I shore do wish I'da been a widow before I got married. It must be somethin' having a pack of mens chasing you. Course I'da still married Piper. You wanna talk to this man?"

No, she didn't want to talk with him. "Take his number, Ruby, and I'll call him. I'm busy right now."

"Yes, ma'am."

Later, looking at the name Ruby had written down, she threw her hands up in disgust. She'd never heard of the man. If she put an ad in the paper saying she'd made her choice, that wouldn't stop it. She'd have to ask Blake to figure a way out of it.

She answered Ruby's knock on her bedroom door. "What is it, Ruby?"

"My Piper said the mens where he works is all talking about you having to get married before a year's up. They said if you choose one of them, that one would agree to help the others support they families. Not including my Piper, mind you. Is that why all these mens is calling here? If you sick of it, I can just tell 'em you already found the man."

"I'd rather you didn't do that. I'm not going to marry a fortune hunter. Period. Maybe I'll keep all these letters and write a book."

Ruby's laughter always seemed to start in the pit of her belly and reverberate from the ceiling. And this time, she gave it full rein.

"What you gon' call it? 'Ducking Work'? Or maybe 'Unearned Income'? I declare these mens is somethin'."

"Or maybe I'll call it 'Wagging The Dog.' "

"And that's just what they's trying to do."

Melinda completed the slate of officers for the board of the Prescott Rodgers Foundation, called them, ascertained their willingness to hold office, and mailed the list to Blake.

"You could have given them to me over the phone," he told her. "You're not avoiding me, are you?"

After years of having to pussyfoot around the truth, from then on she intended to tell it like it was. "You know how it is with me, Blake. Nothing has changed. But I can see that you need a little space, so it's your move."

"Look, I—"

"I don't want to hear any reasons; just let me know when you get it straightened out."

"I . . . I want to see you." His voice reached her as a hoarse whisper. "You . . . you're everywhere. This house is full of you."

"What do you think of the officers I chose?"

"Damn it, Melinda, didn't you hear what I just said?"

Don't do this to me, Blake. Don't make me hurt any worse than I do already. "I heard you, but I'm not listening. I can't."

She'd never heard him sigh, and hearing it now shocked her. "I know what you're saying and why, and I . . . well, I don't blame you. But can't we at least see each other sometime?"

She thought for a moment. They certainly could. "I've just decided I'd like to go to the Urban League's July Fourth dinner dance. Want to take me?"

"I thought the league was sponsoring a picnic down at Kittamaqundi Lake. I threw the invitation in the wastebasket."

"And you obviously didn't read it. If you got an invitation, you're also invited to the dinner dance. The picnic isn't invitational; it's open to the public."

"I'd love to go with you. What's the dress code?"

"Black tie. I'll be wearing a long white chiffon."

"I wouldn't miss it. The local gossipers will have a ball, but don't let that rankle you."

"If I'm with you, they can nose-dive into the lake for all I care. Look, I don't think I need those guards anymore. The house is secure. Having them here is a waste of good money."

Now what had she said? His long drawn-out silence annoyed her. "Blake, you don't have to be so obvious. If you disagree, please say so. After all, you're the one who's running this place."

"Then I say the guards remain until they're no longer needed."

"*Yes, sir!* I have to prepare the brochure explaining the board's purpose and how it will function. See you."

She hung up without waiting for his response, and she wished she hadn't. She hurt so badly. Nothing would make her believe he didn't care for her and care deeply, but she knew that until he worked out whatever was bothering him, he'd pulled the reins on himself and on a relationship with her.

Her mind wouldn't stay on the brochure. She could go out and buy shoes, but she hadn't worn the last pairs she bought when she got into a blue funk. Maybe if she called her mother. She began to dial but hung up before she finished. The phone rang, and she raced to it.

"Hello."

"You sound as if you've been running or exercising. Sit down; we have to talk."

Something began eating at her insides. "What is it, Blake?"

"Sweetheart, I can't explain my behavior, because I don't fully understand it. I know this much: you're precious to me. My body, my emotions, and my heart know what they want, but my head isn't with them, and I've operated on mental power alone ever since I was sixteen."

"Blake, you don't have to explain yourself."

He went on as if she hadn't interrupted him. "Nothing else

would account for my wanting you and caring for you all those years and being able to keep it to myself. You were right, I never planned to consummate what I feel for you, but I . . . I needed you so badly. Don't think I used you; I wanted to give you everything a man could give a woman.''

"And you did, almost."

"Almost?"

"You haven't given me yourself yet."

He didn't deny it. "We need to spend time together, see where we're headed, and I don't mean time working on Prescott's board."

"We're going to that dinner dance. That's a start."

"I'll be at your place around five-thirty that afternoon. It'll take us about half an hour to get to Baltimore."

"I'll see you then."

But he didn't hang up. "Kiss me?"

"Oh, Blake. It's not good enough. Bye."

He'd come around. She didn't doubt it for a minute, and she didn't intend to make it easy for him. She phoned Agnes's Designer Originals.

"Agnes, this is Melinda Rodgers. Do you still have that white chiffon MacFadden gown in size twelve?

"I knew you'd come back for it. It's here."

Melinda thanked her and hung up. "I feel like a teenager," she said aloud. "When I walk in there with Blake Hunter . . . I can hear the buzz right now. In that tux, he'll have women gushing all over him."

She let the phone ring four times before answering it. "Hello." She half expected, hoped to hear Blake's voice, but only silence greeted her ears. Then, breathing, heavy and rhythmic, followed by a man's harsh laugh. She slammed down the receiver. Shaken beyond words. With guards at the doors, he couldn't reach her, so he'd terrorize her by phone. "Not on your neck. You needn't even think it," she said aloud. In the future, she wouldn't lift the receiver unless she knew the caller.

"Thanks, Ruby," Blake said.

He stood at the bottom of the broad staircase and watched Melinda, loveliness personified as she glided down the stairs. She didn't look down at the steps, but gazed into his eyes like someone charmed. And he hoped she was. Her white chiffon gown billowed as she seemed to float toward him. When she reached the bottom, she held out her hand and smiled, but he could only stare at her. Bewitched.

"Hi."

He told himself to get with it, reached for her hand and held it. "You are so beautiful, so lovely."

Her smile widened, and her lashes lowered over her dreamy eyes, light brown pools of enticement that could make a man do things he'd regret. He wanted to take her back up those stairs and love her senseless.

"You look wonderful," she said. "I expect I'm going to have to fight off the females tonight."

"What about me?" he asked as they started for the door. "You don't think the guys out there tonight are going to let me have you to myself, do you?"

She laid her head to one side and looked at him from beneath those long lashes. "If you don't want me to dance with anybody else, just say you don't, and it'll be your arms only."

Fortunately, they'd cleared the front steps or he might have tripped. "Slow down, Melinda. If I ever heard a loaded remark, that was it."

She slipped her arm through his as they walked half a block to his car. "Loaded or not, a simple yes or no will do it."

He helped her fold her skirt across her knees, hooked the seat belt, and closed the door. As he walked around the car, she reached across the driver's seat and unlocked the door for him. He could get used to the company of a woman like her.

Easing the car away from the curb he remembered her comment. "You want me to respond to that remark? Come on, Melinda. If I don't say no, my name is Mudd. Right?"

He glanced toward her as a smile frolicked around her lips. "Something like that. By the way, how many women invited you to take them to this affair?"

"Two. You and Rachel what's-her-name. I've already disappointed a few by declining such invitations, and they don't ask me anymore. Put your hand over here where I can touch it without causing a wreck."

Her hand warm and soft beneath his, the delicate scent of her perfume, and that aura of peace that she never failed to project made him feel like a special man.

"You're a treasure," he said though he hadn't meant to voice his thoughts.

"Thank you. You're not bad yourself."

He hoped she meant that as a compliment. He stopped for the red light and looked across at the Wayside Inn. "Jonas was in my office today, and he said the Wayside Inn recently refurbished its Banneker Room."

"Really? I thought they did that a couple of years ago. It's amazing the pride this town has in Benjamin Banneker."

"Why not? After the Ellicott brothers, he's the town's most famous son. An astronomer, surveyor, and clock maker, the first black scientist this country produced."

"And has he got a family tree! His grandmother was a white slave holder who bought two African men from a slave ship. The same year, 1692, she freed all her slaves and married the slave from that ship. His name was Bannaka. One of her four daughters, Mary Bannaka, married a freed slave, and he took her surname, which they changed to Banneker. She gave birth to Benjamin Banneker, who inherited all of her property."

Blake took the exit off Route 95 and headed for Calvert Street. "The man traveled in fast company, too," Blake continued. "He carried on a steady correspondence with Thomas Jefferson on the injustices of slavery. You can find numerous monuments to Banneker in this part of the country."

"I know, and I'll bet half of the African-American high-school seniors have never heard of him."

"Yeah. And a pity, too. Here we are. Stay put, and I'll go around there and make sure you don't ruin that dress."

She took his arm as they entered the great hall. He'd escorted numerous beautiful women to such affairs, but this one had the eye of every man they passed. From the mirrored wall he could observe her carriage, elegant and graceful. And she paid no attention to her admirers. What a woman!

They'd been given seats at table seven, and it pleased him to see that he'd have Duncan Banks, the noted journalist, for company. Banks stood as they arrived. "Man, I've had my fingers crossed in the hopes we'd have good company. It's great to see you."

He shook hands with Duncan and made the introductions. "Duncan Banks is a friend of long standing, Melinda. This is his wife, Justine Taylor Banks. Duncan and I met in undergraduate days when Morehouse, which was my school, debated Howard, Dunc's school."

"Who won?" Melinda asked.

"They're still debating that question," Justine said. "I'm a psychologist, who's staying home with our two-year-old daughter. In the meantime, I write a syndicated column."

"I teach high-school English and English literature," Melinda said. "Seems to me we're in related fields."

Duncan leaned forward. "Right. Bring her over to see us, Blake."

"Yes, and soon," Justine said. "We could spend a weekend down at our place on the Chesapeake Bay. What about it?"

He looked at Melinda and prayed she'd show enthusiasm for the idea. These people were his closest friends, and he wanted them to love her.

"I'd love that." She turned to him, her eyes bright with excitement. "Can we?"

He nodded, too full of emotion to trust words. He turned and caught Duncan's hard stare and knew that his friend had summed up the situation and reached the right conclusion, that Blake Hunter had finally fallen in love. And there would be questions and more questions. He'd take them as they came.

Duncan's hot gaze roamed over his wife, resplendent in red silk. "Dance with me?" Her smile was that of a woman in love, and she held out her hand to her husband as he approached her.

"How long have they been married?" Melinda asked

"About three years, but being around them is like being on a couple's honeymoon. Deepens your faith in love and marriage."

Her stare spoke volumes. If he didn't know better, he'd say she'd looked right through him. "And your faith in the institution of marriage is shaky?"

"I wouldn't say that exactly but, as a lawyer, I get a constant parade of husbands and wives who behave as if they've never liked, to say nothing of having loved, each other. It makes one wonder."

She leaned back and folded her hands in her lap, exuding an aura of serenity. "What about those who stay together?"

He lifted his left shoulder in a shrug. "I've wondered about that. Whether they're happy or . . ." Leaning toward her, he whispered, "What about you and Prescott? If he had lived, would you ever have asked him for a divorce?"

"You mean if, having made my bed hard, I would have remained in it?"

He reached for her hand and stroked it. "I didn't mean to

be rude. Heck, I don't know why I bothered to ask, because
being the woman you are, you would have stayed to the end.''
    "Yes, I would have," she said, her eyes glistening suspi-
ciously. She blinked rapidly. "Prescott was honorable, and he
deserved my fidelity." Her fingers trembled within his hand.
    Now he'd done it. He stood and held out his arms to her.
"Come here, baby. Come here and let me hold you.''
    "B . . . Blake, there're several hundred people in here.''
    "Then dance with me. Anything just as long as I can get
you into my arms.''
    She stood, and he hugged her to him quickly before taking
her hand and walking with her to the dance floor.

    "I thought you weren't coming tonight.''
    Melinda moved her head from Blake's shoulder and stared
at Ray Sinclair. "Ray, I assume you know Blake Hunter. I did
say I wasn't coming, but I changed my mind.''
    "Mind if I cut in, old man?" Ray asked Blake.
    She nearly laughed aloud when Blake looked around as if
to see where the voice was coming from. "You talking to
me, buddy?" He looked at her, his eyes twinkling in that
mischievous way he had. "Baby, you want to dance with this
fellow?''
    "Me? Why . . . no. I promised you all my dances tonight.''
    "Sorry, pal. The lady says no.''
    Ray Sinclair had a temper, it seemed, and didn't take put-
downs easily. "I see you cut yourself in, Hunter. You're making
sure you're the guy who gets control of old Prescott's fortune.
You may be fooling Melinda, but I'm on to you.''
    Blake missed a step, recovered, and swung her out as if he'd
planned it. Then he stopped the dance. "I will give you a
chance to eat those words, Sinclair, or answer to the charge of

character assassination. Now get as far away from me as you can.''

She was certain he hadn't planned on making a statement that would set the tongues of Ellicott City's gossipers into perpetual motion, but what was done was done. He looked at Ray Sinclair, who seemed unaware that he'd just been threatened with a civil suit. "I mean what I said. You'll regret that remark. Now, go find whoever you came with.''

Evidently deciding to cut his losses, Ray greeted a man who passed nearby and walked off with him, immersed in what had to be a phony conversation.

"I didn't mean to embarrass you," Blake said to Melinda, "but he got off easily. I didn't grow up besting guys with clever words; in my set, we swung our fists. Sinclair was fortunate: It's been years since I settled issues that way; and besides, he showed off in a place and at a time when he knew I wouldn't split his lip.''

"I'm not embarrassed. I just wish it would end.''

"Yeah. I guess you do. Let's finish this one later," he said, referring to the dance and the fact that Ray's ill-timed interruption had sullied the sweetness of being in each other's arms.

"I assume from his remark that he would like to help you comply with the terms of Prescott's will.''

She resisted sucking her teeth, but stopped walking, turned and looked at Blake. "Ray hasn't said that, but after years of treating me as if I were an incurable disease, he's probably heard about Prescott's will, and now he's driving me crazy with his concern for my welfare. Can you think of something I can do to call off these men? They're acting as if I have to pay in order to get married. I don't give a hoot if I—''

His expression, fierce and forbidding, halted her words. Surely the evening was ruined, but he splayed his hand on her back and followed her to their table. As he seated her, he whispered, "For tonight, let's not deal with problems. I want to enjoy being with you. All right?'' His lips brushed her cheek so quickly that she might only have imagined it. She glanced up and saw Duncan's knowing gaze fixed on her.

Duncan's smile was one of indulgence, such as one might bestow on a child. ''Unless you're better at it than the rest of us, don't try winning an argument with Blake. It's usually a waste of time.''

She imagined that surprise showed on her face, because she thought she'd won some points with him. But maybe she hadn't, and issues she'd thought they'd settled would have to be fought out again.

''Come on, Dunc,'' Blake said. ''I'm not that tough. You'll scare her off.''

Duncan let a half smile play around his mouth, and she knew he'd just made up his mind about her. ''I doubt that. I think you've met your match, and it's about time.''

She looked at Justine. ''They're talking over my head.''

''It's a habit of theirs,'' Justine replied, ''but not to worry. They're as dependable as homing pigeons, and they don't surprise you . . . once you get them figured out, that is.''

Melinda looked at Blake, who sat at her left, and what she saw made her heart beat faster, but he quickly hooded his eyes, masking the passion she thought she'd seen. Yet, in that second, he touched her soul and she reached for him, involuntarily. He grasped the hand she held out to him and moved his lips. She didn't know what he said, only that, for him as for her, it was a moment of intense intimacy.

From the orchestra, the sexy growl of a tenor saxophone wailed out the blues, and Blake squeezed her fingers. ''We didn't finish that dance.''

Seconds later, he had her on the dance floor with one arm around her waist and the other around her shoulder. The saxophonist began to play a song about the wonder and beauty of a woman's loss of innocence in the arms of the man she loved, and she put her head against his shoulder while the music and Blake Hunter transported her out of herself.

She tingled with exhilaration, her heart light, as they moved to the beat and the mood of the music, his body shifting provocatively with every step. She told herself she wouldn't give in to him, but he held her close, possessively as if he had the right, and she let him drown her in the seething passion of the moment. Though she fought for control of her senses, his aura claimed her and wouldn't release her. His fingers rubbed circles in the middle of her back, causing waves of excitement to wash over her. She stumbled and missed a step.

"Blake, what's come over you? Are you trying to . . . What are these people going to think about us dancing this way?"

He brushed his lips across her forehead, looked down at her, and grinned. "The men will want to murder me, and the women would like to tear you to shreds. Let them think whatever they like."

"Easy for you to say; I'm the one they'll be talking about."

He stood still and swayed them to the pulsating beat. "Not if Ray Sinclair decides to ignore what I told him. People will talk, Melinda."

"When my father says that, he always adds, 'but make sure they aren't talking about you.' "

The saxophone stopped its wailing and Blake walked them over to the bar at the far end of the ballroom. "He certainly called attention to you last Sunday, or so I'm told."

"Again? I wish he'd stop using me for his examples of a disobedient daughter. Whenever his text begins with the Ten Commandments, I know who he did his research on."

"What would you like?" he asked her when they reached the bar.

"If you're going to dance the way you did on that last number, I'd better stick to ginger ale."

"Didn't you like it?"

"Yes, but—"

His eyes held no mirth, only the look of a man who intended to make himself clear. "If you enjoyed it, that's all I care about. You were with me in every step; in fact, you encouraged me."

"Me? I encouraged you? You did your doggoned best to reduce me to putty out there in front of all these people."

"No, I didn't. I just danced, and you liked it. You swung yourself into me and let me feel every line of your body." He winked, daring her to deny it.

Her bottom lip dropped and she gaped at him, but that didn't faze the man. "Yeah, you liked it," he went on. "Baby, you fit me like a glove, standing or lying down."

"Blake! It's not nice to remind me of things like that."

The bartender put the glasses of ginger ale in front of them, and Blake handed one to her.

"What's not nice? I'm proud of the way you responded to me. Any man would be. So don't get bent out of shape because I bragged about it. I'm only talking to you."

She relented, because her wild surrender in his arms wasn't something a man would forget. She certainly wouldn't. "But I'll bet people can look at me and tell what kind of things you're saying to me."

"Okay." He started to laugh, this new Blake, and she primed herself for a wicked remark. "You're lousy in bed." He pinched her cheek. "That make you feel better?"

"Wait till we leave here."

He laughed and his eyes sparkled as if happiness suffused him. "If you're planning to make me eat those words, we can leave right now."

She sipped her ginger ale, enveloped in his joy. "Oh, you! Your bark is worse than your bite." She'd almost told him that she could be so happy with him, but she knew that such words would have darkened his mood.

His irises seemed to change from light brown to black.

"Don't depend on that. Most times, I don't have a problem with keeping my counsel, but you do strange things to me." He touched her elbow and walked with her back to their table.

The waiters served the dinner, and she toyed with the roast beef, peas, and potato croquettes, but had little interest in the food. Blake wanted space, a chance to deal with his feelings about a relationship with her. As a moral man, he set high standards for himself and, she suspected, for her as well. She knew she loved him and would be happiest if he were her life's mate, but she held out little hope for that. Wanting and needing her, even loving her, wouldn't make him ignore his conscience altogether. He'd capitulated to his libido and made love with her, but she'd bet that when he was alone with his thoughts, he thrashed himself for having done it.

"I hope we can expect you at our place one weekend soon. Our little town of Curtis Bay sits in a tiny inlet at the very edge of the Chesapeake Bay," Justine said, getting Melinda's attention. "The water's great right now, and the place is idyllic." She glanced at her husband. "Perfect setting for lovers. I hope you'll come."

Melinda couldn't help looking at Blake for his reaction. "I'm all for it," he said. "How about it, Melinda?"

Was he admitting to his friends that they were lovers? The man needed a good talking to. Then he grinned sheepishly, as if he'd read her thoughts, and she didn't care that his friends knew they'd been intimate. "Say when," she said, directing the words to him. "I'd love to go."

"We'll let you know," he said to Duncan. "Maybe a couple of weeks from now."

Later, Blake stood in the foyer of her house, holding her right hand and smiling down at her as if she were priceless. "I'm enjoying our time together this evening, and I want us to spend more time in each other's company, this kind of time."

"You mean—"

"I mean being friends, getting to know each other, giving us a chance to find out whether we want to continue what we started. We know we want each other but . . . well, for me, that's not quite enough."

She scrutinized his face, his whole demeanor, and saw only the honesty that was so much a part of him. "Thanks for the company. I wouldn't have thought you'd be such an erotic dancer. But come to think of it—"

"Whoa. I thought you didn't want to talk about that, but if you do . . ."

She held up both hands, palms out. "All right, all right. I take it back. Give a kiss and go home."

His hands grasped her shoulders, and his mouth brushed her lips, but when she parted them, he didn't give her his tongue, but squeezed her gently and withdrew. "Honey, you know where that leads. I'll call you tomorrow."

She watched as he paused on the steps and spoke with the guard, then strode across the street, got into his car, and drove off. Blake Hunter enthralled her, but from then on, she planned to try and keep that to herself.

Blake reread the agenda for the board's first meeting and prepared for fireworks. In a few minutes, the group would assemble in his office. He answered the door and was relieved that Martha Greene was the first to come. If Melinda had arrived first, their being together in his office would have been more fuel for the wagging tongues. Melinda and the others walked in shortly thereafter, and after reading the relevant portion of Prescott's will, Blake asked Melinda to open the meeting.

She thanked them for coming and for their willingness to direct the foundation. "I have appointed the following officers," she told them, and though Blake didn't hear grumbling, disapproval mirrored itself on most of their faces.

She named the officers and added, "Blake Hunter, accountant and chief executive officer. The officers will serve for a term of two years, except that, as executor of my husband's estate, Mr. Hunter shall serve permanently as accountant and CEO."

"It's customary for the board to elect its own officers, isn't it?" Martha Greene asked, clearly offended by having not been given a post.

Blake shook his head. "As executor of the will, it was my decision to make. This was simpler."

He thought the meeting surprisingly free of conflict, but for him, the wonder of it all was the smooth way in which, as president, Betty Leeds handled it. She smiled at a potential troublemaker and then proceeded to ignore him. He was going to enjoy working with the Prescott Rodgers Foundation's board of directors.

The meeting adjourned and, as he was telling Betty Leeds good-bye, half of his sentence remained unuttered, and his mouth dropped open. Melinda Rodgers was walking out of his office in what appeared to be animated conversation with Alice Pride. And, apart from "hello," she hadn't said one word to him since she'd walked in the door.

The next morning, she called almost as soon as he walked in the office. He hoped she called to explain ignoring him the previous morning, but if she knew she'd done that, she didn't consider it worthy of mention.

"Blake, I know it won't be easy, but you have to find a way to call off these guys who want to marry me for Prescott's money."

"Now wait a minute. You're asking me to announce that you've chosen the guy, or that you're engaged? Is that it?"

"Blake Hunter, you are not dense, so stop pretending that you are. I want these men to leave me alone, and since you're in charge of . . . of all this, do something to get rid of them. Just don't tell them I've already chosen someone."

"Why not? What're you saying? You're getting married or aren't you?"

Her tone carried an icy veneer. "I will not have anybody think I'd marry a man for the sake of an inheritance."

"But if you don't get married within the next seven months, you *will* lose it, and I'll be unable to help you."

He could almost feel the arctic air blasting him through the wires. "You're some piece of work. Good-bye!" She hung up.

He understood people; that was part of his job. But he'd never understood what made women tick, starting with his mother. Why couldn't Melinda just come right out and tell him what she wanted him to do? He took the mobile phone off its cradle and dialed her number.

"What's this all about, Melinda? Yesterday morning, you walked in here, stayed for two hours, and all you said to me was hello and thanks. You didn't even bother to say good-bye. If anybody's a piece of work, seems to me it's you."

"Yesterday morning, I was keeping temptation away from you, since that's what you seem to want."

"Don't hand me that. What could happen in the presence of Martha Greene and the rest of that bunch, huh?"

"You want space; I'm giving you space."

She was hell-bent on driving him up the wall. He walked over to the window and looked down on Columbia Pike at the white oak trees swaying in the breeze. Why couldn't she . . . ?

"Melinda, stop pretending. I'm facing the conflicts I have about a committed relationship with you, and you know that. It's not settled in your mind, either, so—"

"You can't speak for me, Blake. I know what I want and don't want. Now will you please call off these wolves? How'd you like it if a string of women asked you to marry them so they could hop on a gravy train? If you don't put a stop to it, I'm leaving town. I'm fed up."

He took a deep long breath before letting the air out of his lungs. "I'll do my best, but right now, I can't imagine what that will be if I can't say you've made a choice."

"You'll think of something. This whole will was an act of . . . of . . . I'll be in touch. Good-bye."

The heaviness around his heart surprised him. "Be careful, Melinda. If one of us is in pain, the other is subject to feel it. Not many people have experienced feelings as powerful as those we share. So don't trash this. I certainly will not. Bye."

"It all depends on you, love. I know where I stand. Bye."

His sharp whistle split the air as he walked back to his desk and placed the phone in its cradle. He wished he could say the same.

Chapter Seven

The Reverend Booker Jones sipped the last of his morning coffee, the one cupful that he allowed himself each day, since more than one would be a sinful indulgence, and patted his wife's hand.

"They've ignored me and all I stand for in this community, Lurlane. My own child didn't want me on her board of trustees."

Lurlane squeezed his hand, though she knew that nothing short of an appointment to the board of the Prescott Rogers Foundation would console him. "Dear, you know if she put you on that board, she'd have to put a preacher of every faith and denomination on it. Then what would she have? A duplication of our annual conference of religious leaders."

He swallowed a forkful of grits and scrambled eggs and waved the fork at her. "What's wrong with that?"

She smothered a smile. "As much as you complain that in fourteen years, the conference has never passed a unanimous resolution, how can you ask?"

His stare disconcerted her, and his lips quivered, not in anger, she knew, but from the pain of rejection. "The Lord will bring down my enemies. Every last one of them will perish for what they've done to me." He got up from the table and went to the phone. "I don't even have a grandchild. The boys are so busy making money that they don't send here, and look at Melinda. Twenty-nine, almost thirty years old and not a child to show for it. The Lord told us to be fruitful and multiply."

"Back then, there weren't more than a couple of million people on earth, Booker. Now, there're more than six billion. Seems to me like there's been too much multiplying."

"You'll have to pray about that," he told her, dialing Melinda's number.

"Booker, the poor child has enough problems. That will specifies twelve board members, and she's already chosen them. There can't be more."

He hung up. "She could've put our Paul on that board. Her own brother, and a professor, too."

Though she hurt for her husband, she believed Melinda had done the right thing. "Board members have to be residents of Ellicott City. Remember?"

With pursed lips and a deeply furrowed brow, he paced the floor. She wished he wouldn't upset himself so much over things he couldn't control. He went back to the phone, and she knew he'd chosen another target.

"You cooked up this whole thing, Hunter," he said, "because you intend to keep Melinda for yourself and walk off with all that money. Not as long as I breathe. You hear me?"

He stared at the receiver, and he didn't have to tell her that

Blake Hunter had hung up on him. When he reached for the phone again, she stopped him with a gentle tap on his shoulder.

"Don't call her when you're angry. She has enough to worry about."

With Ruby at the market, Melinda answered the phone. "Hello."

"My name is Arthur Hicks. Is this Melinda Rodgers?"

Exasperated, she rolled her eyes toward the ceiling and blew out a harsh breath. She'd fix him. "Yes. What can I do for you?"

"Well, somebody told me you was lookin' for a husband and you'd settle some ... er ... funds on him soon as he married you. I'm strong, healthy, and good lookin', and I ain't got no er ... re ... sex diseases. How long would I have to stay married to you?"

Melinda held the receiver at arm's length and stared at it. Then her anger dissolved into uncontrollable laughter.

"What's the matter. What you laughing at?"

"Sorry," she said, when she could control the laughter. "I was laughing at a guy named Blake. That deal is off."

She hung up, got in her car, and headed for Columbia Pike. Maybe when she signed Prescott's property over to him, Blake would get the message. And when women started chasing him for it, he'd understand how it hurt to be the object of a money hunt.

"How nice to see you, Melinda," Irene said when she opened the door. "Come right in." Had Irene's smile been malicious, or did she imagine it?

"He's in there," Blake's secretary said. "Go on in."

After hesitating for a second, Melinda opened the door

to Blake's inner office and stopped in her tracks at the sight of Rachel leaning across Blake's desk, her face inches from his.

She blinked. "What's going on here?"

Rachel jerked around toward the door, startled. But she quickly summoned her aplomb, straightened up, and patted her hair as if to suggest that it had been disarranged.

Then she smiled. "Hi, Melinda."

I'm not falling into that trap, Melinda said to herself. *She needs a reality check if she thinks she's made me jealous.*

"Hi, Rachel." She forced a friendliness that she didn't feel. "Make any headway since you've been here?" She had the pleasure of seeing bright red creep over Rachel's fair skin.

"I don't know what you're talking about," Rachel said.

"Yes, she does," Blake cut in, not bothering to hide his amusement. "But everything's exactly as you left it."

That was music to her ears, not that she'd thought differently. "I need to speak with Blake, privately," she said to Rachel. "If you wait out there with Irene, we could have lunch together. Want to?" She sounded bitchy, but she couldn't resist getting some of her own. She'd deal with Rachel later, too.

Blake stood. "Would you excuse us, Rachel?"

At least he didn't give a reason. She stepped aside as Rachel approached on her way out and smiled broadly, though Rachel looked at her with what could only be described as guilt.

"Irene, would you please show Ms. Perkins out? And next time, be sure I've given her an appointment." He flipped off the intercom and looked at Melinda.

"Which do you believe? What you saw or what I said?"

She tried to make herself smile, but it didn't work. Instead, her bottom lip dropped and stayed there as his seriousness registered. She mentally snapped her fingers; he wanted absolution. He stepped around the desk, took hold of her shoulders, and stared into her face.

"I need the answer to that question."

A fast quip sat on the end of her tongue, but she couldn't utter it. Blake Hunter was dealing with a deep uncertainty and the pain that went with it.

"I know Rachel's aggressive, and I know she's interested in you."

"Meaning what?"

"I believe you. Why wouldn't I?"

He continued to gaze into her eyes, triggering a swell of passion, and though she fought it with every ounce of willpower she could muster, she swayed toward him. He needed no further inducement to lock her in his arms.

"Blake, think. Think. You're pulling me under, but you're not ready for it."

His lips brushed her eyelids, nose, and cheeks, and she struggled beneath the power of his onslaught. "Honey, listen to me. Please. Oh, Blake. Don't make me care more than I do when you're so uncertain about us."

The unsteadiness of her voice emphasized her distress. "Don't. Don't let me love you."

But her words were lost to the storm that raged within him and that burned in his fiery gaze. "I need you."

Then his mouth settled on hers, thrilling her and shocking every nerve in her body. She parted her lips and groaned in pleasure as he filled her with his velvet tongue, searching, probing and claiming what he knew belonged to him alone. When he gripped her buttocks and pressed her to him, she tried to raise her body to fit his. She had to . . . to feel him, to know that he needed her the way she needed him. But immediately, he backed away from her.

"I've never used that sofa over there for anything other than sitting," he said with a wry smile, "but, woman, you make me feel things and do things that surprise the hell out of me. I want to take you over there and love you, and I want it so badly it hurts. But I can't make myself do that, and you wouldn't allow it."

She didn't look at him. He had her on fire, and by the time she would have realized where she was, the act would have been completed.

He tipped up her chin. "There could never be anything between me and Rachel Perkins or between me and any other woman, so long as you're in my life."

She stared at the carpet. "That reminds me why I came here. I want to sign off that will. The board is operational now, and I'm not going through with the rest of it." She sliced the air above her head. "I've had it up to here with that will. Do what you have to do. I don't know what got into Prescott." She walked away, turned, and walked back to him. "Imagine his insisting that I find a husband and get married. Was he mentally okay when he wrote that?"

"He was, and furthermore, you know he was. That clause is the one he insisted on most. He was as lucid as you are right now, so you can't contest it."

"I can't . . ." She stared at him for a long minute. "Be seeing you." She had to get out of there before she said something she needn't bother taking back.

Blake watched as she nearly ran from his office. She hadn't been angry about Rachel, and he supposed he ought to be thankful for that, but something had to be done to ease the friction between them. Making love had left them needing another kind of resolution, a meeting of minds. With that, they could be soul mates. But that wouldn't happen if he couldn't get to the bottom of her cavalier attitude toward that enormous fortune.

Either Prescott had given Melinda money from a source he didn't know about—and that was certainly possible—or she wanted to prove to the people of Ellicott City that she didn't marry a sixty-eight-year-old man for his money. But to throw away millions? Shaking his head in bemusement, he dialed Wayne Roundtree in Baltimore. That's what she wanted, so he had to do it.

"What can I do for you, buddy?" Wayne asked him.

Blake explained about the will and Melinda's request.

"You sure that wouldn't attract more men?"

"That's possible and it's a problem, man. She's fed up, and I don't blame her, but she won't let me announce that she's made a choice."

"And she's right," Wayne said. "Whoever she married, even years from now, would be considered that choice."

Blake's heart constricted, and he had to struggle to get his breath. "I . . . uh . . . hadn't thought of that, but I've gotta do *something.*" He thought for a few seconds. "All right. Run a short story and end it with a statement saying she decided to forfeit the will rather than marry a man she doesn't love. Just tell the truth."

He'd forgotten the possible damage that one of Wayne's whistles could do to an eardrum. Wayne reminded him. "Who'll believe that? If *you* didn't tell me it's true, I wouldn't even print it," Wayne said. "Man, that boggles the mind."

"Yeah. Mine too."

"Okay, check the front page, lower right-hand corner, day after tomorrow."

"Thanks, man. I owe you one."

She'd probably be ready to eat fire when she saw that story on the front page of *The Maryland Journal,* but that was what she'd said she wanted. He didn't question his sense of relief or the smile that lingered on his face for the next few hours.

"What is this I'm seeing, girl?" Booker Jones asked his daughter, holding a copy of the *Maryland Journal* inches from her eyes. Apparently having decided that the phone wasn't adequate for what he had to say, he'd driven to Melinda's house and banged on the door with such force that Tillman, the guard, had restrained him.

"It's true," Melinda told him, "but I didn't write the story printed in that paper."

"Then who did? No. Don't tell me he's busy plotting to take over and get control of all your money." With his hands clasped at his back, he paced the length of the living room. "Lawyers. I never did trust 'em. Bunch of crooks."

She wouldn't have put the story on the front page, but at least it was where you couldn't miss it. And it must be working, because she hadn't had a call all day.

"Papa, you're misjudging Blake. He did what I told him to do."

He glared at her, his eyes fierce and threatening. "If you fool around and lose that money, I'll . . . I'll disown you."

How could he get so angry about money, which he claimed to be the greatest source of evil? His Adam's apple bobbed furiously above his white clerical collar, as he looked at her.

"At least think of your mother. I do what I can for her, but you don't know how happy I'd be if she could have a little time to herself, to enjoy her life, be her old self." He looked into the distance, as though caught up in a dream. "She deserves the best, more than I'll ever be able to give her, considering my small congregation." He wasn't posturing now, but battling tears.

"Papa, I . . . I don't know what to say."

Suddenly, without another word, he turned abruptly and rushed out of the house.

She called her mother. "Mama, please see if you can calm Papa. He's so upset that I'm afraid for him."

Lurlane didn't seem concerned. "Well, don't be. He's pretty strong. Besides, he tells the church folk that money's the root of all evil, and I tell him he ought to practice what he preaches. Is there anything between you and Blake Hunter?"

"*What?*" she gasped. "Who said so?"

"Honey, you two have been the talk of this town ever since that Urban League shindig. Is it true?"

Was it? Melinda asked herself. "We're trying to work out our feelings for each other. We . . ."

She could imagine her mother rolling her eyes when she said, "I don't speak Greek, Melinda. What is he to you?" Lurlane Jones never let up till she had what she wanted.

She didn't lie to her mother. "I . . . uh . . . I love him, Mama."

"And what about him?"

She told the truth as she knew it. "I think he loves me, but he isn't sure about a relationship between us."

"Then I'm glad that story's in the paper today. You ought to marry Blake Hunter. I'd like to know what he's got against a relationship with you. There wasn't anything going on between the two of you while your husband lived, was there?"

She gave Lurlane a synopsis of what had happened since they'd first seen each other, omitting the time they made love.

"Well, child, that's a hot potato. You be careful. Men don't buy what you give 'em for free, and Blake Hunter's no different, I don't care how good a man he is."

She didn't want to talk about Blake, not with her mother or anyone. They'd come to terms or they wouldn't. Whatever happened, there'd never be another man in her life. "Mama, have you forgotten that I'm a recent widow?"

Evidently unimpressed, Lurlane replied, "You lost your best friend, and I sympathize with you. But you listen to me. If you lost Blake Hunter, you wouldn't be acting so brave; you'd be dying inside, and everybody would know it."

"You're being melodramatic, don't you think?"

Lurlane pooh-poohed the remark. "Why do you think Prescott put those strange clauses in his will? He wanted you to get married, and that business about the foundation meant working knee to knee with Blake Hunter. I'm not so sure he didn't have Blake in mind for you. Prescott loved you, though I'd bet my neck he never once kissed you, except for that peck on the cheek at the wedding ceremony, not to speak of—"

"Mama, don't you think you're overstepping?"

"Sure I am, but I've made you think, and that's all I wanted."

She told her mother good-bye and went to the den to go through the morning mail. One envelope with long, back-slanted handwriting got her attention because it didn't have a return address. She opened it. Yet another threatening letter, one that bore a handwriting different from the first one. She stared at words that were meant to unnerve her and dialed Blake's number.

"What does it say?"

She read, "You can put a dozen guards around your house, but I intend to get what's mine." It was unsigned. She described the handwriting.

"It's either forged or someone is trying to camouflage his handwriting," he said. "I'll be over to look at it."

"When?" She could have kicked herself for letting him know she was anxious to see him.

"Now, if you're not busy. I'll finish this brief in a couple of minutes. Did you see the *Maryland Journal* today?"

She should have called to thank him, and she would have if seeing the story on the front page hadn't vexed her. "Yes. Thanks. I hope it works."

*   *   *

She opened the door for Blake, looked at him, and told herself to turn off her emotions. She'd brought the letter down with her so he'd know he wasn't making a social call. At least, she hoped that was the message he'd get.

He looked at her, gave a slight half laugh, and said, "Mind if I come in?"

"Oh, yes. Yes, of course." She creased the side seam of her skirt with her right hand, shifted her weight from one foot to the other, and rubbed her left arm.

"Is it too much to ask if I could have a seat?"

Irritated at his self-assurance and his deliberate effort to let her know that he detected her nervousness, she got back her normal cool persona and strolled into the living room, giving him the impression that he could follow or stay where he was. He walked in and sat down. She knew he'd won their tug of wills when he asked if she'd like him to leave.

"You haven't looked at the letter," she said and didn't try to keep the testiness out of her voice.

He shrugged in that casual, I-don't-care way that he had; then a friendly heart-stopping smile eclipsed his face. "I didn't know. You seemed kind of, well . . . uncomfortable." He opened the letter and read the short note, then studied the envelope for what seemed to her an inordinate amount of time.

"Well?"

"I'm not a handwriting expert, but I'm convinced it's a man who's trying to fake his own handwriting. I can have this evaluated, if you'd like."

She crossed her knee and swung her right foot, a habit she'd begun as a teenager when she had to listen to one of her father's long and rambling lectures. Now swinging that foot helped steady her nerves.

She nodded. "And maybe fingerprints too?"

He shrugged again. "Well, if you want me to, but I don't think that will tell us much. This person apparently knew Prescott, so he might not be a criminal, in which case his fingerprints wouldn't be on record."

She stopped swinging her foot and leaned forward. "You know, this is the third threat I've received in the past few weeks."

"And you didn't tell me?" he roared.

"I figured that with the guards here and the other new security measures, the place is impenetrable."

"This isn't Fort Knox, and when you leave the house, you're at the man's mercy."

"If he knows something of his is in this house, why doesn't he stop the stealthy business and ask me for it?"

"Good question. It's my guess that Prescott didn't think the man was entitled to whatever it is he thinks he has a claim on, so he plans to steal it. I'll tell the guards to be extra cautious. Well, if that's all, I'll be going."

He stood and she had no choice but to follow him to the door. By pretending he had no interest in her as a woman, he was getting some of his own back, and she had only herself to blame. She had wanted to see him, but she'd been ashamed to let him know how much and, instead of greeting him warmly, had been overly cool.

It rankled her that he could look at her dispassionately, as if he had no personal interest in her, the way he was looking at her right then.

"Now that your story is on the front page of the region's biggest newspaper, what are your plans for complying with the conditions of the will?"

"I don't have any," she said, laying back her shoulders and letting her defiance show in her bearing.

He leaned against the wall beside her front door and seared her with a stare that nearly disoriented her. "If I let you walk

away from all this . . ." He flung his arms out as if to encompass
her home and all that would be hers. "Prescott was my client,
but we were also close friends, and he trusted me to see that
his wishes were carried out to the letter."

"If the two of you were so close, you must know why he
tried to force me to get married. If he didn't trust me with his
fortune, why should I care what happens to it?"

"You don't believe what you're saying. Look, Prescott was
a self-made man. He got where he was by working hard night
and day. No one helped him or even comforted him when he
needed it. You were the first person to share his life, and even
that was superficial. So don't think unkindly of him."

She glared at him. "Can you see me forcing myself to be
intimate with a man I don't care for in order to inherit what is
rightfully mine? From what you know about me, can you envis-
age that?"

"Where in that will does it say it has to be a man you don't
care for? It specifies that you marry within a year of the funeral.
In a year's time, a person could fall head over heels in love."

If she wasn't already in love with a man who didn't consider
himself a candidate, her treacherous heart seemed to shout. "In
the nearly five years of our marriage, Prescott showed me only
gentleness and considerateness. I never dreamed he had this
mean streak."

"He wasn't mean. I tried to talk him out of that clause, but
he insisted on it. 'I know what I'm doing,' I remember him
saying, 'and it'll all turn out just the way I want it to. You'll
see.' Those were his exact words."

She waved her hand in dismissal, because she no longer
cared about the inheritance, though she meant to see the foundation grow and flourish. "So he knew I wouldn't hold still for
it, didn't he? Well, it's no skin off my back. I wasn't born into
wealth, and Prescott didn't live the life of a rich man. I won't

miss it.'' She slapped her hands together as if to wipe them clean of the entire affair. ''It's history.''

''By the way,'' he said, and put his hand on the doorknob, ''Martha Greene complained that she should be paid for sitting on the board. I told her what the will specifies, and said we'd be sorry if she decided to resign.''

''But she can't. I'd have to start interviewing again.'' Her hand went to her mouth, and she supposed her eyes widened to twice their normal size when it occurred to her that Martha Greene might have accepted membership in order to undermine the foundation. She said as much to Blake.

''Maybe. I'm not so sure. She likes prestige, and this board will have that. But if you want to talk to her, to try and persuade her, go ahead.''

She couldn't believe her ears. ''You mean you didn't do that?''

''Definitely not. She's already got an inflated opinion of herself. I just let her know she'll miss something.''

''Like what?''

He told her about the reception he planned for the board. ''It's on me.''

''But . . . but why?'' Her father's words drummed in her ears. With effort, she pushed them aside. ''That's expensive.''

''My pleasure. You changed your mind about spending a weekend at Curtis Bay with Duncan and Justine?''

''No, but since you hadn't mentioned it, I figured you'd changed *your* mind.''

He took his hand off the doorknob and stepped closer to her. ''Before I commit myself to anything—I mean anything—I make certain that I want to do it. It may take me a while to get to that point—in fact, it usually does—but once committed, I'm not likely to change.'' His gaze flickered with a fire that she knew well, but only briefly. ''Do you understand what I'm saying?''

She nodded. Nothing had ever been clearer; his words were a reflection, no, a translation, of his behavior with her. Her heart beat faster, and it softened, as she had known it would. She reached up, kissed him quickly on the cheek, turned, and rushed up the stairs. If he touched her, she would explode.

"You may speed up those stairs, but when you get to the top, you'll wish you were down here with me." His words brought her to a halt, and she stood on the stairs with her back to him. "It doesn't matter how much space you put between us, where you go or how long you stay there, you'll come back here to me, because I'm in your blood just as you're in mine."

She whirled around. "Of all the . . . the—"

He didn't wait for her to find the words. "You're going to have to deal with this, just as I am. It isn't what we feel for each other that's in question; we're both clear on that. Our problem is doubt. Your doubt and my doubt."

"Speak for yourself."

"That I am. You're uncertain of me and my objectives."

"How can you say that?"

He raised his right hand as if to ward off more words. "For what other reason would your behavior toward me be so inconsistent?"

"And yours isn't?"

"We react to each other. I do or say something that makes you question me. The same happens with me. I thought I had worked it out while you were in Italy, but this . . . this uncertainty surfaced again." He walked to the bottom of the stairs and gazed up at her. "Are you willing for us to try and get to know each other? Really know and understand each other?"

She took a couple of steps down toward him and stopped. "You can make the sun shine, the moon rise, and stars burst in my head, and you can make me so damned mad I can't see. I'm not so dense that I have to take a course in order to understand you. Be yourself. Lay all your cards on the table, and I won't have a problem reading you.''

He put his foot on the bottom step. "Don't you come up here," she whispered. "Don't . . ."

He took the steps three at a time, picked her up, and carried her to the top. "You tell me I can make the sun shine and expect me to turn around and walk out of that door? That's proof you don't understand me. Put your arms around me.''

"Blake . . . th . . . this is crazy."

"I know it, baby. I know it. Kiss me.''

She looked up into his hungry eyes and parted her lips, but he only gazed down in her face until she wanted to scream her need to be in his arms. And then his mouth possessed her, his big hands gripped her shoulder and her hips, and at last she had the gratifying hot thrust of his tongue. She clung to him as he savored every crevice of her mouth. She wanted, needed more. Frantic for all of him, her hand went to his belt buckle. Immediately, he broke the kiss and cradled her gently in his arms.

"It isn't enough for me either, but I promised myself I'd give us a chance, and I mean to do that. Will you help me?''

Still drunk on him, she closed her eyes, took in a deep breath, and expelled it slowly. "If you tell me how, I will.''

"That's what I mean by getting to know each other.''

She wanted to tell him she knew he wasn't sure of her honor and integrity, but if she did, he wouldn't lie about it, and that would be the end. So she'd wait.

"I'll have to play it by ear," she said and meant it. This man refused to compromise where his needs were concerned, and who could blame him?

"All right. I'll get an expert to look at this letter, and then I want to have a word with Ruby.''

"You don't think she—"

"No, but she might be able to tell us something about the

people who knew Prescott and visited him before you and he were married. She's worked here for more than twenty years." He hugged her. "I'll be in touch."

She listened until she heard the lock click on the front door; then she went into her room to try and sort out her feelings. But the phone rang almost at once, disturbing her thoughts.

"I see Hunter's wound you around his little finger." Ray Sinclair's voice came to her without the obsequious sweetness she'd once heard in it. "Too bad. I'll bet you didn't know you're playing second fiddle to Lacy Morgan."

"I'm what? You must have read the *Maryland Journal* this morning. You gave it your best shot, Ray, you and a bunch of other money hunters, but be a sport and let it lie. If you don't, I may publish the names of the men who tried to get on that gravy train."

"I'll sue you."

"Really? Your messages are still on my answering machine. Good-bye, Ray."

She hung up and grabbed her stomach as pains shot through it. Lacy Morgan had the looks and body of a sex siren and the aristocratic bearing of a sovereign. *Only an idiot would think a man with Blake's looks and achievements would be unattached,* she said to herself. But he'd taken her to the gala and the way he'd danced with her and held her on that dance floor had been nothing less than a public statement. She had to console herself with that knowledge.

Half an hour later, her phone rang again, and she had an impulse to ignore it. After several rings, she answered.

"This is Tillman out front, Ms. Rodgers. A man's been driving past here in a rented Chevy. I got a look at him through me field glasses, and I'll try to photograph him with the zoom lens on me camcorder. Just wanted to let you know."

"Thanks, Mr. Tillman. I hope he drives past again."

"Oh, he will. He's been past here a dozen times already. Be in touch."

Just one more thing to deal with. She'd married and lived with Prescott Rodgers and known almost nothing about him apart from what he'd shown her of his personality. Maybe she'd been naive in marrying him.

She looked at the program she'd outlined for the board's next meeting. A television and radio campaign to enroll functionally illiterate adults in literacy classes and the disbursement of funds for after-school remedial reading programs. Maybe if she proposed that the board appoint Martha Greene chairperson of the media campaign . . . She went to the phone and paused. Better see what Blake thought of that. Martha could be a pain.

"Martha's trying blackmail," Blake said. "She wants an office on the board. Nothing will convince me that that status-conscious woman will resign from the board of the Prescott Rodgers Foundation. Forget about it and see whether she comes to the next meeting."

She told him about Tillman's phone call.

"Yes. He phoned me, and I expect we'll have something to go on. With these fingerprints, the handwriting, and some pictures, we ought to be able to figure out who this guy is and what he wants. Where's Ruby?"

"She's off on Thursday afternoon. She'll be in tomorrow."

"I hope she can identify the man. Of course, we may be dealing with two different men. Duncan wants us to come out this weekend. How about it?"

"Well, I . . . I guess I need to get away from this town's stifling heat."

His lengthy silence served as a reprimand. "Any other reason why you'd consider going there with me?"

She couldn't help laughing. "Certainly not because of your . . . uh . . . magnetism or that commanding aura of yours. You have a great pair of hands, but I wouldn't think they'd have any bearing on my decision to spend a weekend with you. I love the water. Yes. That could be it.''

She heard him clear his throat. ''You have a way of getting fresh with me when I'm nowhere near you. But, lady, I will remember your words. A great pair of hands, indeed!''

''I always did take my punishment well. Just ask my folks.''

''Punishment? Is that the way it strikes you?''

Laughter bubbled up in her, and she let it out and with it the terrible tension that had dogged her since he'd left her house earlier that day. ''Honey, what's in a name? Whatever you call it . . . Being with you is . . . magical. Hang up. I have a lot of work to do.''

''Same here. I'll be by for you shortly after noon on Friday. Kiss me?''

She made the sound of a kiss, hung up, and congratulated herself for not having asked him about Lacy Morgan.

Blake read again the analysis of the handwriting on the letter Melinda gave him. The writer was not a schizophrenic, but a man trying to hide his identity. The fingerprints weren't on record. So, as he'd suspected, the man wasn't a convicted criminal, but if he tried getting into that house again—with or without a key—he'd go to jail. No doubt, he'd had at one time a business relationship with Prescott, who must have kept papers in his home that he hadn't shared with his attorney. He'd have to speak with Melinda about that.

He packed his bathing, surfing, and fishing equipment in the trunk of his car, went back inside, and called Ethan.

''How's the new job?'' he asked the boy. He'd gotten him away from that poolroom as quickly as he could.

''It's great. My boss says he'll buy my books and pay my transportation to and from night school if I'll do what you do.''

''What's that?''

"He wants me to talk to kids about what happens when you get into trouble and go to jail and how to stay straight. I told him I'd do it."

Some made it and some, like Lobo, wouldn't. Ethan had the drive to become a respectable citizen. "I'm proud of you, Ethan," Blake said. "If you need me, you know my cell phone number."

"Thanks. Hang in there."

"You bet, and you do the same."

He'd better call his mother and tell her where he was in case she needed him. Finding her in good health and high spirits heightened his anticipation of the weekend and what it might bring for Melinda and himself. He meant to keep an open mind about her and let the chips fall where they may.

At a quarter of twelve he parked his car in front of her door. "I have something for you, sir," Tillman said to Blake as he walked up the steps to Melinda's front door. "Pictures I took with me camcorder. You can look at 'em in there on the TV. I don't think he knows I took 'em because he's driven by here twice today."

"Thanks. If he continues, I'll suggest to Mrs. Rodgers that she indict him for harassment."

"That's what it looks like to me, sir," Tillman said.

When Blake rang the doorbell, his breathing quickened in anticipation of the sight of her. She opened the door, smiled up at him, and everything around him seemed to glow, but he needed more. All night, he'd wrestled with her words, "an inheritance that's rightfully mine," and doubts about her reasons for marrying his friend had once more filled his head almost to bursting until it ached.

"Aren't you coming in?" she asked.

How fresh and beautiful she was in that yellow sundress! "Hi. Where's Ruby? I want to show you two something. Could you turn on the VCR so I can hook up this camcorder?" They sat down to watch, and when the green Chevy came into view, Blake froze the frame.

"Recognize this man, Ruby?"

Her answer was a good while coming, so he glanced at her and saw that she was concentrating intensely. Finally, she said, "Can't say as I do, Mr. Blake, though he do remind me of the picture Miz Melinda showed me. Still, they's a little somethin' familiar 'bout that face. It's just that the parts don't go together."

Now that was something to think about. "What about you, Melinda? Recognize him?"

She also took her time answering. "He's the man who came to this door before I went to Italy and who I caught on the surveillance camera. I'm sure of it."

He flicked off the camcorder. "Yes. From that sketch you drew, I thought as much."

"Not long after I come here to work for Mr. Rodgers, he had a friend what used to visit pretty often, usually on the weekend," Ruby said. "He stayed in the guest room and come and went pretty much as he pleased. I thought they was working together on somethin'. But that man had salt-and-pepper hair, almost white, and wore black horn-rimmed glasses. What keeps reminding me of him is this man's eyebrows."

"Do you remember that man's name?" Melinda and Blake asked simultaneously.

"Sure 'nuff. I seed him and fed him often enough. Reginald Goodwin or maybe Goodson. No. It was Goodwin."

Ruby slapped her thighs and got up from the chair. "I ain't said they is the same, and I ain't said they ain't. But you don't 'spect to see two different men with bushy eyebrows arched up like that, lest they's father and son. Wouldn't even happen with two brothers what wasn't twins."

Blake looked long and hard at her. Ruby was a smart woman.

He'd have that angle investigated. "You've been a great help," he told her.

Reaching for Melinda's hand, he asked her, "Ready to go?"

She nodded, absentmindedly, he thought. But what woman wouldn't be disturbed learning that her husband hadn't shared with her things that were important to him?

Chapter Eight

Blake drove along Route 40 thinking of the tapes that Melinda had selected for the drive to Curtis Bay. Blues, jazz, and Mozart. He glanced quickly in her direction.

"You didn't happen to bring any Joe Williams CDs, did you?"

" 'Every Day I Have The Blues,' " she said and promptly put it on.

That song always gave him a lift, even though it was blues, and as he always did when he heard it, he sang along with Joe, straight through the hair-raising ending.

"I would never have dreamed it," Melinda said. "My Lord, you can sing, and the blues at that. What else do you want to hear?"

If it hadn't been so hot, he'd have rolled down all the windows and let the breeze blow over him and around him. He felt good. "Play anything you want to. Say, you didn't bring 'Early One Morning,' did you?"

"I don't get in my car without it. Buddy Guy's the man. You bet I brought it."

He put the car on cruise control and let the moment have its way with him. "I want to go through your music. You wouldn't own a recording of 'Carmina Burana,' would you?"

She slid further down in the bucket seat, folded her arms, and closed her eyes. The picture of contentment. "I have worn out two LPs, and I just bought a CD recording a couple of weeks ago. Don't tell me you like that too."

He could hardly believe it. "Honey, I shave by that music."

He reached over and stroked the back of her hand. "Maybe this thing between us isn't so implausible as it seems."

Then she said something that shook him to the core of his being. "Is that why you don't believe in it? Because you think it's inconceivable?"

He switched off the cruise control and slowed down. "Is that what you think?"

She nodded. "You want to believe, but you're not there yet. You take a giant step forward, but something happens, I don't know what, and then you take a step and a half back. Did you realize that?"

"There's some truth in that, I suppose, but what's in my heart never wavers." From the corner of his eye, he glimpsed the broad grin playing around her mouth.

"Maybe one day you'll tell me exactly what's in your heart. Keeping a lid on what's in mine is becoming a problem."

He wished they were holding hands and walking right then. It was a strange way to strengthen their understanding of and feelings for each other, sitting in a moving vehicle and hardly touching.

"We're almost there," he said, "and I don't even remember

when I turned into Route 695. Let's exit at the foot of the
Francis Scott Key Bridge and walk along the bay. Right now,
I feel confined.'' Her head snapped around and she stared at
him.

"That's right. It's the one thing I can't tolerate: being where
I don't want to be. And right this minute, I want to feel the
fresh breeze.''

"You mean you want to feel free.''

"I want *us* to be out there, just the two of us, alone with
nature. Sometimes I walk along the Patapsco River, usually
around sunset, letting the cool air refresh me. It's invigorating.''

He brought the car to a halt and got out. She met him as he
walked around to open her door. With her hand in his, he
walked down to the edge of the Chesapeake Bay to stroll the
path that he'd walked alone so many times. How different it
seemed now as they walked hand in hand.

Not far from shore, one fish and then another jumped out of
the water as if they were playing leapfrog, and she tightened
her fingers on his. "Did you see that? Those two fish?''

"Yeah. Sometimes, late in the day, they put on a show. I've
promised myself I'm going to find out why they do it. When
I see that, I put my fishing gear away; at least on the Patapsco
River, if they're jumping, they don't bite. Out on the bay, they
seldom jump.''

"You love the water, don't you?'' she said. "So do I. It's
liberating. Makes me feel free. Uninhibited.''

Water gave him that same sense of oneness with nature. He
felt as if he floated in a sea of contentment. Everything seemed
so right, so perfect as they strolled beneath the shade trees. He
stopped walking and faced her.

"Sometimes, like this minute, I feel in my gut that you're
the woman for me. And for all time. Whether we're teasing,

arguing, mad at each other, or making love, I'm fully alive when I'm with you. And then, that certainty will slip away from me. Can you understand that?''

She nodded, but he didn't see how she could understand what puzzled him about himself.

Her gaze was soft and her face had that tenderness, that sweetness of expression that made him want to lay his head against her breast and feel her arms around him.

''I suspect something in your past, your childhood perhaps, causes you to need a guarantee before you'll take a chance on us, and on other things, too, I imagine. But, Blake, there's no guarantee when it comes to a relationship with another person, not even if that person is your parent. You know that.''

He walked with her to a bench that rested beneath a huge willow tree whose branches hung low in picturesque splendor. ''Let's sit here out of the sun for a minute. Are you too warm?''

''No. The breeze is wonderful.''

He slung his right arm around her shoulder and held her hand with his left one. ''You may have touched on something important. I wouldn't swear to it one way or another, because I don't spend time trying to figure why I do or don't do a thing. But if I was scared to take a chance, I wouldn't have a bachelor's degree, not to speak of a doctorate.''

''Until a few months ago when Ruby told me about your childhood, I had assumed from the way you carried yourself that you came from a wealthy family. You were the most polished man I'd ever had close contact with.''

''I learned from my teachers, my classmates, from men to whom I delivered packages in their posh offices. My father didn't have time for the niceties; he worked twelve or fourteen hours every day except Sunday, and when we kids weren't in school, we had to work along with him. Life was rough. Hard. When I look back, it seems unreal.''

As if she divined his needs, her arms went around him and the love she gave seeped into him, a healing potion. "But you stepped over every obstacle. You should be proud. I'm proud of you."

He thought of Lacy, of her whining and superficiality. Melinda was real. He could lose himself in her, but it wasn't the time or place for that, so he focused on her words. "I don't think I'm exceptional, only that I wanted it so badly I would have worked at any job, made any sacrifice to escape that harsh life."

She drew back and looked him in the eye. "Since we're learning each other, help me understand this: you're so hard on people. Why?"

"I can't tolerate people who're not prepared to earn what they get, who want the rewards without working for them, who cry about how bad their lot is without doing anything to improve it. If you call that hard, I'm hard."

She seemed pensive, as though musing over his words and their meaning. "Not many people are as strong as you are. For all my father's blustering, he's never seemed strong to me, not even when I was a child."

He stood, suddenly aware that the strength he projected was a part of his attraction for her. He said as much.

She grinned. "You kidding? When I first looked at you, I wasn't seeing strength. Come on, let's walk a little."

"I'm not going to ask what you did see, because you won't tell me."

"Hmmm. I just said 'Oh, Lord, please don't do this to me. I'm a married woman.' "

Laughter rumbled within him and he let it out with joy. "That's exactly what I said, except that I reminded the Lord that *you* were a married woman."

He looked up at the willow branches that drooped almost to the ground and urged her closer. She gazed up at him with lips parted, and he flicked his tongue across them, waited to savor the torture of anticipation, and then plunged into her. When she pulled him deeper, tremors plowed through him from his head to the soles of his feet. He jerked back and stared at her, and all that he felt for her leaped from his lips of its own accord.

"My God, you move me to the pit of my gut."

"If we could only open ourselves up to whatever comes, just think how special it would be."

He nodded, and started with her to the car, his head splitting with anxiety. Even if they cleared every other hurdle, she'd never forgive him if she knew it was he who'd insisted that she couldn't inherit Prescott's estate unless she set up that foundation. He'd known Prescott's preoccupation with illiteracy and how it circumscribed people's lives, but he hadn't been overly concerned about that problem when he wrote that clause in the will. He'd done it because he hadn't believed that a twenty-five-year-old woman would marry a man Prescott's age for any reason other than money, to loll around in luxury as long as the man lived and to be rich when he died.

He didn't return to the highway, but drove along the side road near the water. "We ought to do this more often," he said. "There's something irresistible about wide open spaces. One day, I'm going to have a house on a hill with God's green earth, trees, and water as far as I can see. A place where my kids can romp undisturbed and unafraid, where I can see daybreak in the morning and moonrise in the evening."

His gaze took in the stately willow trees, shrubs, and black-eyed Susans that lined the roadway. Beauty as far as he could see. One couldn't help but feel the power and beauty of nature.

She must have felt it too, for she asked, "Are you telling me you want to go back to your roots?"

"Heavens, no! But I don't want my children skipping rope on concrete. What about you?"

"I've only lived in Ellicott City and College Park, Maryland, where I attended the university. But I can imagine the delight of feeling the morning dew cool under your toes. Does Duncan have grass around his lodge?"

"He sure does, but don't expect a rustic old lodge; his place is a lodge in name only. You'll see in a few minutes. We're less than a mile from Curtis Bay Hamlet. It's a tiny place at the edge of the Chesapeake Bay, right on the water."

He drove up to the two-story, redbrick house and parked. "Here we are."

She got out and gazed around. "You're telling me, this isn't a lodge! It's your quintessential upscale dwelling."

He took their things out of the trunk and started toward the house. "Where's everybody?" she asked.

"Probably at the beach. Or maybe they didn't get here yet." He opened the door with his key. "How many bedrooms do you and I need, one or two?"

"Since that's not a serious question—"

He interrupted. "Just checking. But you're right next door to me, so keep those coals bedded down." He couldn't help laughing when she exhaled sharply and stuck her fists on her hips. "Okay, okay. Just teasing. You're right there." He pointed to the open bedroom door at the top of the stairs. "See you later."

As far as she knew, she'd never walked in her sleep, but she didn't remember ever having slept that close to temptation, either. She unpacked, hung up her clothes, opened the window, and looked out at the Chesapeake Bay. The curtains flapped in the breeze and she stripped, flung her arms wide, and let the cool salty air caress her naked body. She heard his steps, dashed to the closet, and put on a robe, but he didn't pause at her door. She stretched out on the bed, testing it for comfort, and a knock on her door awakened her nearly two hours later.

"Are you all right?" Justine called to her. "I've begun to worry."

She got up and opened the door. "I guess this is what happens when you're not used to fresh air. I'm fine. Thanks for having me."

"We're delighted. Come on down and meet our daughter."

She scrubbed and buffed her face, put on a pair of white shorts, a yellow blouse, and white espadrilles, let her hair down, and skipped down the stairs. Voices led her to the patio on the shaded side of the house, where Blake stood and walked toward her as she stepped onto the patio.

"I almost whistled," he said, "but I figured I'd better be on my good behavior." He stepped to within inches of her, took her hand, and smiled down into her face. "You're so lovely and so . . . so perfect in that getup."

She knew that what she felt right then blazed on her face, but she didn't care. Not with this black Adonis towering over her within kissing distance, telling her she looked great. His fawnlike eyes darkened to obsidian, and his Adam's apple moved rapidly while he looked at her. Mesmerizing. His masculine aura swirling around her like sea foam in a storm. If she didn't corral her thoughts, what he read on her face wouldn't be conducive to polite, company patter.

Her effort to do so didn't succeed. All she could think of as he stared down into her face was the way she'd felt when he lay embedded deep within her, rocking her to the stratosphere.

Teasing and taunting until he forced her to give herself up to him. Driving her out of herself until she died a little.

She watched his breathing quicken, his stance widen, and his pupils dilate, and didn't doubt that he'd read her thoughts. Then, as if to suggest that he'd bewitched her deliberately, he winked, and she knew he'd brought himself under control.

Determined not to let him get the better of her, she reminded him of his earlier admonition to her. "Keep the coals bedded down? Is that what you said? Take some of your own advice."

He laughed, and oh, how she loved to see him open up and let the joy flow out.

"I never saw you laugh so freely and so much until I got back from Italy. Now you laugh a lot, and I love to see it."

He took her hand. "Come around here and meet Tonya. I'm her godfather, and I want you to know that I can do no wrong."

She stopped. "Who's her godmother?"

Both of his eyebrows shot up. Then a grin spread over his face. "Leah, Wayne Roundtree's wife. Why?"

She winked at him. "Just checking."

As soon as he picked up the child, her little arms encircled his neck, and she kissed his cheek repeatedly. "Unca Bake," she said as he walked with her over to where Melinda stood. It was a picture that she could not have imagined.

"Hello, Tonya." She reached for the child, but Tonya wouldn't leave Blake.

"This is Melinda," he told Tonya. "I want you to like her."

Tonya scrutinized her, decided she wasn't interested, and focused her attention on Blake. "She'll come around."

"Maybe," Justine said. "She loves men. I suspect that's due to her passion for Duncan. She idolizes him."

Duncan rounded the side of the house and hopped up on the patio. "Glad you could join us, Melinda. I see you've met my daughter."

"She's a darling, the image of Justine," Melinda said.

He glanced at his wife and grinned at what she surmised was a private joke. "She is that, all right, though I was the last person to see it. I thought we'd cook out tonight. Tomorrow morning, we can go fishing." He looked at Blake. "Unless you'd like to take Melinda for a cruise."

"I'd love that, provided she wants to get up early."

"You name the time. I'd love a boat ride," she said.

"Okay. Leave here at five-thirty?"

When she hesitated, Justine said, "I'll lend you my alarm clock. The bay is heaven that time of morning when you're out there almost all alone. You can make coffee after you get on board."

Melinda reclined in a lounge chair and watched Blake play with Tonya, listened as he exchanged ready quips with Duncan and Justine. Lighthearted, witty, and playful. A different man. She looked up and saw Justine watching her and wasn't surprised when the woman took a seat beside her on the lounge chair.

"Something tells me you're wondering who this Blake is. Right?"

"Pretty close. How did you guess?"

"For weeks, I've watched him unwind. He seems to laugh just because it feels good to do it. Oh, he reverts occasionally, but that doesn't last long."

"He's softened. I don't know what happened, but I love seeing him like this."

"Duncan believes this is the real man, that he buried this side of himself while he made his way up."

"But I've known him for five years, and—"

"Maybe he's changed because he doesn't have to fight so hard with himself."

"What do you mean?"

"My guess is that you're at the center of this. You're a free woman now, and he needn't feel guilty because he wants you."

A gasp escaped her. "He told you about that?"

"He shared his feelings with Duncan, because they're close friends, and he needed one, believe me. I first noticed this new playfulness and even frivolity in him when you were in Europe. He must have come to terms with himself. You're good for him. Very good for him."

"Blake, can you get the potatoes to roasting and throw the salad together? This'll be ready in about fifteen minutes or so," she heard Duncan say.

"Excuse me," Justine said. "I'd better take Tonya. If Blake puts her down, she'll scream. I think she feels she owns him. Be back in a minute."

If playfulness in Blake surprised her, seeing that chef's apron over his white Bermuda shorts challenged her credulousness. She blinked her eyes a few times, getting used to the picture, enjoying the sight of him picking over meslun lettuce leaf by tiny leaf.

"We turn in early," Justine told her after dinner, "because we get up with the sun, but make yourself comfortable. I'll put the alarm clock on your night table." She reached for Duncan's hand. "Come on, husband, I have a few things to say to you."

And the right to say them, Melinda thought. She watched Duncan kiss his wife on the side of her mouth, take her hand, and then, as if he'd already forgotten his guest, glance over his shoulder at them and murmur, "Night."

She didn't want Blake to read her thoughts, to know what seeing that woman leave them to enjoy married bliss with her husband made her feel, didn't want him to know she envied Justine Banks. So she closed her eyes, but he seemed to draw her gaze the way a flame draws a moth, and she opened them and looked at him. There was no mistaking the blazing fire in his now obsidian orbs or what this signified. Suddenly frightened at the power he held over her, though he probably didn't imagine it, she found the strength to look away from him and get up from the chair.

"S . . . since I have to get up before five o'clock, I think I'd better turn in. See you tomorrow morning."

"Yeah. I have to put some ashes on what's left of that fire, so you go on in. I'll . . . uh . . . be out here on the patio when you come down in the morning."

He turned away, and she knew he didn't think he could risk a good night kiss. She certainly couldn't. She paused on her way upstairs. Hadn't Blake seen Duncan pour half a bucket of ashes on those coals? Maybe he was doing that to take his mind off what he really wanted.

First one thing and then another conspired to interfere with her getting a good night's sleep. The infernal clock ticked mercilessly beside her ear, counting off the seconds of the rest of her life. She hated ticking clocks because she didn't like being reminded constantly of her mortality. Exasperated, she put the clock under the bed where she couldn't hear it. In a few minutes, she dozed off to sleep, where Blake awaited her with his taunting and teasing, offering himself to her and then withholding what he knew she so longed for. Furious with him, she bolted upright and was getting out of bed to give him the reprimand he deserved when she awakened, realized she'd been dreaming, and fell back in bed. Defeated. Finally, she slept.

Melinda managed to get safely down the stairs with barely open eyes and make her way to the patio where Blake leaned against the railing, alert and smiling, looking as though he'd already swum a few laps. With her eyes closed, she shook her head slowly and carefully. As heavy as her head felt, in her clouded state, she could easily damage it.

"Hi," she said, "don't tell me you're a morning person."

"Hi, yourself. Guilty as charged. And you're not."

She swayed toward the wall. "No, sir-ree. I've been congratulating myself ever since I realized I'd gotten my eyes open."

"I see your sense of humor is working before sunup. Have you noticed that we're identically dressed?"

"Really? What am I wearing? As far as I'm concerned it's still night. I did well to recognize you."

His left hand went to his chest in a gesture of feigned humility. "Woman, I'm crushed. We're wearing white slacks and sneakers and light blue, collared T-shirts."

"Thank God I'm decent."

He took her hand and started to his car. "The boat's only a few blocks away, but considering your . . . er . . . condition, I wouldn't dare suggest you walk that far."

She could feel the breeze as he sped along the little road beside the shore. "At this rate, I'll wake up," she said.

"It's a bit chilly, but Duncan keeps sweaters on the cruiser. You'll be comfortable." He grinned. "Yep, if I have to keep you warm with my body."

"At five-thirty in the morning, give me blankets."

He drove up to the dock, got out, walked around, and opened her door. "You *are* sleepy, if you didn't rush out of this car before I could get around here."

He stood inches from her, letting her feel the electrifying magnetism of his hot gaze. "I'd enjoy the pleasure of awakening you about this time one morning and seeing how you respond when it's me and not the clock that arouses you."

She shrugged, aware that he jostled her, but lacking the energy to defend herself as she normally would. "Even *I* know the answer to that," she said.

"And . . ."

"And I'd wake up. I might sleep past daybreak, but definitely not past sunrise."

Obviously he remembered that she'd said he could make the sun shine, as his laughter seemed to swell joyously until he doubled up with mirth, thrilling her with the joy he communicated to her. She could listen to him laugh forever. His eyes sparkled and his white teeth gleamed, and she thought what a pleasure it would be if she could stay with him always.

He sobered up, let his fingers rest gently at her elbow, and said, "Now you're waking up.

"Here we are," he said, walking up the gangplank to the sleek, thirty-foot cruiser. He turned and waited for her. "This is the *Tonya Girl*. Let me give you a hand."

But she stood still, her eyes wide as she stared at it. "This is Duncan's boat? I thought it was something small like a fishing boat with maybe an outboard motor. Good grief, you could spend the night in this thing."

"Want to?"

"I . . . I don't know. I've never been on a boat before, much less slept on one. You know how to operate this thing?"

"You betcha. Duncan and I learned to navigate this baby when he put the down payment on it. Justine is learning too. Come on. I'll make some coffee, and then we'll get going."

He brewed a pot of coffee and toasted some bagels, which they consumed as they stood on deck. Minutes later they headed for the open bay. She stood beside him admiring his deft handling of the helm. What else did he do that she didn't know about?

"Blake, tell me about yourself. Out here in Curtis Bay, you're a different man. So free, relaxed. I'd even say loose. Are you happy here? Is that it?"

She hadn't meant to make him frown, but he did. "Loose? I don't know. Happy? I could be. Maybe this lifestyle suits me. I hate being confined, and out here . . . well, I wish I could explain it. Happy will have to do, I guess."

"My Lord, look at that." Colors began to streak across the sky. Blue, red, gray, and orange, mingling, dancing, and suddenly competing for space and position. They gazed in awe as the orange and red streaks battled for prominence until bright red streaked across the horizon and the sun broke through the clouds.

His hand gripped her elbow, and she looked up and saw the fierce look on his face. "You told me I made the sun shine. Do you remember that?"

Of course she did, but she only looked at him and said nothing.

"Did you say it, or didn't you?"

"I said it."

When he grabbed her shoulders, she knew he meant business. He'd let her go the night before, and he'd do it now if she wanted it that way. He stepped back and stared down at her, his hands balled into fists, his stance wide, and his nostrils flaring. She looked at his pectorals, prominent beneath his blue T-shirt, and saw his Adam's apple move rapidly. His breathing quickened, and she could smell the sizzling man in him, feel his hands possessing her body, and taste him. Yes, she could taste him. Her gaze met his and hot pinions of desire shot arrow-straight to the center of her passion. She wanted to . . . to . . . Frustration gripped her and she closed her eyes.

"Come here, Melinda. I need you, baby."

Her eyelids flew open and her lips parted, but she couldn't move and couldn't speak. If he'd only . . . "Can't you just . . ."

"Let me know if you want me. Tell me. I still ache from last night. Do you want to make love with me?"

"Yes. Yes." With her arms open, she sped to him, and he wrapped her close to his body.

"I'm crazy for you. Do you hear me? I'm on fire for you."

Why didn't he move, kiss her, do something? "Isn't there a bed downstairs?" she asked him.

She glimpsed the wild savage expression on his face just before he lifted her and ran downstairs with her. "What about the boat?'' she asked as he opened the door to the captain's quarters.

''I dropped anchor. Kiss me. Honey, open your mouth and kiss me.''

She reached for his belt and pulled his shirt from it, ran her fingers beneath it, up his chest to his sensitive pectorals, and felt the shivers that raced through him. He held her head and plunged his tongue into her mouth, simulating the act of love until she began to undulate against him, demanding more. She knew he wouldn't be delicate this time, that he'd been strung out with desire for her so long that he'd just take what she gave. When she stepped away from him and pulled off her T-shirt, he reached for her, pulled her nipple into his mouth, and suckled her until her escalating moans echoed in the distance.

She fell across the bed and raised her arms to him, and within seconds, he was there with her wrapped in her arms. He tugged her slacks and panties over her hips and threw them aside, then quickly disrobed. She slid down beneath him and kissed his belly, flat, hot, and all male.

''No, baby. I can't handle that.'' He pulled her up, locked her hands above her head, and took his pleasure in her breast, sucking, nipping, kissing, and pinching until she thought she'd go mad. He kept her hands immobilized above her head, and with his lips fastened to her nipple, she felt his fingers trail slowly down to her feminine center. Her entire nervous system shimmered, out of control, and she squirmed, twisted, and flailed in frustration until his talented fingers reached their goal. She raised her body to hasten contact with his hand and feel that unbelievable fullness begin to gather inside of her and drive her crazy. She gave no thought to her dancing hips as he strummed her as a lyrist plays a lyre.

''Blake. Oh, Blake. I can't take more. You've got to—''

''You're not ready yet, baby.''

''I am. I am.''

His fingers danced faster in pursuit of their goal, tantalizing, teasing, and stripping her of her will. When his lips covered her own, she eagerly opened to his searching tongue and moaned in pleasure as he possessed every centimeter of her mouth.

Then he tugged at her nipple, released it, and gazed down into her face. "You like that, don't you?"

"Yes. Yes. I love everything you do to me."

He sucked the other one until she let out a keening cry and the liquid of love flowed over his fingers.

"Blake. Honey, please get in me. *Get in me!*"

"All right, sweetheart." He slipped on a condom and rose above her with his gaze fastened on her eyes. "Take me. Take me in."

She clutched him with her fingers, and in her haste to receive him, raised her body for the sweet thrill of his thrust. He found his place within her, sank home, and at last, he lay deep within her where he belonged.

Her heart took off when he smiled down at her and said, "Relax now."

"I will. I will."

With one hand beneath her buttocks, he shifted his hips and began to thrust. "Relax, honey, and don't hold back. Let it go, baby. Give yourself to me."

She quit struggling for release, locked her ankles across his hips and her arms around his waist, and moved with him. Right away heat seared the bottom of her feet and she thought she would surely die when the swell of climax threatened and then eluded her. He increased the pace and the pinching and squeezing began, but he drove faster and faster until she cried aloud.

"Blake. Oh, Blake, love me. Love me." He thrust powerfully, demanding her submission, until she erupted into ecstasy.

"I do. I do," he said and, draining himself of his essence, he collapsed in her arms.

She looked at his head on her breast and swore that no other man would touch her. He was hers and she wasn't going to let him go.

"How are you feeling right now?" he asked her.

"Queen of the world. I don't think I've been happier. What about you?"

"Unbelievable, sweetheart. Unbelievable."

"I want to sleep, but if we don't go back, they may think we stole the boat," she said.

"Not hardly."

"Then what *will* they think?"

The grin that played around his mouth was answer enough, but he made it crystal clear. "They'll think we're doing whatever it is lovers do." He slipped his hands beneath her hips and squeezed her closer to his body. "Mind if I get some juice? I'm kind of hungry. I'll be right back."

She put her hands over her head and stretched long and lazily. Gazing toward where he'd lain seconds earlier, she imagined the pleasure of awakening beside him every day for the rest of her life. With his pillow clutched to her breast, she smelled his scent, then buried her face in the sheet and inhaled the must of their lovemaking. She couldn't get enough of him.

"I brought you some orange juice."

She pulled herself up and leaned on her right elbow. "Thanks. We didn't eat breakfast. A bagel is nothing. I'm starved."

"I can cook some bacon and scramble two or three eggs. Okay?"

Was he serious? She supposed her disbelief was mirrored on her face, because he set the juice glass on the little table and stared at her.

"What is it? You want to go back?"

Beg him? Having learned that there were more effective ways, she lay back on the bed, patted the space beside her, and then stretched her body suggestively. She didn't purr, but if he didn't get the message soon, she would.

"You want me to—"

She threw aside the sheet in an unmistakable invitation for him to join her. "I thought you said you're a morning person," she needled, when he slipped between the sheets and joined her.

"Yeah, but after what you did to me a few minutes back, I'm not my normal self."

She leaned over him, and when her nipples grazed the hair on his chest, her pulse skittered and the echo of her escalating heartbeat hammered in her ears. She brushed his lips with a soft kiss, then his eyes and his neck. She wanted to explore him, every inch of him. The sparkles of anticipation in his wonderful eyes was all the encouragement she needed, and she let her palms graze his pectorals, barely touching them. His breathing accelerated, and she twirled her tongue around first one nipple and then the other until his body jerked upward. Her fingers trailed down his body, and she assured herself of his readiness, then wrapped her arms around his waist and kissed his belly, cherishing every inch of him until he began to squirm out of her embrace. But she gripped his thighs and loved him.

"Baby, watch that," he yelled, reached down and pulled her from him. "Whew. That was close," he whispered as if to himself.

He reached down for the packet that lay beside the bunk and she shielded him, then he pulled her on top of him and positioned her legs so that she straddled him, open to his penetration. He tested her for readiness, found what he needed there, and drove home. It was fast, furious, and powerful. Then he flipped them over, smiled down at her, and loved her until she screamed aloud her satisfaction and he collapsed, shattered, in her arms.

He levered himself on his forearms. "I'm too heavy for you."

But she clasped him to her, fighting off the unease she already felt that he might slip away. "You're not too *anything* for me; you're what I need."

She could feel his love then, as he gazed into her eyes, open and vulnerable. Flaccid within her. "You're precious to me," he said, his voice a cracked, hoarse whisper. "But so many hurdles. So much ..." He attempted to withdraw from her, but she held him.

"It's so good, holding you this way."

But he separated them nonetheless, leaving her bereft of the protection she'd felt while he lay within her. "One thing I know, Melinda, this isn't going away any time soon, probably never. I have to come to terms with it. You may already have done that; I don't know."

He still had questions, did he? Well, so did she. "What's Lacy Morgan to you?"

He sat up. "Is that a serious question, or are you changing the subject?"

"Serious question."

"I dated her a few times because I was interested, but that quickly petered out. After that, she invited me several places and I went with her. Twice. Then I called a halt to it. She's tenacious, and doesn't want to let go. I have never been intimate with her and don't plan to be. That answer your question?"

She let out the breath she'd been holding. "Sure does."

"Now, what about us? If you're not going to get married by next March, that means giving up your inheritance. If that's what you're thinking of doing, I'd like to know why."

"Let me out of this bed," she said, throwing the sheet off her nude body.

He restrained her with an arm around her shoulder. "That's not an idle question. I want to know why and I think I'm entitled to an answer." His voice softened, pacifying her with its warmth and masculine tenderness. "Baby, don't put bricks in our path. It's hazardous enough as it is. Talk to me."

"I already told you I can't marry another man I don't love, not even if he's a friend, sweet and kind to me. I don't want money that badly."

"Is that your only reason?" His eyes mirrored intense anxiety, and she could see that he held his breath. But could she open her soul to him when he hadn't told her he loved her? She let her hand caress his cheek.

"Do you think I could lie this way with any man but you?"

He sucked in his breath. "Could you?"

"I can't even imagine it."

He wrapped his arms around her and pressed gentle kisses to her lips, eyes, cheeks, and forehead, cherishing her with such tenderness that she couldn't hold back the tears. She knew she'd love him forever.

Shortly after noon, they sat on deck eating the breakfast of scrambled eggs, bacon, and toasted bagels that he'd cooked. "I feel like I could eat a horse," he said, getting up from the table. "Let's see if there's any fruit in the refrigerator. Woman, you gave me a workout."

She swallowed her coffee and yawned with as much dignity as she could muster. "We don't want to mention what you did to me. Say, do you know, we never did see the sun come all the way up?"

"But did it rise?"

"Honey, you made a miracle. Who would believe the sun could rise half a dozen times in the same morning?"

Joy suffused him, and he supposed she could see it in his eyes, the smile on his face, and in the movements of his body. "Yeah. How 'bout that?"

He loped downstairs to the galley for whatever additional

food he could find. How could you love a woman with every atom of your being right down to the recesses of your soul if you weren't sure you trusted her integrity? Maybe he was the problem, not she.

The refrigerator yielded frozen ice cream sandwiches and fresh peaches, and he found a bunch of ripe bananas on the counter. He collected his treasures along with some paper napkins and dashed back upstairs. She wasn't going anywhere, but he still couldn't wait to get back to her.

"It's one-thirty," she said when they'd finished eating and cleaned the galley. "They'll think we drowned."

"Quit worrying about what they think. They want us to enjoy ourselves. You think I'd rather fish with Duncan than be here with you?"

"Hope not," she said and pulled the straw hat down until it almost covered her eyes.

"Where's the linen closet? I want to change the bed in the captain's quarters."

He tipped up the brim of her hat, and ran his index finger down the bridge of her nose. He had to touch her someplace and, if they were ever going to turn that boat around and head back, her nose was the safest place. A cloud covered the sun, and he looked up. He didn't like what he saw, so he dashed downstairs to alert Melinda that they had to lift anchor and go. She stood beside the bunk bed holding their soiled sheets close to her body, her eyes closed and an expression of rapture on her face that zonked him. He felt the rush of blood to his loins, but he had to control it, because that sky held threatening clouds.

"Honey, we have to hurry." Her eyes flew open and she gaped in surprise, but he took care not to let her know he'd shared that moment with her. He made the bed while she found the laundry bag and put the sheets in it.

When they got on deck, he saw that the sky had darkened

and the clouds hung lower, and goose pimples popped out on his arms. He'd never been on that bay in a storm, not even with Duncan at the helm. He pulled anchor and headed for shore, but in less than five minutes, he heard the roar of thunder.

Chapter Nine

At the first clap of thunder, he knew he had trouble on his hands, probably the fight of his life, one that would test his nerve and fortitude—not to speak of his skill—until he anchored that boat in Curtis Bay harbor.

If I get there, he said to himself. A glance toward where Melinda sat minutes earlier made him do a double take. Where on earth was she? The deck chair in which she had been sitting was empty and he hadn't seen her go down the steps. Forced to concentrate on navigating the boat, he couldn't leave the helm and look for her. His heart slowed down to a stop when lightning streaked across the horizon, a blazing light as far as he could see, and the loudest, most threatening noise he'd ever heard roared right over his head.

He looked around. Not another boat in sight, and that left him alone on that vast bay. a sitting duck for lightning strikes.

He did the only thing he could do, opened the throttle as far as it would go in a daring attempt to race ahead of the storm. Where the devil was Melinda?

He reached into the cabinet below the helm, got the foghorn, and called, "Melinda, are you all right? Come here where I can see you."

Lightning danced across the horizon in a spectacular display of nature's graphics, and thunder roared and crashed over and around him, booming its awesome power. His flesh seemed to crawl as the sky loomed black and dangerous, and he'd never seen the waters of the bay so dark and ominous. Suddenly, the wind rose and the dark water seethed in a newly menacing turbulence, so that the *Tonya Girl* began to roll. He grabbed the foghorn and called Melinda again.

"Baby, I can't leave the helm. Come where I can see you and know you're all right. Do you hear me?"

At last he heard a voice, but the high, whipping wind carried the sound away from him, so he turned toward it, and when he did, he saw her white pants silhouetted in the afternoon darkness.

"Melinda!"

"Blake. Honey, will we . . . will we make it?"

He couldn't guarantee it, not with the weather and water conditions deteriorating by the second.

"I'm giving it my best shot. You all right?"

"I'm . . . uh . . . I'm fine. Just trying to get used to the way the boat's rocking."

Lightning bounced off the water all around the *Tonya Girl*. *Any minute now, we'll get a strike,* he said to himself.

He noticed that she'd wrapped her arms around her middle, evidently trying to stave off the tremors, and he didn't blame her for being scared; he wasn't exactly jumping for joy himself. Thunder rumbled in the distance, and he knew that within seconds it would blast over his head and all around them. As he expected, another blinding light flashed around them, and then the thunder crashed so violently that it almost deafened him. He pulled Melinda to him with one hand while gripping the helm with his other one. She burrowed into him.

"We'll make it, baby. We've got to." She covered her ears with her hands, and he hurt for her. "Go on back down before it starts raining."

She looked up at him. "If you can stand up here in this, so can I, and I'm not leaving you. I went down to the ladies' room, not to get away from the storm."

"I thought you were afraid of these storms."

"I am. It's childish, but I'm petrified of lightning."

"Then go back—"

"I'm not leaving you here alone. You may need me."

He didn't argue because he wanted her where he could see her and know that she was safe. "If I can just get us there before it rains, though it's so close I can smell it."

"Me too. How can it be so dark this time of day? It's so eerie that it's almost . . . you know . . . exciting. Wonder what causes this?"

"Beats me. I couldn't stand my ninth-grade geography teacher, so I didn't listen to anything she said, which may account for my ignorance about the elements."

"Why didn't you like her?"

"She was mean to me. She didn't respect me because I was poor, couldn't dress like the other kids, and didn't have time for school plays and other extracurricular activities. One of the first things I did when I got my law degree was look her up and send her an announcement. I got a bang out of that."

Drops of rain sprinkled their bodies. "Would you look under there and get those yellow slickers, please? I almost forgot about them." She did as he asked, and they'd barely put them on when a deluge pelted them.

He saw a searchlight in the distance about where he figured

the marina would be. Surely Duncan wouldn't stand on the dock in that dangerous electric storm. He eased up on the throttle, reducing speed. *I hope that light isn't a mirage,* he said to himself. But as he neared it, he didn't see any other lights and guessed that there'd been a power outage. But his only concern was getting Melinda into Duncan's house unharmed. Lightning blazed around them, and the thunder blasted his ears, but he thought only of the safe harbor within his reach. The darkness slowly receded as rain pelted them. They'd endured twenty-five minutes of pure terror.

"Baby, we're almost there. We've made it." He eased into Duncan's assigned berth, cut the motor, clasped Melinda to him, and held her. Torrents of rain drenched the slickers they wore, but there by the boat's helm, they held on to each other, mute.

"Good Lord, you gave us a scare."

She turned at the sound of Duncan's voice. "This is the worst storm I've ever seen on this bay," Duncan said. "You all right?"

She wasn't all right; for the first time since those clouds had suddenly become black, she gave in to her fear. Tremors shook her body, and she knew Blake could feel them even through those heavy raincoats.

"We're all right," she heard Blake say. "But I'll remember that scene for the rest of my life."

"But you made it back here like a seasoned sailor," Duncan said. "As the Bard noted, 'All's well that ends well.' You two go on to the house. I'll secure the *Tonya Girl.*"

She followed Blake's gaze upward. "Would you believe that?" he asked. "Now that we're safe, it's beginning to look like two-thirty in the afternoon." He shifted his gaze to her face. "If you're okay, I'd like to help Duncan with this. It'll only take a couple of minutes."

His arms still held her, and as she looked into his face, at the caring and deep concern it expressed, she knew she would be dealing with a different man, one who knew exactly what he wanted, but would have to scale high hurdles in order to force himself to achieve it. But that didn't bother her because, now, she knew him. If he'd mastered that boat in his death-defying battle with the storm, he would master Blake Edmund Hunter.

They didn't speak to each other while he drove the few blocks to Duncan's house. Talk would have been anticlimactic. They had deftly communicated their feelings in those moments when their emotions had been raw and their hearts bare.

"You were wonderful," she said later when they stood on the back porch pulling off their raincoats.

She couldn't figure out why he was reluctant to accept her compliment, but he was. When he looked at her, his smile barely touched his lips. "You're the one. You told me you were afraid of lightning, yet you stood there in the midst of those petrifying flashes because you thought I might need you." He tipped up her chin with the index finger of his left hand. "In that storm, a lot of men would have been shaking, terrified. You're an awesome woman."

She didn't want to be awesome. She wanted to be the woman he loved. "You're dynamite on the water," she said, seeking levity. "I'd like to settle with you in a houseboat, or any kind of boat. Something tells me you dance your best dance on the waves."

"Not quite," he said, and a shadow covered the gleam that had brightened his eyes. Surely there wasn't room for sadness after what they'd just come through. "Not quite," he said again.

The back door swung open, and Justine rushed to them. "I thought I heard you down here. We've been out of our minds with worry." She looked at Blake. "Did you have any problems?"

He rubbed the back of his neck, pursed his lips, and seemed to muse over his answer. "Problems? You bet. It wasn't just the weather, though that was awesome. I had to battle the churning in my stomach and, yeah, my faith. If you've ever been tested, you know what I mean."

She nodded. "If you know my story, you know I've been there. The important thing is that you're safe."

" And that you will never again forget that cardinal rule." Blake spun around at the sound of Duncan's voice.

"Rule?" Melinda asked.

"Never take a boat out on this bay or any other body of water without checking the weather forecast. This is August, man. We can get a storm every afternoon. I should have warned you, but . . . ahem . . . I expected you back by eight o'clock this morning."

"Now, honey, you're meddling. We wanted them to enjoy themselves."

Duncan looked at his wife and winked. "And they didn't disappoint us either, baby."

Justine's smile broadened into a full, lusty laugh. "Sorry, Melinda, Duncan didn't mean to embarrass you. We can have lunch whenever you're ready."

Melinda looked at Justine. Deadpan. "Embarrass me about what?"

When Blake nearly doubled up in laughter, she lifted her chin, laid back her shoulders, and strutted past Justine into the house. "You're as nutty as a pecan grove, all three of you," she flung over her shoulder to the chorus of laughter that followed her.

Blake sat on the edge of his bed thinking of their ordeal in the storm. Through it all, he'd been outside of himself, dealing with it as if only Melinda were threatened and he had no duty to himself, only to her. But for a second after he reached the marina, the bottom had nearly fallen out of him when he reflected on the extent of the danger. *I've got to get back to Ellicott City and clean up the mess back there,* he said to himself. *I want my life in order.*

After changing into a short-sleeved yellow sport shirt and white Dockers, he shoved his feet in a pair of sandals and loped down the stairs.

"We're eating in the kitchen," Justine said. "The sun's out, and it's too hot and muggy to eat on the patio."

Blake sat beside Tonya's high chair, and immediately she held out her arms to him.

"Uncle Blake has to eat, Tonya," Duncan said, but the child ignored him and reached for Blake.

Eating with Tonya in his lap would tax his ingenuity as well as his dexterity, but he loved to hold her. "She'll cooperate, won't you, Tonya? Going to be good?' he asked her.

She nodded and reached for him again. "I'm good. Unca Bake, pease kiss," she said.

He unbuckled her and took her into his arms, and she bounced and bubbled with laughter. Then she kissed his cheeks. He looked at her. "You give me something special," he heard himself say to Tonya, though he knew she couldn't understand. With her folded in his arms, he let himself enjoy the love she gave him.

He hadn't meant to look toward Melinda, but her gaze drew him as surely as a magnet draws steel. In her eyes, he saw a longing that aroused in him a desire to have her for himself alone and for all time. He'd felt it before but never with such intensity. If only he could let himself go with her. She pleased him as no woman ever had, but he didn't please himself, not even in their torrid lovemaking just before the storm. He winked at her, and she lowered her gaze.

* * *

Sunday night when he parked in front of Melinda's door, he knew she didn't expect him to come in. "This has been a wonderful weekend," she said. "I'm so full. It's as if I'll bubble over any minute."

Immediately anxious for her, he took her hand. "I hope this doesn't mean you're unhappy."

Her eyes widened. "Unhappy? Not one bit. Maybe the opposite. It's . . . I don't know. Maybe I feel as if I finally have a handle on things, though I can't imagine why. But I'm definitely not unhappy."

"I'd better check things out with Tillman. Sit here for a minute. Okay?"

It was not Tillman, but a man who introduced himself as Robinson who stood guard. "Where's Tillman?"

"His wife's having a baby. I'm his replacement." He asked the man for his ID, checked it, and probed, "Who's at the back?"

"Hawkins."

Seemed all right, but he had to be sure. He walked back to the driver's side of his car, leaned against it, and called Hawkins on his cell phone, keeping an eye on the fellow who called himself Robinson.

"Hawkins speaking."

"Hunter. Where's Tillman?"

"At the front door, as far as I know. Why're you asking?"

"This isn't Tillman on the door. Walk around the side of the house with your gun handy, but be cautious." He called the police next and then the company from which he'd engaged the two guards.

"We don't have a Robinson on our roster, Mr. Blake," the receptionist said, "and Tillman hasn't asked for leave. I'll send the police at once."

"I've already called them."

He didn't want to get too far from Melinda, because he didn't know the intruder's goals, and relief spread through him when Hawkins appeared with his gun showing.

"Where's this—"

The moment Robinson heard the second male voice and saw the gun, he dashed from the steps, ran to the side of the property, and jumped over a cluster of shrubbery. Hawkins fired his first shot in the air and the second one missed as Robinson dashed to his left, over the bushes and out of sight.

"I've never killed a man," Hawkins explained to Blake. "I'm sorry, but I aimed for his leg, and I guess I missed." He looked down at his gun. "I've never missed before."

"What's the matter?" Melinda shouted, jumping from his car. He grabbed her. "It's all right. Just stay right here. The guy might fire back."

"What guy? This is my house, and I want to know what's going on."

He held her in spite of her agitation. "That wasn't Tillman on duty, and we don't know where Tillman is. I suspect foul play, but we can't be sure yet."

The sheriff's car drove up and behind it a squad car. When told of the problem, the sheriff turned to the policeman. "I was telling you just this morning that Ellicott City is not a dull town. Lots of things happen here."

"Yeah," the policeman said, "a regular Madison Square Garden." He recorded the particulars. "I'll put a watch on this house," he told Melinda, "but you be careful who you open the door for."

"What about Tillman?" Blake and Melinda asked in unison.

"We'll find him."

"I got a good look at that guy who calls himself Robinson. The man even had proper ID," Blake told the officer.

"How about coming with me, tell our artist what he looks like, and we'll take it from there."

Blake shook his head. "I can't leave here until the agency sends a replacement for Tillman."

After another hour, while he alternately assured Melinda it wouldn't happen again and fought his fear that it would, he remembered the camera. She hooked it up to the television and rolled the tape. Pictures of the man from every angle. She reversed it. Robinson walked up to Tillman and seemed to ask questions. After a minute, Robinson shook hands with the guard and left. The camera swept the gardens and the street. And then Robinson walked back up the front steps, attempted to open first the door and then the windows, none of which would yield entry. He then positioned himself in front of the door. Tillman was nowhere to be seen.

"What do you think?" Blake asked Melinda.

"I'm not a detective, but I believe he either drugged or poisoned Tillman during that handshake."

"But where do you think he went? He didn't just vanish."

She shook her head. "It takes the camera almost five minutes to complete that half circle. Whatever happened took place when the camera was pointed in the opposite direction."

"I'll buy that. As soon as the new guard arrives, I'll take the tape to the police."

Melinda answered the phone. "It's the agency chief. You want to speak with him?"

He took the phone from her. "No, we don't know where Tillman is."

When questioned, the chief said, "Tillman is a widower. So that business about his wife having a baby was a lie. I'm sending Mrs. Rodgers one of our detectives. He won't stand at the door, but will park across the street and sit in his car. He should be there in half an hour. His name's Jonathan Gordon."

He told Melinda what he'd learned, and then it hit him.

Robinson was waiting for Melinda to return alone, hopefully after dark. There was something in that house that someone wanted, and it was valuable. He'd bet Melinda didn't know it was there. How many times had he represented a woman who had a serious problem because she hadn't familiarized herself with her husband's business deals? He hoped his faith in Prescott hadn't been misplaced.

After speaking with Gordon for half an hour, he'd satisfied himself as to the man's professionalism. "I'm going now," he told Melinda, "but I'll have my cell phone with me every minute. If you need me, call that number. If there's a problem call Gordon and then phone me. All right?"

"I'll be fine, Blake. But starting tomorrow morning, I'm going to try and find out what this is all about."

"I agree that you have to, but before that, could we have a talk? I may have some ideas."

"Tomorrow?"

"Call me as soon as you're ready to start your day. And don't worry. If you're uncomfortable about . . . what happened to Tillman today, say so, and I'll stay with you for as long as you want me to."

She stepped closer to him, placed her hands on his shoulders, and looked into his eyes. That familiar warmth headed for its inevitable home in the pit of his belly, but he knew he had to control it, and he did.

"What is it? You want me to stay?"

"You know I do. But it's not the solution. I'm a hot enough topic in this town as it is."

Her mouth was so soft and sweet, glistening in its pouting fullness, and her eyes had that dreamy look that could start his blood on a fast journey to his loins like molten lava rushing down the slopes of a volcano.

He sucked in his breath and ordered his libido under control. "If you can't sleep, come stay with me."

She laughed, and the weight of her predicament lifted from his shoulders. "If I stay with you, I'll sleep?" she asked him. "Don't make jokes."

"I have a guest room."

To his amazement, she laughed aloud. "Yeah. Right. Who'd be sleeping in it?"

He wrapped his arms around her and hugged her. "You walk in your sleep? What on earth was I thinking?"

Her lips grazed his cheek and when she looked at him, a hint of wickedness gleamed in her brown eyes. "The board meets Tuesday, and I can see Martha purse her thin lips and say, " 'When I want to reach you, Melinda, should I call you at Mr. Rodgers's home or Mr. Hunter's home?' "

He laughed, not because it amused him, but because the light banter cheered her up. "I'd better be going. Don't forget to call me if you need me. Idly, his fingers stroked the smooth Italian marble that outlined the fireplace in the Rodgers's living room. He hadn't previously noticed its uniqueness. He studied it for a minute. *A hefty sum of money went into that,* he said to himself. And the house contained three of them on the first floor. He made a note to examine his records and find out when they were purchased.

She walked with him to the door, and he held her briefly for a kiss. Once outside, he called the guard at the back of the house as a check, and spoke with the detective who sat in a dark green car in front of Melinda's house. Then he took the tape from Melinda's surveillance camera to the police station, waited while an officer made a copy, and went home, taking the original tape with him. He'd be remiss as a lawyer if he gave up the only evidence of Robinson that he had.

Melinda walked into Blake's office at exactly ten o'clock Tuesday morning, half an hour before the board's scheduled meeting. "You sounded so serious on the phone," she told him. "What's up?"

He sat on the edge of his desk, and she knew he'd done it so that their talk wouldn't seem formal, though it dealt with business. "I want you to go through Prescott's papers. I know what's here, but if he kept important papers at home, you're the only person who has the right to examine them. I was his lawyer and friend, but someone knows something I don't know. I'm convinced that he withheld information from both of us, and we need to know what it is. I don't know what you'll be looking for, but I'll bet anything that you'll know when you find it."

"But . . . but that's like invading his privacy. I mean—"

"There's something in your house that a person wants badly enough to try breaking in and maybe to harm your guard. Aren't you even curious?"

Her eyebrows shot up. "I hadn't seen it that way. Come over and let's do this together in case I don't know it when I see it."

He stroked his chin as he mused over her suggestion, not sure he wanted to wade through another man's secrets, especially those of his friend.

"You sure that's a good idea? If he'd wanted me to know about it, he would have entrusted me with it."

"On the other hand, whatever it is—and we don't know that there *is* anything—could have taken place before he met you. Right?"

"Possible. Can we get started this week?" He pressed the intercom. "Irene, how's my docket for Thursday?"

"Friday is your only clear day this week, and I have two requests for appointments for that day. Shall I make them?"

"I'll let you know." He flicked off the intercom. "How's Friday?" She agreed, reluctantly, he thought, and wondered whether she anticipated something unpleasant. "I won't be in Friday," he told Irene.

Martha Greene was first to arrive for the board meeting, and as far as Melinda was concerned that signaled the tenor of the deliberations, as the members couldn't agree on anything except the date for the next meeting. Throughout the bickering and jostling for status, Blake remained silent, his long graceful fingers strumming the table as he watched each participant. With luck, she thought, Martha Greene would finally accost Jonathan Riley, the school principal, and they could leave. She couldn't have had a worse disaster even if she'd put her father on the board. After forty minutes, she asked Betty Leeds to close the meeting.

"Don't worry," Betty assured Melinda, "whenever you get this crowd together, they scrap and argue at first, but eventually they get down to business. Martha's a troublemaker, but she understands the importance of this foundation and its work."

"What do you think?" Melinda asked Blake after the others left.

"It's to be expected. They're all prima donnas. The foundation exists, registered and with a tax-exempt status. If it doesn't work with this group, we'll change."

"I thought they were uncooperative because of me. I can feel Martha's hostility."

"Then I'll get rid of her."

She grasped his right wrist. "Oh, no. She doesn't intimidate me, though she tries. When I'm ready, I'll put her in her place."

His left hand grazed her shoulder with such gentleness she could hardly resist stepping into him and knowing again the comfort of his arms and the sweetness of his mouth. She must have telegraphed to him her feelings, for she saw the sudden blaze in his eyes.

"I don't feel like teasing myself," he said. "I always want

you, but when you let me see that you need me—the way you did just then—I know I'm in trouble.''

"You can kiss me, can't you?'' she asked him, enjoying knowing that the man she wanted desired her.

He looked at her and slowly a grin curled around his lips. "You witch.'' With his arms locking her to him, he pressed a quick kiss on her mouth. "If you don't get out of here, I'll have to take the day off.''

She held up both hands, palms out. "All right, all right. See you Friday.''

"I'm going to see my mother tomorrow, but I'll be back tomorrow night. My father didn't leave a will, and we've had one heck of a time settling my mother's affairs. I hope I can clear things up tomorrow. If you have a problem, call the agency.''

"Will do. Good luck down in Six Mile. Here's a kiss.'' She hadn't meant to let him feel her frustration, and when he stepped back and looked at her as though puzzled, she said, "It's . . . I didn't know I was going to do that. See you Friday.'' With that, she rushed from the office.

Blake glanced at his watch, a twenty-year-old, five-dollar Timex that he kept to remind himself of leaner days, put his briefcase in his desk and locked it. He trusted his secretary, but he didn't want to give her the burden of keeping her mouth shut about information clients had given him in confidence.

"Be back at one-thirty, Irene.''

After dashing to the elevator only to see the door close as he arrived, he sped down the four flights of stairs. Long strides took him to Mill Towne Tavern three blocks away. He'd pounded into Ethan's head the importance of being on time, and he'd almost made himself late for their meeting.

He imagined that he gaped when he saw the boy striding

toward his table dressed in a business suit. He stood and extended his hand, stunned by the change in his protégé.

"Ethan, you're a brand-new man," he said, getting recognition of the change out of the way as quickly as possible.

"Thanks, Mr. Hunter. They're paying me real good for those lectures, so I bought this suit. Would you believe soon as I showed up looking like this, the principal raised me from five eighty-five to eleven-fifty an hour."

"Sure I believe it. You think I don't enjoy wearing jeans, a sweatshirt, and a baseball cap?" He pointed to his white shirt and red and blue paisley tie. "I put this stuff on because I want to be taken seriously."

"Yeah," Ethan said, "but I get tired of this stupid tie strangling me."

"It's working."

"Looks like it. They said the kids talk about what I say in their social science class. One girl cried when I told them what it was like to be in a place where you couldn't eat until somebody fed you and even the toilet wasn't private. Last week, the principal sent me to that high school near the post office. Mostly white kids over there, and they were all upset because a boy in their school just got a twenty-five-year sentence. I did the best I could, but I felt real bad for them. Sick, man. Like walking dead."

He ordered crab cakes, french fries, and a green salad and noticed that Ethan ordered the same. "Do they serve Cokes in here?" the boy asked. Tentatively.

"Sure." He ordered a Coke for Ethan and iced tea for himself. He thought of Johnny and Phil. If only they would turn out as well as Ethan. Later, he shook hands with the boy and promised they'd have lunch again soon.

"Thanks," Ethan said. "I'm glad I had this suit. This is the first time I ate in a place like this." He raised his hand for a high five. "You da man, Mr. Hunter." The boy strode down the street, and for the first time, Blake didn't see Ethan's arrogant swagger. He didn't know when he'd felt so good about someone else's life.

His early flight the next morning brought him to Birmingham at nine-twenty. Once he'd settled in his rental car, he headed back in time. Back to the place that reminded him how far he'd come and what he'd accomplished. As he drove along the two-lane road, his heart bled for the old black women in their wide straw hats chopping autumn corn in the broiling sunshine and humidity. One woman wiped her sunburned neck with a bath towel that she kept wrapped around her waist. He looked the other way, hoping to chase the memory of his own days chopping corn in the scorching heat, and his gaze fell on the men, women, and children who crawled along rows of string beans, harvesting them by the basketful. He hoped they earned more than the thirty-five cents per five-peck basket that he made as a twelve-year-old.

He crossed the brook, the one bit of picturesque scenery he'd enjoyed as a boy, and when he'd learned how to fish and often taken home a sizable catch, his father hadn't minded the time he spent there. Dreaming. As he drove up to his mother's house, no longer an unpainted shack in need of repair, but a glistening white bungalow with green shutters and awnings, he remembered that whenever one of them came home from school or the fields where they'd been working, she always greeted them at the door. He smiled as she stepped out on the porch before he cut the motor. Her arms enveloped him and he understood again the meaning of the word home. Home, the place where one could count on unconditional love. Immediately, he asked himself if he could find that with Melinda.

"It's so good you're here. Come on in," she said. "I'm all ready to go."

He asked how she managed alone. "Emotionally, I mean."

"I get a call from one of you children almost every evening, and the ladies at church . . . well, you wouldn't believe how faithful they are. I'm hardly ever alone on the weekends." She waved her hand around to encompass all she saw. "And you can see that I have more than I need."

"Anything you need done here in the house?"

"Thanks, but John did what was needed last weekend. I'm fine."

After a lunch of fried ham, crackling corn bread, string beans stewed with smoked ham hocks, and butter beans with okra, he told her, "You're lucky if I don't stretch out and go to sleep. I haven't had a meal like that since the last time I was home."

"Don't you want some peach pie?"

"Sure I do, but where will I put it?" He looked around. "You can't know how happy I am that you're so comfortable and that Papa could enjoy the last years of his life."

She walked with him to the glass-enclosed, air-conditioned back porch and sat with him in the swing. "What about you, son? John and Callie have someone in their lives. I don't know if it's permanent, but at least they're not alone. Have you found someone special?"

"I think I have," he said, "but it's so complicated." He told her about Melinda and her marriage to Prescott Rodgers. "I want to believe in her integrity. I need to believe it, but whenever I do, something happens to shake my faith."

She took his hand. "Do you love her?"

He nodded. "I don't doubt that, at least."

"Then why can't you ask her questions and accept her answers? Ask her how she came to know him and what their agreement was about their marriage."

"She's told me, and I believe her." He told his mother about the will.

"What would you have done if she'd found someone and told you she was getting married?"

He heard the groans that eased from his throat and the words of truth that came from his lips. "I don't think I would have let her do it. I don't know what I would have done, but I'd have stopped it."

"And she'd have lost the inheritance."

"Thank God it didn't come to that."

She shook his arm as if to make certain he heard her. "Are you going to make her give it up?"

He turned and looked at her. "What choice do I have?"

A long sigh escaped her. "I never dreamed that a stupid person was capable of getting a law degree from Columbia University. I thought that was an Ivy League school."

His head spun around, and he eyed her until she got up and left the porch. "I'm ready to go when you are," she threw over her shoulder, and walked on into the house singing "Precious Memories."

At the office of the county clerk in Birmingham, they settled the material legacy of Woodrow Wilson Hunter's life. Then, Blake drove his mother back to Six Mile and accepted the peach pie that she gave him to take home.

"Maybe in the winter you'll come up to Ellicott City and spend a few weeks with me."

Observing him closely, she said, "All right. I wouldn't promise, but I want to meet that girl."

"Melinda."

"Nice. I hope she's like her name."

He thought for a minute. "She is." He hugged his mother, got in the car, and headed for the Birmingham airport.

On an impulse, Melinda drove to her parents' home after she left Blake's office. She had expected to find her mother alone, but her father answered the door.

"So you came by to lick your wounds, did you?" he said before she could greet him.

"I don't understand," she said, and that was the truth.

"I hear tell your board meeting this morning was a flop. Martha screwed the bunch of you. If I'd been there, I would have shut her up quicker than she could say 'ugly.' Don't stand out there. Come on in."

Her father was tall and lanky, and she had to reach up to kiss his cheek. "Papa, when I get good and tired of her, you'll hear about it. Where's Mama?"

"She's at the senior center arranging a birthday party for one of 'em. She doesn't have enough to do here." He rubbed his chin and looked at his hand as if to examine the damage done by the stubble. "And wouldn't you think that poor ninety-seven-year-old woman is bored with birthday parties by now? Same old tasteless cake and—"

She stared at the merriment dancing in his brown eyes and interrupted him, though she knew he hated that. "Papa, you are meddling with that poor woman. Do you know her?"

He rolled his eyes and looked toward the heavens. "Do I? Ever since I could crawl. I wonder if she's still chewing Sir Walter Raleigh pipe tobacco." He shook his head. "Never knew where she'd spit."

"She lived near your folks?" This was getting interesting. If she'd ever caught him in such a frivolous mood, she didn't remember it.

"Right across the street. She'd sit on that old front porch and beg everybody who passed. 'Gimmie little somethin'. God'll bless you.' Spitting and begging. We used to go out the back way and steal up the other street where she couldn't see us."

In her mind's eye, she could see her grandparents and parents tipping stealthily in and out of their own home, and all of a sudden, giggles poured out of her. Uncontrollable.

"Why is she living at the seniors' home, Papa?" Melinda asked after she gained control.

He put his hands in the back pockets of his slacks. "She outlived all of her kin and most everybody else she knew when she was able to get around. Who's going to help her, other than my wife? Everybody who remembers her is scared of getting spit on."

He headed for the kitchen, opened the refrigerator, and poured two glasses of lemonade. "Here. Have a seat," he said. "Daughter, I don't want you to fool around and waste your fortune. If you don't want it, give it to somebody who needs it. That's your Christian duty." She should have known he would get around to that.

"Papa, would you expect me to marry a man just so I could get money? I'd have to share a bed with him, Papa, and I can't do that."

He cleared his throat. "Well, when you put it like that, it sounds awfully bad. But I keep thinking there's a reason why Prescott tacked that rider onto his will. He wasn't my favorite person, but he wasn't stupid or foolish. Now you think about that."

"I will, Papa. I promise." She kissed his cheek, and for a man who hated to be touched, he smiled and patted her shoulder. She left him, wondering if he'd had a vision of his imminent demise.

If only she didn't have to tackle Prescott's things. She'd never been in his walk-in closet, though she'd looked in it a time or two, and his clothes still hung there. The thought of sifting through all that, plus Lord knows what was in the basement, was sick making. She'd planned to ask Rachel to help her, but since Blake suspected they might find secrets, that wouldn't be clever. She hated to ask her mother, because she had too much to do as it was.

She stopped in Ludie's Good Eatings, around the corner

from the Ellicott City B&O Railroad Station Museum, the oldest railroad station in the United States, to buy some homemade raspberry jam.

"Rachel," she said, "what a nice surprise. I was just going to eat lunch alone. Can you join me?"

Rachel appeared to think it over. "Okay. Maybe we need to air out some things. I called you Friday night, but Ruby said you'd gone away for the weekend. Mind if I ask where you went?"

They took a table in Ludie's outdoor café in the back of the store and ordered lemonade. Melinda didn't want to give up Rachel's friendship, and now was as good a time as any to find out whether the woman planned to continue her pursuit of Blake.

"I spent the weekend on the Chesapeake Bay and got caught in an electric storm while I was out on the water. I'll never forget it."

"You weren't by yourself."

"No, thank goodness."

"I'm glad you're safe. I know I haven't acted like it, but you're still my best friend. Like you said, I just have this terrible habit of getting interested in men who don't show an interest in me. I want you to know that I . . . I took your advice, and I'm getting help for it. I don't think it's pathological because I hardly ever think about Blake these days."

Melinda searched Rachel's face for evidence that she was fabricating the story and saw none. "I'm glad, because I also want us to be friends. We couldn't be, though, if you decided to go for Blake. He's . . . He's very important to me."

"I know that, and I know he's interested in you. I can't imagine what got into me, Melinda."

They ate their club sandwiches and ice cream and prepared to leave. "I hear Martha Greene trashed the board meeting yesterday morning. If I were you, I'd kick her off. She's such a busybody. She'll give you trouble as long as she's on that board.''

Melinda's father claimed that a dog who brings a bone will carry a bone. Rachel was her friend, but in Ellicott City, gossip ruled, and being the first to tell something could put your status on a par with that of the mayor, at least temporarily. She changed the subject.

"I'm considering adding my brother Paul, not as a board member, but as an advisor to the board. He's just what that board needs.''

"That'll upset some of them.''

Melinda's shrug, long and leisurely, indicated that she didn't care. "Let it. They're all convinced that I'm a woman of questionable virtue, so they'll probably say I violated the terms of the will. To them, I'm a scarlet woman. They have no proof, but that's what they think. I'm not going to waste time trying to please them.''

She bade Rachel good-bye, glad that they'd mended their relationship. However, she had never been one to learn a lesson a second time, and she intended to keep a little distance between them.

As she turned into her garage, Gordon, the detective, got out of his car and walked over to her. "Mrs. Rodgers, I thought you'd like to know we've located Tillman.''

Chapter Ten

Around seven-thirty that evening, Blake turned off Route 40 into Ridge Road and headed home. Six blocks from his house, his cell phone rang, and he pulled over to the curb because he didn't talk on the phone while driving if he could avoid it.

"Hunter."

"This is Gordon, Mr. Hunter. I'm going off duty in half an hour, and a guard named Mitchell will replace me. We've located Tillman, and you'll get a full report in a day or two."

A day or two! "I just got back in town, Gordon, and I'll be over there in ten minutes. I don't want to wait 'a day or two' to find out what happened to the man. This is important."

"Okay. I'll wait here for you."

Blake swung the Cougar around, and in less than ten minutes parked in Melinda's driveway. The detective walked around to meet him.

"What happened?"

"We don't really know. Around one o'clock today, Tillman came to himself sitting in a park in Alexandria, Virginia. He had no identification, no money, and he was hungry. He hailed a Virginia park policeman who took him to a police station. He remembers shaking hands with a man who asked him for directions, but nothing after that until he came to himself on that park bench. The police called the agency, verified his story, and the agency sent a guy to bring him back here."

"In other words, our man drugged Tillman when he shook his hand."

"Looks like it. I won't be shaking anybody's hand unless I know 'em," Gordon said. "You can put your life on that."

"Does Mrs. Rodgers know this?"

Gordon nodded. "I told her as soon as we heard from Tillman."

She might be uneasy, maybe even frightened. "Thanks. I'll see how she's doing. Let me know when Mitchell arrives."

He phoned Melinda. "Hi. Gordon told me what happened. I'd like to speak with you. Would you please open the door?"

"I'll be right down."

After telling her what he knew of the case, he added, "Instead of starting on sorting out Prescott's papers Friday, I think we'd better begin tomorrow if you haven't planned anything more pressing. I'll clear my appointments."

Strains of fatigue showed in her sweet face and in the slope of her shoulders, and it pained him to tax her more, but he wasn't satisfied as to her safety, not even with around-the-clock guards. Guards that were expensive Band-Aids on a problem the dimensions and dangers of which they couldn't even guess.

"I realize this may be getting to you, honey, but we have to find out what the guy's after. I'll be with you all the way."

She patted his arm, though with little apparent enthusiasm. "I know you will. All right. We'll start tomorrow. Incidentally,

I'm going to ask my brother, Paul, to serve as permanent advisor to the board. If he's there, they won't behave as they did yesterday.''

"He's straitlaced?''

She laughed, obviously enjoying a private joke. "He likes to make other people toe the line, although if he ever toed it, I wasn't there to see it. He's efficient. You'll like him.''

"If he's like you, I will. Kiss me, and don't lay it on thick; I'm tired.''

Her eyes sparkled in that devilish way that fascinated him and made him want to explore every facet of her. "I'm not. Why should I bother if I can't do it like I want to?''

"I'm not going to ask you to explain that. Kiss me, woman.''

"Hmmm,'' she said and raised her arms to him at what seemed like a snail's pace. Her fingers skimmed the side of his face, moved slowly to his neck and then to the back of his head, taking her time as if postponing the minute she would reach her goal. He waited, and heat began to sear his loins as he anticipated the second that she would open her mouth to him. Just before she parted her lips, she glanced up at him, and let him see the desire in her eyes, heating him to boiling point. He squeezed her to him, held her head, and plunged into her. When she gripped his hips, locking him to her body, he rose against her. She battled him for his tongue, got it, and sucked it deep into her mouth. He'd promised himself it wouldn't happen again until he'd cleared his mind of doubt about her and could give himself to her totally. But she moved against him, letting him know that she needed him, and he jumped against her belly. Fully aroused.

"Melinda, baby, I don't think—''

"I need you.''

She loosened his tie and slipped it from his neck, and tremors raced through him at the thrill of her fingers unbuttoning first his shirt, then unhooking his belt and reaching for his zipper.

Having a woman undress him until she had him naked, an experience he'd last had when he was four years old, sent his libido into high gear and his blood racing through his veins. She unzipped him, and he took the packet from his pocket and let his trousers drop to the floor. He stepped out of them and kicked them aside, never taking his gaze from the heat and excitement in her eyes.

With one hand, she let the strap of her sundress fall to her left elbow, exposing one full and glistening globe, and he didn't try to control the wildness that flared up in him like a raging storm. Then she locked her gaze to his own and lowered the other strap, baring herself fully to his pleasure. He stared at her, mesmerized, as her tongue moved slowly around her lips, dampening them.

"Kiss me. Love me. Drive me out of my mind," she murmured.

Captivated, he unzipped the dress and let it pool at her feet, exposing all but her lover's gate, hidden from his eyes by the skimpiest of red bikinis. Erotic. She was an aphrodisiac wiggling in his arms, and he hardened against her belly.

For a minute, he fought the savage, uncivilized, and unfamiliar hunger gnawing his insides.

She whispered, "Darling, I'm—"

The drunken sheen in her eyes hurled him over the edge, and he swallowed the remainder of her words in his kiss, picked her up, and looked around. Everything seemed to swim before him, to merge, chair into sofa, window into wall, floor into ceiling, as desire ravaged his nervous system. He knelt with her on the carpet in front of the fireplace, but he sensed at once that she wanted command, handed her the condom, and rolled over on his back. She peeled off his bikini underwear, shielded him, and straddled his body, her beautiful breasts inches from his hungry mouth. He suckled her left one and fondled the right breast until she moaned and squirmed above him. Excited at her brazenness, he let his fingers trail down her body past her navel to her secret folds and found her damp and ready. Quickly, he penetrated her heat, and she moved upon him until he was helpless beneath the onslaught of her merciless motions. He sucked her breast into his mouth and stroked her back and her buttocks, and still she rode him. Her quivers, squeezing and pumping, began, dragging him out of himself, possessing him, sucking him in like quicksand until he threw his arms wide and shouted in surrender. Nothing remained of his own as he gave her the essence of his loins and of himself. She leaned forward and kissed his lips, as moisture from her eyes dripped onto his cheeks.

He lay beneath her, stunned and shattered, depleted of energy. It cost him an effort even to open his eyes, but he had to look at her, at this woman who had finally brought him to heel, in whose body he had at last lost the will to resist and had finally enjoyed the glory of complete fulfillment and total release.

"How do you feel?" he asked her. "You had me in such a fog that I couldn't make sure I'd . . . that you got what you needed. Did you get straightened out?"

Her arms went around his shoulders, and she hugged him and kissed his neck. "You mean release? Yes, I had that. Thank you. But you gave me something more than that, more precious." She smiled through the tears that rolled down her cheeks. "You . . . I don't quite know what happened, but I felt you were mine. At the end there, you'd never given yourself to me like that. . . ."

He kissed the tears that rolled down her cheeks. "Why are you crying?"

"I . . . I'm not crying. I'm . . . I'm just . . . happy."

He closed his eyes, separated them, and held her in his arms. No doubt about it, he had to get to the bottom of the mysteries surrounding her because he couldn't see beyond the place she occupied in his heart.

Minutes later, he said, "I've never felt this way before."

She didn't answer nor did she caress him. When he could no longer stand her silence, he leaned over and looked into her face to gauge her mood. Her eyes were closed, and her breasts rose and fell rhythmically as he observed her in peaceful sleep. This sweet and tender loving woman. He grazed her lips with his own, and she opened her eyes.

"I need to go home. If I'm coming here tomorrow morning, I have to write a brief and draw up a contract before I sleep tonight."

With her hands over her head, she yawned and stretched, long and leisurely. "I could help."

"I don't doubt that you'd want to, but on this night with you in my house, my mind wouldn't be on contracts and legal briefs. I wouldn't sleep a wink and neither would you. So I'll see you in the morning."

For once, he didn't find his work inviting as he dragged himself away from her. "Every time I'm with you," he whispered, "I find something else that endears you to me even more." Covering her with her sundress, he said, "Stay where you are. I'll be here around ten."

He knelt and brushed her mouth with his own, then held her gaze as she stared at him with luminous eyes, her feelings bare. Humbled by what she'd given him and what her eyes promised, he sucked in his breath and left, wondering at his luck.

Later that night, lying in bed, Melinda mused over their lovemaking, trying to figure out what had happened that night that was so different from the other times they'd made love. At the beginning, he'd been slow to cooperate, as if he didn't like their reversed positions. And then he'd caught fire, transmitted it to her and literally abandoned himself to her, moving as she moved until, at the end, he'd given himself over to her.

She hadn't known a person could experience what she felt when his body shook with release and he lay vulnerable and bare in her arms. Happy. She'd never been so happy. Was it the beginning of a new day for them? She turned out the light and slept soundly.

At ten o'clock the next morning, dressed in a red T-shirt, stretch jeans, and sneakers, she opened the door for Blake, who picked up the *Maryland Journal* and handed it to her.

"Good morning, Mrs. Rodgers," he said and walked in past her.

Her eyes widened, and the bottom dropped out of her belly. Had last night been something she dreamed? She spun around to confront him, and the glare in her eyes dissolved into a grin. That six-foot-four-inch, one-hundred-and-ninety-pound man stood there open, vulnerable, and almost scared. One thing was certain, he looked as if he were defenseless, that he needed protection. Her first reaction was, *What a great time to have my way with him.* She couldn't control the mirth that poured out of her in peals of laughter.

"Something's funny?"

She straightened up as best she could. "Uh, yes . . . I mean no. I mean . . . I'm not going to . . . to get out of line. Besides, I can't. Ruby's here."

It was the best she could do, but that didn't erase his frown. "I just want to make sure we spend the day doing what we're supposed to be doing."

"And when did we ever do something we weren't supposed to be doing?"

At that, his vulnerableness evaporated, his face took on a dark and thunderous expression, and his eyes seemed to shoot fire. "You know exactly what I'm talking about."

In other words, don't play with him this morning. "Coffee's ready. Want some toast or a crumpet? Have you had anything to eat?"

The thunderclouds disappeared, and his eyes sparkled with the smile that always made his face beautiful. "I had orange juice. A cup of coffee would make me human."

Her eyebrows went up. "Lord, let me get that coffee." She went into the kitchen and asked Ruby to bring them coffee on the sun porch. "Mr. Hunter will be helping me here in the house today."

"All right. I knows what he likes. I'll bring the coffee. For the rest, give me 'bout ten minutes."

Blake finished the buttermilk biscuits, grits, scrambled eggs, and sausage and sipped his third cup of coffee. "Ruby knows how to feed a man. This was wonderful, like being home with my mother." He took a sheet of paper from his shirt pocket. "Unless you know what's in the basement, I mean what's on the inside of every box and piece of furniture, I suggest we start there."

She put her right elbow on the table and propped up her chin. "I can see that this may take days."

"It may, but if there's an alternative, I don't know what it is."

"Okay, let's get with it. We're in the basement," she called to Ruby.

"Yes, ma'am, Miz Melinda. What time y'all gonna be wantin' lunch?"

"One o'clock will be fine?" She looked at Blake, and he nodded.

"One o'clock," she called to Ruby.

"I haven't spent a lot of time down here," she said, opening a big seaman's trunk. They found rolls of parchment containing diagrams of chemical processes drawn in different colors of ink.

"Wonder why this wasn't locked?" she asked, more herself than Blake.

"That occurred to me too."

An ancient Aetna cedar chest that might have been inherited from Prescott's mother revealed several silver trays, a silver flatware service for twelve, blackened with age and neglect, and linen tablecloths and napkins. She'd attempted to open the chest once while Prescott was alive, but it had been locked. She mentioned it to him, but he didn't open it. She told Blake as much.

"He might have unlocked this chest and the trunk when he realized he was terminally ill. That would make sense," Blake said.

By lunchtime, their search had yielded nothing that might tell them why a man wanted to get in that house.

"What's next?" Blake asked after they'd eaten. "Feel like going through his personal things?"

"I don't feel like it, but we have to do it. Let's start in the den, and if we don't find anything there, we'll check the bedroom."

Finding nothing in the den, they went to his bedroom, which was as Prescott left it when he went to the hospital.

"I don't feel right going through a man's personal things," Blake told her. "I'll just sit in here with you."

She didn't feel like it either, but it had to be done. "I wish I could drop the whole thing."

Around four, Ruby walked into the room with a tray of iced tea and oatmeal cookies. "I don't know what you lookin' for, but the one place he always kept locked from the time I come here was that closet across the hall beside Miz Melinda's room. I ain't never seed it unlocked."

Blake tried the doorknob. "It's locked. Got a screwdriver and pair of pliers?" he asked Ruby.

"In the closet on the back porch. I'll be right back with 'em."

"I'll get them." He opened the closet door and gasped. Rows

of cassettes obviously arranged in an order understandable to their owner. "Come here, Melinda, and look at this."

"Well, I'll be . . ." she said when she could force a sound from her lips.

She remembered Prescott having told her, "That's my old chemical stuff in there. I keep it locked, because that's all behind me now."

"Let's take a couple from the top and play them," she said.

Blake jumped to his feet when he heard his voice. Prescott had taped their conversation about his funeral arrangements. "What the hell! He didn't have to do that. I gave him a signed statement of everything he'd agreed to. I thought the man trusted me."

So Blake didn't know. She stopped the tape, pulled a chair over to where he sat, and took a seat beside him. "You didn't know that Prescott had dyslexia and couldn't read or write? He could barely sign his name, and sometimes he got the letters in the wrong order."

"What? You're telling me that . . . I knew that man well for seven years. He was one of my first clients, and we were close friends. Now you're telling me—"

She placed a hand on his arm. "Did you ever see him write or read anything?"

He thought for a long time, bemusement mirrored on his face. "Only his signature, and I once teased him about that, suggesting that he should have been a doctor. I remember my uneasiness at his response: 'I wish I could have been. It was my childhood dream.' He was so solemn." Blake shook his head.

"Blake," she said, pressing his wrist with her hand, "it's because of that affliction that I knew Prescott." She told him how they met and about the conditions he offered for marriage. "I was so glad to be out from under my father and to have a friend whose company I enjoyed. Yes, the comfort of his home attracted me, because I had spent a couple of hours a day with him for nearly a year before he mentioned marriage, and I knew the place. You must know the terms of our marriage, since you were his attorney.''

"He didn't share that with me. Unable to read and write. That boggles my mind. A brilliant man. Think what he might have done and who he could have become if he'd been literate.''

"I've thought of that many times. I'm the only person in this town who knew, or so I think. He remembered whatever he heard and saw, compensating for his handicap.''

Blake stretched out his legs and locked his hands behind his head, deep in thought. "Whenever I invited him out to lunch or dinner, he gave me an excuse for wanting to eat here at home. And now, I see it was because he couldn't read a menu.''

She got up. "Let's see what else we'll find.'' More cassettes revealed that Prescott recorded all of his business conversations and everything about his work, including his inventions.

"Let's finish this tomorrow. I've had a surfeit of chemical terms, stuff I haven't thought of since my first year in college.''

"What time tomorrow?'' she asked.

"Same time. Okay?'' She nodded, and he laughed. "You're going to behave yourself tonight, baby, because Ruby is here.''

"She's not my mother.''

A grin began around his bottom lip and strayed up to those eyes that she adored. "No? Well, for tonight, at least, she's mine, and I am circumspect around my mother. Come here, and keep the heat down.''

"You're joking. That's like pouring oil on a fire and expecting it to die out. How'm I supposed to keep it down when you're a human generator?''

"Try. You'd be surprised at what you can do with a little self-control.''

"Says you. I had over twenty-nine years of self-control. You let this bird out of the cage, honey, and you needn't expect her to fly back in there willingly.''

He grasped her shoulders and smiled. Sweet. Lord, she adored him. "You like it out here, do you?" he asked her, barely containing the grin.

"If I need self-control, you could use a little ego deflation." She reached up and grazed his mouth with her lips. "Don't expect this often. But since I wore you out last night, I'm letting you off.''

His laugh, full throated and rippling with mirth, excited and thrilled her. "I don't accept challenges, baby, when they're aimed at bending my will. I'm on to you. Kiss me."

Just as she leaned into him, his fingers gripped her waist, and he set her away from him. Then he brushed her lips, her cheeks, and her eyelids with such tenderness that she felt chastened and, in a symbol of remorse, rested her head on his shoulder.

"I don't just want you," she whispered. "I care for you. See you tomorrow morning."

He gazed into her face until she became giddy from the pounding of her heart and the lurching of her pulse. "And I care for you," he said. "A whole lot."

He released her then, and loped down the stairs. "What's for breakfast in the morning?" he called to Ruby, who responded, "Same thing, Mr. Blake. You know I knows what you likes."

Melinda heard the door close. He cared for her. How could she go through with her plan to leave Ellicott City as soon as the board was functioning smoothly? How could she leave Blake?

He spoke with Mitchell, the guard, for a few minutes, got in his car, and headed home. In the kitchen, he took a pepperoni pizza from the freezer and put it in the microwave. Totally at loose ends, he wandered through the living and dining room until he heard the microwave's beep. With a bottle of Pilsner and the pizza, he sat in front of the TV and tried to eat his dinner. Something was totally out of kilter and he hadn't put his finger on it. While surfing TV channels, he passed Chris Rock, all teeth and smiles, and flicked back, because something the man said pricked his memory. He thought he'd heard the comedian say that lonely women didn't do wicked things because they were too desperate. Rock was already on another subject. Blake flicked off the TV and got another Pilsner.

The telephone interrupted his mental meandering. "Hi, Callie," he said after hearing her voice. "What's up?"

"I just talked with Mama, and I thought she seemed kind of down." They talked for a while, and he promised to visit their mother the following weekend.

"You don't have to. I'm going there for the week. Just give her a call. Maybe she's lonely."

He imagined she was, but she didn't appear to be when he called her, so he satisfied himself that he could stay with Melinda until they finished searching Prescott's effects. Imagine spending a lifetime hiding illiteracy. He nearly jumped from his chair. Rather than cheat Prescott, Melinda had befriended him, and Prescott had adored her. Whenever she was in the room with them, Prescott's gaze had followed his wife's every move with an expression that was nothing short of adoration. How could Blake have been so wrong? But why was she so lackadaisical about that inheritance? It didn't make sense.

He spent an hour and a half in his office before going to Melinda's house. Ruby greeted him. "Your breakfast is ready, and I got some good old hot buttermilk biscuits I made this morning. I loves cooking for mens. Miz Melinda don't eat enough to keep a bird flying. You come on in the sun porch. I'll tell her you here."

After breakfast, he kissed Ruby on each cheek, took Melinda's hand, and the two of them streaked up the stairs. "With luck, we'll get at least a clue out of these cassettes."

After listening to each one, they labeled it. "Let's check out some of these," she said, pointing to the bottom of a row.

"You have no claim to this process." It was Prescott's voice, though much younger than in recent years. "I told you about it, thinking you were a friend, and you have the gall to claim partnership!"

"You read this contract and signed it, making me your legal fifty/fifty partner not only in that film-processing fluid, but in the company we'll set up to produce it," a male voice replied.

"Don't be a fool, Reginald. I don't sign contracts, and that is not my signature."

"Nobody will be able to tell the difference. Nobody on the face of this earth. I worked for you for five years and got a pittance compared to what you stashed away. I'll get my share or else."

"I can afford to forget about that fluid and let it die right where it is, a sketch on my drafting table. I don't need another penny, and before I'll let you cheat me out of my work, I won't develop it. You and I are finished. If you don't want to be sued for blackmail, stay out of my life."

Blake looked at Melinda. "Blackmail? What . . . What a mess. This fellow, Reginald, must have discovered that Prescott couldn't read."

They played the last of the tape: "Light green on yellow parchment. The end."

They stood as one. "The trunk," they said simultaneously and headed for the basement.

"Here it is," he said, after unrolling the diagram that was clearly the work of a chemist. Tubes, glass globes, Bunsen burner, and cylinders drawn in intricate architectural fashion, with an assortment of colors that were evidently for identification.

They stared at each other. "This is it," she said. "What else could it be?"

"Let's put it back for now. The next thing is to ask Ruby what she knows about the man named Reginald."

"Why y'all want to know?" Ruby asked.

"We're trying to straighten out all of Prescott's affairs," Melinda said, and he gave her points for discretion.

Ruby sat down. "I told you 'bout him, didn't I? He was the last friend coming here till Mr. Blake here come to dinner that first time. A few years 'fore that, Mr. Reginald practically lived here. I tell you that man done et more of my food than Mr. Rodgers ever et."

"Did he ever come here when my husband wasn't home?" Melinda asked Ruby, and he could see the anxiety in her face.

"All the time, Miz Melinda. He kept a lot of his things up there in that closet of yours."

"Did you like him?" he asked her, hoping to get a clue as to the man's personality.

Ruby lowered her head. "No, sir. He thought he was better'n me."

He thanked her and let his hand graze her shoulder. "Nobody's better than you are, Ruby, and anyone who thinks so is your inferior."

He'd seen Melinda vexed, but not angry, and the fury blazing in her eyes now as she asked Ruby, "What was his last name?" surprised him.

"Goodman or Goodwin, I think. I never remembers for sure, Yes. Reginald Goodwin. But Mr. Rodgers ain't had nothin' to do with him in years."

"What did he look like?" Melissa asked her.

"Real ordinary, except for them thick eyebrows. He wont young, 'cause his hair was salt and pepper, almost silver. But he sure had plenty of it. And he wore them black, horn-rimmed glasses what made him look like a professor."

She'd mentioned those eyebrows when she saw Tillman's camcorder photo of the man who drove by the house in a green Chevrolet. Blake went upstairs and called the police station.

"This is Blake Hunter. Brick, you remember the picture of that man who drove by Melinda Rodgers's house in a green Chevrolet? Yeah. Could you get an artist to change that picture to gray hair and eyebrows and black horn-rimmed glasses? Great. I think we may have him."

After hanging up, he said to Melinda, "I'd lock that cassette up if I were you. Better still, if you have a blank cassette, I'll copy it for you. You may have to give the original to a prosecuting attorney." He copied it and gave them both to her. "Don't forget the board meeting Monday morning."

She stared at him, or was that a glare? "Today is Friday, and you're telling me what will happen on Monday? That's three days from now."

Where was his head? "When it comes to mixing business and pleasure, I'm rough around the edges. Never done it before."

She parked her fists on her hipbones and looked at him from slightly lowered lashes. "What were you mixing with me Wednesday night on the living room floor? Oh, yes. And that kiss last night that knocked my socks off, you do that for all your clients? If I'm getting my signals mixed, please forgive me."

He walked over to her and wrapped his arms around her. "Baby, will you stop acting out and have dinner with me tomorrow night? I was going to call you, but if leaving like this raises your dander, I'll just save myself a phone call. If I get here around seven, will you open the door?" He didn't want to laugh as he watched her deflate, but he couldn't help it.

Her faced softened, and she began to laugh. He stroked her, soft, warm, and sweet in his arms, and when she reached up and kissed him, joy suffused him. "Honey," he said, "we don't have to hit the pinnacle every single time we're together, do we? The thought of you has had me keyed up for so long, I wouldn't mind unwinding, but I'd have to do it slowly. Want to spend a weekend at Cape May? The water's still great.''

With her face relaxed and a smile playing around her lovely brown eyes, he didn't think he'd ever seen her look so mischievous. "You are one sweet-talking con man.'' She pinched his nose. "I'll let you know. See you tomorrow at seven.'' He kissed her cheek and left, satisfied that he'd get a warm welcome the next evening.

"Miz Melinda, is that Reginald what's-his-name been up to somethin'? I tell you I never did trust that man, and I told Mr. Rodgers that more'n once.'' She rambled on, not waiting for an answer. "Mr. Blake ain't staying for dinner? He such a good eater. I loves to cook for him. Well, I guess it's a bunch of veggies and a piece of broiled fish again tonight,'' she grumbled. "At this rate, I'll lose my skills.''

She didn't want to give Ruby too much information. She trusted her, but Ruby would tell Piper who would tell . . . "Ruby, I hadn't touched Mr. Rodgers's things, and I'm fortunate that Mr. Hunter offered to help me sort them out. After a while, I'll do some entertaining, and you'll have a chance to show off your cooking. Is that better?''

"Shore is.''

Melinda went up to her room and telephoned her brother. "Paul, I want you to do something for me,'' she said after they had talked for a while. She explained about the will. "Everybody in this town is convinced that if I'd been a decent woman, I wouldn't have married Prescott. Now I've formed the board, and they're being disrespectful. I can't make you a member of the board, but I want you to be permanent advisor. We hope to meet once a month, and I'll ask Blake Hunter, the executor of Prescott's will, to pay your travel expenses. With you there—"

"You won't have one thing to worry about. I'll see that they shape up."

"Monday morning at ten?"

"Sure. Meet me at the airport at nine."

Monday morning at ten-fifteen, Melinda walked into Blake's conference room, Paul at her side, looked around, and enjoyed a private joke. Martha Greene nodded slowly and pursed her lips as if to say, "Didn't I tell you so?" and Melinda didn't doubt that everyone present except Blake expected her to announce that she'd be marrying the man at her side, her inheritance now ensured.

She walked over to Blake, who had stood when she entered the room. "Mr. Hunter, this is my brother, Professor Paul Jones." After introducing each board member, she grasped Blake's arm, held it, and said softly, "Paul, this is Blake."

She turned around, looked at them, and nearly laughed at the disappointment on their faces. "Ms. Leeds, Paul will be permanent advisor to the board and will attend all of its meetings. Paul, Betty Leeds is board president."

Melinda didn't miss the wry amusement in Betty's face and tone as she opened the meeting. Martha Greene picked up her discussion of rules of procedure where she'd left off at the previous raucous meeting.

"Parliamentary wrangling is out of place here," Paul said. "Let's get down to business." He looked at Betty. "Madam president, go right ahead."

Melinda watched in awe at the orderly interventions and discussion. Even Martha asked permission to speak.

After the meeting, Blake congratulated Paul. "She said you'd do it. Neither she nor I could have put Martha in her place, since the woman is suspicious of us both. I'm glad you're with us."

"I think I'm going to enjoy it, but I need all the advice you care to give me. I'm a professor of civil engineering. This stuff is Greek to me."

She felt good. They liked each other. "Let's get some lunch."

"Great," Paul said. "How about Fisherman's Creek?"

They walked the four blocks to the air-conditioned restaurant, and the sun, hot for early September, made the short hike nearly unbearable.

"I don't believe this," Melinda said.

"You don't believe what?" Blake asked her.

"That's Rachel waiting in line for a table, and she's alone. I'm having lunch with her here tomorrow."

"So it is." He paused, as though in deep thought. "Why don't you ask her to join us?"

She stared at him for a minute, and then asked Paul, "Do you know Rachel Perkins?"

"I don't think so." Melinda pointed Rachel out to him. "No, I don't," he affirmed, "but I wouldn't mind meeting her."

Blake looked at her, grinned, and shrugged. "Go ahead. One man's poison . . ."

When the four of them were seated, Melinda said, "Rachel, you know Blake. This is my brother, Paul."

She couldn't believe her eyes. Paul was attracted to Rachel. "Why did you want her to join us?" she whispered to Blake.

"Because I saw him watching her and figured he'd like to meet her. Wasn't I right?"

"Yes, and she doesn't seem immune."

After lunch, she took Rachel's arm. "I'm so glad we ran into you. Let's be in touch." But Rachel, apparently flabbergasted, just nodded. "See you later," Melinda called to Paul, knowing that he'd either stay with her or with their parents, or go immediately back to Durham, North Carolina, where he lived and taught.

"First time I've known Rachel to be speechless," Melinda said to Blake, as they walked toward her car.

"That'll be interesting to watch. I gather he isn't married."

"No. He's single. Wonder what Papa will say about that?"

"Irene told me your father sent practically everybody in Ellicott City to hell Sunday morning," Blake said. "Did you hear the sermon?"

She shook her head. "Mercifully, I overslept."

"Apparently, somebody stole a woman's pocketbook or snatched it, I don't know which, while the woman was in a booth in the church's ladies' room. From what I heard, he said that if the person doesn't confess and give it back, he'd commend their soul to the devil."

"And he'll do it, too. When may I give this board over to Betty Leeds and go on with my life like the rest of the local citizenry?"

He pulled in his top lip, took a deep breath, and let it out slowly. "Are you telling me you've done all you plan to do in fulfillment of this will?"

"Exactly."

He kicked at the pavement with the toe of his left shoe. "In that case, you have to work with me to decide how to dispose of the estate among charitable organizations, or help me decide on one. And let's keep this under wraps."

"Whatever you say. You're the boss."

"Yeah. Right. I'll call you after I go to the police station to see what the artist did with that photo."

He gazed into her eyes, and she had the impression that he was trying to communicate something to her, something for which he didn't have words, or had them but wasn't ready to use them. *Lord, please don't let me imagine things,* she said as she slowly became enmeshed in his masculine aura. Standing on Columbia Pike Road beneath a broiling sun, the man in him leaped out at her and her breathing accelerated. He must have seen the desire that gripped her, because his eyes held an answering torch. She burned with the need to touch him, to be in his arms.

"Blake, honey, I—"

"It's all right. It just means that we . . . there's more to this than either of us realized. He squeezed her hand and smiled before walking off, but if she'd ever seen a more wooden, forced smile, she didn't recall it.

At home, she made a list of things she needed, and decided to shop for them around six o'clock when the day began to cool. She'd better track Paul down and find out whether he planned to have dinner with her.

She phoned her mother. "Mama, has Paul gotten over there yet?"

"My Paul? He's in town?"

"Yes. He's helping me with the foundation. He'll call you."

She hung up. Wow! She didn't want to call Rachel so she'd play it by ear. If he was hungry, they'd eat out.

When Blake called, his words disturbed her. "If Ruby's there, we'd like her to come to the police station and look at this photo."

"Blake, honey, I'd rather Ruby didn't get involved in this."

"So would I, but that can't be helped. If she doesn't come voluntarily, she'll get a summons. You want me to talk with her?"

"I'll drive her down there."

"Ain't no problem, Miz Melinda. If anybody done something they oughtna, they needs to be punished. Just let me get my umbrella. This sun is too much."

Ruby made a positive identification of Reginald Goodwin, and a judge issued a warrant for his arrest. "But he wasn't the goon who drugged Tillman," the chief of the detective agency said after Tillman examined the photo.

"But he knows who did it," an officer said, "and we'll get both of them."

Melinda took Ruby back to her house and drove to the shopping mall. She stepped out of the office-supply store at dusk, put her packages in the trunk, started around to the driver's side of the car, and screamed. A man lay sprawled supine between her car and the one in front of it. The mall's security arrived, detained her, and called the nearest police station.

"Well, if you didn't hit him," the officer said after she'd pleaded her innocence for twenty minutes, "you'll have an opportunity to prove it."

At the station house, she phoned Blake. "I'll be there in a few minutes."

"The man was dead when the ambulance arrived," the policeman told Blake when he arrived.

"I was in the mall for nearly two hours," Melinda said. "You can check the time of my purchases from the cash register receipts."

"All right, ma'am. If we can get hold of that judge, you'll be free to go soon as you post bail."

"I'll take care of that," Blake said. "Let me have those receipts. I wouldn't get too upset about this if I were you. The coroner will establish the time of death, and you'll be exonerated. Tonight, you go home with me."

He called the night guard and explained that Melinda wouldn't be home. Then he took her home with him.

The next morning, Blake searched for the coffee filters. He was going to throw out the pot and all the filters. He didn't like that coffee, and he hated to give it to Melinda. He looked up and nearly laughed as she strolled into the kitchen wearing his cotton robe. "Where are you in that thing? For a minute there, I thought my robe walked in here under its own steam. Take a seat. I'll have this blasted coffee ready in a few minutes."

"Not like that, you won't. You have to put the filter in that gadget that's shaped like it, place the two over the pot, put the ground coffee in the filter, and *then* pour boiling water over it.''

He looked from her to the filter. "You're kidding."

"Definitely not."

"Maybe this stuff will finally taste like coffee." He lit the oven. "While those biscuits are warming, I'll cook some bacon and scrambled eggs. Or would you rather have some bran flakes?''

"Hmmm. A man who can cook. I could get used to this."

"And I've got a few other things I'd like you to get used to.''

She raised soft round eyes to him, and he worked hard at steadying his nerves. She trusted him now, but he wouldn't bet on how she'd feel about him if she knew the role he'd played in drawing up that will. He didn't want to think about it.

Chapter Eleven

"No wonder you didn't bring the paper inside," Melinda said to Blake as they left his house. She pointed to the headline: *Melinda Jones Rodgers arrested for hit-and-run driving and possibly murder.*

"I didn't know about that." He frowned in displeasure. "I hadn't seen it."

Last night when he'd comforted and cherished her, making no demands, she'd thought her world had at last righted itself. And now this. "But you must have expected it. How can they say I hit the man and ran away? When I found him lying there, I stayed and called the police. What are these people trying to do to me?"

His arms eased around her as if to ward off the late October chill, but it failed to temper her rising anger. "Until I married, people avoided me because I was the daughter of Booker Jones, righteous judge of everybody in town. After I married, people shunned me because they decided I'd hoodwinked an old man and married him for his money."

"Melinda. Sweetheart, don't. Stop it. You're innocent, and I'll prove it."

She moved from the circle of his arms. "And those ridiculous stipulations in that will, as if I'd been a lousy wife and had to do penance in order to inherit what I hadn't known existed. Prescott neither acted nor lived like a rich man."

"Where are you going?" he asked when she hastened down the steps.

"Home. It's mine at least for the next six months."

"I'm taking you home."

She didn't feel the joy that always pervaded her when his arms went around her, and she knew he realized it. They didn't speak during the short drive to her house. Feeling alienated and misrepresented, she didn't try to pretend camaraderie.

Blake stopped in front of her house, put the car in park, and left the motor running. "You tell me you care for me, but in this crisis, you shut me out. Let me know when you feel you can talk to me. Be seeing you." He didn't get out to open the door for her and accompany her up the walkway to the house as he always did.

As she opened the car door, she stopped, turned, and faced him. "As Prescott's lawyer, why did you let him do this to me? Give the money to the Belly Dancers of the World. Whoever. I don't care. Thanks for bringing me home." She didn't wait for his answer.

Tillman stood at the door, and she greeted him as one would an old friend. "I'm so happy you're safe," she said.

"Thank you, ma'am. I sure learned me lesson. From now on, I won't be shaking hands with any man but me brother. I'm lucky I got me life."

"Anyone snooping around this morning?"

"Not a soul, ma'am."

She put her pocketbook and the newspaper beside the vase of yellow, orange, and white chrysanthemums that adorned the table in the foyer and went to the kitchen to speak with Ruby.

"I shore was glad you left that note on the icebox." Ruby always referred to the refrigerator as the icebox. "I'd a been outa my mind. You didn't see them morning papers, did you? I declare these people is something nasty."

"I saw *The Illustrated,* that muckraking scandal sheet, and that was enough."

"Humph," Ruby said and put her hands on her hips, signifying the onset of a diatribe against somebody or something. "What they says on the inside is worse'n the headlines. I'd like to take a stick and go up against the heads of them people on that paper."

"Thanks." She didn't wait to hear more, but when she reached the foyer, she couldn't resist opening the paper.

Scarlet woman shows her colors

Widowed less than a month, Melinda Rodgers advertised for a husband. If that weren't enough, she made a spectacle of herself on a public dance floor. And now, she's accused of knocking a man dead and failing to stop and call for help. Maybe old Prescott Rodgers knew what he was doing when he made it difficult for her to inherit his fortune.

She left the paper on the table and trudged slowly up the stairs, wondering what she'd done to deserve a public flogging such as that one. She rubbed her forehead to ease the sudden pain. If only she hadn't mistreated Blake that morning. He deserved her trust and caring, but after seeing that headline, she didn't have it to give. Longing to make amends, she welcomed the ring of the phone and rushed to answer it, hoping that it was he.

"Hello." She held her breath as she waited for his voice, but it was Rachel who responded.

"Hey, girl. What's up?"

"Rachel! I ought to be asking *you* that. How are you getting on with Paul?"

"Oh, Melinda. He's . . . He's super. I've never met a man like him. Sweet as sugar and absolutely no nonsense."

"That's Paul, all right. Are you . . . uh . . . in touch with him? Often, I mean?"

The voice softened to a purr. "He calls me all the time, and for once I don't feel as if I have to . . . you know . . . go after him. It's a great feeling. Look, I called to say I'm sorry about . . . about all this mess. If you need me, just pick up the phone."

She thanked her, and they talked for a while, but her mind wasn't on the conversation, and she soon said good-bye. *Do what's right and take your medicine, girl.* She phoned him.

"Hello, Melinda. What can I do for you?"

At such times, she wished caller ID had never been invented. Well, only honesty worked with Blake.

"You . . . you can forgive me. I shouldn't have taken my misery out on you."

His silence was deafening, and she had no choice but to wait for the verdict. After what seemed like hours, he said, "No, you shouldn't have taken it out on me, and you shouldn't have walked off with my newspaper either."

" Blake—"

"Just don't shut me out, Melinda. I want to be there for you when you need me. Are you coming to the board meeting tomorrow morning?"

"I'll be there."

"Don't let the stories in these papers drag you down. As soon as this case is settled, we'll get a retraction, or we'll sue for damages in civil court."

Winding the telephone cord around her right wrist absent-mindedly, she heard him and didn't hear him. "All I want right now is to get away from here and shake the Ellicott City dirt off my feet for good."

"You can walk off and leave me"—she heard the snap of his finger—"just like that?"

A strange tiredness seeped into her and she sat down on the bed with a sense of hopelessness. "I may not have a choice," she said and realized that she was offering him an opportunity to give her a reason to stay.

What he said was, "You will have a choice. The question is whether you'll take it."

Her nerves quickened in anticipation. "I'd appreciate a little plain English, Blake. Break it down for me so I'll know exactly what you said."

"I'm in deep. If you leave here, I'll go get you. You belong to me. You understand that? You're mine."

By the time he uttered the last word, she was standing on her feet with her left arm tight around her middle and her mouth agape. When she could collect her wits, she said, "Does that mean you no longer doubt me and mistrust me?"

"It means when I'm arm's length from you, you're too far away. You told me the circumstances of your marriage, and you gave me the proof. You said you wouldn't have deceived Prescott, that you would never have divorced him. I believe you. My gut feeling is that you're honorable, and that's what I'm going to hold on to until you disprove it."

"What a thing for you to tell me on the phone."

"I would have told you this morning, if you'd given me the chance. When your head starts to rule your heart, the way it does sometimes, let yourself remember what you and I are like when we're locked together the way God intended us to be. That ought to tell you that nothing's going to keep us apart for long.''

''Are you telling me you've finally sorted things out, that *your* heart is finally ruling *your* head?''

''I doubt that will ever happen, and it doesn't have to. Last night, for the very first time, you slept in my arms. All I wanted was your contentment and safety. You must have realized that I was on fire for you, but you were more important to me than satisfying my need to make love with you. So why should you be surprised to learn that I feel this way about you?''

''Blake, I'm full to the brim. Oh, honey, I need you, but Ellicott City is beginning to suffocate me.''

''Then we'll take that trip to Cape May where we'll be alone. Are you willing to try and get rid of everything that stands between us?''

''Yes. I want that more than anything.''

''All right. I'll make the reservations. See you in the morning.''

She hung up, and for a long time she couldn't move. Had he told her she didn't have to marry in order to receive her inheritance, or was he saying *they* should marry? *Or did he even realize what his words implied?*

Blake knew what he'd said to her, because he hadn't spoken on impulse. Sleep had come in spurts, fitful, the night before when she lay so peacefully and trusting in his arms. He'd ached with desire, but he hadn't let that bother him. What kept him from sleeping was his fear of rolling over on her, of crushing her with his big body, and of not being awake to soothe her if she awakened alarmed and needing him. While he'd cuddled her as if she were a baby, it had struck him forcibly that his reservations about her integrity were excuses not to let himself love her, not to give himself. He'd known all along that if he opened his heart fully to her, he wouldn't want to live without her. Maybe if he reread Irene's dictations of Prescott's own words stipulating the second condition in that will, he'd find an out for her, because she didn't intend to fulfill it. Furthermore, he wasn't about to give her up to another man.

He answered his cell phone. "Hunter."

"Say, Blake, this is Phil. Me and Johnny passed our tests, and we're going to regular eleventh grade classes. We already got parts in the school play, and Johnny's testing for the debating team. It's a gas, man."

He could hardly believe what he heard, that six months could bring such a change. "I'm proud of you both. Soon as I can manage it, we'll spend a Saturday afternoon doing whatever you guys want to do."

"I can tell you right now. Make it Sunday so we can see either the Ravens or the Redskins."

"Right. I'll get the tickets. Heard anything from Lobo?"

"Our counselor said he got in a nasty fight over at the Hagerstown prison where they sent him. We're not in touch with him."

One more life down the drain. "I'll let you know about the football game. Stay in touch."

Irene's notes didn't tell him anything new. Melinda either fulfilled both terms of that will or he had no choice but to give the money to charity. He lifted his shoulders in a shrug. Prescott had tied his hands, and he'd done it deliberately.

He walked into his conference room the next morning to find Martha Greene already there and ready to pounce.

She didn't waste time on preliminaries. "Melinda Rodgers shouldn't be in charge of a foundation that's so important to this community. Who's going to respect anything run by a woman blasted by every paper in town? Imagine! Running away and leaving a man to die. And that's just one of her cute little tricks. As executor of that will, it's your duty to put her off this board.''

"Good morning, Miss Greene," he said and watched her blanch at his reprimand for not having greeted him more politely. He told his temper to take a walk, leaned back in his chair, and looked her in the eye.

"Prescott Rodgers's will stipulates that, without Mrs. Rodgers, there will be no foundation. Anything else?"

Her pursed lips and jutting chin betrayed her hostility, but if she pushed him, even a little bit, he'd give her the obvious alternative.

"Yes, there is," she said between clenched teeth. "I don't see why I should spend my precious time working on this committee for free."

He showed his teeth in what he supposed passed for a grin. "You knew when you agreed to serve that the will requires board members to volunteer their service. You said you wanted to enhance literacy and education in Ellicott City. Changed your mind?"

"Well, I have to think about it. I'll bet I'm not the only one of us who doesn't like being used like this."

So she planned to stir up trouble. "I don't know what you've got against Mrs. Rodgers, but she discharged her responsibility when she established the board. It exists in fact and in law. Nothing you do about it will affect her personally. If you don't want to serve . . ." He let it hang.

"I'd hate for you to miss the reception I'm planning as an occasion to introduce the board members to the community." Let her digest that.

Blake stood when Melinda and Paul arrived. He knew his gaze devoured her and that Martha would broadcast what she saw as soon as she left his office, but he was powerless to withhold the evidence of his adoration. He walked toward them.

"Hello, Melinda. Good to see you, Paul." Paul's quizzical glances from Melinda to him told him that he'd bared his feelings. Suddenly, he didn't care. Still, relief spread through him, when the other board members arrived and he could concentrate on business rather than on Melinda. He didn't want to subject her to the gossip that would begin even before the meeting closed.

"What about at least paying expenses for board members?" Martha began. "We ought to be remunerated, but if that's not legal, Mr. Hunter has to take care of what it costs us to attend these meetings."

"If any of you spends more than a dollar for gas getting to and from these meetings," Paul said, "let me know, and I'll gladly reimburse you out of my own pocket. Now, let's get down to business."

At the end of the discussions, Blake stood and thanked them for their work on behalf of the community. "Saturday after Thanksgiving, I'll host a reception for the board, at the Dumbarton Hotel ballroom, to let the citizens of Ellicott City know what you're doing for them. Black tie." He looked at Martha. "This is my treat. The will doesn't allow frivolous use of the money available to the board."

Paul's wide grin gave Blake enormous satisfaction. "If any one of you plans to resign," Paul said, "we need at least a week's notice. Several people are anxious to get on this board."

Martha must have known that everyone looked at her, for she busied herself looking over her papers and left without telling anyone good-bye.

"What do you think?" Paul asked Blake when the three of them left the office.

"She won't resign, because she doesn't want to be left out. This board is the latest status symbol. I hope you'll be here for the reception."

"Sure thing. What about guests?"

Blake couldn't stop the laugh that floated out of him. He'd bet on the woman's identity. "You mean Rachel?"

"Uh . . . why, yes. How'd you know?"

"I got my information the same way you got yours this morning."

"You mean about you and my sister?"

He slipped his arm around her waist. "Who else?"

"Blake, we're walking on Main Street," Melinda said.

He tightened his grip. "I know what street it is."

Paul made a show of looking at his watch. "I'd better hurry. I promised Rachel I'd meet her at one, and I have to stop by to see the folks before I head back to Durham. You two have a good time."

As they walked into a nearby restaurant, Melinda looked at Blake from beneath lowered lashes and said, "At least Paul doesn't have a problem with our being together. Don't you think it'll be cool in Cape May this time of year?"

"We may not be able to swim, but it's warm enough still for walking. Would you rather go somewhere else?"

She stopped and looked into his eyes. "I just want to be with you."

He put his hands in his pockets to keep them off her. "And you say *I* chose a bad time to say what I feel. If I had you alone right now, you wouldn't be standing on your feet."

Her wink, slow and impudent, challenged his control, and when she said, "What would I be standing on?" he laughed for want of a better way to slow down his racing heart.

He ate half of the hamburger he'd ordered and noticed that she barely touched hers. "You take my breath, my appetite, my caution—"

"Good grief," she said, "here comes Papa. I didn't know he ate here. And he's made up his face to reproach me right here in this restaurant. Let's go—"

He interrupted. "Let him try it."

"Well, now, miss, you're playing hookey from school. You ought to be thankful they haven't fired you after that trick you pulled. Leaving a man for dead. I'm ashamed of you."

Never had Blake wanted a piece of a man so badly. His fists ached for a spot beside Booker Jones's head. "How does it feel to be the only righteous person in Ellicott City? You must get lonely for company. Don't you know everybody in this restaurant is staring at you while you make a spectacle of yourself?"

"How dare you?" Booker said between clenched teeth.

"Don't challenge me. Don't even think it. If you weren't Melinda's father, I'd have a few things to say to you and they wouldn't be pretty. Whatever you have to say to her, say it in private."

Taken aback, Booker looked at Blake with alarm. "I'll say what I like; she's my daughter."

"But you don't protect her. I do and I will, even from you. You haven't asked her what happened, so I assume you don't care. I can't wait to see you eat crow." He paid the bill, left a tip, and held out his hand to Melinda. "Are you ready to go?"

"Yes. Good-bye, Papa." She walked around him as if to avoid the appearance of disrespect. "I don't let myself be humiliated when he acts like this," she said as they left the restaurant. "He thrives on an audience, and he did this a lot when I was a teenager."

He noticed that she looked straight ahead, avoiding eye contact with anyone in the restaurant. "I think he needs badly to be accepted," she said with a sigh, "but he doesn't know how to get people to like and accept him."

He looked down at her with a compassion that he knew she read in his eyes. "I'm beginning to understand that you've been through a lot. I thought I had a wretched childhood because

I was treated almost as a workhorse, but I see that yours was no more pleasant than mine, only different.''

"He can be so harsh, Blake, and the next hour or so, he's kind and thoughtful. I love him, but I've never felt free to express it as I'd like.''

"Your mother loves him?''

"She sure does, and he loves her, or at least, that's what she says. I need a different kind of love.''

He knew that, and he intended to give it to her. "We'll talk later,'' he said. "Try not to let this upset you.''

The smile didn't make it to her eyes. "It won't. I'm used to his public posturing.''

She might be used to Booker's taunts and accusations, but why couldn't she tell him it hurt, as it surely must? He wondered if she'd ever open herself to him, if they'd ever trust each other enough to expose their doubts, fears, and pain. He was almost there; if she'd trust him, he'd knock down walls to meet her halfway. He slapped his left hand against his forehead. The private investigator he'd hired hadn't gotten back to him. He wanted a report.

Melinda left school at three-thirty, shopped for groceries and wiled away the time, dreading being alone. Ruby greeted her at the door with the look of one thoroughly harassed.

"What's wrong, Ruby?''

"Nobody knowed where you was. The police been after me to go down to the station, but I told them I wasn't going noplace till you come home.''

"What did they want?''

"They got this man down there for me to identify. Suppose I fingers that man and they lets him loose. If it's Goodwin, I wouldn't trust him far as I could throw him. What you think I should do?''

"I'll go with you."

"Seems to me like you wouldn't want to see them cops after what they done to you."

"It's not settled yet. Let's go."

"That ain't Reginald Goodwin," Ruby told the policemen. "I ain't never seen that one before."

"Are you sure?"

"Course I'm sure," she said, bristling. "I'd recognize Reginald Goodwin anywhere, and ifn' I ever heard him talk, there wouldn't possibly be no doubt. You can't miss that nasal twang of his."

Melinda watched the perplexity on the policemen's faces. "Could he be an accessory? If he's innocent, why won't he look me in the face?" she asked them.

"Good question," the detective said. "You're free to go, buddy, but don't move from that address and don't leave town. If you do, you'll be in trouble."

"Yes, sir." The man sauntered out, yanking at his oversize jeans as he went.

"I don't trust that one," the detective said.

"Neither do I," Melinda told him. "He is not the man who rang my bell late one night and who I later caught on my surveillance camera."

"No," Ruby said, "and he sure ain't the one heading up the steps toward Mr. Tillman in that scene the camera took. They's somebody else in this."

The detective walked with them to Melinda's car and thanked them. "But we'll get whoever it is we're looking for. You can be sure of that."

She whirled around and tugged at the detective's sleeve. "Did you ask Tillman if he could identify the man?"

The detective shook his head. "That guy is miles from the

description Tillman gave of the man who slipped him that drug. Don't worry. We'll stay on it.''

"Yes," she said. "I suppose he is."

When they returned to Melinda's house, Paul was talking with Tillman. "What are you doing with guards around the house?" he asked Melinda.

"Tell you later," she said, opened the door, and walked in with him.

"I thought I'd spend the night with you. I'm hanging around town this weekend."

Her eyes widened, and she nodded her head as though acknowledging a fact. "I'd have thought you'd stay at Rachel's place."

"We haven't gotten that far. You know me. I don't rush into anything I might get stuck in."

"If you ask me, you can get stuck even if you don't rush into it."

"You talking about yourself and Blake? When did that start?"

She gave him an edited history of the relationship. "I didn't stand a chance from the minute I saw him, but I'm proud that as long as Prescott lived, Blake didn't guess how I felt."

"My hat's off to both of you. What's holding you back now?"

"I'm still a recent widow, Paul. The local citizenry thinks I'm a gold digger, and now there's the chance I'll be tried for hit-and-run driving."

"Yeah. Papa was ranting about it this afternoon. I told him he should be ashamed of himself for castigating you, that he should be supporting you. Mama told him the same. Is this holding Blake back?"

"No. He's with me in all of this." She told him about the mystery man who wanted access to Prescott's invention.

"Good Lord. You're getting it from every side. I'm glad you

have Blake; he's a good man. You giving up your inheritance? If you love Blake, you can't marry some Joe just to get that money."

"And I never intended to, but Blake doesn't seem to realize it's possible to marry me."

"He will. If you don't believe it, walk off and see what happens."

"He said something to that effect. How're things with you and Rachel? Wait a minute. Let me answer the phone.

"Yes?"

"Our friend's driving by again. I alerted the police and Mr. Hunter. Just want to let you know," Tillman said.

She thanked him. "Where were we? Oh, yes. Rachel. What about her?"

Paul propped his right foot across his left knee and closed his eyes. "I think a lot of her. A lot of things about her suit me, but there's still much more to be discovered. I'm keeping my fingers crossed."

"I hope it works for you."

"Y'all come an' eat," Ruby called. "I cooked a nice dinner 'cause mens always eats good." After a meal of fried Norfolk spots, braised celery, jalapeño cornbread, grilled eggplant, green salad, and sour cream lime pie, they waited in the living room where Ruby preferred to serve the coffee.

"Play something," Paul said.

"I haven't played the piano since Prescott passed away, I—"

"Come on," he said, "that man was crazy about you. He'd want you to play or do anything that made you happy. Play something rousing like Sinding's 'Rustle of Spring.' "

She sat down, rubbed her hands together, and was soon lost in the music; as she finished one composition, she began another. Finally, her fingers and arms sore from that workout after not having practiced for months, she stopped, lowered her head, and closed her eyes. Startled by the applause, she looked around to see that Blake and Rachel had joined her and Paul.

"I couldn't leave the music," Paul explained, "so I asked Rachel to come over here."

"And I came as soon as Tillman reached me with the news that Goodwin or someone like him is on the prowl again. I never heard you play like that. You were always subdued, but this . . . this was as if the music had been locked inside of you and you suddenly let it fly free. It was . . . it was magical."

A loud noise suddenly rang out.

"Good gracious, what was that?" Rachel asked as she moved closer to Paul.

"Get in the back, all of you," Blake said. "That was a gunshot."

"Melinda, what's going on?" Rachel asked, obviously welcoming the opportunity to clutch Paul's arm.

Blake answered his cell phone. "Thanks, Tillman."

"A guy's been harassing Melinda, driving up and down the street past the house. Tillman just shot the man's tires up, and he's on his way to jail," Blake said. "Nothing to get upset about."

Melinda thanked Blake with her eyes. She hadn't wanted to explain the situation to Rachel, but considering Paul's interest in her friend, she wanted to be as gracious as possible. Who knew? Rachel might become her sister-in-law.

"It ought to be safe to leave," Paul said to Rachel. "You must be starved."

"Not exactly," she said, and Melinda's head snapped around. Who was this Rachel? The one she knew would have screamed at the sound of a gunshot, and would certainly have grumbled and held her belly if she couldn't eat dinner at six-thirty. According to her watch, it was nine o'clock. She glanced at her brother, whose gaze devoured the woman beside him, and hoped he'd found what he'd been looking for.

They left arm in arm, but the room seemed no less crowded. How large a man Blake seemed standing in front of her chair! The open-collared T-shirt, black jeans, and black leather jacket emphasized his heady masculinity and enhanced the aura of danger that always clung to him. She patted the place beside her on the sofa, and he sat there.

"I was here ten minutes after Tillman called me. Thank God I was home. Seems the guy had been casing this house for the past hour and a half. You and Ruby will have to go to the police station again tomorrow morning."

She looked down at her hands when she realized she'd been squeezing and unsqueezing her fists. "I figured we'd have to do that. You think this is the end of it?" It wasn't tension, but anger that she needed guards to ensure her safety from a man her late husband had once trusted.

He draped an arm around her shoulder and warmed her with a quick squeeze. "Who knows? If he identifies the man who drugged Tillman, that might end the danger, but we still don't know how far he'd go to get that invention—provided he *is* the guy we're after—or what we're in for legally."

"The more brazen he gets," she said, "the more determined I am that he won't get his hands on that design. He's not dealing with a woman who'll cringe in a corner and beg for mercy." That wonderful laughter rumbled in his throat and spilled over. How she loved to hear it.

"The thought of you cringing anywhere is mind-blowing." He stopped laughing and turned to her, as serious as she'd ever seen him. "We have the ammunition to send him to jail for a long time, but even if he gets ten years, with that invention, he'd be rich when he got out and young enough to enjoy the proceeds. We have to make certain that every one of his henchmen involved in this is with him behind bars."

He was telling her that he would stand by her through whatever she faced. Her eyes must have communicated the love she nurtured for him in her heart, for his own eyes glistened with tenderness. She gripped his arm, and those eyes she loved darkened into obsidian pools of desire. Knowing what would come next, she pressed her hand against his chest in warning.

"Paul's spending the night with me."

With disbelief mirrored in his eyes, he looked toward the ceiling. "Maybe you believe that, but it's not what I saw when he got up to leave. Want to take bets?"

She shook her head. "No, because I have the advantage. I know him. He's enough like you that he's prepared for every eventuality long before it comes."

"Yeah? Then, I'd better leave right now, sweetheart. What I need would take all night, if not longer. See you in the morning around nine."

She walked with him to the front door. "Maybe—"

A wicked grin crawled over his face in slow motion. "Oh, no. I'm not letting that straitlaced brother of yours challenge me tomorrow morning." He kissed the tip of her nose. "See you in the morning."

She stood at the half-open door, watching Blake talk with Tillman, and used as much restraint as she'd ever mustered when she managed not to call him back.

The next morning, Ruby's jovial manner deserted her as soon as she learned that another trip to the police station awaited her. "When is I gonna get this silver polished and these ovens cleaned?" she grumbled, mostly to herself. But when Blake arrived, put his arm around her, and thanked her for her willingness to help, whatever displeasure she'd felt dissipated like a puff of smoke in the wind.

"You knows I'd do anything I can to hold up the law, Mr. Blake." Her smile was luminous. "We just got time for me to give you a little breakfast."

Melinda stared at the two of them. Who'd have guessed it? Ruby Clark was a man's woman, loved being around them and doing things for them, and Blake knew it. If she gave Goodwin bad notices, he deserved it.

At the station house, Ruby's deference to men was nowhere in evidence. She stared at the man sitting beneath the light in the examining room and laughed. "Well. Well, Mr. Goodwin. You ain't looking down your nose at me now, is you? You ain't gonna catch me sitting under no light with the police grillin' me. I'm good as you is now, ain't I?"

The detective touched Ruby's arm. "You say this is Reginald Goodwin, the man Tillman photographed with his camcorder? This is the same man?"

"Yes, sir. Same man what had the run of Mr. Rodgers's house for years, coming and going as he pleased. Even had his own key. It's him, all right."

"You're sure?" Blake asked her.

"He's dyed his hair, but he can't hide them eyebrows and that mole on his nose. You know, I'd forgotten about that mole. It's him."

"Officer, I want this man arrested for entering my house without permission, unlawfully, and for harassment," Melinda said.

The detective nodded, and looked at Goodwin. "Do you know a man who goes by the name of Robinson?"

Goodwin glared at the officer. "Do you think I'm foolish enough to answer any of your questions without a lawyer?"

Ruby jumped up and clapped her hands. "Shore is him. Shore as you born. It ain't possible I'd forget that twang of his, not even if fifty years had passed."

"We're almost there," the detective told them as they left. "We've posted Mrs. Rodgers's reward for information leading to arrests in this case. My hunch is that someone's being paid to steal something in your house. As long as he's out here, you'd be wise to keep those guards stationed at your doors."

As they walked to his car, Blake's arm around her waist

communicated more than the protectiveness she sensed whenever he touched her. What she felt in his caress now was far deeper, exceeding even possessiveness. It was as if, in that one gesture, he said, "You and I are together in this and all things." Not knowing how she should respond, whether she read him correctly, she merely accepted the sweetness of the moment.

He drove Ruby back to Melinda's house and, when Melinda would have gotten out of the car, he detained her. "Let's go over to the Patapsco, sit on the banks and talk."

The autumn leaves were at their most brilliant hue that Saturday morning, dazzling in colors of orange, red, brown, purple, and gold. Evergreen pines stood out among them, asserting their authority in nature. Blake and Melinda had their choice of benches facing the rapidly rushing water and chose one several feet from a huge boulder.

Melinda took in her surroundings and wondered why she didn't go there often. "It's so beautiful here, so peaceful and serene," she said, and couldn't help musing over the sense of rightness she suddenly had about her relationship with Blake. If there was such a thing as fate, she had a hunch she'd met it.

"That's why I wanted us to come here. It's another world." From now on, he intended to avoid making mistakes with Melinda. He took her hand and held it close to his body.

"I ought to have told you this before, but . . . well, I engaged a private investigator to track down whoever hit that man you found lying beside your car. It's obvious to me that whoever did it parked beside you not too long after you left your car. If that coroner knows his job, your cash register receipts will be all we need." He adjusted his trouser leg and draped his right foot across his left knee. "I'm also going to tell him to locate this guy, Robinson. As long as he's loose, we can't relax."

"I know. Whoever he is, he's getting paid to commit a crime.

I don't think Goodwin will reveal the man's identity, because he's hell-bent on getting that invention."

He put an arm around her. "Let's not dwell on that right now. If you don't want to go to Cape May, we can go to the Virgin Islands, the Bahamas, or—"

"I want to go to Cape May. We don't have to swim."

Ray Sinclair, who had been watching the couple from afar, came up to them and said, "Well, well. If it isn't the lovers. Sorry about your ... er ... accident, Melinda. Everybody's talking about it; the poor man had a wife and four kids. You—"

Blake told himself not to lose his temper. "Shut up, Sinclair," he said, getting to his feet and towering over the man. "You heckle Melinda one more time, just one more word, and you're going to see stars. You've got a lot of nerve, brother."

"Don't tell me you'd start a brawl right here in public. Not the high-minded Mr. Blake Hunter."

"That's what you think, huh? Well, let me tell you something: as a teenager in Atlanta, I knew every street man in that city, and they knew me. Nobody bothered me, because the reputation of my fists preceded me wherever I went. Get that?" He slapped his right fist into his left palm. "Don't mess with me, man."

"You don't have to get uptight."

He shoved his hands in his pockets, away from temptation. "Just beat it.

"What I need you to understand," he said to Melinda, as if Ray Sinclair hadn't interrupted him, "is that I want us to have some time together, but only if you want it and wherever you want it, whether that place is here or in the Antarctic. You said you couldn't lie in another man's arms, and I don't want anyone but you. But we don't know whether that's enough."

He could feel her tense. "Haven't we been over this before?"

"I seem to recall that we have, but that was months ago

when . . . when joining our bodies was the most pressing thing we felt. It's more than that now. Haven't you considered whether we can make a life together? I have.''

''Yes, it's been on my mind a lot, but your insistence that I find a husband in order to satisfy the terms of that will confused me.''

He let out a long breath. ''I hope you don't think it didn't bug the hell out of me. I was doing what Prescott wanted, but you've convinced me the price is too high, and I accept that.'' He rubbed his chin with his free hand. ''I don't believe I would have let you do it.''

''I couldn't do that to myself a second time. I'd known Prescott for more than a year, and he was a gentleman, but . . . there is no fortune worth what I would have faced.''

''It's getting toward lunchtime,'' he said. ''Want to go to the Mill Towne Tavern?''

Her face mirrored her disappointment. ''Ruby would never let me forget it. She's prepared lunch, which she hates doing, since I won't consume those high-calorie meals she loves to cook. If I don't show up to eat it, I'll never hear the end of it.''

''By the way,'' he said, and winked to push his point. ''Was Paul still asleep when we left your place this morning? I'd have thought he wouldn't miss that fantastic breakfast Ruby cooked.'' He barely managed to control a laugh when she pursed her lips, frowned, and managed not to look at him.

''You didn't think I'd forget it, did you? From the look in Paul's eyes, Rachel didn't stand a chance. I'll let you know when I'm ready to collect on that bet.''

''Oh, you! A gentleman doesn't press his advantage.''

He had to laugh; he couldn't help it. ''Tut, tut. What gentleman led you to believe that? Surely, you're not so gullible. From now on, I intend to press every advantage you give me.''

''Don't be so cocky. I may not give you any.''

He pinched her nose. "Then I'll make my own advantages. Woman, can't you see I'm getting desperate?"

She looked up at him, and he wondered at her seriousness. "Do you think Rachel's right for Paul?"

"You can't judge another's needs. If she floats his boat, he'll let us know soon enough."

Falling leaves drifted down around them, and for reasons he didn't examine, he picked up a handful of golden, red, and purple ones from the boulder near where they sat, made a bouquet of them, and handed them to her. If ever eyes bore stars, hers did at that moment. He'd never kissed a woman in full view of anyone who wanted to look, but he had to feel the sweetness of her mouth.

Her lips clung to his. He broke the kiss and stared down into her eyes. "I love you."

She gaped as though in surprise, but he hadn't meant to say it right then, so he didn't elaborate. With her hand in his, he strolled with her back to his car, oblivious to Ellicott City's gossiping citizens.

Chapter Twelve

He meant it; she knew he did. He hadn't said it in the grip of passion and, as usual, he'd been the epitome of sobriety. He'd looked her in the eye and told her in a voice unsteady with emotion that he loved her. Somehow, though, she didn't feel like shouting for joy because in spite of all that had passed between them, he still belonged to himself alone. Yet, they were closer in that moment than when they made love. He communicated to her a caring that she hadn't received from anyone else except, perhaps, her mother. She thanked Ruby for her lunch of shrimp salad on lettuce leaves, sliced tomatoes, whole wheat toast, and tea.

"Don't thank me," Ruby said. "Only reason I concoct that stuff is so I don't have to go out and find another job. I declare, Miz Melinda, real food ain't gonna kill you."

"You're a dear," Melinda said. "You make the best shrimp salad I ever ate, and I've eaten a lot of it."

Ruby folded her hands in front of her and allowed herself a moment of modesty. "You go 'way from here, Miz Melinda. I never made that for anybody but you, but if you likes it . . . Course, I'd rather cook real food, but for a nice person like yourself . . ." She let it hang.

Melinda's laughter filled the room, pouring out of her, and with it the tension she'd felt since Blake's declaration of love that noon.

"Ruby, if you ever want to take acting lessons, I'll be glad to spring for them," she said and hurried up the stairs so she wouldn't hear the woman's comeback.

When she was home on Saturday afternoons during the school term, she usually wrote letters, did lesson plans, checked her clothing, or took care of some personal matters. She didn't want to do any of that, and she didn't feel like reading. On an impulse, she called her mother.

"Have they found that hit-and-run driver yet?" her mother wanted to know. "Anybody with sense would know you're too responsible a person to go off and leave a man for dead. Besides, you're the one who called the police."

Melinda didn't want to go over that again. "The police are still looking. How's Papa?"

"Well, I guess he's worried about all this news. You know how he is."

Did she ever! "I'll see you at church Sunday," she told her mother after they'd talked awhile.

Before the Sunday service was over, however, she wished the thought hadn't occurred to her. Booker Jones was on the warpath. "God sees you even if I don't. You can hide from your parents, your siblings, friends, husbands, or wives, and from the law, but not from the Lord. Your sins will find you out. And if you don't confess and repent, you will surely burn eternally in hell fire and brimstone. The Lord does not like ugly.''

He looked directly at his only daughter and shook his finger. ''I do not except anybody under the sound of my voice.''

Melinda tuned him out along with the amens and yes, Lords that encouraged him. ''If you weren't sitting here,'' she whispered to her mother, ''I might get up and leave. I ... oh, I don't know.''

''Don't stay on my account,'' Lurlane said. ''If I wasn't married to him, I might go with you.''

''What a spectacle that would be! Half the people in this town seem to think I'm a sinner beyond redemption. I refuse to give them or him the satisfaction of seeing me stalk out of here.''

She stayed until the last amen, but after she got home, she ignored the ringing phone, certain that the caller was her father bent on reemphasizing the thinly veiled accusations he made during his preaching.

''Miz Melinda,'' Ruby called, ''it's Mr. Blake on the line.''

She rushed to the phone. ''Hello, Blake.''

''Hi. I need to see you about something. Mind if I come over in a few minutes?''

Why would she mind? ''Of course not. See you in a few minutes.''

That didn't sound right. She changed into brown slacks and a burnt-orange cowl-neck sweater, twisted her hair into a French knot, and looked around for something to do while she waited for him. It was then that she made the decision that would prove momentous in her life. Every afternoon after school she would work at straightening out the closets, sorting and packing for charity everything that had belonged to Prescott, except his cassettes and the plans he'd stored in that trunk. She heard the doorbell and hastened down the stairs.

She opened the door for him, and shock at his somber expression curled her nerve ends. "Blake! What is it? What's the matter?"

He put an arm tight around her and walked with her into the living room. "Sit down here with me, honey," he said, pointing to the sofa. "The detective called me. The coroner's report placed the man's death at eleven minutes before you bought that blouse, your first purchase that night. We're not in the clear."

Her breath lodged in her throat, and she had to cough before she could breathe. "I was in that store a long time looking for a blouse to wear with my beige suit. The clerk will testify that I tried on at least four before I settled for the one I bought."

"I hope you remember who she was."

"I certainly do. Her left eyelid drooped noticeably. She's worked there a long time."

"All right. Eleven minutes isn't a lot, but it may prove crucial, and especially since the detective I hired can't find anything about the person who might have done it. I'm going to see that clerk this evening. I hope she's on duty today."

"I hope so too, Blake. I don't see how I could be charged with something I didn't do."

"It happens all the time, but the evidence here is so flimsy that I don't believe it'll stand in court." He looked at his watch. "I have an appointment a few minutes from now. I'll be in touch." He brushed her lips with his own, locked her to him for a second, and was gone.

To Blake's chagrin, the clerk didn't want to get involved. "I don't want nothin' to do wif no law. I don't know nothin', didn't see nothin', and didn't hear nothin,' " she said. Nineteen years old, he surmised, a dozen earrings in her ears and enough makeup to last a normal woman for a year. Not a good witness.

"Would you rather I subpoena you?" he asked her.

She observed him from the corners of her eyes. "I still won't know nothin'."

He produced the receipt. "According to this, you're the clerk who handled the sale."

Her shrug was nothing less than callous. "That don't mean I remember it."

He tried another tactic. "You ever been jailed for drug use?"

Her eyebrows shot up and her bottom lip dropped. Then she said, "You're just fishing."

"And you'd better stay clean. I mean clean as a saint."

He had the pleasure of seeing her wither and knew he had her where he wanted her. "I'll be in touch," he promised, though he made it sound like a threat.

His unease about the case mounted steadily. No lawyer wanted to go to court with a single, recalcitrant witness, but he had to work with what he had. And Melinda wasn't going to spend a minute behind bars for that crime. He told his investigator to find out everything about the witness. He didn't know what he'd do with the information, but he believed in being ready for all eventualities.

He got in his car and phoned Lieutenant Cochrane, the police detective, on his cell phone. "This is Hunter. I need to see you as soon as possible."

"I'll be here for another couple of hours. Come on over."

"I'm laying my cards on the table," Blake told the lieutenant at the station a short while later. "I have a witness, but she's scared of law enforcement officers. She may have a record."

"Who is she?"

"She's the clerk who sold Mrs. Rodgers the first purchase she made that evening."

"I see. She's . . . Not now, Ken," he said to the officer trying to get his attention.

"But, Lieutenant, this old lady is either hysterical or she's killed somebody."

Lieutenant Cochrane spun around and Blake followed him, his adrenaline flowing at high speed.

"Where is she?" Cochrane asked.

Blake saw her then, at least eighty-five years old, wringing her hands, and her dim eyes reflecting the pain she felt.

"Are you the officer I have to speak to?" Cochrane nodded.

"Well, I did a horrible thing. Lord knows I didn't mean to, but I ran away, because I was scared. I've been so upset I can't sleep and Sunday, Reverend Jones said that if I don't confess and ask forgiveness, I'm lost."

"Come over here, ma'am," Cochrane said. "Have a seat. What did you do?"

"Well, it was night, and I can't see so good at night. When I went to park, I didn't see the man till it was too late. I hit him when he was getting out of his car, and I backed up and drove out of the parking lot. I never did do my shopping."

"What time was this?"

"About seven or a little after. I'm not sure. Will I have to go to jail?"

"I doubt it, but you will certainly clear someone else's name."

"Yes, sir. That's one reason why I couldn't sleep. People said such awful things about her when it was me that did it. I'll have to ask her to forgive me like the reverend said."

Lieutenant Cochrane walked over to where Blake stood making notes. "There's your case. We'll take it from here."

"You're not going to prosecute that poor woman, are you?" Blake asked him.

"The fault is with the law. If she can't see when it's dark, she shouldn't be driving at night, but she isn't forced to take a test for night blindness. Too bad."

"No word on who's in cahoots with Goodwin?"

"Nothing, and the man won't budge, but I haven't given up."

Blake raced to his car and headed for Melinda's house. When she opened the door, he picked her up and twirled around and around with her. "It's settled, sweetheart. It's settled."

"What's settled?"

"An old lady confessed to hitting that man. Poor woman didn't see him."

"What woman? Who?"

He hugged her over and over. "I didn't get her name. It's all over, thank God." But, no it wasn't, he reflected. Three newspaper editors were going to print a retraction and an apology to Melinda on the front page, and he intended to write the accompanying editorial about newspaper slander and muckraking himself. It they didn't print it, he'd sue. But that could wait for another time. The sparkle in her eyes and the joyous glow on her face were too beautiful to spoil, and that's what he'd do if he shifted the focus to a campaign for retribution.

Suddenly, a frown creased her forehead, chasing the glow from her face, darkness displacing sunshine. "I wonder why she decided to confess. She's probably in real trouble now."

"What can anybody do to an old woman? Anyway, we can thank your father for this. Seems he—"

"Thank my father?" Her face, indeed her entire demeanor suggested that he might not be rowing with both oars. "What did he do other than castigate me, accusing me of murdering a man without asking me if I did it? If he preached my funeral, he'd probably blame me for dying."

"Well, recently he preached one of his 'Sinners at the Angry Gates of Hell' sermons about burning in hell if you didn't confess your sins and ask forgiveness. Scared the poor old lady to death."

She slapped her hand over her mouth and stared at him. "Wait a minute. I was in church last Sunday morning, and I heard that. Well, I'll be! I was so mad, I could hardly keep myself from walking out. Looks like some good came of it. I'll have to call and thank him.''

''Thank him? Or serve him a plate of crow?''

''Come to think of it, I'd enjoy . . . No, I'd better not do that. It would be just the cue he'd need to give me an hour-long sermon about forgiveness. I'll call him.''

Blake had thought it over and didn't see how it could be avoided unless she gave her father an out. ''You mind if I invite him to the reception I'm giving for the board? It's safe. I'll introduce the board members, but there won't be any speeches. If there were, Martha Greene and your father would make me wish I'd never thought of a reception.''

He might yet wish that, but she didn't see how she could countenance her father's exclusion from such an important social event. ''Of course, I don't mind. Be sure the invitation includes Mama. I'm going to enjoy dressing her up like a glamour girl and watching his reaction.''

The grin began around his lips and got broader and broader until it enveloped his face and he laughed aloud. That wonderful laugh that warmed her all over and nourished her soul. ''In that case, will you be my date for the evening? With Booker's gaze glued to his wife, he'll be less likely to focus on me. He thinks my interest in you is mercenary, and he had the temerity to tell me so.''

She thought about that for a minute and, in her mind's eye, she saw her father's posturing, using his clerical collar as an excuse to be overbearing. He wanted so badly to be liked, to be accepted. Why couldn't he realize people would like him if he were less strident and not so judgmental?

''I think I'd better go see him and thank him for that sermon and for accidentally getting me cleared of those charges.''

He shrugged as if he didn't think much of the idea. ''I suppose that's better than fighting with him, but I don't want to hear that he accused you or bullied you. You understand?''

She nodded. "He won't."

She didn't go to church the next Sunday, not as a show of independence, but because she couldn't take the chance until her father knew the charges against her had been dropped. Instead, she timed a visit to her parents' home to coincide with her father's after-lunch rest period, when he listened to music, usually Monteverdi or Bach, classical music with religious themes. She often wondered why he preached "gospel" sermons, but rarely listened to gospel music.

"I'm so happy it's over," Lurlane said, as tears streamed from her eyes after learning that one of their parishioners had confessed to the crime. "Your father's in the study where he usually is this time of day. Don't be too hard on him, child. You know he'll beat himself to death about it for months to come."

"He ought to have a good talk with himself before he points his finger; a little humility would be good for him."

"I know," Lurlane said, as she brushed out her long, stringy hair, "but he's a good man, just misguided sometimes like all the rest of us, you and me included. Remember that."

She wondered what made Lurlane Jones so faithful to a man who had so many visible flaws. Maybe one day, she'd get the courage to ask her. She opened the door of the study, and her gaze fell on her father, his hands clasped across his still slim waist and his eyes closed as though in reverence. It seemed a pity to interrupt his reverie.

"Papa. How are you? It's me, Melinda." She walked over and placed a kiss on his cheek. Risked it, ignoring then as she always had, his feelings about such things, though he accepted it from her.

"Sit down, girl, and enjoy the music. When you listen to Bach, you have to thank God for your ears. If I ever get to Germany, I'm going to that little church in Leipzig and see the organ he used when he composed all this wonderful music.

He's been dead since 1750, and not a day goes by that somebody somewhere doesn't play his music."

She sat in an overstuffed chair facing him. "Papa—"

"Wait while I put on the Brandenburg Concerto Number Five. It's my favorite, you know."

Her antennae shot up. Her father had the sensors of an animal in the wild, and he suspected she'd come to speak to him about his sermon the previous Sunday when she'd contemplated walking out of church. Well, he wasn't going to hamstring her by portraying himself as a harmless music lover.

"Papa, I think you'll be happy to know that one of your parishioners, a woman of about eighty-five or so, confessed to the police that she struck the man found lying beside my car, and that she ran away because she was scared. Seems she can't see well at night."

He flicked off the CD and sat up straight in the recliner. "What woman are you talking about?"

"I didn't get her name." She described her and related what Blake had told her of the confession.

"Mittie Williams. Can you beat that? Maybe I do some good in this town."

She rolled her eyes toward the ceiling. "I don't think that's been disputed, Papa, but I'd appreciate your telling the congregation about it next Sunday, so they'll all know it wasn't me."

"You're saying I should announce you've been exonerated? You think that's called for?"

"Yes, Papa, I do. You shook your finger at me, accusing me of I don't know what, and what had I done? Nothing. You're always making examples of me. I'm tired of it, and if you keep it up, I'm going to join another church."

"You'd do that to your father?"

How many times had she seen that cloak of innocence without recognizing it for what it was? Not anymore. "Yes, Papa. I don't get anything out of the sermon when I'm mad, and you make me angry. Just tell the folks the Lord answered your prayers, and the police found the person who did it. Closed subject.''

"I never thought you looked at it that way. I've been trying to help you.''

She stared at him in disbelief. He actually believed that. She got up, walked over, and kissed his cheek. "I'd better go. Sorry to interrupt your music.''

He stood and waved a hand as if to dismiss the idea. "Oh, that! It's good to spend a few minutes with you. Come back soon.''

Lurlane waited for her in the living room. "How'd it go? It kinda worried me that he stopped the Brandenburg, much as he loves it.''

She looked at her mother, anxious for her husband and her daughter. "Fine, Mama. I think he just gets carried away sometime. See you in a day or so.''

Lurlane raised an eyebrow and headed for the study.

"Mama!'' Lurlane turned around with a look of expectancy on her face. "I'm coming over tomorrow and take you shopping. I'll call you.''

"Won't that be nice. I need a couple of housedresses.''

Housedresses. Not this time, Melinda vowed.

Blake didn't intend to let tension between Booker and himself ruin his party, so he dialed Booker's number.

"This is Blake Hunter. I'm having a reception for Prescott Rodgers Foundation board members the Saturday night after Thanksgiving, and I want you to be there.''

"Any special reason?''

"Yes. I want to introduce the board members to the town's leading citizens, and that automatically includes you and Mrs. Jones.''

Booker cleared his throat. "Well—"

He didn't want to hear the word no, so he interrupted. "I can imagine you've preached many sermons on letting bygones be bygones, and I think that's appropriate in our case. Besides, I want Melinda to be happy, and that means having her family there."

"That so?"

He wanted a little urging, did he? "Yes, sir. Paul's coming."

"You know? Haven't been to a real social event in years. People seem afraid to invite me."

"Well, I'm not. You'll go in my car. We'll be at your house at six-thirty."

"Now, that will be just lovely. Lurlane needs a night out in company." His voice warmed to a melodious baritone. "Yes, she'll love it. Thank you."

"My pleasure." He hung up, satisfied that Booker wouldn't feel the need for public posturing.

Two weeks later, the Saturday night after Thanksgiving, Melinda paced the floor in her bedroom, occasionally glancing at herself in the mirror, not certain that a long red, shimmering silk sheath was the appropriate attire for a widow. But six and a half months after Prescott's death seemed long enough to deck herself out in white, beige, or navy blue. Prescott had forbidden her to wear black, claiming that the color drowned her personality. At last, the doorbell rang. She draped her silver-fox stole around her shoulders and took one last look in the mirror. She wanted to look perfect this night. The stole, her silver shoes and bag, and the diamond and blue-pearl earrings that hung from her earlobes complemented the red dress. *They can whisper about me all they want to, but they can't say I don't look great.*

With that assurance, she left the room and headed for the

stairs. She took a step down, looked at Blake, and stopped. She couldn't close her mouth. He was resplendent in a black tuxedo with a white shirt, red cummerbund, handkerchief, studs, and ruby cuff links.

"Hi," he called to her. "Somehow, I figured you'd wear red."

She let herself breathe and drifted toward him. At the bottom step, he reached for her hand. "You look fantastic," he said. "Honey, you're a dream walking."

"You don't think the red is too much? You know how—"

"You know what they say. Never let 'em see you sweat. Show you don't care. To me, you look great. Perfect."

"Thanks. You look wonderful. Everybody will think we planned what we'd wear."

"Yeah. Next time we'll make sure."

"What's this?" she asked when she saw the limousine.

"Think I'd expect my best girl to sit in the front seat and get her dress wrinkled?" The chauffeur seated them in the stretch limousine, got in, and drove off. "Er . . . we're picking up your parents; then we're going by Rachel's to get her and Paul."

"You planned all this behind my back? I hope Rachel isn't wearing red."

She felt his arm ease around her shoulders. "If she is, so what? Neither she nor any other woman will look as good as you do, no matter what she's wearing."

Happiness suffused her. "I'd put my head on your shoulder if I didn't think I'd muss my hair."

The car stopped. "Be back in a minute," Blake said, and she wondered whether her father had raised a ruckus when he saw her mother dressed for the evening.

"You both look real nice," Booker said when they were on the way to Rachel's house.

Melinda nearly swallowed her teeth when she saw her

father's grip on her mother's hand. "She made me rent a tuxedo. First time I ever got into one of these things. If I had refused, I expect she'd have filed for divorce. Such a commotion! Hunter, don't make the mistake of letting a woman know you're putty in her hands. Sooner or later, she'll take advantage of you."

Blake cut a quick glance at Melinda. "Well, sir, that's one of those things that sneaks in before you know it." He turned up the light, and she stared at her mother who seemed ten years younger and glittered like starlight, her silver-gray ball gown and silver accessories set off with a short, stylish hairdo and flawless makeup.

"Mama, if I'd met you in the street, I don't think I would have recognized you."

Booker's dry "I certainly would have. This is the way she looked when I was trying to get her—the town belle—to marry me" brought a smile from Lurlane.

"I might have looked like this once," Lurlane said, "but that was so long ago that even I'd forgotten it."

"Well," Booker said, "we're going shopping next week and buy you some clothes, and from now on, somebody else is going to do the housework. The Lord didn't intend for us to hide what he gave us."

Melinda managed to squelch the laughter that bubbled up in her throat. Her father was so turned on by his wife that he hadn't noticed the berry-red dress his widowed daughter wore. She'd always thought Paul handsome, and she knew he looked good in a tux, but with Rachel wearing a navy-sequined gown and Paul in a navy blue tux and accessories, they made a dashing pair.

"This looks serious," Blake whispered to Melinda when he got in the car.

"Anybody else coming?" Booker asked.

"No," Blake said, "but a few friends will join us at our table."

"I didn't know you two were seeing each other," Booker said, his mood jovial. "I'm glad somebody's seeing Paul. It's time I had some grandchildren, but my four children don't seem to be thinking along those lines." Still holding Lurlane's hand, he put his free arm around her shoulder. "You think we ought to run a contest to see which one on them has a child first?"

Lurlane leaned away from her husband in order to look into his eyes. "If you embarrass them, they might not let you know when they have them. We're going to have a wonderful time and not get personal."

Booker blessed them with a smile and pointed to his wife. "She told me I had to behave myself tonight."

Melinda stared at her parents. What on earth had come over Booker Jones? She whispered the question to Blake.

"I think that's probably the way he was when they were young and in love," Blake said softly, "before he settled into the small-town preacher's persona. Seeing her young and lovely brings it all back to him. I wouldn't have missed this for the world."

"You may be right. She's a shock to me, so I can imagine how it affects Papa."

"I rather doubt that," he said dryly.

The limousine arrived at the hotel, and as they started in, the first person Melinda saw was Ray Sinclair. "Did you invite him?" she asked Blake.

"Of course not. He's probably hanging around to see who the guests are."

But he couldn't have been more wrong. "I figured you were sore at me," Ray said to Blake, "but can't we just let bygones be bygones? It seems everybody's invited but me."

Blake raised an eyebrow. "Good evening, Sinclair. Sorry about that."

She hoped Ray didn't decide to get revenge for the snub, but she wouldn't put it past him.

Blake introduced his group to Justine and Duncan Banks, who awaited him at his table.

"Who's looking after my godchild?" he asked them.

"Mattie," Duncan said. "Only problem is that Tonya treats Mattie as if she's a big doll that changes hair color several times a day."

By the time Blake accustomed himself to the new Booker Jones, Melinda smiled at him and said, "May I please have a Bloody Mary?"

He nearly spilled his club soda. What they would drink and whether they'd drink it in the reverend's presence hadn't occurred to him. *You're slipping up, man. The woman has bamboozled you,* he told himself.

"But you don't drink."

Her smile was that of an innocent, but he wasn't fooled. "It goes with my dress."

"Listen, honey," he pleaded. "Everything's going great. You don't want to test your father's mettle here in front of everybody, do you? Why do you think I'm drinking club soda?"

She winked at him. "Probably because you're chicken."

Never one to shirk his responsibility, he leaned toward Booker. "Sir, I haven't asked everyone what they want to drink, but I think I ought to ask whether you'd be offended if I ordered drinks for those who want it?"

He wished Melinda would breathe while they waited for Booker's answer. "I'll just have a glass of ginger ale with a little bit of lemon, thank you. I'm not responsible for anybody's soul tonight but my own. My wife will probably want a glass of wine, though. I remember that in our day, she used to love champagne."

"Then I'll have champagne," Duncan said.

"Me too," Justine and Rachel choroused.

He looked at Paul and Melinda, Booker's children. And with the most pleading look he could muster, beseeched Melinda to join with the others.

"All right, all right. Champagne," she said at last.

"And you, Paul?"

"I'm going with the flow, man. Champagne."

He ordered ginger ale with lemon and two bottles of Veuve Cliquot champagne, and released a long, deep breath. Thank heavens Booker hadn't rocked the boat. He found Melinda's hand and squeezed her fingers. She turned to him, her eyes shining with a look that was for him alone, and he thought his heart would burst. The waiter filled their glasses with champagne, and placed the ginger ale in front of Lurlane, but Blake hadn't noticed until Lurlane said to the waiter, "Whatever gave you that idea?"

She pointed to her husband. "He's the teetotaler at this table."

Blake would have skipped the toast in deference to Booker, but Lurlane raised her glass. "Thank you, Blake, for arranging this party. It's . . . it's wonderful."

"And thank you for giving Lurlane this opportunity to shine like the beauty she's always been," Booker said and took a sip of his ginger ale. "I don't know when I last saw Melinda look so beautiful, either. Truth is, I doubt I ever did."

Blake glanced at Paul, who arched both eyebrows when Booker added, "There're four beautiful women at this table. Makes a man proud."

"Right on," Duncan said, and lifted his glass first to his wife and then to the group.

Blake promised himself he'd say a prayer of thanks first chance he got. He excused himself. "It's time I introduced the board members."

He began by saying there would be no speeches, that he only wanted to thank the board members for helping him carry out Prescott Rodgers's wishes by serving on the board of the Prescott Rodgers Foundation. He asked each one to take a bow when introduced, and it didn't escape him that Martha Greene, who wore an expensive white ball gown, bowed to each corner of the room and took three times as long doing it as was necessary. He introduced Paul as the board's advisor, and made a show of thanking Booker for giving the foundation his blessing, though it only occurred to him at the last minute, for Booker had done no such thing. Yet, the man stood and bowed, acknowledging the applause with smiles and a wave of his hand. Oh, the power of human vanity, Blake thought. Because of that one gesture, Booker Jones had become his ally.

The three strolling violinists he'd chosen from a concert bureau in Baltimore strolled from table to table playing whatever the guests requested. At their table, the leader asked Booker's preference.

"You're going to request one of the Brandenburg concerti," Lurlane whispered, in a tone that said maybe he shouldn't.

"Why not?" Booker asked. "Can you give us a little of Number Five?"

As if they had waited all evening for the opportunity, the three musicians smiled with obvious delight and played the first movement to wild applause.

"Doesn't hurt to reach for the sky once in a while," Booker preened. "Good for the soul even if you don't make it."

"It's a good thing you didn't hire a belly dancer," Paul said to Blake. "A man can take just so many shocks in one evening."

Booker cut a glance toward his son. "Since you'll probably still be here tomorrow, I look forward to a visit from you and Miss Perkins. You shouldn't keep such a lovely woman to yourself."

Paul's white teeth glistened against his high brown complexion as he smiled the smile of a happy man. "Not to worry, Papa. We'd planned to do precisely that."

"I bet something's cooking between those two," Melinda whispered to Blake. "He's here every weekend, and he doesn't stay with me."

Duncan lifted his glass. "Here's to the women we love," he said and looked at Paul as if to see whether he'd drink to that toast.

With a grin as wide as Blake had ever seen, Paul raised his glass in Duncan's direction. "Brilliant move, man."

After the waiters served a meal of cold, smoked sable, filet mignon or chicken cordon bleu, roast potatoes, green beans, meslun salad, and vanilla ice cream with raspberry sauce, Blake thanked his guests and asked them to support the foundation's work.

He didn't know when he'd enjoyed a public gathering so much. He'd have to think about this other side of Booker Jones. Maybe all the man wanted was acceptance. Then, too, a woman who looked as Lurlane Jones did could bring out the best in any man. It was something to think about.

After taking his guests home, he settled back in the limousine with Melinda's hand tight in his. "I feel good about this evening. What about you?"

"It's no wonder. You did yourself proud, and I'm still trying to digest it. I think my mother just taught me a lesson. She always said Papa loved her deeply, but I never saw it until tonight. He wanted the occasion to be special for her, because she looked so special, and something tells me she won't be looking dowdy any time soon."

"She's a beautiful woman and, tonight, she gave him back his youth."

The car stopped in front of Melinda's house. "I'd like to continue this evening," he said, "but I dare not risk walking out of your house tomorrow morning in this tuxedo." The thought of leaving her didn't sit well with him, but he didn't want to compromise her. "Can I see you tomorrow night?"

She nodded. "Come on in for a few minutes."

With her sweet and inviting smile, the scent of her perfume teasing his nostrils and the décolletage of her fiery red dress exposing the tops of her lush mounds, he felt the sexual heat begin a slow rise in his blood. And when she squeezed his fingers as they walked up the path to her door, his blood pounded in his ears. He told himself that there was always tomorrow, but that didn't diffuse the desire that had begun its mad race to his loins.

He nodded to the guard, took her key, opened the front door, and closed it. He had himself in check, he'd swear to it, but she looked up at him with her big, soft brown eyes, telling him without words that he was king of the hill, and he lifted her, locked her to him, and plunged his tongue into her mouth. Her soft breasts rose and fell against his chest, and he held her closer until he could feel her hard nipples through the fabric of his shirt. Half insane with desire, his fingers slipped into the top of her dress and she flung her head back as if in ecstasy, her breath short and fast. Crazed with want, he pulled her breast from the confines of her dress and suckled her.

She cried out, "You can't leave me like this."

Shocked at his loss of control, he worked at covering her breast with the revealing dress until she laughed at his fumbling.

"Wait here," she said. "I'll be back in a few minutes."

He thought she'd gone to make herself presentable, but ten minutes later, she was back wearing a red woolen dress.

"My coat's in the closet here," she said. "Ready to go?"

His pulse took off like a runaway train. "You're ... You bet I am."

* * *

If he'd thought he was leaving her to twist and turn in a rumpled bed alone all night, he didn't know her. From the time she'd seen him standing at the bottom of her steps waiting to take her to the reception, she'd had her own plan for the evening's end. As she put her toothbrush, deodorant, and fresh underwear in her pocketbook and changed her dress, her mind focused on the evening's magic.

To her surprise, her mother had welcomed enthusiastically the idea of spending the day in a Baltimore spa being made over. "That dress you got me needs some glamour," Lurlane had said. "In my day, I didn't take a backseat to any woman anywhere."

She'd learned something wonderful about her parents, too, and she had Blake to thank for it. She suspected her mother could teach classes in the ways to handle a man. Booker Jones had made his children proud.

"I couldn't imagine being away from you this night," she told Blake, as they got into the limousine and headed for his house.

He stretched out his long legs, one of the luxuries the limousine offered. "Nor I, you. Not after that session in your foyer a few minutes ago. I'd have left, but with feet of lead." He opened the bar and poured them each a glass of champagne. "It's getting to the place where I never want to be away from you, not even for a minute. " He locked arms with her as they took the first sip.

When she leaned against his shoulder, he put their glasses in the wine rack, tipped up her chin, and gazed into her eyes. She sucked in her breath at what she saw in him then and parted her lips for his tongue. His kiss was quick and hot.

"I want to be able to walk into my house," he quipped. "When you get going, your heady kissing can cripple a man."

He took the champagne from the limousine's bar and handed her the two glasses. Then he leaned forward and placed a kiss at her throat, sending tremors arrow straight to her feminine core. He opened the door to his house with his free hand, locked it after them, and turned on the light.

"You want to sit down here for a while?" he asked, and she knew he was merely being polite. She didn't need further affirmation that he was a gentleman; she needed what he'd been promising her all evening.

"What for?" she said, wondering at her new brazenness. "We can drink it upstairs."

He hung her coat in a closet, got a tray for the wine and their glasses, and held out his hand to her. "Come."

At the top of the stairs, he asked her, "Am I being presumptuous in assuming that you'll share my room tonight?"

For reasons she didn't understand, laughter pealed out of her. When she managed to control it, she let her finger brush gently over his jaw, feeling the beginnings of stubble and glorying in the masculine feel of it.

"Don't you know how much I love to be with you?" She didn't think she'd ever get used to the joy of knowing that the man she loved and desired loved and wanted her.

The expression in his eyes nearly unglued her, and a wild recklessness overcame her, as it always did when she knew he was going to make love to her. She told herself to let him take the lead. He put the champagne bottle and glasses on a table in the hallway, picked her up, and carried her to his room. A small lamp on his dresser, obviously capable of little more than a night glow, bathed his face in a soft mellow radiance when he turned it on, and she watched, fascinated, as he walked to her in that loose-jointed sexy way of his, a slight smile on his lips. When he reached her, his fingers stroked her right cheek and she looked up into the fierce, blazing storm in his eyes.

Unstrung by the sweet and terrible hunger he stirred in her, she grasped his arm to steady herself. If knowing what to expect hadn't been sufficient, his masculine scent and his powerful male aura possessed her, stripping her of her strength and making her will his will. His arms gripped her to his body and she stared into the dark desire of his mesmerizing eyes.

"You're everything to me," he whispered, his voice hoarse and minus its deep, velvet vibrato. "Do you love me?"

"Yes. Yes, I love you."

His mouth was on her then, hot and demanding, shattering her reserve until she grasped his hips, straining for what she needed to feel. His answer was the rise of his sex against her belly, letting her feel the force of his passion until, of their own volition, her hips shifted against him. But he stilled her and cherished her mouth, her eyes, and her cheeks with his lips. She wanted his hands on her naked skin so badly that she thought she'd scream. In desperation she moved her breast from left to right across his chest, and at last his precious fingers rubbed her tortured nipple.

"Blake. Honey, please."

He unzipped the red dress, and when she stepped out of it, flung it across a chair, though the busy fingers of his left hand never ceased stroking and caressing her.

"Blake!"

"Yes, sweetheart." He lifted her breast from the scant bra, pulled it into his mouth, and started the pulling and sucking that drove her crazy. She heard her moans and was helpless to control them. He picked her up, wrapped her legs around him, and let her feel him, all of him, never taking his lips from her breast. When she tried to force his entry, he lay her on the bed and stood looking down at her while he tore out of his clothes. Then he shielded himself for her protection and joined her.

"I'm going out of my mind," she told him.

"But we've got all night, baby. It's our first night like this. The other time, we didn't make love."

"But—"

"Shhh. Just let me love you. Let me have you." He kissed her shoulders, her breasts, and her belly, skimming his fingers on the insides of her thighs as though oblivious to her frantic movements. Then he hooked her legs over his shoulder and tortured her with his lips and tongue until she screamed, "Oh, Lord. I can't stand it."

He rose above her, and she brought him to her, raised her hips, and welcomed him as he drove home. Immediately the heat he'd built within her burst into a flame, and the powerful clenching began as he rocked her. Enthralled by his passion and enmeshed in the violent, frenzied storm he built around her and in her, she thought she'd die. Her body gave itself up to him, and he soon sucked her into a vortex of passion, refusing to release her until they both shouted aloud their eternal love, and he lay defenseless and vulnerable in her arms.

For a long time, he breathed deeply, his head on her breasts and his weight braced on his forearms. Thinking him asleep, she stroked his back in a soothing fashion, ran her fingers lightly over the tight curls on his head, caressing him as one would a baby. Cherishing him.

"I can't let you go out of my life," he said. "I can't. I just can't."

Was he asleep? Did he know what he was saying? She continued stroking, and words of endearment slipped through her lips.

"My darling. My love," she whispered.

Suddenly, he hardened within her, raised himself up and looked into her face. "There's so much unfinished business between us, but no matter. I won't give you up." He gave her shoulders a gentle shake. "Do you understand what I'm saying to you?"

Tension gathered inside of her, and her heart fluttered madly.

"I don't want you to give me up," she said. "There's no one else for me. There never was."

She felt the tremors that raced through him, and hot needles of desire stabbed relentlessly at her feminine center. He put an arm around her shoulder, his other hand beneath her buttocks, his lips to her breast, and rocked them both to the world that was theirs alone.

Chapter Thirteen

"I would have preferred to spend this afternoon with you," Blake told her, when he called around noon, "but I have to attend Ethan's first public talk on adolescent rebellion and delinquency. This won't be a talk to young people of his own age as he's done in the past, but to an assemblage of their parents at the local YWCA, and he needs support and encouragement. He phoned me a couple of minutes ago and asked me what would happen if he backed out."

"He can't do that. If he does, he may make a habit of it."

"That's what I told him. Look, sweetheart, I hate not to see you today, and especially after what we shared last night. Ethan thinks he isn't up to this, but I know he is, and I have to be there for him."

"It's all right, darling. I'll see you tomorrow morning at the board meeting. However, I don't advise you to catch my eye, because I know I'll give it all away."

"I don't care what they see; I'm through hiding my feelings. Stay sweet."

"You, too. Bye."

She'd been too discombobulated to consider church that morning, and she knew that with her mind on the night before in Blake's arms, she wouldn't have heard a word of her father's sermon. Feeling guilty, she wished she'd gone if only to let him know that she appreciated his graciousness at Blake's party. On an impulse, she got into her car and drove to her father's house.

"I was disappointed not to see you in church this morning, girl," he said. "You're just in time for a bite to eat. Come on in. Your brother's here with his Rachel."

She leaned forward to kiss him on the cheek and nearly froze when he put both arms around her for a brief hug. She could hardly believe it when he said, "You looked good last night, just like your mother when she was your age." Maybe she ought to pinch herself to see if she was asleep. Wasn't he going to lecture her about her sinfulness and the hell she faced for not attending church?

He walked with her to the living room with his hand grazing her shoulder, offering the warmth she'd longed for since she first knew herself. "Wish the other two were here," Booker said when they sat down to dinner, their midday meal. "I don't know when we last had all our children here with us. Why don't we plan a family reunion?"

She caught Paul's gaze and saw his concern. Was their father sick and preparing for his imminent demise? What had caused this . . . this reaching out, this considerateness? She looked at their mother, but Lurlane didn't seem concerned. Instead, she wore the serene expression of a happy woman.

"What a wonderful idea!" Lurlane said. "We could plan it

for Paul's birthday." She looked at Rachel. "We're a small family. My only sister never married, and I didn't have any brothers. Booker has a brother, Rafe, but he's in Alaska getting rich and can't leave his gold long enough to do more than eat and take a short nap. I expect he sleeps with one eye open. We can't count on him, nor his only child, a daughter, who married a Frenchman and lives somewhere in Provence, France."

"Where's his wife?" Rachel asked, sitting forward, her interest piqued.

"Miriam?" Booker asked with a short snort. "She got tired of that gold years ago. Said she couldn't eat it, drink it, wear it, nor sleep with it."

Rachel turned to Paul. "Where do you stand on gold?"

Paul shrugged eloquently. "Me? Greenbacks suit me fine. If Uncle Rafe had a warm, loving woman, he wouldn't spend so much time thinking about gold."

A secretive smile floated over Rachel's face, broadcasting her self-satisfaction and contentment that Paul wouldn't be chasing money at her expense. Lurlane looked from Rachel to Paul, then glanced at her husband, who was also watching them. Booker Jones took his wife's hand, leaned back, and closed his eyes, the picture of contentment. She wished she knew how to interpret her father's unusual behavior.

She nearly sprang from her chair when Booker stood, looked around the table, and asked them, "Anybody want coffee? A meal like this one deserves a good cup of coffee."

"Zip it up, Mindy," Paul said, reminding her of their childhood, when he'd tell her to shut her mouth. With eyes wide and her mouth gaping, it wasn't the first time she'd wished for her brother's poker face.

"Mama, what's come over him?" she whispered, as her father headed toward the kitchen to get coffee for everyone.

A smile drifted over Lurlane's face. "Thanks for the evening gown and accessories and the day at the beauty spa."

"You mean—"

"I mean he just discovered that he can be a loving man and still serve God. He also noticed that nobody got high and misbehaved last night, in spite of all the alcohol consumed at that party, and most of all, the people applauded him. I don't know when he's been so happy. He needs to get out among people more."

She stared at Lurlane. "You sure that's all there is to this? Mama, this is a different man."

"I know, and isn't it wonderful? I think it started when you told him you weren't going to our church anymore, that his sermons made you mad and resentful. He talked about that for the rest of the week, and I think it forced him to so some self-searching."

"But, Mama," Paul said, "I told him practically the same thing when he launched into that diatribe against Melinda with no proof whatever. And look what happened. The charges have been dropped."

"That's another thing. He preached about that this morning, and he meant for Melinda to hear what, for him, was an apology, but she wasn't there."

"Good Lord, I should hope not," Paul said, a wicked gleam dancing in his eyes.

"Last night put a cap on it," Lurlane told them. "He was so happy that Blake introduced him the way he did. Your father isn't used to having people applaud him. When he talked about it after we got home, I thought he would cry."

"I don't suppose you'd share the real reason for this with your children," Paul said, "but you can tell Rachel."

"Sure," Lurlane said dryly, "and she won't breathe it to a soul, not even in her prayers."

"Well, here we are," Booker said, returning with the tray of coffee, milk, and sugar.

It didn't escape Melinda that Rachel rushed to his aid when he looked around for a place to put the tray.

"Let me help you with that, Reverend Jones," she said, and placed the tray on the sideboard.

Anybody could see that Booker Jones wasn't accustomed to serving anything, Melinda thought, but after thirty years of watching her mother work herself to a frazzle with no help from her husband, only the Lord knew how glad she was to see him try.

"Can I drop you and Rachel somewhere?" Melinda asked Paul as they left their parents' home.

"We're going to Rachel's place. Since I have to be at the board meeting tomorrow morning, I won't go back to Durham till tomorrow evening." She noticed that he held Rachel's hand, and she wanted to ask him so many questions, but it wasn't the right time.

"Do you think Papa's all right? I never saw such a change in a man."

"Know what I think?" Rachel said. "Something's happened between him and your mother. I sensed a kind of renewal. They've been married for thirty-five years, and today he held her hand and looked at her as if he'd just fallen in love."

"Yeah," Paul said, "and they must have had a talk, too, because I noticed she didn't jump up and tell him she'd get the coffee. She sat there like a queen and let him do it."

"We'd better have a family reunion," Melinda said. "If John and Peter walk in on this alone, they'll think our parents have gone into mental decline."

"I never dreamed your father could be so . . . so charming. I was always scared to death of him, " Rachel said, "but he's actually . . . uh . . . He's nice."

Paul opened the back door of Melinda's Mercury Sable and held it for Rachel. "I'll say this much; I don't know what got into him, but whatever it is, it works for me."

He walked around to the driver's side of the car where Melinda wiped away fragments of dry leaves caught beneath the windshield wipers. "I'm staying with Rachel tonight. We'll talk after the board meeting." He opened the door for her and got in the back with Rachel. "It isn't often a man has such a sharp chick for a chauffeur. How about driving along the Patapsco?"

She ignored his quip and was about to tell him she wasn't going that way when she remembered it had been there that Blake told her he loved her. She parked near the big boulder and the bench where she'd sat with Blake. Maybe the spot would work a miracle for Paul and Rachel.

"Want to get out and breathe the fresh air?" she asked them.

"No," Paul said, "but you can."

She turned around and gave him a level look. "I should stand out there in the cold while you make out in this warm car? Don't let it enter your mind."

He shrugged and wrapped his arm around the woman beside him. "Just testing the water, sis. No need to get out of joint."

With the days growing shorter, night fell early, so she took them home. As long as her nemesis remained at large, she wouldn't travel alone at night. If the police didn't find Goodwin's accomplices soon, she'd board up the house and leave, because her tolerance for guards at her front and back door was diminishing hourly.

Blake hadn't expected the board members to behave differently that morning, but they did. Even the mayor, who obtained Blake's permission to sit in on the meeting, refrained from asking him whether Melinda had given up the idea of marrying in order to get her inheritance. And a good thing. He had hardly a modicum of tolerance for His Honor, and even less for the idea that some other man would touch any part of Melinda.

Martha Greene rose at the start of the meeting. "Thank you so much, Mr. Hunter, for that wonderful reception you gave for the board members. I'm sure I speak for all of us when I say it was the biggest thing ever to happen here in Ellicott City and an honor to the board and the Prescott Rodgers Foundation."

He smiled, showing the measure of graciousness that the comment required, but he wished the hell she'd sit down. As much trouble as she'd caused him, her tightly shut mouth was all the peace offering he needed.

"Thank you, Mrs. Greene," he said. "We'll start as soon as Mrs. Rodgers arrives."

She walked in with her coat on her arm and her skin glowing from the chill of the brisk wind. He didn't care what any of them said, did, or thought as he walked to meet her and took her coat.

"Consider yourself kissed," he whispered. "I mean from head to toe."

The panic mirrored on her face didn't elicit remorse; rather, the joy inside of him brought a sparkle to his eyes along with the memory of her as his lover.

"We were waiting for you, Mrs. Rodgers," he said. "Where's Dr. Jones?"

"Paul's parking the car. We couldn't find a parking space, and it's cold, so he let me out in front of the building."

None of the board members mentioned Booker Jones's attire and behavior at the reception, and if any of them noticed that Melinda had been Blake's date, none broached the subject. But the devil would have his day; after the meeting, the mayor took him aside.

"It looks as if she isn't doing a thing about getting married, so I'm putting you on notice. This city deserves the largest share of that money, and I'm prepared to go to court to get it."

"Frank, you've known me how many years? Seven? You ever know me to dodge a confrontation? Man, I thrive on the kind of challenge you just threw at me. I'm going by the terms of that will. To the letter. Prescott left instructions as to what I should do if Melinda didn't fulfill the terms of the will. Giving you the money is nowhere in that document. Besides, what did this town ever do for Prescott Rodgers but reject him?"

Frank's face screwed itself into an angry snarl. "I'll see you in hell."

"Hardly. I don't expect to be there."

Frank Washington had sounded desperate, which meant he needed money for more than the city's operation. As Blake headed for Melinda's car, he dialed his private investigator on his cell phone.

"See what you can find out about the financial dealings of Mayor Frank Washington. Soon."

When he reached his car, he asked Melinda, "You going to school now?"

"I took the day off for the board meeting and so I can drive Paul to the airport. That's where we're going now."

He walked around to the passenger's side and shook hands with Paul. "Looks as if things are coming together for you, man. Rachel's a fine woman."

"I think so, too, Blake, and I notice there've been some changes between you and Melinda. I wish you the best. She holds out for what she believes in, so you have to . . . well, just hang in there."

"Tell me about it. I had five rough years to look but not to touch or even reveal what I felt. I'm not in this now for fun."

"I didn't think so, man."

"From this conversation, anybody would think I'm not here," Melinda said.

"Then pretend you're not," Paul said.

"I'll call you this evening," Melinda told Blake, ignited the engine, and headed for Baltimore.

He went back to his office, ruminating about the Jones family, Prescott Rodgers, and the man who'd tried to blackmail Prescott into giving away a fortune in an invention. And he thought about his feelings for Melinda and how long he'd have to wait until she was his forever.

The last thing he expected was a call from Booker Jones. "Blake, if I may call you that," Booker began, "I'm worried about those guards at Melinda's house. Haven't the police found out *anything?*"

Blake sat down, draped his left foot over his right knee, and collected his thoughts. "We have the man who's behind it, and we suspect he's the one who got into Melinda's house while she was in Italy. However, we're certain he has an accomplice or two, and until we find them we don't want to go to court."

"I expect you're on top of it. I . . . uh . . . want to thank you for inviting me and my wife to that reception. It's . . . Well, you couldn't imagine the good it's done. I hope you're willing to let go of the past."

Who *was* this guy? "Of course, sir, and I thank you and Mrs. Jones for coming."

Now what? He heard Booker clear his throat and wondered whether the man's preceding conversation had been a prelude to less palatable words.

"Blake, I'm still worried that Melinda won't someday regret passing up her inheritance. She told me she couldn't live in a loveless marriage, and I don't blame her. Besides, after what I saw between the two of you Saturday night, she'd be stupid to do it. I . . . uh . . . hope you can find a way to see that she gets what's rightfully hers. You will, won't you?"

It appeared that the man's conversion hadn't changed his character completely. Blake ran his hands back and forth over his hair. "Booker, I swore in a signed affidavit that I'd carry out the terms of that will to the letter. I've racked my brain, and so far, I haven't found a legal escape.''

Booker's sigh sounded as if fear had pushed it out of him. ''Look after her as best you can. She can be stubborn; always was like that. I looked at her Saturday night.'' For a long minute, he didn't continue. Then he said, as if in reverence, ''She was never that beautiful before; looked exactly like her mother did at that age. Well . . . it's good talking with you. Lurlane sends regards. God bless.''

Blake stared at the phone long after the man hung up. He'd give anything to know what had caused the change in Booker Jones. He knocked his left fist into the palm of his right hand. Booker was right; those guards were merely a bandage on a serious wound. They had to catch the man who drugged Tillman before he harmed Melinda.

Melinda parked in her garage, locked it, and started to the front door. When a dampness brushed her face, she looked up at the gray November sky and the tiny flakes that heralded the coming of winter. No one could expect men to stand beside her door and freeze in the snow and blustery wind.

''You'll have to come inside, Mr. Tillman. I can't allow you and Mr. Hawkins to stand out here in this weather.''

He touched his hat with his finger. ''Thanks, ma'am, but it's not too bad today. Later, we may have to sit in the car, but we'll manage. I'm not one to back away from doing me job.''

She went into the kitchen, and because Ruby wasn't there, she made a pot of coffee and took a mugful to each of the guards. ''If you get cold,'' she told them, ''come inside.''

She put on a shirt and an old pair of pants and got to work on the closet, telling herself she'd finish sorting, storing, and dispensing with Prescott's effects before Christmas. She listened to the tapes while packing his clothes for delivery to local charity thrift shops. Suddenly she stopped, ran to the radio and reversed the tape, certain she hadn't heard it properly.

Blake's voice came to her clear and strong: "You ought to make it a condition. People don't appreciate what they get for free, but if you make them earn it, they're more likely to cherish it. Besides, it will be your legacy to the community."

"Spell it out," Prescott said. "What would she have to do?"

"I'm talking about a foundation that would support literacy. Give her a year in which to set it up, put together a board of directors, and get a working plan to promote literacy in Ellicott City."

"And if she doesn't?" Prescott asked, his voice communicating a wariness. "Then what?"

"She wouldn't inherit, but my feeling is that she could do it easily. She's smart."

"Yeah. I know she is. All right. I accept that. Make certain that the foundation supports both literacy and reading disabilities, and the help should be available to everybody who needs it. Got that?"

"Right. Consider it done."

"Now," Prescott said, "I have another condition that's very dear to me, but we'll talk about that one another time."

Melinda sat down without looking for the chair and landed on the floor. *"How could he?"* So she didn't deserve what she hadn't earned! How could he claim to have loved her from the minute he first saw her, yet say she should earn her inheritance and then force her to do it. When she thought of what she'd gone through trying to set up that board . . . Well, he was in for a surprise. She could do without that inheritance *and* him.

I can't stand duplicity, she said to herself. *I don't care how much the sun sets in him. It could rise in him for that matter. He can't tell me he loves me and cook up that kind of torture for me.* She got up and slammed the lid on the box of clothing. *The hell with Blake Edmund Hunter!*

From the window of Prescott's bedroom, she stood with her faced pressed to the glass, watching the snow fall thicker and thicker as her tears streamed silently from her chin to her blouse. She wanted to be rid of Blake and everything that reminded her of him and of the hours in his arms when he'd loved her to distraction. How could he do such a thing?

Increasingly outraged, she put on a heavy sweater and went to the front door. "Mr. Tillman, you and Hawkins are discharged as of now. There's no longer any need for your service. I appreciate your help and protection, but you may both leave now."

He stared at her with eyes wide and mouth open. "But, ma'am, they haven't caught the guy who—"

"Those are my last words on the subject, Mr. Tillman. Thank you."

She closed the door, locked it, and went back up the stairs. She couldn't decide whether to call Blake and give him a piece of her mind or wait till he kept their appointment and confront him.

Chapter Fourteen

"What do you mean, you dismissed Tillman and Hawkins?" he screamed into the phone, unable to believe she'd said it. "Have you gone out of your mind? That guy could be watching everything that happens in your house, every person who goes in there and comes out. Those guards are going right back there. This day!"

"Now you listen to me," she yelled right back. "It's my house until May the eleventh, and until then I'll do as I please with it. They're out. Gone. Caput. Period."

"Melinda, sweetheart, what's come over you? Why are you doing this?"

"*Why?* Because you're no longer running my life. All this talk about loving me from the minute you first saw me, and you could make my husband agree that I should establish that foundation in order to earn the right to inherit what was rightfully and legally mine, or else. Earn it? How did you know I hadn't already earned it? You didn't. You didn't know we had a marriage of convenience. I don't ever want to see you again.'' She hung up.

The weight in his chest pulled him down into the nearest chair. Half an hour earlier, he'd been thinking of ways to make a future with her a reality. Now the issue was as dead as the gold standard. Why hadn't he told her? After they'd discovered Prescott's way of taking notes, he should have known she'd eventually come across a cassette that contained his prophetic remarks. He pulled himself up, walked from one end of his den to the other, looked out the window at the season's first blizzard, and hoped the weather would discourage anyone who wanted to break into her house. He considered calling her father, but discarded the idea.

Finally, he phoned Lieutenant Cochrane and reported what she'd done.

''I'll send a squad car past there every so often for as long as the weather will permit. It's already too thick and too deep for all but especially equipped cars.''

''I hear you. I'd go over there, but it's almost impossible walking or riding. Thanks for whatever you can do.''

He'd never felt so helpless. She'd cut him out of her life without giving him a chance to defend himself or to explain that when he and Prescott discussed that will, she was Prescott's wife, and in those days he didn't let himself harbor romantic notions about her. He kicked his prized Turkish carpet with the toe of his left shoe. If that was the way she wanted it, she could have her wish, and it wouldn't kill him. He headed for the refrigerator to get a bottle of beer, opened the door, and suddenly their shattered relationship took its toll, shortening his breath, and he let the refrigerator take his weight. Like hell it wouldn't kill him.

He told himself to get it together, opened the beer, got a bag of chips, and sat down to watch the Giants-Redskins Monday-night football game. Who'd be calling him on his cell phone at eight o'clock on the evening?

"Hunter."

"Got some news for you, sir." His antennae went up. His private investigator never identified himself.

"What is it?"

"The mayor's been dipping into city coffers. Seems he likes to go to out to Pimlico and play the horses. The man's credit rating is nil, he's overcharged on five credit cards, and, like I said, he's helping himself to the city till."

"Thanks, man. Keep up the good work." At least he didn't have to worry that the mayor would bring suit over Prescott's will. He made a note to get a copy of the man's credit rating.

"And another thing," the investigator continued, "Goodwin was just seen talking to a man who'll do anything for money, but that's all I could get."

"Goodwin's out on bail?"

"Evidently, for the last two days, at least."

"Do you know that man's name?"

"My informant wouldn't give it, which means the guy plays rough. I'm trying to find out more."

"When was Goodwin seen talking with that man?"

"Day before yesterday, around four-thirty in the afternoon at Pim's Bar. That's it. Be in touch." He hung up.

Blake waited about ten minutes and rang the number from which his investigator called. As he'd expected, his informant had used a pay phone. The man was being very careful. He phoned Lieutenant Cochrane at the police station and relayed the information.

"Thanks. I'll have a patrol car spot Mrs. Rodgers's house."

But that didn't satisfy him. She was in that house alone. Vulnerable. He caught himself just before he threw the telephone receiver against the wall. Why had she picked a day like this one to do such a foolish thing?

He flipped on the television and was treated to the sight of cars stalled and, in accident after accident, cars crumpled like accordions. He didn't care if Melinda said she didn't want to see him again. He put on the hip boots he wore when trout fishing, dressed in layers of sweaters, an overcoat, heavy scarf, woolen cap, gloves. and goggles, got the walking cane he used when hiking, locked his door, and set out for Melinda's house. He had to make it; her life might depend on it.

What a job! Melinda filled two pillowcases with boots, shoes, and house slippers, tied them, and placed them in the hallway. She didn't like going through the pockets of Prescott's pants and jackets, but she had to do it, and in no time, she found thirty-two dollars in coins and bills. She thought of the drawers in his bedroom furniture, threw up her hands, and decided to call it a night.

Somewhere downstairs, the sound of crashing glass and of a heavy object slamming against a piece of furniture sent a chill through her and goose pimples popped up all over her body. For a minute, fear rooted her to the spot, but she recovered, grabbed a brass bookend, and rushed to the top of the stairs. She thought she screamed, but she didn't hear a sound, as a hand reached through the broken glass panel beside the door and strained toward the key chain. She dashed down the stairs and slammed the bookend against the intruding hand with such force that the would-be intruder screamed in anguish. With her adrenalin pumping at top speed, she forgot her fear, picked up the hall phone, and punched in the precoded number for the police station.

Minutes later, she heard a knock on her door but, rather than answer it, she turned out all of the downstairs lights and stood at the bottom of the stairs, shivering from the blast of cold air that swept through the broken glass pane.

She answered the phone. "It's the security agency at your door, ma'am, Tillman, Hawkins, and Gordon. Can you open up?"

She'd forgotten that her house was wired to the agency's office. With the chain on, she cracked the door, saw Tillman, and opened it.

"You don't know how glad I am to see you," she told them. "Did you catch him?"

"We didn't," Hawkins said. "Policemen were putting him in a police car as we drove up. Fortunately, we have this John Deere snow shovel hooked to the front of the truck. An ordinary car can't move in this stuff. The snow is so deep the man couldn't run."

"Did you recognize him?" she asked Tillman.

"Yes, ma'am, I sure did."

"Now who could that be?" she asked when the doorbell rang again.

"I'll get it," Lieutenant Gordon, the agency's detective, said, drew his gun, and opened the door.

"Blake!"

"Mr. Hunter. Come on in," Gordon said. "You just missed the commotion."

"Hardly," Blake said, his voice and demeanor the epitome of gloom. "That guy spun around right into my arms. Fortunately the police patrol appeared, because he carried a thirty-eight revolver with a silencer." He pulled off his cap and gloves. "As cold as I am, it was all I could do to hold on to him until the policemen could cross the street and handcuff him."

"We don't think it's safe for her to be here alone tonight," Gordon said. "The guy who's behind this is out there free to finish the job himself."

Blake looked at her then, his sadness as obvious as a flashing neon sign. "It's up to Mrs. Rodgers."

If she hadn't seen in his eyes the bleakness of the wintry weather that surrounded them, she might have turned her back, but no matter what he'd done, she loved him. He'd braved the most fierce storm she had ever witnessed, because he feared for her well-being, and how right he'd been.

"You'd better get warm," she said. "I'll run some hot water, so you can get your body temperature back to normal."

"Sure you want to do that?" he asked.

The three men looked from her to Blake, obviously aware that more was going on than what they saw and heard. "We'd better patch up this pane," Gordon said. "You got any cardboard boxes, heavy paper, and tape?"

She thought for a minute. "I think there's some plywood in the basement. Prescott had planned to build a storage closet down there, but didn't get around to it. I'll show you."

She glanced at Blake and saw him shiver. "First I'd better help Mr. Hunter get warm. Come on up to the guest room." She said it pointedly, and for a minute she thought he'd leave.

Instead, he thanked the three men and, as if reluctant to do so, walked slowly behind her up the stairs. At the top, she asked him, "How long did it take you to walk here from your house?"

"Three hours."

"I'll help you out of those clothes," she said, reaching for the buttons on his coat.

"I'll manage. If you'll just put some hot water in that tub, I'll—" He staggered toward the bathroom, and she ran to him, but he held on to the door, sending her the message that he didn't want her help. Unstrung by the obvious incapacity of the man who was, to her, the personification of strength, she sped down the steps and asked Tillman to go up and see if Blake needed help.

"Maybe you could show me that plywood, ma'am," Gordon said. "Stay here, Hawkins. We can't leave that window unattended."

While Gordon and Hawkins boarded up the broken window, she made coffee and ham sandwiches. With Blake in mind, she opened four cans of chicken stock and combined it with pieces of chicken breast, chopped green pepper, and noodles. It wouldn't win a prize in a gourmet magazine, but if you were half frozen, you wouldn't sneeze at it. She put some of Ruby's brownies and chocolate chip cookies on a tray and put that on the table with the sandwiches. By the time Tillman came downstairs, she'd set the breakfast-room table for five.

She didn't want to appear overly anxious about Blake, but she couldn't help it. "How is he?"

"I'd say not so good. He insisted on a shower, which was dangerous, because he could hardly stand up straight. Hypothermia is a serious thing, and you don't get over it by fighting it."

"And that's what he's doing?"

"Yeah."

"Where . . . I mean, what is he doing now?"

"He's lying across the bed, but he said he'd be down in a minute. If you could take him something hot . . ."

"I will. The three of you go in there and eat something. I'll be back in a few minutes."

She put a bowl of soup and the remainder of the meal on a tray along with a napkin and serving utensils and took it upstairs to him. He took his time answering her knock, so she opened the door and walked in without his invitation.

She pulled a chair to the side of the bed, put the tray on it, and sat down beside him. The chill she felt wasn't from the weather, but the frosty reception he gave her. He sat up, with effort, she noticed, and looked at her. "You said you never wanted to see me again. What are you doing up here?"

Taken aback by his blatant hostility, she bristled. "My reason is the same as the one you had for walking here in this blizzard and subzero weather. Now don't give me a hard time. If you don't eat this, you're going to be awfully sick."

He grasped the coffee mug in his long, slim fingers, took several quick swallows and looked around him as if seeing the room for the first time. "You must have decorated this room. Lilac and rose. Soft and feminine like you. And almost like your bedroom."

She supposed her alarm at his reference to her bedroom must have been reflected on her face, for he said it with what was just short of a sneer, "Oh, yes. Your bedroom. I remember everything about it, not the least of which was the way you writhed under my body."

"That's not worthy of you, Blake."

He held the cup to his lips with both hands and drained it. "Then you'll forgive me, Mrs. Rodgers, if I'm not myself tonight."

Refusing to be baited, she put the tray on the bed. "This isn't the best soup I ever made, but it's filling, and you need to eat. If I bring you a pair of Prescott's pajamas, will you stay here tonight?"

"I don't sleep in pajamas. Anyway, where would I sleep?" he asked, eating the soup.

Where did he think? Though it pained her to see him lethargic and weak, his baiting annoyed her and she swung around, a glare on her face.

"Sleep any doggoned place you please."

He finished the soup, pushed the tray away from him, and eased back onto the pillow. "And if it pleases me to sleep with you?"

"Weak as you are, it wouldn't make an iota of difference," she shot back. "I have to go down and give those men something to eat. Be back after a while."

"I'll stay tonight," Tillman said, "and Hawkins will be here tomorrow morning. How's Mr. Hunter?"

"About forty percent of his normal vigor. I hope he'll remain here tonight."

"He needs rest, a lot of it," Hawkins said. "I'll be here when you get up in the morning, ma'am."

She told them good night, went upstairs to deal with Blake, and found him beneath the covers fast asleep.

Aware that Ruby wouldn't be able to come to work, she got up at seven, dressed, and went down to the kitchen to cook breakfast for herself and Blake. She phoned Hawkins, who was responsible for the front door that morning, and asked if he'd come in for breakfast.

"I already ate, ma'am, but I sure would like a cup of coffee."

They talked for a few minutes; then he stunned her with the information that Blake had left.

"What? You mean he walked home?"

"No, ma'am. I came in the truck and Tillman drove it back to the agency. On the way, he dropped Mr. Hunter off at his house. Worked out fine."

"Why ... uh ... that's wonderful. I hope he manages to rest today."

"Seemed a hundred percent when he left here."

"I'll have the coffee for you in two minutes," she said, and came close to adding that she'd like to have Blake Hunter's scalp. How could he leave without saying good-bye? She had a mind to ... Why should he say good-bye? Hadn't she told him she never wanted to see him again? She put the coffee in a thermos, went to the door, and waited until Hawkins, who sat in the agency's car, walked across the street to the house.

"Thanks, ma'am. I know you'll be glad when your problems are over, but after this job, my next assignment will seem like punishment."

"Punishment comes in a lot of forms, Hawkins, but it's least bearable when the source is close to you."

"Tell me about it. It's my middle name."

She didn't ask him to elaborate; she had her own problems to deal with, and considering how hard she'd prayed for sleep the night before and still hadn't had one wink of it at seven that morning, she was in for a rough time. Breaking off from Blake was a matter of words, but getting him out of her soul would take a lot more.

Her pulse kicked into a mad race when the phone rang, and she had to fight for calm before answering it. "Hey, girl. Imagine no school today and probably none tomorrow," Rachel said, her spirits obviously high.

"Too bad Paul went back to Durham yesterday." She didn't feel like bantering. The letdown at hearing her friend's voice and not Blake's stunned her.

"You in the dumps? What's going on with you and Blake?"

If you got a headache, did that mean you had problems with your man? She asked Rachel as much.

"Honey, a headache wouldn't make you sound like that. You've had the wind sucked out of you. What's the matter?"

She took a deep breath and summoned her patience. "Rachel, I don't think you want to know. When I get it all straightened out, I'll broadcast it to all my friends."

"Whoa there. Sorry I butted in."

"Somebody tried to break in on me last night and almost made it. That, and I don't know how many other problems, aren't likely to make me want to dance."

"I guess not. I'm sorry. I told you to let me know if you needed me, but you never have. I'd offer to come stay with you, but I figured Blake was keeping you company."

Blake. Always Blake. "When's Paul coming back?"

"Soon as the airport opens, I guess."

"Are you two making plans?"

"It's getting to that point. I hope I have your blessing, Melinda. If Paul and I got married, you'd be my sister."

Best news she'd had all day, because she suspected Rachel wasn't in a position to tell all of it. "Paul's my favorite sibling. If you make him happy, how could I not be happy myself? I'm glad you two found each other."

"I love him, Melinda. For the first time in my life, I'm in love. I don't know what the problem is between you and Blake, but you love each other. Anybody can see it. If he needs forgiveness, forgive him. That man's worth loving."

"My grandfather used to say, 'Talk's easy done, but it takes money to buy land.' A small thing to some is a behemoth to others."

"Be stubborn and see if he comes crawling. Not in a million years."

Blake swore he'd never again serve as executor of anybody's will. He'd done it a dozen times, but this one was more than he'd bargained for. After telephoning first Ethan and then Phil and Johnny and satisfying himself that they were all right, he phoned his mother, because he knew she'd worry if she saw that snow in the television newscasts.

"You promised to come visit me. I know you said you'd come this winter, but you don't have to wait till then."

"I promise I'll be up there the first part of the year. I've joined a sewing club, and we're making sweaters, mittens, scarves, and caps for homeless children. These will be the only Christmas gift some of them will have."

"If you're enjoying it, great. You need anything?"

She told him she didn't. "You don't seem to have your usual energy. Is anything wrong? What about that girl?"

He should have known she'd ask about Melinda. "I wish I

knew the answer to that. I had great hopes but, well . . . that's life.''

Her loud gasp was as much evidence as he needed that she had hoped for a different outcome of his relationship with Melinda. ''You can't patch it up?''

''I don't know.'' He gave her the essence of the problem. ''I think she's devastated and hurt. I'm sorry, but that doesn't solve anything.''

''But you're not giving up. That's not a bit like you. Besides, being mad with you doesn't mean she's stopped loving you.''

He had to laugh when he remembered Melinda sitting on the side of the bed holding a spoonful of that awful, strange-tasting soup to his mouth. ''I know she loves me, and I probably should have told her of my part in the wording of that will. I didn't get a chance to explain before she gave me a taste of her vituperative tongue, and—''

''Oh, for goodness' sake. We've all said things when we were angry that we later wanted to take back. You can be rigid when you believe you're right, and this time, I'm not sure you are.''

Neither was he. He told her good-bye and hung up. He had to get to his office and prepare for his encounter with the mayor. A desperate man made a worthy opponent, but he was forearmed, and right now he'd welcome a good fight with just about anybody. He put in a call to the sanitation department to check the condition of the streets and learned that if he shoveled his driveway, he could drive to within a block of his office. He brought out the snowplow he hadn't used in four years and went to work. Two hours later, he walked into his office.

He tried to work, but a restlessness pervaded him and he found himself pacing from his desk to the window and back. Eventually, anger replaced his discontent, and in a fit of temper, he telephoned her. But like a dream at daybreak, the anger vanished when he heard her voice, and the only things that mattered were his need of her and whether she loved him.

"Melinda, this is Blake."

"I know. Your breakfast is still on the table where I'd already put it when I learned that you'd been home for nearly an hour."

"If you're mad at me, why would you cook breakfast for me?"

"Because you risked your life for me last night, and I was raised to be grateful for kindness."

"No kidding." He didn't mean to sound sarcastic, but *grateful for kindness* indeed. "I expect you were taught forgiveness, too."

"That's something you have to ask for. Even the Lord demands that."

"Can I see you?"

"I . . . uh . . . I don't think so. You don't know what a torture this whole thing is for me. There've been times when I've actually disliked Prescott, believed he wasn't the man I'd thought. If I was so precious to him, how could he have done this to me? I don't want his money. Blake, I wish you well, but I . . . I still hurt. Bye."

He had to dig into himself, force himself to work, using all his power of concentration, and yet she dashed across the page on which he wrote, laughing, mocking. When at last he finished the draft, he thought of calling her again and telling her he'd done it in spite of her. The idea brought a laugh from him and, with it, the reminder that before he'd opened himself up to her, he'd rarely laughed. She'd given him laughter and so much more.

On the way to his car, he passed the drug store, the only establishment open for business, thanks to Ellicott City's first blizzard in twenty years. His glance caught something in the window and on an impulse he went in and bought it. He had it wrapped in lavender paper and tied with a rose-colored bow, stopped by her house, and asked Tillman to give it to her. If that didn't move her, he'd find something that would.

"Mr. Hunter asked me to give you this, ma'am," Tillman said, handing her a small lavender-colored shopping bag.

"Thanks. " She said it almost absentmindedly, as if neither that nor anything else interested her.

Blake had never given her a gift, and her curiosity sent her barreling up the stairs to her room, where she sat down, calmed herself, and tried to steady her fingers enough to open it. Her gaze focused on the little box wrapped daintily in her favorite colors, and her heart constricted. If only . . . She loosened the bow, eased the ribbon off the paper, opened the box, and stared at the tiger-striped kitten half the size of her hand. He'd chosen a happy little cat that had the slightest suggestion of arrogance, its head tilted upward and its tail up high and curved forward as if it didn't give a hoot. She opened the envelope and read *Her name is Lindy, because she reminded me of you. Love, B.*

"I will not cry. I don't care what he does, I will not cry," she said aloud as moisture dampened her cheeks. She put the kitten on her night table and went back to the drudgery of sorting out the remainder of Prescott's effects. She couldn't call him, because she'd break down if she did, and she didn't want to give in to him. She wanted to forget about Blake, Prescott, and that will and get on with her life. But it was not to be; both had found nesting places in her mind and refused to move.

The following day, with the streets still clogged with what had once been snow but was now ice, school remained closed, and she continued the task of going through her late husband's things. The most difficult job still faced her, for she hadn't touched his bedroom. She heard a loud pop like the sound of a firecracker and rushed to the back window just as a man jumped from the fence into the street. She called Tillman and told him what had happened and, because she knew he'd report it to Blake, she phoned him.

"Thanks for the kitten," she said. "I'm trying to figure out what it is about that little cat that reminds you of me."

"Shouldn't be too difficult. That cat says if you like it, fine; if you don't, tough. And like you, she's so graceful."

"Anyway, I think she's cute. There's something I . . . maybe ought to tell you about." She described the incident. "It happened just a minute ago."

His silence rang in her ears. After a minute, he said, "Thanks for telling me. I expect Tillman's trying to phone me right now. It seems as if Goodwin's getting reckless, and that's what we've been waiting for. He's discovered that there's no guard at the back and he'll try it again, so I'm calling the agency and ordering a guard for that post."

She didn't protest, because she realized dismissing the guards hadn't been a wise move; indeed it could have cost Blake his life. She pulled air through her teeth. Blake. Always Blake. It could have caused *her own* demise.

"Do what you think best," she heard herself say and added, "I'm not used to the taste of crow, but if I have to eat it . . ." She let the thought speak for itself.

"I wouldn't ask for your humility," he said, "not now, not ever, no matter what transpires between us. All I ask is your understanding and a chance to—"

"Please, Blake, I'm not ready to deal with that yet. I'm . . . I'm . . . I put so much of myself into it that I need to breathe a different air for a while."

"Are you telling me you don't . . . that you're no longer interested? If you are, make it plain."

She was irritated by her own inconsistency, her inability to get her heart in sync with her head; anger threatened to sharpen her tongue and she had to exert great effort to control it.

"You want to know where you stand, and I don't fault you for that, but I . . . I need time."

"You're saying you haven't given up on us entirely?"

She told herself he had a right to probe, but that she was entitled to stand her ground. "Blake, you're a smart man. You know how I feel about you, so stop pushing me. Put yourself in my place, and see if you wouldn't feel betrayed."

"All right. Let me know when you have a change of heart. But don't wait too long. I'm going to call Lieutenant Cochrane at the police station and see what they're doing about Goodwin."

"Maybe that wasn't Goodwin."

"I've thought of that. Could be another of his henchmen. Mind if I drop by there tomorrow evening?"

"I may be in school."

"School's closed for the remainder of this week. Well?"

"I'll be here." She could have kicked herself, but she admitted to herself that she wanted to see him.

"Around six. See you then."

She put away her lesson plans at around five that evening, showered, dressed, and still had half an hour to burn before Blake arrived. After pacing the floor for a few minutes, she sat down at the piano and began to play Liszt's Hungarian rhapsodies. Tension seeped out of her muscles, and the stress she hadn't recognized eased from her mind. She closed her eyes and let the music wash away her cares. A kaleidoscope of brilliant colors, ever changing, dancing and flying, exploded in her head as she mastered the keyboard, unaware of all but the music, out of herself. Lost now, somewhere in time, her fingers produced Liszt's magical Rhapsody Number Four in D Minor. When at last she played the final note and an eerie hush was all she heard, she glanced at her watch. Twenty minutes past six. How could it be? Blake was never late.

The doorbell rang and she went to open the door. "Hi," she

said, her animosity gone, a casualty of the music she'd just played.

"Hi," he said. Banal greetings that served as poor substitutes for dashing into each other's arms.

"I didn't want to disturb your wonderful playing, so I waited out here until you finished the piece. You are certainly accomplished."

She walked with him to the living room and offered him a seat. "I should play more often. Music does wonders for me."

He handed her a small package wrapped in rose-colored paper and tied with a lavender velvet bow. "You shouldn't do this, Blake. You're seducing me."

He looked her in the eye and didn't smile. "That's my intention; it's what this male-female thing is all about. But in the meantime, I hope I'm pleasing you."

Before she could answer, his cell phone rang. "Hunter. No, he's dangerous. I'll alert the police out back."

"What is it? What's going on?" She was doggoned if she'd be treated as if she were a helpless child to be kept out of harm's way.

"After your call yesterday afternoon, we set a trap for the guy. He thinks nobody's guarding the place, but in addition to the agency's guards, you have six cops hiding out. When you stopped playing, I had exactly one minute to get inside this house. We'd put the word out that the day guards would leave and that the night guard at the front door was supposed to be there at six, but was in school and always got there between six-fifteen and six-thirty."

"I could have walked right into it. Thanks for not telling me."

"With a detective at each door, there wasn't a chance."

"What was the noise I heard yesterday afternoon, that popping sound out back just before that man jumped over the fence?"

"The guy tried to blow off the back door, but that crude, handmade stick of dynamite he used didn't detonate."

A peculiar fatigue settled in him and around him; he was tired of the fencing, one-upmanship, and discontent, but he had to wait until she came to terms with his having had that clause inserted. He stared at her, wanting to ask how she could be so soft and sweet, how she could give herself up to him so completely, and now be so unyielding.

"I suppose he's in custody now," he said, "but we'd better stay put for a while in case there are any shots."

"Then, maybe I'd better go upstairs out of the range of gunfire. Gee," she said, swung around, and reached for the package, as if suddenly remembering it. "My Lord, look at this! A mahogany and mother-of pearl miniature baby grand." She shook her head in wonder. "Blake, this is . . . I can't believe . . . this is fantastic."

His grin took her aback momentarily, because he hadn't smiled much recently. "Does that mean you like it?"

She raced to him, threw her arms around his neck, and hugged him, and he grasped her to him in a fierce caress. Nervous and self-conscious about her impetuousness, her "Thanks" was barely audible and she moved away from him.

The doorbell rang. "I'll get it," Blake said.

"All clear, Mr. Hunter. He left here in the squad car protesting that Goodwin set him up. Won't he be surprised to see Goodwin when he gets downtown? I don't think they'll be greeting us at Christmas."

"You bet. Thanks, Lieutenant. I'll be down to the agency tomorrow to take care of the bill." He turned to her. "Open the piano, why don't you?"

She lifted the lid and found that the piano was a music box that played the tune, "If I Loved You." At the music's end, she looked up into eyes that shone with love, and her heart seemed to stampede in her chest.

"It's precious, Blake. I've never had one before, and you knew I'd love it."

"I hoped. You're safe now. I'll be in touch."

Gazing at his departing back, she wondered whether he'd come because as executor of the estate, he thought it his duty, or because he wanted to protect her. Then she looked at the music box that she still held in her hand, put it to her lips, kissed it, and wandered in the direction of the kitchen. She had to eat, but the thought of food nearly sickened her.

Chapter Fifteen

Blake usually completed his Christmas shopping before the first of December, but with Christmas only days away, he hadn't managed to buy more than a few gifts. He told himself that he'd been too busy preparing a brief for the trial of Goodwin and his two cohorts, but he'd never been successful at fooling himself. Everything in his life was dragging along like a car with two flat tires. He found a brown leather jacket for his brother, a matching Burberry raincoat, umbrella, and rain hat for Callie, his sister, and a red velour robe and slippers for his mother. He went to the smoking section to look for pipes and remembered. It would be their first Christmas without his father.

With the gifts in shopping bags, he browsed through the store. Nothing he saw looked like her. During the past three weeks, he'd sent her scented candles, a tiny pink satin pillow on which were embroidered the words *What about tonight?*, and a silver chain on which hung a silver key inserted into a silver heart. She'd responded with *Thank you* on scented, personalized notepaper. He didn't care if she didn't call, because those notes told him she didn't trust herself to talk with him. He walked through the book and record department and stopped. At last, he'd found what he wanted.

At home, he took the packages to his den, just as his phone began to ring. He picked it up and heard the mayor's voice.

"Blake, this is your mayor. The whole town knows that Melinda Rodgers isn't trying to find a husband. According to Ray Sinclair, she's on record as saying she's not going to marry anybody, and I'd think he'd be the best candidate, so he should know."

He took a deep breath and decided to let Frank Washington hang himself. "You're suggesting I should start parceling out this man's effects before the deadline for Melinda's compliance with the will. You're a lawyer and an elected official and you're suggesting I break a legal, registered will?"

The mayor's breathing accelerated as if he'd been frightened. "No, you know I'm not saying that, Blake. But she's not going to find a decent man to marry her, not in this town, so you might as well plan now to give that money to the city."

He'd been sitting on the edge of his desk, and he bounded up and nearly snatched the phone wire from its socket. "What the hell do you mean by that statement? Where do you get off with assassinating her character?"

"Now, now, Blake. There're things you don't know. I wouldn't want this to get back to Mrs. Washington, but I know more about Melinda Rodgers than you'd think. I've been having an affair with her for years, and I wouldn't be surprised if I wasn't the only one."

"You're lying, Frank, and I'm the one man who can prove it. Now, let me tell you what you've *really* been doing for

years.'' He repeated what his private investigator had discovered and which he himself had documented. ''You either eat
that lie or I'll give the facts, documented and with a signed
affidavit, to the daily paper tomorrow morning. What'll it be?''

''You can't prove—''

''Give me your fax machine number, and I'll send you
copies.''

''Don't expose me, please, Blake. I never touched her, not
once. I—''

''I know you haven't, but you'd malign her. Don't expect
mercy from me.'' He hung up. That took care of the mayor.

He couldn't leave Ellicott City without giving her the gifts
he'd bought for her and knowing that she wouldn't be alone
on Christmas Eve. He packed his bags, put them in the trunk
of his car, and drove to 391 College Avenue. Darkness had
already set in at five-thirty in the afternoon, and his spirits lifted
when he saw the wreaths glowing from her door and windows.
At least she'd gotten the Christmas spirit. She answered the
door at once, and he was gratified to see that she'd taken the
precaution first to look through the peephole.

''Hi.''

He gazed at her, a sight for his sore eyes, lovely in a red
jumpsuit.

''Hi,'' he said. ''I couldn't leave town without seeing you
and wishing you a Merry Christmas. Did you dress a tree?''

''Uh-huh. Want to see it?''

He followed her into the living room, and when she flicked
a light switch, the six-foot balsam fir—beautifully decorated
with red, green, and silver bells, fairies, angels, munchkins,
and the like—glowed beside the lighted fireplace. A warm, cozy
environment where a man could love a woman to distraction. He
opened the shopping bag and placed two packages under the
tree.

Her mouth worked the way it did when she was struggling

for composure, but he figured it best to pretend he didn't notice. "Thanks for the presents. Would you ... er ... like some eggnog or some mulled wine?"

"I can't have more than a sip, because I'm driving to the Baltimore airport. Mulled wine will be fine."

She brought a glass for him and one for herself and sat in a beige overstuffed chair facing him. "Cheers. Will you be with your folks in Alabama for Christmas?"

She already knew the answer to that. He nodded. "It's our first Christmas without our father, and we'll all be there to give our mother moral support, though I'm not so sure she needs it. She's a strong woman." He sipped the wine and looked at his watch. "I'd better get moving. You'll be with your family, I suppose."

"Yes. We're having a family reunion. I ... uh, hope you have a wonderful Christmas."

She walked over to the tree and picked up a package wrapped in a golden brown iridescent paper and tied with a brown ribbon. He looked at the package, then at her. She'd said his eyes were that color. Was she telling him something?

"Thanks for remembering me," was as much as he could manage. The scene, barren of warmth, lacking all he'd envisioned for the holidays, cut him to the quick.

She walked with him to the door, and he didn't think he'd ever seen her so subdued, nor would he have expected it. "Have a good time." She looked down at her feet and said, "Drive carefully, and get back safely."

She wouldn't look at him, and he'd learned early to seize the moment. If he hadn't he wouldn't be where he was.

"Do you care whether I get back here in one piece?"

She didn't look at him, so he tipped up her chin with his fingers, forcing her to let him see her eyes. The pain in them nearly rocked him on his heels.

"Melinda. Oh, Melinda! Sweetheart, don't ... Don't do this

to us." He opened his arms, and the feel of her soft, sweet body tight in his embrace sent shocks reverberating throughout his system.

Her arms went to his shoulders, and she gripped him with more force than he would have imagined she could muster. He hungered for her mouth, but when he attempted to kiss her, she lowered her head.

"I'm . . . I'm . . . Go on home," she said, "and when you come back, maybe we can talk."

"I'll be back on the thirtieth, can we spend New Year's Eve together?"

"I. . .yes, I want that."

He couldn't leave as things were. "Can't you . . . kiss me?"

He watched her struggle with her inner conflict, but he'd waited a month, and he'd wait as long as he had to. She was his, and he meant to let her know it.

"Kiss me," he whispered. Slowly she raised parted lips to his, and he plunged into her. Shudders plowed through him and tremors shook him as he wrapped her to his body. She battled him for his tongue, and he'd have given her the world if he'd owned it. Her breath came short and fast as she feasted on his tongue. He thought she'd devour him, and he didn't care. Then, as if she'd come to herself and realized what she was doing, she braced her hands against his chest. He released her.

"It won't go away for me either, sweetheart," he said. "I'll barely make my flight, and Callie's meeting it. Be here for me when I get back."

She nodded but didn't answer, and he realized she'd surprised herself when she went into his arms. Nothing had changed, and when he got back, he'd bring that home to her forcibly.

* * *

He sat at the Christmas dinner table with his family, thinking of the warmth and love that surrounded him, and he was almost happy. He and Melinda should have been together, but their course wasn't yet smooth. At least he knew she still loved him; he'd take it from there.

"I was hoping you'd bring Melinda with you," his mother said. "You must have gotten it straightened out, because you've hardly stopped laughing since you've been here." John and Callie stopped eating and focused their attention on him.

"It's better, and it'll get better still."

"How the mighty have fallen," John said, raising his glass. "Here's to Melinda." As his mother and sister joined in the toast, he thought: *Just wait till next year.*

Melinda sat with her parents and her brothers, John and Peter, waiting for Paul and Rachel to arrive for Christmas dinner. "Melinda, you have to find a way to keep your money. If you don't want it, divide it among those who need it, but it would be a crime to let it go to the city and state," Booker said.

"I know, Papa. Blake said he's trying to find a way, and I believe him."

"Of course," Lurlane said, "but you have to help him."

She stared at her mother. "What can *I* do?"

Lurlane rolled her eyes. "This is twice recently you've given me reason to wonder about your intelligence."

She was saved the trouble of answering, for Paul arrived with Rachel, who greeted them with her left hand stretched out in front of her. Melinda ran to her friend and hugged her.

"We're engaged," Paul announced. He greeted his parents, hugged his brothers, and kissed Melinda. "Get your act together, Mindy. Guys like Blake don't show up in this town every day."

Lurlane poured a glass of eggnog for Booker, and then laced the remainder with rum. She knew that none of her children would mention the added kick. But Booker decided he'd like a second glassful.

"Just spit it out, Papa," Melinda said when he tasted it and made a face. "That way, it can't make you high."

Booker glared at her. "Young lady, I want you to know that a teaspoon of liquor isn't likely to make me unsteady. I have stronger willpower."

His four children stared at him, each wondering at his calm acceptance of rum in the eggnog and his failure to spoil their day by sending their souls to hell.

Lurlane raised her glass. "Merry Christmas, all of you." She turned to her husband. "Thank you, my dear, for being the man I married." To Rachel, she said, "Welcome to our family, my daughter."

With the aroma of roasting turkey, buttermilk biscuits, and sweet potato pie filling the house, Lurlane took her husband's hand and started toward the dining room. "Dinner's ready."

"I'd like a word with you, girl," Booker said to Melinda after dinner, and she followed him into his study. Normally, he'd have said whatever he thought in the presence of the others, and she couldn't help being grateful that if he was going to say something that would embarrass her, he'd at least do it in private.

Apprehension settled over her as she followed him, fearing he'd cap a wonderful day with a lecture. "What's happened between you and Blake?" he asked, surprising her. "How come he's where he is and you're here? I know what was going on just a month ago, so this doesn't make sense."

She sat down, weary from fighting herself and lonely for Blake, and told him she'd broken off the relationship and why.

He paced in front of her, his thumbs in his vest pocket, as when he was about to preach. "I can't believe what I'm hearing.

If there was nothing between you, it was his sacred duty to protect his client's interest, not yours. So what if he didn't tell you; was he obligated to tell you how that will was written? Even if he wronged you, what did I teach you since you were born? What? Tell me.''

''You said if we don't forgive, we're lost, and that the person who bears the grudge has a bigger burden than the one against whom the grudge is held.''

''You're the one holding the resentment. So am I right? Aren't you miserable?''

''Yes, sir.''

His arm grazed her shoulder in a gesture of affection that, six weeks earlier, would have startled her. ''Don't ruin your life for spite. Don't be too small a person to forgive. Blake's a good man, and he loves you. Get it straightened out. You hear me?''

''I want to, but I can't figure out how.''

He half-closed one eye and raised his eyebrow above the other one. ''I don't believe you. You have to know you can get that man to do anything you want him to do. If you have a problem with it, talk to your mother.''

She kissed his cheek. ''Thanks, Santa Claus.''

She didn't want to seem too anxious, but every time she heard a car pass her house, she bounded toward the door, slowed down, walked back into the living room, and sat down. She figured that, in the last half hour, she'd lost fifteen pounds jumping up at the slightest sound and sitting back down. Finally, the doorbell rang. She inspected her appearance in the hall mirror, checked her right wrist to make sure her Fendi perfume was working, and made herself walk slowly to the door. After looking through the peephole, she yanked it open.

''Hi,'' she said, as casually as she could. ''Come on in.''

But Blake apparently didn't have games in mind. He stepped in, kicked the door closed, took her in his arms, and brushed his lips across hers.

"Hi," he said. "Thanks for the beautiful cuff links. Did Federal Express bring you a flat envelope today?"

"I don't know. Ruby can't get over the habit of putting the mail on Prescott's desk, and I haven't been in the den today."

"Would you mind checking?" As she started for the stairs, she glanced at him over her shoulder. Hmmm. He was not a worried man. If anything, he was as self-assured as Paul's old peacock. She ran up the steps as fast as her long, slim black skirt would allow and, a minute later, returned with the envelope.

He took the cassette from his own envelope. "I have a feeling we each got one and that they're identical," he said, "but we can play them both."

"Why do you think what's on here is important?"

His eyes sparkled with the glint that always gave her a warm feeling. "There's a note on mine that says 'copy two,' and the return address says 'Estate of Prescott Rodgers, care of Attorney J. L. Whittaker.' I'm executor of the estate, so this is something he deliberately withheld from me."

He put the cassette on. "Sit over here with me. If we don't want to hear it, we can at least comfort each other."

She snuggled up to him, shamelessly, maybe, but she'd missed him so much. "Blake, I'm . . . I'm so sorry I messed things up. I mean, I was mad, but I didn't have to act like I did. And all these little presents you sent me, and the book of poems. I've almost worn out that CD of Brook Benton love songs. I'd never heard of him. He's wonderful. Here's something I got for you," she said, handing him a box.

He opened it, and then his wonderful laughter filled the room. "I'll be doggoned. A necktie with your telephone number on it. Now that's clever!" .

"I bought it in case you decided not to accept my request for forgiveness."

"Don't tell me. You've been talking with your father."

She figured her expression was deprecating at best. "Play the cassette."

He hit the button, and the cassette rolled a full minute before they heard his voice.

"Dear Blake and Melinda,

"I instructed Whittaker to deliver duplicate copies of this tape to the two of you on December the thirty-first of this year. By now, it's clear to both of you that Melinda won't marry a man just to get an inheritance. I inserted that clause because it would force the two of you to accept the fact that you love each other. I knew it from the start, and I loved both of you the more for your strength and virtue, your refusal to dishonor me. You belong together, have from the moment you met. I didn't care a hoot about that foundation, Blake, but I accepted the idea, because it would make it necessary for you and Melinda to spend a lot of time in each other's company. I'm certain that, by now, my scheme has worked because your attraction to each other is so strong. Melinda, my dear, the inheritance is yours. Blake is yours as well. Love him with all your heart. Prescott."

She didn't try to stop the tears, much as she hated to cry, and soon wrenching sobs poured out of her. "I th . . . thought all kinds of me . . . mean things about him for inserting that clause, and he only wanted to help us get together."

"Shhh. It's over now. Please. Honey, stop it. Don't sob like that. I can't stand it. I—"

He hooked an arm under her knees and the other around her shoulders and pulled her into his lap. "Honey, please stop it."

The feel of his lips caressing her eyelids, her ears, neck, and face filled her with another kind of emotion, the drive to explode in passion. Her fingers traced his jaw, his forehead, his cheeks, and his bottom lip.

"Kiss me, Blake. Kiss me as if you mean it."

Immediately that fiery storm she knew so well raged in his eyes, but he gazed at her for the longest time while his eyes seemed to grow stormier and wilder by the second.

"I once told you that if you made love with me, there'd be no turning back," he said, "and if you take me up those stairs with you, you're making a commitment. Is that clear?"

She slid off his lap, stood, and reached for his hand. In a second, he was on his feet and had her locked in his arms with the hard tips of her breasts rubbing against his chest. He brushed his hand across one turgid nipple.

"Yeah! You missed me."

His lips came down on hers in a powerful statement of possession, and she welcomed his velvet tongue into her mouth. Lord, she needed him so badly. Standing on tiptoe, she fastened her hands to his buttocks and pulled him to her.

"Slow down, hon," he said, "I'm short of control tonight."

"I don't want your control. I want to know who you are, and if you're uncorked, I don't care."

He stared at her. "You don't know what you're saying."

He had a wild, feral look now, a little scary, but she wanted him like that, without the polish and the suave lawyer's persona. She wanted down-to-earth, gut-bucket man. As if he read her mind, he picked her up and dashed up the stairs. At the top, he reached for the zipper on her blouse and had if off her by the time he got her into her room. She unzipped her skirt and stepped out of it.

"Good Lord," he whispered, as his gaze swept over her body, bare but for the tiny red bikini panties. He picked her up, dumped her onto the bed, knelt beside it, and slowly, methodically pulled the panties down her legs, kissing every spot they touched. He stood then and took his time getting out of his clothes, never taking his gaze from her.

"I'm going to help myself to you this night," he said, almost to himself. After putting his clothes and her skirt and blouse across a chair, he walked back to the bed and stared down at her. She could see him swallow the liquid that accumulated in his mouth. When she crossed her knees, his familiarity with her body told him desire had begun its strumming in the seat of her passion, and he jumped to full readiness. She opened her arms to him and a loud, hoarse groan escaped him.

She wanted wildness, and he let her have it, plunging his tongue into her mouth and showing her what was to come. He nipped her lip and her ears, and bathed them with the tip of his tongue. His fingers skimmed her arms, neck, and shoulders, teasing her though he had to know she wanted his mouth on her breast. Frantic for it, she put her hand on his head and led him there, and he went at her as if he'd been starved for the taste of her. He suckled vigorously, and stroked the other one until she cried out loud.

"Honey, I need you inside of me." She felt his hand skim her belly and held her breath for that second when he'd touch her and she'd start aching for more. He stroked slowly, driving her nearly mad, until she began to undulate wildly. Frustrated, she slapped his buttocks, and his fingers began their dance, turning her into the earthy, primitive female she knew only when she was in his arms. She swung her hips up to him, but he wouldn't be rushed. She thought she'd die if he didn't get inside of her.

Out of her mind with desire, hot arrows of need pounding her feminine center, she reached for him, but he moved away and continued his onslaught. Sucking vigorously and stroking the diamond between her legs. Love's liquid dampened his fingers, and when he rose above her, she sheathed him with the condom he'd placed on the night table.

"Look at me, baby. You belong to me now. No other man exists."

"Yes. Yes, I'm yours. I—"

He plunged into her hot and furious the way he'd taught her to like it, and within minutes he had her out of control, not certain where she was or how she got there. He stroked with the fury of a fast-moving train, claiming, possessing. He seemed to crawl as he moved up higher, shocking her senses with a feeling she hadn't known before, triggering the awful deathlike fullness. She wanted to die of the half pain, half pleasure, and then he locked her to him with steellike arms. "We're together this time. Give yourself up to me. Let me have you."

He stroked powerfully, until that sweet and awful explosion plowed through her.

"Blake. Blake. I love you, I always loved you," she gasped, shattered by the loving.

He screamed her name, "Melinda. Melinda, my love, my life," and came apart in her arms.

He lay that way for a long while, and she had time to wonder how she'd been so foolish. After about twenty minutes, he raised his head from her breast and looked at her.

"You knocked the stuffing out of me just now."

"It's what you deserved. You did something to me you hadn't done before."

"You weren't committed to me before. I was breaking ground for the future. I want to marry you, Melinda. I had hoped we could announce it this Christmas, but—"

"Would have been nice, too. Paul and Rachel announced their engagement at my parents' house Christmas Day."

He braced himself on his forearms and stared down at her. "Did you just agree to marry me?"

"I sure did. I'm honored, even if you didn't get on your knees to ask me."

"Considering where I am right now, that would be impossible."

"Oh, Blake, I'm so happy."

His smile, so brilliant and sweet, confirmed his words. "I love you now, and I will forever."

"Wait a minute." She remembered the will and its bequeathal of millions. "What will we do with all that money?"

"Whatever you like," he said, nibbling at her breast. "With all these poor people in Ellicott City, spending it won't be a problem. Happy New Year, sweetheart."

"Happy New Year, darling."

Dear Reader:

Greetings! This is my first romance novel and my first letter to you in this, the third millennium. I hope it began as well for you as for me, and that SCARLET WOMAN enriched your life in some way, if only to give you a couple hours respite from the problems of daily living. And I hope, too, that Melinda and Blake will have a place among your favorite romance couples. Love and romance are to be treasured. Having that special person in our lives, there for us through every crisis, and sharing with us our joys, dreams, and successes, are blessings beyond measure. It is soul sustenance of the rarest kind. This is the pinnacle of living, and I find inexplicable pleasure in leading the strong and supportive yet gentle and vulnerable hero and the capable, loving heroine to this fountain of ecstasy. During the months that I spend with these people, they are real, live beings who exist in the world that I create for them. That so many of you embrace these characters is a source of immense satisfaction to me. Thank you also for making SECRET DESIRE such a stunning success. I appreciate your support.

Don't forget to write. I answer every letter and E-mail promptly. E-mail: GwynneF@aol.com; Web page: http://www.gwynneforster.com. Letters may be addressed to me at P.O. Box 45, New York, NY 10044. Please include a self-addressed, stamped, legal size envelope if you would like a reply.

I wish each of you many blessings.

Fond regards,
Gwynne Forster

ABOUT THE AUTHOR

Gwynne Forster is a best-selling and award-winning author of eleven romance novels and four novellas. *Romantic Times* nominated her first interracial romance, AGAINST THE WIND—which Genesis Press published in November 1999—for its award of Best Ethnic Romance of 1999, and nominated Gwynne for a Lifetime Achievement Award. The Romance In Color internet site gave AGAINST THE WIND its Award of Excellence and named Gwynne 1999 Author of the Year. FOOLS RUSH IN, which BET Books published in November 1999, received the *Affaire de Coeur* magazine award for Best Romance with an African-American Hero and Heroine. Her books won that award in 1997 and 1998 also. Her January 1999 book, BEYOND DESIRE, is a Doubleday Book Club, Literary Guild and Black Expressions club selection.

Gwynne holds a bachelor's and master's degree in sociology and a master's degree in economics/demography. As a demographer, she is widely published. She is formerly chief of (non-medical) research in fertility and family planning in the Population Division of the United Nations in New York and served for four years as chairperson of the International Programme Committee of the International Planned Parenthood Federation (London, England). These positions took her to sixty-three countries. Gwynne sings in her church choir, loves to entertain, and is a gourmet cook and avid gardener. She lives with her husband in New York City.

DIALOGUE AND LITERATURE

DIALOGUE AND LITERATURE

Apostrophe, Auditors, and the Collapse of Romantic Discourse

MICHAEL MACOVSKI

New York   Oxford
OXFORD UNIVERSITY PRESS
1994

Oxford University Press

Oxford   New York   Toronto
Delhi   Bombay   Calcutta   Madras   Karachi
Kuala Lumpur   Singapore   Hong Kong   Tokyo
Nairobi   Dar es Salaam   Cape Town
Melbourne   Auckland   Madrid

and associated companies in
Berlin   Ibadan

humca

Copyright © 1994 by Oxford University Press, Inc.

Published by Oxford University Press, Inc.,
200 Madison Avenue, New York, New York 10016

Oxford is a registered trademark of Oxford University Press

Chapter 5 first appeared in *ELH* 54 (Summer 1987) and is reprinted by
permission of The Johns Hopkins University Press.

Library of Congress Cataloging-in-Publication Data
Macovski, Michael Steven.
Dialogue and literature : apostrophe, auditors, and the collapse
of romantic discourse / Michael S. Macovski.
p. cm.   Includes bibliographical references (p.   ) and index.
ISBN 0-19-506965-X
1. English literature—19th century—History and criticism—Theory, etc.
2. English literature—20th century—History and criticism—Theory, etc.
3. Discourse analysis, Literary.
4. Romanticism—Great Britain.
5. Reader-response criticism.
6. Dialogue.   I. Title.
PR457.M33   1994   820.9′008—dc20   91-2886

INDEXED IN   EGLI

987654321

Printed in the United States of America
on acid-free paper

For Deborah, with love

Acknowledgments

If on some level critics always write about their own lives, then this book reflects my own history of dialogue—my critical engagements with readers, texts, and listeners. First among these respondents was Andrew L. Griffin, who originally sparked the idea behind this study, and then guided it through formulation, development, and completion. It was he who not only encouraged my interest in literary auditors, but also inspired my love of Romantic literature.

Both during and after this initial writing, Frederick Crews stood out as another crucial supporter of this book, as mentor, advisor, and teacher. Early incarnations of the text were also enriched by discussion and friendship with Vincent Dunn, Pamela Ferguson, Annette Lareau, Victoria Smith, and Gina Sosinsky. Finally, during the last stages of revision and rethinking, Caryl Emerson engaged my argument with insight, warmth, and vigor. I have been amazed at her ability to combine humane exchange and "active understanding" in the true spirit of dialogic criticism.

Indeed, since critical discourse is at least as interactive as the literature discussed in this study, I also want to thank the scholars whose work often influenced mine, including Stuart Curran, Don H. Bialostosky, Michael Holquist, Paul Magnuson, Beth Newman, Gary Saul Morson, Charles Rzepka, and Susan Wolfson. These voices resonate through many parts of this work in ways that no customary modes of citation can capture.

All of these wise friends and scholars were generous enough to point out the critical path; how I finally made my way is a matter of my own responsibility.

My other debts extend beyond language. They are owed to Deborah Tannen.

Contents

Abbreviations

AR   Coleridge, Samuel Taylor. *Aids to Reflection and the Confessions of an Inquiring Spirit*. London: George Bell and Sons, 1890.

Journal   Shelley, Mary W. *Mary Shelley's Journal*. Edited by Frederick L. Jones. Norman: Oklahoma University Press, 1947.

NB   Coleridge, Samuel Taylor. *The Notebooks of Samuel Taylor Coleridge*. Edited by Kathleen Coburn. 4 vols. New York: Pantheon, 1957–1990.

Poetics   Bakhtin, Mikhail. *Problems of Dostoevsky's Poetics*. Translated by Caryl Emerson. Minneapolis: University of Minnesota Press, 1984.

Prose   Wordsworth, William. *The Prose Works of William Wordsworth*. Edited by W. J. B. Owen and Jane Worthington Smyser. 2 vols. London: Oxford University Press, 1974.

"Response"   Bakhtin, Mikhail. "Response to a Question from the *Novy Mir* Editorial Staff." In *Speech Genres and Other Late Essays*, translated by Vern W. McGee, edited by Caryl Emerson and Michael Holquist, 1–7. Austin: University of Texas Press, 1986.

"Speech"   Bakhtin, Mikhail. "The Problem of Speech Genres."
                In *Speech Genres and Other Late Essays*, translated
                by Vern W. McGee, edited by Caryl Emerson and
                Michael Holquist, 60–102. Austin: University of
                Texas Press, 1986.

"Text"   Bakhtin, Mikhail. "The Problem of the Text in Lin-
                guistics, Philology, and the Human Sciences: An Ex-
                periment in Philosophical Analysis." In *Speech
                Genres and Other Late Essays*, translated by Vern
                W. McGee, edited by Caryl Emerson and Michael
                Holquist, 103–31. Austin: University of Texas Press,
                1986.

I

Romantic Formalism and the Specular Lyric

1

Knowledge, Rhetoric, and Authority: Toward a Theory of Romantic Dialogue

> Each epoch, each literary trend and literary-artistic style, each literary genre within an epoch or trend, is typified by its own special concepts of the addressee of the literary work, a special sense and understanding of its reader, listener, public, or people.
>
> In each epoch certain speech genres set the tone for the development of literary language. And these speech genres are not only secondary (literary, commentarial, and scientific), but also primary (certain types of oral dialogue — of the salon, of one's own circle, and other types as well, such as familiar, family-everyday, sociopolitical, philosophical, and so on). Any expansion of the literary language that results from drawing on various extraliterary strata of the national language inevitably entails some degree of penetration into all genres of written language (literary, scientific, commentarial, conversational, and so forth) to a greater or lesser degree, and entails new generic devices for the construction of the speech whole, its finalization, the accommodation of the listener or partner, and so forth.
>
> Bakhtin, "The Problem of Speech Genres"

I

This book conceives of literary discourse as a composite of voices — interactive personae that not only are contained within the literary text but extend beyond it, to other works, authors, and interpretations. Within this schema, literary characters interact not only with individual voices but also with other discourses themselves – political, religious, and historical. A given speaker engages not only fellow characters but his or her own past, present, and future as well. It is this pluralistic, transtemporal rhetoric that defines the nature of literary dialogue. Yet to conceive of literature in this manner is also to reconsider our notion of literary meaning, our formulations of authorial intention, invention, and above all, originality. For both the production and the interpretation of aesthetic meaning become, in this context, social acts – collaborative inventions derived from multiple viewpoints. When we speak of literary voices, then, we envision not a circumscribed text but a socially constituted event – a convergence of vocative perspectives, rhetorics, and idioms. According to this view, literary meaning is rendered not by a single speaker, nor even by a single author, but is communally constructed and exchanged. It is not declaimed but incrementally accrued in time and space. It is neither focal nor detached but processive, accretive, and multireferential.

That the subtitle of this book names Romantic discourse is meant to suggest the proliferation of this dialogic meaning, form, and interpretation in the literature of that era. While such features are found in a variety of literary periods, the manifestations of dialogue are particularly pronounced during the Romantic epoch. The present study accordingly traces the evolution of this concept within Romantic literature, beginning with the first-generation poets of the period, and extending to those nineteenth-century prose works most often treated as "Romantic": *Frankenstein*, *Wuthering Heights*, and *Heart of Darkness*. As is often noted, such works share a common concern with both the integrity and history of the self, with that individuation of the "I" that characterizes Romantic discourse. What this book suggests, however, is that such an emphasis on individuation must be reconsidered in light of those voices located outside the Romantic self. If previous approaches have focused on the strictly internal aspects of a single narrative consciousness, the present study stresses the interaction between this self and separate others, between discrete voices in dialogue. Such voices are seen not as interior, solipsistic aspects of an insular "I" but as idiolectal entities – voices distinct from the self. What ultimately distinguishes this approach, then, is that it provides a social model: only the distinct outsideness of these voices can enable exchange. Whether such voices signify actual characters within the text or less defined representations of exterior perspectives, the point is that they remain rhetorically differentiated and therefore capable of genuine interchange. Deprived of such distinction – such as when the "I" threatens to merge or fuse with these exterior voices—all dialogue is silenced.

Hence to conceive of such voices as limited to either a single psyche or a single corporeal frame is to miss the multireferentiality of the model—a model founded primarily on the writings of Mikhail Bakhtin. Although these voices may be subsumed at times, or even migrate to a primary speaker, their language remains peripheral to the ego, rhetorically distinct, and multiple. In defining this external language, we speak not of the "Other" but of others: a proliferating matrix of tongues. In a Romantic context, moreover, these others are often represented by literary auditors—designated listeners who, though they may appear undefined, essentially enable the rhetoric of interaction. Although such listeners are only one manifestation of external voices, their incorporation within the Romantic text comes to instantiate the language of dialogue—that concurrent articulation of the various liaisons, invocations, and discourses of the period.

II

This articulation of exterior voices further leads us to question the prevailing critical belief in a solipsistic Romantic self, and to suggest instead that this "I" must be defined in relation to discrete others. Of course, this is not to deny the operation of interior voices, what Bakhtin variously refers to as "interior dialogue" or "microdialogue" (*Poetics* 74, 212). If it is misguided to ignore the voices that externally surround the self, it is equally mistaken to assume that the ego itself is internally univocal and autogenic. As Bakhtin's formulation stresses, however, this micro-"other" (or "second voice") within interior dialogue necessarily retains the separateness and distinctiveness of an "*outside* voice," an externalized "*other* person" (213, emphasis added). It is dialogue, in fact, that enables a literary character to represent, within himself, this external "other"; in Bakhtin's terms, only "*dialogue allows him to substitute his own voice for the voice of another person.*" In this sense, even the interior monologue of a given character is "dialogized," in that it contains the "anticipated responses of others" (214, 74). Hence "all words in it are double-voiced, and in each of them a conflict of voices takes place. . . . Dialogue has penetrated inside every word, provoking in it a battle and the interruption of one voice by another" (214, 74–75).

We should bear in mind, though, that even this inner voice—

this dialogized "second voice" — is by definition "only a substitute, a specific surrogate for the actual voice of another person" (*Poetics* 254). In other words, this "*substitute*" or "second" voice must be distinguished from those that constitute a genuine other — from what Bakhtin terms the "third voice, the direct voice of the other" (214). A given character thus encompasses three distinguishable types of vocal elaboration: first, "his 'I for myself' . . . ; [second,] his fictitious 'I for the other' (reflections in the other), that is, [his] second substituting voice; and finally the genuinely other voice" or "third" (217; cf. 214). Although the manifestations of these voices may vary from text to text, we must stress that "there can be no question of synthesis; one can talk only of the victory of one or another voice, or of a combination of voices in those places where they agree. It is not the idea as a monologic deduction, even if dialectical, but the event of an interaction of voices" that is crucial (279).

We can say, then, that literary dialogue includes a given literary character's interaction with both these "second" and "third" voices. Indeed, the incorporation of such voices at times constitutes a meliorative act on the part of a particular narrator. If the internally limited self remains isolate and enclosed, the outwardly directed ego achieves externalization by literally extrapolating a separate other, in what might be called an extreme form of projection. Such externalization involves not self-division but self-generation — a progenitive act in which a speaker, "like Prometheus, creates (or rather re-creates) living beings who are independent of himself and with whom he is on equal terms" (*Poetics* 284). This Promethean creation effectively enables a poetic speaker to stand outside himself: by "looking inside himself, he looks *into the eyes of another* or *with the eyes of another*" (287). At the same time, this ability to endow a discrete other further applies to temporalized versions of oneself, including former and anticipated images of the ego. In such cases, the capacity to envision one's past and future selves as distinct others becomes another form of the externalization we are discussing. As we shall see in Chapter 2, even Wordsworth's chronotopic invocations of his former "I" — what he refers to in *The Prelude* as his "two consciousnesses" — can be reinterpreted in terms of these exteriorized others.

In thus conjuring former versions of his own ego, even an apparently isolated speaker can sustain the externality requisite for dialogue. Here, what may appear to be internal fragments of a once unitary "I" may in fact be discrete voices, as opposed to divided or fragmented aspects of a single psyche. In this context, we must also reconsider the concept of the fragmented self in the Romantic period—the idea that the speaking "I" comes to splinter or disperse within the literature of the era. For although this study recognizes what might be called the plurality of the Romantic ego, it defines such plurality, here again, in terms of contrastive voices retaining the distinctiveness and completeness of an "outside" other. Such a plurality derives not from fragmentation but from multiplicity, a relational ensemble of social tongues. Hence what earlier approaches have termed the dispersal of the Romantic "I" may be evidence less of any psychological breakdown than of the manifold interactions among autochthonous others. If we speak of the presumed fragmentation of the Romantic ego, we must envision a proliferation that is less pathological than rhetorical, a propagation of vocative exchange. It is less a division than an expansion, in that the identity and language of the ego must encompass a diversity of "outside" registers.

What these dialogic effects have in common is a move away from insularity. In Bakhtin's terms, such an approach seeks "not an analysis of consciousness in the form of a sole and single *I*, but precisely an analysis of the interactions of many consciousnesses. . . ." (*Poetics* 287). The focus of this book is accordingly not on the composition of an interior psychomachia but on the delimitation of the social self. Each chapter revises the idea of the dissociate ego, and looks instead toward its exteriorized moorings. It is this external mooring, in fact, that has the capacity to organize the divided self, coordinate its components, and thereby alleviate its fragmentation. Such externalized voices can actually define the boundaries of the fragmented ego—delineating its margins, orienting its contexts, and enacting its uniqueness. Without such boundaries, the self becomes amorphous, unsubstantial, and monologic.

Within this revisionary account of the Romantic ego, then, the self's exterior alliances become more vital than its internal machinations, since the actual definition of the self occurs at the junctures of this externalized exchange—along the boundaries of the "I." We must accordingly stress, in Bakhtin's terms, "[n]ot that which takes place within, but that which takes place on the *boundary* between one's own and someone else's consciousness, on the *threshold*. And everything internal gravitates not toward itself but is turned to the outside and dialogized, every internal experience ends up on the boundary, encounters another, and in this tension-filled encounter lies its entire essence" (*Poetics* 287). Again, a "person has no internal sovereign territory, he is wholly and always on the boundary; looking inside himself, he looks into the eyes of another or with the eyes of another." In this sense, Romantic discourse is necessarily "turned to the outside and dialogized," looking beyond strictly "internal experience." Such discourse is, in the broadest sense, specular, in that it sees with "the eyes of another" — in that it attempts an expanded prospect, a panoramic view beyond the autotelic ego. Such an "I" is, in the end, neither internally unitary nor externally circumscribed.

III

Recent criticism concerning Romantic genres has begun, in fact, to reconsider the historical notion of a circumscribed Romantic "I" — that "autotelic subjectivity" defined by an internally singular consciousness.[1] In examining both lyric poetry and Romantic narrative, such studies point to their "intersubjective" or "transsubjective" viewpoints, multiple perspectives marked by manifold voices, tonal diversity, deictic shifts, and most prominently, the rhetoric of apostrophe. According to these approaches, apostrophic tropes create several divergent points of view within a single narrative, giving voice to invocative forms that perform several thematic functions. Those poetic effects discussed most often include summoning up the voices of both the dead and of Death itself, especially through epitaphic apostrophe[2]; presenting a speaker's words as the metonymic voice of Nature, particularly as a vocative river or breeze[3]; and establishing the identifiable, rhetorical position of the apostrophic voice in order to substantiate a narrator's self.[4] For each of these diverse poetic functions, apostrophe enables the lyric poet to represent unknown or even hostile forces as vocal manifestations of a polyphonic world.

That such studies would focus on Romantic genres is not surprising when we consider that many Romantic poems present a literary exchange in which one figure is cast as a listener. While poems like the "Epistle to Dr. Arbuthnot" depend upon our sense of implicit reciprocation, Romantic lyrics usually depict a less mutual situation in which a speaker addresses an unanswering companion, bird, or painted figure. The revolutionary volumes that effectively initiate the period, including the *Songs of Innocence, Songs of Experience*, and *Lyrical Ballads*, build upon this apostrophic form. In the former collections, it shapes such poems as "The Lamb," "The Tyger," "The Little Vagabond," and the "Introduction" stanzas; in the last volume, it provides the foundation for the "Rime," "Anecdote for Fathers," "We are Seven," and "Expostulation and Reply." The prevalence of this rhetorical address becomes all the more apparent when we begin to consider its formal variations in the most compelling lyrics of the period, including "Tintern Abbey," "Nutting," "Frost at Midnight," "The Eolian Harp," "This Lime-Tree Bower My Prison," and much of "Dejection: An Ode." Even the later verse of these first-generation poets tends to allude to a designated addressee for a poetic speaker's narrative, as in Coleridge's "Phantom or Fact" or the final books of *The Prelude*. Of course, the individual configurations of such poems may vary considerably; while most listeners appear before their respective speakers as direct, face-to-face respondents, a few stand as auditory surrogates, representing an imagined public, hero, or ideal. In other cases, an author may actually blur the line between speakers and listeners; many Romantic works, for instance, consist of several concentrically framed tales, with speakers eventually becoming listeners to other, more deeply embedded stories. Indeed, the question of who listens and who narrates becomes a complex one in these texts, since they are often built around a series of speaker/listener paradigms. In each case, however, the rhetorical consequences of these poetic interlocutors bring out such prevalent Romantic concerns as audience epistemology, object relations, and temporal dislocation.

At the same time, we should also consider that both these thematic concerns and the apostrophic form that supports them extend well into the second-generation era, and that the resurgence of the figure in both Keats's and Shelley's poetry further underscores its pointedly Romantic affinities. In these later works, the invention of an addressee serves to convey a speaker into an idealized realm, so that designating an other becomes an act of imaginative expansion. For Shelley in particular, this apostrophic endeavor actually maps out a new world, a newly defined rhetorical space that momentarily transports him out of self. As he states in the motto to "Epipsychidion," "The soul that loves projects itself beyond the created world and creates in the infinite a world all its own, very different from this obscure and fearful abyss." As Shelley's language suggests here, however, this transported "soul" continually threatens to abjure its crucial separation from the "created world," to remain instead in a world that *is* "all its own" — self-regulated rather than externalized. On such occasions, instead of extrapolating these multiple, "infinite" others, the poet's "I" actually merges with them — thus eradicating the possibility of dialogic exchange, and leading to his rhetorical "annihilation." Hence in the well-known apotheosis to "Epipsychidion," Shelley describes how "We shall become the same, we shall be one / Spirit . . . / One hope within two wills, one will beneath / Two overshadowing minds, one life, one death, / One Heaven, one Hell, one immortality, / And one annihilation" (573-74, 584-87). Later, in "Adonais," he attempts a similarly apocalyptic immersion, this time in the elegiac other represented by Keats; in this poem, he again concludes, "No more let Life divide what Death can join together" (477).

If Shelley has difficulty differentiating this "soul out of my soul," Keats too addresses an other as part of a failed attempt to envision an inspirited netherworld, to construct a distinct entity within a noumenal realm. His many apostrophes to the nightingale, the urn, and the knight-at-arms — as well as the formulaic invocations of Homer, Chaucer, Boccaccio, and the Muses — can accordingly be read as attempts to invoke this visionary realm. Yet these poems further suggest that the barrier between him and this ineffable world is silence. Hence in "The Fall of Hyperion," where the Poet attempts to "tell [his] dreams" to another, we learn that the "fine spell of words alone can save / Imagination from the sable charm," from that sense of "dumb enchantment." In this narrative, such "telling" takes the form of an attempted dialogue with Moneta, an exchange that ultimately founders on the paucity of human response: "I had no words to answer," says the speaker, "for my tongue, / Useless, could find about its roofed home / No syllable of a fit majesty / To make rejoinder to Moneta's mourn. / There was a silence. . . ." As the poem progresses, this muteness in an addressee reflects that of the Titans, "Listening in their doom for Saturn's voice" — or that of Saturn himself, whose "bow'd head seem'd listening to the Earth, / His ancient mother, for some comfort yet." Despite Moneta's humanized translations, the speaker becomes not an interlocutor but an observer; in the end, such godlike interchange proves "Too huge for mortal tongue, or pen of scribe," and the poem breaks off unfinished.[5] Even before this, in "The Eve of St. Agnes," Madeline longs for a similarly invocative connection between speaker and listener, for she equates her lover's silence with the "be-nightmar'd" duplicity of her dream: "'Ah, Porphyro!' said she, 'but even now / Thy voice was at sweet tremble in mine ear, / . . . Give me that voice again. . . .'" In a parallel manner, Lorenzo also seeks, as he says, to "tell my love all plain" to the object of desire. As "Isabella" opens, "he inwardly did pray / For power to speak; but still the ruddy tide / Stifled his voice" — a silencing that also foreshadows his later quest for an avenging auditor, when his specter is "striving, in its piteous tongue, / To speak as when on earth it was awake, / And Isabella on its music hung." Although the potential for locating a listener diverges markedly in such examples, even Keats's early works posit a spoken pursuit of aural recognition: Endymion, too, like the speaker in "Epipsychidion," desires to speak with his auditory lover, his "second self." As his story concludes, he accordingly asks Echo to "hear, and sing / This ditty to her!" Yet it is this impetus toward conflation with the listening other, with this "second *self*," that ultimately comes to disable dialogue for the younger Romantics, and — as we shall see in the coming chapters — to distinguish such late Romantic rhetoric from the more delineated, externalized dialogues of Wordsworth and Coleridge.

IV

The recurrence of the apostrophized listener in these poems thus begins to suggest a rhetoric of Romanticism. It is this rhetoric that first led M. H. Abrams to define the Romantic lyric as a "sustained colloquy, sometimes with himself or with the outer scene, but more frequently with a silent human auditor, present or absent" ("Lyric" 527). For Abrams, such an apostrophe "captures remarkably the qualities of the intimate speaking voice" within the "dramatic mode of address to an unanswering listener" (531, 533; cf. 553–56). Yet this "silent human auditor" suggests not only a rhetoric of "address" but a poetics of dialogue — a poetics in which a speaker's words are actually constructed in relation to proleptic response. As Paul Magnuson has noted, such a poetics emerges from the "vital and dynamic relationship between speaker and auditor" — the sense that there "cannot be segregated and isolated utterances."[6] Generally speaking, the rhetorical inclusion of even a mute listener implies the form of a dialogue, with its attendant notions of reception, affect, and potential for response. Indeed, the incorporation of the Romantic addressee as a metonymic listener within the text sets up the formal configuration of "co-respondence" — the structure, at least, of a communication. Romantic apostrophe accordingly becomes a rhetorical synecdoche or figure for dialogue — even if this form remains vestigial or unspoken.

Hence contemporary theories of dialogue formulated by Bakhtin, Hans-Georg Gadamer, Michel Foucault, and Jürgen Habermas delineate the rhetorical implications of even these silent, implied colloquies. Yet before examining such theories individually, we should bear in mind that the history of Romantic criticism has long associated the period with poetic encounters, philosophical dichotomies, and the epistemological conflict between subject and object. Although these dichotomies never qualify as actual dialogue, such studies have located suggestive precursors to the kind of language we are defining. Often, for instance, they usefully identify a given poem's dynamic as a specific movement between self and designated object; yet at the same time, they normally fail to recognize this object as that multiple other who is by definition external and rhetorically instrumental. Similarly, while they may insightfully envision this poetic dynamic as an interpretive quest or investigation, they usually misrepresent it as the kind of structured dialectic that moves toward a definitive conclusion.

Still, such approaches do point toward certain philosophical dichotomies that serve as signposts to more rhetorical issues. Earl Wasserman, for instance, locates such a dichotomy in Romantic opposition to the rationalist speculations of a pre-Kantian canon. "What Wordsworth, Coleridge, Keats, and Shelley chose to confront more centrally and to a degree unprecedented in English literature," he writes, "is a nagging problem in their literary culture: How do subject and object meet in a meaningful relationship?" (Gleckner and Enscoe, 335). Later, Abrams explicates this Romantic dichotomy in terms of "ego and the non-ego, spirit and other," and the "interactions" between "individual human selves." "Fichte, Schelling, and Hegel," he writes, "begin with an undifferentiated principle which at once manifests itself in the dual mode of subject and object, whose interactions (in and through individual human selves) bring into being the phenomenal world and constitute all individual experience, as well as all the history of mankind . . . " (*Supernaturalism* 91). He then goes on to suggest "how this metaphysics of subject-object interaction parallels the exemplary lyric form" in which "an individual confronts a natural scene and makes it abide his question, and the interchange between his mind and nature constitutes the entire poem . . . " (92). Still later, Abrams looks beyond this formal colloquy between "mind and nature" to include among his lyrical objects the "absent friend," one who in turn personifies a given speaker's "interchange with an outer world" (277).[7]

Abrams's characterization of the nineteenth-century "I" in terms of "spirit and other"—a function of the speaker's "interchange with an outer world"—begins to suggest why the Romantic self cannot be regarded as an asocial entity. We should bear in mind, however, that discussing this social self in terms of "subject and object"—with a focal "I" taking precedence over a given "thou"—tends to obscure the egalitarian nature of dialogic interaction. Bakhtin's formulation emphasizes an "analysis of the interactions of many consciousnesses; not many people in the light of a single consciousness, but precisely an analysis of many equally privileged and fully valid consciousnesses" (*Poetics* 287). As part of this equipoised rhetoric, moreover, these "interactions" also recall the tendency for dialogue to shift repeatedly from consciousness to consciousness, alternating among various voices. Here again, such interactions may appear to resemble other classic characterizations of Romantic form — particularly those interactive forces that Stuart Curran has termed "opposing impulses" between general themes such as "virtue and vice, honor and shame, freedom and tyranny" (185, 80). For Curran, such opposition manifests itself as what he refers to as "dialectical form," the interpretive aesthetic that alternates between "contraries," "contradictory elements," and the "stark and irreconcilable antitheses" that constitute Romantic irony (66, 185, 81–82). In the context of dialogue, however, we must stress that this interpretive process alternates not so much between abstract themes as between the poetic voices that represent them — between the recognizable utterances that instantiate not dialectic but dialogue. We must accordingly stress that, contrary to some of the previous formulations, dialogue is less abstract than rhetorical, less thematic than personified, and less bilateral than multiplex — encompassing the "interactions of many consciousnesses."

Here again, then, we must take care to distinguish dialogue from the normative view of Romantic thought as a dialectic alternation between opposites or contraries. Indeed, as we move toward the present era of Romantic commentary, several studies begin to blur this distinction — to characterize such thought both as a mentalistic alternation within a single mind and as an exchange with an apparently "separate" embodiment, presumably with the potential for rhetoric and response. In his classic study of Wordsworth's "*via naturaliter negativa*," Geoffrey Hartman begins by characterizing the Wordsworthian lyric as a "product of two kinds of [interior] consciousness . . . ordinary and supervening, which gather in tension around the precipitating image" (16). Yet in describing this "dialectical factor," Hartman goes on to discuss it as an "apostrophe" from the poet to a "separate consciousness" (16, 12, 17). Although such an apostrophe can be "addressed either to an auditor or to himself," the speaker's viewpoint takes on an "outward-directed" character in which the "usurping consciousness . . . becomes its own subject as it were, and so retains momentarily a separate existence" (7–8, 16). While he ultimately leaves open the question of whether this "separate existence" constitutes a distinctly externalized voice, Hartman depicts such an encounter as an impulse toward "response" and "communion" — as a rhetorical movement in which this impulse "spreads sociably from one person to another over great spaces of fantasy and solitude. . . . [I]t transcends the finitude of self and the fixity of self-consciousness" (7–8, 15). It is significant, finally, that for Hartman the coincidence of these features takes on the dimensions of a paradigm. Although such a combination "is not a genre originally, it is a specific rhetorical form whose rise and modifications one can trace and which significantly becomes a genre in the Romantic period" (11).

Hartman's characterization of this poetic encounter with a "separate consciousness" is particularly suggestive for a reformulation of the Romantic lyric as dialogue. His description is especially noteworthy for its insistence that this poetic consciousness "blends outward-directed feeling and inward-going thought" — that it can encompass both responsive figures (such as an implied listener or reader) and the internal perspectives of the poet (12, 8). Still, the scope of Hartman's study prevents him from examining the dialogic roles of the Wordsworthian other, especially as these roles take on particular maieutic functions in the early lyrics. We must recognize, moreover, that this "separate consciousness" represents not an individual, "usurping" "subject" but a host of former voices and selves.

Hence previous conceptions of nineteenth-century interlocutors tend to foreshadow some aspects of their dialogic nature while missing others. Several such studies manage, for instance, to look beyond the traditional belief in isolated poetic speakers, arguing instead for a language that "fuses them with that which is outside themselves — other persons, other times, other cultures" (Martin 28). Yet in recognizing this turn toward "that which is outside," the same study never considers that the alleged "fusion" between "I" and other would necessarily preclude rhetorical exchange — and thereby discount the dialogic modes so prevalent throughout the century. Still other studies tend to focus, here again, on internal relations within the fragmented subject — on what they call the "divided self" — while ignoring its externalized liaisons with distinct others. According to this view, the multiple voices that characterize nineteenth-century texts indicate not dialogue but "internal division," "double consciousness," and the "war within." Characters like Victor and the monster "become . . . indistinguishable" halves of an "essential identity."[8]

When such studies do recognize the rhetorical independence of these voices, they still tend to limit both its provenance and origins to the mid-Victorian era — to restrict its purview to those genres normally associated with the post-Romantic years.[9] As a result, they tend to reduce the Romantic "I" to a "discretely boundaried" and "complete whole," leading to a "unitary" and organically contained self (Martin 25, 24, 133). In defining the Romantic subject according to a restricted notion of Coleridgean organicism, such approaches argue for a Romantic belief in the "sovereignty of the self," in a sense of "symmetry" and "closure" that bespeaks the "integrity of the individual" (29, 25, 28; cf. Miyoshi xvi, 28–29, 53–54, 83–84). Such approaches begin, of course, with M. H. Abrams's "'expressive' theory of romanticism, which emphasizes the poet as source and validation of the poem," in contrast with the "older 'pragmatic' theory, which is concerned with the effect of the poem on its readers." They go on to contrast Victorian poetics with a "Romantic poetry [that] seemed too inward, too asocial."[10]

Yet as we have noted, several more recent, revisionary views of the Romantic speaker have come to question this notion of the organically whole and bounded "I" — a notion that, given the radical appropriation of others in such lyrics as the Conversation poems, falls far short of describing even Coleridge's subjects, much less those in works by Wordsworth, Blake, or Shelley. One need consider only the pronounced disjunctions between distinct voices in *The Prelude* — or the ironized distance between narrators and characters in Blake's *Songs* — to recall that such poems neither envision nor desire a synthesis among multiple subjects. Indeed, the extrapolation of a speaking "I" beyond the confines of an isolate self might well be taken as a formal principle of Romantic discourse. The alleged divergence between Romantic and Victorian conceptions of the ego accordingly suggests a difference more in degree than in kind, for in fact both eras belie the fiction of an autotelic ego with a commensurate reach beyond the contained self.

V

A poetics of the nineteenth-century "I" must accordingly begin with the idea of consubstantial voices. What Abrams calls the "interaction" between "individual human selves" prefigures a Romantic encounter between speaker and listener, voice and response, interior ego and exterior world. At the same time, moreover, we must bear in mind that such encounters and "interactions" lead not to accord and reconciliation but to dissociation and estrangement. Rather than confronting an object amenable to representation, the Romantic subject comes up against what, in Blake's terms, "is not too Explicit" — what Pater, in looking back upon the era, describes as "things unlikely or remote" (Gleckner and Enscoe, 23). As a result, the relation between subject and object comes to represent an aporia, a scene of uncertainty in which the Romantic "I" can neither apprehend nor construct an ideal world. In characterizing this misapprehension, Jerome J. McGann suggests that "in a Romantic poem the realm of the ideal is always observed as precarious — liable to vanish or move beyond one's reach at any time" (*Ideology* 72). The scene of this poetic reaching is thus one of "contradiction, conflict, and problematic alternatives," one in which "transcendent and ideal subjects" must "occupy areas of critical uncertainty" (72-73). In contrast to the empiricism of the previous century, this uncertainty emerges as Romantic irony, the philosophical skepticism that gives rise to a poetry "deliberately open-ended and inconclusive."[11]

What is striking about this Romantic encounter with uncertainty — with "contradiction, conflict, and problematic alternatives" — is that it manifests itself as what I refer to as Romantic dialogue: those misinterpreted conversations, unanswered addresses, bogus receptions, and other disjunctions between speakers and listeners that distinguish nineteenth-century literature. The epistemological crises of the period are expressed not only as an iterative motif but as a formal construct. To speak of Romantic dichotomy and contradiction is to speak the language of literary polarization, the narrative estrangement between "I" and "thou." Such problematic dichotomies are accordingly rehearsed, reinterpreted, and finally reformulated as literary dialogue. Generally speaking, the shifting claims and borderland conflicts of the poetry are played out in the rhetorical arena of such dialogue.

If we characterize Romantic epistemology in terms of dialogue — the rhetorical form that *perpetuates* itself through continual repulsions and attractions — we are also linking this rhetoric with the Romantic concept of organic form and developmental process. Such a process shapes, for instance, an essay like Hazlitt's "The Fight," in which the involved machinations leading up to the eventual prizefight (finding a site, securing lodgings, introducing contestants) take precedence over the event itself. Underlying such narrative structures is the organic concept of evolution and development, what Schlegel calls the process of "becoming." "The romantic ["universal"] kind of poetry," he writes, "is still becoming; that, in fact, is its real essence: that it should forever be becoming and never be perfected."[12] As Anne K. Mellor has noted, Schlegel's depiction of this incessant development represents the generative alterations of thought itself. Elsewhere he writes, "Never will the mind that knows the orgies of the true Muse journey on this road to the very end, nor will he presume to have reached it; for never will he be able to quench a longing which is eternally regenerated out of the abundance of gratifications." The eternally regenerating mind will accordingly *"begin again and again from the beginning."* Such an act of resynthesis defines the poetic "journey"—much as the dialogic retellings of, say, the Mariner's tale become a poetic act in themselves.[13] In such cases, the philosophical process of "becoming" is rhetorically represented as a dialogic movement of continual regeneration.

These examples from Hazlitt and Schlegel thus depict the recursive nature of Romantic thought, the inexorable renewal of cycle and process. It is this continually resynthesizing action that is ultimately reformulated as the alternating voices of dialogic form—a structure that Schlegel himself saw as the conversation of "divergent opinions" in order to shed "new light upon the infinite spirit of poetry."[14] That this structure is continually "infinite," "new," and "divergent" further characterizes dialogue as a self-generating rhetoric, predicated upon the renewed responsiveness of the utterance. "The word," writes Bakhtin, "always wants to be *heard*, always seeks responsive understanding, and does not stop at *immediate* understanding but presses on further and further (indefinitely)" ("Text" 127). In pressing beyond this immediate understanding, the word engenders yet another response, perpetuates that dynamism of strophe and antistrophe, question and response, that underlies dialogic form. In this context, then, the question looks not to an answer but to the perpetuation of interrogative form, the rhetorical protraction and kinesis of dialogue.

This concept of the word that "presses on further and further," that continually queries yet another respondent, begins to suggest the investigatory motivation behind the impetus to dialogue. Such an interpretive intention is in effect the motive behind the ongoing, regenerative quest we have been discussing, since it acts as a method of sustaining continuous inquiry. Put another way, we can say that the Romantic view of an inexorable process, representing interpretive contradiction as an ongoing interchange between "I" and "others," is formally manifested as a move toward Romantic dialogue. We would do well to turn, then, to a more comprehensive critique of Bakhtin's theory of dialogue, for he has formulated and developed what is perhaps the most extensive approach to the form and its implications.

VI

This theory of dialogue begins with the "utterance," what Bakhtin calls the "unit of speech communication."[15] Such utterances, as the originary constituents of human discourse, go to make up "speech genres," those "relatively stable types" or forms that derive from the spoken word. Bakhtin then goes on to divide speech genres into two forms, "primary (simple) genres that have taken form in unmediated speech communion," and "secondary (complex) speech genres — novels, dramas, all kinds of scientific research, major genres of commentary, and so forth [that] arise in . . . comparatively highly developed and organized cultural communication (primarily written) that is artistic, scientific, sociopolitical . . . " ("Speech" 62). Regarding primary speech genres, for instance, Bakhtin suggests that oral "dialogue is a classic form of speech communication," the genesis of vocative forms (72). More significantly, however, he stipulates that secondary genres (including literature) "absorb and digest" the primary, establishing a definitive link between spoken dialogue and primarily written forms. Such written forms are in many cases "a conventional playing out of speech communication and primary speech genres" (72; cf. 62). We can say, then, that literary language draws on these primary genres, transposing and reinterpreting the rhetoric of spoken forms. Such a reinterpretation or exchange accordingly leaves its mark on a variety of written modes, including literary genres: "Any expansion of the literary language," Bakhtin continues, "that results from drawing on various extraliterary strata of the national language inevitably entails some degree of penetration into all genres of written language (literary, scientific, commentarial, conversational, and so forth) to a greater or lesser degree. . . ." At the same time, this inter-"penetration" between the literary and extraliterary also results in a gradual transformation of communicative discourse, since it "entails new generic devices for the construction of the speech whole, its finalization, the accommodation of the listener or partner, and so forth" (65–66).

* * *

This "accommodation of the listener or partner" is central both to Bakhtinian thought and to our analysis of literary dialogue. For what Bakhtin calls the "addressivity" of speech genres posits the dynamic reception of any utterance, the continual resounding of dialogic echoes and resonances through a series of respondents. "An essential (constitutive) marker of the utterance," he writes, "is its quality of being directed to someone" ("Speech" 95). The present theory of dialogue thus defines the word as always already containing its own response: in the context of "addressivity," narration necessarily assumes and takes into account its reception. "The entire utterance is constructed," he goes on, "in anticipation of encountering this response" (94). What is more, such anticipation includes a narrator's cognizance of not only his auditor's response but also his own narration as *itself* responding to its rhetorical precursors. In Bakhtin's terms,

> Each utterance is filled with echoes and reverberations of other utterances to which it is related by the communality of the sphere of speech communication. Every utterance must be regarded primarily as a *response* to preceding utterances of the given sphere (we understand the word "response" here in the broadest sense). Each utterance refutes, affirms, supplements, and relies on the others, presupposes them to be known, and somehow takes them into account. (91)

Addressivity thus locates the "listener or partner" directly within the dialogic matrix: each narrator both reacts to and generates a corresponding field of rhetorical resonance.

If we return to literary texts, then, and to the many dialogues within Romantic literature, we find this addressivity represented in terms of a textual audience, an internally incorporated auditor who, as we have noted, becomes a surrogate for dialogic form. We have further noted that this form persists even when a given auditor remains silent, implicit, or for the moment forgotten. Bakhtin specifically includes within his typology of addressees an "indefinite, unconcretized *other*," undelineated by verbal acknowledgment or overt rhetorical markers ("Speech" 95). Here again, the very position of an auditor implies the structure of a dialogue, with its consequent implications and resonances. As Bakhtin writes elsewhere, "Being heard as such is already a dialogic relation" ("Text" 127). Even the mute listener, then, stands as a figure for literary addressivity. Hence in Romantic literature, the recurrence of silent witnesses like Dorothy

Wordsworth, Hartley Coleridge, Charles Lamb, and even Wordsworth and Coleridge still enacts and sustains a poetics of dialogue.

These auditors further represent several nineteenth-century versions of a poetic trope that spans the continuum of literary history.
"Each epoch," writes Bakhtin, "each literary trend and literary-artistic
style, each literary genre within an epoch or trend, is typified by its
own special concepts of the addressee of the literary work, a special
sense and understanding of its reader, listener, public, or people"
("Speech" 98). In the Romantic era, moreover, this "special concept
of the addressee" focuses on listeners who, if they are not always
addressed in the "language of men," nonetheless communicate in the
form and style of quotidian dialogue, in what Bakhtin terms the "familiarization of styles." Wordsworth's avowed attempt to write in
what he terms "simple and unelaborated" forms that "in no respect
differ from the most unimpassioned conversation" parallels Bakhtin's
discussion of familiar, "intimate genres and styles [that] are based on
a maximum internal proximity of the speaker and addressee" (*Prose*
1:124, 154; "Speech" 97). When Wordsworth advocates an aesthetic
characterized by unelaborated style and conversational form, his formulation closely resembles Bakhtin's notion of a familiar, immediate
style that assumes the rhetorical position of an addressee. In both
cases, the conversational "familiarization" of literary language derives
from dialogic forms, from those structures that invoke even implicit
addressees. As Bakhtin concludes, "Familiar and intimate genres and
styles (as yet very little studied) reveal extremely clearly the depen-
dence of style on a certain sense and understanding of the addressee
. . . on the part of the speaker, and on the addressee's actively responsive understanding" (97).

Hence much as Wordsworth values a poetry based on familiar,
unelaborated style, what he calls "ordinary conversation," Bakhtin's
idea of dialogue is a poetics unencumbered by prescriptive definitions
of formal language and convention. Bakhtin reminds us that the "familiarization of styles opened literature up to layers of language that
had previously been under speech constraint" ("Speech" 97). At the
same time, we know that Wordsworth's stylistic revolution challenged
both the literary and political beliefs of his era; here again, such
a revolution parallels Bakhtin's description of how unconventional
language comes to supplant established poetic forms. He writes,
"When the task was to destroy traditional official styles and world
views that had faded and become conventional, familiar styles became
very significant in literature" (97). According to this view, both familiar and intimate styles — the ones most prevalent in dialogic forms —

become a force in literary history, a movement that seeks to revamp poetic form, to recreate literary expectations. Here, too, such a movement recalls Wordsworth's own attempt to challenge the "present state of the public taste," those "known habits of association" and convention that govern a reader's expectations of poetic narrative and diction (*Prose* 1:120, 122). In this context, Wordsworth's "familiar" language, his recurrent incorporation of an addressee, and his overall deployment of literary dialogue become ways of rewriting "traditional official styles and world views that had faded and become conventional." We can locate Wordsworth within a general Romantic tendency to challenge these "traditional official styles," to redefine poetic style by incorporating dialogic genres within literary language. In every era, Bakhtin suggests, "certain speech genres set the tone for the development of literary language" ("Speech" 65).[16]

In considering this "development of literary language," moreover, we should ask not only how the Romantic era usurps "traditional official style" but also how it illustrates the capacity of the utterance to incorporate and reconstitute other voices. Not only does the poetic speaker anticipate his addressee's response but the individual utterances of each are actually "aware of and mutually reflect one another" ("Speech" 91). In this sense, the

> speech experience of each individual is shaped and developed in continuous and constant interaction with others' individual utterances. This experience can be characterized to some degree as the process of *assimilation*—more or less creative—of others' words. . . . Our speech, that is, all our utterances (including creative works), is filled with others' words, varying degrees of otherness or varying degrees of "our-ownness," varying degrees of awareness and detachment. These words of others carry with them their own expression, their own evaluative tone, which we assimilate, rework, and re-accentuate. ("Speech" 89)

It is this capacity for the creative assimilation of others' voices — for reworking utterances from even disparate places and times — that illuminates Romantic notions of temporal unity, elision, and recovery. In Bakhtin's terms, "Two utterances, *separated from one another both in time and in space*, knowing nothing of one another, when they are compared semantically, reveal *dialogic relations*," even if their topics overlap only tangentially ("Text" 124, emphasis added). These "dialogic relations" constitute a kind of linguistic matrix or echo chamber, a complex whole that concatenates even widely separate voices. "Each word," Bakhtin goes on, "contains voices that are sometimes infinitely distant, unnamed, almost impersonal . . .

almost undetectable, and voices resounding nearby and simultaneously" (124). In Romantic terms, this convergence of disparate voices
recalls Wordsworth's notion of an aural continuum, of "memory
. . . as a dwelling-place / For all sweet sounds and harmonies." Such a
"dwelling-place" of voices amounts to a rhetorical lineage, connecting
expostulation and reply over many generations.

Because of this capacity of dialogue to assimilate utterances from
distant periods, the form also recalls de Man's definition of the rhetoric of Romantic temporality — that capacity for language to mediate
time, to place the prelapsarian child in view of the bereft adult. For de
Man, Wordsworth's poetic language stresses this moment of temporal
transition from one world to the other, this "state of suspension" in
which "time finds itself preserved, without losing the movement of
passing away which makes it real" (*Rhetoric* 55, 54, 56). As a result,
such language enables the Romantic poet to keep "sight of that im-
mortal sea / Which brought us hither," a sea of primal echoes and
aural "glories." Although nothing can bring back the hour of primor-
dial knowledge, poetic dialogue represents a kind of verbal linkage, a
series of rhetorical echoes that connect remembered past with present
utterance. This mnemonic "utterance," writes Bakhtin, "is a link in
the chain of speech communication, and it cannot be broken off
from the preceding links that determine it both from within and from
without, giving rise within it to unmediated responsive reactions and
dialogic reverberations" ("Speech" 94). It is this "dialogic reverbera-
tion" from "preceding links" that attests that the poet "Can in a moment travel thither, / And see the Children sport upon the shore";
although one can never abridge time, one can reclaim it in the form
of rhetorical resonance, through a dialogic liaison that essentially
elides temporal distinction. In a sense, then, dialogue represents the
"faith that looks through death," the linguistic recovery of that "primal sympathy / Which having been must ever be."

This link with a rhetorical past, with a primal "other," again
enables the poet to represent responses from a variety of temporal
eras. We must bear in mind, however, that these rhetorical responses
are a function not of any identifiable reader but of dialogue itself. As
a result, the analysis of these dialogic responses differs significantly
from those approaches known collectively as reader-response theory.
In the present context, the addressee is less an index of reader response
than a representation of dialogue: a synecdoche for the interactive
voices that constitute a text. These voices include an author's imagined
respondents, incorporated auditors, and other representative characters — personae who, though they may provide various examples of

reading, suggest that a writer often reassigns or rotates this role among a cast of speakers and listeners. More to the point, then, are those few studies that have begun to conceive of the internal auditor not as a reader-surrogate but as one among many reactions within a textual chorus.[17] Yet even when such auditors are absent—when a work offers no direct, textual evidence of audience reception—it is still contained within a matrix of response, a network that not only situates its internal voices but locates itself in relation to other, separate works as well. The response to a given text accordingly includes not only readers or reader-surrogates but also other texts themselves. Reviews, synopses, and even hearsay constitute a dialogic arena of co-respondence. According to this view, the incorporated addressee embodies not a particular reader's response but an array of mutually responsive voices. The addressee bespeaks a composite text, a polyphonic discourse in which call and response are indistinguishable, in which each response is itself a "call." Taken together, they compose a field of mutually resonant utterances.

Instead of limiting literary auditors to the domain of reception, then, dialogics strives to encompass a much broader spectrum of those rhetorical relations associated with a text. Bakhtin begins, for instance, by characterizing the speaker's discourse as a *"product of the social interaction of three components: — the speaker* (author), *the listener* (reader), and *the one of whom* (or of which) *they speak* (the hero)" ("Discourse" 17). In this sense, all listeners become interlocutors, voices within a tripartite linkage of social utterance. It is crucial to recall, moreover, that Romantic discourse specifically stresses these listeners—along with their dialogic implications—by portraying them as *actual characters* within the text. Although the Romantic work will occasionally invoke a disembodied reader, the overwhelming majority of these auditors are identified as rhetorically incarnate—manifested in the language of deictics, demonstratives, and prolepsis within the text. Unlike the "Dear Reader" allusion of so many Victorian novels, Romantic literature seeks to instantiate dialogue by explicitly inscribing a listener's position into the text.

VII

If we go on to consider the actual language of Romantic dialogue, we come to recognize that our normative conceptions of conversational call-and-response soon collapse. If we consider the alleged "response" of, say, the child addressees in "We are Seven," "Anecdote for Fathers," or even "The Idiot Boy," we begin to see that such interlocutors offer neither reciprocation nor corroboration, nor even assent. Auditors like the stricken Wedding Guest, the indifferent Babe, and the nominally pensive Sara represent not a language of complementarity but a rhetoric of resistance. Indeed, *what is most striking about Romantic auditors is that they are agons*, that they effect an epistemology of opposition. Although the addressivity of the utterance posits an interlocutor's reception, Romantic dialogue offers a countervailing "response" in which a listener misjudges, denies, or recoils from a respective narrator. Similarly, in the novels we are considering, nearly every listener fails to apprehend what he hears. Characters like Victor Frankenstein, Lockwood, and Marlow's listeners on the Thames have gone down in literary history as auditory boors, incapable of discerning the imaginative power of the stories they hear. They emerge as either uninformed, uncomprehending, or enigmatically silent. More surprisingly, such bogus listeners often become the lens through which we view our primary narrator, as if these authors had incorporated an intentionally skewed frame of reference into their works. Generally speaking, while dialogue persists during these literary encounters, communicative exchange does not. Indeed, we might begin to draw a distinction here between dialogue and colloquy— a dichotomy in which colloquy connotes reciprocal exchange while dialogue signifies a broader set of rhetorical interactions that proceed despite verbal imbalance, conflict, and agonism.

Of course, in some ways this auditory agon recalls the process of poetic revisionism discussed by Harold Bloom, that "influential" mode by which authors rewrite their forebears in a patricidal regress of "poetic misprision."[18] Bloom defines this poetically agonistic "spirit . . . as contesting for supremacy, with other spirits, with anteriority, and finally with every earlier version of itself" (*Agon* viii). In this sense, such an overtly combative "contest" has much in common with the kind of thwarted interaction we are defining. Yet within many Romantic works, we must also consider those agonistic relations that involve a less eristic expression of bafflement, dismay, and even silence. Such resistance involves the desire not just to "swerve from inherited words" (21) but, in a larger sense, to respond to them— to include them within the broader linguistic context of dialogic reaction, anticipation, and what Bakhtin sees as projective addressivity. Within this latter context, then, literary agons not only respond to previous utterances but anticipate future ones as well: they address not just "anteriority" but also a kind of proleptic posterity, in the form of expected rejoinders, rhetorical premonitions, and presumptive response. Such transtemporal responsiveness derives, moreover, from a model of actual interchange, from "dialogic intercourse among people" (*Poetics* 111). As such, its operations extend beyond the primarily textual "misreading" stressed by Bloom and look instead toward the more broadly dialogic "event," toward interactions that include the spoken word, the act, and even culture itself (279).

According to this approach, then, the primary mode of agonistic interaction is neither Freudian nor psychological but, rather, historically Socratic and linguistically dialogic. Indeed, within this latter context, poetic agonism takes on a pointedly rhetorical purpose in sustaining both ongoing, investigative openness and Socratic anacrisis: the "provocation of the word by the word." Here again, such rhetoric deploys agonism not just to "contest for supremacy" but to "dialogize thought, . . . carry it into the open, turn it into a rejoinder, attach it to dialogic intercourse among people" (*Poetics* 111).

Such dialogic agonism follows directly, moreover, from the history of classical forms. Walter J. Ong has traced such formal opposition not only to the classical study of "rhetoric" and "logic" but also to what he terms the "adversativeness of language and thought" (*Fighting* 34). For Ong, the addressee countermands a respective speaker in order to perpetuate a cycle of "qualification." In his formulation, "the ultimate paradigm or model" for such qualificatory exchange

> is . . . conversation itself, dialogue about a particular matter, in which each statement by one interlocutor needs qualification from the other interlocutor's statement in order to move toward fuller truth. Dialogue entails a certain negativity, for there is always at least some subtle negative element in any articulated dialogic response. . . . This negative element is a response to the limitations of the original statement. And the response requires further qualification from the first interlocutor. There is opposition here but no head-on collision, which stops dialogue. (*Fighting* 32)

Ong's version of "dialogic response" here presupposes a listener's "negativity," a rhetorical skepticism that stems from a cultural disposition toward "dispute or verbal struggle" (*Fighting* 34).[19] At the same time, he notes that the classical "Greek fascination with the agonistic structures of speech and thought spread and continued through the West," and underscores the particularly Western manifestations of this formal struggle. Within this cultural framework, the Romantic interpretation of these "agonistic structures" constitutes part of the history of nineteenth-century rhetoric.[20]

It is not extraordinary, then, that this tradition of Romantic skepticism would manifest itself in the form of a particular poetic rhetoric. Susan J. Wolfson, for instance, has located such skepticism in the poetic question, whether it be syntactically expressed or rhetorically subsumed. In either case, such "questions show the poet trying to apprehend mystery, to explore regions where familiar paths of understanding are blocked" (25). She then goes on to suggest how, in response to these questions, any "answers, if they are accessible, are often ambiguous, inadequate, unstable, or so tidy as to appear to parody rather than confirm the desires they satisfy" (21). In the present context, moreover, it is this notion of the bogus "answer"—the "ambiguous, inadequate, unstable" response—that also illustrates what we have been calling the agonism of Romantic dialogue. For the agonistic auditor actually embodies the dubitable answer, that adversative quality of dialogic response. Such a listener in fact demonstrates the impossibility of any ultimate, synoptic answer, or of any conclusion to the maieutic process. However diverse these oppositional auditors appear—whether they manifest an unstable reaction, a "subtle negativity," or a more overtly agonistic challenge—they will necessarily inhabit those interrogatory "regions where familiar paths of understanding are blocked."

VIII

Hence the poetic question, in conjunction with the blocked answer, comes to incarnate Romantic agonism. We should not assume, however, that this unanswered query signifies the end of the poetic process, the impossibility of poetic comprehension, or the futility of the interrogative mode. Nor should we simply stop at the prevalent conclusion that these bogus responses bespeak some general fallibility of language, some semiotic gap between representation and phenomena. Instead, we would do well to consider dialogue from at least two distinct perspectives. On one hand, we must recognize that dialogue may nominally collapse—in the sense of a conversational breakdown or similar rift within normative exchange. Yet on the other hand, we have noted that such breakdowns may betoken not discoursal failure but dialogic agonism, in that the actual operations of dialogue will often continue to operate. Hence dialogue may *collapse* in the sense that it ceases to entail balanced, equilateral exchange, or at times even the rudiments of communication; yet such collapse need *not* signify *failure*, since the meliorative processes of dialogue — including its potentially hermeneutic and ontological effects — will proceed despite the lack of mutually corroborative interlocutors.

Such ongoing processes will include, then, the kind of agonistic questioning we have begun to discuss. By maintaining the form of poetic interrogation — the structure of recurrent question followed by inadequate answer — the Romantic work sustains an exegetical process of interpretation and understanding. Before analyzing the dynamics of this process, however, we must further distinguish it from several other investigatory forms of rhetoric, grouped loosely under the rubric "dialectic." Although these latter forms also operate more or less interpretively, we shall find that the assumptions behind them differ markedly from those of dialogue.

Within the various historical accounts of classical rhetoric, "dialectic" has emerged as a relatively imprecise, catchall term that frequently suggests a closure-directed, consummate argument with deductive intent. To begin with, then, we must stress that such a conclusive notion of dialectic is fundamentally opposed to the ongoing, open-ended form that we have defined as dialogue, particularly in its Bakhtinian formulation. If dialectic is the rhetoric of argument — a specifically terminal form — then dialogue is the language of dynamic, continuing interchange. Indeed, Bakhtin specifically links the ongoing nature of the latter with the accretive "process" of "Socratic dialogue" — as distinguished from the Platonic bastardization that "transformed [it] into a simple form for expounding already found, ready-made irrefutable truth," a pedagogical "form for training neophytes" (*Poetics* 110). In contrast to the "already found, ready-made" truisms established by Platonic dialectic, Bakhtin stresses the ongoing construction of knowledge, an epistemological openness that he traces to the "Socratic method of dialogically revealing the truth." Such a method holds that knowledge belongs not to an "exclusive possessor," but "is born *between people* collectively searching for truth, in the process of their dialogic interaction" (109, 110).

This distinction between the dynamic, collective generation of truth and the static possession of preexistent meaning — between dialogue and dialectic — runs throughout Bakhtin's writings on language. If one form presumes a "dialectical synthesis" between thesis and antithesis, we have seen that in dialogue "there can be no talk . . . of any sort of synthesis. . . . It is not the idea as a monologic deduction, even if dialectical, but the event of an interaction of voices" that is central (*Poetics* 279). This emphasis on the co-constructed "event" again suggests that, for Bakhtin, the process of generating an idea takes precedence over the idea itself, over the fully evolved content that is central to Platonic forms. Instead, Bakhtin again emphasizes the "interrelation between perceiving human beings, created by the varying degrees of their participation in the idea" — a participation that, in the Platonic context, is "ultimately extinguished in the fullness of the idea itself" (280). By way of further differentiation, he goes on to suggest that if dialectic presumes a bilateral exchange between co-occurring speakers, dialogue can take place among a diversity of distant voices and discourses. As we shall see in our discussion of Wordsworth, this capacity for dialogue to extend diachronically, across both time and space, distinguishes it from any conventional notions of real-time dialectic. Within a Bakhtinian universe at least, then, dialogue and dialectic function as antipodes.

Yet to eliminate the many forms of dialectic language entirely from this study would be to ignore a rhetoric that sheds light on several crucial features of Romantic literature. For even as the Romantics came to mistrust linguistic signification, they hypostatized *historical* rhetoric — including not merely the formal "reconciliation of opposites" and "contraries" but also the mode that "does not stop at *immediate* understanding but presses on further and further (indefinitely)" ("Text" 127). It is this latter dynamic that characterizes the relentless Romantic quest, explicitly sustained by the presumed responses of a designated listener. We have noted that such unending, irreconcilable exchanges differ vastly from the kind of finalized arguments that are normally associated with conclusive forms of dialectic.

Here again, however, we should further distinguish this truncated dialectic from the more genuine, original rhetoric promulgated by Socrates. As we have suggested, the notion of a peremptory, closure-directed dialectic actually comes down to us through Plato, who in translating Socrates' dialogues into the fixed medium of print is forced to misrepresent the ongoing, open-ended, and processive nature of the form. In Socrates' original formulation, the fundamentally oral quality of dialectic precluded any such notion of a forced, premature conclusiveness. On the contrary, the very immediacy of the form ensured that any interlocutor could continue the process of response, interrogation, and qualification within an ongoing search for viable premises. If persuasion was a by-product of such a process, it came not in the form of coerced finality but as a participatory agreement concerning provisional truth. According to this concept of dialogue, then, philosophical meaning is represented not as a unilateral lecture or document but as a jointly created, jointly sustained process: an aggregation of voices. Meaning is not proclaimed but constructed, fashioned, and revised. It is best depicted not as a record but as an action, extending beyond the boundaries of the closed text. As Tullio Maranhão has noted in describing this specifically "open-ended" process, "truth was not unilaterally and monologically asserted by a text or speech, but was generated in the dialogical exchanges between two or more truth seekers." Socrates "chose dialectic and dialogue because . . . knowledge could be restituted to the interior of man, and the habitude of its awakening could grow in real situations—not in the absence of one of the parties, momentarily represented by a text" (235, 171, 221).[21]

Throughout this study, then, I posit a Bakhtinian "rhetoric" that extends beyond those classical forms associated with Platonic supremacy, public competition, and monologic authority. In his "Discourse on the Novel," Bakhtin deplores such notions of rhetorical singularity and closure, in favor of a more comprehensive model that, while it may include agonism, nevertheless insists upon the multivoicedness of ongoing exchange and pluralistically generated meaning. My own analyses of figures and tropes are thus intended to invoke and elaborate this more comprehensive model of polyphonic rhetoric. Again, though, Bakhtin's description of discourse may still overlap with certain classical formulations. As Don H. Bialostosky and others have noted, Bakhtin's notions include several aspects of the situational, epideictic, and deliberative aspects of formal rhetoric (cf. "Criticism"). In the same way, I shall demonstrate that Bakhtin's characterization often partakes of the kind of ongoing agonism and Socratic perpetuation that recall particular classical traditions.

IX

It is this cogeneration of collective meaning—this interpretive quest for "knowledge" in the actual "exchanges between two or more truth seekers"—that underlies the process of Socratic dialogue as originally formulated. Here again, such a process reveals much about what we have begun to call the interpretive impetus behind Romantic dialogue—an impulse manifested, first, in the aforementioned use of questions, and second, in the dialogic representation of orality. Indeed, both characteristics prove to be central to a yet another approach to interpretive rhetoric — one that, though it deploys the term *dialectic*, serves as a forerunner to our conception of Romantic dialogue. In this schema, Hans-Georg Gadamer begins with much the same figure that Wolfson sees as quintessentially Romantic: the interrogative mode. "Discourse that is intended to reveal something," he writes, "requires that that thing be opened up by the question. For this reason, the way in which dialectic proceeds is by way of the question and answer or, rather, by way of the development of all knowledge through the question" (326).

For Gadamer, moreover, this dialectic discourse is again agonistic by definition: he predicates the form upon the unanswered question, the ongoing dialogue between inexorable query and flawed response. Within Romantic rhetoric, then, we might reconsider the poetic figure of the recursive question or narrative: when Coleridge's Mariner, for instance, is compelled to respond to the Guest's ineluctable question ("Why look'st thou so?"), his response constitutes not so much a reply as a retelling, a provocation to further inquiry. In Gadamer's terms, "Dialectic, as the art of asking questions, proves itself only because the person who knows how to ask questions is able to persist in his questioning, which involves being able to preserve his orientation towards openness. The art of questioning is that of being able *to go on asking questions* . . . " (330; cf. 331). In the context of dialogue, we can say that the agonistic respondent originates this process of interrogative exchange: the recursivity of the specifically disputed question sustains the dialogic process.

Gadamer's emphasis on "discourse that is intended to reveal something" is thus useful for our return to dialogue. His analysis enables us to formulate, in fact, a constitutive feature of the latter: that dialogue is inherently hermeneutic, a struggle toward the "development of all knowledge through the question." Though the dialogic equivalent of such "development" is at once halting, unending, and provisional, it is nevertheless related to what Gadamer calls the "process of question and answer, giving and taking, talking at cross purposes and seeing each other's point [that] performs that communication of meaning which, with respect to the written tradition, is the task of hermeneutics" (331). Here, too, such a hermeneutic "task" casts dialogue as its potentially interpretive method, even as it reveals this method to be interminable and self-questioning. Within the "written tradition" of poetic discourse, moreover, the literary rendering of this dialogic process is itself an epistemological act, a way of retelling and resynthesizing the world for an other. Bakhtin repeatedly points out, for instance, the "role of these others, for whom my thought becomes actual thought for the first time (and thus also for my own self as well)" ("Speech" 94). Elsewhere, Bakhtin's reading of Marx and Engels's *German Ideology* stresses the same concept, in which "only thought uttered in the word becomes a real thought for another person and only in the same way is it a thought for myself" ("Text" 127). Dialogue with the other thus reconstitutes unformed notions into "thought," and modulates them into ongoing interpretation. Again, Ong's formulation suggests that all narrative statement "needs qualification from the other interlocutor's statement in order to move toward fuller truth" (*Fighting* 32).

This hermeneutic motive behind dialogue, this rhetorical "move toward fuller truth," becomes particularly pertinent in the context of nineteenth-century form — which, as we have suggested, enacts the epistemological process of addressing "contradiction, conflict, and problematic alternatives." Such an interpretive enterprise actually distinguishes the prominent literary forms of the century, including such major frame narratives and addresses as *Frankenstein, Wuthering Heights*, and *Heart of Darkness*. For the narrative apostrophes in these works form part of a similarly epistemological process, a dialogic act of interpretation applied to such textual problems as Victor's Prometheanism, Heathcliff's alien casuistry, and Marlow's mendacity. Instead of leaving us with only circumscribed vision, such addresses actually keep the possibility of interpretation open by sustaining a rhetorical process of understanding, by enacting a series of hermeneutic forms. In such cases, apostrophic form functions not only as an interrogative trope but also as a heuristic method.

X

We have also suggested that this heuristic dimension of dialogue is grounded not only in the interpretive tradition of the reiterated question but in the ongoing, spoken nature of Socratic exchange as well. It is no coincidence, moreover, that the Romantics would gravitate toward this oral form, and attempt to transcribe its characteristics within literary discourse. When Wordsworth redefines poetic diction in terms of "ordinary conversation," "everyday" words, and the "language of men," he is attempting to represent at least some qualities of

oral dialogue within his written verse. Generally speaking, the Romantics' recurrent concern with conversational encounters, colloquial
diction, and the "spontaneous" immediacy of the impassioned imagination reveals a desire to inscribe the language of orality into their
printed discourse. Such a desire accounts for the tendency of the
Romantic text to "absorb and digest" the spoken language, to establish a "communality" of literary voices, and thereby to link utterances
"separated from one another both in time and in space" ("Speech" 62,
91; "Text" 124). Their prefaces, essays, and other commentary on
language betray a pained mistrust of the written word, an attempt to
reach beyond the dead letter of the static text, to locate poetry within
the interactive orality of vocative forms.[22] Hence, in Gadamer's terms,
"that which is handed down in literary form is brought back out of
the alienation in which it finds itself and into the living presence of
conversation" (331).

Thus the Romantic desire to reconstitute oral discourse suggests
what Bialostosky, in characterizing Wordsworth's narrative diction,
terms a "poetics of speech." For Bialostosky, such a formulation distinguishes Wordsworth's poetry as a representation of vocalization,
in which a narrator is either "speaking himself [or] repeating the
speech of his characters" (*Tales* 12). Unlike the Aristotelian concept —
where poetry imitates many forms of dramatic "action" — Wordsworth's definition follows the Platonic imperative in which "there is
only the representation of telling or talking" (15). Following the work
of Barbara Herrnstein Smith, Bialostosky goes on to discuss lyric
poems as fictive representations of actual utterances — works that,
though they retain their status as representational artifacts, are nonetheless "to be understood first *as* possible voices speaking the way
natural human voices do" (17). In Smith's terms, such lyrics "typically
represent personal utterances"; more generally, she suggests that the
"various genres of literary art — for example, dramatic poems, tales,
odes, lyrics — can to some extent be distinguished according to what
types of discourse — for example, dialogues, anecdotes of past events,
public speeches, and private declarations — they characteristically represent" (8; cf. 30). For Wordsworth, then, poetry takes its cadence
not (as Coleridge believed) from an abstracted concept of poetic meter
and decorum but from human speech itself.[23]

It is this foregrounding of the human speech event, moreover,
that also accounts for the Romantic emphasis on both agonistic form
and "ordinary conversation." In Ong's words, "The fate of agonistic
structures is tied in with the history of *verbalization*. . . . Words are

essentially oral events. They came into being in sound. They can never be totally disconnected from sound. To realize the meaning of a word, including the written or printed word, one must refer it somehow to the oral world, directly or indirectly, in speech or in imagination" (*Fighting* 26, emphasis added). Here again, Ong goes on to link such orality with the tradition of verbal contest and forensic opposition. "Historically," he writes, "some of the most conspicuous manifestations of adversativeness in the human lifeworld across the globe have been in speech itself. In distant ages, speech, together with thought, was a highly combative activity, especially in its more public manifestations — much more combative than we in our present-day technological world are likely to assume or are even willing to believe" (*Fighting* 34). In reconsidering nineteenth-century genres, then, we can say that the Romantic preoccupation with specifically oral encounters, interrogative rhetoric, and conversational oppositions locates these works in the "oral world," whether "directly or indirectly, in speech or in imagination." Indeed, we can often characterize Romantic writing in terms of those figures, tropes, and terms that describe spoken discourse. Even when such terms are used metaphorically, as often occurs in Bakhtin's works, they nevertheless identify particular oral effects and parallels — features that, at the same time, serve to illuminate the qualities of literary dialogue.

XI

If dialogue embodies the epistemological struggle to fathom nineteenth-century irony, we have also suggested that it can represent an endeavor to comprehend the self, the boundaries of the Romantic "I." Literary dialogue seeks to address internal dilemmas by including them within an externalized exchange; as such, it operates not only as a hermeneutics of nature but also as an exegesis of the ego. This ontological effect emerges most explicitly, moreover, in the speaker's attempt to delineate the self before a listener. As Bakhtin writes, "I am conscious of myself and become myself only while revealing myself for another, through another, and with the help of another. The most important acts constituting self-consciousness are determined by a relationship toward another consciousness (toward a *thou*)" (*Poetics* 287). What Bakhtin calls "self-consciousness" thus becomes a function of dialogue, a form of verbal demarcation.

In order to foster this impetus toward selfhood, the Romantic speaker struggles to enact a parallel "relationship toward another consciousness." Here, too, the narrative address takes on ontological implications, since it is the very presence of this listening consciousness that defines the speaking self. Alterity thus acts to bound and delimit the conscious "I," which in turn develops incrementally during the process of addressing a "Thou." Indeed, for poets such as Coleridge, the locating of this definitive "Thou" is tantamount to selfhood; for him, the ego's "Consciousness" is a function of an externally directed "Conscience." He writes, "But for my conscience—i. e. my affections & duties towards others, I should have no Self—for Self is Definition . . . & is knowable only by Neighbourhood, or Relations" (*NB* 2:3231). What Coleridge refers to as the "Boundary" of the "Self" is thus defined by a conscience "towards others," a delineation consisting of close "Relations." Such "Relations" essentially distinguish the individual "Consciousness" and make it "knowable." As a result, when these relations with the other are manifested as dialogue, they become the rhetorical equivalent of an ontological "Boundary." In this sense, dialogue enables the ego to emerge within a process of contrast, differentiation, and eventual divergence.

It is this ontological process, moreover, that distinguishes the Romantic view of consciousness. Charles Rzepka has astutely noted that "self-consciousness requires the presence, real or imagined, explicit or implied, of another" (6). The self is accordingly "individuated by the minds of others, whose consciousness of me and of the world we all inhabit is fundamental and axiomatic to my self-definition" (16). For Rzepka, moreover, these others "embody" the ego as a perceivable self, individuated and objectified by an exterior consciousness. He goes on to say that "embodiment, the sense of possessing a body that others can perceive and recognize, is a prerequisite of self-consciousness and a sense of the real."[24]

Yet if the inclusion of others confers this notion of self-embodiment, we must also recognize that the self-affirming effects of this encounter derive from its specifically *linguistic* nature, its potential for colloquy. In this context, the ontological potential of Romantic form inheres not in the duality between subject and object but in the language that mediates between them—in the process of verbal dialogue. The "I" seeks both differentiation and delineation during the process of rhetorical interchange with an other. Here again, the arena of self-definition is not psychomachy but dialogue—since only the linguistic relation between "I" and "thou" can hypostatize the self. As Bakhtin writes, "In dialogue a person not only shows himself outwardly, but *he becomes for the first time that which he is*—and, we repeat, not only for others but for himself as well. *To be means to communicate dialogically*" (*Poetics* 252, emphasis added). According to this view, the ego engenders itself through a series of linguistic interchanges with an other. "Life," Bakhtin goes on, "by its very nature is dialogic. To live means to participate in dialogue: to ask questions, to heed, to respond, to agree, and so forth" (*Poetics* 293). The self thus effects its separateness by enabling dialogic contrast, by invoking and provoking an other.

That dialogue can thus define each of us as ontologically separate or unique is a function not only of its contrastive features but again of its orality. In this context, we can say that the oft-cited individuation of the Romantic self results in part from its association with an identifiable voice, since only the particularized voice can endow the "I" with an individual character or "face." Indeed, Romantic preoccupations with the recognizable self make it especially crucial to avoid the anonymity associated with the voiceless, faceless text. Deprived of such voices, the dialogic text takes on the depersonalized quality of what Bakhtin deplores as abstract dialectic and impersonal argumentation. Such depersonalization results when we "[t]ake a dialogue and remove the voices (the partitioning of voices), remove the intonations (emotional and individualizing ones), carve out abstract concepts and judgments from living words and responses, [and] cram everything into one abstract consciousness" ("Notes" 147). Only the definitiveness of voices—replete with "living words," "intonations," and "responses"—can act to "individualize" consciousness.

Hence the indications of orality, vocalization, and responsiveness within dialogue serve to demarcate and personalize the "I"—to give it, in effect, a face. In considering such dialogue *within literature*, however, we must bear in mind that these oralistic, "individualizing" effects emerge not because dialogue actually records the transcriptive character of an extant voice but because its essentially literary power is designed to fabulate such effects. In elaborating on the "voice" of literary dialogue, then, we must distinguish it from a mimetic record of its vocalized counterpart—from what Paul de Man refers to as its "phenomenalization" ("Voice" 55). Although dialogic praxis stresses the particularity of distinct speakers within a specific context, its literary version stands as a representation of such phenomena—as a rendering of the voice. Although it appropriates the signs of conversational exchange, it is in fact reproducing such scenarios, with all the linguistic slippage and nonphenomenal word-play of a written figure. It entails not transcription but inscription. Indeed, we have noted that even seemingly direct invocations to a reader extend beyond any referential signs of reader response, beyond the virtual "act of reading." It is in this sense, then, that we can agree with de Man's contention that the phenomenal "claim for vocal presence" is misguided, since the lyric, at least, never intends to describe verifiable voices with any phonological "accuracy of actual observation" (56, 61). In his terms, the genre as a whole "does not describe an entity," but rather seeks to allegorize it by means of rhetorical or "linguistic figuration."

With this last reference, however, de Man comes up against an antipathy between figurative rhetoric and dialogue. For, as Bakhtin has noted, the tendency to discuss rhetorical figuration in terms of fixed tropes has traditionally defined them as single-voiced — and as therefore fundamentally divergent from the necessarily plural and distinct voices that constitute dialogue. Yet even in specifically literary contexts, these dialogic voices are necessarily derived from multiple speakers who can be neither subsumed nor represented by the normally unitary figure of the trope. Hence while it would be mistaken to discuss literary dialogue in terms of a transcribed voice, it would be equally illusory to confine it to the monologic figure of the univocal trope.

Both the advantages and disadvantages of de Man's approach emerge when he extends his discussion to the rhetoric of address. His remarks prove to be particularly relevant to the present study's concern with apostrophe ("prosopopoeia" in classical terms), which he characterizes not as an address to an actual reader but as a figural interaction of "purely verbal" "systems" — a function of those semantic relations and "verbal plays" that remain exclusive to the realm of language (59, 60; cf. 55). For de Man, the apparent verisimilitude of prosopopoeia derives not from its adherence to a particular referent but from a kind of "hallucinatory effect" based on the "wiles of rhetoric" (63, 64). The very etymology of the figure affirms this departure from the referent; in de Man's terms, "*prosopon-poiein* means to *give a face* and therefore implies that the original face can be missing or nonexistent" (57).

In terms of the present study, however, we must also recognize that the figure of apostrophe is derived from interactions between authentic interlocutors — between speakers who are, as we have noted, necessarily distinct, plural in number, and defined by the voice. Within this framework, rhetoric becomes the study of quotidian exchange and the conversational scene, of interactions that are by definition both multifocal and multivocal. And, here again, the authenticity of such interaction will be reflected even when it is transposed and represented within literary contexts, such as the inscribing of apostrophe. Indeed, it would be a mistake to suggest that such prosopopoetic figures discount the extancy of the voice. As the foregoing etymology implies, "to give a face"—including the gateway or mouth of vocal expression—is to include the feature that is the very synecdoche of vocal interaction. This association reflects the sense in which all rhetoric must echo the voice from which it ultimately derives. As a result, though it would be a misnomer to characterize this literary voice as anything other than a figure—as anything more than (in de Man's terms) an "arbitrary" signification—it is nevertheless linked both metonymically and synecdochically to actual exchange. As de Man himself suggests, "The phenomenal and sensory properties of the signifier have to serve as guarantors for the certain existence of the signified and, ultimately, of the referent" ("Voice" 62).

To sustain this "existence of the signified," then, prosopopoeia is a figure that *plays* on authentic interaction; it is one of the few rhetorical tropes that is inherently personal. Indeed, all such dialogic rhetoric—and in particular apostrophe—is founded upon this authentic, anthropomorphically based exchange. Only this foundation can delimit, in de Man's terms, the "'here' and 'now' of the poem" ("Voice" 62). While literary dialogue cannot incorporate the referential, transcriptive aspects of authentic interaction, Bakhtin does suggest that it can inscribe the textual correlatives of these social dynamics. Here again, in discussing the relation between relatively "complex" (including literary) genres and what he calls "primary" (including spoken) genres, he states that the former "absorb and digest various primary (simple) genres that have taken form in unmediated speech communion. These primary genres are altered and assume a special character when they enter into complex ones. They lose their immediate relation to actual reality and to the real utterances of others" ("Speech" 62). Again, literary genres tend to "absorb and digest" the forms of "unmediated speech communion." At the same time, however, such absorption is not without literary transmutation. Much as de Man stresses the "nonreferentiality" (63) of figures like apostrophe, Bakhtin maintains that the elements of spoken rhetoric "lose their immediate relation to actual reality" when they are inscribed as written forms—such as literary dialogue. By imprinting the diversified (and unpredictable) scenes of conversational interaction, such dialogue can juxtapose, reorient, and realign them in combinations that would be impossible in the phenomenal world. By inditing the various registers of spoken discourse, literary dialogue necessarily reframes, recontextualizes, and reinterprets them within the verbal play of printed rhetoric.

Still, one of the central tenets of this book is that the Bakhtinian formulation actually accounts for the depiction of *social process* within literary rhetoric—for the dynamics of interactive discourse—more than does de Man's notion of figuration. Accordingly, when this study speaks of an externalized voice or other, it refers not to the phenomenalism of an "external referent" but to the linguistic expression of social externalization—to a transposed, translated, and thereby reinterpreted interaction among now literary voices. When we speak of rhetorical "presence," we refer not to empirical vocalization but to a linguistic recasting of worldly intercourse.

XII

To consider dialogue as a whole, then, is to consider a concept that extends beyond the phenomenal, beyond the oralistic, and beyond the formal. As we have noted, Bakhtin's analysis characterizes dialogue in terms of a speaker's "self-consciousness," invention, and "thought"; in doing so, it reaches beyond formalism to suggest the actual effects of, and reasons behind, this structure—to suggest, for instance, its specifically ontological and interpretive consequences for the poetic "I." Such effects are a direct result of what we have called the extrapolation of the poetic subject, its capacity to reach beyond its autotelic confines. In particular, the present study argues that the nineteenth-century externalization of the "I" manifests itself as a desire for dialogic form—for a rhetoric that is at once ontological, hermeneutic, temporal, and above all, agonistic. Put another way, the Romantic subject attempts to instantiate the dialogue that can interpret the self, delineate its origins, and define its temporality—by giving voice to those adverse voices surrounding the "I." Here again, this augmentation of the Romantic ego is best characterized not as self and other but as a more inclusive matrix of manifold utterances: a rhetorical acknowledgment that the Romantic subject is delimited by conflicting resonances, that it actually consists of and is constituted by a profusion of voices, intertextual and intratextual, spoken and written, remembered and anticipated.

* * *

The implications of this poetics of dialogue for Romantic literature become apparent when we begin to examine its manifestations in the first-generation poems of the period, particularly those by Wordsworth and Coleridge. These poets — the subject of Part I — exemplify the Romantic preoccupation with fractured and discrepant voices, with voices that define their very being in terms of their agonistic relation to one another.

Part I analyzes the significance behind this agonistic relation between interlocutors, behind the particularly disparate personae that characterize Romantic dialogue. At this point, however, the comparison between Wordsworth and Coleridge leads us to a crucial distinction in the ways that they deploy this poetic agonism. In Wordsworth's case, the recalcitrance of child addressees in such lyrics as "We are Seven" and "Anecdote for Fathers" represents not a radical disjunction but a kind of rhetorical dissonance. Indeed, the gap between speaker and listener often manifests itself as a partial opportunity — a mode of knowing what can and cannot be known. It accordingly becomes a locus of didacticism, as speakers claim to "learn" the opaque insights of leech-gatherers, vagrants, and child-seers. However vexed this learning appears, it nevertheless takes the form of a communication, and is thus amenable to halting attempts at identification, pedagogy, and rapprochement. At the same time, this flawed communication can also become a model for reading in these lyrics: poetic auditors often personify the lack of traditional judgment and inhibition that Wordsworth (in describing the many children in *Lyrical Ballads*) refers to as imaginative "idleness." Such listeners come to represent the combination of latent curiosity and "wise passiveness" that the poet sought to inculcate in his readers. In this sense, Wordsworthian resistance between speaker and auditor presents itself as a heuristic, an attempt to demonstrate that the "understanding of the Reader must necessarily be in some degree enlightened." Although agonism persists, Wordsworth is nonetheless *"creating* the taste by which he is to be enjoyed" (*Prose* 1:127 [1850], 3:80).

For Coleridge, however, the situation differs drastically. While he professes a similar attitude toward his readers, he in fact represents a more divisive struggle between an intransigent auditor and a cryptic speaker. If the gap between Wordsworth's speaker and listener is a dissonance, that between Coleridge's interlocutors is an *aporia* — an unapproachable disjunction that denies all attempts at didacticism or rapport. As the following chapters show, the Coleridgean auditor provides neither corroboration nor reception but a means toward exposure — what the notebooks refer to as "Outness." In a poem like the

"Rime," for instance, we can read the Mariner's address to his aural interpreter as an attempt to effect this symbolic "Outness" and exposure. Although Coleridge clearly distinguishes himself from the Mariner, the poem enacts his own desire to expose what he variously refers to as his "secret lodger" or "hidden vice": the "Origin of moral Evil." While Wordsworth seeks to "endure and note / What was not understood," Coleridge attempts to "eloign and abalienate" this secret lodger, to bare it before the other (*Prelude* 14:335-36). He accordingly represents this exposure as a form of flawed confession (the Mariner asked the Hermit to "shrieve" him, to "wash away the Albatross's blood"). As the "Rime" suggests, however, the Hermit's inability to expiate the Mariner resembles the Guest's failure to comprehend him; in both cases, Coleridge represents a poetic address that ultimately fails to enable understanding. He needs to posit a counteractive listener, utterly at odds with his poetic protagonist.

In this sense, Coleridge's poetics become the paradigm for agonistic dialogue. The auditors represented in his poems provide the most explicit model of the poetic agon — a model that applies variously to many nineteenth-century works. In proposing this view of Coleridge's interlocutors, then, we question the prevailing one, which defines them as corroborators or "vicarious" representatives of his personal fears. Instead, it is his need for externalization — for the rhetorical expression of proleptic exposure — that defines his conceptions of conscience and self, and that challenges previous assumptions about the solipsism of the Romantic "I." At the same time, moreover, it is this same Coleridgean disjunction between speaker and listener that begins to explain the hermeneutic gaps in those prose works most often regarded as "Romantic" — the works considered in Part II of this study. As that section will demonstrate, it is this paradigmatic disjunction between interlocutors that ultimately accounts for the introduction of an interpretive figure into works like *Frankenstein, Wuthering Heights*, and *Heart of Darkness*.

2

"The Language of My Former Heart": Wordsworth, Bakhtin, and the Diachronic Dialogue

> It is necessary, first of all, to single out specifically the aspect of man's essential *becoming*.
>
> Bakhtin, *Speech Genres and Other Late Essays*

> They are as a creation in my heart;
> I look into past time as prophets look
> Into futurity. . . .
>
> Wordsworth, MS Fragment

> The tension between the narrative and the apostrophic can be seen as the generative force behind a whole series of lyrics. . . . In lyrics of this kind a temporal problem is posed: something once present has been lost or attenuated; this loss can be narrated but the temporal sequence is irreversible, like time itself. Apostrophes displace this irreversible structure by removing the opposition between presence and absence from empirical time and locating it in a discursive time. . . .
>
> Apostrophe resists narrative because its *now* is not a moment in a temporal sequence but a *now* of discourse, of writing.
>
> Jonathan Culler, "Apostrophe"

I

In reconstructing the history of such seminal lyrics as the Intimations Ode and "Tintern Abbey," Wordsworth scholars of the past decade have increasingly alluded to a continuum of influence—a matrix of commentary and response including, most prominently, Coleridge's own Ode and letters, but also works by Milton, Gray, Dryden, Burns, and others. Such a continuum — what Thomas McFarland has called a "symbiosis" or "intertwined" development — manifests itself as a variety of intertextual influences, distinguished by their relative proximity to or distance from the poem in question. In Paul Magnuson's view, for instance, this intertextuality amounts to an "extended lyric sequence or lyric dialogue," in which we can examine the "relationships between Coleridge's and Wordsworth's texts as though they were *one work*," as in fact Coleridge refers to them (*Wordsworth* 4). For Gene W. Ruoff, such textual relationships are similarly constitutive — part of a "confluence of diverse waves of influence" — though, unlike Magnuson, his "reading of the lyric sequence sees parody as a fundamental device" (16, 15). Yet whether these relations derive from parodic rewritings of a recent past, table-talk conversations with a contemporaneous poet, or Bloomian struggles with more distant, psychodynamic antecedents, such influences have come to define a kind of hermeneutic genetics in which interpretation emerges from a lyric's contextual history. For Wordsworth's Ode in particular, recent interpretations tend to construe the poem as a response to preceding historical traditions, involving, say, the erotic pastoral of the Renaissance or the carnivals of revolutionary France. Indeed, critics have differed markedly on whether such histories are actually elided or hypostatized by the premises of the poem (cf. Ruoff 284–88).

Still, whether such historical and cultural traditions are repudiated by the Ode — or whether (in Ruoff's terms) it constitutes an actual "recovery of human time" — we must recognize that these poems specifically apostrophize a vocal past, that they are essentially in dialogue with disinterred cultures. As such, we can view other lyrics by Wordsworth as extensions of this dialogue with temporality, this pendant desire both to meliorate and to thwart the "recovery" of history. What the following chapter argues is that such historical concerns are enacted within the rhetorical arena of Wordsworth's lyrics, so that they partake of such dialogic tropes as prosopopoeia, proleptic response, and poetic agonism. In this context, dialogue becomes the objective correlative of historical invocation: the tortuous relation to history is manifested as a linguistic recuperation of extinct voices.

We begin by suggesting, then, that Wordsworth's attempt to triangulate a relation between cultural history, his private past, and the poetic speaker is inscribed in the text as dialogue. We must ask, however, how such antecedents and influences are actually incorporated within Wordsworth's rhetoric—how he not only alludes to but also finally conjures and rewrites this personal history. We must also consider why such influences often manifest themselves as his most immediately invoked "others"—that is, as the Wordsworthian reader. And finally, we must reconsider the poetic roles of this Wordsworthian other, especially as they take on particular forensic, oralistic, and heuristic functions within the confines of lyric dialogue.

II

We can begin to address such questions if we consider that Wordsworth's celebrated concern for his readers' "taste" is in fact part of a larger desire to represent that vast "confluence of diverse waves of influence"—that externalized influence on the reflexive persona. We must accordingly bear in mind that Wordsworth's frequent exhortations to his audience extend far beyond any immediate concerns about reader response. Indeed, although we know that Wordsworth cared passionately about his audience's "immediate pleasure," recent criticism has also uncovered his more arch designs upon his readers: a desire to remold their "savage temper," to put them through paces that might reshape their "degrading thirst after outrageous stimulation (*Prose* 1:128, 130).[1] Unlike Byron, who sought to coax, delight, and educate by parodic example—to foster an essentially Horatian relation with his audience—Wordsworth's more overtly directive intention was to challenge "certain known habits of association." He felt it his "duty" not only to redirect the "public taste" but also to transmogrify the very language of poetry, the arbitrary and capricious habits of expression practiced by neoclassical lyricists.[2] Hence while we may question Keats's sense of being "bullied into a certain Philosophy" by Wordsworth, we must agree that the latter's aesthetic "has a palpable design upon us" (*Keats's Letters*, 2/3/1818). At the same time, moreover, we must consider that Wordsworth's preoccupation with both readers and other "external things" indicates not only didactic intention but ontological need as well—a need to orient the self in reference to external others, to "recall [himself] from this abyss of idealism to the reality" of the external world (*Poetical Works* IV:463). As Charles Rzepka has noted, Wordsworth seeks to "make for himself a real place in the temporal and finite world . . . —a place in history, which is to say, in the world of others" (32).

What is most striking, however, about this desire for an "external existence" is that it manifests itself in the very rhetoric of Wordsworth's poetry, in its linguistic form and genre. While numerous studies have plumbed his definition of poetic diction, less attention has been paid to the actual shape and dialogics of his lyrics. For in order to instantiate his affective "design," Wordsworth's rhetoric often incorporates the most immediate audience for his poems — those poetic respondents and auditors who listen within his works. Though few of his lyrics directly address a "reader" (as in "Heart-Leap Well," "Simon Lee," and "The Idiot Boy"), a remarkable number enact an actual dialogue between speaker and auditor — a spoken interchange that often represents Wordsworth's projections of a hypothetical audience. In portraying the various "tastes" or responses he envisions, he constructs a poetic microcosm — a literary encounter that replicates what he calls his "terms of engagement" with a reader. Such engagements emerge, moreover, in the form of both specific addresses to a respondent and more indirect, broadly aimed invocations. At the same time, they extend beyond mimetic analogues of reader response to more polyphonic representations of poetic voices. For example, in poems like "Anecdote for Fathers," "We are Seven," and even "The Idiot Boy," Wordsworth personifies these readerly "terms" not only with his child interlocutors — the direct addressees in these works — but also with those adult respondents who initiated the exchange. Such lyrics accordingly implicate a diversity of potential audiences, represented not only by internal addressees but by poetic speakers as well. In other poems, including "Expostulation and Reply," "The Thorn," and "Goody Blake and Harry Gill," these encounters demonstrate response to a manifestly baffling or enigmatic figure, who in turn becomes a locus for speculative dialogue. Finally, in poems like "Tintern Abbey," "To My Sister," "Simon Lee," and "The Tables Turned," Wordsworth insinuates only the shadow of response, portraying it proleptically within a silent addressee. Although such lyrics vary markedly in both affective intention and linguistic structure, each enacts poetic dialogue as an allegory of reading and interaction.

That Wordsworth would return time and again to this dialogic form raises questions not only about his formal rhetoric but also about his poetics as a whole. We must ask, for instance, whether such dialogue is in fact a poetic *techné*, sign, or genre. How does it correlate with Wordsworth's diverse theories of language, including his excurses on poetic diction and affect? We must also consider whether these issues bear not only on the *Lyrical Ballads* but on the many other works that feature Wordsworthian dialogue — including the lesser-known lyrics (such as "The Fountain" and "Two April Mornings") and several major narratives ("Lucy Gray," "Resolution and Independence," the Intimations Ode, and even *The Prelude*, the epic address to a "Friend"). Finally, we must also ask whether Wordsworth's rhetoric incorporates not only the exterior voices of his audience but his mental dialogues concerning the problematic issues addressed in his lyrics. In this context, we will also be asking whether Wordsworth's dialogic rhetoric functions as an interpretive process, enabling him both to bring forth and to project his diverse, often contradictory beliefs, and to play them off one another. According to this approach, Wordsworth gives voice to potential audience reaction in order to externalize private dilemmas as dialogue.

III

We can begin to answer the foregoing questions by locating Wordsworth's particular concept of dialogue within his more synoptic ideas about language and poetic inspiration. When he asks, for instance, "What is a Poet?" he immediately goes on to say, "To whom does he address himself? And what language is to be expected from him?" (*Prose* 1:138 [1850]). In this and other passages, Wordsworth repeatedly refers to the poetic vocation as an act of "address," specifically constructed so as to be "universally intelligible" to a common audience (*Prose* 1:124n, 128). Throughout the ancillary comments and successive editions of *Lyrical Ballads*, he reiterates this notion of mutual intelligibility by stressing a theory of lyric dissemination. Although these communicative intentions often conflict with his more subjective poetics, he is nevertheless preoccupied with conveying his notions of reception and taste. When he discusses his depiction of imaginative power, for instance, Wordsworth speaks of the "satisfaction of knowing it has been communicated to many hundreds of people" (*Prose* 1: 150). Earlier, he lauds those edifying passions that can be most "forcibly communicated," explaining "that the understanding of the being to whom we address ourselves . . . must necessarily be in some degree enlightened" (*Prose* 1:124, 126). To ensure such enlightenment, Wordsworth calls for a poetry "well adapted to interest mankind permanently" (*Prose* 1:158). He thus posits a poetics of communicative intention, predicated upon a community of reception. Such communication is represented, here again, by the poetic dialogue, the language of interchange.

This is not to say that communication proceeds with equanimity in the Wordsworth canon, nor that dialogue ever develops symmetrically. Indeed, the many unanswered questions and cryptic responses in poems like "Anecdote for Father" and "We are Seven" suggest that interchange often derails its own intentions. We should recall, though, that such interchange still implies the *form* of a dialogue, that its rhetorical situation signifies at least potential response. What is more, such rhetoric necessarily keeps open the possibility of bilateral exchange, of questions and answers — of a self-generating inquiry. Hence in such poems as "The Tables Turned" and "To My Sister," Wordsworth addresses a clearly recalcitrant "Friend," prejudiced by "toiling reason," "endless strife," and other "joyless forms." Yet it is the apparent resistance of his studious auditors that becomes the rhetorical impetus for ongoing dialogue, the very occasion for further questions. It is the projected denials and proleptic reactions of such addressees that sustain dialogic form.

Thus Wordsworth's references to a poetics of communication suggest more about his interest in agonistic dialogue and contextualized addressees than about his need to educate particular readers. Indeed, we might best characterize his wish to be "universally intelligible" as a desire not so much for communication as for contextualization — for what Bakhtin calls the contextual "utterances of the other speakers." In discussing his own view of contextualized language, for instance, Bakhtin distinguishes it from what he refers to as the decontextualized "sentence": "The sentence itself," he writes, "is not correlated directly or personally with the extraverbal context of reality (situation, setting, prehistory) or with the utterances of the other speakers . . . " ("Speech" 73). By acknowledging the "utterances of *other* speakers," one establishes an external "context" — an amalgam of conversational, cultural, and situational features that serves to orient speakers within a *potentially* communicative framework. Indeed, it is this linguistic acknowledgment of others — this capacity for implicit connections with diverse voices — that leads Bakhtin to define the utterance as the "*real* unit of speech communication" (71, emphasis added). Much as Wordsworth advocates poetic subjects that can be "forcibly communicated," Bakhtin stresses such communication as the "essence" or object of the utterance (68). In this sense, Wordsworth's deployment of the poetic addressee actually represents his "*necessary* relation to *other* participants in speech communication," his "direct relation to others' utterances." Wordsworth emphasizes this "direct relation" between disparate utterances not only to demonstrate his own "engagement" with his readers but also to suggest a more expansive dialogue with what he calls the "public taste" — including those who will learn of his work only through hearsay. The recurrence of dialogic form suggests that, for Wordsworth, poetic language is "communicative" in the sense of being linguistically encompassing — connecting not only diverse readers but manifold characters and distant voices as well. As Bakhtin puts it, the utterance encompasses more than a single "speaker's individual discourse," more than a solitary "man's need to express himself." It extends beyond unitary articulation to embody the entire "communicative function of language" (67).

In a parallel manner, Wordsworth's rhetoric also underscores the potential for universal reception based upon linguistic inclusion and mutuality. Indeed, it is in response to the question concerning "what *language* is to be expected" of the poet that he invokes the paradigm, a "man speaking to men" — a phrase implying not only an affective community, but, more significantly, a *lingua franca* that might unite it (*Prose* 1:138 [1850]).[3] Coleridge's critique notwithstanding, we know that Wordsworth valued a public language that would eventually expand his projected audience.[4] What is less frequently noted, however, is that the origin of this language is a "man speaking," that Wordsworth envisions the "real language of men" in spoken or vocal terms (*Prose* 1:130; 1:142–43 [1850]).[5] In his appendix to the 1800 preface, he extols a poetic language "really *spoken* by men, language which the poet himself had *uttered* when he had been affected by the events which he described, or which he had *heard uttered* by those around him" (*Prose* 1:161, emphasis added). Wordsworth's one caveat to this assertion is that, in poetic usage, what he calls "ordinary" spoken interchange will normally appear more "unusual" than it would in its more quotidian contexts. He insists, however, that its overall form and tone "in no respect differ from the most unimpassioned conversation" (*Prose* 1:154). We have, in the broadest sense, a man *conversing* with men.

Hence vocalized "conversation" and utterance begin to emerge as Wordworth's idealization of poetic form. If he often falls short of this model — "only selecting from the real language of men" — he nevertheless stresses this spoken diction within his poetic "purpose" (*Prose* 1:143 [1850]; 1:158, 122). Only by introducing such vocal forms can Wordsworth locate those "simple and unelaborated expressions," that "plainer and more emphatic language" that distinguishes the sentient poetry of noble passions. Only such speech can capture and "imitate" the "spontaneous overflow of powerful feelings" (*Prose* 1:124, 126). Wordsworth accordingly stresses what he calls the "immediate," face-to-face nature of these dialogues that underlie his poetic language: he intends "to keep the Reader in the company of flesh and blood, persuaded that by so doing I shall interest him" (*Prose* 1: 130). However impracticable this vocative model eventually proves, it nonetheless pervades both Wordsworth's theoretical vision and his poetic praxis.

We have noted, moreover, that this concern for the vocative dimension of poetry manifests itself in Wordsworth's choice of poetic form—his predilection for what he calls "*ordinary conversation*" (*Prose* 1:161, emphasis added). If the diction and dialect of *Lyrical Ballads* are only rarely colloquial, the structure and rhetoric of the poems often take the bilateral *form* of conversation—of that dialogue "uttered by men in real life" (*Prose* 1:138 [1850]). And although such dialogues scarcely reproduce an idiom "really spoken by men," they regularly parallel the shape of this "ordinary conversation." Indeed, the recurrence of dialogic form throughout the *Lyrical Ballads*—despite the many inadequate and even absent addressees implied—suggests that a potentially bilateral figure is central to Wordsworth's concept of the "real language of men."

IV

We are now in a position to examine Wordsworth's poetry in light of Bakhtin's analysis of "communicative function," oral "speech genres," and other features of dialogic form. We can begin with what are perhaps the most explicit examples of dialogic rhetoric in the Wordsworth canon, "Expostulation and Reply" and its pendent piece, "The Tables Turned." For even the latter poem—although it excludes the actual words of one interlocutor—contains a proleptic response. As we have noted, even the silent addressee remains, in Bakhtin's terms, an "indefinite, unconcretized *other*," one who continues to represent a listener's "silent responsive understanding" ("Speech" 95, 69). Consider, for instance, the following excerpts:

> Up! up! my Friend, and quit your books;
> . . . .
> Come forth into the light of things,
> Let Nature be your Teacher.

She has a world of ready wealth,
Our minds and hearts to bless —
Spontaneous wisdom breathed by health,
Truth breathed by cheerfulness.

One impulse from a vernal wood
May teach you more of man,
Of moral evil and of good,
Than all the sages can. (1, 15–24)

In these and other such passages, the dialogic rhetoric of the poem emerges explicitly with Wordsworth's emphasis on the second-person address ("May teach you," "your Teacher"), impersonal invocation ("my Friend"), and copious imperatives ("come," "up," "quit," "hear," "come," "clear," and so on). What is remarkable here, though, is not the appearance of these polyphonic signs so much as Wordsworth's exploitation of them for his particular ends. In this case, the dialogic viewpoint of the poem actually enables Wordsworth to sustain two distinct and contradictory approaches to the tendentious didacticism that finds its most complete expression in the "Essay, Supplementary to the Preface" (1815).

In that essay, Wordsworth traces a literary genealogy of "bombastic" poetry in order to demonstrate for his readers the principles of "sound judgment," "true discernment," and aesthetic "Taste" (*Prose* 3:73, 63, 81). He thereby claims to obviate these readers' "misconceptions and mistakes," and to regenerate their inchoate "sympathies" (3:64). Yet, as is often the case with Wordsworth, the lyrics serve to problematize the theory. If we consider a poem like "The Tables Turned," we find that Wordsworth both affirms and contests this pedagogical view of his reader's "misconceptions," and that he prevents us from correlating either perspective with a particular character in the poem. When his speaker, for instance, suggests, "Let *Nature* be your Teacher," Wordsworth appears to impugn the kind of overt didacticism that characterizes the supplementary "Essay," and to argue instead for a less actively acquired "lore." Throughout the lyric, he takes pains to mock this dissective, intentional nature of analytical knowledge. Yet, as Paul Sheats has noted, we cannot regard such unilateral positions as a "solemn summary of Wordsworth's doctrine of nature." In particular, the dialogic form of this poem doubles back upon itself, offering a more equivocal (and literally multivocal) approach to the problem of didactic art.[6] On one hand, the speaker abjures any outright, personified "Teacher" in favor of a more wisely passive process, a "heart / That watches and receives." On the other hand, however, the same speaker actually becomes this manifest "Teacher," usurping "Nature" and ventriloquizing her in order to instruct his listener about definitive "truth," "wisdom," and "moral evil and good" (20, 12, 19, 23). It is he, not "Nature," who speaks his own "Truth breathed by cheerfulness," a "wisdom breathed by health." Although he eventually qualifies this "meddling" approach to knowledge, he nevertheless takes on Nature's role and intends to "teach" (22), to convey designated insights to both "our minds and hearts" (18). Indeed, the heart that "watches and receives" is best exemplified not by William but by Matthew's *opposing* position within the interchange—by the addressee who, while he may be intent on reading the "sages," has passed the better part of the poem listening without rejoinder. Generally speaking, Wordsworth manages to suspend both viewpoints by casting his poem in the form of a dialogue: while he questions the analytical methods of his bookish auditor, he deploys the address form to expose the precariousness of his speaker's own preceptive rhetoric. In the penultimate stanza of the poem, Wordsworth accordingly stresses this dichotomy by compressing these antithetical positions into a dialogized narrative voice: the turn to the plural person here ("We murder," "Our meddling") suggests the necessary dialogue between seemingly incompatible voices.

We can say, then, that Wordsworth's apostrophe to a particular listener enables him to represent a necessarily bilateral process—in this case, a pluralistic alteration between didactic intention and its more "spontaneous" counterpart (19). To sustain this process, he incorporates the addressee as a kind of rhetorical placemarker: by portraying a listener who watches and receives, he represents both immediate reception and future response. Such a formulation requires not verbal corroboration but participatory reception, the acknowledgment that Bakhtin refers to as tacit "understanding" ("Speech" 68, 69). On occasion, this understanding may appear so passive as to be functionally absent; yet it ultimately becomes rhetorically crucial to Wordsworth's speakers. As we have noted, even an addressee's seemingly passive understanding is "inherently responsive." "Any understanding," writes Bakhtin, "is imbued with response and necessarily elicits it in one form or another" (68). It is essentially "responsive understanding with a delayed reaction"—delayed yet continually anticipated (69). Even Wordsworth's silent addressees, then, represent the kind of "response" that prolongs interchange. Hence "Expostulation and Reply," too, calls for an addressee's "wise passiveness": "wise" in that he can respond even silently, and "passive" only insofar as he suspends overt reaction while sustaining dialogue. Here again, only the heart that "receives" can constitute what Wordsworth terms a "reply," the poetic impetus to further exchange (15).[7]

V

If we turn to Wordsworth's companion poem, then, we find that both the expostulation and the reply proceed without muting one another. While this poem appears to favor William's reply as the first-person frame of reference, Wordsworth again implicates both sides of the poetic exchange. Here, too, each voice sustains dialogue by retaining a "passiveness" that not only enables the *other's* "responsive understanding" but also is a response *in itself*. In "Expostulation and Reply," however, Wordsworth actually recreates dialogue by giving voice to both interlocutors — and then implying, in Sheats's words, that "neither of the two speakers can be regarded as his philosophical spokesman" (209). As a result, Wordsworth again turns to the plural pronoun to suggest this rhetorical alliance of divergent voices within a single dialogue: "We cannot bid the ear be still; / Our bodies feel, where'er they be, / Against or with our will" (18–20; cf. 22–23, 28). As Don H. Bialostosky has demonstrated, such rhetoric suggests that "Expostulation and Reply" "comes closer to balance than any other poem in the 1798 collection" (*Tales* 131–32; cf. Sheats 209, 188).[8] Wordsworth accordingly puts in dialogue both Matthew's erudite "spirit breathed / From dead men to their kind" and William's more corporeal sensibility in which "Our bodies feel, where'er they be, / Against or with our will." To balance William's immediate contentment, Wordsworth presents Matthew's historical perspective:

> "Where are your books? — that light bequeathed
> To Beings else forlorn and blind!
> Up! up! and drink the spirit breathed
> From dead men to their kind.
>
> "You look round on your Mother Earth,
> As if she for no purpose bore you;
> As if you were her first-born birth,
> And none had lived before you!" (5–12)

We must also ask, however, why Wordsworth would include within this rhetorical balance what is certainly anathema to him: a view promoting the ratiocinative knowledge of "dead men" with an over-zealous sense of "purpose" (8, 10). Similarly, why would he devote nearly half his lyric to an opponent who derogates "William's" natural piety as a vain desire to "dream [his] time away"?

If we consider the poem as dialogue, however, we can begin to reexamine such questions, for in this context Matthew's dyspathic address is no mere foil but a rhetorical testament to the efficacy of William's words. To begin with, we should bear in mind that William characterizes his words as a "reply" (15)—that he predicates this position on its relation to a preceding turn. In Bakhtin's terms, such an "utterance is a link in the chain of speech communication, and it cannot be broken off from the preceding links . . . " ("Speech" 94). As part of this linkage, he states that an "essential (constitutive) marker of the utterance is its quality of being addressed to someone, its *addressivity*" (95). Yet Bakhtin also suggests that these "preceding" utterances are not only linked to present speech but also actually "determine it both from within and from without" (94). Hence "the role of *others* for whom the utterance is constructed is extremely great." We can say, then, that the utterance looks both backward and forward, that it both replies to former speech and addresses coming response.

It is this dual reliance on "preceding" utterance and anticipated response that accounts for both Matthew's recriminatory address and William's responsive reply. If we regard the latter's "reply" as part of an ongoing dialogue—as a "link in the chain of speech communion"—then even Matthew's agonistic expostulation becomes crucial. In a sense, his antithetical position can be said to buttress William's re-active "reply," for if the latter is to signify anything, it must also encounter those "responsive reactions" "for whom the utterance is constructed." William's words acquire meaning only in the context of that dialogic linkage, that "communion" of discourse from which they arise; they take their sense only in relation to the collectively shared interchange that engenders them. Put another way, Matthew's anticipated response provides the rhetorical orientation that actually upholds his interlocutor William's meaning. Hence even William's central stanzas, while appearing merely to parry Matthew's protest, are shaped by the dialogic structure of their joint discourse:

"Nor less I deem that there are Powers
Which of themselves our minds impress;
That we can feed this mind of ours
In a wise passiveness.

"Think you, 'mid all this mighty sum
Of things for ever speaking,
That nothing of itself will come,
But we must still be seeking?

"—Then ask not wherefore. . . ." (21–29)

Here, William's use of apostrophic forms ("Think you," "ask not") is a grammatical representation of his initial attempt at dialogue, of the "heart that . . . receives." His final stanzas are themselves reactions to a collective discourse; in Bakhtin's terms, such responses are "determined . . . by others' utterances on the same topic to which we are responding or with which we are polemicizing" ("Speech" 91). We must remember, Bakhtin goes on to say, that

[u]tterances . . . are aware of and mutually reflect one another. These mutual reflections determine their character. . . . Every utterance must be regarded primarily as a *response* to preceding utterances of the given sphere (we understand the word "response" here in the broadest sense). . . . The expression of an utterance always *responds* to a greater or lesser degree, that is, it expresses the speaker's attitude toward others' utterances and not just his attitude toward the object of his utterance. (91–92)

We can conclude, then, that Matthew's initial remarks and implied, proleptic reception actually constitute those "mutual reflections" and "preceding utterances" that go to make up the "communality of the sphere of speech communication" (91). Matthew's stanzas accordingly signify the "addressivity" of William's words, their capacity to bring forth response—and thereby to generate dialogue.

VI

Matthew's expostulation further engenders dialogue by way of another trope: the question. Take, for instance, the investigatory introduction to the poem:

"Why, William, on that old grey stone,
Thus for the length of half a day,
Why, William, sit you thus alone,
And dream your time away?

"Where are your books? . . . " (1–5)

This succession of queries establishes not only Matthew's agonistic stance but also the interrogative origins of dialogue in the poem. As Susan Wolfson has demonstrated, such queries force the "rhetoric of answers into the domain of the question"; they "drive the constructive faculty of the imagination even as they subvert or challenge the results with continued motions of inquiry" (20, 31). In the context of dialogue, too, this interrogative rhetoric is not only hortatory, but revelatory—part of what Gadamer calls the "development of all knowledge." As we have noted, he suggests that the "structure of the question is implicit in all experience. We cannot have experiences without asking questions. . . . Discourse that is intended to reveal something requires that that thing be opened up by the question. For this reason, the way in which dialectic proceeds is by way of the question and answer or, rather, by way of the development of all knowledge through the question" (326).

Here, Gadamer's use of the term *dialectic* implies not Platonic closure but ongoing inquiry. For him, moreover, the very process of questioning is hermeneutic: it is the impetus for "discourse that is intended to reveal something," intended to "open up" experience. If we apply this formulation to Wordsworth's poem, we find that Matthew's first, seemingly banal questions actually generate the poetic equivalent of Socratic dialogue—the oral form that is intrinsically interpretive. In a similar manner, Matthew's two following, conditional queries ("As if she for no purpose bore you; / As if you were her first-born birth") further perpetuate this underlying interrogative drive, this incipient inquiry (10–11). Here again, "Dialectic, as the art of asking questions, proves itself only because the person who knows how to ask questions is able to *persist* in his questioning, which involves being able to preserve his orientation towards openness. The art of questioning is that of being able to go on asking questions, ie the art of thinking" (Gadamer 330, emphasis added). Hence Matthew's capacity "to go on asking questions" again sustains the interpretive direction of the poem, its hermeneutic "openness." When William, in contrast, attempts to truncate this process, his presumably

"wise" admonition comes to resemble not insight but suppression — an
end to the interrogative "seeking" that his interlocutor first initiated:

> "— Then ask not wherefore, here, alone,
> Conversing as I may,
> I sit upon this old grey stone,
> And dream my time away." (29-32)

With this final stanza, then, William both paraphrases and reduces
Matthew's seminal question, as if to end the poem with an allegedly
culminative answer that might obviate the entire interrogative process.
His words thus circumvent dialogue in the same way that his divisive
dash in this passage cuts off Matthew's potential response to the previous inquiry. Even William's one rhetorical question ("Think you
. . . we must still be seeking?") effectively silences the "art of asking
questions" — and thereby stifles dialogue — since it actually denigrates
"seeking" while seeming to offer a genuine query. As the poem ends,
only William's final reference to "Conversing" hints at the now diminished process of inquiry.

It is this premature breach of inquiry, then, that subverts the
meliorative tone of William's "reply." At the same time, Wordsworth
casts doubt upon the principle of poetic closure by suggesting that the
process of dialogue, of ongoing query, would perpetuate itself if not
for William's false conclusion. That Wordsworth would purposively
deflect any conclusive rejoinder in these pendent poems is not surprising, moreover, when we consider that they perpetuate an issue that
dogged him throughout his life: the question of a potential bridge
between William's natural contemplation and Matthew's intellectual
"seeking" — the problem, more generally, of whether "Love of Nature"
is in fact "Leading to Love of Mankind."[9] In Wordsworth's later
poetry, this problem raises further questions about the relation between "minds and hearts" (18), between "what they half create, / and
what perceive," and between the synthetic and experiential modes of
imaginative being. It is the desire to modulate between the poles of
such dichotomies that leads Wordsworth both to dialogue form and
to its interpretive potential. In Gadamer's terms: "Precisely this is
what characterises a dialogue . . . : that here language, in the process
of question and answer, giving and taking, talking at cross purposes
and seeing each other's point, performs that communication of meaning which . . . is the task of hermeneutics" (330).

VII

This process of "giving and taking" takes another direction in a radically different poem by Wordsworth: "Tintern Abbey." Yet his most renowned poetic address is in fact rarely treated as one, with the result that the final, apostrophic paragraph of the narrative has only recently come under critical scrutiny.[10] Before we consider this concluding section, though, we must first bear in mind that such invocations never actually authorize Dorothy as a potential speaker, that they never engage her in what Wordsworth terms "ordinary conversation." It would be misleading, then, to suggest that this final section exculpates Wordsworth from what commentators since Coleridge have described as the "poet's excessive involvement in . . . personal experience."[11] At the same time, however, we must also acknowledge that the culminative address casts "Tintern Abbey" within a particular rhetorical mode—a mode that, if it does not lend Dorothy Wordsworth a voice, still *represents* her voice as the instantiation of dialogue. If the female interlocutor is relegated to "other" within "Tintern Abbey," Wordsworth's rhetoric nevertheless incorporates her as that "separate consciousness" essential to Wordsworthian invocation.

Indeed, in order to reexamine the concluding section, we must bear in mind that the entire poem is an invocation, a series of apostrophes that constitute a call to dialogue. The very impulse for the poem in fact emanates from Wordsworth's initial invocation of the "wild secluded scene" identified in the poem's title, the catalogue of "beauteous forms" that acts as a point of reference for his personal metamorphosis. As the poem proceeds, Wordsworth stresses his dialogic intent by reconjuring this scene with both demonstrative pronouns (3–16) and recurrent personification: "How oft . . . have I turned to thee, / O sylvan Wye! thou wanderer thro' the woods. . . ." Next, after invoking further reveries about the scene, he goes on to address a succession of former selves (67–83). Lastly, in the final section of the poem, his most explicit invitation to dialogue emerges in the verse paragraph to Dorothy, and it is in this section that the dialogic force of the poem becomes clear.

Wordsworth's first invocation to Dorothy establishes her as both an aural and a visual presence in the poem:

> For thou art with me here upon the banks
> Of this fair river; thou my dearest Friend,
> My dear, dear Friend; and in thy voice I catch

> The language of my former heart, and read
> My former pleasures in the shooting lights
> Of thy wild eyes. (114–19)

Here, with his initial address to his sister ("in thy voice I catch / The language of my former heart"), Wordsworth establishes the mnemonic origins of the poem. Paul Sheats, for instance, explicates these lines as a "return to sensation," in which Wordsworth envisions his own youth in Dorothy's "voice" and "eyes." As a result, Wordsworth first remembers and then "redeems" this past, "relinquishing what he has lost"; by the end of the poem, such a process enables him to abjure his youth without derogating "former pleasures" (240, 239). Yet we must also consider that Wordsworth accomplishes this mnemonic redemption through a poetic recovery of past voices, a process that enacts memory in the form of a rhetorical recapitulation. To begin with, when he finally manages to "catch" that "language of [his] former heart," Wordsworth redefines the sense of apostrophe we have heretofore seen in the poem. While earlier invocations address inanimate, unresponsive images (hedge-rows, farms, and cottage-ground), this one adjures a living persona, a potentially reciprocal interlocutor who actually embodies a "language" he can "read" or "catch." In this context, Dorothy's capacity for response identifies her as a presumptive interlocutor, rendering her both answerable and answering. This potential reciprocity manifests itself even more pointedly in the vocal or spoken nature of Dorothy's "language," for she specifically emerges as a "voice" (116, 148), a speaker of "all sweet sounds and harmonies" (142). As an addressee, too, Dorothy is all the more answerable because she can hear and be heard with the immediacy of the spoken word. Unlike the mute, enigmatic signs addressed earlier in the poem — those "wreaths of smoke / Sent up, in silence" — Dorothy's vocative endowment acts as a harbinger of dialogue. At the same time, her vocal acumen, this sensitivity to "all . . . sounds," also presages her later ability to apprehend the "still, sad music of humanity" that Wordsworth attempts to reconcile both to her and to himself.

By stressing the orality of his interlocutors, Wordsworth casts their discourse as dialogic "utterance" — as utterance that, if it is heard by another, will necessarily encounter "responsive understanding." Despite Dorothy's silence, moreover, the allusions to both her "voice" and her act of listening become figures for this dialogic response. As we have noted, even a silent auditor can represent such response, since the act of understanding is by definition responsive. As Bakhtin

puts it, "An utterance is not always followed immediately by an artic-
ulated response. An actively responsive understanding of what is
heard . . . can remain, for the time being, a silent responsive understanding (certain speech genres are intended exclusively for this kind
of responsive understanding, for example, lyrical genres) . . . "
("Speech" 68–69). Such "responsive understanding" is accordingly associated with even the mute addressee, that "indefinite, unconcretized
other" who nevertheless remains party to a dialogue. Here again,
"When the listener perceives and understands the meaning (the language meaning) of speech, he simultaneously takes an active, responsive attitude toward it. . . . Any understanding of live speech, a live
utterance, is inherently responsive . . . " (68). Hence when Wordsworth presents Dorothy as a "voice" — and as one who "understands
the meaning . . . of speech" — she becomes "inherently responsive,"
part of a proleptic dialogue.

What is most remarkable about Wordsworth's choice of the "utterance" form, however, is the capacity of such a language to give
voice to the past — to enable him to address his former selves, to recall
his past voices as if they were themselves interlocutors. Although he
can never return to these former voices, he momentarily manages to
retrieve the "sounding cataract" of his youth, the "coarser" sounds of
his "boyish days," and the "sweet sounds and harmonies" of his dialogues with Dorothy.[12] He thus invokes Dorothy not merely because
she resembles "his juvenile self" but because her position as an apostrophized "voice" becomes a rhetorical mode of reclaiming other
voices from the past. Dorothy's depiction in terms of a "voice" or
utterance thus serves an historical function, for such an address enables Wordsworth to disinter his personal chronology in the form of
multiple voices, silenced long ago.

VIII

Wordsworth thus exploits the capacity for dialogue to link past and
present voices — to associate the authenticity of a past event with its
present reconstruction. His autobiographical works in particular juxtapose the actual time of a remembered event with the poet's present
act of recounting, the former self in contrast with the currently experiencing "I." That Wordsworth would deploy this dualistic view of
personal narrative is not extraordinary when we consider that it characterizes the seminal autobiography of the period, Rousseau's *Confes-*

sions. There, Rousseau writes: "By surrendering myself at the same time to the memory of the impression received and the present feeling, I shall paint a double picture of the state of my soul, namely at the moment in which the event occurred and at the moment I described it."[13] This "double picture," encompassing both "memory" and the "present feeling," helps to define Wordsworth's rhetoric of temporality. As several critics have noted, he seeks to create not a discrete, independent past but one filtered through retrospection, reflecting the orientation of a narrative ego.[14] In the context of the present discussion, however, we must recognize that it is Wordsworth's use of dialogue that enacts this contact between past outlook and present interpretation. For if his poetry often presents a bifurcated perspective, it is his form that links them within a single exchange — as if dialogue had enabled Wordsworth's present voice to speak directly with his previous ones. According to this view, Rousseau's "double picture" takes the form of a double voice, a series of dyadic exchanges between present consciousness and former self. In "Tintern Abbey," for instance, Wordsworth's narrating voice — the present "breath of this corporeal frame" — comes to echo and engage the river of his youth — that "soft inland murmur" of his primal language, his original voice. Together, such cross-temporal voices establish what he later calls the "power of harmony" (47). Wordsworth is thus able to depict both the narrating "I" and the experiencing "I" as potentially interactive utterances — poetic manifestations of what Bakhtin calls the continuity of the "chain of speech communion" ("Speech" 94).

Indeed, we can better understand this Wordsworthian notion of transtemporal narrative if we briefly consider what Bakhtin describes as the diachronic quality of the utterance — the temporal link between all spoken language. "Utterances are not indifferent to one another, and are not self-sufficient," he writes. "Each utterance is filled with echoes and reverberations of other utterances to which it is related by the communality of the sphere of speech communication" ("Speech" 91). This "communality" of "echoes and reverberations of other utterances" thus amounts to a kind of oral intertextuality, a linguistic continuum that cuts across chronological boundaries. As we have seen, Bakhtin stresses that "each individual utterance is a link in the *chain* of speech communion. It . . . reflects the speech process, others' utterances, and, above all, preceding links in the chain . . . (93, emphasis added). If we reconsider Dorothy's position in light of this temporal continuity, we find that Wordsworth invokes her as a rhetorical link in this dialogic continuum of past and present utterances.

When he represents her in terms of a recognized voice or individual utterance (116, 148), he suggests that her invoked "language" (117) forges a link in the chronological "chain" of verbal resonance, a connection that "cannot be broken off from preceding links [and] . . . dialogic reverberations" (94). His own address to Dorothy accordingly locates him within a chain of "preceding" memories, for she is a repository or "mansion" for preceding voices; he sees her "memory . . . as a dwelling-place / For all sweet sounds and harmonies," resonating from many voices in his past. Much as they share a succession of common memories, he envisions their pasts in terms of a shared vocal history—a jointly held, vocative "existence" (149). Wordsworth thus exploits the possibilities of dialogic form in order to draw on a linkage of voices that can recall his lost "feelings . . . / of unremembered pleasure." By rhetorically conjoining his sister's past with his own, he constructs a timeless dialogue that can oppose the more ephemeral and "dreary intercourse of daily life."

Wordsworth's dialogue with his sister thus constitutes a kind of temporal isthmus. It locates him on a durational midpoint, a moment of transition between past and present. Paul de Man describes such a midpoint when he writes that "the essential moment above all other poetic moments is that of the transition," the moment "in which the movement of passing away curiously joins with a condition of remaining" (*Rhetoric* 55–56). By enacting this transitional moment, Wordsworth essentially puts the present in dialogue with the past: he interprets what passes from the vantage of what remains. In this sense, it is the dialogic moment that essentially enables the poet's historical consciousness. As de Man goes on to say, such a moment "lends duration to a past that otherwise would immediately sink into the nonbeing of a future that withdraws itself from consciousness" (64).

Despite this historical dialogue, however, Wordsworth remains troubled by that time and place "where I no more can hear / Thy voice." Although the hearing of another's voice can reenact past discourse—can in fact "re-voice" past dialogues—he nevertheless questions whether he can initiate such a reclamation.[15] Wordsworth accordingly seeks not only to recover his former voices but also to extend his discourse into the "*future*" (65)—beyond that prospective era when, either through estrangement or death, he loses the voice of his dialogic past.[16] What Wordsworth envisions in Dorothy, then, is response hereafter: the extrapolation of his past voices into the future. He thus attempts to ensure that she will never "forget" the present interchange (149, 155), that she will echo and respond to his vocal "exhortations":

> . . . thy mind
> Shall be a mansion for all lovely forms,
> Thy memory be as a dwelling-place
> For all sweet sounds and harmonies; . . .
> . . . with what healing thoughts
> Of tender joy wilt thou remember me,
> And these my exhortations! Nor, perchance —
> If I should be where I no more can hear
> Thy voice . . .
> . . . —wilt thou then forget
> That on the banks of this delightful stream
> We stood together. . . . (139–42, 144–51)

In this passage, Wordsworth prolongs dialogue in the form of Dorothy's verbal "memory," joint "thoughts," and future response. As Bakhtin puts it, "The entire utterance is constructed, as it were, in anticipation of encountering this response" ("Speech" 94). For Wordsworth, this act of "anticipation" allows him to count on potential reception, to look to "subsequent links in the chain of speech communion — and thereby to ensure an imaginative extension of dialogue. By incorporating response in the form of a voice, he can essentially project an anticipated exchange, *ventriloquizing* it as a known form.

In the final section of "Tintern Abbey," then, Wordsworth's singular pronouns again give way to the plural (124, 126), signifying a joint discourse within Dorothy's memory — a projected reconstitution of the present dialogue "in after years" (137). As part of this projected discourse, his own love will not only live on but also intensify, extended far beyond the present interchange: "With warmer love — oh! with far deeper zeal / Of holier love." As the poem closes, moreover, this poetic projection enables Wordsworth to create a prospective voice — to embody, in effect, a proleptic self. His own voice can perpetuate itself in anticipation of Dorothy's "responsive understanding," for she stands as the representative of a succession of future listeners. Even "If," as he says, "I should be where I no more can hear / Thy voice," her rhetorical position as a poetic addressee will nevertheless allow him to perpetuate his dialogic liaison with a "past existence" (149). Since, as he suggests, present dialogue also contains the germ of coming exchanges, Wordsworth knows that "in this moment there is life and food / For future years" (64–65). The process of anticipated dialogue thus inveighs against rhetorical "absence" (23, 157), so that "after many wanderings, many years," the present "intercourse" will live on in the language of "both."

We are thus in a position to re-evaluate the frequent references both to Wordsworth's abortive memory and to his essentially mnemonic relation to the past. For in the context of the present discussion, such attempts to bridge gaps between past and present testify neither to the vagaries of Wordsworthian memory nor to the nineteenth-century desire to locate a fixed past. Such Romantic commonplaces, while certainly operative, are in fact functions of what we have been calling the dialogic linkage between disparate utterances, between voices that actually diverge in both space and time. Within this schema, the attempted abridgements of temporal linearity become part of a larger, specifically *linguistic* act of interpolation — defined by a rhetoric of quotation that is both antecedent and anticipatory, revisionary and proleptic. Wordsworth's invocation of a bereft past thus serves to demonstrate the Romantic concept of the interactive utterance, in which language is both responsive and enactive, perceptive and creative. According to this approach, Wordsworth deploys language not to remember the past so much as to conjure it; poetic discourse is seen not as a mnemonic reference to particularized events but as an unfixable, dynamic continuum — an echoic rhetoric in which temporality is neither captured nor abridged, but extrapolated.

IX

"Tintern Abbey" thus plays on the twin features of dialogue form: in apostrophizing Dorothy, its language becomes both invocative and prophetic, capable of both disinterring buried voices and deploying them within a projected future. Generally speaking, Wordsworth's poetic form enables him to elide temporal boundaries, to hail past and future selves — and, in a sense, to apostrophize time itself. Indeed, addressing not only a particular addressee but also a larger, more generalized concept is central to Bakhtin's idea of dialogue. In "Tintern Abbey," for instance, Wordsworth addresses not only Dorothy but also something more extensive — what Bakhtin generally refers to as a "superaddressee," a "third party." If his apostrophe to Dorothy constitutes dialogue with a "second party," Wordsworth's inclusion of this party encompasses a more synoptic exchange. As Bakhtin puts it,

[I]n addition to this addressee (the second party), the author of the utterance, with a greater or lesser awareness, presupposes a higher *superaddressee* (third), whose absolutely just responsive understanding is presumed, either in some metaphysical distance or in distant historical time. . . . In various ages and with various understandings of the world, this superaddressee and his ideally true responsive understanding assume various ideological expressions (God, absolute truth, the court of dispassionate human conscience, the people, the court of history, science, and so forth). ("Text" 126)

This "third" or "superaddressee" thus represents an extrapolation of the speaker's more immediate, "second party" interlocutor – an "ideological" expansion inherent in dialogic form. For the speaker, this "higher," immanent addressee epitomizes reception, the "understanding" that suggests not only direct communication with another but a more profound connection with an objectified principle as well. For Wordsworth, in fact, one manifestation of this "higher" principle, this superaddressee, is *temporality itself*. Such consummate reception enables him to address his entire temporal "existence" (149), including what he calls the disturbing "presence" of his later, more somber concept of memory (cf. 88-102). By taking this "higher," more distanced view of his past – of his "thoughtless youth" – he ascends to the vantage of "elevated thoughts," a "sense sublime / Of something far more deeply interfused." At the same time, moreover, Wordsworth's address to this higher "ideology" also partakes of a more global dialogue within literary history: that collective interchange between Romantic writers and their ideological precursors, including those fallen poets who represent commensurate anxieties about both literary influence and personal mutability.[17] If, as Bakhtin suggests, "in various ages . . . this superaddressee . . . assume[s] various ideological expressions" ("Text" 126), then one higher ideology addressed in the nineteenth century is the fear that "that time is past" (83). This historical orientation accordingly places Wordsworth's address within more general nineteenth-century dialogues concerning mutability, history, transition, and the various personifications of memory and prophesy.[18]

We can thus reconsider Wordsworth's language as an elision of chronology itself, a process of using apostrophe not only to conjure former selves but actually to displace temporal boundaries as well. "Tintern Abbey" is, in fact, an example of just such a process: beginning with the "Banks of the Wye" in his title, Wordsworth addresses a primal "scene" (6) in order to reincarnate first his "boyish days," then his "thoughtless youth," and ultimately his "future years." Even before the direct address to his sister, he employs dialogic rhetoric both to recover lost "recognitions" and to conjure new ones — as if to demonstrate this form's diachronic potential, and to prepare for his final act of reclamation through Dorothy. In this sense, "Tintern Abbey" is itself a "link in the chain of speech communication."

X

If we can read "Tintern Abbey" as a dialogue, we are also in a position to reconsider the poem's many manifestations of "uncertain notice" (19) — those interrogative tropes, strained apostrophes, uneasy qualifiers, and other features that take on the force of questions. As we have noted, such questions bespeak the manifest doubt that underlies many of Wordsworth's early lyrics. In "Tintern Abbey," such hortatory indications as "if" and "perchance" — addressed primarily to Dorothy — serve to dispute the poet's claim of "cheerful faith" (133; cf. 112, 143, 147). As Wolfson demonstrates, these markers stand as evidence of Wordsworth's latent self-questioning, the state of misgiving that underlies even the most steadfast conclusions and resolute "therefores" of "Tintern Abbey" (65). In the present context, however, we must recognize that these questionings again constitute an interpretive act, a investigatory attempt to denominate what is "nameless," to "read" an "unintelligible world" (34, 117, 41). As we have seen, any object of interpretive discourse "requires that that thing be opened up by the question," by a bilateral process of dialogic queries (Gadamer 326). In Wordsworth's case, many personal dilemmas are expressed as a poetic process of addressing queries to an other. His poetic dialogues accordingly become a rhetorical mode of personal interpretation. When he asks, for instance, "If this / Be but a vain belief," he not only suggests the dubitable nature of belief in a "living soul" but also enacts a process of interpreting this "mystery," a process of constructing belief by querying another (49-50, 38). As we have seen in his invocation to Dorothy, Wordsworth prolongs this interpretive discourse in a series of speculative inquiries concerning their future lives and coming dialogues:

> *If* solitude, or fear, or pain, or grief,
> Should be thy portion, with what healing thoughts
> Of tender joy wilt thou remember me,

And these my exhortations! Nor, *perchance* —
. . . wilt thou then forget
That on the banks of this delightful stream
We stood together. (143–46, 149–51, emphasis added)

Such rhetoric underlies Wordsworth's heuristic attempt both to know what he is and to "paint / What then I was." In making Dorothy the object of his queries, he proceeds beyond "uncertain notice" to glimpse what is "almost suspended" (19, 45). Only by apostrophizing this "unintelligible world" can he begin to "see into the life of things" (49).

To read "Tintern Abbey" as an attempt at dialogue, then, is to trace a movement toward an enabling rhetoric — a movement that proceeds not only in the culminative address but also in a structural shift toward interchange during the course of the poem. At the same time, this structural development of the poem actually parallels Wordsworth's own development from a perceptual, imagistic discernment of nature to a linguistic apprehension of it. We have noted, for instance, how in both the initial address to the river scene (5–21) and the following memory of this boyhood "landscape" (22–46), Wordsworth depicts the "beauteous forms" of nature as perceived images, muted and shrouded in "silence" (18). As the poem goes on, he continues to depict nature in predominantly imagistic terms, as a "picture of the mind" composed of "daylight" and "darkness" (51–52) — of visual "landscape" and immediate "recognitions," both "Their colours and their forms" (79). It is indeed a scene devoid of "any interest / Unborrowed from the eye" (82–83), a sensual appropriation derived from the "dizzy raptures" of "thoughtless youth" (85, 90). Yet as the poem devolves past its midpoint, such imagism begins to fade. Although this shift is neither progressive nor consistent, we nevertheless follow an evolution beyond imagistic cognizance — in much the same way that Wordsworth's apprehension of his world evolves beyond those perceptions derived "from the eye." The poem moves, in fact, toward what Wordsworth earlier terms an "eye *made quiet* by the power / Of harmony" (47–48, emphasis added). Such "harmony" is accordingly understood only within the *linguistic*, bisensate "world / Of eye, and ear," within the imaginative world that can metaphorically hear the "still, sad music of humanity" (105–6, 91). We can say, then, that the world of music, harmony, and the discerning ear is requisite for Wordsworth's audible "language of the sense" (108) — the verbal figure that, if it cannot picture Wordsworth's "unintelligible world," can at least "guide" us aurally within it. In the end, Wordsworth comes to translate and interpret nature in terms linguistic as well as visual, in his own particular language of the sense. Only such a translation can give voice to the "language of [his] former heart" — much as only verbal "intercourse" can sound the evocative "voice" of dialogue.

3

Coleridge, the ''Rime,'' and the Instantiation of Outness

> The first task is to understand the work as the author himself understood it, without exceeding the limits of his understanding. . . .
>
> The second task is to take advantage of one's own position of temporal and cultural outsideness.
>
> Bakhtin, "Notes Made in 1970–71"

> "'Tis no common rule,
> Lycius," said he, "for uninvited guest
> To force himself upon you, and infest
> With an unbidden presence the bright throng
> Of younger friends; yet must I do this wrong,
> And you forgive me."
>
> Keats, "Lamia"

I

The many unanswered questions about the "Rime" have given rise to a remarkable evolution of critical response. During the nineteenth century, these questions led most commentators to eschew any speculative theories that went beyond textual explication of the poem. This prehermeneutic trend had, in fact, its own peculiar history, but it ended with the well-known essays of the 1930s and 1940s in which Robert Penn Warren and Maud Bodkin began to interpret the persistently questionable events of the poem (the slaying, the blessing, the reanimation, and so on) in symbolic terms. The course of such interpretations — and the reactions against them — follow the tortuous evolution of New Criticism itself, yet we should note that these readings set the stage for several decades of progressively more calculated accounts of the "Rime" and its baffling sequence of events, including analyses based upon Coleridge's protean Christian and Platonic beliefs. The most recent decade, however, has seen a determined — if inconsistent — turn from this interpretive legacy of what Frances Ferguson calls a "craving for causes" and answers.[1] Although these recent critics hardly constitute a consensus, they would seem to agree that the events of the Mariner's puzzling story result in neither a "redemption" nor a "sacramental vision," as both Warren and J. B. Beer had suggested.[2] On the contrary, as Paul Magnuson has noted, "If the inspirited bodies and the circling of the spirits around the sun represent a resurrection and establishment of order in the universe, as both Beer and Warren suggest, clearly the Mariner does not participate in it" (*Poetry* 77). Magnuson goes on to say that our "problems in reading the final sections come finally from Coleridge's uncertainty about the nature of evil and innocence and the possible means of redemption for someone who has suffered as the mariner does" (82). "Coleridge's confusion" can accordingly be seen as a kind of whipping boy for certain "problems in reading" (82).

Thus, the present generation of critics seems inclined to let the problematic mysteries and open questions in the "Rime" live a life of their own, and indeed there is much to be said for this approach to interpretation. Certainly the narrative itself is a labyrinth of false maps and traces: the reason suggested for the Mariner's killing the albatross is — as Ferguson and others have noted — "insufficient" ("Reader" 620), and the slain bird's varying effects on the augural weather leave us — along with the mariners — asking whether the killing was "right" or "hellish" (101, 91). Ferguson also goes as far as to say that our entire experience of reading the poem "seems to present us with an impasse" (634). Yet if the poem intentionally does confront us with an "impasse," we must still ask how Coleridge might have expected us to respond to such an interpretive predicament. If, as she notes, "perhaps no other writer in English worries more concertedly than Coleridge about deluding his readers" (630), then why would he present us with a sequence of events that at first appears to be either a Christian redemption, a Platonic allegory, or a casuistic lesson — and then turns out to undermine all such dubitable interpretations? And finally, if these apparently unanswerable questions are inseparable from the elusive beauty of the poem, we must still ask what they say about Coleridge's more general aesthetic of poetry.

In addressing such questions, I will suggest that they do not so much indicate Coleridge's contradictory values as they reveal his theories of poetic dialogue, response, and epistemological possibility. We can trace these theories of dialogue by beginning with what would appear to be the most immediate audience for the "Rime": those incorporated witnesses and auditors who listen to the narrative perforce. Indeed, many of the unresolved questions cited are a result of what I consider the central structure of the narrative: a rhetorical disjunction between listeners and speakers. And although these listeners can hardly be said to resemble actual readers, I would also argue that their responses represent a gesture to the reader of the poem — an index of designated response. Finally, I will suggest that this broken colloquy is distinctly Coleridgean, that both his poetry and prose are characterized by dialogue between two divergent and unequal points of view.

II

Those few studies that consider Coleridge's frequent use of apostrophe tend to see his auditors as embodying what the speaker himself longs for in various lyrics.[3] According to this view, the listener is a potential corroborator, a respondent used by Coleridge to represent an ideal that he cannot attain. Hence for Paul Magnuson, Coleridge's delights are "vicarious" since "his joy is that of contemplating those who are not subject to the loss and isolation to which he is subject" (*Poetry* 17). Magnuson goes on to say that these more fortunate "others" enable Coleridge to verify the ego, in that the "goal of a properly individuated self . . . could be attained only with the realization of . . . first, the assurance that the self is grounded in a reality outside the self, a reality that can be embodied in objective symbols in nature and, more importantly, in other persons . . . " (5). For W. J. Bate, this vicarious joy again depends on another, since the "unconfident Coleridge . . . became most completely alive and the resources of his mind most open when he could talk or write vicariously: when he could speak on behalf of another, as a champion or defensive critic, or appropriate and embellish arguments from another . . . " (37). Thus, in Bate's view, Coleridge takes on a "habitual role as usher — as benevolent and understanding usher for whom the release, the happiness or confidence, the opportunity for insight, are either given or presumed to be possible only to another" (50).

   Such readings of the "vicarious" Coleridge are especially valuable for their recognition of the poetic auditor as his dialogic object, ideal, or "goal" within many of the major lyrics. Magnuson notes, for instance, that (except in "Reflections on Having Left a Place of Retirement") auditors like the "Wordsworths, Lamb, and Hartley Coleridge are at the center of the vision in the other Conversation Poems, while Coleridge enters only vicariously into their experiences" (*Poetry* 18). And although Magnuson means this to apply primarily to the eight conversation lyrics, we should not be surprised that his observation has resonance for another poem written during the same few years — namely, the "Rime." There, as in the conversation poems, Coleridge stresses the central auditor's reactions at certain focal points in the narrative, most notably in the introduction and conclusion to the poem. There, too, the Guest seems to exemplify some designated reaction to the Mariner's tale, even insofar as he is "sadder and wiser" when it concludes.

Yet the idea that these poems are attempts to bridge a gap between an "unconfident" speaker and an idealized auditor leads to some troubling conclusions. For one thing, auditors such as Sara, the Guest, or even Asra seem unlikely candidates for this firm ground of "reality outside the self," much less for corroborators or favorable listeners. For another thing, both Magnuson and Bate acknowledge that these auditors actually participate in repudiations of their respective speakers.[4] According to such interpretations, we might suggest that any serious attempts to bridge a narrative gap, any searches for a corroborator, are, in a sense, rhetorical failures — that those poems in which a narrator fails to achieve communion with his addressee are in some way unsuccessful. Yet we know, as M. H. Abrams has pointed out, that a poem like "The Eolian Harp" "initiated the English vogue for" the "greater Romantic lyric," and that this poem eventually became the prototype for such triumphs as "Frost at Midnight."[5] Why, then, would Coleridge organize some of his most compelling poems around these halting interchanges between a speaker and listener? Why, indeed, do such broken colloquies recur persistently throughout the "Rime"? And finally, why would his poetry specifically call attention to these dialogic disjunctions?

III

To answer these questions, we should first consider the exact nature of the narrative dialogue within the "Rime." In part I, for instance, we should note that Coleridge uses nearly half of the section's nineteen stanzas to establish the presence of the Guest, to create a narrative situation that we are apt to recall whenever the rhetorical circumstances of the poem are invoked. To set off this scenario, the first five stanzas are told from an external narrator's point of view, allowing us to observe the initial encounter, the Guest's early resistance, and the Mariner's seemingly hypnotic "power of speech." During these early stanzas, we find that we cannot ignore the Guest's responses, for not only do they provide our first description of the Mariner's appearance (3, 11) but they also begin to suggest that the Mariner's particular curse *must* lead to a "tale" or address to an auditor, a fact confirmed only later in part VII.[6]

It appears, then, that Coleridge took pains to introduce the "Rime" to us as a dialogue with a definite "other." In the 1798 version of the poem, he stresses the presence of this "other" with the following parallelism:

> Never sadder tale was told
> To a man of woman born . . .
>
> Never sadder tale was heard
> By a man of woman born. . . . (366–67, 370–71)

As the 1800 narrative progresses, this rhetorical pattern continues to develop: although the frequency of the Guest's interjections diminishes, his dialogic responses to the tale he hears become increasingly evident in the Mariner's proleptic reactions to him. When the Guest hears, for instance, that the lifeless crew "uprose"—and immediately responds with his customary "I fear thee"—the Mariner seems to anticipate both his misinterpretation and the consequent need for an attempted explanation: "Be calm, thou Wedding-Guest!" he says,

> 'Twas not those souls that fled in pain,
> Which to their corses came again,
> But a troop of spirits blest. (345–49)

In such exchanges, Coleridge reinvokes the rhetorical situation of the poem in order to call attention to the overall issue of interpretive dialogue. For him, the Guest's bogus interpretations and oblique responses serve to sustain an investigatory process; indeed, it is the rhetorical presence of this resistant "other" that perpetuates the dialogue so essential to hermeneutics. As Bakhtin suggests, such an interpretive process requires the "role of these others, for whom my thought becomes *actual thought* for the first time (*and thus also for my own self as well*)" ("Speech" 94, emphasis added; cf. "Text" 127).

Put another way, such "thought" is a direct result of the Guest's deluded queries—part of what Gadamer calls the other's ability to "persist in his questioning," to "go on asking questions" (330). Hence when the Guest advances a series of antithetical responses, he sustains a heuristic discourse within the poem, one that implicates not only the Mariner but also Coleridge himself. When he recoils, for instance, at the prospect of a revivified crew, he represents a probable but specious interpretation of the Mariner's tale. At the same time, however, this dialogic response enables Coleridge to describe an alternative interpretation, one based not on an indulgence of preconceived beliefs but on a flight of imagination. We learn that the "troop of spirits" is indeed "blest," in that

> . . . when it dawned—they dropped their arms
> And clustered round the mast;
> Sweet sounds rose slowly through their mouths,
> And from their bodies passed.
>
> Around, around, flew each sweet sound,
> Then darted to the Sun;
> Slowly the sounds came back again,
> Now mixed, now one by one. (350–57)

What the Guest saw as a group of ghosts has been reinterpreted as a host of "sweet" messages, singing an "angel's song" (365).

This form of dialogic reinterpretation occurs again in part IV, after the Mariner describes the death of the crew (216–23). In this passage, the Guest hypothesizes that the skeletal Mariner perished with the rest of his spectral crew (224–29); the Mariner accordingly responds, "Fear not, fear not, thou Wedding-Guest! / This body dropt not down" (230–31). Here again, however, such a turn addresses a hermeneutic problem: the Guest, it seems, is unable to imagine that the Mariner's punishment is not his death, but his survival—which in effect allows for the recursive nature of his story. Generally speaking, such misreadings by the Guest serve to transform the "Rime" into an interpretive act: they direct us beyond his protests to Coleridge's notion of dialogue.

This pattern of interpretive dialogue is further complicated by the fact that certain phenomena in the poem beggar all interpretation, no matter how imaginative. We learn that many actual questions asked in the "Rime" must necessarily go unanswered. Indeed, what seems to be the seminal event in the narrative (the Albatross's death) is itself presented as a spurious answer to an impossible question: after the Mariner first describes the bird's portentous behavior, the Guest asks, "Why look'st thou so?" (81). The Mariner's reply ("With my cross-bow / I shot the Albatross") is scarcely an answer, much less an explanation; it raises still more queries about both his motive for the act and its ultimate effect (cf. 91–102). In fact, the Mariner's entire narrative is, in its first telling, only a dubious answer to that germinal question asked by the Hermit:

> "Say quick," quoth he, "I bid thee say —
> What manner of man art thou?"
>
> Forthwith this frame of mine was wrenched
> With a woful agony,
> Which forced me to begin my tale;
> And then it left me free. (576–81)

Here again, the Mariner's storytelling never qualifies as an answer to the proffered question. And that the Hermit should be party to this broken exchange only serves to underscore its collapse. For it is the Hermit who not only "loves to talk with marineres" (17) but is also portrayed as the sacerdotal figure able to "shrieve" the Mariner (512, 574). If the "godly" Hermit is here to grant absolution, then the Mariner's tale is a failed confession, a failed attempt to convey the meaning of an unexplained crime.

Thus, although the hermeneutic effects of the poem persist, the assumed rapport between a storyteller and his listener breaks down in the "Rime" to become a series of rhetorical disjunctions. In the 1798 version, Coleridge seems to insist on this disjunction by having the Mariner repeatedly punctuate his tale with the cry "Listen, Stranger!" — a refrain that only calls attention to the Guest's botched attempts to "Listen," precisely because he is a "Stranger" to the Mariner's meaning (cf. 11, 45, 49, 205, 362). In both versions, then, the Mariner's final direct address to his auditor ("O Wedding-Guest! this soul hath been . . . ") is never answered, and we are left with a description of the Mariner that only repeats the one in the first stanza (618–19), as if to keep us on the framed outskirts of the receding tale.

In a parallel manner, the two "Voices" of the poem — which presumably control the Mariner's ordeal — nevertheless discuss it in a similar succession of questions and nonanswers (398, 410–13, 422–23). Although the "first voice" repeatedly asks how the enchanted ship can move "so fast" (412, 422), it receives only an intrinsically unsatisfying explanation about the moon (414–21) or the kind of "soft response" (411) that has by now become familiar in the poem: "The air is cut away before, / And closes from behind" (424–25). Such elliptical responses, moreover, are particularly troublesome in a work that stresses the apparent power of the "voice," including its communicative potential. The power of song seems on one hand to meliorate threatening situations in the poem, most notably when the "good" Hermit "singeth loud his godly hymns" (509, 510) or the dead mariners' voices become like an "angel's song" (365). Yet when the Mariner bites his arm to break his silence, his cry of mercy proves false (160–66, 193), much as his "power of speech" later becomes the ironical source of his punishment (587–90). Finally, we should note that silence, too, manifests these same contradictory implications in the poem.[7]

Underlying this recurrent motif of unanswered questions and failed exchanges is what I would say is Coleridge's more general aesthetic concerning the possibility—and the desirability—of conveying one's deepest impulses to an anticipated interlocutor. We would do well to examine, then, a notion discussed in even his earliest notebooks: the need to define his "outness" in terms of those around him. For we can begin to understand the significance of what he elsewhere refers to as a "conscience toward others" if we consider his own excurses on engaging listeners.

IV

We should first note that although he clearly differs from the Mariner, Coleridge referred back to this figure throughout his life, using it as a kind of thematic touchstone. Kathleen Coburn notes that the many echoes of the "Rime" in Coleridge's notebooks provide "corroboration . . . that the symbolical personal significance of the poem had been deepening for the author himself."[8] Perhaps the most compelling evidence of this "personal significance" is Coleridge's preoccupation with the advisability of narrating his own insights. That he was often spurned by his listeners in person only intensified his ambivalent feelings concerning sympathy, audition, and dialogue—issues that he often grouped under the heading "conscience."[9]

For Coleridge, "conscience" was not merely self-judgment, but self-definition. Between 1807 and 1810, he wrote, "*From* what reasons do I believe a *continuous* <& ever continuable> *Consciousness?* From *Conscience!* Not for myself but for my conscience – i.e. my affections & duties toward others, I should have no Self – for Self is Definition; but all Boundary implies Neighbourhood – & is knowable only by Neighbourhood, or Relations" (*NB* 2:3231). Coleridge's "conscience" – those "affections & duties toward others" – thus provides him with not only a moral framework but an ontological one as well: in clarifying his attitudes about others, he establishes a personal frame of reference, a mental "Boundary" that defines his place in the world. This "Boundary" or limitation in turn distinguishes his "Consciousness" from those around him.[10] We should bear in mind, however, that this "Definition" of self specifies only what Coleridge needs to feel *"toward others"* – not what he expects in return. He says elsewhere, in fact, that "Self in me derives its sense of Being from having this one absolute *Object . . .* " (*NB* 2:3148, emphasis added). While he speaks of those who receive his "affections & duties," Coleridge focuses on himself as source; his "others" are objects in that their own "affections" – their responses as subjects – are problematic for him, an unknown variable in his attempts at dialogue.

Yet what *did* Coleridge want and expect from these "others"? Certainly his desire for affective sympathy has been well documented:[11] the quests for Asra's love and Wordsworth's admiration make for some of the most anguished entries in the notebooks. Indeed, the picture of Coleridge most often put forth by critics and biographers is one of an unwillingly iconoclastic writer, painfully alienated from both friends and family – a poet who craved the artistic acknowledgment of others. Yet we should be careful to distinguish between Coleridge's need for emotional recognition and his more volatile feelings concerning artistic collaboration, advice, and dialogue. Even before his period of prolonged alienation, the idea of writing with – as he once put it – a "sectarian spirit" troubles Coleridge deeply. When he thinks that Wordsworth has "bidden farewell to all small poems," Coleridge applauds him, saying,

> [D]ifference of opinion with his best friends irritated him/& he wrote at times too much with a sectarian Spirit, in a sort of Bravado. – But now he is at the Helm of a noble Bark; now he sails right onward – it is all open Ocean, & a steady Breeze; and he drives before it, unfretted by short Tacks, reefing & unreefing the Sails, hawling & disentangling the ropes. – His only Disease is the having been out of his Element – his return to it is food to Famine, it is both the specific Remedy, & the condition of Health. (*NB* 1:1546)

Clearly, Coleridge would not include this "sectarian spirit" among those requisite "affections & duties towards others." This is not, of course, to say that he disavowed a desire for dialogue; on the contrary, in 1804 he went so far as to ask Dorothy Wordsworth if a poet "gained by repeating to a beloved House-mate [a] Poem" in daily installments or "by storing it up a week or fortnight" (*NB* 1:1830). Yet, among the many contradictory stands Coleridge explores in the notebooks, his feelings about this listening, dialogic "Housemate" stand out as particularly tortuous.

We can trace this ambivalence in many statements he makes about potential interlocutors. Although he writes, "My nature requires another Nature for its support," he goes on to describe this requirement as a fault, since his nature "reposes only in another from the necessary Indigence of its Being" (*NB* 1:1679). However "necessary" this "Indigence" is, it leads to a relationship with "another" that can be characterized only in terms of a harplike "Flute" — a contradictory image that for Coleridge expressed both harmony and disunity.[12] When Coleridge does indulge this feeling of indigence, moreover, it seems that he rarely finds the kind of "support" and understanding he desires. As early as 1802, he writes, "The unspeakable Comfort to a good man's mind — nay, even to a criminal to be *understood* — to have some one that understands one — & who does not feel, that on earth no one does. The Hope of this — always more or less disappointed, gives the *passion* to Friendship" (*NB* 1:1082). While he seeks "some one that understands" him, he nevertheless insists that "no one does"; he can extol the "passion" of "friendship" even as he says that it is "always more or less disappointed." And if he does manage to find a measure of this reciprocal friendship, Coleridge feels that it is continually slipping from his grasp: in an 1803 entry (addressed presumably to Sara Hutchinson), he says, "Fear of Parting gives a yearning so like Absence, as at moments to turn your presence into absence" (*NB* 1:1334).

During the next decade, Coleridge went on to clarify these misgivings about "support," "friendship," and rhetorical "presence." After repeated failures to achieve these "comforts" himself,[13] their assumed necessity becomes suspect: what was once a requirement (*NB* 1:1679) is now a "desirableness" — the "desirableness of having each Soul watched over, as it were, by its Sister — . . . " (*NB* 3:4169 [1812]). The doubts and qualifications in such statements, moreover, have become even stronger:

But then ask what this means? bring it to its true principle of causation! — It will be found neither more or less, than to keep continually + with −, one person with another wholly out of all sympathy with him, & vice versâ, as the young with the aged, the grave with the gay. Now I deny not but this is excellent as a medicine & a discipline, but it is destructive, as a *Diet*, as a regular Scheme. (*NB* 3:4169)

Coleridge appears to recognize that the dialogic "Nature" he once looked to for "support" and "friendship" is necessarily *"out of all sympathy with him,"* a potentially "destructive" watchdog who should only occasionally "discipline" or "check" wayward impulses. Throughout the next several years, his notebook entries suggest that the kind of consummate dialogue or friendship he had envisioned is virtually impossible to achieve; he comes to "examine . . . the multitude of causes that make men delude themselves & attribute to Friendship what is only a . . . similarity of Pursuit, or even mere dislike of feeling one's self *alone* in any thing" (*NB* 3:4175). But "supposing [Friendship]" he goes on to say, "as real as human nature ordinarily permits, yet how many causes are at constant war against it −," including "violent irruptions, unobserved yet constant wearings away by dispathy &c. . . . The influence of wives, how frequently deadly to Friendship − . . . by direct incroach, & perhaps intentional plans of alienation − . . . of families, by otherwise occupying the heart − and of Life in general, by the worldly-wise, chilling Effect of prudential anxieties − " (*NB* 3:4175).

According to Coleridge, then, much of "human nature" itself is "at constant war against" the kind of union and friendship that enables colloquy. Even the sacrosanct bond of marriage is tainted − in part because "so *few* . . . can be at once − the attached & Loving − Husband − & the *Friend*" (*NB* 3:4013).[14] Thus, whether he is alluding to "Friendship" or the "parental and . . . conjugal Relation," he sees each as only an "obscure Hope," a "yearning Sigh" − or the *"incorporeity* of true Love in absence" (*NB* 3:4036). For Coleridge, that "happiness incomplete without the happiness of some other" is all too readily transformed into a "Happiness blasted & transformed by incompleteness." He comes to mistrust that "other" who might transform and complete his view of the world − that "sole organ thro' which [he] could enjoy" the "advantages & favorable accidents of Nature, or Fortune" (*NB* 3:4036).

Coleridge's distrust of this "other" becomes all the more apparent in *Biographia Literaria*. He devotes a large part of chapter 12, for instance, to a theoretical defense against those critics who remain "ignorant of his understanding" (Engell and Bate 1:232). As early as chapter 3, moreover, Coleridge chafes at having to address what he calls the "multitudinous PUBLIC," who sit "nominal despot on the throne of criticism" (1:59). Yet his most poignant assessment of this critical other comes in the following passage, where he expresses his consternation that "after having run the critical gauntlet for a certain class of faults which I *had*, . . . I should, year after year, quarter after quarter, month after month . . . have been for at least 17 years consecutively dragged forth by ["anonymous critics"] into the foremost ranks of the *proscribed*, and forced to abide the brunt of abuse, for faults directly opposite, and which I certainly had not" (1:50, 48).

Coleridge's reactions to this "merciless and long-continued" abuse have, of course, been frequently noted. It is perhaps less well known, however, that most of this alleged abuse is an invention — a fiction of vituperative response. For although Coleridge endured several painful reviews, the vast majority of them, fully sixty-three out of ninety, repeatedly extol him (1:50). We must accordingly ask why he would distort such reception, why he would posture as an ostensibly "proscribed" poet. We might consider, in fact, whether such a posture has less to do with Coleridge's oft-cited melancholia than with his notions of poetic response — and whether his critical defenses might actually stem from beliefs concerning the function and value of agonistic reception. Finally, we should consider why Coleridge would essentially fictionalize his role as the recipient of critical attack, as if his stance of rhetorical justification had become a form in itself — a gesture toward dialogue.

Indeed, it would be misguided to say that Coleridge's disavowals of both the critical and the corroborative other indicate a denial of dialogue. Though he eventually mistrusts this other who remains "wholly out of all sympathy with him," he nevertheless seems to need some external presence as the objective of his copious writings. This externality — what he refers to as *outness* — has less to do with corroborative "support" than with a confessional "Outlet" for his inmost thoughts (*NB* 3:3325; cf. 1:1307). Coleridge found, in fact, that he could often meet this need for dialogic "outness" by addressing not a listener but his notebooks themselves. After nearly three decades of sporadic entries, he refers to these books as "the Confidantes who have *not* betrayed me . . . the Friends, whose silence was *not* Detraction, and the Inmates before whom I was not ashamed to complain, to yearn, to weep — or even to pray!" (4:4946).[15] Earlier, in 1808, he begins an excursus on outness with the address, "Ah! dear Book! Sole Confidant of a breaking Heart, whose social nature compels *some* Outlet" (*NB* 3:3325). In the notebooks, then, Coleridge finds a reflective surface for those "painful Peculiarities of [his] nature" (*NB* 3:4166). One of these, he writes in 1811, "I will here record — and my Motive or rather Impulse to do this, seems to myself an effort to eloign and abalienate it from the dark Adyt of my own Being by a *visual* Outness — & not the wish for others to see it —" (*NB* 3:4166). Coleridge implies that if he can manage to record his obscure fears, he can bring them to light, delimit their form — give them, as he says, "visual Outness." It is this need for delimitation, for an external vantage that begins to account for Coleridge's desire for a dialogic "thou." Such externalization is intended to be not so much purgative as creative: for Coleridge, true artists must observe the world from outside themselves in order to re-create "Nature." He writes that the "Artist must first *eloign* himself from Nature in order to return to her with full effect" (*NB* 3:4397). In both passages, the verb *eloign* suggests that in deciding to "absent" or "distance" himself, the artist acquires the dialogic outness necessary to rise above this particular "Nature" (cf. *NB* 3:4397, 4166).

After discussing this requisite outness, Coleridge goes on to say that his revelatory "vision" of buried fears occurs only when they come into "commune with full Consciousness," when he is finally able to expose part of his hidden "nature." We should bear in mind, however, that this exposure is again part of a multivocal process — a function of dialogue. At the same time, moreover, such dialogic exposure never requires definite corroboration. Coleridge again emphasizes that the "motive" for exposing his peculiar nature before consciousness is solely that need for the foregoing outness, and "not the wish for others to see it." Even the silent other, then — what Bakhtin calls the "indefinite, unconcretized other" — can be used for such exposure and outness.

V

Establishing a "*visual* Outness" thus requires an external translation of those "peculiarities" that lie hidden in the "dark Adyt of [Coleridge's] own Being." In order to "eloign" — or, as he puts it elsewhere, to "withdraw" — his "hidden" nature, he must rely on a symbolic expression of his inmost thoughts (*NB* 3:3624). Here, I think, we arrive at the heart of the matter: in the same entry that refers to his notebooks as an "Outlet," he writes,

> in the last minute or two that I have been writing on my writing, I detected that . . . I was only *thinking.* All minds must think by some *symbols*—the strongest minds possess the most vivid Symbols in the Imagination—yet this ingenerates a *want*, ποθον, *desiderium*, for vividness of Symbol: which something that is *without*, that has the property of *Outness* (a word which Berkley preferred to "Externality") can alone fully gratify/even that indeed not fully—. . . . (*NB* 3:3325)

If "all minds must think by some *symbols*," and "the strongest minds possess the most vivid Symbols in the Imagination," then only these "symbols" can reveal the "vividness" of the Coleridgean "Imagination"—those thoughts buried in the "dark Adyt of [his] own Being." Coleridge's mind thus acquires "*visual* Outness" when the symbols he chooses most closely approximate the "vivid" imaginative vision they represent. As he suggests earlier, "Language & all *symbols* give *outness* to Thoughts/& this the philosophical essence & purpose of Language/" (*NB* 1:1387). This lifelong need for a correspondence between internal imagination and an outwardly directed "vividness of Symbol" is expressed most clearly, I think, in Coleridge's late essay on "Symbol and Allegory." There, in discussing the power of biblical symbols, he describes a "system of symbols" that are "consubstantial with the truths, of which they are the *conductors*" (6:29). Such a symbol, he adds, "always partakes of the Reality which it renders intelligible; and while it enunciates the whole, abides itself as a living part in that Unity, of which it is the representative" (6:30). The truly imaginative mind strives to attain this ideal unity of the symbol and the thing symbolized.

We must bear in mind, moreover, that this desire for an externalized, symbolic figure is also part of a larger belief within Coleridgean aesthetics—one that addresses not only his personal need for a listener but also his more philosophical concern with what he terms "natural language." Indeed, many of Coleridge's writings on the symbol explore the possibility of a language that exemplifies a ready correspondence between sign and referent, a language in which symbols bear a causal relation to concepts symbolized. In seeking such a corresponding or "natural" language, Coleridge distinguishes his beliefs from the Lockean school of linguistics, a doctrine that posits the arbitrary status of the sign, and that consequently denies any particularly phonetic or formal link between symbol and referent.

This semiotic affinity between a self-created sign and an external reality carries particular meaning for Coleridge. We must recall, for instance, that he continually harbored profound doubts concerning the validity of any self-created belief, and that he painstakingly questioned each of his personal systems, whether moral, religious, or (as in the present case) linguistic. As a result, the possibility that his internal vagaries could be partially confirmed by an outwardly directed, broadly communicative language tantalizes him, especially in his later writings concerning language. For Coleridge, such a correspondence defines the existence of an *Ursprache*, an ultimately reliable, universally intelligible language that both expresses and hypostatizes one's internal truth.

In the context of the present discussion, then, this emphasis on a linguistic correspondence between inner meaning and external symbol takes on new significance: Coleridge actually represents this semiotic linkage as a poetic correspondence between his internal voice and a dialogic other. In this sense, narrative exposure before a listening other becomes the rhetorical equivalent of that semiotic correspondence between internal belief and external reception, between inner thought and externalized reality—and between private language and public projection. Coleridge's use of poetic dialogue accordingly constitutes a literary emblem of that desire to "eloign" or "draw out" the self, to substantiate its outness before an other. He seeks the externalized symbol in an attempt to enact his concept of outness. Although such externality never becomes actual corroboration, the use of a poetic interlocutor comes to embody his concept of the nonarbitrary sign.[16]

Hence when Coleridge speaks of that "absolute *Union*, which the soul sensible of its imperfection in itself, of its *Halfness*, yearns after" (*NB* 3:3325), he is referring *not to his potential connections with a corroborative other but to a* "Unity" *of the* "*Literal* and *Metaphorical*"—of the represented and the representative (*The Statesman's Manual*, 6:30). The other is not a testimonial supporter so much as an expression of Coleridge's symbolic outness—a hypostatization of an internal need. In order to address the "imperfection" or "*Halfness*" of his "soul," Coleridge directs his feelings toward a symbolic "other."

Later, he comes to describe this otherness as a condition that exists "when the emotions have their conscious or believed object in another" (*AR* 347). Although these internal "emotions" can also have as their "subject" the "individual personal self," Coleridge stresses that they often find expression through a dialogic other — in what he refers to as a relation between the "*alter et idem*, myself and my neighbour" (*AR* 347).

If Coleridge can achieve this corresponding "vividness of Symbol," he believes that the symbolizing imagination will be able both to perceive and describe the world. By creating a recurring symbol, such as a name, for his various perceptions, Coleridge can locate them within his memory — and, consequently, within his imagination. As he says, "The repetition of past Perceptions in the Consciousness is Imagination" (*NB* 3:3605). The clearest explanation of this imaginative naming of the outside world comes in an entry of 1805:

> In looking at objects of Nature while I am thinking, as at yonder moon dim-glimmering thro' the dewy window-pane, I seem rather to be seeking, as it were *asking*, a symbolical language for something within me that already and forever exists, than observing any thing new. Even when that latter is the case, yet still I have always an ["obscure"] feeling as if that new phaenomenon were the dim Awaking of a forgotten or hidden Truth of my inner Nature/It is still interesting as a Word, a Symbol! It is Λογος, the Creator! < and the Evolver! >. (*NB* 2:2546)

In creating a "symbolical language for something within," Coleridge defines his relation to the dialogic other — his verified outness. Only after symbolizing or expressing his "inner Nature" can a "man having long mediated & perceived a certain Truth" find "another . . . foreign Writer, who has handled the same with an approximation to the Truth, as he < had previously > conceived it . . ." (*NB* 2:2546).

Here again, it is the notebooks that often allow him to establish these externalized symbols. In describing his mnemonic process, he writes,

> O! Heaven! one thousandfold combinations of Images that pass hourly in this divine Vale, while I am dozing & muddling away my Thoughts & Eyes — O let me rouse myself — If I even begin mechanically, & only by aid of *memory* look round and *call each thing by a name — describe it, as a trial of skill in words* — it may bring back fragments of former Feeling — *For we can live only by feeding abroad.* (*NB* 3:3420, emphasis added)

In symbolically naming the world, Coleridge is "feeding abroad"; he is taking in the world imaginatively. His "system of symbols" constitutes a external record of those "past Perceptions" of his surroundings—which in turn allows his "Imagination" to function. We witness this onomastic process in one of the more poignant love lyrics from the notebooks:

> I knew you not, I knew not that you were/
> No Voice had made the mind-embodying air,
> Be music with your name—. (*NB* 2:3003)

The "name" here allows Coleridge to know an existence *outside himself*. And because both names in particular—and words in general—make this symbolic knowledge possible, the notebooks themselves become an emblem of Coleridge's apprehension of his world; they represent what he refers to as the "*Light*, which I myself in these very Memorandum Books have tried to make permanent for myself" (*NB* 3:4013). By addressing these "Books" as an outward presence, Coleridge attempts to fix the world as a set of exterior, imaginative symbols. In rhetorical terms, such externality enables a kind of epistemological exchange—what he calls a "mind-embodying" dialogue with the world.

When he addresses a dialogic presence, then, Coleridge focuses on a "system of symbols" that renders his inmost thoughts "visual" to the other. The dialogic address allows him to express these thoughts externally, to turn his mind outward, as he would have to do if he were actually communicating to another. Indeed, the conscious *exposure* of his secret thoughts to this other *necessitates* an external set of symbols—an outness that ultimately permits Coleridge to eloign his hidden self.

VI

When Coleridge manages to enact this form of dialogic exposure, we must also ask exactly what he needs to expose, what might require this seemingly purgative outness. The answer to such a question would begin, of course, with those studies of what is often referred to as the "Gothic" aspect of his poetry.[17] In the "Rime," for instance, Coleridge repeatedly represents the Mariner's animus as a "frightful fiend" (450). The Mariner is thus

> Like one, that on a lonesome road
> Doth walk in fear and dread,
> And having once turned round walks on,
> And turns no more his head;
> Because he knows, a frightful fiend
> Doth close behind him tread. (446–51)

The Pilot, too, deems the returning ghost-ship "fiendish" (538), and several stanzas later his assistant perpetuates the metaphor by referring to the Mariner himself as the "Devil" (569). Earlier, too, such naturalistic symbols as the storm also appear in this guise. The tempest, we learn,

> Was tyrannous and strong:
> He struck with his o'ertaking wings,
> And caused us south along. (42–44)

Even the sun, cross-hatched by the cursed ship, appears to the Mariner "As if through a dungeon-grate he peered / With broad and burning face" (179–80). Such fiendlike images accordingly come to embody much that is "dread" in the poem; as a result, they begin to delineate those personal demons that Coleridge himself needed to draw forth into dialogue.

To examine such demons, we can turn briefly to those confessional writings in which Coleridge attempts to define what he came to call his "secret lodger." In trying to describe this "lodger" as the subject for spiritual "reflection," he states that

> the most frequent impediment to men's turning the mind inwards upon themselves, is that they are afraid of what they shall find there. There is an aching hollowness in the bosom, a dark cold speck at the heart, an obscure and boding sense of a somewhat, that must be kept out of sight of the conscience; some secret lodger, whom they can neither resolve to eject or retain.[18]

This "secret lodger" corresponds with what Coleridge had earlier described as "some hidden vice" that continually threatens him, an undisclosed evil prophesied by an "act of [his] own Spirit, of the absolute Noumenon." However obscure this lodger appears to be, it engenders an "inexplicable feeling of causeless shame & sense of a sort of guilt" (*NB* 3:4166). Of course, part of Coleridge's remorse here is Christian: his allusions to "vice," "immoral practice," and the "unreflecting

Christian" admonish the sinner to "kindle the torch which his Father [has] given into his hands" (*AR* 10). Yet in such passages Coleridge is also struggling with a more perplexing problem: a premonition of a sin that can never be atoned for within his moral "system."[19] Because of its "hidden" nature, this moral transgression seems to be immune to any conventional means of expiation.[20] As we shall see, confessing such a sin to an attendant auditor only brings out the futility of recounting the "secret lodger" to another. In this context, his self-avowed "apprehension" of hidden sin becomes as much a casuistic struggle as an interpretive quandary.[21]

Coleridge's approach to this immanent "Evil" is, as we have noted, to expose it. In his most nightmarish works, such exposure can also take the form of an internalized disclosure—what is in effect an exposure before a projected "conscience." This peculiar process is at the center of *Aids to Reflection*, where Coleridge notes that the foregoing "secret lodger" is usually "kept out of sight of the conscience"; ideally, he says, we should have "sufficient strength of character to be able to draw forth an evil tendency or immoral practice into distinct consciousness, [while] bringing it in the same moment before an awaking conscience. . . . [F]or this very reason it becomes a duty of conscience to form the mind to a habit of distinct consciousness. An unreflecting Christian walks in twilight among snares and pitfalls!" (10). If we would not be "unreflecting," then, we must develop this "habit of distinct consciousness," this conscious exposure to "conscience." For Coleridge, spiritual "reflection" is the "awaking conscience" in the process of *witnessing* a moral dilemma. In order to expose a forbidden "lodger," to "draw forth an evil tendency," we must succeed in "bringing it . . . before an awaking conscience."[22]

It is this process of "abalienating" an opaque lodger, then, that begins to account for Coleridge's use of auditors: his listeners represent the "awaking conscience" hearing the "unhallow'd" practices of a transgressing storyteller. Accordingly, Coleridge often portrays his auditors at odds with an "obscure" speaker: they must endeavor both to unveil this speaker's "immoral practice" and to "draw forth" his buried self. In this context, moreover, we can also say that Coleridge translates internal dialogue into poetic rhetoric. When he pits a dialogic listener against an impenetrable speaker, he represents his own attempt "to eloign and abalienate" personal guilt "from the dark Adyt of [his] own Being"—his attempt at "turning the mind inwards upon [himself]." By creating a dialogic conflict between an addressee and a storyteller, he gives his inner contest with that "hidden vice" a "visual" expression: he can confront "one of the strangest and most painful peculiarities of [his] nature" by "bringing it before" an incorporated listener.

VII

The exact nature of these "painful peculiarities," this hidden lodger, has only recently been recognized as central within a Coleridgean poetics.[23] To bring this poetic "Evil" into relief, though, we must begin with Coleridge's early notions about the intent of narration. In 1797, for instance, a year before Coleridge first published the "Rime," Charles Lamb had advised him to complete an extensive poem on "the Origin of moral Evil."[24] The subject had long been a preoccupation of Coleridge's, and it continued to haunt him long after his poetic efforts had diminished. Although Lamb's suggestion appears to have gone unheeded, several biographers have wondered whether such a poem came to be unnecessary because Coleridge, in composing the "Rime," had for the moment addressed his most immediate dilemmas concerning moral evil (cf. Lockridge 76–77, 265–66; Magnuson, *Poetry* 65–76). In support of this argument, these accounts have pointed to several of the poem's major events as evidence of the Mariner's own casuistic dilemma: his wanton slaying of the bird, his lack of will in blessing the seasnakes "unaware," and his eventual "crime against God."[25]

Such allusions to Coleridge's moral poetics tend to focus on transgressions of human will, on his sense that solipsistic motivation necessarily engenders Satanic pride. As Laurence S. Lockridge has shown, Coleridge traces the pernicious "origin of evil" to the "human will's departure from God's will at the center to the periphery that is self-will" (73). In the "Rime," this human will's "separateness" from the center — and the consequent "alienation," "individuation," and predominance of "self-will" — forestall both a "reunion with God" and with that wedding party or "community the Mariner can never join" (74, 73). In the context of the present discussion, then, this solipsistic or separated will would appear to preclude Coleridge's early efforts at exchange and colloquy. Yet if we consider his later concerns with poetic apostrophe, we must recognize that such willful separation actually enables a kind of rhetorical distance — a linguistic differentiation of voices that instantiates not reciprocal, balanced colloquy but oppositional, agonistic dialogue.[26]

This dialogic differentiation of multiple voices may thus reframe moral concerns about the solipsistic will's evil potential; for the "Rime" in particular, such dialogic multiplicity can redefine questions of moral responsibility. Still, the more common question of moral culpability—including the Mariner's individual accountability for his actions—has become a critical quandary. W. J. Bate, for instance, has suggested that Coleridge deliberately chose a bird (and not a man) as the poem's symbolic victim in order to leave open the question of the Mariner's guilt (59). As Ferguson has noted, moreover, to regard such symbolic acts as the slaying or the blessing as causative events is to sort the "Mariner's experience . . . into a more linear and complete pattern than the poem ever agrees to do" ("Reader" 620). Nevertheless, she—along with most commentators on the poem—continues to insist that "morals are at issue" in the "Rime" (620), an assertion that still leaves us with the nagging question of whether Coleridge's preoccupation with "the Origin of moral Evil" ever found its way into the poem—and, if so, where.

We can begin to address this question if we consider Coleridge's own writings on both moral evil and its sources. In October of 1803, he writes, "I will at least make the attempt to explain to myself the Origin of moral Evil from the *streamy* Nature of Association, which Thinking = Reason, curbs & rudders/how this comes to be so difficult/Do not the bad Passions in Dreams throw light & shew of proof upon this Hypothesis?—Explain those bad Passions: & I shall gain Light, I am sure— . . . " (*NB* 1:1770). Here, recognizing the "Origin of moral Evil from the *streamy* Nature of Association" proves to be a vital concern for Coleridge, one that characterizes even his own mental "Nature of Association." Some two months after the foregoing entry, while lamenting the widespread attenuation of childhood liberties, he says that

> without any reference to or distinct recollection of my former theory, I saw great Reason to attribute the effect wholly to the streamy nature of the associating Faculty and especially as it is evident that *they most labor under this defect who are most reverie-ish & streamy*—Hartley, for instance & myself/This seems to me no common corroboration of my former Thought on the origin of moral Evil in general. (*NB* 1:1833)

Here, too, this "*streamy nature* of the associating Faculty" appears to disturb Coleridge deeply—that empiricist tendency to pile image upon image without adequately discerning the connectives between them (cf. *NB* 3:3342; Magnuson, *Poetry* 60–70). Such connectives, he says, come only with "Reason," which "curbs & rudders" this obsessive flow of imagery. Deprived of this "rudder," the mind moves from impression to impression merely on the basis of the "law of association," a term that Coleridge tellingly reserves for his derogation of "Fancy" as opposed to "Imagination."

In considering these entries from his notebooks, we should further note that Coleridge indicts *himself* as a source of this "associating Faculty" gone awry — a painful accusation that he echoes several times in the commentary of 1803 and 1804.[27] Such "streamy" associations, he suggests, taint not only his mode of thought but that of his speech as well, including the capacity to show another the paratactic links between his rapid-fire images. Hence a year after his discussions of moral evil, he writes:

> There are two sorts of talkative fellows whom it would be injurious to confound/& I, S. T. Coleridge am the latter. . . . The second sort is of those who use five hundred more ideas, images, reasons, &c, than there is any need of to arrive at their object/till the only object arrived at is that the . . . mind's eye of the bye-stander is dazzled with colors succeeding so rapidly as to leave one vague impression that there has been a great Blaze of colours all about something. Now this is my case — & a grievous fault it is/my illustrations swallow up my thesis — I feel too intensely the omnipresence of all in each, platonically speaking — or psychologically my brain-fibres, or the spiritual Light which abides in the brain marrow as visible Light appears to do in sundry rotten mackerel & other *smashy* matters, is of too general an affinity with all things/and tho' it perceives the *difference* of things, yet is eternally pursuing the likenesses, or rather that which is common [between them]/bring me two things that seem the very same, & then I am quick enough [not only] to shew the difference, even to hair-splitting — but to go on from circle to circle till I break against the shore of my Hearer's patience, or have my Concentricals dashed to nothing by a Snore — that is my ordinary mishap. (*NB* 2:2372)

Certainly this entry is a written demonstration of the "talkative" phenomenon described: the rapidly "associating Faculty" that links images on the basis of the fancy, not the imagination. At the same time, Coleridge implies that such associations have grave affective consequences for his interlocutors. Indeed, to corroborate his statement that he often breaks "against the shore of my hearers' patience," we need only turn to Keats's account of Coleridge's excurses:

I met Mr. Green our Demonstrator at Guy's in conversation with Coleridge— . . . I walked with him a[t] his alderman-after dinner pace for near two miles I suppose In those two Miles he broached a thousand things—let me see if I can give you a list—Nightingales, Poetry—on Poetical sensation—Metaphysics—Different genera and species of Dreams—Nightmare—a dream accompanied by a sense of touch—single and double touch—A dream related—First and second consciousness— the difference explained between will and Volition—so many metaphysicians from a want of smoking the second consciousness—Monsters— the Kraken—Mermaids—southey believes in them—southeys belief too much diluted—A Ghost story—Good morning—I heard his voice as he came towards me—I heard it as he moved away—I had heard it all the interval—if it may be called so. He was civil enough to ask me to call on him at Highgate Good Night! (4/15/1819)

I have quoted both Coleridge and Keats at length here in order to underscore the recursive nature of the Coleridgean voice. Indeed, Coleridge's choice of metaphors (the "stream" or wave) is telling here, suggesting as it does an inexorable torrent of recurrent associations, "eternally pursuing the likenesses" or "difference[s]" between "ideas, images, reasons, &c." We can say, then, that it is this self-generative quality of the rapidly "associating" mind that—since it "eternally" threatens to spin out of control—leads Coleridge to fear it as the "origin of moral Evil." He accordingly mistrusts his own "talkative" style of narration because that "great Blaze of colours" threatens to engulf not only his interlocutor but himself as well. It is this engulfment, moreover, that leads him to reformulate his views of the disjunctive dialogues that appear in both his conversational and poetic discourse.

Actual accounts of these skewed dialogues occur at intervals in the forty-odd notebooks kept by Coleridge throughout his life. Here, whenever he calls attention to his associative chains of ideas, he seems to doubt his capacity to pursue any to a viable conclusion, to shape it into an organic entity. He writes:

How far one might imagine all the association System out of a system of growth/ . . . —one tiny particle combines with another, its like. & so lengthens & thickens.—& this is at once Memory & increasing vividness of impression, one might make a very amusing Allegory of an embryo Soul up to Birth!—Try! it is promising!—You have not above 300 volumes to write before you come to it—& as you write perhaps a volume once in ten years, you have ample Time, my dear Fellow!—. . . . (*NB* 2:2373)

The irony here is double-edged, for Coleridge is still genuinely fearful that these digressive meanderings are not only difficult for listeners to follow but "Evil." After rereading both a particularly convoluted entry in his notebooks and then his own copy of a garbled letter to Southey, he writes:

> But I leave it, < as I wrote it > − & likewise have refused to destroy the stupid drunken Letter to Southey, which I wrote in the sprawling characters of Drunkenness/. . . If I should perish without having the power of destroying these & my other pocket books, the history of my own mind for my own improvement. O friend! Truth! Truth! but yet Charity! Charity! I have never loved Evil for its own sake; . . . <no! nor > ever sought pleasure for its own sake, but only as the means of escaping from pains that coiled round my mental powers, as a serpent around the body & wings of an Eagle! < My sole sensuality was *not* to be in pain! − >. (*NB* 2:2368)

The "Evil" here is not only the addiction to opium but also the ranting language it leads to: the "sprawling characters of Drunkenness." Coleridge fervently mistrusts the discursive voice. Yet it is his horror at "Evil for its own sake" that lies behind this preoccupation with the "streamy nature of the associating Faculty" − that "talkative" manner of combining "ideas, images, reasons." In this context, both narration and dialogue become moral issues − the "origin" of discursive "Passion." If we return to the "Rime," then, we begin to recognize something of the rhetorical history underlying the Mariner's dialogue with the Guest. The Mariner's story is, in fact, a dream-vision, narrated in a compulsive trance − a reverie that transfixes the Guest. As such, it resembles that "streamy" narration of the "associating Faculty," what Coleridge sees as that "reverie-ish" mode that is the "origin of moral Evil." We have noted, moreover, that Coleridge stresses this uncontrolled, "reverie-ish" nature of the Mariner's dialogue, including its compulsive recursion and the baffling, "stunned" responses it provokes in the Guest. By emphasizing this "streamy" narration and its trancelike effects, then, Coleridge brings out what I take to be one of the most vexed moral issues of the "Rime": the fallibility of colloquy. We can accordingly agree with those critics who have maintained that "morals are at issue" in the poem; yet we must also conclude that this issue comes up less in relation to the sundry effects attributed to the albatross's death, or the variously redemptive meanings associated with the snakes' blessing, than it does concerning the Mariner's recursive narration as *itself a potential "origin of moral Evil."* It is this narration that the Mariner must expose to another in the form of dialogue.

VIII

Despite this moral concern about both the wildly "associating" voice and its dialogic effects, they nevertheless seem to hold an essential allure for Coleridge, as if they were the source of some dark insight. His peculiarly recursive modes of dialogue persist not only in the notebooks but also in much of the prose published during his lifetime. Indeed, Coleridge seems desperate to continue in this manner, to speak in this self-generative form. Although he dreads such a discursive "Evil," we have also seen him justify his position by asserting that his "sole sensuality was *not* to be in pain." It would seem that for Coleridge, then, dialogue (including even tortuous or perfidious narration) can be, as he says, "a *means* of escaping from pains." Viewed in this manner, his "talkative" form becomes a kind of *confession* — a self-exposure or outpouring that may help him to address the "pain" of "moral Evil."

Coleridge's obsession with this widespread Evil — coupled with his many personal interpretations of Christianity — suggests that some form of confessional mode would eventually enter his writing. As we have noted, he insists that in order to confront this "evil tendency," we must succeed in exposing it, in "bringing it . . . before an awaking conscience" (*AR* 10). In the context of confessional dialogue, however, we must bear in mind that such an exposure must necessarily take place before an "other" who personifies this "awaking conscience" — a surrogate confessor who allows for Coleridge's examination of "hidden vice." In creating this confessional aesthetic, Coleridge begins that "effort to eloign and abalienate [this vice] from the dark Adyt of [his] own Being by a *visual* Outness."

This spiritual context accordingly leads Coleridge to regard his listeners as if they could on occasion expiate him. We have noted that even in his notebooks, an ostensibly soliloquial form, Coleridge addresses a forgiving "friend" who could conceivably have the "power of destroying these . . . pocket books" — someone who is potentially able to understand his outpouring, and thus to absolve him (*NB* 2: 2368). In the "Rime," too, it is this desire for rhetorical absolution that is presumably behind the Mariner's request for a confessor (the Hermit) to "shrieve" him (512, 574). Hence in characterizing the Hermit's sacerdotal status, Coleridge stresses the ability to confess others, to engage in redemptive dialogue: the Hermit is a "holy man" in that "He loves to talk with marineres" and can therefore "wash away / The Albatross's blood" (574, 517, 512–13). Again, the entire first telling of the Mariner's tale comes as part of a dialogic confession:

> "O shrieve me, shrieve me, holy man!"
> The Hermit crossed his brow.
> "Say quick," quoth he, "I bid thee say —
> What manner of man art thou?"
>
> Forthwith this frame of mine was wrenched
> With a woful agony,
> Which forced me to begin my tale;
> And then it left me free. (574–81)

The Hermit's command here ("I bid thee say — / What manner of man art thou?") is more than a frightened request for explanation; it is his prescription for initiating dialogue, his immediate reply to the Mariner's request to be shriven. The command consequently gives rise both to the Mariner's cathartic "agony" and to the confessional tale itself. Much as one would expect from a formal confession, moreover, the witnessed telling also seems to leave the teller morally "free" (581). The Hermit's ritual thus confirms not only his spiritual vocation but also his dialogically necessary role as a designated interlocutor – as one who "must" attempt to interpret the Mariner's "strange power of speech."

Yet we know, of course, that even as the poem concludes, the Mariner is not actually "free." That his tale becomes, in effect, a compulsive chain of repetitions would suggest that the confession is somehow flawed – that concerted dialogue can never lead to final expiation or conclusive ratiocination. Indeed, for Coleridge, confession was not an affirmation of forgiveness and redemption but a never-ending struggle against immanent evil. In arguing for Luther's notion of confession, he writes, "He would have us feel and groan under our sinfulness and *utter incapability of redeeming ourselves* from the bondage, rather than hazard the pollution of our imaginations by a recapitulation and renewing of sins and their images in detail. . . . —I venture to be of Luther's doctrine."[28] In this sense, confessional dialogue fails to become an expiatory exchange, a communication to one capable of "redeeming" the penitent; rather, it represents the speaker's continual exposure before conscience, his ongoing means of "seeing his sin" (*AR* 352). In the same passage, moreover, Coleridge asks, "Is not this sacrament medicine as well as food? Is it an end only, and not likewise the *means*?" (352, emphasis added). Such a confession, then, may never "end" in absolution; it persists as a "means" of drawing forth "sinfulness." In the "Rime," too, we never hear the Hermit's expiatory response to the Mariner's confession; the tale must continue perpetually as a dialogic "means" of exposure.

IX

Thus, if the concept of a "shrieving" presumes the presence of a comprehending listener, we must recognize that Coleridge's poetic dialogues often represent an unsuccessful attempt at such purgation. We can begin to understand the significance of such failed confession if we briefly return to Coleridge's ancillary writings concerning communion with another. In 1802, he writes, " . . . tho' one should unite Poetry, Draftsman's–ship & Music – the greater & perhaps nobler certainly all the subtler parts of one's nature, must be solitary – Man exists herein to himself & to God alone/ – Yea, in how much only to God . . . " (*NB* 1:1554).

Foremost among these necessarily "solitary" "parts of one's nature" seems to be Coleridge's notion of poetic invention. Much as these "nobler" and "subtler" aspects of the personality must be "solitary," the inmost workings of the creative process must also remain an individual concern. They can only rarely be clarified for an interlocutor. Coleridge says as much, moreover, in commenting on Wordsworth's creative endeavors. As we have noted, when Wordsworth seems to be turning from the lyric to the "solitary" task of writing *The Prelude*, Coleridge commends him, saying, " . . . difference of opinion with his best friends irritated him / & he wrote, at times, too much with a sectarian Spirit, in a sort of Bravado. – But now he is at the Helm of a noble Bark. . . ." For Coleridge, it seems, there can be no genuinely artistic collaboration; even Wordsworth, his continual source of inspiration, feels compelled to report, "I had very little share in the composition of [the "Rime"], for I soon found that the style of Coleridge and myself would not assimilate."[29] Again, of course, Coleridge's belief in this autonomy never actually diminishes his personal need for friendship; while he might question the ability of, say, Asra or his daughter to be critics, their affection is indispensable to him.[30] But although Coleridge may require emotional substantiation from these figures, we should recall that this affectionate support never approaches the "sectarian spirit" of invention that he disparaged in Wordsworth. In fact, Coleridge's belief that the "subtler parts of our nature must be *solitary*" suggests that he knows his creative understanding of these "nobler" parts *must* come without the critical aid of an audience, collaborator, or supporter. In a sense, then, the *lack of any "sectarian" corroboration is, for Coleridge, evidence of his contact with this "nobler" nature.*

Given this insistence on the "solitary" poet, it is not surprising that Coleridge would dwell on those dialogic instances in which, as he says, "I break against the shore of my hearers' patience." In the 1804 entry that we have already seen, he attempts to account for this recurrent conflict between himself and his "bye-stander"; the remainder of this passage is now worth reexamining not only because it exemplifies the tortuous exchange he is trying to explain but because it also constitutes a veiled defense of his dialogic effect upon his "hearers' patience." After noting that it would be "injurious" to confuse the "two sorts of talkative fellows," Coleridge goes on to say that he is of the "second sort,"

> those who use five hundred more ideas, images, reasons &c than there is any need of to arrive at their object/till the only object arrived at is that the . . . mind's eye of the bye-stander is dazzled with colors succeeding so rapidly as to leave one vague impression that there has been a great Blaze of colours all about something. Now this is my case—& a grievous fault it is/my illustrations swallow up my thesis—I feel too intensely the omnipresence of all in each, platonically speaking. . . . bring me two things that seem the very same, & then I am quick enough [not only] to shew the difference, even to hair-splitting—but to go on from circle to circle till I break against the shore of my Hearer's patience, or have my Concentricals dashed to nothing by a Snore—that is my ordinary mishap. . . . At Malta however, no one can charge me with one or the other. I have earned the general character of being a quiet well meaning man, rather dull indeed—& who would have thought, that he had been a *Poet*! "O very wretched Poetaster, Ma'am!" (*NB* 2:2372)

Coleridge's last point here is crucial: when, at Malta, he concerns himself with the "charge" of his beleaguered "bye-stander"—and accordingly gives up his characteristic effusions of "ideas, images [and] reasons"—he becomes a "quiet well-meaning man, rather dull indeed." More tellingly, in his eyes he ceases to be a "poet," becoming instead a "poetaster," a parodic image of his former self. The implication is that, however vexed his "hearers' patience" is, Coleridge's poetic process must proceed associatively if he is to create that "blaze of colours" in the "mind's eye." Indeed, even the language here belies the statement that his "talkative" style is a "grievous fault": his interlocutor is, on the contrary, "dazzled" by this "great Blaze of colours," as if the poet's evocation of "spiritual light" were as significant as any bystander's "vague impression."[31] Later, he comes to defend this allegedly "unpremeditated" style as the mark of a "man of superior mind." In "The Speech of Educated Men," he insists that "however irregular and desultory his talk, there is method in the fragments."[32] In both cases, an interlocutor's "vague impression" only testifies to Coleridge's disavowal of the "sectarian spirit"—the public "bravado" that can only inhibit the "solitary" inspiration of poetic invention.

This is not, of course, to say that a bystander's "vague impression" ceases to concern Coleridge, for he is repeatedly involving himself with the epistemological predicament of his interlocutors.[33] Yet even in his later writings, during the period when his audience's moral response was his principal interest, he laments the attenuation of internal "Truth" for public approbation. "To be admired," he writes, "you must make your auditors believe at least that they understand what you say; which, *be assured, they never will*, under such circumstances, if it be worth understanding, or if you understand your own soul" (*AR* 127–28, emphasis added). For Coleridge, the impetus to dialogue must be distinguished from a desire for others' admiration, which he later refers to as the "vanity or the weakness of the pleasure of communicating thy Thoughts & awaking Sympathy" (*NB* 2:2196). In *Aids to Reflection*, he goes on to suggest that when we start to acquire insight and knowledge—beginning at what he calls the "starting-post" of "Truth"—our personal "attainment" should take precedence over this "anxiety to be admired." Coleridge decries those "times when the few who know the truth have clothed it for the vulgar, and addressed the vulgar in the vulgar language and modes of conception, in order to convey any part of the truth" (*AR* 228). Any compromised presentation or explication for others must accordingly be postponed, for both this "anxiety to be admired" and the fear of judgment tend to corrupt any search for "Truth." If "you have appointed the Many as your judges and appraisers," he says, then "your words must be as indefinite as their thoughts" (*AR* 127).

X

Here Coleridge is not, I would say, disparaging "the Many." He seems in fact protective of their responses when he goes on to remind us

that those who succumb to that "anxiety to be admired" are "at once
taxing the patience and humiliating the self-opinion of [their] judges."
He elsewhere insists that, given the conditions appropriate for an
interlocutor, "a sacred Sympathy would at once compel & inspire me
to the Task of uttering the very Truth" (*NB* 2:2196). But Coleridge
also comes to suspect his desire to be "admired" and "appreciated,"
his need for the "Sympathy" that can betray personal conviction. We
begin to see, moreover, why he might scorn such sympathy on the part
of even well-meaning reviewers — to the point of actually fictionalizing
their "gauntlet" of alleged "abuse." Generally speaking, he feels a
need to guard his own process of spiritual reflection and potential "attainment" of the "Truth." If he acquiesces to "the pleasure
of communicating . . . Thoughts & awaking Sympathy," he might
lose the "Tranquillity" of self-contemplation, "& in acquiring the *passion* of proselytism lose the *sense* of conviction" (*NB* 2:2196). The
search for the comprehending "other" can thus undermine a knowledge of self; indeed, the desire "to be compared and appreciated" is
clearly at odds with certain private truths. For as he goes on to ask,
" . . . while your prevailing motive is to be compared and appreciated, is it credible, is it possible, that you should in earnest seek for *a
knowledge which is and must remain a hidden light, a secret treasure*?" (*AR* 128, emphasis added).

With this last quotation, we arrive at what I take to be the essence
of Coleridge's "Truth," and the corresponding problem with corroborative audition: the "knowledge" he alludes to "is and must remain a
hidden light, a secret treasure" — "secret" from even his closest interlocutors. Such "hidden" knowledge is similar to the "secret lodger"
discussed earlier in *Aids to Reflection*: the undefined spectre that
Coleridge refers to as "an aching hollowness in the bosom, a dark
cold speck at the heart, an obscure and boding sense of a somewhat,
that must be kept out of sight of the conscience" (*AR* 9–10). Again,
this "lodger" resembles what Coleridge also describes as "some hidden
Vice" foreshadowed by an "act of [his] own Spirit, of the absolute
Noumenon" (*NB* 3:4166). In both passages, he seems either unwilling
or unable to define this "sense of a somewhat" — a seemingly unusual
omission for someone as given to excursus as he was. Yet I would
argue that Coleridge is here attempting to represent a form of dialogue that is founded upon what is "noumenal," "hidden," and
"secret." He recognizes that, in order to effect such dialogue, his
interlocutors must continue to come up against this noumenal object,
that they must remain agons. It is only agonistic dialogue, moreover —

the process of Socratic query and rhetorical resistance—that can address those "invisible things" invoked in the motto to the "Rime": "I readily believe that there are more invisible than visible things in the universe. . . . The human mind has always circled about knowledge of these things, but never attained it."[34]

The auditor contained within the poem thus becomes a synecdoche for rhetorical resistance, for poetic agonism. It is this resistance on the part of an incorporated auditor that ensures that the poetic speaker will continue to respond, endeavoring to answer an interlocutor's protests and queries. In this sense, agonism serves to perpetuate dialogue. In the "Rime," moreover, this perpetuation of dialogue takes on an interpretive function, in that the ongoing process of question and answer constitutes a kind of poetic hermeneutic. In fact, queries and protests from both the befuddled Guest and the perplexed Hermit (asking, "What manner of man art thou?") effectively recast the Mariner's narrative as a continuing exchange of interrogation and response. Here again, then, Gadamer's analysis of this form applies readily. Although he refers to such a process as "dialectic," he clearly stresses the ongoing interrogation of the form. "Dialectic," he writes, "as the art of asking questions, proves itself only because the person who knows how to ask questions is able to persist in his questioning, which involves being able to preserve his orientation towards openness. The art of questioning is that of being able *to go on asking questions* . . . " (330).

In perpetuating dialogue, then, Coleridge's agonistic interlocutor also impels the process of interpretive questioning. We must bear in mind, moreover, that such a heuristic is grounded not only in the interpretive operations of Socratic exchange but also in the *oral* tradition of narrative poetry—that process whereby bardic poetry is passed on, developed (and once again, reinterpreted) over time. Indeed, as Jerome J. McGann has demonstrated, the "Rime" is historically linked to the early biblical narratives within this oral tradition, to the "idea, which Coleridge explicitly endorsed, that the biblical narratives were originally bardic (oral) poetry which gradually evolved into a cycle of communal literary materials. Embedded in primitive and legendary saga, the Scriptures grew by accretion and interpolation over an extended period of time" ("Meaning" 48). McGann goes on to demonstrate that this oral tradition of biblical exegesis profoundly influenced Coleridge's construction of the "Rime"; he suggests that such an ongoing, oral "cycle" is represented by the "layers" of interpretation inscribed directly within the poem (including the original tale, the editorial gloss, the Mariner's retelling, and even the divergent kinds of diction employed). In the present context, moreover, we can also say that this oral tradition is represented by the explicitly spoken exchange between the Mariner and the Guest — by the actual dialogue inscribed within the poem. Generally speaking, this oral dialogue becomes a poetic embodiment of the rhetorical features we have stressed; it represents, for instance, that ongoing process of oral "accretion and interpolation," propelled by the agonistic stance of several interlocutors. At the same time, we have noted that such poetic exchanges can also represent a hermeneutic process, directly related both to classical dialogue and to the oral tradition of narrative exegesis, through repeated scenes of retelling and relistening.

XI

It is this combination of dialogic processes — interrogative, accretive, and exegetical — that Coleridge brings to bear on the various *aporia*, "invisible things," and noumenal "knowledge" depicted in the "Rime." He seeks to make us aware of a knowledge that can never be "attained" but only "circled about" — that part of the self unavailable to us. As he asks in the poem "Self-Knowledge," "What is there in thee, Man, that can be known? — / Dark fluxion, all unfixable by thought . . . " (6-7). Delphic self-knowledge is, according to Coleridge, beyond our comprehension; consequently, when he discusses this "unfixable" knowledge, he refers to it as an "obscure" premonition, a "vision," an intangible "hollowness."[35] Indeed, his language here reflects a problem in epistemology: although he needs to grapple with the "secret lodger," he realizes that he will never exorcise it. "All notions," he writes, "[remain] hushed in the phantasms of place and time that still escape the finest sieve and most searching winnow of our reason and abstraction." Yet if the "human mind" must continually hover on the edge of this mysterious knowledge, Coleridge nevertheless demands that such mystery be inscribed in the agonism of poetic dialogue. After publishing the 1800 version of the "Rime," he suggests that "Materialists unwilling to admit the mysterious of our nature make it all mysterious — . . . " (*NB* 1:920).

We should not be surprised, then, to find that Coleridge would deploy agonism to instantiate these "hidden" notions in his poetry — this "knowledge which is and must remain a hidden light." What is surprising, however, is that Coleridge would find such hidden knowledge to be a hallmark of what he calls the "grandest efforts of poetry." Yet one year after publishing the "Rime," he wrote in his notebook, "When no criticism is pretended to . . . Poetry gives most pleasure when only generally & not perfectly understood" (*NB* 1:383). For Coleridge, it would seem that this state of "not perfectly" understanding — of keeping the mind dialogically engaged in an ongoing and highly directed search — defines affective "pleasure" in poetry. In elaborating on this definition, he suggests that the "elder Languages were fitter for Poetry because they expressed only prominent ideas with clearness, others but darkly." While an interlocutor can readily grasp these "prominent ideas," he should be able to see that "the others" will remain "not perfectly understood" — that they are "and must remain a hidden light."

Yet for Coleridge it is precisely this dialogic struggle with a "hidden light" that matters, rather than any goal of understanding the "secret" source of such knowledge. The attempt to approach the "incomprehensible," and the *process* we undergo in that attempt, concern him more than the content of this "obscure" "speck at the heart."[36] In fact, his most illuminating commentary on this hidden "lodger" comes in the work entitled *Aids to Reflection*, in which he focuses on the reflective process as a spiritual end in itself: by continually "looking down into" the obscure parts of the self, we sustain a process of spiritual growth, of ongoing discovery. And because the continuation of this reflective process takes precedence over any ultimate explanation, a futile process engages Coleridge at least as much as one that ends in ostensible insight. Accordingly, he presents the Wedding-Guest's failed attempts to fathom the Mariner's tale as an ineluctable process. Similarly, the Mariner's compulsive retellings also represent a dialogic process of reflection, as do Christabel's "vain," unconscious endeavors to tell Geraldine's true story:

> But vainly thou warrest,
>   For this is alone in
> Thy power to declare,
>   That in the dim forest
> Thou heard'st a low moaning,
> And found'st a bright lady, surpassingly fair. . . . ("Christabel" 271–76)

Of course, the precise nature of these tortuous reflections differs. Yet each features a rhetorical process as the means of confronting a secret lodger. It is this process, moreover, that comes to represent Coleridge's own ruminative efforts to expose this lodger. The aim of these works—if we can call it that—is contemplation: although we have "never attained" any "knowledge of these [invisible] things," the motto goes on to remind us that "it is sometimes good to contemplate in the mind, as in a picture, the image of a greater and better world; otherwise the intellect, habituated to the petty things of daily life, may too much contract itself, and wholly sink down to trivial thoughts." It is this reflective contemplation that underlies the process of Coleridgean dialogue.

Thus, while Coleridge recognizes that a failure of understanding will most often "break against the shore of his hearers' patience," he is extraordinary in his belief that this state of "not perfectly" understanding is in fact a condition for great poetry. "The grandest efforts of poetry," he writes, "are where the imagination is called forth,"

> not to produce a distinct form, but a strong working of the mind, still offering what is still repelled, and again creating what is again rejected; the result being what the poet wishes to impress, namely, the substitution of a sublime feeling of the unimaginable for a mere image. I have sometimes thought that the passage just read might be quoted as exhibiting the narrow limit of painting, as compared with the boundless power of poetry: painting cannot go beyond a certain point; poetry rejects all control, all confinement. (*SC* 138)

Great poetry will often be "rejected" by an interlocutor precisely because it conjures the "unimaginable": that "knowledge which is and must remain a hidden light." Such poetry will, however, attempt to offer this secret knowledge even as it is "repelled"—as if the poet were cognizant that a rejection of the "unimaginable" is an indication of its presence. Thus, when Coleridge thinks of an audience for these "grandest efforts of poetry," he envisions neither a corroborator nor even what could be called a "vicarious" participant—that receptive listener onto whom a poet can project his most personal ideals. Coleridge speaks, rather, to a dialogic agon: a voice that he must necessarily struggle against, "creating what is again rejected." Indeed, the continuance of this struggle seems actually to be a precondition for Coleridge's creativity—much as the storm becomes the source of the speaker's inspiration in "Ode: To Dejection." Coleridge accordingly attempts to become a rhetorical "watcher from without," one who eschews the "sectarian spirit."[37]

It is this concept of agonistic dialogue — the rhetorical struggle with "what is still repelled" and "rejected" — that defines the nineteenth-century prose forms considered in Part II. Coleridge's disjunctive rhetoric is, in this sense, paradigmatic, for his interlocutors foreshadow the cleft exchanges that characterize *Frankenstein, Wuthering Heights*, and *Heart of Darkness*. As we shall see, these works adapt and reinterpret the figure of rifted dialogue — particularly in their introduction of an interpretive voice that mediates between such characters as the monster and Walton, Heathcliff and Lockwood, and Kurtz and the Thames listeners. At the same time, however, these works continue to display the kind of dialogic resistance that we have seen in Coleridge's lyrics. Like them, these prose works of the nineteenth century feature a dialogic attempt to confront what Coleridge calls the "unimaginable," the "invisible." Like the figures in Coleridge's "Rime," then, the interlocutors in these latter works must offer a "strong working of the mind," a rhetorical exertion toward outness, in response to their own versions of the poet's "secret lodger."

II

The Novel All Told: Audition, Orality, and the Collapse of Dialogue

> Utterances and their types, that is, speech genres, are the drive belts from the history of society to the history of language.
>
> Bakhtin, "The Problem of Speech Genres"

> And he felt in his heart their strangeness,
> Their stillness answering his cry,
> While his horse moved, cropping in the dark turf,
> 'Neath the starred and leafy sky;
> For suddenly he smote on the door, even
> Louder, and lifted his head: —
> "Tell them I came, and no one answered,
> That I kept my word," he said.
> Never the least stir made the listeners,
> Though every word he spake
> Fell echoing through the shadowiness of the still house
> From the one man left awake:
> Ay, they heard his foot upon the stirrup,
> And the sound of iron on stone,
> And how the silence surged softly backward,
> When the plunging hoofs were gone.
>
> Walter de la Mare, "The Listeners"

4

Three Blind Mariners and a Monster: Frankenstein as Vocative Text

> In ["the last, realistic type of novel of emergence"], however, human emergence is of a different nature. It is no longer man's own private affair. He emerges *along with the world* and he reflects the historical emergence of the world itself. . . . This transition is accomplished in him and through him. He is forced to become a new, unprecedented type of human being. . . . It is as though the very *foundations* of the world are changing, and man must change along with them. Understandably, in such a novel of emergence, problems of reality and man's potential, problems of freedom and necessity, and the problem of creative initiative rise to their full height.
>
> Bakhtin, "The *Bildungsroman*"

> I was exceedingly surprised on receiving so rude an answer from a stranger. . . .
>
> [T]his strange dialogue continued. . . .
>
> Victor in *Frankenstein*

During the years that Mary Shelley revised her dreamt account of a fallen Adam — complete with Edenic allusions to both prelapsarian innocence and Satanic wrath — John Keats was composing his own dream-vision of a fallen god, namely, the titan Saturn, and of his aspiring compeer, Hyperion. In both "The Fall of Hyperion" and its earlier incarnation, Keats portrays a Saturn bereft of his birthright and overwhelmed by another's Promethean ambition, depictions that tellingly recall Mary Shelley's own disconsolate monster. What is striking about these two fallen figures, however, is their predisposition for the word — for dialogue as a modality of empowerment and recovery. Much as Saturn is "listening to the Earth, / His ancient mother, for some comfort yet," so the monster entreats his parent to "listen to me, and grant me thy compassion" (I:325-26).[1] And much as Saturn bemoans his "feeble . . . voice," longing instead for "Voices of . . . proclaim" and "trumpets blown," so Shelley's creature despairs of his inarticulateness, his "harsh . . . voice" — and so seeks to "acquire the art of language," that "godlike science" betokening the "perfect forms" of a divine race (110, 107, 109).[2] In both cases, moreover, the synecdoche representing this fallen self is silence, that ineffable yet divisive barrier between each figure and his lapsed kingdom. In Keats's fragment, for instance, Saturn's enfeebling silence is reflected in the muteness of the poem's narrator. When this narrator reacts to his own muse's godlike address, he has

> no words to answer, for my tongue,
> Useless, could find about its roofed home
> No syllable of a fit majesty
> To make rejoinder. . . .
> There was a silence. . . . (I:228-32)

Like the socially silenced monster, Keats's narrator believes that language alone has the power to spring the imagination, that "every man whose soul is not a clod / Hath visions, and would speak, if he had love, / And been well nurtured in his mother tongue" (I:13-15). "Poesy alone," he suggests,

> can tell her dreams,
> With the fine spell of words alone can save
> Imagination from the sable charm
> And dumb enchantment." (I:8-11)

It is this desire to "tell [one's] dreams" — to impel the self beyond "dumb enchantment" — that motivates the three concentric dialogues that constitute *Frankenstein*. Like Keats's vision, Shelley's narrative is constructed almost entirely of apostrophe: the monster must recount his history to Victor, who in turn conveys it to Robert Walton. The latter then beseeches his sister, Margaret (that eristic figure whose presence frames the novel), "Oh, that some encouraging voice would answer in the affirmative!" (12).[3] In many ways, this hortatory request for an "answer" operates as a kind of formal principle for apostrophe in general — as a motif in which the apostrophic request, surrounded by a narrative frame, looks outward to the frame itself for a meliorative "answer." In this sense, the inner stories contained within each frame are effectively apostrophic pleas, addressed to those characters who listen from the margins of the embedded tale.

Again, however, these dialogic pleas ultimately founder upon a pervasive silence: in response to the monster's entreaty for Victor to "hear my tale," the scientist must respond, "Begone! . . . your words will only exasperate my rage" (96, 165). If we attempt to account for such acts of failed listening, moreover, we find a number of plausible explanations. These accounts usually begin by asserting that works like *Frankenstein* depict either a particular narrator's collapse, the faltering of language itself, or, most often, a paradigmatic act of misinterpretation — what various critics call a "permanently frustrated desire for meaning" or "process of misreading," since the "Creature's fate is to be misread."[4] Although such studies hardly constitute a consensus, they appear to agree that "narrative itself is implicated" or "fails" in *Frankenstein*, that "storytelling itself is . . . a means of displacing and sublimating desire that cannot be satisfied directly."[5] These approaches tend to characterize the narrative exchanges and framed tales within *Frankenstein* as interchanges of "non-meaning," the "inaccessible signified," an "emblem of language's murderous lack of transcendent reference" (Brooks 214, 212, 220). Like Yeats's gyre, such novels are said to have a "central gap," an "absent" or "missing center," since "language never can overcome the gap" "between signifier and signified."[6] According to this view, any narrator's attempt to cross this interpretive gap — such as by apostrophizing an auditor — must necessarily lead either to misinterpretation or to the dissolution of the narrator's self. Indeed, such studies come to regard narrative apostrophe, with its frequent multiplication of invoked voices, as a liability for the self. In appropriating these disparate voices into a single self, apostrophizing narrators often internalize what should remain part of the external world; such speakers thereby effect the very solipsism they appear to escape (Culler 146; Jacobus 175). At the same time, these narrators' attempts to include multiple voices serve only to disperse the self, diffusing and attenuating any potential for a coherent identity.[7]

I

There is, of course, much to be said for these approaches to apostrophe and narrative framing. To be sure, the monster — a central apostrophic narrator in *Frankenstein* — despairs of developing a coherent self, integrated with those around him. What is more, even his attempts to "signify" to another — as demonstrated by his linguistic preoccupations with phonological competence, literary understanding, and cultural communication — fail to clarify his innocence to those around him, to represent his prelapsarian state. He remains, in this sense, unable to name his linguistic beginnings, and must in turn remain nameless himself. He consequently baffles listeners like the De Lacys, who would hear (or "read") his "papers" of origin — and is, according to this view, misread (135).

In what follows, however, I argue that the divergent voices invoked by narrative apostrophe are indications not of dispersal but of the *rhetorical construction of selfhood from multiple voices.* Narratives addressed to such failed listeners as Victor Frankenstein, Felix De Lacy, and the Irish islanders are not so much examples of "misreading" as they are apostrophic attempts to create what the monster refers to as "being." In this context, the succession of flawed interchanges between storytellers and auditors should be considered not as "misinterpretation" but as an *ongoing narrative process* of self-framing and self-decipherment. Hence when characters in the novel seek to "declare [themselves] to the whole world," they are in effect demonstrating what the monster sees as a linguistic "intercourse" essential to "existence" (183, 143). In fact, the many apostrophic declarations to listeners in *Frankenstein* often become calls for this verbal "intercourse," for what Victor refers to as "dialogue" (170).[8] In such Romantic narratives, moreover, apostrophe is itself a figure for dialogue, a synecdoche for this verbal intercourse. Finally, I will suggest that addresses in *Frankenstein* form part of a hermeneutic process, a rhetorical act of interpretation applied to such problems as Victor's Prometheanism and the monster's vengeful murders. In such cases, the dialogic form of the novel functions not only as an ontological key but as a heuristic method.

II

It is this need for both hermeneutic understanding and verbal self-creation that initially leads the monster out of self, in search of a listener. He accordingly turns to language in hopes of persuading potential interlocutors to disregard his monstrosity. After observing the De Lacys, he speaks of his resolve to "become master of their language; which knowledge might enable me to make them overlook the deformity of my figure" (109; cf. 110). The monster sees this linguistic "knowledge" as both overcoming visual horror and displacing his own body-angst. For him, verbal signs must substitute for the signs of the body. Indeed, at one point the monster actually covers Victor's eyes, saying, "Thus I take from thee a sight which you abhor. Still thou canst listen to me" (96). Yet he intends this linguistic facility not just to mask his outward "figure" but to define his internal self. Accordingly, his quest for an affirmative listener becomes his primary motivation in the novel. In fact, the impetus for such a narrative resides in this drive for the other: the monster's central desire is for someone "with whom I can live in the interchange of those sympathies *necessary for my being*" (140, emphasis added). The "sympathies" alluded to here—as well as the bilateral "interchange" that elicits them—are "necessary" in that they confirm one's "being," in that they delimit and animate the ego. As Victor puts it, "We are unfashioned creatures, but half made up, if one wiser, better, dearer than ourselves—such a friend ought to be—do not lend his aid to perfectionate our weak and faulty natures" (1831:232). Behind the narrative interchanges in *Frankenstein*, then, is a need for that extrinsic other who completes our "faulty natures"—"but half made up" in themselves.

Mary Shelley's portrayal of this "necessary" "friend" who can sustain "nature" proves to be tragically prophetic when, in the summer of 1822, she learns of her husband's death by drowning off Via Reggio. The exact meaning of such a "friend" becomes apparent in her first journal entry written after the tragedy:

> . . . all is silent around me. . . . The stars may behold my tears, and the winds drink my sighs; but my thoughts are a sealed treasure, which I can confide to none. But can I express all I feel? . . . Alas! I am alone. No eye answers mine; my voice can with none assume its natural modulation. What a change! O my beloved Shelley! how often during those happy days—happy, though chequered—I thought how superiorly gifted I had been in being united to one to whom I could unveil myself, and who could understand me! (*Journal* 180–81)

Here, Mary Shelley speaks of her husband in much the same way that the monster explains his own desire for a companion. Though *Frankenstein* predates this entry, the passage recalls her creature's abhorrence of solitude. Like him, she needs an other in order to bring forth the isolated ego, to unlock the "sealed treasure" of the self. Her self-affirmation thus derives from self-expression to another; such interchange allows her, as she says, to "unveil myself." In this sense, each address invokes both external and internal voices, for it not only enlightens others but also enables her to "understand" the self—to fathom those "sympathies necessary for . . . being."[9]

Given this need to "unveil" the self before another, to reinvent oneself before one who "answers," it is not extraordinary that narrators in *Frankenstein* would preoccupy themselves with the potential reactions and judgments of a listening witness. For to sustain the engagement of a listener—and thereby to maintain interchange—is actually to construct and perpetuate one's own "being." The three narrators of the novel accordingly become critically aware of the responses to their tales. Victor, for instance, interrupts his excursus on the Promethean "pursuit of knowledge" with the following apology: "But I forget that I am moralizing in the most interesting part of my tale; and your looks remind me to proceed" (51). Later, after telling Walton of his feelings before returning to Geneva, Victor says again, "I fear, my friend, that I shall render myself tedious by dwelling on these preliminary circumstances . . . " (70; cf. 152). Victor's syntax here suggests that affective interchange not only absorbs a listener but also can, as he says, "render [one]self"—remaking the identity of a speaker. The monster, too, feels a need to maintain this self-defining interchange, and he in turn anticipates his auditor's responses: "I now hasten to the more moving part of my story," he says after fully describing the De Lacys (111). The creature is also careful not only to engross his listener with a climactic sequence of events but also to provide those background passages crucial to his narrative: "I must not omit," he says at one point, "a circumstance which occurred in the beginning of the month of August of the same year" (123). And earlier, when he begins to hint at his request for a companion, he says, "I will soon explain to what these feelings tended; but allow me now to return to the cottagers, whose story excited in me such various feelings of indignation, delight, and wonder, but which all terminated in additional love and reverence for my protectors . . . " (117).

In this last passage, however, the monster looks beyond the novel's general concern for auditor comprehension, first by anticipating questions about these painful "feelings," and then by foreshadowing how these sentiments are eventually "terminated."[10] Walton, too, seems to apprehend this deep awareness of the shape and denouement of narrative when he makes a point of telling his sister that Victor's "tale is connected" (207). Both characters thus become concerned with the ratiocinative quality of narrative for an audience's benefit. Underlying such concerns, though, is the suggestion that in recounting comprehensible narrative before an other—in making it appear "connected"—one can essentially compose a coherent self. Put in Victor's terms, narrative apostrophe—that verbal "fashioning" *for* an other—can reconstruct "weak and faulty natures," redefining the "half made up" self.

Hence the attempt to weave together a "connected," progressive tale becomes the very ethos of storytelling in the novel—the rhetorical equivalent of self-creation. As the narratives succeed one another, each speaker reveals an Aristotelian consciousness of progression, a belief in the formal coherence of narrative for a listener. In reading the monster's narrative, we are accordingly asked to trace those "feelings which," as he puts it, "from what I was, have made me what I am" (111). The monster later reiterates his belief in this alleged progression when he refers to his story as an "account of the progress of my intellect," an "account" that seems to offer "progress" to a listener (123). It is this focus on the intelligibility of narrative—on its internal continuity, ratiocination, and affect—that calls attention both to individual auditors and to the overall potential for dialogue in the novel. Only the appropriation of narrative by an other can engender the self. Victor, Walton, and the monster thus attempt to fashion "being' by transforming narration into "interchange," storytelling into "intercourse."

III

The critic who has most clearly formulated this ontological connection between speaker and other (or "friend") is, again, Bakhtin. To speak of that "friend" who completes the "half made up" self—that object who informs "being"—is to speak at once of what Bakhtin calls "self-consciousness." He writes, "I am conscious through another, and with the help of another. The most important acts constituting self-consciousness are determined by a relationship toward another consciousness (toward a *thou*)" (*Poetics* 287). For Bakhtin, this "thou" hypostatizes self-consciousness—which is to say that only such interchange (or "dialogue") can make the self aware of its own distinctness, can actually unveil the self to itself. As we have noted, Bakhtin suggests that "in dialogue a person not only shows himself outwardly, but he becomes for the first time that which he is—and, we repeat, not only for others but for himself as well. To be means to communicate dialogically" (252). Dialogue with the "friend" can thus enact the ego. In the case of the monster, then, recurrent pleas for a "companion" — for "communion with an equal" — signify a desire for self-consciousness, for what he calls his ongoing "existence" (140, 143). Such a companion would enable him "to be," to recognize "that which he is."

Bakhtin explains this view of self-consciousness as a process of juxtaposing self and others. He writes:

> The hero's attitude toward himself is inseparably bound up with his attitude toward another, and with the attitude of another toward him. His consciousness of self is constantly perceived against the background of the other's consciousness of him — "I for myself" against the background of "I for another." Thus the hero's words about himself are structured under the continuous influence of someone else's words about him. (*Poetics* 207)

Here, establishing the self is a contrastive act, a matter of perceiving the other as "background" for identity. The limits of the "I" emerge only amidst contrasts with the "thou." We can say, then, that when the monster begs for that "interchange . . . necessary for my being," he seeks this self-fashioning contrast or "background": he sees that "consciousness of self is constantly perceived against the background of the other's consciousness of him." Early in his narrative, he accordingly refers to this need for a contrastive "consciousness," saying, " . . . I was dependent on none, and related to none" (124). What is more, he immediately goes on to suggest the ontological consequences of this lack of "relation": "Who was I?" he asks. "What was I?" The monster's being ("Who was I?") thus depends on his need for the other ("related to none"): he knows that only in encountering this other will he "become for the first time that which he is." Here again, "to be" — for the monster — "is to communicate dialogically," since only this dialogic presence can sustain his selfhood.[11]

We must further bear in mind that if the monster establishes this "being" in relation to a "companion," he also implies that such delineation of self must be *vocal* or *spoken*. The ego must be overheard in the form of a voice. In the monster's words, it is Victor who literally "*called* me into being," and it is Victor's voice that must be replaced (220, emphasis added). He accordingly bends his entire education toward the purpose of spoken "interview" with the De Lacys (126). Walton, too, stresses the auricular word by choosing to portray Victor's essence as a deeply affecting "voice," a "voice so modulated to the different feelings expressed in his speech" that it transfixes the entire crew (213). For Walton, Victor's "eloquence is forcible and touching" (208), whether it be "tranquil" or "broken" (207). Later, Walton is again moved by the monster's "powers of eloquence and persuasion" (218). Generally, then, the auricular dimension of narrative determines a given narrator's "power" and authority over his audience. In each case, Shelley measures this oral acumen in terms of its rapport, its rhetorical impact on a designated auditor.

Such concerns with "eloquence" and "voice" are also central to Mary Shelley's journal. In the foregoing entry, the metaphor employed in depicting grief — and her own need for the absent other — revolves around her desire for a responding "voice," beyond the tragically "silent" world of her unanswered "sighs" (180). In her comments on self-modulation and the emergent voice, we see that the respondent she seeks is quintessentially a listener — in much the same way that her monster initially longs for someone simply to "Listen" (96). In both cases, being heard tends not only to ensure response but also to enact existence. Listeners accordingly give voice to the isolated mind, enable it to "assume its natural modulation." Only such audition can "answer" the self, can provide the aural response that is "necessary for . . . being."[12]

Because such "modulation" must be heard, then, the self-affirming other in *Frankenstein* is necessarily an auditor — just as the monster's long-sought "interchanges" are necessarily conversation-based, what Bakhtin refers to as "dialogue." "Life," writes Bakhtin, "by its very nature is dialogic. To live means to participate in dialogue: to ask questions, to heed, to respond, to agree, and so forth" (*Poetics* 293).[13] Here again, such participation is represented as a spoken process of questioning, heeding, and rejoining. In the following passage, too, he develops this notion of shaping the ego amidst spoken dialogue, of individuating the self as a "voice." He writes, "To find one's own voice and to orient it among other voices, to combine it with some and to oppose it to others, to separate one's voice from another voice with which it has inseparably merged — these are the tasks that the heroes solve. . . . And this determines the hero's discourse. It must find itself, reveal itself among other words . . . " (239). Once again, the process of defining the self is both oral and contrastive: one must "oppose" one's "voice" to another. In *Frankenstein*, then, the hortatory narratives of Victor and the monster must also "orient [themselves] among other voices"; each must "find itself, reveal itself among" the potential responses of inadequate listeners. Only such interchanges, including the listening that sustains them, can resonate the social self.

Nowhere does this need to "orient" the self "among other voices" become more apparent than in Victor's flawed search for interchange. For Victor implicitly attempts to re-"connect" his shattered life by retelling it before others, reconstituting it in terms of other voices (196). Yet until he finally meets Walton, Victor must stifle this constitutive voice, with disastrous consequences. He determines, for instance, never to reveal the monster's existence to another, in part because his auditors have proven to be consistently incredulous. "I avoided explanation," he says, "and maintained a continual silence concerning the wretch I had created. I had a feeling that I should be supposed mad, and this for ever chained my tongue, when I would have given the whole world to have confided the fatal secret" (182, cf. 245). This feeling that he would "be supposed mad" silences Victor repeatedly; the secret he would have confided in a listener never becomes "explanation" to another (cf. 72, 183, 196–98, 252). Even Elizabeth is divorced from his apostrophic quest for "confidence": "I have one secret, Elizabeth, a dreadful one," he tells her initially; "I will confide this tale of misery and terror to you the day after our marriage shall take place; for, my sweet cousin, there must be perfect confidence between us" (187). Once again, however, Victor's "secret" expression — and the demarcation of self it represents — falls upon deaf ears. In murdering this last of Victor's listeners, the monster consummates his revenge: it consists not only of dismembering Victor's family but also of arresting his rhetoric of being, Victor's dialogue with the world.

Yet Victor's "continual silence" represents not only a response to absent auditors but also a cause or perpetuation of them. If the monster gradually silences his creator's auditors, it is Victor himself who ultimately ignores or denies every potential interlocutor in the novel. He essentially mutes his own world by encountering it without a voice. "By the utmost self-violence," he says, "I curbed the imperious voice of wretchedness . . . " (183). Long after he first learns of Clerval's death, Victor says, "I often sat for hours motionless and speechless . . . " (179). And after failing to engage the Genevan magistrate, he notes that he quietly "retired to meditate" on his plight (198). In each case, this voicelessness traces Victor's gradual loss of being during the novel. It is this same pervasive silence, moreover, that accounts for his oft-cited failure as a responsible creator: Mary Shelley represents Victor's inability to parent the monster as an incapacity to sustain interchange.[14] Hence when he first comes upon his creature out of the laboratory, Victor tells us that "hatred . . . deprived me of utterance" (94); by the end of the novel, the monster too says, "He may not answer me" (217). Victor thus offers the monster the same self-abnegating "answer" that has plagued both of them. And later, Victor's final silence in death proves to be the echo of his life: in either case, he is "unable to speak" (214, 216).

Victor also bequeaths this fatal silence to all those who might respond to the monster's pleas. In warning Walton to shun the creature, Victor says, "He is eloquent and persuasive; and once his words had even power over my heart: but trust him not. . . . Hear him not . . . " (206). And indeed, Walton later denies his capacities as a potential listener for the monster: "I was at first touched," Walton says, "by the expressions of his misery; yet when I called to mind what Frankenstein had said of his powers of eloquence and persuasion . . . indignation was re-kindled within me" (218). Such 'indignation" at the monster's attempted interchange testifies to more than just his deformities, for both Walton and Victor continue to have "bewildered" responses long after they have begun to look past his physical appearance (142, 144). Instead, narrative "eloquence and persuasion" have themselves become suspect for Walton, so that he can hardly react to the monster's call for an "answer": "I attempted to speak," Walton says, "but the words died away on my lips" (217).[15] Here again, the death of all such "words"—of all sustenative "answers"—prefigures the deaths of both Victor and the monster. As we move through the successive narrators and auditors of the novel, silence begets silence.

Denied this vocal connection to the other, the monster too comes to represent a kind of rhetorical solipsism. Without the "communion" that affirms "being," his development of self is painfully stunted: he remains, as he puts it, "unformed in mind" (124). He is in this sense exiled within an inchoate mind, trapped within an echoless purgatory. It is just such entrapment, too, that Mary Shelley herself feared during her periods of isolation. Years later, she would describe in her journal a similar imprisonment within the self: "How painful all change becomes," she writes, "to one who, entirely and despotically engrossed by their own feelings, leads as it were an internal life, quite different from the outward and apparent one!" (183; cf. 203). In this entry, the potential growth and "change" of everyday life become insufferable to those trapped within the self-"engrossed" mind. Banished to this "internal life," lacking all "outward" connection, the self becomes, she goes on, "sterile" and unreceptive; it "distorts" all contact that might lead to interchange with an external other, and ultimately to the constitution of a distinct identity (184).

It is this longing for "outward" connections, for a foil to the "internal life," that underlies the search for an exterior other in *Frankenstein*. Several characters refer to the hermitic self as some demon trapped within them, an internal "hell." Like Milton's Satan, Shelley's monster exclaims, "I . . . bore a hell within me" (132).[16] Victor, too, bemoans this intrinsic demon: "Anguish and despair had penetrated into the core of my heart," he says; "I bore a hell within me" (84). On one level, of course, Victor's painful "hell within" is mnemonic, contained in the recurring scenes of his monster's ruin and havoc. On another level, however, this "hell within" is, for both him and his monster, an image of the interred, dissociated ego—a testament to each character's inability to effect colloquy with his counterpart. Victor's hell thus amounts to a linguistic estrangement from the other, a polarization from a series of potential auditors, including the monster. Hence when Victor says, "I . . . carried about with me my eternal hell," "my own vampire, my own spirit let loose from the grave," his words apply not only to the monster but also to his own seclusion "within," to the "eternal hell" of the internalized self (201, 72). It is thus misleading to focus on the oft-cited conflation of Victor and his creature, the critical position that describes creator and created as pendants of a single psyche.[17] For we have seen that characters' rhetorical *separations* from one another motivate their ongoing quests for listeners, and that even when these quests founder, such separations still keep open the potential for meliorative dialogue.

IV

Hence Mary Shelley decries the 'internal life" in favor of "outward" connections and exterior interchange. It is also crucial, though, to note that in those key passages where she comments on this "hell within," she does so by directly citing her contemporary, S. T. Coleridge.[18] Coleridge's "Rime of the Ancient Mariner," for example, is particularly resonant for her: much as the Ancient Mariner represents his crime as a "frightful fiend," Victor cites parallel passages from the

"Rime," referring to the monster as a "fiend," "vampire," "demon," or "devil" (15, 54). What is most significant about this Coleridgean connection, however, is that Mary Shelley's concept of "outward" interchange—of exposing the "hell within" to an external other—clearly demonstrates what Coleridge refers to as outness. As we have seen, such outness is that process by which he can expose or "withdraw" his "painful Peculiarities . . . from the dark Adyt of [his] own Being . . . " (*NB* 3:4166). Such a process of externalizing inner struggles bears directly on Coleridge's own views of an extrinsic listener; in this context, his "outward" listeners enable him both to present and examine his internal conflicts. Much like the monster, he can delimit the "Peculiarities" of the self only by establishing what he calls an external "Boundary" or "Neighbourhood"—in a word, outness (*NB* 2:3231). Applying this to *Frankenstein*, we can say that even failed listeners represent such outness for the monster: he desires not corroboration by others so much as exposure before an external conscience. In Coleridge's terms, the sole "Impulse" for establishing outness is to unveil or "withdraw" the hidden self—and "not the wish for others to see it" (*NB* 3:4166, 3624). It is the symbolic and rhetorical presence of such listeners, then, that enables the monster to expose his inner self, to demarcate "existence," and thereby to establish "being" (143, 140).

Thus although Coleridge's use of this peripheral other differs from Mary Shelley's, we can locate several crucial links between them. Like Mary Shelley, for instance, Coleridge represents this poetic other as a dubious, often resisting listener (especially in works like the "Rime," "Christabel," and the conversation poems). Both writers also incorporate this listener within a frame-narrative form. And finally, Coleridge's philosophical aesthetics are cited by the many critics who explicate the Romantic origins of *Frankenstein*.[19] It is accordingly no surprise that we can better understand Mary Shelley's portrayal of "existence," "sympathies," and "being" (143, 140) if we briefly examine Coleridge's analysis of the same issues. For both she and Coleridge discuss this being and selfhood in terms of what Coleridge, like Bakhtin, calls "Consciousness." And much as Bakhtin constructs this consciousness "outwardly," Coleridge suggests that defining "Self" is a matter of establishing this "Consciousness" through external others, through a projected "Conscience." It is worth recalling, then, how Coleridge formulates this ontological process. He writes, "*From* what reasons do I believe in *continuous* < & ever continuable > *Consciousness?* From *Conscience!* Not for myself, but for my conscience—i.e.

my affections & duties toward others, I should have no Self — for Self is Definition; but all Boundary implies Neighbourhood — & is knowable only by Neighbourhood, or Relations" (*NB* 2:3231). For Coleridge, then, "Self" is defined as a conscience toward others," a "Boundary" consisting of close "Relations." Such "Relations" essentially distinguish the individual "Consciousness" and make it "knowable." Returning to *Frankenstein*, then, we can say that it is this sense of "Boundary" and "Definition" that the monster hopes to derive from his "affections & duties" toward both the De Lacys and, later, an intimate partner: only his long-sought "Relations" with them can foster what he refers to as his "existence." Hence the monster himself might have said, as Coleridge did, "Self in me derives its sense of Being from having this one absolute Object" (*NB* 2:3148). The monster's external companion ("Object") would thus provide a mental "Boundary," which would in turn define the "Neighbourhood" or distinctness of the ego. Denied this boundary, the creature necessarily loses his "being" and perishes (164). He falls victim to what Coleridge calls "the *incorporeity* of true love in absence" — the "incorporeity" of the "Self" that follows from the loss of "Definition" (3:4036).

V

Throughout *Frankenstein*, Shelley refers to this ontological "Definition," these personified "affections & duties," as "sympathy." We have noted, for instance, that the monster craves those "sympathies necessary for . . . being"; such "sympathies" are again at issue when, before encountering the De Lacys, the monster imagines "lovely creatures sympathizing with my feelings and cheering my gloom" (127; cf. *Letters* 1:204, 2:18, and Marshall). Clerval, too, is praised for his "sympathy" (69), and Victor uses the same term to thank Walton for becoming his auditor (24, 23; cf. 13, 231). Yet "sympathy" in *Frankenstein* designates more than moral receptivity, for such passages ultimately come to suggest that these characters conceive of "consciousness" in social terms — as a quest for community. In the monster's seminal plea to Victor, for instance, this social production of self is demonstrated most explicitly: "Oh! my creator, make me happy," he says, "Let me see that I excite the sympathy of some *existing* thing . . . " (142, emphasis added). Here, exciting "sympathy" in an other becomes a metaphor for "existing," for fabricating a correspondent link with a preestablished collectivity. By instilling human sentiment within a member of this community, the monster can situate himself within it. Hence, evincing communal "sympathy" from another (whether from Victor or some fellow being) becomes the primary impetus behind the monster's narration, for in seeking such affect, he is actually striving to orient the self—to place it within the social world. As he says to Victor, he seeks to locate his consciousness within a human order, to "feel the affections of a sensitive being and *become linked to the chain of existence and events, from which I am now excluded*" (143, emphasis added).[20] If the monster can enter this social "chain of existence and events"—if he can "become linked" to this exchange of sympathy—he will have woven what Bakhtin refers to as the relational "fabric" of the ego. For the monster's desire to enter the social "chain" recalls Bakhtin's notion of social discourse, in which one "invests his entire self in discourse, and this discourse enters into the dialogic fabric of human life" (*Poetics* 293). In this context, then, social "discourse" distinguishes "human life." The ontological development of the self is thus essentially interactive—social in the broadest sense. As Bakhtin goes on to say, the self "must find itself . . . within an intense field of interorientations" (239; cf. "Speech" 94).

In *Frankenstein*, then, the self-affirming other will at times emerge collectively, as what Victor refers to as "society" (1831:254, cf. 167). It should hardly be surprising, then, that this societal impulse would later emerge in Mary Shelley's own life. Two years after her husband's death, she writes, "I like society; I believe all persons who have any talent (who are in good health) do. The soil that gives forth nothing, may lie ever fallow; but that which produces—however humble its product—needs cultivation, change of harvest, refreshing dews, and ripening sun. Books do much; but the living intercourse is the vital heat. Debarred from that, how have I pined and died!" (*Journal* 205). For Mary Shelley, "society" is the "soil that gives forth" identity. If social interchange acts as "cultivation," then its harvest or "product" is the self. Without such interchange, the human soul lacks all fecundity, regeneration, or "health"; it has "died." When Shelley refers to "living intercourse," then, her words take on at least two readings: "intercourse" not only occurs between the "living" but actually designates them as alive, as "ripening" cultivators of the word. For Shelley as for her creature, "living intercourse is the vital heat" of existence.[21]

Throughout *Frankenstein*, this desire for "living intercourse" manifests itself as a narrative search for the "friend." Walton opens his series of letters by describing his own need for the "company of a man." He writes to his sister,

> I have one want which I have never yet been able to satisfy; and the absence of the object of which I now feel as a most severe evil. I have no friend, Margaret: when I am glowing with the enthusiasm of success, there will be none to participate my joy; if I am assailed by disappointment, no one will endeavour to sustain me in dejection. I shall commit my thoughts to paper, it is true; but that is a poor medium for feeling. I desire the company of a man who could sympathize with me; whose eyes would reply to mine. You may deem me romantic, my dear sister, but I bitterly feel the want of a friend. I have no one near me, gentle yet courageous, possessed of a cultivated as well as of a capacious mind, whose tastes are like my own, to approve or amend my plans.[22] (13; cf. 231–32, and Marshall)

This search for what Walton calls the "object" who can "sustain" him heralds the monster's own search for someone to nourish the ego. For Walton, however, this idealized "friend" also serves to integrate the insular self into societal interaction. In the foregoing passage, then, his solipsistic, asocial obsessions with "dejection" must accordingly be tempered and refined by this "friend," his "medium for feeling." Such a medium can "amend" these feelings, socialize them so that Walton too can "become linked to the chain of existence." In this way, he seeks to mitigate what has become an immolating dissociation from both his crew and the society they represent.

That such isolation is anathema within Shelley's world is again clear from her response to it several years later. Soon after Percy's death, her journal reads, "First, I have no friend. For eight years I communicated, with unlimited freedom, with one whose genius, far transcending mine, awakened and guided my thoughts. I conversed with him; rectified my errors of judgment; obtained new lights from him; and my mind was satisfied. Now I am alone—oh, how alone!" (180; cf. *Letters* 1:210, 214, 248; 2:18, 68). Hence much as Walton seeks a "capacious mind" to "amend [his] plans," Shelley's own deceased "friend" has "rectified [her] errors of judgment" and "guided [her] thoughts." Notwithstanding her intense grief—nor her husband's avowed paternalism[23]—she nevertheless views this rectification as a kind of corrective, as if the "friend" can meliorate those asocial "errors" that threaten to circumscribe the self. Such a 'friend' thus proves crucial within the world of *Frankenstein*, where several figures suffer from these asocial impediments: For Walton, this segregation follows from a dangerous intrepidity, extending beyond sane aspiration; for Victor, it results from a Promethean iconoclasm; and for Mary Shelley herself, it derives from an inexorable grief. In each case, though, the absent "friend" has the power to bring the self into what Walton calls "company," what the monster refers to as the desire for a "companion." Such a friend ultimately forges a link to the communal "chain."

VI

If Walton and Victor desire that "friend" who can rectify judgment and socialize the mind, then the abandoned creature's need is commensurately greater. By the time he makes his final demand for a companion, the monster has followed a trajectory that began in early life, with his first request for sustained rhetorical interaction: his long-awaited "interview" with the De Lacys (126). In this episode, the linguistic encounter again takes on ontological significance: the monster views his first verbal exchange as an entry into all human discourse, the decisive act in his search for "society." "It was in intercourse with man alone," he tells Victor, "that I could hope for any pleasurable sensations . . . " (114). "I resolved," he goes on, " . . . in every way to fit myself for an interview with them which would decide my fate" (126). The "interview" or dialogue thus comes to represent the monster's desire for community, exchange, and an individuating "fate"; he appropriately calls it the "hour and moment of trial, which would decide my hopes, or realize my fears" (129).

The forces that lead up to the creature's first dialogue are consequently vital; Shelley details both his painstaking study of language and increasing knowledge of the humanities in order to have the process culminate in this single exchange. Language in particular, as the premise of this interview, stands as the object of the monster's quest; he begins life with a resolute faith in the capacity of language to engender both "sympathy" and "society"—to make him in effect a linguistic member of the species. Much as Clerval's facility with languages allows for his ready interactions with human society, so the monster seeks out language as the foundation of the Edenic community he envisions around him: "I easily perceived," he says, "that although I eagerly longed to discover myself to the cottagers, I ought not to make the attempt until I had first become the master of their language . . . " (109). He then goes on to say, "I formed in my imagination a thousand pictures of presenting myself to them, and their reception of me. I imagined that they would be disgusted, until, by my gentle demeanour and conciliating words, I should first win their favour, and afterwards their love. These thoughts exhilarated me, and led me to apply with fresh ardour to the acquiring the art of language" (110). Here, the lack of physical acceptability, of conformity to any bodily standard, sends the monster in search of a linguistic substitute. In the absence of what we might call a "communal body," he seeks a communal language in which, once again, verbal signs can replace bodily ones. In this passage, then, "acquiring the art of language" leads not only to discourse, but also to social "reception," to "conciliating" interchange — and to the same, self-framing "interview." His first dialogue represents the delineation of the ego in sociolinguistic terms.

The monster's verbal education thus becomes a figure for the linguistic rendering of self. To him, language is a "godlike science" that he "ardently desired to become acquainted with" (107). These "conciliating words," in fact, become the primary concern of all three protagonists in *Frankenstein*. For the monster, they represent the forensics that can presumably convince Victor to create an other. For Walton, they are the basis of his affection for his own admired friend: in depicting Victor as "noble" and "cultivated," Walton says, "although his words are culled with the choicest art, yet they flow with rapidity and unparalleled eloquence" (22). Finally, for Victor, his creature's consummate power within the human community also stems from language; as we have noted, Victor cautions Walton by emphasizing that the monster is "eloquent and persuasive; and once his words had even power over my heart" (206).[24] Each of these characters thus presents language as the currency of liaison — whether it be persuasion, admiration, or "power over" another. For each of them, language is relational, the axes that can locate a given mind in terms of another.

Thus language — educed as "eloquence," "interview," and "persuasive" rhetoric — impels self-invention in *Frankenstein*. In the linguist Clerval, then, we can best observe Shelley's personification of this verbal self-fashioning. Immediately after he matriculates at Ingolstadt, for instance, we learn that Clerval "was no natural philosopher. His imagination was too vivid for the minutiae of science. Languages were his principal study . . . " (64). As the novel proceeds, Clerval's linguistic abilities come to represent not only his articulate interchange with Victor but also a more widely applicable insight into human interrelation. As his name implies, Clerval possesses a clear-sightedness born of imagination, a perspicacity that allows him both to assess his fellow beings and to intuit his place among them. He is, as Victor tells us, "always quick in discerning the sensations of others" (63). Later, Victor goes on to say,

> my health and spirits had long been restored, and they gained additional strength from . . . the conversation of my friend. Study had before secluded me from the intercourse of my fellow-creatures, and rendered me unsocial; but Clerval called forth the better feelings of my heart; he again taught me to love . . . the cheerful faces of children. Excellent friend! . . . I became the same happy creature who, a few years ago, loving and beloved by all, had no sorrow or care. (65, cf. 254)

Here, Clerval's "conversation" prefigures the overall "intercourse of . . . fellow-creatures," thereby precluding the "unsocial" stultification of the mind. Only such "conversation" can "call forth" Victor from self-effacement. It is Clerval, furthermore, who attempts to usher Victor back into society on two separate occasions (once from Ingolstadt, then later from Scotland). This mediatory role ultimately accords with Shelley's portrayal of Clerval as a purveyor of diverse languages, for he is in this sense a translational link between all people, a metaphor for social affiliation. It is this linguistic facility — together with the communal "love by all" it engenders — that begins to reconstruct Victor's dissociated "heart."

This linguistic ability is only one among Clerval's diverse range of interests in the humanities. By focusing on him repeatedly, Shelley shows us an eclectic belletrist — orientalist, linguist, naturalist, and aesthete — "formed in the 'very poetry of nature'" (153; cf. 64, 65, 154). Such interests serve, of course, as a foil to Victor's obdurately scientific pursuits. We must consider, though, that what Clerval's diverse humanistic concerns have in common is the capacity to represent humanity as a unified species, a relatively integrated, organic whole. The humanities in general — and the language "art" in particular — stress the interactive aspects of society: the shared communication, myth, and history that keep each individual "linked to the chain of existence and events." Whereas the predominantly isolated Victor concludes that science or "natural philosophy is the genius that has regulated my [particular] fate" (32), Clerval's study of the humanities underscores what is common to all, what can therefore unite beings into an entity. Hence even the monster (an eventual outcast from this human community) cannot fathom his tenuous place within this social matrix until he pursues the humanities, what he calls the "science of letters" (114). His first knowledge of a book accordingly gives him "insight into the manners, governments, and religions of the different nations of the earth" (114–15); later, after discovering the three volumes in Victor's portmanteau, he learns more about these "large assemblages of men" (124). In such cases, self derives from a cognizance of broadly humanistic connections, associations, and dialogue.

We can accordingly regard the narrative interchanges between characters in *Frankenstein* as representations of "communal" "assemblage," as the rhetorical equivalent of Mary Shelley's own "living intercourse." It follows directly, then, that she would construct her entire novel around a succession of these dialogues, narrative exchanges that enact her premises about community and individuation. The very form of the novel thus tests the possibility of linguistic alliance, the capacity for the ego to emerge in relation to an auricular other.

VII

We can thus reconsider the genre of frame narrative—in particular, the dialogue between apostrophizing narrators and those listeners who constitute framing audiences. For these narratives addressed to an other can be viewed as rhetorical quests for language, society, and the self. We must also recognize, however, that such novels can work through these dialogic quests or processes despite eventual breakdowns in narrative interchange during the story. If language ultimately fails to link the monster to the "communal sphere of speech communion," the fault is not with the form itself—not with "dialogic relations"—but with the monster's exclusion from this dialogic community. If most listeners in *Frankenstein* finally fail to comprehend their respective narrators, the novel nevertheless illustrates those linguistic "interorientations" that can lead to self-definition. Indeed, it is the repeated failure of these attempted communications that prolongs and sustains the ontological process. In this sense, such an address proceeds not in spite of but because of a paucity of genuinely insightful listeners. Instead of suggesting the final undecidability of interpretation in the novel—that the "creature's fate is to be misread"—the breakdowns of listener comprehension in *Frankenstein* represent a narrator's ongoing rhetorical struggle away from reflexivity. Although the monster finally despairs of evincing "sympathy" from his listeners, his search for it has engendered a narrative quest that—in evolving for over one-third of the novel—not only lays bare the dynamics of this self-affirming process but also dramatizes Mary Shelley's point better than any rapport between speakers and listeners could. That the monster's verbal quest for what he calls "society and sympathy" gradually runs aground enables Shelley to demonstrate the necessity of this linguistic process for hypostatizing the ego. The slow erosion of such dialogue thus underscores its inspiriting potential; collapse only intensifies our belief in the urgency of the form.

Mary Shelley consequently stresses the sustained search for listeners by concluding with the monster's failed struggle to engage them. Soon after the foregoing interview, for instance, the monster sees that the De Lacys have "spurned and deserted" him (134). After several other agonizing encounters, he is finally "driven from the society and sympathy of . . . fellow-creatures" (130). Most tellingly, he emerges "friendless" and "unsympathized with" (130, 132). When his attempts to establish dialogue ultimately fail, his deformities take precedence over human sympathy. And once more, Mary Shelley represents this loss of relation by finally rupturing even those rhetorical bonds that sustained the novel itself. As the monster's last narrative closes, his final listener curses him (218), much as the De Lacys deny him the "voice of kindness" (131, 134)—and much as Walton eventually loses Victor's "encouraging voice," that "answer in the affirmative" (131, 12). In this context, frame narrative becomes a symbol for dialogic community: as the later fails, so must the former.

Audition has thus come full circle, since Victor's first reaction to his creature has again failed to become a sympathetic "voice": Victor's initial words to him are "Devil! . . . do you dare approach me," to which the monster answers, "I expected this reception" (94). The novel thereby denies the creature's quest for both "reception" and the communal "chain." Victor's next reply to the monster's entreaty is "Begone! I will not hear you. *There can be no community between you and me . . .* " (95, emphasis added). The long-sought social intercourse or "community" between storytellers and listeners in this novel thus collapses. That the monster never locates a response in either Victor or the De Lacys completes a pattern that begins with his first attempts at linguistic communication: as Victor tells it, "His jaws opened, and he muttered some inarticulate sounds, while a grin wrinkled his cheeks. He might have spoken, *but I did not hear*; . . . I escaped, and rushed downstairs" (53, emphasis added). Here, Victor's failure to "hear" the monster, to become his audience, has actually little to do with the "inarticulate" nature of this attempt to employ language. Long after the monster masters these "sounds" and pleads eloquently for a companion, Victor still proves to be a bogus respondent. "The being finished speaking," he says, "and fixed his looks upon me in expectation of a reply. But I was bewildered, perplexed, and unable to arrange my ideas sufficiently to understand the full extent of his proposition" (140).[25] What this "bewildered" reaction signifies, though, is the miscarriage not of language but of human affinity: in the words of Elizabeth, all "men appear to me as monsters thirsting for each other's blood" (88).

VIII

These "perplexed" and "bewildered" responses, then, account for the monster's conflagration of being. Yet such interchange is not the only rhetoric that comes to disintegrate in the novel. Although we have traced attempts at specifically vocal or spoken colloquy, several characters are asked to accept its written counterpart—inscribed addresses in the form of letters, journals, and diaries. Throughout *Frankenstein*, Mary Shelley incorporates Victor's correspondence from both his fiancée and his father, highlights the letters between Felix and Safie, and even frames the entire tale as a combined journal and letter addressed from Walton to his sister. It would appear that much as the monster must "decypher the characters" of Victor's journal, we as readers must also confront the written versions of exchange in the novel (126). In a similar manner, Shelley also presents Victor's story as a written, twice-removed artifact of spoken narrative. And that we would be left with such an artifact is particularly striking when we consider that Shelley herself regarded writing as a paltry substitute for spoken "intercourse" and "expression." Two years following her husband's death, she writes, "I can speak to none. Writing this is useless; it does not even soothe me; on the contrary, it irritates me by showing the pitiful expedient to which I am reduced" (*Journal* 196). For her, the power of spoken dialogue to "soothe" conscience and ease the self becomes—in written form—a mere "pitiful expedient." "Well, then," she writes, "now I am reduced to these white pages, which I am to blot with dark imagery" (181). Shelley thus reiterates Victor's own suspicions of the written word; as we have noted, he writes, "I shall commit my thoughts to paper, it is true; but that is a poor medium for feeling. I desire the company of a man who could sympathize with me; whose eyes would reply to mine" (13). For both her and her creations, then, writing bastardizes dialogue, that eye-to-eye encounter represented by rhetorical presence, community, and the immediacy of "reply" (cf. *Journal* 180–81).

Yet much as even failed interchanges come to demonstrate the force of dialogue, so writing in *Frankenstein* ultimately comes to represent and embody Mary Shelley's "living intercourse" (cf. *Letters* 1:204). In much of the novel, she manages to instill writing with some of its spoken, dialogic effects by depicting the written word not as an engraved, monolithic log but as a redaction of conversation, a rendering of oral interchange. Her protagonists, in fact, repeatedly focus on the rhetorical presence of the voice. Victor, for one, chooses to preserve not unilateral narrative but transposed "conversation": on learning that Walton has "made notes concerning his history, [Victor] asked to see them, and then himself corrected and augmented them in many places; but principally in *giving the life and spirit to the conversations* he held with his enemy" (207, emphasis added). Walton, too, seems preoccupied with this oral or conversational rendering. After Victor promises to "commence his narrative the next day," Walton writes to his sister, "This promise drew from me the warmest thanks. I have resolved every night, when I am not engaged, to record, as *nearly as possible in his own words*, what he has related during the day. If I should be engaged, I will at least make notes. . . . [T]o me, who know him, and who hear it from his own lips, with what interest and sympathy shall I read [this manuscript] in some future day!" (25, emphasis added). Walton (and by implication Mary Shelley) thus seeks to reproduce the orality of each respective narrator, the sense that each tale offers "his own words." Like Shelley herself, each speaker seeks an answering "voice" that enables his own speech to "assume its natural modulation." *Frankenstein* accordingly reenacts a series of transposed "conversations"—not to privilege them over writing but to stress their interactive, dialogic character. More generally, it is this allusion to the "life" of the spoken word that recalls its aural presence, its interactive immediacy: the sense that oral language is, in Walter J. Ong's terms, a "mode of action" (*Orality* 32; cf. 42, 189). In *Franken-*

stein, then, it is this capacity to act on another, to apostrophize a listener, that preserves the "life and spirit of conversation." What is significant about this vocal imitation is that it enables Shelley to cast her characters' narratives as specifically aural addresses: the tales in the novel are (with Walton's the exception) self-consciously spoken only because they must be heard by an other. By deemphasizing the chirographic quality of each narrator's story, she ensures that we will in effect "hear it from his own lips."

Shelley's emphasis on the oral nature of her narrators' stories thus suggests that the apostrophic form of the novel is more than a vestige of Gothic convention. We have noted, for instance, that *Frankenstein* revolves around three narrators' quests for a "friend," for that integrative community that composes being. We should add, however, that these spoken quests represent *in themselves* the concept of a vocative community. As Ong remarks elsewhere, the "spoken word forms human beings into close-knit groups. When a speaker is addressing an audience, the members of the audience become a unity, with themselves and with the speaker." "Sound forms community," he goes on to say, "as reading alone cannot" (*Rhetoric* 140). In *Frankenstein*, too, it is this notion of a vocally constituted community that motivates the narrators' spoken quests — and begins to explain the oral tropes of Shelley's novel. The monster, for one, often seeks an auricular "unity" with his human audience, a spoken constituency in which the "individual's reaction is not expressed as simply individual or 'subjective' but rather as encased in the communal reaction, the communal 'soul'" (Ong, *Orality* 46; cf. 49).

To enter the communal soul, then, narrators in *Frankenstein* must partake of mutual reaction, a collectivity of response that enables communal relations. Yet what gathers these responses into a communicative matrix is their inherent linkage, their status as what Bakhtin terms "utterances." As we have noted, he suggests that

> every utterance must be regarded primarily as a *response* to preceding utterances of the given sphere (we understand the word "response" here in the broadest sense). Each utterance refutes, affirms, supplements, and relies on the others, presupposes them to be known, and somehow takes them into account. After all, as regards a given question, in a given matter, and so forth, the utterance occupies a particular *definite* position in a given sphere of communication. It is impossible to determine its position without correlating it with other positions. ("Speech" 91)

In Bakhtin's terms, the utterance is by definition part of an interactive unity, an alignment or conjunction of responses; as he says, "Any utterance is a link in a very complexly organized chain of other utterances" ("Speech" 69). Because this "utterance occupies a particular *definite* position in a given sphere of communication," it necessarily links up with the "chain of other utterances." Returning to *Frankenstein*, then, we can say that it is the monster's need to establish this definite position within the chain of utterances that underlies his oral efforts to engage an interlocutor.[26] Here again, he seeks to "become linked to the [vocative] chain of existence and events from which I am now excluded" (143).

In regarding the spoken word, then, the monster seeks to enter an oral "chain of existence," an aural linkage of response. Such response is, in fact, endemic to the aural "process of listening and understanding." As Bakhtin goes on to say, "When the listener perceives and understands the meaning . . . of speech, he simultaneously takes an active, responsive attitude toward it. . . . Any understanding of live speech, a live utterance, is inherently responsive. . . . Any understanding is imbued with response and necessarily elicits it in one form or another . . . " ("Speech" 68). Here, the "understanding of live speech," of oral address, *necessarily* engenders a process of mutual response — an act of exchange. If the monster, for instance, can locate aural reception for "live speech," he will necessarily elicit this communal response, this representative "thou." The spontaneous, vocal nature of "live utterance" ensures a commensurate immediacy and accessibility of response. In addressing this responsive "thou," moreover, a speaker simultaneously constitutes himself as an "I": he defines himself according to a dialogic act. For a speaker like the monster, then, "live utterance" with an other instantiates the self, providing what Jonathan Culler terms the speaker's "poetic presence" during the apostrophic gesture.[27]

IX

Hence even when Shelley's characters are bound by the constraints of the written journal, they attempt to render the oral nature of the utterance, the "life and spirit" of vocal interaction. Although written inscriptions abound in the novel, they often derive from models of the face-to-face encounter. Images of the written word in *Frankenstein* thus come to embody many qualities of the spoken "interchange" that the monster craves. At the same time, such inscriptions also take on the ontological force that Mary Shelley ascribes to this oral dialogue. The recurrence of testimonial letters, for instance, ultimately betokens what both Walton and the monster consider to be sensibility or "existence." In Walton's view, such letters act to substantiate the monster's very life. After hearing Victor's story, Walton writes, "His tale is connected, and told with an appearance of the simplest truth; yet I own to you that the letters of Felix and Safie, which he shewed me . . . brought to me a greater conviction of the truth of his narrative than his asseverations, however earnest and connected. Such a monster has then really existence; I cannot doubt it . . . " (207). In this passage, the written word attests not only to the "truth" of spoken narrative but also to the actual "existence" of its speaker. Such letters essentially invent or "envoice" the monster by enabling him to engage in a kind of proximate interchange—to "correspond" with others by intercepting their displaced addresses. The survival of such correspondence, in fact, comes to represent that coincidence of response that defines a vocative community. The monster accordingly preserves these letters because they serve as a talisman of social identity; they simulate "living" exchange.

Such ontological implications are also evident in the monster's description of Victor's writing the laboratory journal. The creature says to Victor:

> It was your journal of the four months that preceded my creation. You minutely described in these papers every step you took in the progress of your work; this history was mingled with accounts of domestic occurrences. . . . Every thing is related in them which bears reference to my accursed origin; the whole detail of that series of disgusting circumstances which produced it is set in view; the minutest description of my odious and loathsome person is given, in language which painted your own horrors, and rendered mine ineffaceable. (126)

Here again, the written word comes to represent "origin" and "creation." As the monster later puts it, "I learned from your papers that you were my father, my creator . . . him who had given me life" (135). And much as these inscribed "papers" chronicle Victor's role as "creator," their narrative "progress" becomes a written figure for the anatomical development of the monster's self. In such cases, the written word is able to represent both Victor's creative process and the monster's presence; it becomes a "history" of being. In one sense, then, the written journal also takes on apostrophic features: intercepted by the other, it comes to resemble a dialogic form with the capacity to imply selfhood—to "render [one] ineffaceable." In this context, moreover, the self-perpetuating, "ineffaceable" qualities of the written word never follow from its capacity to persist as a permanent, inscribed record (cf. Miller, *Linguistic* 109–12). Indeed, Mary Shelley portrays writing less as a timeless artifact than as an evolving representation of living speech, an impulse toward self-affirming dialogue.

In locating Victor's journal, then, the monster discovers the power of writing to disinter his lost history—to become what Derrida terms a "psychographic metaphor" (*Writing* 220, 22). We have also noted, though, that in *Frankenstein* the written word emerges as a surrogate for orality, a stand-in for the monster's desire for spoken dialogue. While reading Victor's journal to himself, for instance, the creature cries out and apostrophizes, "Cursed creator! Why did you form a monster so hideous that even you turned from me in disgust? . . . Satan had his companions, fellow-devils, to admire and encourage him; but I am solitary and detested"(126). The monster's cry thus reframes the "solitary" context of the written word within a potentially bilateral dialogue. Whether such written language addresses an inadvertent recipient (as does Victor's journal) or an actual correspondent (as does a direct letter), it nevertheless partakes of the ontological impulse that must orally "declare itself" to another process.

X

Shelley's suggestions of orality further echo another, final concern—one less ontological than it is interpretive. For *Frankenstein* seeks to address a series of explicatory dilemmas, including Victor's Promethean desire, Walton's naive adventurism, and the monster's self-justified vengeance. As a result, the novel's spoken dialogues often approximate the form of Socratic dialogue, that exchange of query and response fundamental to interpretive designs. In *Frankenstein*, moreover, such questioning proves particularly seminal, since it impels the monster's entire narrative. We have noted how, after first wandering from Victor's laboratory, he asks, "What was I? Who was I?" (124). With these words, the monster initiates a heuristic process in which he attempts to engage a succession of listeners, ending with his final questioning of Victor and Walton (140, 217).

* * *

The process of such interpretive questioning is, again, best clarified in the work of Hans-Georg Gadamer. As we have noted, he suggests that "discourse that is intended to reveal something requires that that thing be opened up by the question. For this reason, the way in which dialectic proceeds is by way of the question and answer or, rather, by way of the development of all knowledge through the question" (326).[28] In this context, the apostrophic rhetoric of *Frankenstein* can be viewed as part of an interrogative call to an auditor, a call that is in fact more dialogic than dialectic. For Gadamer, moreover, this interrogative quest for knowledge is founded on a specifically vocative model, a live conversational exchange: "Precisely this," he writes,

> is what characterises a dialogue, in contrast with the rigid form of the statement that demands to be set down in writing: that here language, in the process of question and answer, giving and taking, talking at cross purposes and seeing each other's point, performs that communication of meaning which, with respect to the written tradition, is the task of hermeneutics. Hence it is more than a metaphor, it is a memory of what originally was the case, to describe the work of hermeneutics as a conversation with the text. . . . Thus that which is handed down in literary form is brought back out of the alienation in which it finds itself and into the living presence of conversation, whose fundamental procedure is always question and answer. (331)

Here, Gadamer traces exegetical writing to both its interrogative and vocal origins. What is more, his belief that such writing derives from the "living presence of conversation" parallels Victor's desire to preserve the "life and spirit [of] conversations" recorded in Walton's journal. Each recovers the spoken quality of Socratic exchange by grounding this "literary form" in "conversation," "communication," and "dialogue." As Gadamer goes on to say, the "literary form of the dialogue places language and concept back within the original movement of the conversation" (332; cf. 330).

In imitating the oral, multivocal form of conversation, then, this literary form also accomplishes a particular kind of interpretive act — what Gadamer later calls the act of "making fluid and subtle the abstract determinations of thought" (332). It is this fluidity that allows for what we might call literary hermeneutics, that "dissolving and remoulding logic into the procedures of language" characteristic of "genuine conversation" (332–33). Only such language can reshape logic in terms of oral hypothesizing, of ratiocinating aloud by "talking at cross purposes." We can conclude, then, that when Victor and

Walton seek to reclaim the vocal "spirit' of conversation, they initiate the "task of hermeneutics." Indeed, the dialogic shape of the entire novel can be said to replicate this hermeneutic process. If its transcribed exchanges appear to be misreadings, they nevertheless constitute a hermeneutic process, a rhetorical approach to each narrator's analytical quandaries.[29]

Without this rhetoric, storytellers like Victor, Walton, and the monster abdicate as the novel closes. In the words of Walter Benjamin, "Storytelling is always the art of repeating stories, and this art is lost when the stories are no longer retained. It is lost because there is no more weaving and spinning to go on while they are being listened to" (91). In *Frankenstein*, too, the decline of auditor retention and repetition presages the end of oral narrative. The final storyteller in Mary Shelley's novel accordingly pleads for an auditor: "Listen to me, Frankenstein," says the monster—but when audition finally collapses at the end of the novel, each storyteller is silenced forever.

5

Wuthering Heights *and the Rhetoric of Interpretation*

Never seek to tell thy love,
Love that never told can be:
For the gentle wind does move
Silent, invisibly.

I told my love, I told my love,
I told her all my heart;
Trembling, cold, in ghastly fears,
Ah! she doth depart.

Soon as she was gone from me
A traveller came by
Silently, invisibly —
He took her with a sigh.

Blake, "Love's Secret"

I want you to *tell* me my way, not to *show* it; or else to persuade Mr. Heathcliff to give me a guide.

Lockwood in Wuthering Heights

I

Ever since F. R. Leavis first characterized it as a "kind of sport" — an anomaly with "some influence of an essentially undetectable kind" — critics have attempted to locate *Wuthering Heights* within various schools of literary interpretation or detection. To the "barred" doors of the Heights world have come those who see the novel as an allegory of class conflict, a microcosm of generational tension, or a response to Romantic tradition.[1] More recently, however, the last fifteen years have seen critics eschew this tradition of attempted interpretation, of what J. Hillis Miller calls our need "to satisfy the mind's desire for logical order," to "indicate the right way to read the novel as a

134

whole."[2] These latter studies accordingly cite what they variously refer to as the "misinterpretation," "crisis of interpretation," or "conflicting possibilities of interpretation" that allegedly distinguish the novel.[3] Of course, such approaches also differ among themselves. While some attribute this misinterpretation to a particular narrator's "unreliable" point of view, others maintain that *any* path through the novel leads to a "reader's quandary"—since its "multiplicity of outlook" and "surplus of signifiers" demonstrate an "intrinsic plurality." Still others deny even the potential import of such signifiers, insisting that the very language of the novel presents us with a "missing center"; hence even the name of a given character "despotically eliminates its referent, leaving room neither for plurality nor for significance."[4] While these recent arguments scarcely appear unanimous, they would seem to agree that, in Miller's words, "however far inside [the "penetralium"] the reader gets," he will find only "enigmatic signs," "bewilderment," and "ultimate bafflement." "The secret truth about *Wuthering Heights* is," Miller goes on, "that there is no secret truth."[5]

Again, then, the present generation of critics seems inclined to let the problematic mysteries of *Wuthering Heights* live a life of their own, and there is much to support such an approach to interpretation. The tortured relationship, for instance, between Catherine and Heathcliff is inimical to any recognizable casuistic standard; and if some alien morality stands behind Heathcliff's own inconsistent actions, it has yet to be defined. Yet despite the reader's "bewilderment" and even "ultimate bafflement" at such mysteries, it is difficult to deny that the novel is about the act of interpretation itself. Despite its disturbing "crisis of interpretation," we must still recognize that Brontë presents the entire novel as a rendering, as a story reported at one, two, or three removes. The interpretive valuations of characters like Lockwood, Nelly, and Zillah distort nearly every episode of the story we hear, thereby implicating the reader as the last in a framed succession of interpreters.

Much has been made of this peculiarly framed form of *Wuthering Heights*. Several critics, for instance, have suggested that the listeners embedded in the novel are in many ways analogous to actual readers; such studies attempt to liken our interpretations to those of the "normal skeptical reader," and to insist that Nelly and Lockwood, the primary witnesses to the events of the novel, serve to represent this reader.[6] Yet the question of reading in *Wuthering Heights* is surely more complex than this comparison would suggest. We must ask, for instance, how any reader who apprehends the novel can resemble Lockwood, a character universally acknowledged to be an effete bungler, insensitive to the dramatic power of the story he hears. We must also take into account that we hear Nelly's perspective during most of the novel, and sense that she too is not an observer worth emulating. Finally, we must consider what these models of audition say about the possibility for interpreting such characters as Heathcliff and Catherine Earnshaw.

What the foregoing studies have not considered is that the issue of interpretation and response is addressed directly within the text of *Wuthering Heights*—most explicitly by interrogative exchanges between characters but also by the rhetorical form of the novel itself. For the substance of the novel is in effect a succession of addresses directed to designated listeners, a series of witnessed narratives. These addresses include not only Nelly Dean's narrative to Lockwood but also the two climactic exchanges in which Heathcliff and Catherine respectively describe their preternatural union to Nelly (72–74, 255–56). The novel accordingly foregrounds the act of interpretation by framing both characters' experiences within the context of sustained audition.

In fact, in order for these two characters to "let out" (in Catherine's words) their secrets, the presence of an interpreter appears to be vital (70). At the beginning of one interchange, Catherine actually proceeds to restrain Nelly, her auditor (72). Furthermore, Catherine seems determined to incorporate a listener's response into her own evaluation of self. Again and again, she begs Nelly to corroborate her decision to marry Edgar. When Nelly mocks the question, Catherine again demands, "Be quick, and say whether I was wrong"; still later, Catherine pleads, "Say whether I should have done so—do!" (70). Finally, at the end of this broken colloquy Catherine says to Nelly, "Yet you have not told me whether I'm right" (71). Thus, the impetus behind rhetorical interchange here appears to be interpretation: to "let out" one's "secret" is to need it received and judged.

Even Heathcliff displays this need to express his inmost feelings before another, to break his solitude, at least momentarily. During his most extended attempt to describe his relation to Catherine, he says to Nelly, "You'll not talk of what I tell you, and my mind is so eternally secluded in itself, it is tempting, at last, to turn it out to another" (255). Here again, the purpose of audition is to draw out the "eternally secluded" self: to delineate the ego according to social or dialogic correlates. Much as Catherine seeks to "let out" her buried "secret," Heathcliff too attempts to "turn [his mind] out to another" in order to interpret it. In this sense, his request to "turn out" his self to Nelly resembles his earlier plea to Catherine's ghost: "Oh! my heart's darling, hear me *this* time" (33). In both cases, Heathcliff enjoins his listener to "hear" or comprehend the broken "heart"—the fragmented self. And although he eventually attains a form of union with the deceased Catherine, Heathcliff still spends the final days of his life endeavoring to address her beyond the grave and thus transcend both his rhetorical and social isolation.

II

Yet audition ultimately fails Heathcliff, as it does nearly all would-be interlocutors in *Wuthering Heights*; within the dialogic framework of the novel, they must remain "eternally secluded." No sooner has Heathcliff begun the foregoing attempt to "turn out" his mind "to another" than he breaks off, saying, "It is frenzy to repeat these thoughts to you" (255). He then concludes, "My confessions have not relieved me" (256). And such an outpouring to Nelly does indeed resemble an undirected "frenzy," since she proves incapable of any reciprocal response. In recounting Heathcliff's earlier efforts to describe his attendant "spectre," Nelly says, "He only half addressed me, and I maintained silence—I didn't like to hear him talk!" (230).

Nelly's "silence" here indicates a larger pattern of failed audition, for it implies an inability to apprehend those "ghosts and visions" that represent revelation in the novel. When Catherine, for instance, begins to speak of her vision of heaven, Nelly insists, "Oh! don't, Miss Catherine. . . . We're dismal enough without conjuring up ghosts, and visions to perplex us" (72). When Catherine goes on, Nelly cries, "I tell you I won't harken to your dreams, Miss Catherine!" Yet by refusing to "harken" to these revelatory visions, Nelly also misses the pivotal revelation of the novel: the spectral bond between Catherine and Heathcliff, a bond represented primarily by sightings and visions. As one critic has written in describing this mystic bond, "To deny Heathcliff's assurance of Catherine's presence is to deny the novel."[7]

Such denials amount to a kind of analytic deafness: both Nelly and Lockwood attempt to discount what they cannot understand. Thus when Nelly first bungles this auricular role, Catherine responds, in effect, to every interpretative process in the novel: "That's not what I intend," she says, "that's not what I mean!" (73). Even Heathcliff has become a deceived auditor after he "listened till he heard Catherine say it would degrade her to marry him, and then he stayed to hear no farther" (73). We thus begin to see that this failure of interpretation runs deeper than any local misunderstandings of Heathcliff and

Catherine on the part of Nelly. Although revelations are "half-addressed" to listeners, they repeatedly encounter interpretive silence. Here again, whereas exposure may be possible in this novel, colloquy is not.[8]

We are left, then, with the question of why this novel would incorporate a self-consciously flawed model of listening. What is more, why would Brontë emphasize these flawed interpretations by making them the central point of view, the irregular lens through which we see every character in the novel? Why would she actually dramatize a frustrated interchange seen from the position of an uncomprehending observer — as if she had built an intentionally skewed frame of reference into her novel? And if this distorting frame does leave us in what Miller calls "ultimate bafflement," how might Brontë have expected us to respond to such an exegetical predicament? That is, what are we to make of those longstanding critical dilemmas that continue to dog the novel: the unaccountable cruelty and other Gothic events; the frame narrative and representations of reading; and the import of Catherine's climactic statement, "I *am* Heathcliff"?[9] And finally, if these critical problems are inseparable from the elusive beauty of the novel, we must still ask what they say about the status of interpretive possibility in Brontë's world.

We can start to answer these questions of interpretation and response by reexamining what is certainly the most immediate audience for Heathcliff's and Catherine's story: those incorporated auditors who first witness the narrative. I will argue that many of these unresolved questions are a result of what I consider the vital structure of the novel: an epistemological disjunction between listeners and speakers. It is, moreover, precisely this disjunction that blurs the line between speakers and listeners. Indeed, the question of who interprets and who narrates becomes a complex one in this novel, since it is actually built around a pair of speaker/listener paradigms. We have noted, for instance, that while Nelly clearly directs her tale to Lockwood, the most crucial scenes of the novel center around those dialogues in which she herself must play the listener to Heathcliff's and Catherine's revelatory confessions. Nelly must therefore be both teller and listener, for she acts as an interpreter positioned between an unexplained character and an uncomprehending audience. Though she is a storyteller in her own right, she is also a listener attempting to fathom the "history" of an enigmatic Heathcliff (37, 139). And once again, the final listeners in these successions of audience are ourselves, the readers: we receive Lockwood's journal of uncertain destination.

We can thus reconsider *Wuthering Heights* as a convergence of apostrophes, a chain of rhetorical exposures. Indeed, I would suggest that when the speakers of *Wuthering Heights* address a listener, they in effect expose a hidden part of the self—expose it to the interpretation not only of the other but of themselves as well. While most of these interpretations break down during the novel, I ultimately reject the notion that Brontë leaves us with only circumscribed vision and misinterpretation. Instead, I would again argue that the novel continually keeps the possibility of interpretation open by sustaining a rhetorical process of understanding, by enacting a series of hermeneutic forms. For even when these addresses come up against inadequate audition, they nevertheless establish models of ongoing comprehension and interpretation for the reader. What is more, these rhetorical exposures before an other come to represent not only the separate interpretation of self and other but also the actual fashioning of this self in terms of the other. In this sense, the listener's function is both interpretive and ontological.

It is not surprising, then, that these narrative exposures take on different functions at various points in the novel. On one level, I argue that when Brontë uses the narrative address to an auditor as a mode of interpretation, she in effect reenacts the nineteenth-century transformation of confession into self-decipherment. On another level, I show how, elsewhere in *Wuthering Heights*, this narrative exposure takes on attributes of an interpretive dialogue, and is accordingly analogous to such psychoanalytic processes as reconstructing the past and transferring onto an other. I will then expand on Brontë's view of self-interpretation, taking as my model the child's method of mirroring his ego onto an other, and showing how this method illuminates the literary speaker's establishment of his or her own self before an addressee. At other points in the novel, this self-creation results from a character's dialogic interchanges with a listener, which I go on to consider in light of Bakhtin's paradigm of multiple voices. Lastly, I suggest that this nineteenth-century desire to inspirit the self through another is best explained by Coleridge's concept of outness, that state in which he can define the "Boundary" of his external "Self."

III

Though the actual purpose of audition is rarely discussed, many studies note the deployment of frame narrative in *Wuthering Heights*. Still other approaches stress the Gothic elements of the novel (the enigmatic hero, mist-shrouded house, hidden evil, and so on).[10] Yet what such studies miss is that these Gothic features are precisely what gives the novel its framed form, since the Gothic evils actually prompt the need for exposure to another within a narrative frame. Accordingly, Brontë repeatedly invokes this notion of evil incarnate as something grossly inhuman and "unnatural," comparable to a "ghoul" or "vampire" that must be unmasked (258-60). These terms are, in fact, Nelly Dean's impressions of Heathcliff: at one point, she alludes to him as an "evil beast" (94), and even by the end of the novel he remains a "dark thing" for her (260). Charlotte Brontë, in her second preface to the novel, refers to Heathcliff as one "animated by demon life — a Ghoul" (12). It is such a "beast" that must be rhetorically loosed from *Wuthering Heights*.

This demonically represented evil also spawns a host of guilty acts into the novel, which in turn become further motives for narrative confession. Heathcliff, the mysterious locus of the tale, is also the very incarnation of guilt, not only because of his own vengeful action but also because of his relationship to the other characters in the novel. To Mr. Earnshaw, he represents familial disruption and, possibly, the memory of adulterous love; to Catherine, he becomes the image of innocence lost and passion abandoned; and to Nelly, Heathcliff stands as the reminder of her confessed "cowardice and inhumanity" to him, as well as her consequent punishment (39). He thus personifies an almost universal guilt in this narrative, an autochthonous other who returns to haunt nearly every character in the novel. He represents that omnipresent yet hidden incubus that must be verbalized before an interpretive listener.

It is this kind of persistent guilt that helps to explain the need to expose the "beast" within *Wuthering Heights*. For instance, in recounting his dream about Jabes Branderham's invective sermon, Lockwood notes that "either Joseph, the preacher, or I had committed the 'First of the Seventy-First,' and were to be publicly *exposed* and excommunicated" (28, emphasis added). We soon learn, however, that the immoral acts that disturb Lockwood and the preacher prove to be no ordinary Christian sins; Lockwood insists that "they were of the most curious character — odd transgressions that I had never imagined previously" (29). He further contends that Branderham has committed a "sin that no Christian need pardon" (29). Generally speaking, these "odd transgressions" seem to fall outside the realm of evangelical Christian morality; as such, they remain unredeemable by any conventional notion of repentance, absolution, or "pardon" by a listening other.

Brontë works out the implications of these unpardonable sins within the narrative structure of bogus confession. As we have noted, Heathcliff brings this form directly into question when he says, "My confessions have not relieved me" (256). That Heathcliff would refer to these outpourings as "confessions" is particularly telling, for his term reflects a widespread nineteenth-century desire both to adapt and redefine the confessional form.[11] Generally speaking, many nineteenth-century theologians sought to transform the confession from a coercive means of compelling secret truths to a bilateral examination of self — a mutual, two-sided hermeneutic in which both roles are crucial to interpretation. In *Wuthering Heights*, too, both of these roles become crucial within the apostrophic form of the novel, and we would do well to examine each of them separately.

The role of the speaker/confessee in Brontë's novel reflects the nineteenth-century view of confession as self-examination, as opposed to the earlier injunction to provide evidence for external judgment. In Michel Foucault's formulation, "The nineteenth century altered the scope of the confession; it tended no longer to be concerned solely with what the subject wished to hide [from another], but with what was hidden from himself" (66). Earlier religious encounters had stressed an outside witness's role in both interpretation and absolution; now confessional rhetoric was also seen as enabling a speaker to structure his own self-knowledge, his process of learning what was "hidden from himself." Hence in *Wuthering Heights*, when Heathcliff and Catherine deliberately seek to confess their secrets, each is framing these mysteries within a mode of discourse that demands as much decipherment from the speaking confessee as it does from the listening confessor (39, 70). Thus when Brontë depicts both characters deploying the rhetoric of confession, she suggests that each is engaged in a process of revealing the self. Such revelation is not only exposure of self (to another) but disclosure within self as well.

Yet the confession mode still necessitates some external casuistry, however inadequate it appears in *Wuthering Heights*, and herein lies the role of the listener/confessor. This role becomes especially crucial when Brontë ceases "making the confession a test, but rather a sign" (67). For when Heathcliff and Catherine seek to "turn" or "let out" their selves "to another," this rhetorical situation becomes a figure or "sign" for ongoing interpretation. Inasmuch as the presence of Brontë's listeners draws forth what a speaker has "hidden from himself," they reenact this confessional figure. In *Wuthering Heights*, then, the narrative address itself constitutes a sign of interpretive engagement, despite the fact that many of the novel's secrets remain opaque. Confessional narration thus takes on a hermeneutic function: a confessional impulse can be realized as truth only in the presence of a listener who both assimilates and attempts to interpret it. The personal secrets within *Wuthering Heights* can be revealed only within a symbiosis between confessee and confessor, an interchange between self-revelation and external decipherment.

Once again, though, such decipherment is particularly scarce among listeners in *Wuthering Heights*; yet this inability to apprehend the Heights world does not inhibit the dual roles of the confession form. However inadequate the casuistry of Lockwood and Nelly is, it nevertheless keeps the continuing attempt to interpret confession before Brontë's reader. Indeed, when any confessing speaker encounters a failed response, this problematic interpretation may in fact be evidence that a speaker's revelation is taking place; as Foucault notes, confession is a "ritual in which the truth is corroborated by the obstacles and resistances it has had to surmount in order to be formulated" (62).

IV

Narrative addresses in *Wuthering Heights* thus make use of confessional tropes, and thereby enact a rhetorical search for unorthodox notions of relief and pardon. In other passages, however, the addresses in the novel represent a more overt form of interpretation: an enactment of a narrative form that is intrinsically self-analytical. In rhetorical terms, the recurrence of the attempted colloquy in *Wuthering Heights* signifies a proleptic method of interpreting the self, a method best explained in terms of the psychoanalytic dialogue. This heuristic again demands the presence of a listener, even an agonistic one, for he or she is the rhetorical equivalent of the analytic or interpretive figure. Even Lockwood can hold this rhetorical place in the novel, especially since his early request to play the listener to Nelly's narrative actually initiates the analytic form of the novel. Accordingly, it is Lockwood who voices the novel's analytic intention, its interpretive quest to fathom Heathcliff's "curious conduct" and "character" (19, 37), "decypher" Catherine's "faded hieroglyphics" (26), and uncover, in Lockwood's words, "something of my neighbors" (37).

What distinguishes this analytic rhetoric is that it allows characters like Heathcliff and Catherine to effect the kind of projective self-understanding sought during the psychoanalytic exchange. When these characters address an interpretive figure, they necessarily attempt to imagine his listening experience, his process of interpreting their directed address. As one psychoanalyst has put it, "We have overt experience of this [projection] when we say 'I suppose you think that this is. . . .'"[12] In *Wuthering Heights*, we encounter such projection most explicitly when Heathcliff (speaking of Cathy's "startling likeness" to her mother) says to Nelly, "That . . . which *you may suppose* the most potent to arrest my imagination, is actually the least, for what is not connected with her to me?" (255, emphasis added). Heathcliff again makes use of this other-directed rhetoric in attempting to comprehend the "maddening" and "strange change" in himself: again addressing Nelly, he says, "You'll perhaps think me rather inclined to become ["insane"]" (255). Earlier, he wonders aloud to Nelly if his failure to avenge himself "sounds [to you] as if I had been labouring the whole time, only to exhibit a fine trait of magnanimity" (255; cf. 118). Generally speaking, characters engaged in this projective type of self-analysis assume the stance of the other, a position that actually enables them to inhabit an other's critical faculty and apply it to themselves. In becoming the other, they enter the interpretive process; they conjure their own analysis as well as their own listeners.

Hence both Catherine's and Heathcliff's secrets are consciously "half-addressed" to Nelly, despite her avowed preference, as we have seen, to have maintained silence. Their heuristic addresses proceed not in spite of but because of a paucity of genuinely insightful listeners, for Nelly's unresponsive silence enables them to address her as a rhetorical surrogate, an analytic proxy. When Heathcliff, for instance, strives to verbalize the "eternally secluded" self, to "turn it out to another," Nelly's blank silence momentarily helps him to appropriate her angle of vision and substitute a personal perspective: it allows him to "try to describe the thousand forms of . . . ideas [Hareton] awakens, or embodies" (255). Finally, Catherine too depends on Nelly's audition without heeding her response: "Tell me," she demands, "what I've done to grieve [Heathcliff]" (72, 75). Here again, Catherine seeks to know the critical faculty of her listeners in order to distinguish her own. She must "become the other" to interpret herself.

Thus the implied dialogues in *Wuthering Heights* are analytic in that they enable Catherine and Heathcliff to recreate the externality of the other. Yet this analytic form serves another purpose in the novel, one whose function is not so much interpretive as ontological.

For this analytic mode is also particularly suited to historical reconstruction, to the recovery of what Lockwood refers to as Heathcliff and Catherine's "history" (36, 37). Indeed, such analytic exchanges can represent a succession of past dialogues from a given speaker's history. Accordingly, when a character in *Wuthering Heights* manages to initiate such addresses, there are necessarily echoes of parallel conversations buried in his or her past. The attempted dialogue thus disinters a character's rhetorical history, much as the analytic dialogue invokes a series of transferences to figures from an analysand's past. Hence Brontë's dialogic novel essentially exhumes the hidden past of its most impenetrable characters. When Heathcliff, for instance, attempts to "turn out" his mind, he seeks to recover his past dialogues not only with Catherine but also with those unknown listeners who presumably constitute his own hidden past; he exposes his thoughts "to another" in order to revive the "past associations" of his mysterious history (255). And when Catherine repeatedly endeavors to "let out" her "secret" before Nelly (70), she is attempting to evoke a series of interlocutors from her own history, including her absent mother, indulgent father, and, ultimately, the mishearing Heathcliff. In describing her first "fit" or trance, she says,

> Nelly, I'll tell you what I thought . . . I was enclosed in the oak-panelled bed at home; and my heart ached with some great grief which, just waking, I could not recollect. . . . most strangely, the whole last seven years of my life grew a blank! . . . I was a child; my father was just buried, and my misery arose from the separation that Hindley had ordered between me and Heathcliff. (107; cf. 108)

Here again, narrative apostrophe serves to disinter the buried figures in a character's past. Such rhetoric enables Catherine to recover what is "enclosed," to reconsider "separation," in a word, to "recollect."

According to this view, the recreation of dialogue gives voice to a silent history and thereby allows for its reinterpretation. If Heathcliff's truncated dialogues with Nelly represent his desire to hear his earliest historic voice, Catherine's flawed addresses attempt to invoke her father and Heathcliff, the auditors of her first linguistic era. Even Nelly, by sustaining her own narrative address before Lockwood, attempts to impose some contrived order on her past dialogues with both Heathcliff and Catherine. In each case, these characters initiate an interpretive reenactment of past voices—a regress that ultimately extends back to that original dialogue with the self, that confrontation with the other that we experience during the "mirror stage."[13]

This stage is, of course, Jacques Lacan's term for the child's clarification of selfhood by focusing on an other with whom he can identify. The child thereby defines his ego by projecting his own separateness onto an other. Lacan sees this process of self-identification as a mirroring, "a veritable capture by the other . . . 'as in a mirror,' in the sense that the subject identifies his sentiment of Self in the image of the other."[14] It is this mirror-stage confrontation that lies at the heart of many sustained addresses in *Wuthering Heights*, for only in being recognized by the autochthonous other can characters like Heathcliff and Catherine extract their own identities. "The first object of desire is to be recognized by the other" (31), and it is precisely this desire for "recognition" of self in another that in turn prompts Catherine to envision her identity in Heathcliff: "He's more myself than I am," she says to Nelly; "Whatever our souls are made of, his and mine are the same . . . "(72). Later, she adds, "So don't talk of our separation again — it is impracticable" (74). In *Wuthering Heights*, moreover, this primal recognition also takes place in rhetorical terms, which again accounts for the self-defining other's repeatedly taking the form of an addressee. Accordingly, establishing self in the novel is essentially a linguistic act, since only through language can the "other" both manifest itself and provide "recognition."[15]

V

Thus the analytic addressee serves not only to represent the past interlocutors of Heathcliff and Catherine but also to provide them with recognition — the self imaged in the other. In what is perhaps the most explicit account of this projected selfhood, Catherine says to Nelly, "Surely you and everybody have a notion that there is, or should be, an existence of yours beyond you. What were the use of my creation if I were entirely contained here?" (73–74). On one level, of course, Catherine's "existence . . . beyond" refers to Heathcliff: she is explaining a union that eventually defies "separation." Yet on another level, this passage also alludes to a more vital capacity to move outside one's contained existence, to establish creation and being through another. Later, Heathcliff too seeks this externalized identification when, upon learning of Catherine's death, he cries, "Take any form . . . only *do* not leave me. . . . Oh, God! it is unutterable! I *cannot*

live without my life! I *cannot* live without my soul!" (139). Heathcliff
recognizes that "life" inheres in the form of the other, the surrogate
soul.

This ontological connection between speaker and other again recalls Bakhtin's analysis of how dialogue instantiates what he terms
"self-consciousness." When Catherine speaks of that "existence . . .
beyond" the "contained" self, the otherness that enables selfhood, she
recognizes that one is "conscious through another, and with the help
of another." Here, too, the "most important acts constituting self-
consciousness are determined by a relationship toward another consciousness (toward a *thou*)."[16] This "thou" accordingly enables a kind
of linguistic differentiation, an individuation of being. We must again
bear in mind that "in dialogue a person . . . becomes for the first
time that which he is," that "to be means to communicate dialogically"
(*Poetics* 252). Thus dialogue with the "existence . . . beyond" enacts
the ego. It is worth recalling, moreover, that Bakhtin describes this
enactment as a contrastive act — that a speaker's "attitude toward himself is inseparably bound up with his attitude toward another, and
with the attitude of another toward him." As he goes on to say, "His
consciousness of self is constantly perceived against the background
of the other's consciousness of him — "I for myself" against the background of "I for another." Thus the hero's words about himself are
structured under the continuous influence of someone else's words
about him" (207). Consciousness thus dissolves unless projected
against the "background" of the other. The "thou" effectively silhou-
ettes the "I," much as the Freudian ego takes form only in opposition
to the super-ego. Hence when Catherine suggests that her "existence
. . . beyond" the self completes her "own being," she recognizes that
"consciousness of self is constantly perceived against the background
of the other's consciousness of [her]." When she concludes that
Heathcliff is, in her words, "always in my mind — not as a pleasure
. . . but as my own being" (74), she acknowledges that only in engaging the other does she "become for the first time that which [she] is."
In both passages, defining the self requires delimitation, with the
other becoming a "background" for the ego. Catherine accordingly
abhors what she calls "separation" since, again, "to be means to communicate dialogically": only this dialogic presence sustains her selfhood. Invoking Heathcliff, she insists, "My great thought in living is
himself" (74).

Thus "living," for Brontë, requires keeping the other "in mind":
"existence" partakes of the other. In *Wuthering Heights*, moreover,

this other can also manifest itself collectively, as what she calls "society." For instance, although Lockwood pretends to abjure this "society" (13), proclaiming himself a "perfect misanthropist," he ultimately casts his narrative in the form of what he calls "sociable conversation" with Nelly (22). Then, after two days at the Grange, he also acknowledges a need for "social intercourse," and remarks upon Heathcliff's curious antipathy toward "conversation" (35; cf. 17). Heathcliff himself, of course, craves the preternatural "society" of Catherine; yet we should also recognize that, like Lockwood, nearly every character in the novel voices a commensurate need for such social interchange: Cathy, Nelly, and even Joseph each refer to disparate versions of a "friend," "companion," "company," or "union" (249, 247, 265, 250; cf. 38). In each case, the quest for such companions represents the socially connected self. Catherine, for instance, in seeking union with Heathcliff, is actually striving to orient her existence, to place it within the social world. She attempts to locate her consciousness within a human order, to eschew (in Lockwood's words) the "perpetual isolation" of being "banished from the world" (17, 240). Hence this need for social intercourse recalls Bakhtin's notion of polyphonic discourse, in which one "invests his entire self in discourse, and this discourse enters into the dialogic fabric of human life" (*Poetics* 293). Brontë's concept of the self is thus essentially plural, social in the broadest sense. As Bakhtin goes on to say, the self "must find itself . . . within an intense field of interorientations" (239).

We must further bear in mind that if characters establish being through social intercourse, they also stress this delimitation of self as oral or spoken. Once again, the ego must be overheard in the form of a voice. Even Cathy Linton acknowledges Hareton's identity by first assailing his silence, an act that, if he listens, will rhetorically introduce her into his discourse and his life. "Hareton, Hareton, Hareton!" she cries, "do you hear? . . . you must listen to me" (247). For Heathcliff, too, this ontological listening must also precede potential union; as we have noted, his plea to Catherine is "hear me *this* time" (33). Indeed, we have observed that throughout *Wuthering Heights* the self-affirming other is necessarily an auditor, and the foregoing social "interorientations" are necessarily vocative, what Bakhtin refers to as "dialogues." As we have seen, he suggests that "life by its very nature is dialogic. To live means to participate in dialogue: to ask questions, to heed, to respond, to agree, and so forth" (*Poetics* 293). Here again, then, we should keep in mind Bakhtin's concept of how the ego distinguishes itself within dialogue, how it emerges as a "voice." One seeks, he writes, "To find one's own voice and to orient it among other voices, to combine it with some and to oppose it to others, to separate one's voice from another voice with which it has inseparably merged. . . . [T]his determines the hero's discourse. It must find itself, reveal itself among other words . . . " (239). In this passage, self-creation is again a matter of vocative contrast, of counterposing one's voice against another's. In recounting their own stories, then, Heathcliff and Catherine must "orient [them] among other voices"; each narrative must attempt to "find itself, reveal itself among" the dialogic responses of deficient listeners. Here, too, such voices serve to counterpoint the "I," to resonate the social self.

VI

Bakhtin's discussions of this dialogic consciousness of self thus serve to clarify Brontë's concepts of existence and social intercourse. Yet we need not rely solely on modern commentary to expand on this notion of consciousness-in-other. Indeed, the writer who best exemplifies the nineteenth-century concern with the externally defined self, with plural self-consciousness, is Coleridge, whose aesthetics are cited by the many critics who insist on the "Romantic" quality of *Wuthering Heights*.[17] Although his use of an external other often differs from Brontë's, he too represents this ontological other as a dubious listener (especially in poems like "The Rime of the Ancient Mariner" and "Christabel"). As we observed with *Frankenstein*, then, we can better understand Brontë's portrayal of "existence" (73), "conscience" (73), and "being" (74) if we briefly examine Coleridge's analysis of the same issues. Here again, both Brontë and Coleridge discuss "being" in terms of what Coleridge, like Bakhtin, calls "Consciousness." We would do well to recall, then, how Coleridge defines "Self" in terms of an externalized conscience: "*From* what reasons do I believe in *continuous* <& ever-continuable> *Consciousness?* From *Conscience!* Not for myself but for my conscience—i.e. my affections & duties toward others, I should have no Self—for Self is Definition; but all Boundary implies Neighbourhood—& is knowable only by Neighbourhood, or Relations" (*NB* 2:3231). Coleridge again reminds us how "Self" emerges only as a conscience "towards others," a "Boundary" consisting of close "Relations." If we can establish such "Relations," we effectively delineate the individual "Consciousness" and make it "knowable."

Here again, it is this sense of "Boundary" and "Definition" that Catherine derives from her "affections & duties" toward Heathcliff: only he can effectively represent part of what she refers to as "being." Catherine's one explanation of this projected being is thus crucial: "[M]y great thought in living is himself. If all else perished, and *he* remained, I should continue to be; and, if all else remained, and he were annihilated, the Universe would turn to a mighty stranger. I should not seem a part of it . . . he's always, always in my mind – not as a pleasure, any more than I am always a pleasure to myself – but as my own being" (74). What Catherine is suggesting is that Heathcliff, and the external "conscience" he stands for, can actually delimit self in this novel. In embodying her "Boundary" or "Relations," Heathcliff enables her to "continue to be"; in representing her link with "the Universe," he in effect confirms her "being." Again, Catherine herself might have said (as Coleridge did), "Self in me derives its sense of Being from having this one absolute Object" (*NB* 2:3148). In this case, her "Object" defines a mental "Neighbourhood," which in turn defines her place in "the Universe." When she momentarily loses this "Boundary" (during Heathcliff's absence), she necessarily loses her "being" and becomes a spectre (85). Like Frankenstein's monster, she despairs at what Coleridge calls "the *incorporeity* of true love in absence" – the "incorporeity" of "Self" that follows from the loss of "Definition" (*NB* 3:4036).

Catherine's apparent need for this projected existence or "Definition" is again explicable in light of what Coleridge refers to as outness, the state in which he can expose or "withdraw" his "painful Peculiarities . . . from the dark Adyt of [his] own Being" (*NB* 3:4166). For both Coleridge and Catherine can circumscribe the "Peculiarities" of the self only by establishing this definitive outness. Here again, such outness emerges even in the form of feckless listeners, like those in *Wuthering Heights*; they provide not corroboration by others so much as an exposure before conscience. To use Coleridge's terms once again, the sole "Impulse" for establishing outness is to unveil or "withdraw" the hidden self – and "not the wish for others to see it" (*NB* 3: 4166, 3624). Here, too, it is the rhetorical, dialogic presence of such listeners that enables Catherine to expose her self, to demarcate "existence," to "continue to be."

At this point, then, we are addressing what is perhaps the most perplexing critical dilemma surrounding *Wuthering Heights*: the status of Catherine's cryptic statement, "I *am* Heathcliff" (74). For we can now account for this equation by reflecting on what we have been calling Catherine's avowed need for outness, that desire to define "being" in terms of an "existence . . . beyond" one's "contained" self. Thus, in the statement "I *am* Heathcliff," Catherine essentially delimits her existence by locating it in another, by making her outness one with Heathcliff's. It is this notion of outness that also accounts for Heathcliff's last visions of Catherine's spectre, for he is essentially living out her stated description of her externality: "If all perished, and *he* remained, I should still continue to be" (14). And it is this depiction of self-defining, moreover, that also underlies the novel's last ghostly images of Catherine and Heathcliff; by the time of her death, they have at last established this externally hypostatized self-through-other.

As the novel closes, it is this projection of self that finally accounts for the attenuated image of the second-generation union — for in this couple not only does part of Catherine and Heathcliff "continue to be" but a symbol of their rhetorical process of outness necessarily lives on. And when the younger Cathy ultimately asks Hareton to listen, she necessarily provides a vehicle for her own "affections & duties towards others," her own "Definition" of "Conscience" and "Self," her own outness. The legacy of the auditor is thus confirmed.

6

The Heartbeat of Darkness: Listening in(to) the Twentieth Century

> To whom do you think he is writing? For me it is always more important to know that than to know what is being written; moreover I think it amounts to the same, to the other finally.
> Derrida, "Evois"
>
> *Cor Cordium*, "heart of hearts."
> Leigh Hunt's epitaph for Percy Shelley

I

The trajectory of nineteenth-century dialogue ends with the works of Conrad — or, more specifically, with those Marlow narratives that focus on the potential colloquy between narrator and listener. The final words of such core characters as the monster and Heathcliff have by now dwindled to Kurtz's terse pronouncement, "The horror"; more significantly, with this decline in loquacity comes a corresponding intensification of the problem of interpretation. There is precious little left to hear. In the same way, the succession of narrators and listeners in *Frankenstein* and *Wuthering Heights* has dwindled to the essentially singular address by Marlow to the Thames listeners. It is as if this narrowing of the narrative field begins to foreshadow the nonaddress of the stream-of-consciousness novel. And indeed, the notorious unreliability of a narrator like Marlow leads us to ask why Conrad would build his entire novella around a lapsed exchange, an act of interpretation destined to collapse.

This relative unreliability of Marlow as narrator has preoccupied critics from Percy Lubbock to Ian Watt, and no wonder: we witness nearly everything in *Heart of Darkness* from Marlow's perspective, and while we may reject his interpretation of events, it remains difficult to escape his narrative point of view. Commentators have accordingly concentrated on Marlow's narrative foibles: his recurrent mendacity, pious moralizing, and suspect garrulity. What such studies have not considered, however, is that these allegedly untrustworthy traits may be indications less of Marlow's pathology than of his rhetoric—his vocative attempts to provoke a recalcitrant audience into some form of dialogue. If this account is correct, Conrad's oft-cited quotation of Novalis may in fact cut both ways: "It is certain my conviction gains infinitely the moment another soul will believe in it."[1] According to this view, Conrad may intend not only to remind us of potential communion but also to explore dialogues in which "another soul" cannot corroborate or "believe in" a speaker.

II

Despite this potential dearth of corroboration, several critics have rightly observed how Conrad's works foreground the act of apostrophe, of including the other within the narrative gesture. In *Conrad's Romanticism*, for example, David Thorburn notes the potentially bilateral features of narrative, as a given speaker "mediates between the tale and its intended audience." "But in Conrad," he goes on, "and in the Romantic poems that most closely resemble his fiction"

> this mediating role has a special urgency. The gesture of community implicit in any teller's decision to relate a story is acknowledged and lifted to a particular prominence by Conrad's drama of the telling, by his insistent habit of setting the scene in which the telling occurs, . . . of introducing auditors who converse with the narrator and even . . . receive letters from him.
>
> These and similar strategies have their counterpart in Wordsworth's habit of addressing particular speakers—his sister Dorothy and Coleridge especially—in a number of poems. The whole of the *Prelude* is addressed to Coleridge, and it is crucial to the poem's meaning that at key moments Wordsworth speaks directly to him. . . . Coleridge, too, has some important poems—including *To William Wordsworth* and the *Dejection Ode*—in which the speaker implicates a particularized auditor in the spiritual anguish he is evoking.[2] (128–29; cf. 103–4)

Thorburn's recognition of this "particularized auditor" within a dramatized "scene" of telling begins to suggest the potential for Romantic dialogue in Conrad's narratives. In fact, despite a given narrator's lack of corroboration, the genesis of *Heart of Darkness* is actually a longing for audition, for that witness to narration who enables Conradian "conviction" (72). "Kurtz wanted an audience," says Marlow, and indeed, the former repeatedly addresses not only Marlow but the naive Russian as well (56). When asked whether he has had occasion to "talk with Mr. Kurtz," the Russian replies, "You don't talk with that man — you listen to him . . . " (54). Marlow, too, insists upon this drive to "listen," to establish at least the rudiments of dialogue. In the following passage, such dialogue represents the entire rationale for his journey. When he fears that Kurtz has been murdered, he says,

> I couldn't have been more disgusted if I had travelled all this way for the sole purpose of talking with Mr. Kurtz. Talking with . . . I flung one shoe overboard, and became aware that that was exactly what I had been looking forward to — a talk with Kurtz. I made the strange discovery that I had never imagined him as doing, you know, but as discoursing. I didn't say to myself, "Now I will never see him," or "Now I will never shake him by the hand," but, "Now I will never hear him." The man presented himself as a voice. Not of course that I did not connect him with some sort of action. . . . That was not the point. The point was in his being a gifted creature, and that of all his gifts the one that stood out pre-eminently, that carried with it a sense of real presence, was his ability to talk, his words — the gift of expression. . . .[3] (48)

By becoming auditor to this "gift of expression," Marlow hopes to generate the kind of dialogic "discoursing" that has become his "sole purpose" in the novella. He yearns to hear not only Kurtz's utterance but also the articulation it represents — what he repeatedly refers to as the pandemic "voice" at the heart of human darkness.[4] It is this dual desire for such a voice that valorizes the "inestimable privilege of listening to the gifted Kurtz" (48–49; cf. 77).

Such "listening" eventually becomes Marlow's sole access to this revelatory period of his life: each memory turns out to have its own audible "voice." In the following reverie, Kurtz's words blend with the voices of Marlow's entire experience:

> A voice. He was very little more than a voice. And I heard — him — it — this voice — other voices — all of them were so little more than voices —

and the memory of that time itself lingers around me, impalpable, like a dying vibration of one immense jabber, silly, atrocious, sordid, savage, or simply mean, without any kind of sense. Voices, voices—even the girl herself—. . . .[5] (49)

Here, "even the girl," Kurtz's Intended, constitutes part of this collective "voice," this attempted dialogue with the world. Later, too, "her low voice seemed to have the accompaniment of all the other sounds" in Marlow's world (77). As part of this dialogic "accompaniment," he becomes a clearly sympathetic auditor: "I feel I can speak to you," she says, "and oh! I must speak. I want you—you who have heard his last words—to know I have been worthy of him . . . " (77). In speaking with Marlow, then, the Intended also expects to find that "sympathy" requisite for external confession. As Marlow puts it, the "girl talked, easing her pain in the certitude of my sympathy; she talked as thirsty men drink" (77).

Heart of Darkness thus becomes a chain of apostrophes, in which each narration constitutes an attempt at dialogue. Near the beginning of his story, Marlow refers to all history as a "gigantic tale," a tale in that it must necessarily be *told to* a listener (4). To tell a story is to endeavor to engage Kurtz, one's past, or the heart of darkness itself— memories repeatedly represented by the presence of the voice. This emphasis on audibility extends even to Marlow's listeners on the Thames. During most of his tale, Marlow's only contact with them is aural: "For a long time already he, sitting apart, had been no more to us than a voice" (28). Yet for these listeners, Marlow still represents a rhetorical "pilot, which to a seaman is trustworthiness personified" (3). Although such "trustworthiness" is ultimately misplaced, the potential intelligibility and response of this "voice" stands as a kind of guide during Marlow's profoundly "inconclusive" narrative. Much as Victor Frankenstein seeks a "friend" to "regulate [his] mind," such listeners regard Marlow, at least initially, as a dialogic "friend." In the case of the Intended, it is again Marlow who becomes the auditory "friend," by listening both to her and to Kurtz's cryptic account. "Who was not his friend who had heard him speak once?" she asks (77; cf. 76).

For the Intended, in fact, audition amounts to an almost illusory faith. She is "ready to listen without mental reservation, without suspicion, without a thought for herself" (74). In her, such readiness constitutes a boundless "capacity for fidelity, for belief" (76). In this sense, she also demonstrates Marlow's own desire to express "some sort of belief," for she continues to reflect the "unextinguishable light of belief," even as the novella ends (72, 76). Much as Victor avoids a listener's "unbelief" by choosing to address Walton, Kurtz too may find such belief when he speaks to the Intended. What these characters have in common is, to paraphrase Novalis, the need for another soul who believes — for that rapport that might enable colloquy. Although such auscultatory belief finally turns out to be a "saving illusion," it nevertheless represents the rhetorical desire for corroborative response (77).

III

We must bear in mind, however, that the requirements for any conventional notion of conversation or corroboration are never satisfied in *Heart of Darkness*. As the novella proceeds, our expectations for any recognizable communication or reception must ultimately collapse. Hence while dialogue — in the broad sense we have defined it — may prove to be viable, colloquy itself is not. During his conversation with the brickmaker, for instance, Marlow allows his awed interlocutor to believe that company positions are determined by some widespread "influence in Europe" (27). Marlow perpetuates such an illusion "simply because," as he tells his listeners,

> I had a notion it somehow would be of help to that Kurtz whom at the time I did not see — you understand. He was just a word for me. I did not see the man in the name any more than you do. Do you see him? Do you see the story? Do you see anything? It seems to me I am trying to tell you a dream — making a vain attempt, because no relation of a dream can convey the dream-sensation. . . .
>
> No, it is impossible, it is impossible to convey the life-sensation of any given epoch of one's existence — that which makes its truth, its meaning — its subtle and penetrating essence. It is impossible. We live, as we dream — alone. . . . (27–28)

Marlow concludes that his auditors will never understand the nature of his experience; such a story is "impossible to convey," making his endeavor to provoke colloquy a "vain attempt." Such a conclusion is underscored, moreover, when it emerges during Marlow's failed interchange with the brickmaker. Although this station agent begs not to be "misunderstood," Marlow continues to "let him run on" until the agent becomes "exasperated" with Marlow's "unresponsive attitude" (26, 28).

Such "unresponsive" exchanges stem from a general poverty of audition in the novella, as the unscrupulous brickmaker becomes part of a general breakdown in communal rhetoric. As Aaron Fogel has said of *The Secret Agent*, Conrad's nihilistic depictions of communal "sympathy," "tact," and "legal institutional power" belie any notions of sociable conversation or unresisted dialogue (154ff., 227).[6] In this context, Marlow's "young fool" resembles his auditors on the Thames, for each is entrapped by the "normal" desires of a staid society (48). Like the tasteless readers bemoaned in Wordsworth's 1800 "Preface" — readers who prefer verse novels to poetry — Marlow's audience is "moored" by the bland "appetites" and expectations of Britain's "sepulchral city" (72). Upon returning to England, Marlow sees such people "hurrying through the streets to filch a little money from each other, to devour their infamous cookery, to gulp their unwholesome beer, to dream their insignificant and silly dreams" (72). As potential interlocutors, the British appear fundamentally unable to hear and apprehend the "essence of dreams" that Marlow experiences. When he attempts to describe his odd interest in Kurtz, for instance, they sigh sarcastically, prompting Marlow to respond, "This is the worst of trying to tell. . . . Here you all are, each moored with two good addresses, like a hulk with two anchors, a butcher round one corner, a policeman round another, excellent appetites, and temperature normal — you hear — normal from year's end to year's end. And you say, Absurd!" (48). Several pages later, after having again attempted to explain those "powers of darkness" that possess Kurtz, Marlow despairs of reaching his interlocutors, saying, "You can't understand. How could you? — with solid pavement under your feet, surrounded by kind neighbors ready to cheer you or to fall on you, stepping delicately between the butcher and the policeman, in the holy terror of scandal and gallows and lunatic asylums . . . " (50).

IV

Such "kind neighbors," then, "ready to cheer you or to fall on you," represent the possibilities for interchange in *Heart of Darkness*. It is this succession of bogus auditors — interlocutors who remain ignorant, bourgeois, and painfully "normal" — that signifies the breakdown of colloquy in the novella. Although the Bakhtinian implications of dialogue may persist, the idea of narrative as a conveyance or communication implodes. Conrad indicates this implosion, moreover, by impugning the very hallmark of communicative rhetoric: a narrator's eloquence. Hence much as Victor tells Walton to beware the monster's "powers of eloquence and persuasion" (218), Marlow comes to be wary of Kurtz's forensic powers. In place of that "gift of expression," the "voice" that Marlow longs for, he hears Kurtz "hide in the magnificent folds of eloquence the barren darkness of his heart" (48, 69). In this context, Marlow views Kurtz as a succession of "splendid appearances" masking "frightful realities"—a shadow "draped nobly in the folds of a gorgeous eloquence" (75). Marlow goes on to insist that "there was something wanting in him—some small matter which, when the pressing need arose, could not be found under his magnificent eloquence" (58). In *Heart of Darkness*, then, narrative eloquence signifies not disclosure but duplicity: it conceals and suppresses more than it conveys. It accordingly obfuscates those savage emotions that "blazed" at the end of the infamous "Report"—"vibrating with eloquence" (50). And when Kurtz finally does manage to strip these "folds of eloquence" from his terse, final "pronouncement" (72), his message still serves to cast doubt on the potential for colloquy among human beings: "No eloquence," says Marlow, "could have been so withering to one's belief in mankind as his final burst of sincerity" (68).

By the end of the novel, then, the sound of eloquence becomes a veritable parody of exchange. While eloquent addresses literally constitute the novel, each fails to elicit a commensurate reaction, so that narration itself rings hollow. In discussing Kurtz with the Intended, for instance, Marlow begins to say,

> It was impossible not to—
> "Love him," she finished eagerly, silencing me into an appalled dumbness. (76)

Such an interchange, the concluding conversation of Marlow's narrative, is in fact representative, for Marlow's eloquence bespeaks the denial of communion. His encounter with the Intended dissolves into a series of false starts, broken repairs, and bogus readings, each calculated to maintain a "saving illusion" (77; cf. 78). In place of the extended engagements and interpretations of exchange, they are both left in "appalled dumbness."

* * *

Indeed, when such eloquence fails to engender any viable exchange in the novella, we are each of us left in silence. As each successive colloquy founders, silence itself comes to signify the overall muting of reception and disclosure. Much as Frankenstein's epistolary "silence" presages the end of exchange, so Marlow's "silencing . . . into an appalled dumbness" is part of a larger narrative denial. Such a denial does not, however, indicate a calm: this "stillness of life did not in the least resemble a peace" (34). Rather, it is the silence of human community bereft of a voice, what Marlow sees as a "region" approached "by the way of solitude — utter solitude without a policeman — by the way of silence — utter silence, where no warning voice of a kind neighbor can be heard whispering of public opinion" (50).

It is this mute "region," then, that betokens the solitary and circumscribed heart of Africa: Conrad repeatedly invokes this "utter silence" to characterize both the dumb landscape of the novella, and the consequent impossibility of colloquy.[7] As he writes in the 1899 text, such a landscape "seemed to demand a cry, but the unbroken silence that hung over the scene was more formidable than any sound could be" (62).

It is therefore appropriate that Marlow's narrative would both begin and end with this symbolic quiet (3, 79), and that the few encounters that appear sustained would be essentially silent or muted. As the helmsman dies, for instance, his "glance" speaks an "understandable language" for Marlow: "the intimate profundity of that look" is "like a claim of distant kinship affirmed in a supreme moment" (47, 52). So, too, the natives' calls to Kurtz come as "amazing words that resembled no sounds of human language" (68). Though they remain fearfully inarticulate to Marlow — "like the responses of some satanic litany" — they seem to speak readily to Kurtz (68). Here again, however, the alleged exchange proves specious, the victim of Kurtz's rapacious practices and spurious eloquence. Like the silenced skulls that encircle his house, he speaks with the "shrunken dry lips" of "eternal" silence (58). Such colloquies are by definition muted, partial, and ephemeral; in the absence of both language and response, they trail off into an "audible and soothing silence" (65).

V

Yet, in one sense, the pervasive silence in *Heart of Darkness* is itself a response — first, to an eloquence that obfuscates more than it reveals, and then to an audience who misapprehend more than they can fathom. In both cases, moreover, this silence leaves us questioning the limits of interpretation — a question that, as we have seen, recalls the hermeneutic potential inherent in dialogic form. Indeed, in *Heart of Darkness* such potential again takes an interrogative form: Marlow repeatedly asks his listeners, "Do you understand?" and the implication is that they do not (76).[8] This failed interpretation is also re-enacted in the various crossings of diverse languages in the novella. Much as the characters in *Frankenstein* must stumble between Arabic, French, English, and other tongues, those in this novella attempt to make sense of Russian, English, and sundry native languages. "I don't understand the dialect of this tribe," says the Russian, on encountering the natives who serve Kurtz (62). Marlow, too, experiences this difficulty when he makes a "speech in English with gestures" (21), only to have his native audience disregard him the next morning. And Marlow also mistakes the Russian's language for "cipher" (39) — much as Hareton Earnshaw confronts the seemingly unintelligible characters written above his own doorway. As both works end, the path to interpretation — and to interpretive listening — appears to be permanently blocked. Even after Marlow completes his tale, he learns that the "offing was barred" (79), in much the same way that Lockwood finds the gate to the Heights closed upon his return. The various stories in these works are not so much paths to comprehension as they are exposures of what Marlow refers to as "human secrets" (42; cf. 5, 43).

It is this notion of "human secrets" that accounts for the failure of ratiocinative interpretation in *Heart of Darkness*. Just as Coleridge's "secret lodger" remains "obscure" and "out of sight," so Marlow repeatedly refers to his own "human secrets" as "inscrutable" (5, 22, 62) and "incomprehensible" (6, 14, 36, 77; cf. 72). Indeed, in "The Eolian Harp," we learn that "The Incomprehensible" is Coleridge's own term for an unknown God (59). In that poem, too, Coleridge speculates upon the same "invisible things" that we have seen invoked in the motto to the "Rime": "I readily believe that there are more invisible than visible things in the universe. . . . The human mind has always circled about knowledge of these things, but never attained it." Such a concept of noumenal thought — of secret "knowledge" — figures prominently in *Heart of Darkness*, for Marlow too refers to the "hidden knowledge" that surrounds Kurtz's house and person (57).

Of course, part of this knowledge involves what Marlow regards as the "hidden evil" of the human abstract (33), comparable to the "hidden vice" that Coleridge sought to "eloign and abalienate" from his "dark Adyt." For this reason, "the inner truth is hidden — luckily,

luckily" (34). Yet there is another sense in which this inner "knowledge" is, whether "evil" or no, "hidden" and "secret" *by definition*, and therefore inimical to an auditor's interpretation. As Marlow puts it, certain noumenal experiences are "impossible to convey" to any audience, since "no relation of a dream can convey the dream-sensation" (27). He would have his interlocutors sense that "there's no initiation . . . into such mysteries" (6).

Hence no initiation — including the experience of interpretive audition — can ever reveal the "subtle" essence of the "life-sensation." Narration is by definition "inconclusive" since truth itself is "unspeakable" (7, 63). When Marlow does attempt to speak of such truths, his story must accordingly remain "not very clear" (7). In the end, then, Marlow's tales eschew any audible core that might be interpreted by a listener: "To him the meaning of an episode was not inside like a kernel but outside, enveloping the tale which brought it out only as a glow brings out a haze . . . " (5). Since it remains "outside" Marlow's tales, such noumenal "meaning" can never be plumbed by a listener: it is "impenetrable to human thought" (56).

Yet we have already noted that a listener's particular interpretation is normally not the objective of these witnessed narratives; rather, it is the dialogic *process* of exposure that justifies their continuation. Much as the Ancient Mariner must retell his story inexorably, narration in this novella is a recursive act — "interminable" as the two rivers in Marlow's story (3, 38). And indeed, as his story begins, we learn that we are "fated, before the ebb began to run, to hear about one of Marlow's inconclusive experiences" (7); clearly, the tale is only "one of" many that constitute a perpetual process of exposure. Even at the end, Marlow says of Kurtz and the Intended, "I shall see this eloquent phantom as long as I live, and I shall see her, too . . . " (78). No storyteller can ever completely exorcise a "memory," and that is why Marlow must continue to tell his tales. Like the Mariner, his "curse" is in one sense eternal narration — what Marlow in another context terms "eternal condemnation" (76).

Again, however, we must not conclude that such a narrative is devoid of melioration. On the contrary, by repeatedly exposing his "hidden vice" before an audience, Marlow actually partakes of an ongoing process of abalienation, of continual outness. As we have just seen, this necessarily recursive process serves to account for the repetitive attempts at colloquy in the novella. Yet while such recursivity may further the ends of exposure, it comes at the price of repeated rhetorical collapse, flaws that again betoken elisions among shared terms of social inquiry, understanding, and judgment. Marlow, for instance, fails to invoke any shared moral schema with which he might locate Kurtz, for neither moral nor rhetorical standards have any force in this novella. As he says, " . . . I had to deal with a being to whom I could not appeal in the name of anything high or low. I had, even like the niggers, to invoke him — himself — his own exalted and incredible degradation. There was nothing either above or below him, and I knew it. He had kicked himself loose of the earth" (67). In the absence of any common standards to "invoke" or "appeal to," societal judgment erodes. Much as Frankenstein's monster mocks the "sanguinary laws of man," Marlow denigrates the "farcical law" that sends natives up the river without food (41; cf. 17). Earlier, he also satirizes the "outraged law" that enslaves people according to some legalistic "mystery" (16). Generally speaking, those consensual bonds that normally link members of a community are absent from *Heart of Darkness*. In the same way that characters in *Wuthering Heights* and *Frankenstein* focus upon their social solitude — their separation from society — so figures in Conrad's novella dwell upon their own "great solitude" (59), their "lonely desolation" (48) — what Marlow calls his "isolation amongst all these men with whom I had no point of contact . . . " (13; cf. 20, 50, 55, 65 — 66).

In the midst of such mutually enforced isolation, Marlow is amazed to find that many station agents harbor a "philanthropic pretence" about their enterprise (91; cf. 81, 101). Such a pretence is consistent with Kurtz's report on "Savage Customs," including its bald commentary on political extermination and imperialistic desire. In the present context, however, we should also recognize that Conrad's rhetorical disjunctions serve to represent the divisive community of the novella — a divisiveness that echoes both the Branderham episode and Victor's encounter with the Irish. In each of the three works, moreover, the force motivating this socio-rhetorical divisiveness is personified as an endemic "monster," — as a hidden evil that instantiates the failure of colloquy (cf. 65-66, 36, 21, 22-23). The broken interchange thus becomes a rhetoric of flawed community.

VI

The few studies that consider this flawed rhetoric, this overall failure of colloquy, attribute its demise to several interrelated causes. For David Thorburn, the recurrence of this broken rhetoric, both in Conrad's works and Romantic poetry, signifies a general fallibility of language. Such breakdowns reveal the "Romantic preoccupation with the reaches and limits of language," a broad and self-conscious "suspicion of art and of language" (115; cf. 106, 117, 124). He goes on to characterize Marlow's narrative language as inherently "tentative" and "self-doubting," a language that must necessarily "fall short of perfect truth." It is a dialect of failure, one that "registers, above all, a fundamental humility" (118).[9]

For Edward Said, however, this failure of colloquy has a more rhetorical, interactional origin — what he refers to as the "conflict" or "contest" between associated utterances. In Conrad's works, such a contest derives from both a "wanting-to-speak and the need to link a given utterance with other utterances." "The internal continuity of each tale," Said suggests,

> derives from the speaker's self-consciousness as someone producing an utterance that . . . stands against or among conflicting or complementary utterances. In a sense every narrative utterance in Conrad contests another one: Marlow's lie to Kurtz's intended is only the most notable instance of a common enough habit. . . . [T]he reader [can] see Conrad make tension and conflict, and thereby a dynamic narrative texture, out of an utterance at odds with and yet ineluctably linked to other utterances. (102)

The allusion to "conflicting" utterances here recalls Ong's own notion of contestational rhetoric within the Socratic tradition.[10] Yet, like Thorburn, Said traces the rifts between these conflicting utterances to an overall schism or fallibility within language itself. For him, "language fails ultimately to represent intention and, analogously," the "mimetic function of language is sorely inadequate to make us see" (110). Hence the collapse of both "mutual comprehension" and "complete expression" combine to erode the "sense of community between speaker and hearer" (104, 105, 100).

In the context of dialogue, however, we have seen that "mutual comprehension" and rhetorical "community" are neither goals nor requirements. While the desire for corroboration may motivate colloquy, the poetics of dialogue are often founded upon its absence. Indeed, as Fogel has noted, Conradian discourse is by definition based upon "unstable results" and a "mutual failure of realization" (221, 220). For Fogel, moreover, this failure is less a matter of fallible language than of coerced speech — the forcefully elicited articulation that reflects psychological, historical, and political encounters within Conrad's world. Fogel concludes that "in spite of [Conrad's] reputation for writing about solitaries, he is in fact preoccupied with a type of relation that takes place not so much inside the consciousness of relatively isolated persons as between them: forced contractuality. This idea of forced relation becomes most clear in scenes where persons are forced to produce some speech or written language" (219). According to this view, such "forced dialogues" or "scenes of coercion to speak" represent both the "institutional variety" and "historical recurrence" of sociopolitical conflict. In characterizing *Heart of Darkness*, for example, Fogel links this rhetorical force to a "dialogical mood of imperialism, of 'overwhelming the other' by misty imperial words" (19). At the same time, he further locates this effect within the classical concept of "dialogue as coercion and appropriation found in at least some major Greek literature" (236). In this sense, the "combative" quality of dialogue derives from an "'Oedipal dialogic,' . . . in which the inquisitor is violently revealed and punished by the process he institutes" (230).

There is much to say for these accounts of Conradian rhetoric, not the least of which is their recognition of a self-conscious desire to depict rhetorical division, struggle, and contest. Yet whether this divisiveness derives from a consummate fallibility of linguistic representation or a more specifically coercive speech act, we must also recognize that such failed encounters constitute part of a broader process: a dialogic operation. In terms of the present study, they serve both to instantiate and sustain what we have defined as "agonistic discourse": the linguistic structure that depends upon disjunctive rhetoric for the particular kinds of exposure and investigation we have discussed. According to this approach, the foregoing instances of flawed representation have specific textual results, including the particular ontological and hermeneutic effects exemplified in the foregoing chapters. Although a given address may in effect be coerced or forcefully elicited, the act of apostrophizing an other can nonetheless constitute a "communality of speech" — an act of dialogue. And although such encounters may lead to neither normative communication nor mutual reception, they are nevertheless central to a kind of counter-rhetoric that is both self-interpretive and self-fashioning. Such exchanges thus point not merely to the general fallibility and forced nature of language but also to the specific adversativeness of dialogue.

VII

Thus even when Conrad's exchanges bespeak a kind of social discord, we again see that, for many speakers, reciprocal corroboration is simply not the point. In *Heart of Darkness* particularly, the argument for dialogue as a mutual conveyance or explanation actually begs the question. "Mind, I am not trying to excuse or even explain," says Marlow to his auditors; "I am trying to account to myself for—for—Mr. Kurtz—for the shade of Mr. Kurtz" (122). Marlow's narration thus accounts, as he says, "to myself"—without any need to "explain" his address to his listeners. Instead, his concept of such an address is comparable to his attitude toward the river steamer. "No influential friend would have served me better," he says. "She had given me a chance to come out a bit—to find out what I could do. . . . I like what is in the work—the chance to find yourself. Your own reality—for yourself, not for others—what no other man can ever know. They can only see the mere show, and never can tell what it really means" (29). Like his work on the steamer, Marlow's address before an auditor (or "friend") allows him to "come out" of a secluded self, to establish his individual "reality" through an other. And much as Coleridge insists that his sole "Impulse" for exposing his painful lodger is to establish outness—and "not the wish for others to see it"—so Marlow would have his listeners seek not corroboration but, as he says, "Your own reality—for yourself, not for others" (cf. *NB* 3:4166).[11]

This quest for an external "reality," a dialogic other, persists throughout *Heart of Darkness*. In the same way that Catherine Earnshaw envisions what she calls an "existence of yours beyond you"—a self not "entirely contained here"—so Marlow locates "another existence" for himself within the "impenetrable forest" (34; cf. *Wuthering Heights*, 73–74). The narrative address thus allows for an "existence . . . beyond" the solipsistic mind, for a Coleridgean outness that eventually defines the individual "Self." As we have seen, Coleridge himself writes: "Not for myself, but for my conscience—i.e. my affections & duties toward others, I should have no Self—for Self is Definition; but all Boundary implies Neighbourhood—& is knowable only by Neighbourhood, or Relations" (*NB* 2:3231). Because "Self . . . is knowable only by Neighbourhood," one establishes identity by regarding an interlocutor as a "Boundary," as a symbol of "affections & duties toward others." When Coleridge finally manages to effect this outness—this "Boundary" of the self—he is momentarily able to stand apart from his internal "vice," to pronounce judgment upon his "hidden" evil (cf. *NB* 3:3325; *AR* 10).

It is this need to stand outside the self, to pronounce judgment, that motivates the central dialogues within *Heart of Darkness*. Kurtz, for instance, manages a "supreme moment of complete knowledge"

when he briefly recognizes "The horror" for what it is (71). As Marlow
says,

> I was within a hair's breadth of the last opportunity for pronouncement,
> and I found with humiliation that probably I would have nothing to
> say. This is the reason why I affirm that Kurtz was a remarkable man.
> He had something to say. He said it. . . . He had summed up — he had
> judged. "The horror!" He was a remarkable man. After all, this was the
> expression of some sort of belief; it had candour, it had conviction.
> . . . I like to think my summing-up would not have been a word of
> careless contempt. Better his cry — much better. It was an affirmation, a
> moral victory. . . . (72).

According to Marlow, then, Kurtz has finally managed to pronounce
judgment on the darkness of experience, to expose his "secret lodger."
We must bear in mind, however, that such exposure demands the
inscribed presence of a dialogic listener, that witness who enables
"another existence" (34). Again, Marlow stresses that "Kurtz wanted
an audience" (56), and the motley Russian provides one by referring
to Kurtz in the manner noted above: "You don't talk with that man —
you listen to him . . . " (54). And here, too, the "existence . . . beyond" the "contained" mind does not derive from an auditor's potentially corroborative response. On the contrary, in speaking of his
other "existence," Marlow tells his listeners that such externality
comes about only when one has been, as he says, "cut off for ever
from everything you had known . . . " (34).

We can conclude, then, that while a corroborative listener is unnecessary, at times even destructive, to dialogue, the rhetorical presence of
a potential interlocutor is essential. To establish his "existence" apart,
Marlow too requires a witness to "listen to him": someone *to whom*
he can "surrender personally all that remained" of Kurtz's "shade"
(74; cf. 69, 78). He says, "All that had been Kurtz's had passed out of
my hands: his soul, his body, his station, his plans, his ivory, his
career. There remained only his memory and his Intended — and I
wanted to give that up, too, to the past, in a way — to surrender
personally all that remained of him with me to that oblivion which is
the last word of our common fate" (74). Although Marlow eventually
distorts this "last word" for an essentially naive auditor (the Intended), he nevertheless accomplishes a "surrender" of "memory," a
movement toward outness. Like Coleridge's own need for exposure,
he "wanted to give that up," to "bring it before an awaking conscience." Later, Marlow's other listeners (on the Thames) allow for a

deepening of this exposure, this "surrender" to the other. We must bear in mind, however, that in each case such audiences remain nameless. Like the sympathetic Russian, both the Intended and the silent passengers on the *Nellie* have intentionally been left anonymous. We know them only as allegorized figures who encompass everyone: the Lawyer, the Accountant, the Director. Such generalized roles ultimately come to embody each of us, for the rhetoric of these works requires us, too, to partake of dialogue.

In thus engaging us within the dialogic process, moreover, Conrad ensures that we, like his textual auditors, will represent the kind of exposure, surrender, and implicit response that enables hermeneutic inquiry. As Fogel has suggested in discussing *The Secret Agent*, such inquiry is necessarily tenuous, since Conradian dialogue "does not either completely take or completely reject the advice not to inquire" (152). According to this approach, Conrad's hermeneutic enterprise is seen as a process of "coercive and violent inquiry" deriving from Conrad's "ritual dramatic inheritance" — that is, from his relation to those Sophoclean exchanges in which Oedipus literally forces those around him to speak, with catastrophic results (148, 221). In the context of the present study, however, we have stressed not the dramatic but the rhetorical genealogy of dialogue: its philosophical antecedents in the form of Socratic (rather than Oedipal or even Platonic) dialogue. Such a perspective has led us to analyze rifted dialogue less as a drama of coercion than as an action of agonism — of the rhetorical counterpoise that measures dialogue as a hermeneutic endeavor. In this context, moreover, such interpretive inquiry defines dialogue as neither "self-destruction" nor a cause of "tragedy" but as a forward dynamic, a rhetorical attempt to fathom the "voice speaking from . . . an eternal darkness" (77).[12] In the same way, the interpretive act of overhearing is neither "passive" nor disengaged (171) but, in Bakhtin's terms, "actively responsive" — inasmuch as "any understanding is imbued with response and necessarily elicits it in one form or another" ("Speech" 68).

   It is this paradoxically responsive act of "overhearing," then, that finally enables the hermeneutic impetus behind dialogue. Whether this interpretive process operates as an externalized analysis of the self, of a given character's buried past, or of some other textual "darkness," it defines the heuristic potential within dialogue. We must recognize, moreover, that even when naive, ratiocinative interpretation fails in *Heart of Darkness*, the act of dialogue does not. As the novella concludes, Marlow's exposure before the Intended allows for a last kind of dialogic process, involving not burial but recovery—an interpretive, mnemonic recuperation. Long after he has lost Kurtz's "voice," Marlow momentarily recovers it in the "echo of his magnificent eloquence"—in the evocative voice of the Intended (72). As we have noted, he feels that "the sound of her low voice seemed to have the accompaniment of all the other sounds, full of mystery, desolation, and sorrow, I had ever heard—the ripple of the river, the soughing of the trees swayed by the wind, the murmurs of the crowds, the faint ring of incomprehensible words cried from afar, the whisper of a voice speaking from beyond the threshold of an eternal darkness" (77). In speaking with the Intended, then, Marlow briefly conjures that posthumous "voice speaking from beyond the threshold." His contact with this voice establishes dialogue not only with Kurtz's memory but also with his own synoptic experience of human "darkness," with that "accompaniment of all the other sounds, full of mystery, desolation, and sorrow, I had ever heard." Although such contact is subject to duplicity—susceptible to Kurtz's specious "eloquence"—it nevertheless functions as a kind of interpolated dialogue, as a mnemonic exchange with lost voices. Like Wordsworth's projective address to his sister, or Catherine's inclusive cry to Heathcliff, such dialogues serve to disinter the buried voices of a vocative past.

This linguistic disinterment, or vocative recovery, thus serves to underscore the historical dimension of dialogue, its ability to engage the vocal past. As we have noted, such a recovery occurs when a character manages to invoke the past across a "chain" of interconnected utterances—across the continuous, transtemporal chain that constitutes dialogue. In *Heart of Darkness*, this linguistic chain is represented as a diachronic linkage of memories, names, and voices— a historical chain that effectively enables Marlow to connect characters across time, to link up a present figure like the Intended with both the vanished native woman and the deceased Kurtz. Hence in speaking to the Intended about her dead fiancé, Marlow says, "I saw her and him in the same instant of time—his death and her sorrow—I saw her sorrow in the very moment of his death. Do you understand? I saw them together—I heard them together" (76). What Marlow "hears," in fact, is the echo of dialogue across time. Such an echo again accounts for how, even after Kurtz's voice goes silent, Marlow is able to conjure it in death and "even beyond, when," as he puts it, a "long time after I heard once more, not his own voice, but the echo of his magnificent eloquence . . . " (72).

What is most startling about Conrad's language here is that he is representing not merely the associative power of memory, but the actual dialogization of human history—the chain of human utterance. As the novella proceeds, this dialogic chain ultimately links Marlow not only with Kurtz but also with the entire chronology of human events, with that "gigantic tale" (4) that is the narrative of human history. From this perspective, dialogism allows Marlow to speak with the "prehistoric man," with the "night of first ages" (36; cf. 5, 41, 50). Kurtz's abominable "pamphlet" and vocalized "horror" become a linguistic extension—in effect a ventriloquization— of the entire evolution of human darkness. In the same manner, Kurtz's death becomes one in a chain of deaths that go to make up our collective historical memory. As Marlow puts it, "I thought his memory was like the other memories of the dead that accumulate in every man's life—a vague impress on the brain of shadows that had fallen on it in their swift and final passage . . . " (74).

Throughout the novella, moreover, these accumulating "memories of the dead" are further represented in the form of names—"the last word of our common fate" (74). They are invoked, accreted, and passed on in much the same way that mariners drift through time on the ocean current: "The tidal current runs to and fro in its unceasing service, crowded with memories of men and ships it has borne. . . . It had borne all the ships whose names are like jewels flashing in the night of time . . . " (4). For Conrad, only this linguistic "current," this metonymic dialogue, can represent the chain of memories, voices, and names that is history. And only such a linkage can enable us to fathom, to "imagine what particular region of the first ages a man's untrammelled feet may take him into . . . " (50).

VIII

We can say, then, that the audition that frames Marlow's narrative constitutes an aural record of his gesture toward "another existence." Much as Coleridge attempts to "record" his sense of "some hidden vice," Marlow's listeners allow for a continuance of Kurtz's "memory" within that lethean "oblivion which is the last word of our common fate" (74). In attempting to extend dialogue into the future, Marlow seeks a proleptic "utterance" that, in Bakhtin's terms, "is related not only to preceding, but also to subsequent links in the chain of speech communion" ("Speech" 94). In designating these future listeners, he looks to the vocative resonance that "presses on" toward the "last word" ("Text" 127). Hence much as Wordsworth strives to project his dialogue with Dorothy into the rhetorical future, so Marlow endeavors to extend his own recurring "yarns." And much as Walton believes his sympathies "want keeping" by an other, so Marlow uses his audience as a fixed frame of reference for his often digressive memorializing.

As we have noted in the foregoing chapters, moreover, such memorial dialogues can be epistolary as well as auscultatory. Thus, the packet of Kurtz's letters that Marlow delivers up to the Intended can be viewed not only as an artifact of Kurtz's "memory" but as a record of Marlow's discourse — an *extension* of dialogue. Such a record also recalls how the monster produces the De Lacys' letters as testaments to his own narrative "truth." In both cases, written address takes on the same function as witnessed narrative; as Marlow says of Kurtz, "His words will remain" (78; cf. 51).

This endurance of the inscribed address also figures in the many journals and articles alluded to within the novella. When various curiosity-seekers attempt to reconstruct Kurtz's memory, Marlow hands them the "famous Report" concerning "Savage Customs" (74; cf. 50, 73). Later, in referring to Kurtz, Marlow goes on to say, "He had been writing for the papers and meant to do so again, 'for the furthering of my ideas. It's a duty'" (70). Here again, directed writing is regarded as a dialogic address in this novella — as a heard record of "memory," a continual "furthering of . . . ideas" to another. And once again, this written address compares directly with its counterparts within *Frankenstein* and *Wuthering Heights*. In the former novel, Victor insists on editing the written record of his spoken narrative as a specific address to posterity (207) — much as Walton edits it specifically for Margaret and his "future" self (25). In *Wuthering Heights*, Lockwood's journal not only resembles an address in itself but also includes several letters that appear to offer proof of its veracity to some unspecified recipient. The written address thus comes to project a rhetorical audience as immediate as that for spoken narration; each form tends toward a prolepsis of dialogue. Here again, in Bakhtin's terms, the word "does not stop at *immediate* understanding but presses on further and further (indefinitely)."

By the end of *Heart of Darkness*, then, the printed word has appropriated the fluid immediacy of exchange that often characterizes spoken dialogue. We learn that Kurtz has "scrawled" a "kind of note" at the end of his written report, as if he needed to address readers beyond the confines of print — as if they were actual listeners. Indeed, in this context his annotations resemble the Russian's marginal notes to the book on seamanship (39). However privatistic such commentaries become, they nevertheless represent the printed word as a form of externalized dialogue. Much as Lockwood can respond to Catherine's entries along the family Bible's margins, so Marlow's experiences suggest that the printed word can both speak to a dialogic audience and become a witnessed record. In this sense, the books depicted in *Heart of Darkness* must be listened to as much as they are read.

7

Conclusion: Dialogue, Culture, and the Heuristic ''Third''

> A picture held us captive, and we could not get outside it, for it lay in our language and language seemed to repeat it to us inexorably.
>
> Ludwig Wittgenstein, *Philosophical Investigations*

Nearly a decade ago, Paul de Man defined what he called the "Rhetoric of Romanticism" in terms of a "rhetorical analysis of figural language *avant la lettre*" (viii). What the present study suggests is that such rhetorical analysis must account for a rhetoric of dialogue, evolving from the first-generation poets through such narratives as *Frankenstein, Wuthering Heights*, and *Heart of Darkness*. Having mapped such a course, however, we must also recognize that these dialogues diverge greatly from the type. If, in *Frankenstein*, the breakdown of dialogue stems from social myopia and corporeal angst, such misfires in *Wuthering Heights* more often derive from monetarial and class-bound distinctions. Similarly, while various dialogues founder almost immediately (including those between Victor and the monster, or Marlow and the Thames listeners), others proceed unequivocally until some irremediable rift opens between interlocutors (as between Victor and Walton, or Lockwood and Nelly). Finally, such distinctions also emerge along lines of literary history; toward the end of the century, for instance, we have noted how characters who remain largely absent—including both Heathcliff and Kurtz—pose increasingly difficult problems for those who would dialogically interpret them. As the available utterances of such characters become progressively more sparse and cryptic, the dialogues concerning them are correspondingly muted and flawed. Yet despite such distinctions, the point of this book has been to show that the modes and operations of these works constitute a dialogic rhetoric — that the qualities of dialogic discourse inform not only their structures but also their fundamental positions concerning knowledge, interpretation, and the heuristic method itself.

This last subject — the status of dialogue as an inquiry into otherness — stands behind each reading put forth in the foregoing chapters. Indeed, throughout this study, we have stressed the hermeneutic impetus behind dialogue as an interpretive rhetoric that Bakhtin elsewhere compares to his "investigatory" method ("Response" 1, 7). In the literary works we have discussed, auditors deploy such a method to investigate both themselves and some central, noumenal character such as Heathcliff, Kurtz, the Ancient Mariner, or the monster. We have further suggested that this interpretive capacity results in part from the externalized vantage that dialogue provides — from the rhetorical displacement that effectively enables characters to stand outside themselves, to see themselves from the "third" perspective. We are now in a position, however, to discuss this externalized vantage in terms of that investigative stance often sought by cultural anthropologists — an anthropological distance that strives for a kind of cultural otherness.[1] By thus comparing both literary and cultural investigations, we will be able to reframe our foregoing conclusions about interpretive dialogue within the larger context of literary hermeneutics and cultural studies. At the same time, such an approach will enable us to speculate about the implications of literary dialogue for the fields of philosophical methodology and cultural anthropology.

It is not surprising that the anthropological distance noted here would recall the kind of literary rhetoric we have termed outness — the Coleridgean concept that, throughout this study, denotes both an externalized hermeneutic and the exposure of self. At this point, however, the analogy between these two "investigatory" rhetorics comes into focus when we consider the parallel concept of what Bakhtin refers to as "outsideness," in a late essay concerning the relations between literature and culture. Such "outsideness" not only is central to Bakhtin's general concept of cultural inquiry but is also directly applicable, as Michael Holquist has pointed out, to the particular anthropological dilemma of how to compare diverse cultures from a single perspective. "Bakhtin's insistence on the necessary role of outsideness [вненаходимость] in any creative act of understanding," writes Holquist, has a new and crucial "contribution to make to the thorny problem of cultural relativism."[2]

In the context of the present study, moreover, these parallel concepts of critical "outsideness" and cultural inquiry also bear directly on the literary auditor's position within a dialogic text. For it is this heuristic "outsideness," this investigatory distance, that is represented by the externalized listener in dialogue with an "internal" character. Although the focus of this book has been on neither cultural diversity nor that anthropological perspective necessary for understanding culture, we have repeatedly characterized the literary auditor as a representation of this interpretive "outsideness"—of that "otherness" requisite to investigating difference. The auditor's externalized position, often within the outermost layers of several concentric narrative frames, tends to locate him or her in another time, another place— and another worldview. As a result, this external figure is in a unique position to investigate the notorious enigmas of such centrally embedded characters as Heathcliff, Kurtz, and the monster. As Bakhtin puts it,

> In order to understand, it is immensely important for the person who understands to be *located outside* the object of his or her creative understanding—in time, in space, in culture. For one cannot even really see one's own exterior and comprehend it as a whole, and no mirrors or photographs can help; our real exterior can be seen and understood only by other people, because they are located outside us in space and because they are *others*. ("Response" 7)

In literary terms, too, it is the auditor's dialogic position that enables one to confront the "object of his or her creative understanding." As one "located outside" this focus—"in time, in space, in culture"—the external interlocutor is able not only to stand outside a textual enigma but to launch an investigatory dialogue into it. Whether or not such an endeavor actually leads to understanding, it necessarily instantiates dialogue, the rhetorical encounter that, as we have seen, can confront both textual and cultural meaning. Any such "meaning," writes Bakhtin, "only reveals its depths once it has encountered and come into contact with another, foreign meaning: they engage in a kind of dialogue, which surmounts the closedness and one-sidedness of these particular meanings, these cultures" (7).

This desire for an externalized encounter with the "foreign"—for something *outside* "particular meanings" and "cultures"—leaves its rhetorical mark on each of the literary investigations addressed in this study. As we have noted, Coleridge specifically calls for his own version of outness, for that ability to confront a "secret lodger" from outside—to "eloign and abalienate it," as he says, "from the dark Adyt of my own Being." We can now add, however, that this desire to delineate the self's external "Boundary," to seek that "Definition . . . knowable only by Neighbourhood, or Relations," parallels Bakhtin's own belief in an external vantage on cultural knowledge. For the latter, too, writes that the "most intense and productive life of culture takes place on the boundaries of its individual areas" ("Response" 2). Such "boundaries" accordingly define the rhetorical vantage point for both kinds of inquiry, whether into personal "Being" or the "life of culture." In both cases—whether we would investigate an identifiable "area" of culture, or what might be called the unexplored culture of personal "Definition"—our approach must embrace this "outsideness," this view from the "boundaries."

Hence in a novel like *Frankenstein*, we have seen that both Victor and Walton look to the "boundary" of a "friend," to an outsideness that represents an (ultimately broken) attempt at anthropologically understanding the other. Such a boundary might, they feel, "repair the faults" of one's cultural awareness—the knowledge that acts to separate every character from the "foreign" monster. In a parallel manner, Catherine Earnshaw also seeks an "existence . . . beyond" the "contained" self, an exterior vantage that would both contextualize her knowledge of the foreign Heathcliff and thereby delineate her own being. "What were the use of my creation," she asks, "if I were entirely contained here?" Finally, we recall that for Marlow, too, the "meaning of an episode was not inside like a kernel but outside, enveloping the tale." This epistemologically "outside" view of narrative "meaning" is reflected in Marlow's own cross-cultural characterization: for all his British pedigree, he is repeatedly linked to the cultural metonymy of the East. (He narrates, for instance, in the "pose of a Buddha"—"cross-legged," "ascetic," like an "idol.") These associations gradually establish their own kind of anthropological outness, a vantage from which Marlow attempts to illuminate both Kurtz's darkness and the cultural crimes it represents.

What such perspectives have in common, then, is their heuristic separation from a centrally representative character, ethic, or culture. Such separation manifests itself not only linguistically but temporally as well. Wordsworth, for instance, strives for externalization not only by including his sister's vantage point but by rhetorically representing their eventual separation in death—the final outness that results when, as he puts it, "I no more can hear / Thy voice." More surprisingly, we have seen him stress this outness by initiating an actual dialogue with his former selves. Such temporal dislocation also distinguishes the narratives of Walton, Lockwood, and Marlow, each of whom casts his story as a vastly removed "history." Yet what is most remarkable about such histories is not the fact of this broad temporal displacement but the deployment of such separation as a mode of epistemological and, ultimately, cultural investigation. As Bakhtin puts it, "We usually strive to explain a writer and his work precisely through his own time and the most recent past. We are afraid," he goes on, "*to remove ourselves in time from the phenomenon under investigation*" ("Response" 3–4, emphasis added). Such a removal in time, or "temporal distance," is necessary to sustain the outness of cultural scrutiny (cf. 6).

Hence the works we have discussed often emphasize extended periods of time between the recorded past and the narrative present, with investigation proceeding over many decades. Marlow, for instance, begins by likening his subjects of investigation to Roman "conquerors" and "prehistoric" cultures. Lockwood's rhetoric, too, highlights the duration of his narrative, as he follows his protagonists both into the next generation and ultimately beyond the grave. And as we have noted, both Wordsworth and Walton underscore the temporal disjunction between their sisters and themselves; the latter, for instance, suggests that the uncertain path of his letters to Margaret results in a kind of infinitely suspended dialogue. Finally, in all of these cases, our own investigatory separation from the period of each narrative is represented by the emergence of dated journals, archaic inscriptions, and purposively antiquated language.

Thus temporality, too, can entail the kind of literary and cultural otherness requisite to dialogic exchange. Working within a cultural framework, Bakhtin suggests that "such a dialogic encounter of two cultures does not result in merging or mixing. Each retains its own unity and *open* totality, but they are mutually enriched" ("Response" 7). Only such unmixed distinction and discreteness can enable the "investigatory boldness" of an outside viewpoint. Hence if external interlocutors attempt to "merge" or "mix" with a given subject of investigation, they necessarily abjure their outside vantage, their capacity to interpret actively, in favor of a misplaced empathy. In an early essay entitled "The Philosophy of the Act," Bakhtin specifically questions the heuristic results of such empathy. As Gary Saul Morson and Caryl Emerson have noted in discussing this essay, the empathetic stance remains, for Bakhtin, interpretively "unproductive." They write, "In empathy, one tries to merge totally with the suffering other and to experience the world entirely from the other's place. But even if such 'pure in-dwelling' were possible, it would in any case be unproductive, because total identification precludes the capacity to contribute something new: 'in someone else's place I am as without meaning as I am in my own place' ('Act,' 95)" (*Rethinking* 11).

Morson and Emerson go on to distinguish this empathetic stance, or "pure in-dwelling," from what Bakhtin in the same essay terms *vzhivanie*: a "live entering" or "living into." "In *vzhivanie*," they suggest, "one enters another's place *while still maintaining one's own place*, one's own 'outsideness,' with respect to the other. 'I actively live into [*vzhivanie*] an individuality, and consequently do not, for a single moment, lose myself completely or lose my singular place outside that other individuality' ('Act,' 93). From such a relation, something new and helpful can emerge"(11). It is the desire to represent this interpretive "singularity," this hermeneutic "outsideness," that leads the writers discussed in this study to incorporate specifically discrete auditors, distinct characters, into their works. Such exterior auditors remain separate from — and even averse to — a text's internal mysteries in order to construct an external interpretation that is at once "new," distanced, and creative. In confronting an enigmatic Kurtz, Heathcliff, or monster, then, these auditors must eschew the kind of utter identification that subverts heuristic autonomy. Only by sustaining such autonomy — by "maintaining one's own place, one's own 'outsideness,' with respect to the other" — can a listener or reader "enter into" these others, engage them in dialogue, and interpret anew. Indeed, it is this emphasis on discrete, irreducible voices that characterizes the following development in Bakhtin's thought. Morson and Emerson write:

> Later in his life, after language had become central to his thought, Bakhtin was to rethink this concept in dialogic terms as "creative understanding." Dialogic response, he came to write, depends on the irreducibility of both participants. In creative understanding, the reader or listener does not seek to merge with the author of the text. Respecting the author's "outsideness" and "otherness," the reader "lives into" the text and lives alongside the text. "Passive understanding," which is similar to empathy, simply reproduces what is already there; creative understanding, like "live entering," produces something new and enriching. (*Rethinking* 11)

Once again, this need to "live *alongside* the text" — to respect its requisite "'outsideness' and 'otherness'" while still "entering into" it — accounts for the necessarily marginalized positions of such interpreters as Lockwood, Walton, and the Wedding-Guest. For in remaining unable to merge (or even identify) with such alien protagonists as Heathcliff and Catherine, these externalized auditors come to instantiate the kind of cultural distance necessary for "creative understanding," for producing "something new and enriching." In maintaining the "irreducibility of both participants," both external and internal, then, these works effectively engender dialogue. It is not that we are asked to adopt the flawed perspective of a resistant Lockwood, or even of an entranced Marlow; rather, we are asked to partake of their difference, to participate in their outness. It is this cultural outness, moreover, this need both to resist conflation and sustain difference, that accounts for the rhetorically agonistic auditors we have stressed. Here, too, it is agonism itself, the very resistance to conflation, that affirms the otherness of dialogue. Only such a resistance to knowledge can, paradoxically, enable interpretation.

Notes

Chapter 1

1. Rajan (195–96) tests this concept of the "seemingly autonomous lyric voice" against several "intersubjective" narratives of the Romantic era. She comes to question the "illusory unity of a single voice" by comparing it with poems that "turn monologic effusion into dialogue," that "expose lyrical meditation to the dissent of another voice" (200–201, 206). Jacobus (173–77), too, expresses reservations about this alleged monologism: in discussing *The Prelude*, she contends that "Wordsworth has to eschew the very fiction of individual voice which is central to Romantic conceptions of the poet" (176). For her, "Calling the self into being through apostrophe becomes rather a matter of calling another into being; perhaps an 'authorial' voice, but equally, the variety of haunting, threatening, nightmarish, or apocalyptic voices heard throughout *The Prelude*. . . . The voice is always a doubling of self, and more often a multiplication . . . " (175). Hence "far from attesting to unity of origin or a stable identity, voice comes to imply all the destabilizing multiplicity of plural (or ancestral) voices . . . " (175). For Jacobus, then, this "trans-subjective" multiplicity essentially "collapses the entire Romantic fallacy of spontaneous lyric utterance . . . " (176–77).

For comparable reinterpretations of the notion of lyric autonomy, see Lentricchia (109), Kneale (354), and Miller (*Linguistic* 98).

2. Culler (149–54) holds that apostrophe elides both temporality and death by indicating a present, rhetorical act: "it produces a fictive, discursive event" by "replacing a temporal presence and absence with an apostrophic presence and absence" (153, 154). The poet can thus "find, in his poetic ability to invoke [an object] as a transcendent presence, a sense of his own transcendent continuity" (152). The reader, too, partakes of this transcendence, since apostrophe enables him to "blind himself to [the poet's] death by an imaginative act" (154). Miller (*Linguistic* 104–13), too, discusses this linguistic stay against death (although he focuses more on the written word than on spoken apostrophe per se): "Wordsworth's poetry," he writes, "is an epitaph for the work of all the dead poets" (110). On one hand, these poets "have survived by entering proleptically into the space beyond death that is literature"; on the other hand, when the "poet creates his own tombstone

in writing his verse," he "has already departed" (110, 109, 112). Ferguson (*Wordsworth* 155–72), too, discusses how the poet's epitaphic "tombstone" attempts to "stress the links between the community of the living and the community of the dead." For Wordsworth, she writes, the "epitaph 'introduces' the stranger to the implied living consciousness of the speaker, and that living consciousness 'introduces' the stranger to the deceased friend" (158, 159–60; cf. 28–34, 239–50). Kneale (353–54) appears to share this notion of the poet's timeless "tombstone," though he locates his own sense of the "epitaphic voice" in Nature, which "itself is like one giant epitaph, one complex memorial text to be conned by human beings" (354). Regarding Wordsworth, he suggests that the "text acknowledges the passing from living voice to dead letter but seeks to outlive this death through the epitaphic permanence of writing that aspires to the phonocentric immediacy of speech" (355). For Jacobus, such an immediacy of the voice remains tenuous; it does, however, imply "pure presence," whereas "writing, the permanent record of thought, involves both the muting of voice—a kind of deafness—and the death of presence" (178; cf. 170).

  3. Kneale (352–55) views the "*vox naturae*, or voice of nature" as a "combination of apostrophe and imperative,'" "apostrophizing the viewer-listener through an admonishing rhetoric." For him, Nature's rivers and echoes not only bespeak "one giant epitaph" but tend to "first blend with and then usurp the human voice" (354, 353). Jacobus, too, cites "loss of individual identity" as the cost of that "Wordsworthian desire to appropriate the speaking voice of Nature" (171, 170). The "poet's voice" is essentially "subsumed into transcendental Nature" (176). For her, however, this conflation is also an "attempt to render his own [voice] imperishable"—part of the "tension between poetic self-assertion and self-immersion" that characterizes the appropriation of Nature's voice (170; cf. 173, 175–76).

  Culler turns to Percy B. Shelley in maintaining that the "things of earth function as thous when addressed": when such poems "address natural objects, they formally will that these particular objects function as subjects" (145, 140). Such subjectification, moreover, redounds upon the apostrophizing poet, since "one who successfully invokes nature is one to whom nature might, in its turn, speak" (142).

  For a discussion of Nature's language as the apostrophized voice of the divine, see Miller (*Linguistic* 83–86).

  4. Jacobus (172–73, 175, 178, 181) demonstrates how apostrophe can engender "self-presence and voice," the "bringing into being of the poet's voice" (172). It is thus "self-constituting" (172), in much the same way that Culler (142–43, 146) also describes. He, too, suggests that "apostrophes work . . . to dramatize or constitute an image of self," in that "the poet makes himself a poetic presence through an image of voice" (142). For him, apostrophe "evokes poetic presence . . . only in the moment when poetic voice constitutes itself" in relation to a "thou" (142–43). Indeed, both studies stress this apostrophic creation of a vocal "presence" (Culler 142, 152–54; Jacobus

177–78) that transcends death (see note 2). (As I go on to suggest, such poetic presence must also be distinguished from its phenomenal counterpart.)

Rajan (195–96, 207) argues for an "understanding of the self as constituted by and not deconstructed by its differences from itself." She suggests that by incorporating "another voice," poetry can "present the self in interaction with other characters and events." Such incorporation takes lyric beyond the purely monologic by including the "other through which we become aware of the difference of the self from itself."

5. Michael Ragussis offers an insightful interpretation of Keats's use of silence in this poem; see *The Subterfuge of Art* (Baltimore: Johns Hopkins University Press, 1978), 35–69.

6. *Wordsworth* 31. Magnuson further suggests that this textual relationship between speakers and listeners can represent the actual dialogues and textual influences between two distinct poets — so that poetic interchange effectively comes to "duplicate their dialogue within individual poems" (31).

7. Still later, Abrams writes that this lyric form "represents a solitary speaker confronting a particularized landscape, moves through a sustained meditation which is stimulated by the altering visual details, then rounds back to a close which echoes the opening description, but with a difference effected by all that has intervened" (*Supernaturalism* 453). This "rounding back" or framing effect essentially enacts the Romantic subject's encounter with the world, followed by a peremptory return to the self. (For further discussion of this form, see also 92, 271–77, 392.)

8. These citations are taken respectively from Miyoshi xi (cf. x, xii, xiii, 264, 268, 272), 230, and xiv (cf. 29). For his commentary on *Frankenstein*, see 81 and 83.

9. Unlike Miyoshi, Martin traces these multiple voices to midcentury, and thereby minimizes their centrality within a Romantic poetics. He also tends to overstate the "oneness" or "boundaried" nature of the Romantic self, as opposed to the allegedly more fractured or "divided" nature of the Victorian speaker (28, 23). But though I have focused on Martin's fine study in this section, one finds parallel characterizations in a variety of approaches to the nineteenth-century subject. Unlike many such commentators, moreover, Martin at times acknowledges that "Romantic poets confront the conflict between the notion of a divided subject and the desire for unity as directly as Victorian poets do, but their poetic responses are different" (23). Still, such approaches again tend to trace what they see as the "divided self" to either the dramatic monologue or the early nineteenth-century novel. And we have further noted that the term *divided self* is itself problematic, since it fails to acknowledge that the ego may be not divided but defined by the discrete voices of others. In this sense, there never was any "whole" self *to become* divided. (For discussions of *thematic* division within the Romantic lyric, see the illuminating analyses of ironic disjunction and divisive uncertainty by both Wolfson and Mellor.)

We should also bear in mind that Martin's characterization of the dramatic monologue's auditor applies just as readily to an analysis of Romantic dialogue. Hence the Romantic "I' is as cognizant of a "listener's ability to respond" as is his late-century counterpart, suggesting that the Romantic self is likewise "constituted as part of a larger system of relationships and interactions" (132, 133; cf. 29, 31). Similarly, the poetic tropes that support this matrix of interactive relations (including apostrophe and questions) have recently been shown to be central to a rhetoric of Romanticism (see Wolfson, Culler). Finally, we may also question the conclusion that this interactive rhetoric indicates "expected or desired reciprocity" and "exchange" (135, 28). As we shall see in the following chapters, Romantic works more often manifest a desire for agonistic dialogue, with its related capacity to motivate ongoing discourse, to establish hermeneutic rhetoric, and to delineate a speaker's being.

10. The previous two quotations are from Mermin (4, 6), who goes on to trace the tension between the expressive and pragmatic in Victorian poetry—the "real contradiction in the simultaneous demands for unselfconscious sincerity and deliberate communication" (6). Such a "contradiction" also compares with the kind of speaker-auditor relation that I term "agonistic," in which listeners take on the "power to resist" or remain silent (Mermin 9; cf. 2, 7, 11, 14, 155). Indeed, many aspects of Mermin's model apply to what I define as a Romantic dialogics of the auditor, including the primacy of speech and response (2, 6, 14), the auditor's determinative influence on a speaker's discourse (1, 2), and the disavowal of the auditor as a "reader of words on paper" (2).

Still, Mermin occasionally stresses the pragmatic aspect of Abrams's dichotomy—the sense that a poem's auditors gauge "its effect on an audience," on "prospective readers," so that "poems with auditors are about communication" (8). We must bear in mind that although the Romantics, too, cared deeply about communicating with readers, their auditors tend to enact a particular dynamics of conversational discourse rather than the monolithic reactions of a general audience or readership. As we shall see in defining Romantic dialogue, the deployment of auditors is often less affective than rhetorical, in that auditors measure not reader response so much as dialogue's capacity to conjure past selves and instantiate present ones. According to this view, auditors may represent a series of prior or proleptic interlocutors, so that dialogue becomes neither real-time "communication" nor designated "performance" nor even attempted persuasion (8, 11, 7)—but rather a literary *techné*, one that seeks both to elide temporality and effect interpretation.

11. Mellor (6). Mellor further suggests that Romantic irony "posits a universe founded in chaos and incomprehensibility rather than in a divinely ordained teleology."

12. Friedrich Schlegel, *Critical Fragments* from *The Athenaeum* (1798–1800), in *Lucinde and the Fragments*, no. 116. Mellor discusses this passage as Schlegel's call for a "balancing between self-assertion and self-reflection" (16).

13. The final two citations here are respectively from Friedrich Schlegel, *Dialogue on Poetry and Literary Aphorisms*, trans. Ernst Behler and Roman Struc (University Park: Pennsylvania State University Press, 1968), 53; and his *Philosophische Lehrjahre*, 18:283, #1048. Mellor quotes both passages to demonstrate how, for Schlegel, "any theoretical formulation of reality can never be infinite or complete, but only 'an approximation' that must ultimately be transcended by being negated and rejected" (8).

14. Mellor notes Schlegel's use of the dialogue to represent various genres, viewpoints, and aspects of his mental life (22). As I go on to show, moreover, we must also bear in mind that Schlegel's approach to the form diverges from the more diachronic and agonistic views of dialogue later formulated by Bakhtin.

15. "Speech" 73. The following analysis is based upon Bakhtin's late theory, which develops and reinterprets some of the first formulations of dialogue. For a discussion of the relation between these various formulations, see Michael Holquist's introductory essay to *Speech Genres and Other Late Essays*.

16. While this dialogic conception of auditors and audience informs all literary texts, we should again bear in mind that it resonates particularly with such Romantic concepts as philosophical irony and interrogative presence. As we have noted, narration continually presses toward further response, further interpretation, and further questions; it thereby persists in a perpetual state of unresolved query, of imperfect comprehension. It is this perpetual search beyond "immediate understanding," this reaching for even contradictory responses, that delineates the irreconcilable poles of Romantic irony. And it is this everlasting query beyond the present response that sustains the Romantic experimentation with interrogative modes.

17. The first studies to distinguish between levels of response within a taxonomy of audience types include Walter J. Ong, S.J., "The Writer's Audience Is Always a Fiction," *PMLA* 90 (January 1975): 9–21; and Gerald Prince, "Introduction à l'étude du narrataire," *Poetique* 14 (1973): 178–96, which develops the ideas first proposed in his "Notes toward a Categorization of Fictional 'Narratees,'" *Genre* 4 (1971): 100–106. Ralph W. Rader contributes to this taxonomy in referring to what he terms a "dramatic auditor"; see his "The Dramatic Monologue and Related Lyric Forms," *Critical Inquiry* 3 (1976): 131–51. In "Authors, Speakers, Readers, and Mock Readers," *College English* 11 (February 1950): 265–69, Walker Gibson introduces his own concept of a "mock reader," but his formulation never locates this reader as a character within the text. Nor do the related concepts of an "implied reader," proposed by Wolfgang Iser and Wayne C. Booth, include the possibility of intratextual response. More recently, however, Peter J. Rabinowitz's "Truth in Fiction: A Reexamination of Audiences" (*Critical Inquiry* 4:1 [1977]: 121–41) defines four levels of audience response: first, the "actual," "flesh-and-blood" audience; second, the "authorial audience," readers envisioned by a given author who makes "certain assumptions about his readers' beliefs,

knowledge, and familiarity with conventions," and then "designs his work rhetorically for [this] specific hypothetical audience"; third, the "narrative audience," an "imitation" or "imaginary" audience envisioned by a narrator who expects us temporarily to "take on certain minimal beliefs in addition to those we already hold"; and finally, the "ideal narrative audience," the "audience for which the narrator wishes he were writing," who "believes the narrator, accepts his judgments, sympathizes with his plight, laughs at his jokes even when they are bad." Although Rabinowitz never discusses these audiences in terms of fictional characters or various other intratextual voices, his distinctions help to identify those responses that cannot be ascribed to a given reader. In particular, his formulation can be used to describe that dialogic interlocutor who, while operating within the framework or belief system of the "narrative" or "imaginary" audience, is nevertheless defined as the antithesis of a narrator's ideal.

Such approaches begin to indicate the variety of divergent voices that constitute a text, and to suggest that an inscribed auditor often functions in ways other than a reader. Although auditors at times offer an image of reading, they are not necessarily readers themselves, nor even models of reading. And although these listeners can become representations of affective response, they often imply a broader spectrum of dialogic processes. They suggest, in fact, that Romantic discourse employs a *range* of exchanges — including ones besides the reader-speaker relation — and that such a range enacts the various dialogic effects I go on to discuss (such as the rhetorical demonstration of Romantic agonism, skepticism, temporality, ontology, and hermeneutics).

The following chapters further suggest that the use of an incorporated other is less an indication of response than a figure for the dialogic nature of the text — for the entire social context of the utterance. In this sense, we must concur with Frank Lentricchia's critique of the reader-response school, which, as he says, stresses a *"literary* community walled off from the larger enclosures of social structure" (147) — and thereby ignores what Bakhtin views as the broader, social sphere affecting the utterance.

18. Bloom discusses this concept of synoptic influence in both *Anxiety of Influence* and *Agon*; my references here are to the latter.

19. Although the gender differentiations within this cultural perspective are beyond the scope of this study, we should note that this predisposition for dispute varies along sexual lines; for more on this differentiation, see Ong, *Fighting*, especially chapters 2 and 3.

It is also worth noting that Bakhtin distinguishes among a variety of dialogic genres, not all of which operate agonistically (see, for instance, "Speech" 97). What is most significant in the present context, however, is that Romantic dialogue not only emerges in this agonistic mode but actually uses it to perpetuate itself as well. Generally, then, what Bakhtin refers to as listeners' "responsive understandings" does not necessarily require their assent ("Speech" 68–69, "Text" 125).

20. As we have suggested earlier, this rhetoric reveals the Romantics in the act of formulating concepts of philosophical quandary and epistemological doubt. Returning to Schlegel, for instance, we recall that he too deploys dialogue form in order to represent oppositional viewpoints. His own critical "dialogue," he writes, "is intended to set against one another quite divergent opinions, each of them capable of shedding new light upon the infinite spirit of poetry from an individual standpoint, each of them striving to penetrate from a different angle into the real heart of the matter." What distinguishes these "divergent opinions" is that they must remain agonistic, what he elsewhere refers to as "absolute antitheses" (*Athenaeum* 121). As Mellor has noted, "The two opposed principles stay in constant conflict . . . as two opposed voices or personae, . . . which the author carefully balances and refuses to synthesize or harmonize . . . " (11, 18). Here again, however, the kind of dialogue we are considering often goes beyond Schlegel's notion of an exchange between "ideas" or "themes." As we have noted, the notion of a formal dichotomy between "thesis" and "antithesis" runs counter to the Bakhtinian concept of open-ended, nondeductive dialogue.

21. Given the previous discussion, it is not extraordinary that Maranhão would cite, in the first of these passages, Bakhtin's incisive reading of Socratic form (see especially *Poetics* 87–100). See also Maranhão's useful analysis of this dialectic form (219–36), especially his subsequent discussion of its Platonic versions (235).

22. The Romantic suspicion of the written word is compellingly demonstrated in discussions by Kneale, Miller (*Linguistic*), and Ferguson (*Wordsworth*). Although these commentators also recognize the period's ambivalence toward spoken discourse, they nevertheless emphasize a latent desire to recover the salient features of oral language.

23. See Bialostosky (*Tales* 16). Smith defines what she terms "*mimetic* or *fictive discourse*" not only as the "representation of speech in drama, but also lyrics, epics, tales, and novels" (cf. 24–33, 8–9).

Bialostosky also goes on to describe Wordsworth's poetics as one "which lacks the category of medium," in that the poetic deployment of speech will rarely call attention to itself as a consciously constructed artifact (*Tales* 17; cf. Smith 26). In his illuminating second chapter, he further characterizes this Wordsworthian aesthetic in terms of Bakhtin's essay, "Discourse in Life and Discourse in Art." Bialostosky is particularly concerned with the Bakhtinian notion of the "poem as a scenario of an event involving the mutual interrelations of speaker, hero, and listener" — or, as he later puts it, the idea that "tone always involves gestures in two directions, toward the listener and toward the hero" (Bialostosky 44, 75). He also suggests that these "interrelations" constitute "communities of speakers," in that all three parties are assured of a common referentiality. He writes:

> For Bakhtin as for Wordsworth, the . . . words of a speaker always assume and may be taken to imply a listener (even if only an inner listener) who knows what the speaker is talking about, understands the relation in which he stands to the

speaker, recognizes the speaker's intentions, and shares (potentially at least) the speaker's evaluations. Wordsworth's interest in the language of men in low and rustic life makes sense in these terms as an interest in the language of speakers who can take the satisfaction of these conditions for granted. Speaking in a community where speaker and listener enjoy common objects of experience and regular intercourse with one another, Wordsworth's rustic speakers can safely assume that they will be understood by their fellows without needing to elaborate on what they are talking about or where they stand toward their listeners. . . . (40; see also McKusick 112)

This community of "common" discourse proves to be vital within Wordsworth's dialogic poetics. As I have begun to suggest, however, the Romantics also stress the agonistic potential of dialogue, as well as its hermeneutic and ontological implications.

24. 1–2; cf. 10, 13–14. Rzepka's emphasis on corporeal embodiment is also apparent when he suggests that the "identity of the self could not be separated from one's habitual appearance for others or from the responses to one's presence that one habitually came to expect from others" (21). According to this view, self-definition is a quest for "spatial" delineation, a "struggle to test the reality of the finite self in the eyes of others" (16, 22). Though Rzepka maintains that the self cannot be "reduced to a physical thing," his formulation nonetheless presents the body as an objective correlative for both the ego's consciousness and the other's defining perception (18; cf. 15–16).

In the context of the present discussion, however, we should bear in mind that the self seeks not only corporeal or spatial definition but *linguistic* delimitation as well. As the following chapters suggest, self-delineation is a function of not only physical embodiment but also linguistic differentiation from the other. The "I" acquires such delineation, moreover, during the process of interchange with — and opposition to — this other, in the linguistic encounter between speaker and addressee. In this sense, the mode of human individuation is not so much psychomachy as dialogue.

This view of dialogic differentiation also implies a parallel conception of the antipodal other. Whereas Rzepka concentrates on "others who are either sympathetic or are to be made, somehow, nonthreatening," I stress those Romantic dialogues in which a listener is purposively agonistic — a listener whose questioning, incomprehension, and other oppositional stances create an ontological "boundary" for the self (29; cf. 21).

Chapter 2

1. For a compelling account of Wordsworth's affective concerns and their aesthetic motivation, see Andrew L. Griffin, "Wordsworth and the Problem of Imaginative Story: The Case of 'Simon Lee,'" *PMLA* 92 (1977): 392–409. Wordsworth's own exegesis of this readerly design is expressed most thoroughly in his "Essay Supplementary to the Preface" (*Prose* 1:62–84).

2. In distinguishing Wordsworth's "deeply interior" verse from Byron's poetics, Jerome J. McGann writes,

> Wordsworth's "imagination," Byron says, involves him in his private "reveries," which ultimately prevent an engagement with the audience. Wordsworth himself was acutely aware of the audience-problem which his poetry faced, so that he spoke many times of the need for "creating the taste by which [his verse] is to be enjoyed." . . . [I]t was Wordsworth who harped, in his "Prefaces," on the "degraded" character of current public taste.
>
> Thus, Byron's literary argument in the early cantos [of *Don Juan*] based itself on the Horatian idea that the poet had to foster (not "create") a functional and persuasive relation between himself and his audience. (*Context* 78–79; cf. 68–77)

In order to continue "creating" his reader's taste—and thereby confronting this "audience-problem"—Wordsworth incorporates a representation of affective relations, an encounter expressed as dialogue. Although such exchanges often extend beyond the readerly, it is this broadly dialogic rhetoric that ultimately enacts Wordsworth's didactic concerns.

3. McKusick argues that, unlike Coleridge, Wordsworth sought a language of common referentiality by falling back on the alleged uniformity and simplicity of those immersed in "rustic life" (112).

4. See Engell and Bate, *Biographia Literaria*, especially chapters 17 and 18.

5. Although J. Douglas Kneale acknowledges the centrality of vocal forms in Wordsworth's poetry, he goes on to suggest that Wordsworth balances these forms with images of the written word (351). The first book-length study to stress the vocative dimensions of the "man speaking" is Bialostosky, especially 11–31.

6. As Sheats's subtle analysis shows, Wordsworth structures both this poem and "Expostulation and Reply" as a "debate," in which "'William's' enthusiasm is acknowledged and corrected by the form of the poem," by the "antithetical sentiments of the opposing speaker, Matthew" (208–9). Sheats goes on to note that Wordsworth's "views are embodied in the dramatic conflict between human and natural wisdom . . . " (209). We must also bear in mind, however, that unlike "debate," the concept of dialogue recognizes the poem's overtly interpretive intentions, its status as a exegetical process. As I go on to suggest, such rhetoric enables the poem to confront the dichotomy between active and passive modes of knowledge. Unlike debate, moreover, the process of dialogue presupposes no winning or privileged position; instead, it seeks to suspend and sustain a diversity of voices, including those positions that extend across time from a speaker's rhetorical past.

7. We might note in passing that Bakhtin stresses the listener's "responsive understanding" within the broadest possible context: as a way of distinguishing between entire speech genres, a method of defining "specific types of utterances [as] distinct from other types" ("Speech" 69, 61). Such a context extends far beyond strictly rhetorical or literary approaches to speech genres, studies that limit themselves "to such aspects as the relation to the listener

and his influence on the utterance, the specific verbal finalization of the utterance (as distinct from its completeness of thought), and so forth" (61).

8. Bialostosky goes on to describe William and Matthew's "coming to an understanding," a "common faith" in an unobtrusive mode of knowing (*Tales* 132). We must also consider, though, that the dialogic "balance" of the poem is less a stable agreement than a temporary counterpoise between agonistic voices. The rhetorical alliance of the poem signifies not resolution but juxtaposition, a counter-action of opposing tensions that is the impetus for continued dialogue.

9. The tenacity of this problem is apparent in what Sheats sees as Wordsworth's lifelong struggle to "correct and humanize a relationship to nature that threatens to exalt itself above the human condition" (206–7).

10. Both Susan Wolfson and Anne K. Mellor have suggested that Wordsworth's final address to Dorothy is more problematic and revealing than previous readings have considered. Wolfson, for instance, demonstrates how Wordsworth places his sister in an untenable position by regarding her both as an "unchanging text" *and* as a "thinking thing" who "cannot escape knowledge of change" (67). See also her subtle reading of Dorothy's incarnation of William's "future years" (66–69).

11. See Hartman (4), citing (though not corroborating) the collective judgments of not only Coleridge but also Anna Seward and Jeffrey.

12. Sheats has shown how, throughout this section of the poem, Wordsworth "rearranges the past" in order to construct a "past that he can relinquish without protest" (237, 238). At the same time, "Wordsworth reaches out toward a vision of his own past that is also Dorothy's present" (240). In the context of the present discussion, I would suggest that Wordsworth not only reaches toward this parallel between his past and Dorothy's but actually reconstitutes it as a dialogue with her. By addressing his past selves, Wordsworth effectively lends them a voice; as we see in the following discussion, he reclaims the "language of [his] former heart" in order to reinterpret it.

13. Quoted in Lindenberger 140. This dualistic configuration also derives from those confessional forms that distinguish nineteenth-century autobiography—tropes that depict a younger, past "I" confessing to a narrating adult. For an analysis of Wordsworth's adaptation of such forms, see both McConnell and Lindenberger (preface; 140).

14. Both Lindenberger and Sheats, for example, have demonstrated the pervasiveness of this "double perspective" in *The Prelude*. In discussing the foregoing passage, Lindenberger also suggests that for Rousseau this concept of present consciousness impinges directly on his mnemonic past (143). Sheats, too, alludes to this bifurcation in the stolen-boat episode, where the "point of view shifts delicately between that of the boy, who suffers delusion, and that of the adult speaker, who perceives this delusion naturalistically, as the effect of an optical illusion brought on by the boy's own activity" (222).

15. For examples of such acts of verbal reclamation, see Leavy. Using a psychoanalytic model of discourse, he argues that present dialogue can in

effect reenact former conversations through the process of rhetorical transference.

16. De Man comments on this diachronic uncertainty when, in another context, he writes that "the poet's language . . . glimpses its inauthentic past in the light of the precarious knowledge of its future" ("Lyric" 55).

17. For a discussion of this desire to suspend and even leap over their literary antecedents, see Leslie Brisman's concept of the "second birth," in which the Romantics can be said to sustain a dialogue with their ideological precursors, even as they attempt to abjure them.

18. In *Mysteries of Identity*, Robert Langbaum discusses a parallel desire to address a higher addressee; for him, the Romantic period in particular embodies the need for what he terms imaginative "projection" onto an other.

Chapter 3

1. "Coleridge and the Deluded Reader: 'The Rime of the Ancient Mariner,'" *Georgia Review* 31 (1977): 617. Like Ferguson, I suspect the veracity of the "Gloss" as gloss; I have accordingly focused my comments on the two earlier versions of the "Rime" (1798 and 1800).

2. Cited in Paul Magnuson, *Coleridge's Nightmare Poetry* (Charlottesville: University Press of Virginia, 1974), 76.

3. See, for example, W. J. Bate, *Coleridge* (New York: Macmillan, 1968), 55–65.

4. Bate 48–51; Magnuson, *Poetry* 5–6, 11, 58, 72–73, 80, 83–84.

5. *Natural Supernaturalism* 453; cf. 275.

6. All references to Coleridge's poetry are to *The Complete Poetical Works of Samuel Taylor Coleridge*, ed. Ernest Hartley Coleridge (Oxford: Clarendon Press, 1912). Notebook citations are to Kathleen Coburn, ed. *The Notebooks of Samuel Taylor Coleridge*, 4 vols. (New York: Pantheon, 1957–), cited as *NB* in the text. See also Thomas M. Raysor's edition of *Shakespearean Criticism* (London: Constable, 1936).

7. We witness a similar collapse of dialogue in the painful silence of the Mariner's nephew:

> The body of my brother's son
> Stood by me, knee to knee:
> The body and I pulled at one rope,
> But he said nought to me. (341–44)

See also lines 137 and 478, and *NB* 1:1339. Coleridge explores the problem of interpretive silence still more explicitly in the 1798 version of the "Rime."

8. See *NB* 3:4166n; Coburn cites parallel echoes of the "Rime" in *NB* 1:1473n and *NB* 2:1913 and n. The lifelong significance of themes in the "Rime" is further demonstrated by the recurrent notebook references to the "wandering Jew" motif. Yet I would say that the strongest evidence of this "deepening" significance is Coleridge's continual reference to both his listen-

ing audience and the dialogic form they suggest: see, for instance, *NB* 3:4248 and 4169; *Table Talk*, 21 June 1823; *Aids to Reflection* 352.

 9. See, for instance, his reference to both Wordsworth's and Beaumont's uniquely receptive responses (*NB* 2:2193), as well as his elaboration in *NB* 2:2196. See also *NB* 3:4248, where Coleridge instructs his audience to consider whether they understand the ignorance of a celebrated personage — and if they do not, to refrain from any critique. We must also keep in mind his at times distorted image of this allegedly vituperative reader; see Engell and Bate, *Biographia Literaria* 1:50. Perhaps because of this image, Coleridge also reminds himself not to talk as if all listeners were Southey; he insists, however, that given the right occasion, it would be his "sacred duty" to provide an answer to a young inquirer.

 10. Later in the same entry, Coleridge elaborates on these ontological implications of his "Conscience" toward loved ones — that is, the ability of the conscience to ensure his "existing" or "Consciousness." He writes, "*I love* — & more strongly than ever feel that Conscience, or the Duty of Love, is the Proof of continuing, as it is the Cause & Condition of existing, Consciousness" (*NB* 2:3231). The power of this loving conscience to define consciousness is also evident in the late notebook entries, though it has become more of an agonistic relation between self and others. Coleridge writes,

> I remember a similar feeling when I first saw the connection between Time, and the being resisted; Space and non-resistance — or unresisted Action — that if no object met, stopped, or opposed itself to, my sight, ear, touch, or sensitive power, tho' it were but my own pulse rising up against my own thumb, I could have no sense of Time; & but for these or the repetition of these in the reproductive Memory or Imagination, should have no Time. . . . [O]nly by meeting with, . . . so as to be resisted by, *another* does the Soul become a *Self*. What is Self-consciousness, but . . . to know myself at the same moment that I know another, and to know myself by means of knowing another, and vice . . . versa an other by means of & at the moment of knowing my Self. Self and other are as necessarily interdependent as Right and Left, or North and South (*NB* 4:4929).

In *Coleridge the Moralist*, Laurence S. Lockridge further delineates the relation between Coleridge's divergent conceptions of ontological "conscience" and the instantiation of "consciousness" (see especially 124–30). We should also note the religious implications of the term, as in the following: "The one great & *binding* ground of the Belief in God, and Hereafter is the law of Conscience — . . . " (*NB* 3:4060). See also *AR* 343–44, and *The Friend* (2:8).

 11. See, for example, *NB* 1:1679, 1830.

 12. For a discussion of the opposing meanings behind the harp image — including the problematic passivity it represents — see Magnuson, *Poetry* 1–4, 74. It is Coleridge's self-condemned reliance on "another Nature" that ultimately leads to his use of this contradictory image.

 13. See note 9 above, as well as *NB* 3:3232 and Lockridge. For a discus-

sion of Coleridge's political alienation from his neighbors, see Kelvin Everest, *Coleridge's Secret Ministry* (New York: Barnes and Noble, 1979).

14. Coleridge's notebooks document his increasing cynicism about the potential for any dialogic rapport within marriage; cf. *NB* 1:13, 883; 2:2934n; 3:3264 and n., 3265, 3648, 4013, 4110, 4430 and nn., and especially 3729.

15. Later in this entry, Coleridge links these notebooks — his written attempts at outness — with an obligation toward others, or what he refers to as a "Duty towards my Neighbor." Such language accordingly recalls the foregoing definition of "Conscience," in which his "affections & duties toward others" serve to establish "Consciousness." In either case, both emotional and inscriptive outness are necessary to enact the self.

The same entry also stresses Coleridge's "Marginal notes from many . . . old Books and one or two new ones" — notes that provide another form of chirographic outness. (For further discussion of the role of marginal notes, see my analysis in chapter 6.)

16. James C. McKusick offers the best analysis of Coleridge's linguistic concepts; see especially chapters 1, 4, and 5. For further discussion of these approaches, particularly of desynonymization, see Hamilton, Corrigan, and Christensen; for more on the Coleridgean relation between symbol and referent, see Lockridge 183. A more synoptic analysis of Romantic linguistic concepts emerges in the work of Hans Aarsleff (especially pages 345–81). Finally, for the crucial primary sources behind these linguistic positions, see Condillac, Herder, Monboddo, and Rousseau ("Language").

17. For a discussion of Coleridge's "demonic" or "Gothic" motifs, see Tave.

18. See *AR* 9–10 (Aphorism 19). I have compared this "secret lodger," this evil tendency or immoral practice, to what Coleridge in an earlier work discusses as "some hidden vice" that he sought to "eloign and abalienate"; the latter "vice" is described in Coburn. (See especially *NB* 3:4166.)

19. On July 21, 1832, Coleridge spoke of an overall moral "system" and "redemptive process" for "society"; the implementation of this process, he asserts, "I have been all my life doing in my system of philosophy." See *Specimens of the Table Talk of Samuel Taylor Coleridge*, ed. Henry Nelson Coleridge, 1836.

20. A conventional atonement would require, among other things, the transgressor's prior understanding of the consequences arising from his own actions; yet as Ferguson has noted, "In Coleridge's work generally, intention and effect are absolutely discontinuous, and the moral is that morality appears to involve certainty only if you can already know the full outcome of every action before you commit it" (624). She goes on to say that "reading as a *techné* and morals as techniques of behavior . . . become suspect for Coleridge because they imply that experience — and one's interpretation of it — are both stable and repetitive — that one can learn what one needs to know" ("Reader" 627).

21. The pervasiveness of this casuistic problem is again apparent when Coleridge writes of "[t]he desirableness of having each Soul watched over, as it were, by its Sister — Brother by Brother — *so as to prevent or considerably check all growth of Evil*" (*NB* 3:4169, emphasis added). Later in this entry, he implies that this "Evil" is endemic to all societies, requiring a "medicine & a discipline" to keep it in check. Such medical tropes also echo his reference to Wordsworth's "Disease" of trying to convey secret thoughts — a disease for which "both the specific Remedy, & the condition of Health" is the forsaking of the "sectarian Spirit" (*NB* 1:1546). In such entries, the presence of this "hidden vice" is so encompassing that it actually takes on the rhetoric of a pathology. It is not extraordinary, then, that such "vice" would become an impetus for Coleridge's dialogic process of exposure.

22. Coleridge's use of the progressive tense in this passage ("bringing," "awaking," "unreflecting") further testifies to the ongoing nature of this ineluctable dyadic process.

23. See Lockridge (53–77) and Magnuson (*Poetry* 1–17, 71–76).

24. See Magnuson (*Poetry* 65, cf. 66–68) and Bate (46, 59).

25. These three interpretations are advanced, respectively, by Bate (57–60), Magnuson (*Poetry* 74–75, 81), and Warren (27).

26. Although he occasionally overstates Coleridge's rejection of the will's "separateness," Lockridge clearly recognizes that such "alienation will remain even here the essential feature of his moral vision," in that "an act of alienation must precede an act of reunion" (74, 73). Again, though, we must also consider those circumstances in which Coleridge desires neither reunion nor community, but the preservation of rhetorical agonism — the rifted dialogue that, as we have noted, enables particular narrative and interpretive strategies. In this context, Coleridge's interpretive "vision of evil" is not only "projected from within" (76), but enacted from without — by those voices on the margins of his poetic narratives (cf. 77, 67). While the will's position at the "periphery" or circumference may initially signal human errancy, such positioning ultimately expresses the desire for linguistic outness — the poetic position of those "others" who, while they are often dyspathetic toward Coleridge's vision, nevertheless become the cynosure of dialogue.

In characterizing Coleridge's relation to the poetic other, then, we must align several perspectives. To begin with, we must consider Lockridge's superb analyses of moral distance, personal conscience, generalized consciousness, and ontological potential (cf. 99, 152, 183, and especially 124–30). At the same time, however, we must also bear in mind that this relation to the other is necessarily both *linguistic* and *agonistic*. That is, in order to effect dialogue, this relation must first of all be defined in rhetorical terms, as a specifically conversation-based interchange of multilateral response. Secondly, such an other must also remain rhetorically resistant to a given speaker, must become a clearly adversarial interlocutor.

Of course, neither of these formulations is antithetical to Lockridge's analyses (cf. 47, 182–83), for he too is concerned with the relation between

Coleridge's idea of moral evil and the poet's view of language. But whereas Lockridge traces this evil to Coleridge's particular notions of linguistic "abstraction"—and its consequent "power of shielding one from experience" (182)—the present study stresses Coleridge's doubts about specifically narrative recursivity, arbitrary signification, and (as a result of such features) the baffling of one's listeners.

27. Magnuson (*Poetry* 68) notes several of these self-accusations, though he does not apply them to Coleridge's poetic rhetoric. He then goes on to discuss Coleridge's preoccupation with the passive and diseased imagination. In the present context, however, we should also bear in mind that Coleridge regards this rhetorical "disease" as evidence of a particular narrative form—an often meliorative yet incommunicative exposure before an audience.

28. See *Notes on the Book of Common Prayer*, "Companion to the Altar" (reprinted in *AR* 352, emphasis added). For a consonant approach to confession in the "Rime," see Magnuson, *Poetry* 72–74, 76.

29. See Wordsworth's comments to the Reverend Alexander Dyce, dated approximately 1835. In the 1843 headnote to "We are Seven," Wordsworth continues to stress this alienation from Coleridge.

30. Cf. note 9 above. Nevertheless, Coleridge's continual doubts about friendship—the need that necessarily leads to "disappointment"—remain clear in many passages from the notebooks; see especially *NB* 1:1082.

31. Such sentiments are further corroborated, clarified, and developed in the later writings; see especially *AR* 153 and *Shakespearean Criticism* 93–94. All further references to *Shakespearean Criticism* are cited in the text as *SC*.

32. See *The Friend*.

33. See, for instance, the "Essay on Method." Coleridge frequently reiterates this desire to be understood, as both Ferguson ("Reader" 630–31) and others have noted.

34. The translation follows Ernest Hartley Coleridge's edition.

35. Coleridge refers to this premonition as a "vision" in a crucial passage from the notebooks:

> One of the strangest and most painful Peculiarities of my Nature (unless others have the same, & like me, hide it from the same inexplicable feeling of causeless shame & sense of a sort of guilt, joined with the apprehension of being feared and shrunk from as a something transnatural) I will here record—. . . .
>
> It consists in a sudden second sight of some hidden Vice, past, present, or to come, of the person or persons with whom I am about to form a close intimacy—. . . . I see it as a Vision, feel it as a Prophecy—. . . . (*NB* 3:4166)

36. Here again, Coleridge's emphasis on process, on means rather than ends, resembles other aesthetics common to Romantic writers; as in Hazlitt's "The Fight," the path (or method) overshadows the arrival. Such a process underlies the poetic use of dialogue.

37. Coleridge's characterization of Wordsworth as such a "watcher"—a *Spectator Ab Extra*—thus applies to himself as well. For discussion of con-

cepts parallel to this externalization and polarization, see Thomas McFarland, "A Complex Dialogue: Coleridge's Doctrine of Polarity and Its European Contexts," in *Reading Coleridge*, ed. Walter B. Crawford (Ithaca: Cornell University Press, 1979), 56–115.

Coleridge's personal knowledge of this agonistic dialogue derives in part from the social resistance he experienced in his own listeners. He complains repeatedly of such rejections: much as it is "injurious" to confuse the "two sorts of talkative fellows," he feels compelled to protest the "injurious Manner in which men of Genius are treated, not only as Authors, but even more when they are in social Company" (*NB* 3:4248). Indeed, the difficulties which this "Company" has in comprehending him become a lifelong topic of discussion (cf. notes 8 and 9), and he often reflects on the causes of his hostile receptions. He bemoans, for instance, his own lack of selectivity in choosing an appropriate audience; on other occasions, he insists that "a man long accustomed to silent and solitary meditation, in proportion as he increases the power of thinking in long and connected trains, is apt to lose or lessen the talent of communicating his thoughts with grace and perspicuity." For further discussion of this necessarily "solitary" "power of thinking," see "His Prose Style" in *The Friend*.

Chapter 4

1. Rieger 96. All further references to *Frankenstein* are from Rieger's edition and are cited parenthetically in the text. Like Rieger, I have relied primarily upon the 1818 text for the reasons outlined in his "Note on the Text" (xliii). Despite its emendations by others, however, I also consider the 1831 text as both contiguous with, and extending the central ideas of, the 1818 edition. I have accordingly cited the later work when it develops notions essential to the former; all such citations refer to Rieger's "Appendix B" and are indicated in the text.

Citations of Keats's poetry are to Stillinger's edition, and are also cited parenthetically.

2. Such a parallel between the linguistic aporia of both the monster and Saturn runs deep within both Romantic narratives. Each work, for instance, is concerned with the epistemological slippage between the word and the image — between dialogue and what it might visually represent. Hence the narrator of "The Fall of Hyperion" says,

> nor could my eyes
> And ears act with that pleasant unison of sense
> Which marries sweet sound with the grace of form,
> And dolorous accent from a tragic harp
> With large-limb'd visions. (I:441–45)

In a parallel manner, the monster believes that "language . . . might enable me to make them overlook the deformity of my figure" (109).

As I go on to suggest, for both figures dialogue comes to represent what each refers to as the "Godlike" voice—the capacity for exchange both to engender the linguistic emblems of community and to initiate one's ascension within such a group.

3. Although Walton's early request for this affirmative answer is written (rather than spoken), I will go on to suggest that it nevertheless derives from spoken rhetoric and form.

4. The first phrase is from Brooks (213), the rest from Sherwin (888, 890). Brooks further suggests that the "daemon . . . can never fix or pin down meaning" in the novel (220).

5. Newman 148 (157, 143–44). Newman's words here support Brooks's concept of the "permanently frustrated desire for meaning" in *Frankenstein*; they are also consonant with parallel approaches to frame narrative, including J. Hillis Miller's statement that a novel like *Wuthering Heights* frustrates our need "to satisfy the mind's desire for logical order," to "indicate the right way to read the novel as a whole"—since "interpretation always leaves something over" (*Fiction* 52–53, 49). Brooks (217–18) and Miller (*Fiction* 69–70) maintain that the source of these frustrated understandings is the influence of what both term, after Freud, "the uncanny."

6. Brooks (220, 218), Newman (141, 154), Sherwin (884), and Miller (*Fiction* 67, 60, 52) each cite this absent or missing center (of indeterminacy) within the frame narratives they discuss. The final comment on language is also from Brooks (220, 212); although he recognizes the "rhetorical effect" of the monster (212, 209), Brooks nevertheless concludes that the creature's "language is metonymic advance without a terminus" (213; cf. 212, 220).

7. Culler (146) refers to this process as the danger of "radical . . . solipsism" inherent in apostrophe. According to this view, even invocations to Nature perpetuate this self-abnegation, since voices like the river Derwent and Eolian winds continually threaten to subsume the voices of the lyrical "I" (Kneale 353–55; Jacobus 170, 176). Jacobus further suggests that serial apostrophe results not in a "stable identity" but a "destabilizing multiplicity" of voices—one that "can equally take on the daemonic aspect of possession" (175, 174). For Ferguson, similarly, the written connections (epitaphic "echoings") that link a given speaker with the "community of the dead" simultaneously "drive toward an inarticulateness which closes over even the poet and his consciousness" (158, 170). In many of Rajan's readings, too, this "lyrical voice comes up against a repudiation of its feelings that makes us recognize the self-presence of meaning . . . as already an illusion" (195–96). What is more, the pervasiveness of written figures within Romantic poetry repeatedly challenges the spoken character of lyrical apostrophe, especially when the inscribed word outlasts or engulfs its spoken counterpart (Miller, *Linguistic* 108–13; Kneale 351, 357–58; Jacobus 177–78).

8. If this apostrophic form suggests an attempt to establish "existence," we must also recognize that the novel's historical context recapitulates a similar quest for selfhood. We must consider that *Frankenstein* is itself one of those hybrid monsters known as the "Romantic novel"—an oxymoronic

phrase that embodies the tension between the Romantic lyric and the prose form that came to predominate as the century progressed. Each of these influential strains, moreover, carries with it particular ontological implications. On one hand, the lyrical form historically concerns itself with delimiting the boundaries of the subjective "I" within the world (Frye 31–32). On the other hand, the nineteenth-century novel usually endeavors to define its own "I" in relation to the more pluralistic interactions of society at large. In *Frankenstein*, however, both processes of establishing the self take place simultaneously: we witness both the development of the isolated lyric speaker *and* his self-definition during exchanges with listeners.

Frankenstein is, in fact, one of the few examples of the genre to address this formal tension explicitly – to meld aspects of both the lyric and the novel into a single, organic entity. On the purely formal level, for instance, the novel often juxtaposes the story of a single narrator with his continual desire to find a sympathetic listener – to turn his narration into dialogue. Generally speaking, whereas the succession of solitary narrators in *Frankenstein* explores certain Romantic conventions of the solipsistic lyric speaker, the emphasis on the *response* to this speaker – on those characters who both enter into and translate a narrator's argument – resembles the more diffuse interactions of the novel. And whereas the solitary narrator attempts to express his ego with a single voice, his position within *Frankenstein* introduces a polyphonic, contextual dimension to this desire for self.

9. Mary Shelley's personal doubts about "being" also manifest themselves in her correspondence. To Leigh Hunt, she writes, "Well, my dear Hunt, how do you do? I am Mary Shelley I hope – though like the little woman in the story book – I begin to doubt 'if I be I' . . . " (1:244).

We can also consider such correspondence as a record of her desire for the other. In a letter to Edward J. Trelawny, for instance, she writes, "Shut out as I am from all communication with life I feel as if a letter from you would be to me a token sent from a world of flesh and blood to one of shadow" (1:211; cf. 1:341). To begin with, then, communication with the other betokens her very "life," the "world of flesh and blood." If such communication evades her, she loses her ability to penetrate this world, to "learn" its secrets: she writes to Claire Clairmont, "I am silent and serious. Absorbed in my own thoughts, what am I then in this world if my spirit live not to learn and become better?" (1:209). Later, in the letter to Trelawny, she goes so far as to say that such self-absorption saps her creative powers. "I find only solitude," she says, " . . . my imagination then so fond of sharing" (1:212).

Such imaginative "sharing," moreover, not only penetrates the world but also sheds light on the endemic darkness between all humans. Without this interchange, we founder: " . . . blind miserable beings thus we grope in the dark [;] we depend on each other yet we are each a mystery to the other – and the heart which should be in the hand of a *friend*, either shuns the contact, or is disdainfully rejected" (2:18). Denied this discourse with the other, then, the "mystery" between individuals divides them forever. As she goes on to say, "Thus scattered about the world, useless to others, a burthen to themselves, are human beings destined to be—who might be happy, did not a thousand circumstances—tyrannical passions, and want of *sympathy* prevent their ever uniting to any purpose" (2:18; emphases added).

10. Such foreshadowing also figures directly in Victor's narrative style, for he repeatedly alludes both to "frightful events which [he] is about to relate" (171) and to "fears . . . which soon were to clasp" him (191).

11. This reading sees the "friend" as a linguistic expression of the socially defined self—as an "other" in Bakhtin's sense of the term. According to this view, we can presume a rhetorical distance between listening "others" and discrete speakers or interlocutors. Such a "friend" accordingly differs from the Lacanian Other, especially since the latter can either merge with or derive from the speaking self (cf. Sherwin 889, Brooks 213, and my note 20).

12. Mary Shelley's association between this answering voice and the existential "I" becomes most explicit in a letter to Maria Gisborne. She writes, " . . . when L[ord] B[yron] speaks I wait for Shelley's voice in answer as the natural result . . . " (1:204). In such passages, she implies that Shelley's voice might precede him, that vocalization itself might incarnate being. (For further description of the voice's "power of awakening melancholy," see her journal entry of October 19, 1822.)

For a linguistic view of this vocative self-fashioning, see Derrida (*Speech and Phenomena*), who discusses the ontological implications of voice in terms of what he calls "presence," "self-presence," and "ideality." In Derrida's formulations, establishing being (presence) as an ideal form (ideality) demands vocal expression: "the substance of expression—which best seems to preserve ideality and living presence in all its forms is living speech, the spirituality of the breath as *phōnē* . . . " (10; cf. 78). Later, in response to Husserl's description of insubstantiality, Derrida writes that "it remains, then, for us to *speak*, to make our voices *resonate* throughout the corridors in order to make up for [*suppléer*] the breakup of presence" (104).

Derrida then goes on to suggest that the incorporeal, unworldly nature of the voice accounts for its capacity to establish idealized presence. He writes:

> [T]his ideal being must be constituted, repeated, and expressed in a medium that does not impair the presence and self-presence of the acts that aim at it, a medium which both preserves the *presence of the object* before intuition and *self-presence*. . . . The ideality of the object, which is only its being-for a nonempirical consciousness, can only be expressed in an element whose phenomenality does not have worldly form. *The name of this element is the voice.* (75–76)

For Derrida, moreover, this vocal self-presence is complicated by the auditors of *parole*, by those who hear the utterance. Although speakers often establish presence by hearing themselves (102), he goes on to suggest how this process can be represented and replicated with the presence of an auditor: "To speak to someone is doubtless to hear oneself speak, to be heard by oneself; but, at the same time, if one is heard by another, to speak is to make him *repeat immediately* in himself the hearing-oneself-speak in the very form in which I effectuated it" (80; cf. 70, 78, 73 n. 2). It is this chain of vocal self-defining that accounts for the representation of spoken narrative in Shelley's novel.

For further discussions of this ontology of voice, see Porter and Harding.

13. Although Margaret, Walton's sister, is not strictly an auditor, Walton continually implicates her within the kind of ontological, Bakhtinian dialogue I am considering. As I go on to explain, she in effect completes this dialogue even if she never receives the letters Walton is writing.

14. For incisive discussions of Victor as Mary Shelley's revision of a failed parental paradigm, see Moers (90–99) and Poovey. In much the same manner, we can also discuss storytelling as an figurative act of creation. I would stress, though, that the ontological implications of this act derive from its rhetorical foundation — its reference to voice, apostrophe, affect, and interpretive dialogue.

15. Even William Frankenstein — the Rousseau-inspired "beautiful child" whom the monster presumes to be "unprejudiced" and educable — echoes this rejection of attempted dialogue. When the monster cries out, "I do not intend to hurt you; listen to me," the boy never hears his plea (138–39). We must again bear in mind, however, that what becomes suspect here is not narrative so much as its affective intention — its designation for an other, for dialogue.

16. As Rieger has noted, this line echoes Satan's cry in *Paradise Lost*:

Me miserable! which way shall I fly
Infinite wrath, and infinite despair?
Which way I fly is Hell; myself am Hell. . . . (IV:73–75)

In Mary Shelley's terms, however, we can read this internal "Hell" as an emblem of the rhetorically entrapped self.

17. My emphasis here on rhetorical disjunction between self and other differs from the current approach, which argues for a conflation of Victor and the monster: see, for instance, the comments of George Levine, who writes, "So pervasive has been the recognition that the Monster and Frankenstein are two aspects of the same being that the writers in this volume assume rather than argue it" (15; also cited in Sherwin 889). For similar approaches to this assumed conflation, see Miyoshi (83–84), Brooks (214, 207), and Bloom ("Frankenstein"; "Afterword"). For a view of Victor's relation with the monster as less "reducible" to singularity, see Sherwin (889–90), who sees the monster as a "giant form of Solitude, an existence made absolute by its confinement to the hell of being itself."

This linguistic separation between speakers and listeners also helps to account for the novel's frame-narrative structure, since the formal disjunction between story and frame further emphasizes the rhetorical separation between characters — between self and other.

18. Mary Shelley essentially rewrites Coleridge by reshaping the quest motif, as her quotations of "The Rime of the Ancient Mariner" suggest. Her reinterpretation sheds light on not only the monster's search for being but

Victor's and Walton's as well. Walton, for instance, stresses this parallel between himself and the Mariner, saying, "It is impossible to communicate to you a conception of the trembling sensation, half pleasurable and half fearful, with which I am preparing to depart. I am going to unexplored regions, to 'the land of mist and snow'; but I shall kill no albatross, therefore do not be alarmed for my safety" (15). In the later edition, Shelley develops this comparison; there, Walton attempts to comfort Margaret if, in his words,

> I should come back to you as worn and woful as the "Ancient Mariner?" You will smile at my allusion; but I will disclose a secret. I have often attributed my attachment to, my passionate enthusiasm for, the dangerous mysteries of ocean, to that production of the most imaginative of modern poets. There is something at work in my soul, which I do not understand. . . . [T]here is a love for the marvellous, a belief in the marvellous, intertwined in all my projects, which hurries me out of the common pathways of men, even to the wild sea and unvisited regions I am about to explore. (231)

Like the Ancient Mariner, Walton attempts to expose this "belief in the marvellous," this "secret" that he does "not understand." And — like the Mariner — Walton, Victor, and the monster seek out an external, "unvisited" other: they must tell their tales before this listener in order to effect "being."

We can also trace other motifs prevalent in both the poem and the novel, including the protagonists' Promethean desire (15), the omnipresent references to the "fiend" or hidden evil (54), and, as suggested, the frame-narrative form of both works. And we should further note those many episodes that appear to echo Coleridge's language from the "Rime": see, for instance, 160, 167, 169, 203, 205.

For further approaches to this Coleridgean parallel, see Brooks and Newman (145).

19. See, for instance, Sherwin (895, 900–902), Newman (159–60), Rieger (xviii), and note 8 above.

20. For the monster, this "chain" represents the rhetorical equivalent of a constitutive "society" — a verbal matrix that enables the social enactment of self. This social matrix is further suggested by the chain of proleptic addresses in the novel's concentric frames. (For a different approach to this passage, see Brooks's reading of the monster's "chain" in terms of "Lacan's exposition of the 'signifying chain' of language" [208].)

21. Mary Shelley's predilection for "society" is further evident in her letters. Even before her husband's death, she often extols "all the delights of friendly and social intercourse" (1:154). Although she occasionally mentions the pains of such intercourse, she repeatedly refers to the necessity of "friends," correspondence, and a broad social "horizon" (1:146, 169).

22. Mary Shelley develops this notion of the auditor-friend in the 1831 edition: she stresses the "gentle and feminine fosterage" (230) supplied by Elizabeth, Victor's need for someone to have "entered attentively" (231) into his plans, and the search for one "fit to appreciate" (232) a given narrator. Her discussion of the "friend" here also recalls the entire context of "feminine

fosterage" in the nineteenth century: it evokes not only Wordsworth's notion of "female service" in "Michael" but also George Eliot's reinterpretation of the concept in *Silas Marner*. All told, such examples indicate a tendency to envision this sustentative rhetoric in female terms.

23. Percy Shelley's liberties with his wife's manuscript are by now well known, as is her decision to give him "carte blanche to make . . . alterations" (Rieger xviii). We must also bear in mind, though, that her vision of both Nature and the imagination ultimately reinterpreted her husband's views (see Sherwin 900, Newman 159–60). My point here, however, is that her frequent discussions of silence, communication, and the "internal life" affirm the interlocutor's relation to being — the ability of the "friend" to rectify the ego.

24. See Clifford for a divergent approach to this eloquence, stressing verisimilar potential over ontological implications.

25. Victor's final "reply" is, of course, a refusal; yet we must again consider that his dubitable powers of audition follow not from any signal inarticulateness on the monster's part — nor even from a more global failure of language. If the inadequacy of language had caused audition to break down in this novel, then those few passages in which narrators apparently manage to speak plainly and eloquently would meet with commensurate responses. Yet when Justine, for instance, decides to "rest [her] innocence on a plain and simple explanation of the facts" (78), her audience nevertheless condemns her. Indeed, no matter how "plain and simple" an apostrophic "explanation" becomes in *Frankenstein*, the corresponding auditor's response is still not forthcoming. Rather than resulting from the relative skills of individual narrators, the collapse of audition in this novel depends on the breakdown of what Bakhtin calls the self's "field of interorientations" — what I have been calling a community of dialogue.

26. Besides his truncated dialogues with both Victor and the De Lacys, the monster also attempts to engage the first cottagers (100–101), William Frankenstein (139), and the misguided hunter (137).

27. Culler 142–43; cf. 146. In discussing Shelley's "Ode to the West Wind," Culler describes how the apostrophizing "I" might engender response from a "Thou," and thereby "establish its identity as poetical and prophetic voice" (142). See also Jacobus 175, 178.

28. Such questioning is intended to produce not an answer but a continuing exchange — an ongoing process of call and response. As Gadamer says earlier, "Dialectic, as the art of asking questions, proves itself only because the person who knows how to ask questions is able to persist in his questioning, which involves being able to preserve his orientation towards openness. The art of questioning is that of being able *to go on asking questions*, ie the art of thinking. It is called 'dialectic' . . . " (330). *Frankenstein*, too, is constructed so as "to go on asking questions": beginning with the monster's "Who was I?" (124), the novel initiates a series of interrogative exchanges that terminate in his final crescendo of queries: "Was there no injustice in this? Am I to be thought the only criminal, when all human kind sinned

against me? Why do you not hate Felix, who drove his friend from his door with contumely? Why do you not execrate the rustic who sought to destroy the saviour of his child?" (219). Soon after this, all questions stop, and the monster abandons his quest.

29. Such dialogic exchanges ultimately set the standard for what Justine refers to as "interpretation" (78). If "interpretation" founders in the novel, such a failure again represents not the end of language but the sundering of this dialogic community — the rhetorical consensus that interprets when "any circumstance appears doubtful or suspicious" (78). It is here, I think, that the potential interpretations in the novel falter — at the eventual failure of the communal rhetoric that enables auditors "to understand the full extent of [a] proposition" (140).

Chapter 5

1. For an indication of this extraordinary range of readings — a range so contradictory that it begins to suggest a problematic approach to interpretation — see Richard Lettis and William E. Morris, eds., *A Wuthering Heights Handbook* (New York: Odyssey Press, 1961); Miriam Allott, ed., *The Brontës: The Critical Heritage* (London: Routledge and Kegan Paul, 1974); Miriam Allott, "The Brontës," in *The English Novel: Select Bibliographical Guides*, ed. A. E. Dyson (London: Oxford University Press, 1974), 218–45; Alastair G. Everitt, ed., *Wuthering Heights: An Anthology of Criticism* (London: Frank Cass, 1967); as well as the criticism selected in William M. Sale, Jr., ed., *Wuthering Heights: An Authoritative Text, with Essays in Criticism* (New York: Norton, 1963). My citations of the novel refer to this edition; see page 17 for the reference to the "barred" doors of the Heights world. (I have also adopted the practice of using "Catherine" to designate Catherine Earnshaw, and "Cathy" to refer to her daughter by Edgar Linton.)

Regarding the novel's Romantic characteristics, I have summarized research on this aspect of *Wuthering Heights* in note 17.

Finally, Leavis's observation also accounts for the unusually disparate attempts to approach this novelistic "sport" and trace its "undetectable" influence; he briefly mentions the novel in *The Great Tradition* (1948; reprinted, New York: New York University Press, 1973), 27.

2. See J. H. Miller's *Fiction and Repetition* (Cambridge: Harvard University Press, 1983), 52–53, 49. The remainder of Miller's comments cited in this section are from an earlier version of his chapter on the novel: "*Wuthering Heights* and the Ellipses of Interpretation," *Notre Dame English Journal* 12 (1980): 85–100.

For a survey of what I see as the prevailing approach to the novel during the past fifteen years, see note 3.

3. The three phrases are, respectively, from Allan R. Brick, "*Wuthering Heights*: Narrators, Audience, and Message," *College English* 21 (November 1959): 81, reprinted in Lettis and Morris, 219–20; Carol Jacobs, "*Wuthering*

Heights: At the Threshold of Interpretation," *Boundary 2* 7 (1979): 68; and
Peter K. Garrett, "Double Plots and Dialogical Form in Victorian Fiction,"
Nineteenth-Century Fiction 32 (1977): 8. Although Brick's essay predates the
period I am discussing, it too partakes of the hermeneutical approach that
has prevailed during the past fifteen years. A brief glance at the titles of these
studies – see Donoghue, Jacobs, and Sonstroem (cited in notes 4 and 17) –
again suggests this approach. See also Elizabeth R. Napier, "The Problem of
Boundaries in *Wuthering Heights*," *Philological Quarterly* 63 (1984): 96, 97;
and Peter Widdowson, "Emily Brontë: The Romantic Novelist," *Moderna
Sprak* 66 (1972), who notes that his essay "is not intended to circumscribe the
range of interpretation of *Wuthering Heights* (which is splendidly impossible
anyway)" (3).

    4. Those studies that attribute the novel's problems of interpretation to
its narrator's "unreliability" include Gideon Shunami, "The Unreliable Narrator in *Wuthering Heights*," *Nineteenth-Century Fiction* 27 (1973): 449–68;
and Jacqueline Viswanathan, "Point of View and Unreliability in Brontë's
Wuthering Heights, Conrad's *Under Western Eyes*, and Mann's *Doktor Faustus*," *Orbis Litterarum* 29 (1974): 42–60.

    The phrases "reader's quandary" and "multiplicity of outlook" are from
David Sonstroem, "*Wuthering Heights* and the Limits of Vision," *PMLA* 86
(1971): 59, 61; the phrases "surplus of signifiers" and "intrinsic plurality" are
from Frank Kermode, "A Modern Way with the Classic," *New Literary History* 5 (1974): 434, 425. See also J. Hillis Miller, *Fiction and Repetition*, who
writes that the "act of interpretation always leaves something over. . . . This
something left out is clearly a significant detail. There are always in fact a
group of such significant details which have been left out of any reduction to
order. The text is over-rich" (52).

    Both Miller (67) and Jacobs (note 3) argue that the language of the
novel leaves us with a "missing center" (56).

    5. "*Wuthering Heights* and the Ellipses of Interpretation," 92. Miller
goes on to revise this sentence in *Fiction and Repetition*, where he writes that
"there is no secret truth which criticism might formulate" as a "principle of
explanation which would account for everything in the novel" (51). Despite
this revision, however, he then goes on to say that "it is impossible to tell
whether there is any secret at all hidden in the depths" of *Wuthering Heights*
(69). And although he speaks of the reader's "process" and "effort of understanding," he repeatedly stresses the "baffling of that effort" – since an "interpretive origin . . . cannot be identified for *Wuthering Heights*" (53, 63). Yet
if Miller dwells on that "remnant of opacity which keeps the interpreter dissat-
isfied" (51), I argue that the rhetorical force of those hermeneutic forms
enacted in the novel counterbalances this opacity. Although such concerns
are finally distinct from Miller's, he is clearly aware of them when he writes
that opacity keeps "the process of interpretation still able to continue" (51–
52) and that "the situation of the reader of *Wuthering Heights* is inscribed
within the novel in the situations of all those characters who are readers [and]
tellers of tales" (70).

6. See, for instance, Carl R. Woodring, "The Narrators of *Wuthering Heights*," *Nineteenth-Century Fiction* 11 (March 1957): 298–305, reprinted in Sale's edition of the novel (338–43). See especially 315, 338, 340. Woodring comes closest to the concerns of this study when he writes: "If he [Lockwood] seems inane, he suffers from the inanity his author attributes to the average London reader into whose hands her book will fall. In his introduction to the the Rinehart College Edition, Mark Schorer follows Garrod in interpreting the original plan of the novel as the edification of a sophisticated and sentimental prig, Lockwood, in the natural human values of grand passion. Rather, Lockwood reacts for the normal skeptical reader in appropriate ways at each stage of the story and its unfolding theme" (340). Woodring, however, never explains his use of the term "normal skeptical reader," nor does he mention why Brontë would feel the need to represent such a reader's reactions in this particular novel. We must also ask how readers since 1847 have read the novel: do they share reactions that have been widely recognized to be inadequate to the novel? Such questions, I would say, can be addressed only if we consider the status of listeners in the novel. See also Clifford Collins, "Theme and Conventions in *Wuthering Heights*," *Critic* 1 (Autumn 1947): 43–50, reprinted in Sale's edition of the novel (309–18). Collins maintains that "Lockwood not only exhibits the reactions that may be expected from the ordinary reader (thereby invalidating them, for his commentary is carefully shown to be neither intelligent nor sensitive), but he is representative of urban life and by origin unfitted for the tempo of life about the Heights" (315). Yet I would say that, for reasons that I will make clear, the reactions of more than just the "ordinary reader" inform the frame structure of the novel. And I would add that *Wuthering Heights* is less about the incompatibility of "urban life" and the Heights than about interpretive rhetoric and the epistemological chasm between listeners and narrators.

7. See Walter E. Anderson, "The Lyrical Form of *Wuthering Heights*," *University of Toronto Quarterly* 47 (1977–78): 120.

Of course, most characters in this novel *do* deny its visionary premises (as represented by its spectral symbols), and in doing so they deny not only the novel but the very possibility of interpretive audition as well. Lockwood, for instance, not only repulses the ghostly Catherine's return to Heathcliff (30) but also fails to understand how this vision of Catherine resonates throughout the narration he hears from Nelly. He seems unaware of the connection between his waif-haunted nightmare and the later "confession" by Heathcliff: "The moment I closed my eyes, she was either outside the window, or sliding back the panels" (230). On an earlier occasion, Lockwood calls Heathcliff's belief in Catherine's ghost "folly" (33)—a term that Nelly later uses to describe Catherine's revelations (74). Indeed, when Catherine herself begins to describe her phantasmal union with Heathcliff, Nelly can only respond, "I won't hear it, I won't hear it! . . . I was superstitious about dreams then, and am still" (72). Later, Heathcliff's encounters with "ghosts and visions" prompt the same fearful response from Nelly: "Mr. Heathcliff! master!" she cries, "Don't, for God's sake, stare as if you saw an unearthly vision" (261). And when Nelly encounters the child who claims to have glimpsed the deceased lovers, she insists that "he probably raised the phantoms from thinking" (265). By the end of the novel, Nelly regards even her own dreams as lapses into "superstition," which, as she says, continued until "dawn restored me to common sense" (260).

We should also note that Lockwood's general incapacity for response precludes reaction not only to the visionary mysteries of Heathcliff and Catherine but even to the "fascinating creature" who earlier shows interest in him (15). "I 'never told my love' vocally," he says; and when he finally does prompt a "return" from her, he reports, "I . . . shrunk icily into myself, like a snail; at every glance retired colder and farther" (15). Once again, Lockwood's silence obviates any rhetorical return.

Finally, Edgar too becomes the victim of broken colloquy when he demands of Catherine, "Answer my question. . . . You *must* answer it. . . . I absolutely *require* to know"—only to hear her order him from the room (101–2).

8. As I go on to argue, it is this exposure that sustains both the ongoing process of interpretation and the vitality of rhetorical form. This is not to say, though, that the novel discounts the fallibility of the interpretive process, including its potential for flawed judgment and moral caprice. Even Nelly seems at times to recognize this possible failure, for after condemning one of Catherine's explanations, she adds, "Though I'm hardly a judge" (73). And indeed, the entire issue of judgment as interpretation is a questionable one within *Wuthering Heights*: the Branderham episode, for example, erupts into a chain reaction of misfired auditions. First Lockwood renounces his listening role and attacks the offending narrator; then the congregation itself appears to misjudge its leader's account of Lockwood and falls upon one another. And response in *Wuthering Heights* is patterned after Lockwood's audition during this sermon—a botched audition that Branderham, with appropriate inclusiveness, refers to as "human weakness" (29). In the end, Branderham's casuistry also proves to be flawed, for his "judgment" is actually retribution when he cries, "Execute upon him the judgment written" (29).

Generally speaking, the listeners in *Wuthering Heights* indulge in seemingly arbitrary moral judgments; like Branderham, each has "his private manner of interpreting" (29). Because of this moral subjectivity, no interpretation can transcend another: as Nelly puts it to Lockwood, "You'll judge as well as I can, all these things; at least, you'll think you will, and that's the same" (152). Without interpretive standards, then, audition becomes a punishment with narration the trial. Listeners accordingly become the objects of judgment in this novel; like Lockwood, they are "condemned to hear" what they can never understand (29).

9. See Anderson (note 7) for a reading of Catherine's celebrated statement. For discussions of other critical dilemmas mentioned here, see the anthologies listed in note 1 (esp. Lettis and Morris).

10. Numerous studies of the novel allude to its "Gothic" character; see,

for instance, James Twitchell, "Heathcliff as Vampire," *Southern Humanities Review* 11 (1977): 355–62; Peter McIverny, "Satanic Conceits in *Frankenstein* and *Wuthering Heights*," *Milton and the Romantics* 4 (1980): 1–15; Ronald A. Bosco, "Heathcliff: Social Victim or Demon?" *Gypsy Scholar* 2:21–39; Judith Weissman, "'Like a Mad Dog': The Radical Romanticism of *Wuthering Heights*," *Midwest Quarterly* 19 (1978): 383–97; Emilio de Grazia, "The Ethical Dimension of *Wuthering Heights*," *Midwest Quarterly* 19 (1978): 176–95; as well as the references to the Gothic listed in Patrick Diskin, "Some Sources of *Wuthering Heights*," *Notes and Queries* 24 (1977): 354–61; and Miriam Allott, "The Brontës," in *The English Novel: Selected Biographical Guides*, ed. A. E. Dyson (London: Oxford University Press, 1974), 218–45. Several of these studies also suggest that the Gothic novel may have redefined the frame narrative form.

11. See Michel Foucault, *History of Sexuality*, trans. Robert Hurley (New York: Pantheon, 1978), esp. 66. All quotations are from Hurley's edition.

For a more detailed history of this shift in confessional rhetoric, see Walter H. Conser, Jr., *Church and Confession: Conservative Theologians in Germany, England, and America, 1815–1866* (Macon: Mercer University Press, 1984), esp. 8–9, 99–160; Frank D. McConnell, *The Confessional Imagination: A Reading of Wordsworth's Prelude* (Baltimore: Johns Hopkins University Press, 1974); and Henry C. Lea, *History of Auricular Confession and Indulgences in the Latin Church*, vol. 3 (Philadelphia: Sea Bros., 1896).

For analysis of the psychological aspects of confession—in terms of the two roles I discuss—see Terrence Doody, *Confession and Community in the Novel* (Baton Rouge: Louisiana State University Press, 1980); Theodor Reik, *The Compulsion to Confess: On the Psychoanalysis of Crime and Punishment* (New York: Farrar, Strauss and Cudahy, 1959), 304, 270; Erik Berggren, *The Psychology of Confession*, Studies in the History of Religions, vol. 29 (Leiden: E. J. Brill, 1975); Walter J. Koehler, *Counseling and Confession* (St. Louis: Concordia, 1982); and Paul E. McKeever, *Theology 77*, (Washington, D.C.: Catholic University of America Press, 1953).

Emily Brontë's own religious attitudes toward forgiveness and confession are discussed in Clement King Shorter, *The Brontës: Life and Letters* (New York: Haskell House, 1969). (I would also note in passing that not only Heathcliff but also Catherine and Nelly refer to their effusions as "confessions" in various passages of the novel [39]).

12. Stanley Leavy, *The Psychoanalytic Dialogue* (New Haven: Yale University Press, 1980), 40. The most pertinent discussions of psychoanalytic rhetoric, as it informs narrative structure in general and literature in particular, include Leavey, esp. 39–41, 55, 80, 86; Roy Schafer, "Narration in the Psychoanalytic Dialogue," in *On Narrative*, ed. W.J.T. Mitchell (Chicago: University of Chicago Press, 1981), 25–50; and Robin Tolmach Lakoff, "When Talk Is Not Cheap: Psychotherapy as Conversation," in *The State*

of the Language, ed. Leonard Michaels and Christopher Ricks (Berkeley: University of California Press, 1980), 440–48.

For linguistic studies of the necessarily bilateral aspect of interpretation within dialogue, see William Labov and David Fanshel, *Therapeutic Discourse* (New York: Academic Press, 1977); Frederick Erickson, "Listening and Speaking," in *Languages and Linguistics: The Interdependence of Theory, Data, and Application*, ed. Deborah Tannen (Washington, D.C.: Georgetown University Press, 1986), presented at Georgetown University Round Table on Languages and Linguistics, 1985; and R. P. McDermott and Henry Tylbor, "On the Necessity of Collusion in Conversation," *Text* 3 (1983): 277–97.

13. See Jacques Lacan, "Le Stade du miroir," reprinted in *Ecrits* (Paris, 1966). I am applying Lacan's model selectively here, with particular emphasis on his discussion of the infant's ontological development. See also Lacan, *The Language of the Self*, trans. Anthony Wilden (Baltimore: Johns Hopkins University Press, 1968), 100, 163, 166, 172–74, 200. Unless otherwise noted, all references to Lacan are to the Wilden edition.

14. See Lacan, "Propos sur la causalité psychique" (1950), p. 45; quoted in Wilden p. 100, n. 27.

15. Lacan 9. In Lacan's terms, such linguistic recognition is a function of what he calls the "Word"—that abstract sign of the analysand's individual "response," his discreteness. "What I seek in the Word," he writes, "is the response of the other" (63). In *Wuthering Heights*, I would say that the interpretive listener represents this linguistic "response of the other": when characters like Catherine, Nelly, and Heathcliff seek out listeners, they seek the linguistic interpretation ("response") that identifies the self ("recognition"). Many studies, of course, have cited examples of such linguistic interpretations in *Wuthering Heights*, including the instances of Hareton's reading, Nelly's censorship, and Lockwood's decipherment and naming process; see, for instance, Jacobs (note 3), 99; Ian Gregor, "Reading a Short Story: Sequence, Pace, and Recollection," in *Reading the Victorian Novel: Detail into Form*, ed. Ian Gregor (Totowa, N.J.: Barnes and Noble, 1980); and J. Hillis Miller, *Fiction and Repetition*. What these studies have not noted, though, is that such linguistic interactions can use the "response of the other" to establish the self. In Lacan's words, "Language, before signifying something, signifies for someone" (76–77). Self-affirmation in *Wuthering Heights* is literally the articulation of the self to the other.

16. *Problems of Dostoevsky's Poetics*, trans. Caryl Emerson (Minneapolis: University of Minnesota Press, 1982), 287. Although for Bakhtin dialogues between self and "thou" may take place internally, he nevertheless depicts them in terms of the spoken word.

17. For studies that apply Coleridge's theory and poetry to the novel, see, for instance, Denis Donoghue, "Emily Brontë: On the Latitude of Interpretation," in *The Interpretation of Narrative: Theory and Practice*, ed. Morton W. Bloomfield (Cambridge: Harvard University Press, 1970), 105–33,

esp. 114; and Widdowson (note 3), 1–9 (esp. 4, on the "Rime"). My references to Coleridgean theory are from Kathleen Coburn, ed., *The Notebooks of Samuel Taylor Coleridge* (New York: Pantheon, 1957–61), and are cited by volume and page number parenthetically in the text.

The most provocative applications of general Romantic ideology to the novel include Alan S. Loxterman, "*Wuthering Heights* as Romantic Poem and Victorian Novel," in *A Festschrift for Professor Marguerite Roberts*, ed. Frieda Elaine Penninger (Richmond: University of Richmond Press, 1976), 87–100; and Widdowson (note 3). For more theoretical treatments of Romanticism in relation to the novel, see J. Hillis Miller, *The Disappearance of God* (New York: Schocken, 1965), 160; Walter L. Reed, *Meditations on the Hero: A Study of the Romantic Hero in Nineteenth-Century Fiction* (New Haven: Yale University Press, 1974); Weissman (note 10); Alain Blayac, "A Note on Emily Brontë's Romanticism in *Wuthering Heights*," *Cahiers Victoriens et Edouardiens* 3 (1976): 1–6; and Donoghue (above), 113, 115. Studies that discuss the novel directly in the context of Romantic poetry include John Hewish, *Emily Brontë: A Critical and Biographical Study* (New York: Macmillan, 1969); and Miriam Allott, *Novelists on the Novel* (London: Routledge Paperback, 1968), 169. Other research briefly notes this Romantic context for the novel, but chooses not to dwell on its particular implications: see Q. D. Leavis, "Introduction to Charlotte Brontë's *Jane Eyre*" (Harmondsworth, U.K.: Penguin, 1966), 25; Patricia Meyer Spacks, *The Female Imagination* (New York: Knopf, 1975), 134; Muriel Spark and Derek Stanford, *Emily Brontë: Her Life and Work* (New York: J. Day, 1959); and E. A. Baker, *The History of the English Novel*, vol. 8 (New York: Barnes and Noble, 1968), esp. 11–29, 64–77, and preface.

Still other approaches cite the Romantic qualities of the novel but then go on to characterize it as transitional to (or indicative of) the Victorian era; see, for instance, David Sonstroem (note 4); Loxterman (above), 93; and even Arnold Shapiro, "*Wuthering Heights* as a Victorian Novel," *Studies in the Novel* 1 (1969): 284–95. I would stress that those who see the novel as a response to Romanticism also serve to locate the work within the general rhetorical and philosophical currents I am discussing (see, for instance, Nancy Armstrong, "Emily Brontë In and Out of Her Time," *Genre* 15 (1982): 243–64, esp. 260, 262, 259).

Chapter 6

1. As Thorburn has noted, Conrad emphasizes this passage in both the epigraph to *Lord Jim* and the climax to *A Personal Record*.

2. Such subtle readings serve as a precursor to any dialogic interpretations of Conradian narrative, especially in regard to Romantic traditions. At the same time, however, we have seen that this dialogic form is frequently agonistic, an adversarial rhetoric in which the literary encounter functions as both personal exposure and ongoing heuristic. Such an approach differs from

Thorburn's view of these encounters as "gestures of inclusion and sharing," "gestures designed to create an alliance of shared feeling that will bind the speaker and his sense of what is important and humanly true to the validating sympathies of another person." According to this reading, Conrad's prototypical interlocutor is not an agon but an index of both "validating sympathies" and "spiritual company." His "most characteristic situation [is] a kind of partnership – a meeting or joining together of two characters, one young and inexperienced, the other usually older, whose role is that of guide or teacher" (129).

Thorburn is clearly aware of the limits to this "joining" or "partnership," as he suggests in describing Conrad's overall "suspicion of art and of language" (115; cf. 106, 117, 124).

3. As Ong has suggested, Marlow's partial knowledge of Kurtz comes only by way of this *vocal* "mediation" and "interpretation" – by way of dialogue. "By far most of Marlow's contacts with Kurtz are indirect," he writes, "mediated by others – in stories, in responses to his anxious questions, in mementos or souvenirs of various sorts, including bits of personal property left by Kurtz at his death – and thus readily subject to Marlow's interpretation, to accommodation to his own needs" ("Conrad's Darkness" 157).

4. On this voice, see 78, 80, 134–36, 138, 146, 148. As colloquy fails in the novel, however, this vocative dimension of Conrad's semiotics is finally muted.

5. For a discussion of "voice" as a modernist sign of subverted "identity and presence," see Vincent Pecora, 1001 and *passim.*

6. Fogel's illuminating description of a "forced overhearer" who "stands outside the context of actual events, but at the same time, and perhaps as a result, amplifies, exaggerates, and overreacts," has much in common with this study's characterization of rifted dialogue (171). Yet whereas Fogel tends to link such features with post-Romantic movements (170), we have viewed this adversativeness of dialogue within a wider framework that encompasses not only the Lake poets but also the various traditions of hermeneutic rhetoric, developmental ontology, and philosophical outness that they illustrate.

7. For further instances of this semiotic link between silence and the Congo, see 4, 20, 26, 29, 33, 35, 38, 40, 54, 57, 62, 65 – and, in another context, 39.

8. References to this collapse of mutual understanding are legion; see, for instance, 7, 27, 28, 36, 40, 60, 65, and 69. For the significance of the Intended's pivotal question, see Ong, "Conrad's Darkness," 154, 157.

9. Jerry Wasserman, too, traces the collapse of both naming and colloquy in the novella to a more global failure of language. He suggests that, for Marlow, "names, words, language in general, the province of the Europeans, are artificial, farcical, or absurd" (329; cf. 332).

For Vincent Pecora, however, such a failure derives from the dubitable ability of the human voice to signify "identity and presence" (1001). In Pecora's subtle study of the novella, Conrad's history emerges as an "investigation of the spoken word as the proof and sign of an inviolable human presence in the world"—an investigation that ultimately leads to a subverted "belief in the identity affirmed by this voice" (1000, 1009). Pecora then goes on to situate this failure in terms of two phenomenological traditions. Regarding the first of these—the "problem of the philosophical subject"—he demonstrates German idealism's inability "to reproduce in rationally viable terms the notion of personal identity" (994). In the second case, he documents the modernist critique of "intentionality, of one's ability to say what one means" (996). What both approaches amount to, then, is a "critique of voice as the sign of presence," a failure of the "cultural need to articulate the concept of personal identity" (994, 1001).

Yet for Pecora, such breakdowns are again related to a more synoptic failure of language—to what happens when "modern man" has "denied any transcendental signified and displaced language from its semantic moorings" (996). At the same time, his study focuses on the absence signified by voice itself—on the actual lack of any clear "identity affirmed by . . . voice"—rather than on those absences represented by the failed *interaction* of *multiple* voices. His concerns lie ultimately with the "ambiguity in the ontological status of the voice" (996) rather than with any rhetorical implications of voices in dialogue. For my own view of ontological orality, see pages 33–38.

10. Indeed, Said's incisive analyses serve to identify a host of dialogic features within Conradian discourse. Besides this allusion to the combative encounter, his description here of the associative utterance, "ineluctably linked to other utterances," coincides with Bakhtin's contention that the "utterance is a link in the chain of speech communication" ("Speech" 94). This linkage suggests that, in Said's terms, such "narrative no longer merely assumes listeners" but "dramatizes them as well" (101). Finally, much as Bakhtin rests his formulation on the proliferation of spoken (primary) genres, Said stresses the actual scene of colloquy, the sense that Conradian "narrative is presented as utterance, something in the actual process of being spoken" so that the "content of what is said need not by definition be as important or clear as who says it, why, and how" (101). Conrad can thus "stage his work as a writer" by "redispersing, then reassembling, language into voices" (99).

11. For a consonant approach to Conrad's passage, see Thorburn 123.

12. See Fogel 151, 177; Fogel's astute analysis recognizes some of the hermeneutic dimensions of Conradian dialogue when he discusses the latter as a forced production of "truth," a coercive "scene . . . in which question and answer are asymmetrical to each other" (225–26).

Chapter 7

1. I am indebted here to Michael Holquist, whose essay "Bakhtin and Beautiful Science: The Paradox of Cultural Relativity Revisited" locates dialogism within the contexts of both cultural anthropology and a more general philosophy of science. We might note in passing, moreover, that not all

cultural anthropologists seek to maintain this externalized vantage during their field research; see, for instance, Stoller and Olkes.

2. Holquist (forthcoming). In focusing on Bakhtin's analyses of cultural inquiry and critical "outsideness," Holquist reframes the problem of cultural relativity in terms of a universal, somatic standard—a "third term that would let the outside observer of any two versions of socially constructed reality judge between them."

Works Cited

Aarsleff, Hans. *From Locke to Saussure: Essays on the Study of Language and Intellectual History*. Minneapolis: University of Minnesota Press, 1982.

Abrams, M. H. "Structure and Style in the Greater Romantic Lyric." In *From Sensibility to Romanticism: Essays Presented to Frederick A. Pottle*, edited by Frederick W. Hilles and Harold Bloom. New York: Oxford University Press, 1965.

_____. *Natural Supernaturalism*. New York: Norton, 1971.

Allott, Miriam, ed. *Novelists on the Novel*. London: Routledge Paperback, 1968.

_____. *The Brontës: The Critical Heritage*. London: Routledge and Kegan Paul, 1974.

_____. "The Brontës." In *The English Novel: Select Bibliographical Guides*, edited by A. E. Dyson, 218–45. London: Oxford University Press, 1974.

Anderson, Walter E. "The Lyrical Form of *Wuthering Heights*." *University of Toronto Quarterly* 47 (1977–78): 120.

Armstrong, Nancy. "Emily Brontë In and Out of Her Time." *Genre* 15 (1982): 243–64.

Baker, E. A. *The History of the English Novel*, vol. 8. New York: Barnes and Noble, 1968.

Bakhtin, Mikhail. "Discourse in Life and Discourse in Poetry." In *Bakhtin School Papers*, translated by John Richmond, edited by Ann Shukman, 5–25. Russian Poetics in Translation No. 10. Oxford: RPT Publications, 1983.

_____. *Problems of Dostoevsky's Poetics*. Edited and translated by Caryl Emerson. Minneapolis: University of Minnesota Press, 1984.

_____. *Speech Genres and Other Late Essays*. Translated by Vern W. McGee. Edited by Caryl Emerson and Michael Holquist. Austin: University of Texas Press, 1986.

_____. "Response to a Question from the *Novy Mir* Editorial Staff." In *Speech Genres and Other Late Essays*. Translated by Vern W. McGee. Edited by Caryl Emerson and Michael Holquist, 1–7. Austin: University of Texas Press, 1986.

_____. "The Problem of Speech Genres." In *Speech Genres and Other Late Essays*. Translated by Vern W. McGee. Edited by Caryl Emerson and Michael Holquist, 60–102. Austin: University of Texas Press, 1986.

_____. "The Problem of the Text in Linguistics, Philology, and the Human Sciences: An Experiment in Philosophical Analysis." In *Speech Genres and Other Late Essays*. Translated by Vern W. McGee. Edited by Caryl Emerson and Michael Holquist, 103–31. Austin: University of Texas Press, 1986.

_____. "From Notes Made in 1970–71." In *Speech Genres and Other Late Essays*, translated by Vern W. McGee, edited by Caryl Emerson and Michael Holquist, 132–58. Austin: University of Texas Press, 1986.

_____. "K filosofii postupka" [Toward a Philosophy of the Act]. In *Filosofiia i sotsiologiia nauki i tekhniki*. Soviet Academy of Sciences (Moscow: Nauka, 1986), 80–160. Excerpted and partially translated in *Rethinking Bakhtin*, edited by Gary Saul Morson and Caryl Emerson. Evanston: Northwestern University Press, 1990.

Bate, W. J. *Coleridge*. New York: Macmillan, 1968.

Beer, John B. *Coleridge the Visionary*. London: Chatto and Windus, 1959.

Benjamin, Walter. "The Storyteller." In *Illuminations*, 83–109. 1955. New York: Harcourt, Brace and World, 1968.

Berggren, Erik. *The Psychology of Confession*, Studies in the History of Religions, vol. 29. Leiden: E. J. Brill, 1975.

Bialostosky, Don H. *Making Tales: The Poetics of Wordsworth's Narrative Experiments*. Chicago: University of Chicago Press, 1984.

_____. "Wordsworth's Dialogic Art." *The Wordsworth Circle* 20 (1989): 140–48.

_____. "Bakhtin and the Future of Rhetorical Criticism: A Response to Halasek and Bernard-Donals." Paper presented at the Modern Language Association meeting, Chicago, December 28, 1990.

Blayac, Alain. "A Note on Emily Brontë's Romanticism in *Wuthering Heights*." *Cahiers Victoriens et Edouardiens* 3 (1976): 1–6.

Bloom, Harold. Afterword to *Frankenstein*. New York: New American Library, 1965.

_____. "Frankenstein, or the Modern Prometheus." *Partisan Review* 32 (1965): 611–18. Reprinted in *The Ringers in the Tower*. Chicago: University of Chicago Press, 1971.

_____. *The Anxiety of Influence*. New Haven: Yale University Press, 1973.

_____. *Agon: Towards a Theory of Revisionism*. New York: Oxford University Press, 1982.

Bodkin, Maud. "A Study of 'The Ancient Mariner' and of the Rebirth Archetype." In *Archetypal Patterns in Poetry: Psychological Studies of Imagination*, 26–89. New York: Oxford University Press, 1934.

Booth, Wayne C. *The Rhetoric of Fiction*. 2d ed. Chicago: University of Chicago Press, 1983.

Bosco, Ronald A. "Heathcliff: Social Victim or Demon?" *Gypsy Scholar* 2 (1974): 21–39.

Brick, Allan R. "*Wuthering Heights*: Narrators, Audience, and Message." *College English* 21 (November 1959): 81. Reprinted in *A Wuthering Heights Handbook*, edited by Richard Lettis and William E. Morris, 219–20. New York: Odyssey Press, 1961.

Brisman, Leslie. *Romantic Origins*. Ithaca: Cornell University Press, 1978.

Brontë, Emily. *Wuthering Heights*. Edited by William M. Sale, Jr. New York: Norton, 1972.

Brooks, Peter. "'Godlike Science/Unhallowed Arts': Language, Nature, and Monstrosity." In *The Endurance of Frankenstein: Essays on Mary Shelley's Novel*, edited by George Levine and U. C. Knoepflmacher, 205–20. Berkeley: University of California Press, 1979.

Christensen, Jerome. *Coleridge's Blessed Machine of Language*. Ithaca: Cornell University Press, 1981.

Clifford, Gay. "*Caleb Williams* and *Frankenstein*: First-Person Narrative and 'Things as They Are.'" *Genre* 10 (Winter 1977): 601–17.

Coleridge, Henry Nelson, ed. *Specimens of the Table Talk of Samuel Taylor Coleridge*. 1836.

Coleridge, Samuel Taylor. *Aids to Reflection and the Confessions of an Inquiring Spirit*. London: George Bell and Sons, 1890.

_____. *The Complete Poetical Works of Samuel Taylor Coleridge*. Edited by Ernest Hartley Coleridge. Oxford: Clarendon Press, 1912.

_____. *Coleridge's Shakespearean Criticism*. Edited by Thomas M. Raysor. 2 vols. Cambridge: Harvard University Press, 1930.

_____. *The Notebooks of Samuel Taylor Coleridge*. Edited by Kathleen Coburn. 4 vols. New York: Pantheon, 1957–.

_____. *The Collected Works of Samuel Taylor Coleridge*. Edited by James Engell and W. Jackson Bate. 16 vols. London: Routledge and Kegan Paul; Princeton: Princeton University Press, 1979–.

Collins, Clifford. "Theme and Conventions in *Wuthering Heights*." *Critic* 1 (Autumn 1947): 43–50. Reprinted in *Wuthering Heights: An Authoritative Text, with Essays in Criticism*, edited by William R. Sale, 309–18. New York: Norton, 1963.

Condillac, Etienne Bonnot de. *An Essay on the Origin of Human Knowledge Being a Supplement to Mr. Locke's Essay on the Human Understanding*, translated by Thomas Nugent. London: J. Nourse, 1756.

Conrad, Joseph. *Heart of Darkness*. Edited by Robert Kimbrough. New York: Norton, 1971.

Conser, Walter H., Jr. *Church and Confession: Conservative Theologians in Germany, England, and America, 1815–1866*. Macon: Mercer University Press, 1984.

Corrigan, Timothy. *Coleridge, Language and Criticism*. Athens: University of Georgia Press, 1982.

Culler, Jonathan. *The Pursuit of Signs: Semiotics, Literature, Deconstruction*. Ithaca: Cornell University Press, 1981.

_____. "Apostrophe." In *The Pursuit of Signs: Semiotics, Lit erature, Deconstruction*, 99–123. Ithaca: Cornell University Press, 1981.

Curran, Stuart. *Poetic Form and British Romanticism.* New York: Oxford University Press, 1986.

de Grazia, Emilio. "The Ethical Dimension of *Wuthering Heights.*" *Midwest Quarterly* 19 (1978): 176–95.

Derrida, Jacques. *Speech and Phenomena.* Translated by David B. Allison. Evanston: Northwestern University Press, 1973.

———. *Writing and Difference.* Translated by Alan Bass. Chicago: University of Chicago Press, 1978.

Diskin, Patrick. "Some Sources of *Wuthering Heights.*" *Notes and Queries* 24 (1977): 354–61.

Donoghue, Denis. "Emily Brontë: On the Latitude of Interpretation." In *The Interpretation of Narrator: Theory and Practice,* edited by Morton W. Bloomfield, 105–33. Cambridge: Harvard University Press, 1970.

Doody, Terrence. *Confession and Community in the Novel.* Baton Rouge: Louisiana State University Press, 1980.

Erikson, Frederick. "Listening and Speaking." In *Languages and Linguistics: The Interdependence of Theory, Data, and Application,* edited by Deborah Tannen. Washington, D.C.: Georgetown University Press, 1986. Presented at Georgetown University Round Table on Languages and Linguistics, 1985.

Everest, Kelvin. *Coleridge's Secret Ministry.* New York: Barnes and Noble, 1979.

Everitt, Alastair G. *Wuthering Heights: An Anthology of Criticism.* London: Frank Cass, 1967.

Ferguson, Frances. "Coleridge and the Deluded Reader: 'The Rime of the Ancient Mariner.'" *Georgia Review* 31 (1977): 617–35.

———. *Wordsworth: Language as Counter-Spirit.* New Haven: Yale University Press, 1977.

Fogel, Aaron. *Coercion to Speak: Conrad's Poetics of Dialogue.* Cambridge: Harvard University Press, 1985.

Foster, Dennis A. *Confession and Complicity in Narrative.* Cambridge: Cambridge University Press, 1987.

Foucault, Michel. *History of Sexuality.* Translated by Robert Hurley. New York: Pantheon, 1978.

Frye, Northrup. "Approaching the Lyric." In *Lyric Poetry: Beyond New Criticism,* edited by Chaviva Hosek and Patricia Parker, 31–37. Ithaca: Cornell University Press, 1985.

Gadamer, Hans-Georg. *Truth and Method.* New York: Continuum, 1975.

Garrett, Peter K. "Double Plots and Dialogical Form in Victorian Fiction." *Nineteenth-Century Fiction* 32 (1977): 1–17.

Gibson, Walker. "Authors, Speakers, Readers, and Mock Readers." *College English* 11 (1950): 265–69.

Gleckner, Robert F., and Gerald E. Enscoe, eds. *Romanticism: Points of View.* Englewood Cliffs, N.J.: Prentice-Hall, 1970.

Gregor, Ian. "Reading a Short Story: Sequence, Pace, and Recollection." In

Reading the Victorian Novel: Detail into Form, edited by Ian Gregor. Totowa, N.J.: Barnes and Noble, 1980.

Griffin, Andrew L. "Wordsworth and the Problem of Imaginative Story: The Case of 'Simon Lee.'" *PMLA* 92 (1977): 392–409.

Habermas, Jurgen. *Communication and the Evolution of Society*. Boston: Beacon Press, 1979.

Hamilton, Paul. *Coleridge's Poetics*. Stanford: Stanford University Press, 1983.

Harding, Anthony John. "Speech, Silence, and the Self-Doubting Interpreter in Keats's Poetry." *Keats-Shelley Journal* 35 (1986): 83–103.

Hartman, Geoffrey H. *Wordsworth's Poetry, 1787–1814*. Cambridge: Harvard University Press, 1987.

Hazlitt, William. "The Fight." *New Monthly Magazine* (February 1822).

Herder, Johann Gottfried. *Essay on the Origin of Language*. In *On the Origin of Language*, translated by John H. Moran and Alexander Gode. New York: F. Ungar, 1966.

Hewish, John. *Emily Brontë: A Critical and Biographical Study*. New York: Macmillan, 1969.

Holquist, Michael. "Bakhtin and Beautiful Science." In *Dialogue and Critical Discourse*, edited by Michael Macovski. New York: Oxford University Press, forthcoming.

Iser, Wolfgang. *The Implied Reader: Patterns of Communication in Prose Fiction from Bunyan to Beckett*. Baltimore: Johns Hopkins University Press, 1974.

Jacobs, Carol. "*Wuthering Heights*: At the Threshold of Interpretation." *Boundary 2* 7 (1979): 49–71.

Jacobus, Mary. "Apostrophe and Lyric Voice in *The Prelude*." In *Lyric Poetry: Beyond New Criticism*, edited by Chavia Hosek and Patricia Parker, 167–81. Ithaca: Cornell University Press, 1985.

Keats, John. *Complete Poems/John Keats*. Edited by Jack Stillinger. Cambridge: Belknap Press of Harvard University Press, 1982.

_____. *Letters*. Edited by Charles Armitage Brown and Jack Stillinger. Cambridge: Harvard University Press, 1966.

Kermode, Frank. "A Modern Way with the Classic." *New Literary History* 5 (1974): 415–34.

Kneale, J. Douglas. "Wordsworth's Images of Language: Voice and Letter in *The Prelude*." *PMLA* 101 (May 1986): 351–61.

Koehler, Walter J. *Counseling and Confession*. St. Louis: Concordia, 1982.

Labov, William, and David Fanshel. *Therapeutic Discourse*. New York: Academic Press, 1977.

Lacan, Jacques. *Ecrits*. Paris: Editions du Seuil, 1966.

_____. "Le Stade du miroir." Reprinted in *Ecrits*. Paris: Editions du Seuil, 1966.

_____. *The Language of the Self*. Translated by Anthony Wilden. Baltimore: Johns Hopkins University Press, 1968.

———. "Propos sur la causalité psychique." 1950. Reprinted in *Ecrits*. Paris: Editions du Seuil, 1966.

Lakoff, Robin Tomach. "When Talk Is Not Cheap: Psychotherapy as Conversation." In *The State of the Language*, edited by Leonard Michaels and Christopher Ricks. Berkeley: University of California Press, 1980.

Langbaum, Robert. *The Mysteries of Identity: A Theme in Modern Literature*. New York: Oxford University Press, 1977.

Lea, Henry C. *History of Auricular Confession and Indulgences in the Latin Church*. 3 vols. Philadelphia: Lea Brothers, 1896.

Leavis, F. R. *The Great Tradition*. 1948. New York: New York University Press, 1973.

Leavis, Q. D. "Introduction to Charlotte Brontë's *Jane Eyre*." In *Jane Eyre*, by Charlotte Brontë. Harmondsworth, U.K.: Penguin, 1966.

Leavy, Stanley. *The Psychoanalytic Dialogue*. New Haven: Yale University Press, 1980.

Lentricchia, Frank. *After the New Criticism*. Chicago: University of Chicago Press, 1980.

Lettis, Richard, and William E. Morris, eds. *A Wuthering Heights Handbook*. New York: Odyssey Press, 1961.

Levine, George. "The Ambiguous Heritage of *Frankenstein*." In *The Endurance of Frankenstein: Essays on Mary Shelley's Novel*, edited by George Levine and U. C. Knoepflmacher, 3–30. Berkeley: University of California Press, 1979.

Lindenberger, Herbert. *On Wordsworth's Prelude*. Princeton: Princeton University Press, 1963.

Lockridge, Laurence S. *Coleridge the Moralist*. Ithaca: Cornell University Press, 1977.

Loxterman, Alan S. "*Wuthering Heights* as Romantic Poem and Victorian Novel." In *A Festschrift for Professor Marguerite Roberts*, edited by Frieda Elaine Penninger. Richmond: University of Richmond Press, 1976.

Lubbock, Percy. *The Craft of Fiction*. New York: Viking Press, 1957.

Macovski, Michael, ed. *Dialogue and Critical Discourse: Language, Culture, Literary Theory*. New York: Oxford University Press, in press.

Magnuson, Paul. *Coleridge's Nightmare Poetry*. Charlottesville: University Press of Virginia, 1974.

———. *Wordsworth and Coleridge: A Lyrical Dialogue*. Princeton: Princeton University Press, 1988.

Man, Paul de. *The Rhetoric of Romanticism*. New York: Columbia University Press, 1984.

———. "Lyrical Voice in Contemporary Theory: Riffaterre and Jauss." In *Lyric Poetry: Beyond New Criticism*, edited by Chavia Hosek and Patricia Parker, 55–72. Ithaca: Cornell University Press, 1985.

Maranhão, Tullio. *Therapeutic Discourse and Socratic Dialogue*. Madison: University of Wisconsin Press, 1986.

Marshall, David. *The Surprising Effects of Sympathy: Marivaux, Diderot, Rousseau, and Mary Shelley.* Chicago: University of Chicago Press, 1988.

Martin, Loy D. *Browning's Dramatic Monologues and the Post-Romantic Subject.* Baltimore: Johns Hopkins University Press, 1985.

McConnell, Frank D. *The Confessional Imagination: A Reading of Wordsworth's Prelude.* Baltimore: Johns Hopkins University Press, 1974.

McDermott, R. P., and Henry Tylbor. "On the Necessity of Collusion in Conversation." *Text* 3 (1983): 277–97.

McFarland, Thomas. "A Complex Dialogue: Coleridge's Doctrine of Polarity and Its European Contexts." In *Reading Coleridge*, edited by Walter B. Crawford. Ithaca: Cornell University Press, 1979.

———. *Romanticism and the Forms of Ruin.* Princeton: Princeton University Press, 1981.

McGann, Jerome J. *Don Juan in Context.* Chicago: University of Chicago Press, 1976.

———. "The Meaning of the Ancient Mariner." *Critical Inquiry* 8 (1981): 35–67.

———. *The Romantic Ideology: A Critical Investigation.* Chicago: University of Chicago Press, 1983.

McIverny, Peter. "Satanic Conceits in *Frankenstein* and *Wuthering Heights.*" *Milton and the Romantics* 4 (1980): 1–15.

McKeever, Paul E. *Theology 77.* Washington, D.C.: Catholic University of America Press, 1953.

McKusick, James. *Coleridge's Philosophy of Language.* New Haven: Yale University Press, 1986.

Mellor, Anne K. *English Romantic Irony.* Cambridge: Harvard University Press, 1980.

———. Introduction to *Romanticism and Feminism.* Bloomington: Indiana University Press, 1988.

Mermin, Dorothy. *The Audience in the Poem.* New Brunswick: Rutgers University Press, 1983.

Miller, J. Hillis. *The Disappearance of God.* New York: Schocken, 1965.

———. "*Wuthering Heights* and the Ellipses of Interpretation." *Notre Dame English Journal* 12 (1980): 85–100.

———. *Fiction and Repetition.* Cambridge: Harvard University Press, 1983.

———. *The Linguistic Moment.* Princeton: Princeton University Press, 1985.

Miyoshi, Masao. *The Divided Self: A Perspective on the Literature of the Victorians.* New York: New York University Press, 1969.

Moers, Ellen. *Literary Women.* Garden City, N.Y.: Doubleday, 1976.

Monboddo, James Burnet, Lord. *Of the Origin and Progress of Language.* 2d ed. 6 vols. Edinburgh: Balfour and Cadell, 1774–92.

Morson, Gary Saul, and Caryl Emerson. "Introduction." In *Rethinking Bakhtin*, edited by Morson and Emerson. Evanston: Northwestern University Press, 1990.

Napier, Elizabeth R. "The Problem of Boundaries in *Wuthering Heights*."
    Philological Quarterly 63 (1984): 96, 97.

Newman, Beth. "Narratives of Seduction and the Seductions of Narrative:
    The Frame Structure of *Frankenstein*." *ELH* 53 (Spring 1986): 141–63.

————. "The Writer's Audience Is Always a Fiction." *PMLA* 90 (1975):
    9–21.

————. "Truth in Conrad's Darkness." *Mosaic* 11 (Fall 1977): 151–63.

————. *Fighting for Life: Contest, Sexuality, and Consciousness*. Ithaca:
    Cornell University Press, 1981.

————. *Orality and Literacy: The Technologizing of the World*. London:
    Methuen, 1982.

Pater, Walter. "On Classical and Romantic." Excerpted from *Appreciations*,
    by Walter Pater, 241–61. New York: Macmillan, 1889. Reprinted in
    Romanticism: Points of View, edited by Robert F. Gleckner and Ger-
    ald E. Enscoe, 19–25. Englewood Cliffs: Prentice-Hall, 1970.

Pecora, Vincent. "*Heart of Darkness* and the Phenomenology of Voice."
    ELH 52 (Winter 1985): 993–1015.

Poovey, Mary. "My Hideous Progeny: Mary Shelley and the Feminization of
    Romanticism." *PMLA* 95 (May 1980): 332–47.

Porter, James I. "Saussure and Derrida on the Figure of the Voice." *MLN*
    101 (1986): 857–94.

Prince, Gerald. "Notes toward a Categorization of Fictional 'Narratees.'"
    Genre 4 (1971): 100–106.

————. "Introduction à l'étude du narrataire." *Poetique* 14 (1973): 178–96.

Rabinowitz, Peter J. "Truth in Fiction: A Reexamination of Audiences."
    Critical Inquiry 4 (1977): 121–41.

Rader, Ralph W. "The Dramatic Monologue and Related Lyric Forms." *Criti-
    cal Inquiry* 3 (1976): 131–51.

Ragussis, Michael. *The Subterfuge of Art: Language and the Romantic Tradi-
    tion*. Baltimore: Johns Hopkins University Press, 1978.

Rajan, Tilottama. "Romanticism and the Death of Lyric Consciousness." In
    Lyric Poetry: Beyond New Criticism, edited by Chavia Hosek and
    Patricia Parker, 194–207. Ithaca: Cornell University Press, 1985.

Reed, Walter L. *Meditations on the Hero: A Study of the Romantic Hero in
    Nineteenth-Century Fiction*. New Haven: Yale University Press, 1974.

Reik, Theodor. *The Compulsion to Confess: On the Psychoanalysis of Crime
    and Punishment*. New York: Farrar, Strauss and Cudahy, 1959.

Rousseau, Jean Jacques. *Confessions*. Paris: Pléiade, 1951.

————. *Essay on the Origin of Languages*. In *On the Origin of Language*,
    edited by John H. Moran and Alexander Gode. New York: F. Ungar,
    1966.

Ruoff, Gene W. *Wordsworth and Coleridge: The Making of the Major Lyr-
    ics, 1802–1804*. New Brunswick: Rutgers University Press, 1989.

Rzepka, Charles. *The Self as Mind: Vision and Identity in Wordsworth,
    Coleridge, and Keats*. Cambridge: Harvard University Press, 1986.

Said, Edward W. "Conrad: The Presentation of Narrative." In *The World,* the Text, and the Critic, 90–110. Cambridge: Harvard University Press, 1983.

Saussure, Ferdinand de. *Course in General Linguistics*. Edited by Charles Bally and Albert Sechehaye. Translated by Wade Baskin. New York: McGraw-Hill, 1966.

Schafer, Roy. "Narration in the Psychoanalytic Dialogue." In *On Narrative*, edited by W.J.T. Mitchell, 25–50. Chicago: University of Chicago Press, 1981.

Schlegel, Friedrich. *Philosophische Lehrjahre*. In *Kritische-Friedrich-Schlegel-Ausgabe*. 22 vols. Paderborn and Munich: Ferdinand Schoningh, 1958–.

_____. *Dialogue on Poetry and Literary Aphorisms*. Translated by Ernst Behler and Roman Struc. University Park: Pennsylvania State University Press, 1968.

_____. *Critical Fragments* from *The Athenaeum* (1798–1800). In *Friedrich Schlegel's Lucinde and the Fragments*. Translated by Peter Firchow. Minneapolis: University of Minnesota Press, 1971.

_____. *Critical Fragments* from *The Lycaeum*. In *Friedrich Schlegel's Lucinde and the Fragments*. Translated by Peter Firchow. Minneapolis: University of Minnesota Press, 1971.

Shapiro, Arnold. "*Wuthering Heights* as a Victorian Novel." *Studies in the Novel* 1 (1969): 284–95.

Sheats, Paul D. *The Making of Wordsworth's Poetry, 1785–1798*. Cambridge: Harvard University Press, 1973.

Shelley, Mary W. *The Letters of Mary W. Shelley*. Edited by Frederick L. Jones. 2 vols. Norman: Oklahoma University Press, 1944.

_____. *Mary Shelley's Journal*. Edited by Frederick L. Jones. Norman: Oklahoma University Press, 1947.

_____. *Frankenstein; or, The Modern Prometheus*. Edited by James Rieger. Indianapolis: Bobbs-Merrill, 1974.

Sherwin, Paul. "*Frankenstein*: Creation as Catastrophe." *PMLA* 96 (1981): 883–903.

Shorter, Clement King. *The Brontës: Life and Letters*. New York: Haskell House, 1969.

Shunami, Gideon. "The Unreliable Narrator in *Wuthering Heights*." *Nineteenth-Century Fiction* 27 (1973): 449–68.

Siskin, Clifford. *The Historicity of Romantic Discourse*. New York: Oxford University Press, 1987.

Smith, Barbara Herrnstein. *On the Margins of Discourse: The Relation of Literature to Language*. Chicago: University of Chicago Press, 1978.

Sonstroem, David. "*Wuthering Heights* and the Limits of Vision." *PMLA* 86 (1971): 51–62.

Spacks, Patricia Meyer. *The Female Imagination*. New York: Knopf, 1975.

Spark, Muriel, and Derek Stanford. *Emily Brontë: Her Life and Work*. New York: J. Day, 1959.

Stoller, Paul, and Cheryl Olkes. *In Sorcery's Shadow: A Memoir of Appren-*

ticeship among the Songhay of Niger. Chicago: University of Chicago Press, 1987.

Tave, Katherine Bruner. *The Demon and the Poet: An Interpretation of "The Rime of the Ancient Mariner" According to Coleridge's Demonological Sources.* Salzburg, Austria: Institut für Anglistik und Amerikanistik, Universität Salzburg, 1983.

Taylor, Mark C. *Altarity.* Chicago: University of Chicago Press, 1987.

Thorburn, David. *Conrad's Romanticism.* New Haven: Yale University Press, 1974.

Twitchell, James. "Heathcliff as Vampire." *Southern Humanities Review* 11 (1977): 355–62.

Viswanathan, Jacqueline. "Point of View and Unreliability in Brontë's *Wuthering Heights*, Conrad's *Under Western Eyes*, and Mann's *Doktor Faustus*." *Orbis Litterarum* 29 (1974): 42–60.

Warren, Robert Penn. "A Poem of Pure Imagination: An Experiment in Reading." In Coleridge, *The Rime of the Ancient Mariner, with an Essay by Robert Penn Warren.* New York: Reynal and Hitchcock, 1946. Reprinted in *Selected Essays.* New York: Random House, 1958.

Wasserman, Jerry. "Narrative Presence: The Illusion of Language in *Heart of Darkness*." *Studies in the Novel* 6 (1974): 327–38.

Watt, Ian. *Conrad in the Nineteenth Century.* Berkeley: University of California Press, 1979.

Weissman, Judith. "'Like a Mad Dog': The Radical Romanticism of *Wuthering Heights*." *Midwest Quarterly* 19 (1978): 383–97.

Wesling, Donald. "Difficulties of the Bardic: Literature and the Human Voice." *Critical Inquiry* 8 (1981): 69–82.

Widdowson, Peter. "Emily Brontë: The Romantic Novelist." *Moderna Sprak* 66 (1972): 1–9.

Wittgenstein, Ludwig. *Philosophical Investigations.* New York: Macmillan, 1958.

Wolfson, Susan J. *The Questioning Presence: Wordsworth, Keats, and the Interrogative Mode in Romantic Poetry.* Ithaca: Cornell University Press, 1986.

Woodring, Carl R. "The Narrators of *Wuthering Heights*." *Nineteenth-Century Fiction* 11 (March 1957): 298–305.

Wordsworth, William. *The Poetical Works of William Wordsworth.* Edited by Ernest de Selincourt and Helen Darbishire. 5 vols. London: Oxford University Press, 1940.

———. *The Prose Works of William Wordsworth.* Edited by W.J.B. Owen and Jane Worthington Smyser. 2 vols. London: Oxford University Press, 1974.

Index